“一切民族、
肤色、
野蛮、
文明、
语言……”

PENGUIN

LITTLE BLACK

CLASSICS

独自在黑夜的海滩上

On the Beach at Night Alone

［美］沃尔特·惠特曼　著

郑远涛　译

中信出版集团 | 北京

图书在版编目（CIP）数据

企鹅经典：小黑书．第三辑：汉、英 /（英）简·奥斯汀等著；夏星等译．-- 北京：中信出版社，2019.6

书名原文：Penguin Little Black Classics

ISBN 978-7-5217-0407-5

Ⅰ．①企… Ⅱ．①简… ②夏… Ⅲ．①世界文学－作品综合集－汉、英 Ⅳ．① I11

中国版本图书馆 CIP 数据核字 (2019) 第 072172 号

企鹅经典：小黑书　第三辑
独自在黑夜的海滩上

著　　者：［美］沃尔特·惠特曼
译　　者：郑远涛
出版发行：中信出版集团股份有限公司
（北京市朝阳区惠新东街甲 4 号富盛大厦 2 座 邮编 100029）
承 印 者：北京楠萍印刷有限公司

开　　本：787mm × 1092mm　1/32　　印　　张：45.75　　字　　数：756 千字
版　　次：2019 年 6 月第 1 版　　印　　次：2019 年 6 月第 1 次印刷
京权图字：01－2018－6477　　广告经营许可证：京朝工商广字第 8087 号
书　　号：ISBN 978－7－5217－0407－5
定　　价：149.00 元（全 10 册）

目录

候鸟

／

普遍性之歌[1]

一

来呀，缪斯说，
为我唱一首没有诗人唱过的歌，
为我歌咏普遍性吧。

在我们这广阔的地球中，
深不可测的厚度和熔渣之间，
它中心的中央安然包裹着、
栖息着完美的种子。

每个生命或多或少享有它的一份，
一切出生都是它的出生，掩藏不掩藏，种子都在等待。

二

看啊！目光犀利而卓然挺拔的科学，

1. 写《普遍性之歌》前，惠特曼经受了一些个人生活的考验，包括中风瘫痪和丧母之痛。此诗重申了他的信仰，也反映出他研读黑格尔哲学受到的影响。（说明：书中脚注除特别标明的之外，均为译者注。）

如同从高峰上俯视着现代人，
不断地发出绝对的律令。

但再看啊！灵魂，超乎一切科学之上，
历史由于它一层层环绕了地球，
整个星河由于它在天空上转动。

经过漫长周折的螺旋之路，
（如同海上一条因风转舵的船）
部分的由于它向恒常的汇流；
真实的由于它向理想的趋近[1]。

由于它，神秘的演化
不但令正义合理，也令我们称之为邪恶者合理。

从无论什么样的面具底下，
从溃烂的巨大躯干之中，从奸诈和诡计和泪水之中，
将出现健康和欢乐，普遍的欢乐。
脱开病态的和浮浅的主体，脱开恶劣的多数，人和
　　国家的变化无穷的欺骗，

1.“真实”者，指世间存在的各种殊相；“理想”者，指普遍性的事物共相。

如电、没有污染，分劈着、充盈着一切，
只有良善是普遍的。

三

在疾病和哀愁丛生的群山之上，
一只无拘无束的鸟儿永远展翅悬停着，停着，
高高地处在更纯净、更快乐的风中。

从最浓重的缺憾的云翳那里，
永远会放射一道完美的光，
闪现天堂的荣耀。

对着潮流和习俗的争吵，
对着巴别塔般的喧嚣、震耳欲聋的狂欢，
一缕清音，依稀可辨，安抚着每一个间歇，
那是最终的合唱，来自某个遥远的海岸。

啊，蒙福的眼睛、快乐的心，
能看见、能认识宏伟的迷宫中

一条细细的指引之线。[1]

四

而你，阿美利加[2]，
你为了宏图的顶点、它的理想和它的成真，
你为了这些（并非为你自己）而来临。

你也包围一切，
拥抱着、提携着、迎接着一切，你也通过崭新的大道，
向理想趋近。

别的大陆上局限的信仰、过去的伟大，
不是给你的，你拥有自己的伟大，
属灵的信仰和广博，吸收着、容纳着一切，
适合一切人的一切。

一切，一切追求不朽，

---

1. 希腊神话中，英雄忒修斯凭借阿里阿德涅交给他的线团，循着细线前行，走出迷宫。
2. 本书出于声韵与音节字数的考量，统一使用“阿美利加”来翻译 America，而不用美利坚或美国。

爱如同静静包裹万物的光，
大自然的改善福佑万物，
花儿、时令的果实、神圣和从不爽约的果园，
形态、事物、各种生长、各种人性，都在成熟为精
　　神的形象。

神啊，为了让我能歌唱那个理想，
请向我，向我所爱的男女赐予这不灭的信仰，
不管你从整体[1]中保留什么，也请赐予我们
蕴含在时间和空间中的对你蓝图的信念，
健康、和平、普遍的拯救。

它是否是一个梦？
不，但没有它则是梦，
辜负它，生命的传承和财富就是个梦，
全世界都会是一个梦。

---

1. “整体”的原文 ensemble 是超验主义的概念，这股思潮认为万物都包含宇宙的缩影。惠特曼受超验主义代表人物爱默生影响很深。

开拓者！啊，开拓者！

　　来呀，我脸面黝黑的孩子们，
排好队形，准备好你们的武器，
手枪带上了吗？锋利的斧子带上了吗？
　　开拓者！啊，开拓者！

　　因为我们不能在这里徘徊，
我们必须前进，亲爱的，我们必须一马当先，
我们是年轻力壮的民族，别的民族全依靠我们，
　　开拓者！啊，开拓者！

　　啊，你们青年，西部的青年，
如此性急、充满活力，充满男儿的骄傲和友情，
我清楚看见了你们，西部的青年，看见你们大步当先，
　　开拓者！啊，开拓者！

　　年长的民族止步了吗？
他们在大洋彼岸暮气沉沉，不再学习了吗？
我们来扛起这永恒的使命、责任和课业吧，
　　开拓者！啊，开拓者！

我们将过去的一切抛在身后，
一个更新、更强的世界，多种多样的世界，豁然开朗，
我们抓住这鲜活健朗的世界，劳动和行进的世界，
开拓者！啊，开拓者！

我们的分遣队源源不断进发，
走下悬崖，穿过关隘，攀上陡峭的山岭，
我们在未知的道路中征服、占据、冒险、勇闯，
开拓者！啊，开拓者！

我们砍倒原始的森林，
我们截停江河的流水，我们摇动大地，钻探内里，
我们测量广阔的原野，我们在处女地垦荒，
开拓者！啊，开拓者！

我们是科罗拉多的男人，
从巨大的山峰，从庞大的齿形山脉和高原，
从矿井和沟壑，从狩猎的小径上，我们来了，
开拓者！啊，开拓者！

从内布拉斯加来，从阿肯色来，

我们是内陆中部的人种，从密苏里来，与大陆血脉
　　相连，
伙伴们扣紧彼此的手，所有的南方人，所有的北方人，
　开拓者！啊，开拓者！

　啊，不可阻挡，不知停歇的民族！
啊，大家都可爱！对大家的柔情令我胸口作痛！
啊，我伤怀而又雀跃，我欣喜若狂地爱着大家，
　开拓者！啊，开拓者！

　举起那伟大的母亲般的女主人，
高高地摇动着娇巧的女主人，比一切灿烂如星的女
　　主人都高，（你们全都低下头吧，）
举起有獠牙并且好战的女主人，严峻、冷漠、武装
　　的女主人，
　开拓者！啊，开拓者！[1]

　看，我的孩子们，勇敢的孩子们，

---

1. 读者若觉得这四行突兀难解，可以查看乔万尼·巴蒂斯塔·提埃坡罗（Giovanni Battista Tiepolo）绘于18世纪的著名穹顶画《行星和大陆的寓言》中的美洲一幅，那里便有一个作为美洲化身的“女主人”。

看在我们后方的蜂拥人群的分儿上，我们决不能退
　　　　让或动摇，
以往世代的数以百万的幽灵在我们身后皱眉催促，
　　开拓者！啊，开拓者！

　　前进又前进，紧簇的队伍，
永远有增补，死者的位置被迅速填充，
穿越战斗，穿越战败，依然前行而永不停止，
　　开拓者！啊，开拓者！

　　啊，在前进中死去！
我们当中有人委顿而死吗？时候到了吗？
那么我们在行进中死去正当其时，缺口会迅速填补！
　　开拓者！啊，开拓者！

　　世界上所有的脉搏，
各就各位地以西部运动的拍子，为我们跳动，
有单独有联合，稳稳地移向前方，全为我们，
　　开拓者！啊，开拓者！

　　生活中复杂多变的盛会，
所有的形态和展览，所有干活的工人，

所有的水手和陆上的人，所有的主人和奴隶，
开拓者！啊，开拓者！

所有不幸的沉默的恋人，
所有在监狱坐牢的人，所有的义人和恶人，
所有欢喜的人，所有哀愁的人，所有活着的人，所有垂死的人，
开拓者！啊，开拓者！

我也跟我的灵魂和肉体，
组成好奇的三者，我们在路途上跋涉、游荡，
穿过死荫之地的这些海岸，幽灵们紧紧相随，
开拓者！啊，开拓者！

看，那迅疾滚动的星球！
看，它四周的兄弟星球，所有一簇簇的恒星和行星，
所有灿烂的白昼，所有多梦的神秘之夜，
开拓者！啊，开拓者！

这一切关乎我们，和我们同在，
它都是为了初始而必要的劳作，后继者尚在胚胎中等待，

我们这今日向前的队伍，我们开辟着行进的道路，
　　开拓者！啊，开拓者！

　　你们啊，西部的女儿！
你们啊，青春的和年长的女儿！你们啊，母亲们和
　　　　妻子们！
你们千万不要失散，在我们的队伍里你们团结向前吧，
　　开拓者！啊，开拓者！

　　潜伏在大草原上的歌手！
（别的大陆上裹着尸衣的诗人呀，你们已完成工作，
　　　　可以歇息了，）
很快我会听见你们来临的婉转歌喉，很快你们会起
　　　　来跟我们同行，
　　开拓者！啊，开拓者！

　　不是为了甜美的娱乐，
不是靠枕和软鞋，不是宁静的日子和学者的生活，
不是安全乏味的财富，寡淡的享受对我们无用，
　　开拓者！啊，开拓者！

　　贪嘴的宴饮者总是在宴饮？

肥胖的沉睡者总是在睡觉？他们锁门上闩了吗？
我们的餐食粗糙如故，毯子铺地而眠，
　　开拓者！啊，开拓者！

　　夜幕降临了吗？
近来的路是否太过辛苦？我们是否气馁地停下过，在
　　　　路途上垂头打盹儿？
但是我让你们在小径上休息短短的一小时，放空身心，
　　开拓者！啊，开拓者！

　　直到随着号角的吹响，
黎明远远地发出呼唤——听！我听见它嘹亮清楚的
　　　　呼声，
快呀！赶到军队的前头！——快呀！冲上你们的位
　　　　置，
　　开拓者！啊，开拓者！

给你

不管你是谁，我只怕你行走的是梦中的道路，
我只怕这些所谓的现实即将从你的脚下和手中消融。
即便此刻，你的五官、欢乐、言谈、房子、职业、举止、烦恼、蠢事、装束、罪行，也已经散逸离开你，
你真正的灵魂和肉体出现在我面前，
它们摆脱了事务，摆脱了商业、店铺、工作、农场、衣服、房子、购买、出售、进食、饮酒、受苦、死亡。

不管你是谁，现在我把手放在你身上，你来做我的诗，
我以嘴唇俯近你的耳朵低语，
我爱过很多女人和男人，但是都没有我爱你这么深。

噢，过去我拖沓又迟钝，
我许久以前就应该径直向你奔来，
我早就应该仅仅叨念着你，我早就应该仅仅歌唱着你。

我会离开所有人来创作你的赞美诗，
没有人曾经了解你，但是我了解你，

没有人曾经公平地对待你，你也未曾公平地对待自己，
没有人觉得你处处完美，只有我觉得你完美，
没有人不会把你放在次要位置，只有我这个人决不同意把你放在次要位置，
只有我一人看见你内在的潜能，不让任何主人、所有权人、优越者、上帝凌驾于你。

画家们画出人头攒动的群体和一切的中心人物，
从中心人物的头部放射金色的光轮，
但是我画出无数的头部，画笔下却没有一个不带着金色的光轮，
从我的手从每个男人和女人的大脑中它流泻出来，永远灿烂。
啊，关于你，我能唱多少壮阔和荣耀的歌！
你还不知道你是什么，你一生都在自己身上酣睡，
你的眼皮大部分时间就像闭着一般，
你做过的事已经在滑稽模仿中回来，
（你的节俭、知识、祈祷，如果不在滑稽模仿中回来，还能怎样回来？）

滑稽模仿并不是你，

我看见你潜藏在其下和其中，

我在无人追逐你的地方追逐你，

沉默、书桌、轻佻的表情、黑夜、日常习惯，如果这些对别人和你自己构成一重重的掩盖，你对于我却是没有掩盖的，

刮净的脸、游移的眼神、不纯净的肤色，如果这些阻挡着别人却并不阻挡我，

光鲜的衣着、畸形的体态、烂醉、贪婪、早死，我把这些全都抛在一边。

凡是男人或女人具有的天赋，你无一不具备，

凡是男人或女人具有的贤德和美好，也同样存于你身上，

别人身上的任何胆量或毅力，也同样存于你身上，

任何等待着别人享受的快乐，也同样等待着你来享受。

至于我，我什么也不给任何人，除了我谨慎交给你的，

每当我咏唱任何人，乃至上帝的荣耀之歌，那都是我为你唱的荣耀之歌。

不管你是谁！要不顾风险获取你自己的一切！

这些东方和西方的气象跟你相比都平淡无奇，
这些广阔的草原、滔滔不息的江河，你就像它们一样广阔而滔滔不息，
这些天昏地暗、狂风暴雨、雷霆、大自然的运动、分解时显现的挣扎，你是掌控它们的男女主宰，
你就是大权在握的男女主宰，掌控着大自然、狂风暴雨、痛苦、激情、分解。

镣铐从你的脚踝脱落，你找到可靠的独立，
无论老少、无论男女，粗鲁、卑微、被其他人拒绝，你不管什么本性都传播你自己，
穿过出生、生命、死亡、埋葬，通路都齐备，没有一样缺少，
穿过愤怒、丧失、野心、无知、厌倦，你凭着本性举足落步。

法兰西，合众国的第 18 年[1]

一个伟大的年份和地方。
一声粗嘎不协调的新生的尖叫传出，比什么都更深
　　地触动母亲的心。

我行走在我的东部海岸上，
听见那小嗓子隔着浪涛传来，
看见那神圣的婴儿在她醒来的地方哀哀啼哭，炮声
　　隆隆，咒骂声、嘶喊声、建筑物的倒塌声不绝，
阴沟中流淌的血、一具具尸体、成堆的尸体、被死
　　囚车运走的尸体并不那么令我恶心，
屠杀的碾压并不那么令我绝望——频频齐发的枪弹
　　并不那么令我震惊。

我苍白、沉默、冷峻，我能对那种常年积怨的报复
　　说什么？

1. 此诗写于 1860 年，是美国南北战争（1861—1865）爆发前夕，当时的社会气氛已是山雨欲来（参见《流星的一年》）。惠特曼在诗中想象远在他出生之前的一个年份——法国大革命时期“革命法庭”活动到达高潮的 1794 年，那年是美利坚合众国成立的第 18 年。

我能期求不一样的人性?
我能期求人民有木头和石头的品性?
还是期求正义在命运或时间中得不到伸张?

啊，自由！啊，你是我的伙伴！
这里也有火光，有霰弹和斧子的储存，以备必要的
　　时候拿出来，
这里也压抑已久，却永远不会被摧毁，
这里也终会奋起反抗，杀气腾腾、慷慨激昂，
这里也要求着彻底的清算。

所以我要拿起笔向海的那边遥遥致敬，
我并不否认有血红可怕的降生和洗礼，
但是我记得所听见的小嗓子的啼哭，于是我无比信
　　任地等待，不管要多久，
从今以后我要为一切土地维护那个遗留的事业，心
　　怀悲哀但雄辩有力，
我带着爱意把这些话语送去巴黎，
猜想那里有些歌曲作者将会明白我的含义，
因为我猜想法兰西依然有音乐的潜流，滔滔汩汩，
啊，我已经听见乐器在拨动，响声很快就会淹没一

切干扰的杂音，
啊，我觉得东风吹来了一首胜利和自由的进行曲，
它传到这里，使我欣喜得如痴如狂，
我要快快把它变作言辞，说明它的真意，
我还要为你唱一支歌，我的女人[1]。

1. “我的女人”原文为法语 ma femme，也表示“我的妻子”，这里指拟人化的民主理想。

我和我的全部[1]

我和我的全部，永远在锻炼，
为了抵受冷和热，为了举枪能瞄准，为了航船，为了
　　骑马，为了生育出众的孩子，
为了随时清晰地说话，为了在普通人中间感到亲切，
也为了在大地和海洋情势可怕时站住脚跟。

不为了做一个刺绣工，
（永远会有许多刺绣工，我也欢迎他们，）
却为追求事物的本质，并追求男子和女子的内在。

不为了雕出装饰品，
却为了用潇洒自如的刻刀凿出许多无上神明的头和
　　四肢，为了合众国使他们得以行走和说话。
让我用自己的方式，
让别人去生成律法，我不要理会律法，
让别人去歌颂杰出的人并支持和平，我支持骚动和
　　冲突。

---

1. 此诗可说是惠特曼创作观的阐述，他将《草叶集》视为以文字表达的全部自己。

我不歌颂杰出的人，我对公认最高明的人也当面指责。

（你是谁？是什么让你一生偷偷地内疚？
你要回避自己的一生？你要在翻拣和闲话中度过一生？
你是谁，念念叨叨地死记硬背，年份、页数、语言、往事，
至今也意识不到你没法儿恰当地说一个词儿？）

让别人去完成范例吧，我从来不完成范例，
我像大自然一样用无穷的律法来开始篇章，新鲜现代而持久。

我不把什么当作义务给予，
别人作为义务给予的，我作为活生生的冲动给予。
（我要把心的行动作为义务来给予吗？）

让别人去解决问题，我什么都不解决，我唤起无法回答的问题，
我看见并触摸的他们是谁，他们怎么样？
这些像我一样的人怎么样？他们用温柔的直接和迂回的路线吸引我贴近。

我呼吁世界不要轻信我朋友们的讲述，而要像我一样，聆听我的敌人，
我要求你永远拒绝那些要解说我的人，因为我也解说不了自己，
我要求不要因我建立任何理论或学派，
我要求你潇洒地离开，就像我做的那样潇洒地离开。
在我之后，远景！
啊，我看见生命并不短促，而是悠长得难以计量，
从此我在世界上行走，贞洁，自持，清早就起床，稳健地成长，
每小时都是未来几个世纪的精子，还属于更久以后的世纪。

我必须紧紧跟上空气、水、大地的这些不断的教诲，
我感受到我没有时间可以浪费。

流星的一年（1859—1860）[1]

流星的一年！沉思的一年！
我要用回顾的文字系定你的一些事情和征兆，
我要歌唱你的第 16 届总统任期的竞争，
我要歌唱一位高个子的白发老人，如何在弗吉尼亚
　　登上绞刑架，
（我就在左右，咬紧牙关默默站着，观看，
我站在你身边，老人，当时你平静冷漠，只是年纪
　　和没有愈合的伤口使你颤抖着，登上了绞刑架；）
我要在我丰富的歌曲中歌唱你各州的人口普查报告，
那些人口和产品的报表，我要歌唱你的航船和运载
　　的货物，
曼哈顿骄傲的黑船纷纷来了，有的满载移民，有的

1. 此诗写于 1865 年美国南北战争结束时。诗中回忆的总统竞选是 1860 年林肯对道格拉斯的宣战，林肯当选总统。被处死的老人是美国起义领袖、废奴主义者约翰 · 布朗，处决时间在 1859 年 12 月。年轻的英格兰王子指维多利亚女王的长子爱德华（后来的英王爱德华七世），1860 年 10 月他 18 岁，到访纽约，惠特曼的日记中有记载。伟大东方号是著名的英国铁制蒸汽轮船，1860 年首次航越大西洋，6 月末抵达纽约。“预感不祥的一年”一语指当时战争已如箭在弦上的气氛。

装着黄金从巴拿马地峡来,
我要歌唱这一切，我要对所有前来的人表示欢迎,
我也要歌唱你，英俊少年！年轻的英格兰王子，我
欢迎你！
(你可曾记得你和贵族随从们经过曼哈顿的汹涌人群?
我站在人群中，只对你依依不舍地注目；)
我也不要忘了歌唱那条大船开进我海湾的奇观,
伟大东方号形体匀称而庄重，她以600英尺[1]的身长,
开进我的海湾,
她迅速地行驶，被无数的小船包围，小船我也不忘
歌唱;
不忘北方出现的不期而至的彗星，闪耀在天宇,
不忘奇异浩大的流星队伍，炫目而清晰，在我们头上
笔直飞行,
(一瞬间，只有一瞬间，队伍在我们头上划过一簇簇
超凡的光球,
然后离去了，沉没在黑夜中，不见了；)
对这些骤然来去的事情，我歌唱——我借着它们的

1. 一英尺约为 25 到 34 厘米。——编者注

微光来照亮并拼凑这些颂歌，
你的颂歌呀，啊，善恶杂陈的一年——预感不祥的一年！
彗星和流星的一年，短暂又奇异——看！这儿还有一个也同样短暂又奇异！
既然我匆匆地掠过你，很快要坠落不见，这首歌是什么呢？
我除了是你的一颗流星还是什么？

因为前人

一

因为前人，
因为我的父系母系和以往各时代的积累，
因为那些倘若没有，就不会有今时此地之我的一切，
因为埃及、印度、腓尼基、希腊和罗马，
因为凯尔特人、斯堪的纳维亚人、阿尔比人和撒克
　　逊人[1]，
因为古时的海上冒险、法律、手工技艺、战争和旅行，
因为诗人、北欧诗人、萨迦、神话和神谕[2]，
因为奴隶的售卖，因为狂热者，因为吟游诗人、十
　　字军和修道士，
因为我们来到这个新大陆之前的那些旧大陆，
因为那些日益衰落的王国和国王，

---

1. 这一行诗里全是古意盎然的名称。阿尔比恩（Albion）是大不列颠岛最古老的名称，阿尔比人（Alb）即阿尔比恩的居民。

2. 北欧诗人原文为 skald，在维京人时期，他们是斯堪的纳维亚（北欧）地区传诵英雄传奇的诗人，萨迦（saga）是北欧从前用来流传神话、史诗和英雄故事的文学类型。

因为那些日益衰落的宗教和神父，
因为从我们自己眼前的大海岸回望而去的小海岸，
因为向前奔去终于到达现在的数不清的年头，
你和我已经抵达——阿美利加已经抵达，正在创造
　　今年，
今年！它推动着自己奔向数不清的未来岁月。

二

啊，但是这无关岁月——而是关于我，关于你，
我们触碰所有的法律并估量所有的前人，
我们是北欧诗人、传神谕的人、修道士和骑士，我
　　们容纳了他们还大有余地，
我们站在无始无终的时间之内，我们站在恶与善之内，
一切围绕我们转动，黑暗和光明同样多，
太阳和它的星系围绕我们转动，
它的太阳，它太阳的太阳，全都围绕我们转动。

至于我，（矛盾的、狂躁的，身处暴烈的日子中间，）
我有所有人的意念，我是所有人并信仰所有人，
我相信唯物论是真的，唯灵论是真的，什么我都不

排斥。

(我忘了什么吗？忘了过去的任何东西吗？
到我这里来，不管是谁，不管是什么，直到我给你承认。)

我尊重亚述[1]、中国、条顿[2]和希伯来人，
我接纳每一个理论、神话、神和半神，
我清楚从前的故事、圣书、族谱都是真的，没有例外，
我坚信过去的每一天都非得那样不可，
决不可能胜过它实际的样子。

而今天则一定是这样，阿美利加一定是这样，
今天和阿美利加决不可能胜过它们实际的样子。

1. 亚述：兴起于两河流域的国家。公元前 8 世纪末，亚述帝国逐步强大，先后征服了小亚细亚东部、埃及等地，亚述人在两河流域频繁活动约两千年，后失去霸主地位，不再有独立的国家。——编者注

2. 条顿：古代日耳曼人的一个分支，公元前 4 世纪时分布在易北河下游的沿海地带，后来逐步和日耳曼其他民族融合，后世以条顿人泛指日耳曼人及其后裔。——编者注

三

以各州的名义，以你和我的名义：**过去**，
以各州的名义，以你和我的名义：**现在的时间**。

我知道过去伟大，未来也将会伟大，
我知道两者奇异地接合于现在的时间，
（为了我展现的他，为了平凡的普通人，如果你是普通人，这便是为了你，）
今天我所在之处，你所在之处，就有一切时日、一切民族的中心。
民族和时日对于我们曾经衍生的、将要衍生的一切意义也尽在其间。

百老汇大街的庆祝游行[1]

一

从大洋西边的日本来了
彬彬有礼、脸颊微黑、带两把佩剑的使节，
他们靠坐在敞篷四轮马车上，没有帽子，面无表情，
今天驱车穿过曼哈顿。

自由啊[2]！我不知别人是否看见我的所见，
在队伍中跟日本贵族们一起的，还有跑腿的人，
走在后面，流连在前面、周围，或在行列中前进，
但是我要给你唱一首亲身见闻的歌，**自由**。
当百万双脚的曼哈顿自由自在走下她的人行道，
当声如惊雷的礼炮用我喜爱的豪迈咆哮叫我抖擞，
当浑圆的炮口从我喜爱的浓烈硝烟中吐出它们的敬意，
当火光闪烁的礼炮使我精神大振，云霞在我的城市

---

1. 此诗最初发表于 1860 年 6 月 27 日的《纽约时报》，纪念 11 天前在纽约市百老汇大街上欢迎访美日本使团的庆祝游行。
2. 原文是 Libertad，惠特曼习惯用这个西班牙语单词的大写来表示拟人化的自由。

上空蒙了一层如纱如影的华盖，
当数不清的华丽杆子，码头上的密林，彩色缤纷，
当每一条盛装打扮的船都把她的旗帜升到最高，
当信号旗低垂而沿街的窗户挂下彩带，
当百老汇被行走和驻足的人完全占领，最是密密麻麻，
当房屋的正面万头攒动，当千万双眼睛同时盯住一个
　　方向，
当来自岛国的客人们行进，当游行队伍前移到视线
　　之内，
当传召令发下，当等候数千年的答案有了回应，
我也站起身，回应着，走下人行道，汇入人群，和大
　　家一同注视。

二

神采飞扬的曼哈顿！
阿美利加的同志们！东方，终于到我们这里来了。

到我们，到我的城市中间，
我们高峻的大理石屋顶和美丽的铁构建筑分列两旁，
　　中间的大街走着游行队伍，

今天地球另一端的人来了。

女创世者来了，
语言的巢穴、诗歌的传递者、远古的遗民，
脸色红润，思虑深沉，出神陶醉，激情炽热，
香气蒸腾，衣裳宽大而飘逸，
有黝黑的面容，有专注的灵魂和闪亮的眼睛，
梵天的子民来了。

看呀，我悦耳的歌！游行队伍中的这些那些都向我
　　们闪现，
队伍随着移动而变化，像个神奇的万花筒在我们眼
　　前移动变化。

因为不只有使节或来自岛屿的晒黑的日本人，
轻巧沉默的印度人出现了，甚至亚细亚大陆也出现了，
　　它的过去，它的死者，
在如夜如晨的朦胧中发生的奇观和无法索解的寓言，
包裹着的奥秘，古老而未知的蜜蜂，
北方，闷热的南方，东方的亚述，希伯来人，最古的
　　古人，

巨大而荒凉的城市，滑行的此刻，所有这些那些都
在庆祝的游行中。

地理学，全世界，都在其中，
大洋[1]，成群的岛屿，波利尼西亚，更远的海岸，
今后你要面向的海岸——你呀，自由！你金色的西
海岸和它遥遥相对，
那里的国家和它们的居民，千百万人一起奇妙地身
临此地，
拥挤的集市，两侧或尽头都神像成行的庙宇，和尚、
婆罗门和喇嘛，
官老爷、农民、商人、机械工和渔夫，
歌女和舞女、沉醉迷狂的人、宫禁里的皇帝，
孔夫子自己、大诗人和英雄豪杰、战士、各个种姓，
所有人，
聚集成群，从四面八方涌来，从阿尔泰的山岭，
从西藏，从中国的四条蜿蜒长流的大江，
从南方的许多半岛和仿佛大陆般的岛屿，从马来西亚，
这些以及属于它们的一切都向我清楚显现，被我领会，

1. 当指太平洋。

我也被它们领会，被它们友爱地拥抱，
最后如同在这里一样我歌咏他们所有人，自由！为了
　　他们也为了你。

因为我也扬起了声音加入这游行的行列，
我是歌手，我在盛会之上发出洪大的歌声，
我歌咏我那西海上的世界，
我歌咏远方众多的海岛，密集如满天的星辰，
我歌咏那空前壮阔的新帝国，在灵视之中看见了它，
我歌咏女主人阿美利加，我歌咏一个更高的权威，
我歌咏一千座新兴的城市，将要在那些海岛群中拔
　　地而起，
我的帆船和蒸汽船在群岛中间穿梭，
我的星条旗在风中拍动，
商路打开了，沉睡的几个世纪结束使命，民族再生，
　　再次青春，
人生、事业都恢复了——目标我不知道——但是古
　　老的亚洲一定会更新，
从这一天开始被世界包围。

三

你呀，世界的**自由**！
你将会千秋万代稳坐当中，
因为今天亚洲的贵族从一边来到你面前，
因为明天英国女王要从另一边派她的长子来见你。

迹象在倒转，地球被合围，
圆环已合拢，旅程已结束，
盒子盖只是微微打开着，香气却从整个盒子里喷涌
　　而出。
年轻的自由！对待那可敬的亚洲、一切的母亲，
你从今以后要始终体贴而热情，因为你就是一切，
向那个越过群岛向你发来消息的远方母亲俯下你骄
　　傲的头吧，
就这一次俯下你骄傲的头吧，年轻的**自由**。

那些孩子向西漫游了那么久吗？跨过那么宽广的地
　　方吗？
自乐园[1]以来迷茫的世世代代向西闯荡了那么久吗？

1. 即伊甸园，象征人类最初纯真原始的状态。

多少个世纪为了你、为了某些原因，朝那个方向不断前行而不为人知？

时代都理由充分，它们已大功告成，现在它们也应该被掉转方向，从那边朝你行来，

自由呀，时代现在也应该看在你的分儿上，顺从地向东挺进。

海流

/

出自晃荡不停的摇篮[1]

出自晃荡不停的摇篮，
出自学舌鸟的喉咙、往复如梭的音乐，
出自九月的午夜，
荒芜的沙地和远处的田野上，起了床的孩子独自游
　　荡，光着头，光着脚，
沐浴在一阵阵洒落的光晕下，
俯临着影子们像是活的一样交缠扭摆的神秘游戏，
走出了荆棘和黑莓生长的灌木丛，
记忆中的那只鸟，在我耳边唱过歌，
记忆中悲伤的兄弟，让我听见过一阵阵高低起伏的
　　歌声，
从迟迟升起又胀鼓鼓的仿佛含着泪水的半个黄月亮
　　底下，
从薄雾里最先响起的那些渴望和爱的乐音，

1. 这是惠特曼自传性的名篇，像歌剧（启迪惠特曼开创其自由体的艺术形式）一般层次繁复，大开大阖。诗中有几个独立又有所交融的声音，分别为成年时的诗人、学舌鸟和童年时的诗人，大海则以暗示向童年时的诗人发出话语。

从我心中一千个永不停息的应答，
从自此苏醒的无数词句，
从那个比什么都更强大更悦耳的词语，
从词句如今又开始重返的故地，
就像一群飞鸟，啁啾、腾起、从头顶掠过，
匆匆被送到这里，趁着一切还没有被我忘却，
一个男人，由于这些泪水又成了小男孩，
扑倒在沙地上，面对海浪，
我，痛苦和欢乐的歌手、连接今天和未来的人，
接纳一切暗示来运用它们，但又迅速地跃过它们，
为一件往事歌唱。

从前在鲍玛诺克[1]，
当空气中飘着丁香的芬芳，五月的草正在生长，
从亚拉巴马来了两个披着羽毛的客人，
双双落在海岸上的荆棘丛里，
他们的窝，有四只浅绿带褐色斑点的蛋，
每天那雄鸟在附近飞来飞去，

1. 鲍玛诺克：纽约州长岛的印第安语名称，惠特曼出生在那里，他对这个能唤起他童年回忆的名称情有独钟。

每天那雌鸟蹲在窝里，安安静静，眼睛发亮，
每天，我这好奇的男孩，从不走得太近，从不惊动
　　他们，
小心地窥察着、吸收着、转译着。

闪呀！闪呀！闪呀！
倾注你的温暖，太阳！
我们晒太阳，双双做伴。

双双做伴！
风吹向南，风吹向北，
白天明亮，夜晚黑暗，
家乡，或者远离家乡的河流山脉，
只要我们相守，
就一直唱歌，忘记时光。

突然有一天，
上午雌鸟没有蹲在鸟巢里，
也许被捕杀了，她的伙伴不知道，
下午也没有回来，第二天也没有，
再也没有出现。

从此以后整个夏天在大海的声音中，
在黑夜里满月当空而天气较平静的时分，
在波涛哗哗汹涌的海上，
或者白天在丛丛荆棘之上，
我时常看见那只遗留的雄鸟飞过，
听见那来自亚拉巴马的孤独客声。

吹吧！吹吧！吹吧！
海风狂吹鲍玛诺克的海岸吧；
我等呀等，直到你把我的伙伴吹回来。

是的，当星光闪烁，
他彻夜站在长满青苔的木桩尖上，
几乎就在海浪的拍拍打打中，
孤单的歌手，奇异而催泪。
他呼唤他的伙伴，
他倾吐的心声，人类中只有我懂得。

是的，我懂得我的兄弟，
别人也许不懂，但我一直珍重每一粒乐音。
因为我不止一次懵懵懂懂地溜到海滩，

安静，避开月光，把自己藏在阴影里，
现在还记得那些模糊的形状、回响、种种声音和景象，
浪花破开的白手臂不知疲倦地挥舞着，
我，光脚的孩子，被风吹动着头发，
倾听了很久很久。

倾听来保存、来歌唱，时而转译乐音，
来追随你的歌声，兄弟。

抚慰！抚慰！抚慰！
后浪紧紧地抚慰着前浪，
又被下一个浪紧紧地拥抱、拍打，
但是我所爱的不抚慰我了，不抚慰了。

低垂的月亮，迟迟升起，
它那么迟缓——噢，我想它是重负着爱情，爱情。

啊，大海疯狂地扑向陆地，
怀着爱情，爱情。

啊，黑夜！我看见的莫不是我的爱侣在浪花里翻飞？
我在那白浪里看见的小黑点是什么？

嘹亮！嘹亮！嘹亮！
我嘹亮地呼唤你，我的爱侣！
我抛出我高亢清晰的声音越过波浪，
你一定知道在这里的是谁，是谁，
你一定知道我是谁，爱侣。
低垂的月亮！
你黄褐色脸盘上的暗点是什么？
啊，就是她的形状，我伙伴的形状！
月亮啊别再扣留她，还给我吧。

陆地！陆地！噢，陆地！
不管我转向何方，噢，我想你可以交还我的伙伴，
　　只要你肯，
因为不管我望向何方，我都好像是依稀看见了她。

啊，上升的星星！
也许我渴望的那个也会升上天空，和你们一同升起。

啊，喉咙！啊，颤动的喉咙！
发出更清晰的声音越过空气！
穿透树林、大地，

我渴望的那个一定在某地切盼着听见你。

放声歌唱吧！
寂寞此地，黑夜之歌！
孤单爱恋之歌！死亡之歌！
在那迟缓的、消殒的黄月亮下面歌唱！
啊，在月亮下，在她几乎沉入大海的地方！
啊，不顾一切的绝望之歌。

但是轻些！压低！
轻些！让我只是呢喃吧，
你呀，喧嚣的大海，请你也停一停，
因为我相信我听见了伙伴正在什么地方回应着，
那么微弱，我得安静，安静地听，
但不能彻底安静，那样她可能不会立即来我这儿。

来这儿呀爱侣！
我在这儿！这儿！
我只用这刚能听见的歌声向你宣告我自己，
这轻柔的呼唤是给你的，我的爱，给你的。
不要上当去了别的地方，

那是风的呼啸，不是我的声音，
那是翻飞的、翻飞的浪花，
那些是树叶的影子。

噢，黑暗！噢，徒然！
噢，我多么苦闷多么哀伤。

啊，天空中月亮旁边的褐色光晕，低垂在海上！
啊，海中散乱的倒影！
啊，喉咙！啊，搏动的心！
我彻夜无效地唱着，无效。

啊，过往！啊，快活的日子！啊，欢乐的歌！
在空中，在树林，在田野上，
爱过！爱过！爱过！爱过！爱过！
但是我的伙伴不再，不再跟着我了！
我俩不再双双。

咏叹调沉寂了，
别的一切都还继续，星光闪闪，
风在吹，鸟的乐音在久久地回响，

凶猛的老母亲[1]不断发出她愤怒的呻吟，
在鲍玛诺克岸边沙沙作响的灰色海滩上，
半个黄月亮变大了，耷拉着，下垂着，几乎贴到大海
    的脸，
男孩心醉神迷，波浪戏弄着他的赤脚，空气撩拨着
    他的头发，
长久禁闭在心里的爱，现在自由了，现在终于轰然
    爆发了，
咏叹调的含义，耳朵、灵魂，迅速地将它储存，
奇异的眼泪淌下脸颊，
三者[2]在那里对话，各有各的言说，
低声部是狂野的老母亲在不断地叫着，
阴冷地应和着男孩的灵魂的提问节奏，嘶嘶吐出某
    个淹没的秘密，
回答那起步的诗人。
不是精灵就是鸟了！（男孩的灵魂说，）
你真是在对你的伙伴唱歌？还是其实是对我？

---

1. 惠特曼常用老母亲来喻指大海。他写诗有时喜欢采用一些法文词，法文中“母亲”（la mère）与“大海”（la mer）同音。

2. 三者指雄鸟、大海和孩子。

因为，那时是个孩子，我舌头的用处还在沉睡，现在
　　却听见了你的话语，
现在我一瞬间知道了我为何而生，我觉醒了，
已经有一千名歌手、一千首歌，比你的歌更清晰、更
　　嘹亮，也更哀伤，
一千种婉转的回声被我内心的生命振起，永不消亡。

哦，你这孤独的歌手，只身唱歌，投影出我的未来，
哦，孤独的我在倾听，我将会永远不息让你不被遗忘，
我将永远不会逃避，永远不会有震颤的回声、
有不得满足的爱的呼喊被我听而不闻，
我将永远不再是那一夜之前的平静的孩子，
在那下沉的黄月亮照临的海边，
使者在那里被唤醒，看见了火，甜蜜的内心地狱，
未知的渴求，我的天命。

啊，给我线索！（它潜伏在这黑夜的某个地方，）
啊，如果我可以得到那么多，再多给一些！

就一个词吧，（因为我能征服它，）
那个最终的词，超乎一切的词，

不着痕迹，送来了——它是什么？——我在倾听；
你低语着的就是它吗，海浪，一直是它？
从你晶莹的浪沫和潮湿的沙中来的就是它？

大海对此回答，
没有延宕，没有匆忙，
一整夜都在对我低语，在天亮前已十分清楚，
喃喃对我说着那个低沉悦耳的词：死亡，
一再地说死亡，死亡，死亡，死亡，
嘶嘶发出的美妙音调，不像那鸟鸣也不像我这孩子
　　的激动心跳，
却渐渐向我一个人贴近，在我脚边簌簌响动，
从那里平稳地爬上我的耳朵，轻柔地冲洗我的全身，
死亡，死亡，死亡，死亡，死亡。

这我没有忘记，
但对于我那幽暗的精灵和兄弟，
在鲍玛诺克的灰色海滩月光下给我唱的歌，
我将它和一千首应答的歌任意融合，
使我自己觉醒于那个时刻的歌，
海浪传来的那个词是开启它们的钥匙，

那钥匙关乎最甜蜜的歌和一切的歌，
那强大悦耳的词，悄悄爬上我的脚——
（或者像一个老婆婆晃动着摇篮，衣裳发出好闻的气
　　味，在旁边弯腰，）
大海给我的低语。

当我跟生命之海一同退潮

一

当我跟生命之海一同退潮，
当我在熟悉的海岸漫步，
当我行走在那里，涟漪不断冲洗着你，鲍玛诺克，
细浪沙沙涌上来，嘶哑地响动，
那里凶猛的老母亲不断哭叫着被风浪放逐的人，
这秋日傍晚默想的我，向南方凝望，
内心放电般流动的豪迈诗情一度将我抓住，
那个追踪脚下百千行[1]的精灵将我凭附，
沉渣积在海的边缘，代表地球上所有的水域和所有
　　的陆地。

我被深深吸引，目光从南方转回，垂下，追随那些
　　狭长的堆集，

1. 原文 lines 可能暗指诗行，惠特曼有多首涉及漫步的诗，这似乎是他获取灵感的一种方式。

谷糠、麦秆、碎木片、海草、海胶[1]，
浮渣、闪亮岩石的鳞屑、咸莴苣的叶子——潮水的
　　遗留，
几英里的行走，另一侧响着波浪破开的声音，
当时当刻，鲍玛诺克令我想起物我一致的古老观念，
你这鱼形的岛呀，你向我呈现过这些，
当我在熟悉的海岸漫步，
当我内心带电、行走着寻思题材的时候。

二

当我再走向不熟悉的海岸，
当我倾听那哀歌，遇难的男男女女的声音，
当我吸进向我扑来的不可触及的微风，
当神秘莫测的海洋对着我席卷而来，越来越近，
我也最多不过像是一点冲上来的碎片，
一些沙子和死去的叶，差可收集，
收集、糅合我自己于沙子和碎片之中。

---

1. Sea-gluten（海胶）是惠特曼生造的复合词，可能指海中动物的黏稠分泌物或富含蛋白的动物组织。

啊，困顿、受阻、弯腰贴近地面，

我由于自己曾经胆敢张嘴而深感压迫，

现在已知道我发出过的所有吹嘘都对我反唇相讥，我从来不曾理解自己的身份和本质。

在我所有狂傲的诗歌面前真正的我从未被触碰，被表露，完全不可即，

退缩在远处，用戏仿祝贺的手势和鞠躬嘲弄着我，

对我写下的每个词遥遥发出一串串反讽的笑声，

默默指着这些歌，再指指下面的流沙。

我感受到我没有真的明白过什么，哪怕只是一样东西，这是谁也做不到的，

大自然在这里利用海的景象对我拨弄，射中我、刺痛我，

因为我曾经胆敢张嘴唱歌。

三

你们这两个海，我向你们逼近，

我们都一样喃喃地责备着卷起沙子和漂流物，不知原因，

这些小碎片确实代表你们和我和所有的人。

你这脆弱的海岸，布满一道道残渣，
你这鱼形的岛，我取用脚下的一切，
父亲[1]，属于你的就属于我。

我也这样，鲍玛诺克，
我也有过破灭的泡沫，经过漫漫无边的漂流，被冲
　　上你的岸滩，
我也只是一道漂浮的碎屑，
鱼形的岛，我也在你身上留下小小的残骸。

我扑向你的胸膛，父亲，
我紧紧地贴着你，让你不能松开我，
我牢牢抱住你直到你给我一个答案。

亲吻我，父亲，
用你的嘴唇抚慰我，就像我抚慰那些我爱的人，
当我拥抱着你，请用气息对我说我所羡慕的喃喃之
　　中的秘密。

---

1. 父亲喻指生养了诗人的鲍玛诺克岛，与大海母亲相对，可能也兼指和诗人关系疏离的生身父亲。

四

退潮吧，生命之海，（水流将会回来，）
不要停止你的呻吟，凶猛的老母亲，
不断地为被你放逐的人哭叫吧，但不要害怕我、拒绝我，
当我触摸你或向你收集，不要那么嘶哑而愤怒地对着我的脚沙沙涌上来。

我对你和所有人心怀温柔，
我为自己而收集，也为这个幽灵，它俯视我们前进的方向，追踪我和我的全部。

我和我的全部，散乱的堆集、小小的尸体，
浮沫，雪一般白，泡影，
（看，从我僵死的嘴唇终于流出渗出物，
看，那五光十色在闪亮，在滚动的，）
一团团麦秆、沙子、碎块，
因许多互相矛盾的情绪而浮游至此，
来自风暴、长久的沉寂、黑暗、汹涌，

默想着，思索着，一口气息、一滴咸泪、一抹液体或
泥土，
全都一样出自无穷尽酝酿翻腾的过程，
一两朵疲软的花，已破败，也照样漂浮在浪头上，随
波逐流，
大自然呜咽的哀歌也照样对我们播送，
云中的号角也照样在我们所来的地方吹响，
我们，捉摸不定，不知自己从何方来到这里，在你
面前散开，
你在那高处或行或坐，
不管你是谁，我们也在你脚下零落。

泪水[1]

泪水！泪水！泪水！
黑夜里，孤独时，泪水，
在白色海岸上滴落，滴落，被沙滩吮干，
泪水，一颗星星也不闪，处处幽暗而荒凉，
从蒙头人的眼睛里流出潮湿的泪水；
啊，那幽灵是谁？那幽暗中流泪的影子是谁？
那不成形状的一团，弯着腰，蹲在沙滩上的是什么？
涌流的泪水，抽泣的泪水，挣扎，间杂着喘气的放声号哭；
啊，暴风雨，凝聚了，升腾了，在海滩一带横冲直撞！
啊，狂野阴森的黑夜暴雨，挟着风——啊，狠狠地喷射！
啊，白天里那么文静有礼的幽灵，面容平和，步子沉稳，
但在无人看见的黑夜，你肆意地飞驰——啊，海洋也

1. 英文 tear 既表示裂口（名词）、撕裂（动词），也表示眼泪，此诗利用了词义的这个叠合来组织意象。

搅乱，

迸裂出泪水！泪水！泪水！

给军舰鸟[1]

你先在暴风雨之上一夜沉睡，
再抖擞巨大的翅膀腾空醒来，
（冲破了风暴？你越过它向上飞升，
安歇在天空，天空是推你摇篮的奴仆，）
如今蓝色的一点，远远地遨游太空，
迎着这里甲板上的光线我对你仰望，
（我是个斑点，茫茫世界中浮游的一个微粒。）

在远远的海上，
一夜惊涛将船只的残骸零散地搁在岸边以后，
如今重新出现快乐宁静的白天，
玫瑰色轻盈的黎明、闪耀的太阳，
一大片蔚蓝清澈的长空里，
你也重新出现了。
你天生是大风的对手，（羽翼占满身体，）

---

1. 惠特曼依据法国史学家儒勒·米什莱的一首诗作的英译本而改写成此诗。早在尚未出版《草叶集》的年轻岁月，惠特曼已读过米什莱的著作，颇受其熏陶。

能应付天空大地大海和飓风，
你驭风而行的船从不收帆，
接连数日、数周也不知疲倦、继续向前，穿过空间，
　　在诸域旋转，
黄昏时俯瞰过塞内加尔，早晨就到了阿美利加，
你在闪电和雷云中间游戏，
在这些之中，在你的体验中，你拥有我的灵魂，
何等的快乐！何等的快乐属于你！

在船上的舵轮旁

在船上的舵轮旁，
一个年轻舵手小心地操纵航向。

透过浓雾，海岸上哀哀响彻着
一口海洋钟——啊，是波浪摇动的一口警钟。

啊，你给了很好的提醒，你这口钟在暗礁旁鸣响，
鸣响，鸣响，警告船只不要误撞翻沉。

因为舵手啊，警惕的你在意那响亮的告诫，
拨转了船头，满载的货船张着灰色船帆顺应风向，加速离去，
雍容美丽的船带着她所有的珍宝加速离去，欢快又安全。

但是那只船，不朽的船啊！船上的船啊！
肉体的船，灵魂的船，一直航行，航行，航行。

在黑夜的海滩上

在黑夜的海滩上，
站着一个孩子和她的父亲，
观看着东方，秋季的天空。

在那幽暗的高处，
贪婪吞噬的云，埋葬云，一团团黑压压地张开，
阴沉而迅速地横扫天空压下来之际，
在东方依然余留的一带澄辉中间，
升起了大而静穆的众星之王朱庇特[1]，
离它不远，略高一点的地方，
游动着纤巧的七姊妹星[2]。
孩子握着父亲的手从海滩仰望，
那些埋葬云胜利地下降，顷刻间就要吞食一切，
她静静地哭了。

别哭，孩子，

---

1. 即木星。
2. 即金牛座的昴宿星团。希腊神话中，七姊妹星是肩负天宇的阿特拉斯的七个女儿。

别哭，我的宝贝，
让我用亲吻擦掉你的泪水，
那些贪婪吞噬的云的胜利不会长久，
它们不会长久地占有天空，它们吞食星星只是一个
　　幻象，
朱庇特会出来的，耐心点，过天晚上再看，七姊妹星
　　会出来的，
它们是不朽的，所有这些银色和金色的星星都会再
　　次闪光，
大的星星和小的星星都会再次闪光，它们会长存，
巨大而不朽的恒星、长存而默想的卫星都会再次闪光。

那么，我的小心肝，你只为朱庇特难过吗？
你只惦记被埋葬的星星？

有一点什么，
（我用嘴唇抚慰着你，低声加一句，
我给你最初的一个暗示、难题和言外之意，）
有一点什么甚至比星星更为不朽，
（许多埋葬，许多日日夜夜，正在过去，）
有一点什么甚至比灿烂的朱庇特更能长存，

比太阳或任何旋转的卫星更长，

也长过光采夺目的七姊妹星。

海水之下的世界

海水之下的世界,
海底的森林, 千枝万叶,
海莴苣、大片的苔藓、奇异的花和种子、茂密的缠结、
　　罅隙孔穴、粉红色的草皮,
斑斓的彩色, 淡灰和绿、紫、白、金, 光线穿透海水
　　的游戏,
无声的游泳者置身岩石、珊瑚、海胶、杂草、丛生植
　　物中间, 还有游泳者的食物,
懒惰的生物在那里悬浮觅食, 或贴近海底慢慢地爬行,
抹香鲸上到海面喷出气体和水花, 摆动尾鳍玩耍,
目光呆滞的鲨鱼、海象、海龟、毛茸茸的海豹, 还有
　　魟鱼,
那里有激情、战争、追逐、种群、海洋深处的景象、
　　海里众生呼吸的浓稠空气,

从那里转换到这里的景象，转换到像我们一样行走

此界的生物所呼吸的轻快空气，

再从我们这里转换到另种生物行走的其他界域。

独自在黑夜的海滩上

独自在黑夜的海滩上，
当老母亲来回摇晃着吟唱她那沙哑的歌，
当我看着明亮的群星闪烁，我想到万千宇宙和未来的钥匙[1]。

一种茫茫的相似将万物勾连，
一切星球，长成的、未长成的，小的、大的，那些恒星、卫星、行星，
一切空间的距离，不管多宽广，
一切时间的距离，一切无生命的形态，
一切灵魂，一切活着的肉体，尽管它们从不相同，或处于从不相同的世界，
一切气体的、液体的、植物的、矿物的演变，游鱼、走兽，
一切民族、肤色、野蛮、文明、语言，
一切曾经存在或可能存在于这个星球，或任何星球上的个体，

1. “钥匙”（clef）一词为法文，意思是可以用它解开宇宙的奥秘。

一切生命和死亡，一切过去、现在、未来，
这种茫茫的相似贯通它们，历来就贯通着，
也会永远地贯通它们，并紧致地把持和包围它们。

给所有大海、所有船的歌

一

今天来一曲简短粗朴的宣叙调[1]，
关于航行四海的船，各有特殊的旗帜和信号旗，
关于船上无名的英雄——关于远远散开望不到边的
　　海浪，
关于飞溅的浪花，还有呼啸或吹动的海风，
源于这些产生的一首歌，唱给各国的水手，
一波波，如同潮水。

关于少壮和年老的船长，还有伙计，和所有无所畏惧
　　的水手，
关于那极少一撮人，精挑细选，沉默寡言，从不为
　　命运所惊讶，从不因死亡而惶恐，
是你呀，老海洋，你静静地千里挑一，选择了他们，
大海你及时地拣选了族人，联合了各国，
声音沙哑的老保姆，他们受你哺育，象征着你，

1. 宣叙调又译朗诵调，原指歌剧里介乎歌唱和说话之间的演唱方式，与咏叹调相比，宣叙调着重叙事，旋律简单。

像你一样无可屈服、桀骜不驯。

（不管在海上还是陆地，英雄们从来零零星星地出现，
这血统始终保有而从未丧失，虽然稀罕，却留着足够的种子。）

二

大海啊，招展你那些各国不同的旗帜！
招展各色各样的信号旗，始终让人看见！
但是请你在一切之上为你自己和人类的灵魂特别保留一面旗，
一个用精神织就而代表万国的徽号、人类昂扬超越死亡的标志，
代表一切勇敢的船长和一切无所畏惧的水手和伙计，
也纪念一切忠于职守而沉入海底的人，
这是他们的记忆，由一切无所畏惧的老少船长编织而成，
一面普世的信号旗，在一切时代轻灵地飘扬，俯临着所有勇敢的水手，
所有大海、所有船。

巡行巴尼加特[1]

张狂又张狂的风暴，大海翻滚着巨浪，
咆哮不停的风，低声部永不间断地发出嗡嗡，
一阵阵恶魔般的笑声刺耳地鸣响，
浪、风、午夜，最野蛮的三位一体鞭打着，
那边黑影堆里乳白色的梳子[2]纷纷扫下来，
凶猛的雪片斜打着海滩的冰棱和沙子，
灭绝的东风穿过那里的幽暗扑袭着，
穿过锐利的旋风和飞澜警惕而坚定地前进，
（那远远的东西！是条翻沉的船？红色信号灯是否在
　　闪烁？）
海滩的冰棱和沙子不知疲倦地漫游直到黎明，
坚定地、缓慢地，穿过无休无止的沙哑咆哮，
沿着被那些乳白色梳子扫出的午夜边缘，

1. 巴尼加特是新泽西州的一个长达 30 英里的海湾，惠特曼晚年住在新泽西州肯顿，有时会到访此地。原诗为十四行商籁体，每行均以现在分词 -ing 形式来结尾；不计括号部分的问句，全诗始终没有出现陈述句的谓语动词，从头到尾用状语成分来描述情态，紧张感十足。
2. Comb 可以表示梳子，也可以表示鸡冠或蜂窝状的东西，这里暗喻浪头。

一群迷蒙、怪异的形体，挣扎着，跟黑夜对抗，
那野蛮的三位一体在警觉地注视。

在海船后面

在海船后面，在呼呼的风后面，
在桅杆和绳索拉紧的灰白船帆后面，
底下，千万个波浪在奔走，高高抬着脖子，
不停地向着大船的航迹流动而去，
海洋的波浪们汩汩冒着水泡，惬意地东张西望，
波浪，起伏的波浪，形状不定，高高低低，你追我赶，
欢笑而轻快，跑着弧线，奔向旋转的急流，
那里是大船的航行和转向把海面破开的地方，
大大小小的波浪便在那汪洋中热切地流动，
在海船过处的航迹中，波浪在阳光下闪耀、游戏，
一支混杂的队伍，带着无数斑斓的泡沫和碎片，
追随着雍容疾驰的船，追随她的航迹。

译后记

/

这本小册子分为两个部分，共十九首诗。惠特曼晚年亲自编订了《草叶集》（1891—1892）最终版，企鹅出版社从中摘选两个相邻而完整的子集《候鸟》《海流》组成了这个微型选本。

《候鸟》探索了不同类型的运动变化，有宇宙从缺陷趋于完美的进程，有美国向西的开拓，有自我身份的追寻，也有历史的波澜、文明的盛衰。这组诗并不包含惠特曼的代表作，但是它视野宏大，富于诗人早期作品的特色，自有动人之处。《海流》则喻示着诗人创作重心的转变：基调从开拓精神、唯物论和个人性走向了内省、唯灵论以及同物无虑的信仰。而自《草叶集》问世以来，恐怕

《海流》就比《候鸟》更能抓住读者的心，它语调亲密，多用诗人童年记忆中的大海、沙滩、星月、飞鸟组织意象，探索那“勾连万物”的“茫茫相似”（《独自在黑夜的海滩上》）。诗与诗环环相扣，回味深长，头两首《出自晃荡不停的摇篮》《当我跟生命之海一同退潮》早已成为经典，值得一读再读。

十几年前，由于成长和爱情的经历，我被惠特曼的一些诗深深打动，翻译过诗人最终收录在子集《芦笛》的一组十二首诗以及另一首自传性的名作 *There Was a Child Went Forth*（标题拙译为《有一个孩子脱颖而出》）。《草叶集》在我国已经有多个全译本，选译本更难计数，我本来以为自己不会再动翻译惠特曼的念头了。文学译本有时代性，此番企鹅出版社希望用新文字来呈现这位 19 世纪大诗人的风貌，我考虑后愿意尝试。翻译它，从准备到译成不过短短几个月，却重新燃烧起我对惠特曼的热情。译稿完成对于我大概不会是结束，而是一个新开始。

无论选择与否，我们都走在前人铺过的路上（见本书《因为前人》一诗）。我事先挑选了两个颇受好评的《草叶集》全译本作参考，工作之中也将它们展卷置于案头。我借鉴了这些译本的样式和语调，有时遇到特别优美灵巧的处理，自问无法更进一步或别开生面的时候，就沿用了前辈的译法。为此，我要郑重向这两位前辈译者——邹仲之先生和已故的赵萝蕤先生致以谢忱和敬意。然而，任何译本都只是一种诠释，原文才是译者的圣经。我对每首诗的主题、词义、句法、韵律都独立推敲，任何细节均不欲盲从前贤，务求从原著中得到肺腑之中的感情共鸣及理性体会才落笔。翻译有时像是跟作者对话，但这次翻译与其说是惠特曼和我的对话，不如说是四方（他、三位译者）隔着时空的交谈，只不过我只记录了自己的心得。当下读来，我满意这份记录，但是选手并不能同时做裁判。本人在原诗理解和风格再现方面跟前辈有何差异，在文字取舍间可能有何得失，我不想自己举例，感兴趣的读者可以自行比较。盼望大家慷慨赐教，推动惠特曼中译的继续进步。

本书的编辑白姗提了许多细致而宝贵的意见，令译稿得有寸进，也要向她道谢。

除了上述两个译本，此书的注释、译后记里对本书两组诗的阐释，还参考了 Routledge 出版社 1998 年版《惠特曼百科全书》、Norton 出版社的英文《草叶集》，并其他几部英文传记和研究专著。

惠特曼自由奔放的诗篇给人潇洒的印象，却绝非随意散漫的创作：从他36岁时自费出版薄薄一册的《草叶集》首版开始，到72岁临终前发表极厚重的第九版《草叶集》定本，数十年之间，诗人屡次仔细修改自己的每首作品，使技法趋于成熟、内容趋于饱满，有手稿和不同版次为证。如果说诗在翻译中折损属于必然，那么我也努力追随了前人的脚步来减少折损，力求从形式和精神两方面趋近原作。惠特曼擅长以“你”呼唤读者，常令人在当下看见自己，肉体灵魂都感受到他的永在。希望我的工作没有辜负诗人的一片苦心。

郑远涛2018年5月记于美国西海岸

（时为惠特曼出生月、他诞辰的第199周年）

企鹅经典：小黑书　第三辑

21. 漂亮的卡桑德拉
[英] 简·奥斯汀

22. 温顺的女人
[俄] 陀思妥耶夫斯基

23. 猫与维纳斯
[古希腊] 伊索

24. 黄昏之读
[英] 查尔斯·狄更斯

25. 一个可怕的故事是如何被一条普通的屠夫的狗公之于众的
[德] 约翰·彼得·黑贝尔

26. 亚瑟·萨维尔勋爵的罪行
[英] 奥斯卡·王尔德

27. 伊凡·伊里奇之死
[俄] 列夫·托尔斯泰

28. 我们为何为同一件事哭和笑
[法] 蒙田

29. 我的生命是一杆上实弹的枪
[美] 艾米莉·狄金森

30. 独自在黑夜的海滩上
[美] 沃尔特·惠特曼

Penguin Little Black Classics Vol. III

21. JANE AUSTEN
    The Beautifull Cassandra

22. FYODOR DOSTOYEVSKY
    The Meek One

23. AESOP
    The Cat and Venus

24. CHARLES DICKENS
    To Be Read at Dusk

25. JOHANN PETER HEBEL
    How a Ghastly Story Was Brought to Light by a Common or Garden Butcher's Dog

26. OSCAR WILDE
    Lord Arthur Savile's Crime

27. LEO TOLSTOY
    The Death of Ivan Ilyich

28. MICHEL DE MONTAIGNE
    How We Weep and Laugh at the Same Thing

29. EMILY DICKINSON
    My life had stood a loaded gun

30. WALT WHITMAN
    On the Beach at Night Alone

‘All nations,
colors,
barbarisms,
civilizations,
languages . . .’

WALT WHITMAN

On the Beach at Night Alone

Contents

BIRDS OF PASSAGE

Song of the Universal

1

Come said the Muse,
Sing me a song no poet yet has chanted,
Sing me the universal.

In this broad earth of ours,
Amid the measureless grossness and the slag,
Enclosed and safe within its central heart,
Nestles the seed perfection.

By every life a share or more or less,
None born but it is born, conceal'd or unconceal'd the seed
is waiting.

2

Lo! keen-eyed towering science,
As from tall peaks the modern overlooking,
Successive absolute fiats issuing.

Yet again, lo! the soul, above all science,
For it has history gather'd like husks around the globe,
For it the entire star-myriads roll through the sky.

In spiral routes by long detours,
(As a much-tacking ship upon the sea,)
For it the partial to the permanent flowing;
For it the real to the ideal tends.

For it the mystic evolution,
Not the right only justified, what we call evil also justified.

Forth from their masks, no matter what,
From the huge festering trunk, from craft and guile and
    tears,
Health to emerge and joy, joy universal.
Out of the bulk, the morbid and the shallow,
Out of the bad majority, the varied countless frauds of men
    and states,
Electric, antiseptic yet, cleaving, suffusing all,
Only the good is universal.

3

Over the mountain-growths disease and sorrow,
An uncaught bird is ever hovering, hovering,
High in the purer, happier air.

From imperfection's murkiest cloud,
Darts always forth one ray of perfect light,
One flash of heaven's glory.

To fashion's, custom's discord,
To the mad Babel-din, the deafening orgies,
Soothing each lull a strain is heard, just heard,
From some far shore the final chorus sounding.

O the blest eyes, the happy hearts,
That see, that know the guiding thread so fine,
Along the mighty labyrinth.

4

And thou America,
For the scheme's culmination, its thought and its reality,
For these (not for thyself) thou has arrived.

Thou too surroundest all,
Embracing carrying welcoming all, thou too by pathways
  broad and new,
To the ideal tendest.

The measur'd faiths of other lands, the grandeurs of the
  past,
Are not for thee, but grandeurs of thine own,
Deific faiths and amplitudes, absorbing,
  comprehending all,
All eligible to all.

All, all for immortality,
Love like the light silently wrapping all,
Nature's amelioration blessing all,
The blossoms, fruits of ages, orchards divine and certain,

Forms, objects, growths, humanities, to spirtual images
 ripening.

Give me O God to sing that thought,
Give me, give him or her I love this quenchless faith,
In Thy ensemble, whatever else withheld withhold not
 from us,
Belief in plan of Thee enclosed in Time and Space,
Health, peace, salvation universal.

Is it a dream?
Nay but the lack of it the dream,
And failing it life's lore and wealth a dream,
And all the world a dream.

Pioneers! O Pioneers!

Come my tan-faced children,
Follow well in order, get your weapons ready,
Have you your pistols? have you your sharp-edged axes?
Pioneers! O pioneers!

For we cannot tarry here,
We must march my darlings, we must bear the brunt of danger,
We the youthful sinewy races, all the rest on us depend,
Pioneers! O pioneers!

O you youths, Western youths,
So impatient, full of action, full of manly pride and friendship,
Plain I see you Western youths, see you tramping with the foremost,
Pioneers! O pioneers!

Have the elder races halted?
Do they droop and end their lesson, wearied over there beyond the seas?
We take up the task eternal, and the burden and the lesson,
Pioneers! O pioneers!

All the past we leave behind,
We debouch upon a newer mightier world, varied world,
Fresh and strong the world we seize, world of labor and the march,
Pioneers! O pioneers!

We detachments steady throwing,
Down the edges, through the passes, up the mountains steep,
Conquering, holding, daring, venturing as we go the unknown ways,
Pioneers! O pioneers!

We primeval forests felling,
We the rivers stemming, vexing we and piercing deep the mines within,
We the surface broad surveying, we the virgin soil upheaving,
Pioneers! O pioneers!

Colorado men are we,
From the peaks gigantic, from the giant sierras and the high plateaus,
From the mine and from the gully, from the hunting trail we come,
Pioneers! O pioneers!

From Nebraska, from Arkansas,
Central inland race are we, from Missouri, with the continental blood intervein'd,
All the hands of comrades clasping, all the Southern, all the Northern,
Pioneers! O pioneers!

O resistless restless race!
O beloved race in all! O my breast aches with tender love
for all!
O I mourn and yet exult, I am rapt with love for all,
Pioneers! O pioneers!

Raise the mighty mother mistress,
Waving high the delicate mistress, over all the starry
mistress, (bend your heads all,)
Raise the fang'd and warlike mistress, stern, impassive,
weapon'd mistress,
Pioneers! O pioneers!

See my children, resolute children,
By those swarms upon our rear we must never yield or falter,
Ages back in ghostly millions frowning there behind us
urging,
Pioneers! O pioneers!

On and on the compact ranks,
With accessions ever waiting, with the places of the dead
quickly fill'd,
Through the battle, through defeat, moving yet and never
stopping,
Pioneers! O pioneers!

O to die advancing on!
Are there some of us to droop and die? has the hour come?
Then upon the march we fittest die, soon and sure the gap
is fill'd,
Pioneers! O pioneers!

All the pulses of the world,
Falling in they beat for us, with the Western movement beat,
Holding single or together, steady moving to the front, all for us,
Pioneers! O pioneers!

Life's involv'd and varied pageants,
All the forms and shows, all the workmen at their work,
All the seamen and the landsmen, all the masters with their slaves,
Pioneers! O pioneers!

All the hapless silent lovers,
All the prisoners in the prisons, all the righteous and the wicked,
All the joyous, all the sorrowing, all the living, all the dying,
Pioneers! O pioneers!

I too with my soul and body,
We, a curious trio, picking, wandering on our way,
Through these shores amid the shadows, with the apparitions pressing,
Pioneers! O pioneers!

Lo, the darting bowling orb!
Lo, the brother orbs around, all the clustering suns and planets,
All the dazzling days, all the mystic nights with dreams,
Pioneers! O pioneers!

These are of us, they are with us,
All for primal needed work, while the followers there in
embryo wait behind,
We to-day's procession heading, we the route for travel
clearing,
Pioneers! O pioneers!

O you daughters of the West!
O you young and elder daughters! O you mothers and you
wives!
Never must you be divided, in our ranks you move united,
Pioneers! O pioneers!

Minstrels latent on the prairies!
(Shrouded bards of other lands, you may rest, you have
done your work,)
Soon I hear you coming warbling, soon you rise and tramp
amid us,
Pioneers! O pioneers!

Not for delectations sweet,
Not the cushion and the slipper, not the peaceful and the
studious,
Not the riches safe and palling, not for us the tame enjoyment,
Pioneers! O pioneers!

Do the feasters gluttonous feast?
Do the corpulent sleepers sleep? have they lock'd and
bolted doors?
Still be ours the diet hard, and the blanket on the ground,
Pioneers! O pioneers!

Has the night descended?
Was the road of late so toilsome? did we stop discouraged
nodding on our way?
Yet a passing hour I yield you in your tracks to pause
oblivious,
Pioneers! O pioneers!

Till with sound of trumpet,
Far, far off the daybreak call – hark! how loud and clear I
hear it wind,
Swift! to the head of the army!–swift! spring to your
places,
Pioneers! O pioneers!

To You

Whoever you are, I fear you are walking the walks of dreams,
I fear these supposed realities are to melt from under your feet and hands,
Even now your features, joys, speech, house, trade, manners, troubles, follies, costume, crimes, dissipate away from you,
Your true soul and body appear before me,
They stand forth out of affairs, out of commerce, shops, work, farms, clothes, the house, buying, selling, eating, drinking, suffering, dying.

Whoever you are, now I place my hand upon you, that you be my poem,
I whisper with my lips close to your ear,
I have loved many women and men, but I love none better than you.

O I have been dilatory and dumb,
I should have made my way straight to you long ago,
I should have blabb'd nothing but you, I should have chanted nothing but you.

I will leave all and come and make the hymns of you,
None has understood you, but I understand you,
None has done justice to you, you have not done justice to yourself,

None but has found you imperfect, I only find no
    imperfection in you,
None but would subordinate you, I only am he who will
    never consent to subordinate you,
I only am he who places over you no master, owner, better,
    God, beyond what waits intrinsically in yourself.

Painters have painted their swarming groups and the
    centre-figure of all,
From the head of the centre-figure spreading a nimbus of
    gold-color'd light,
But I paint myriads of heads, but paint no head without its
    nimbus of gold-color'd light,
From my hand from the brain of every man and woman it
    streams, effulgently flowing forever.
O I could sing such grandeurs and glories about you!
You have not known what you are, you have slumber'd
    upon yourself all your life,
Your eyelids have been the same as closed most of the
    time,
What you have done returns already in mockeries,
(Your thrift, knowledge, prayers, if they do not return in
    mockeries, what is their return?)

The mockeries are not you,
Underneath them and within them I see you lurk,
I pursue you where none else has pursued you,
Silence, the desk, the flippant expression, the night, the
    accustom'd routine, if these conceal you from others or
    from yourself, they do not conceal you from me,

The shaved face, the unsteady eye, the impure complexion,
if these balk others they do not balk me,
The pert apparel, the deform'd attitude, drunkenness,
greed, premature death, all these I part aside.

There is no endowment in man or woman that is not tallied
in you,
There is no virtue, no beauty in man or woman, but as
good is in you,
No pluck, no endurance in others, but as good is in you,
No pleasure waiting for others, but an equal pleasure waits
for you.

As for me, I give nothing to any one except I give the like
carefully to you,
I sing the songs of the glory of none, not God, sooner than
I sing the songs of the glory of you.

Whoever you are! claim your own at any hazard!
These shows of the East and West are tame compared
to you,
These immense meadows, these interminable rivers, you are
immense and interminable as they,
These furies, elements, storms, motions of Nature, throes of
apparent dissolution, you are he or she who is master or
mistress over them,
Master or mistress in your own right over Nature, elements,
pain, passion, dissolution.

The hopples fall from your ankles, you find an unfailing
sufficiency,
Old or young, male or female, rude, low, rejected by the
rest, whatever you are promulges itself,
Through birth, life, death, burial, the means are provided,
nothing is scanted,
Through angers, losses, ambition, ignorance, ennui, what
you are picks its way.

France, the 18th Year of These States

A great year and place.
A harsh discordant natal scream out-sounding, to touch the mother's heart closer than any yet.

I walk'd the shores of my Eastern sea,
Heard over the waves the little voice,
Saw the divine infant where she woke mournfully wailing, amid the roar of cannon, curses, shouts, crash of falling buildings,
Was not so sick from the blood in the gutters running, nor from the single corpses, nor those in heaps, nor those borne away in the tumbrils,
Was not so desperate at the battues of death – was not so shock'd at the repeated fusillades of the guns.

Pale, silent, stern, what could I say to that long-accrued retribution?
Could I wish humanity different?
Could I wish the people made of wood and stone?
Or that there be no justice in destiny or time?

O Liberty! O mate for me!
Here too the blaze, the grape-shot and the axe, in reserve, to fetch them out in case of need,
Here too, though long represt, can never be destroy'd,
Here too could rise at last murdering and ecstatic,
Here too demanding full arrears of vengeance.

Hence I sign this salute over the sea,
And I do not deny that terrible red birth and baptism,
But remember the little voice that I heard wailing, and wait
with perfect trust, no matter how long,
And from to-day sad and cogent I maintain the bequeath'd
cause, as for all lands,
And I send these words to Paris with my love,
And I guess some chansonniers there will understand them,
For I guess there is latent music yet in France, floods of it,
O I hear already the bustle of instruments, they will soon
be drowning all that would interrupt them,
O I think the east wind brings a triumphal and free march,
It reaches hither, it swells me to joyful madness,
I will run transpose it in words, to justify it,
I will yet sing a song for you ma femme.

Myself and Mine

Myself and mine gymnastic ever,
To stand the cold or heat, to take good aim with a gun, to sail a boat, to manage horses, to beget superb children,
To speak readily and clearly, to feel at home among common people,
And to hold our own in terrible positions on land and sea.

Not for an embroiderer,
(There will always be plenty of embroiderers, I welcome them also,)
But for the fibre of things and for inherent men and women.

Not to chisel ornaments,
But to chisel with free stroke the heads and limbs of plenteous supreme Gods, that the States may realize them walking and talking.
Let me have my own way,
Let others promulge the laws, I will make no account of the laws,
Let others praise eminent men and hold up peace, I hold up agitation and conflict.
I praise no eminent man, I rebuke to his face the one that was thought most worthy.

(Who are you? and what are you secretly guilty of all your life?
Will you turn aside all your life? will you grub and chatter all your life?
And who are you, blabbing by rote, years, pages, languages, reminiscences,
Unwitting to-day that you do not know how to speak properly a single word?)

Let others finish specimens, I never finish specimens,
I start them by exhaustless laws as Nature does, fresh and modern continually.

I give nothing as duties,
What others give as duties I give as living impulses,
(Shall I give the heart's action as a duty?)

Let others dispose of questions, I dispose of nothing, I arouse unanswerable questions,
Who are they I see and touch, and what about them?
What about these likes of myself that draw me so close by tender directions and indirections?

I call to the world to distrust the accounts of my friends, but listen to my enemies, as I myself do,
I charge you forever reject those who would expound me, for I cannot expound myself,
I charge that there be no theory or school founded out of me,
I charge you to leave all free, as I have left all free.
After me, vista!
O I see life is not short, but immeasurably long,

I henceforth tread the world chaste, temperate, an early
riser, a steady grower,
Every hour the semen of centuries, and still of centuries.

I must follow up these continual lessons of the air, water,
earth,
I perceive I have no time to lose.

Year of Meteors (1859–60)

Year of meteors! brooding year!
I would bind in words retrospective some of your deeds
    and signs,
I would sing your contest for the 19th Presidentiad,
I would sing how an old man, tall, with white hair,
    mounted the scaffold in Virginia,
(I was at hand, silent I stood with teeth shut close, I
    watch'd,
I stood very near you old man when cool and indifferent,
    but trembling with age and your unheal'd wounds you
    mounted the scaffold;)
I would sing in my copious song your census returns of the
    States,
The tables of population and products, I would sing of
    your ships and their cargoes,
The proud black ships of Manhattan arriving, some fill'd
    with immigrants, some from the isthmus with cargoes
    of gold,
Songs thereof would I sing, to all that hitherward comes
    would I welcome give,
And you would I sing, fair stripling! welcome to you from
    me, young prince of England!
(Remember you surging Manhattan's crowds as you pass'd
    with your cortege of nobles?
There in the crowds stood I, and singled you out with
    attachment;)

Nor forget I to sing of the wonder, the ship as she swam up my bay,
Well-shaped and stately the Great Eastern swam up my bay, she was 600 feet long,
Her moving swiftly surrounded by myriads of small craft I forget not to sing;
Nor the comet that came unannounced out of the north flaring in heaven,
Nor the strange huge meteor-procession dazzling and clear shooting over our heads,
(A moment, a moment long it sail'd its balls of unearthly light over our heads,
Then departed, dropt in the night, and was gone;)
Of such, and fitful as they, I sing – with gleams from them would I gleam and patch these chants,
Your chants, O year all mottled with evil and good – year of forebodings!
Year of comets and meteors transient and strange – lo! even here one equally transient and strange!
As I flit through you hastily, soon to fall and be gone, what is this chant,
What am I myself but one of your meteors?

With Antecedents

1

With antecedents,
With my fathers and mothers and the accumulations of past
ages,
With all which, had it not been, I would not now be here,
as I am,
With Egypt, India, Phenicia, Greece and Rome,
With the Kelt, the Scandinavian, the Alb and the Saxon,
With antique maritime ventures, laws, artisanship, wars
and journeys,
With the poet, the skald, the saga, the myth, and the
oracle,
With the sale of slaves, with enthusiasts, with the
troubadour, the crusader, and the monk,
With those old continents whence we have come to this
new continent,
With the fading kingdoms and kings over there,
With the fading religions and priests,
With the small shores we look back to from our own large
and present shores,
With countless years drawing themselves onward and
arrived at these years,
You and me arrived – America arrived and making this
year,
This year! sending itself ahead countless years to come.

2

O but it is not the years – it is I, it is You,
We touch all laws and tally all antecedents,
We are the skald, the oracle, the monk and the knight, we
easily include them and more,
We stand amid time beginningless and endless, we stand
amid evil and good,
All swings around us, there is as much darkness as light,
The very sun swings itself and its system of planets
around us,
Its sun, and its again, all swing around us.

As for me, (torn, stormy, amid these vehement days,)
I have the idea of all, and am all and believe in all,
I believe materialism is true and spiritualism is true, I reject
no part.

(Have I forgotten any part? any thing in the past?
Come to me whoever and whatever, till I give you
recognition.)

I respect Assyria, China, Teutonia, and the Hebrews,
I adopt each theory, myth, god, and demi-god,
I see that the old accounts, bibles, genealogies, are true,
without exception,
I assert that all past days were what they must have been,
And that they could no-how have been better than they
were,

And that to-day is what it must be, and that America is,
And that to-day and America could no-how be better than
they are.

3

In the name of these States and in your and my name, the
Past,
And in the name of these States and in your and my name,
the Present time.

I know that the past was great and the future will be great,
And I know that both curiously conjoint in the present
time,
(For the sake of him I typify, for the common average man's
sake, your sake if you are he,)
And that where I am or you are this present day, there is the
centre of all days, all races,
And there is the meaning to us of all that has ever come of
races and days, or ever will come.

A Broadway Pageant

1

Over the Western sea hither from Niphon come,
Courteous, the swart-cheek'd two-sworded envoys,
Leaning back in their open barouches, bare-headed,
impassive,
Ride to-day through Manhattan.

Libertad! I do not know whether others behold what I
behold,
In the procession along with the nobles of Niphon, the
errand-bearers,
Bringing up the rear, hovering above, around, or in the
ranks marching,
But I will sing you a song of what I behold Libertad.
When million-footed Manhattan unpent descends to her
pavements,
When the thunder-cracking guns arouse me with the proud
roar I love,
When the round-mouth'd guns out of the smoke and smell
I love spit their salutes,
When the fire-flashing guns have fully alerted me,
and heaven-clouds canopy my city with a delicate
thin haze,
When gorgeous the countless straight stems, the forests at
the wharves, thicken with colors,
When every ship richly drest carries her flag at the peak,

When pennants trail and street-festoons hang from the windows,
When Broadway is entirely given up to foot-passengers and foot-standers, when the mass is densest,
When the façades of the houses are alive with people, when eyes gaze riveted tens of thousands at a time,
When the guests from the islands advance, when the pageant moves forward visible,
When the summons is made, when the answer that waited thousands of years answers,
I too arising, answering, descend to the pavements, merge with the crowd, and gaze with them.

2

Superb-faced Manhattan!
Comrade Americanos! to us, then at last the Orient comes.

To us, my city,
Where our tall-topt marble and iron beauties range on opposite sides, to walk in the space between,
To-day our Antipodes comes.

The Originatress comes,
The nest of languages, the bequeather of poems, the race of eld,
Florid with blood, pensive, rapt with musings, hot with passion,
Sultry with perfume, with ample and flowing garments,

With sunburnt visage, with intense soul and glittering
eyes,
The race of Brahma comes.

See my cantabile! these and more are flashing to us from
the procession,
As it moves changing, a kaleidoscope divine it moves
changing before us.

For not the envoys nor the tann'd Japanee from his island
only,
Lithe and silent the Hindoo appears, the Asiatic continent
itself appears, the past, the dead,
The murky night-morning of wonder and fable inscrutable,
The envelop'd mysteries, the old and unknown hive-bees,
The north, the sweltering south, eastern Assyria, the
Hebrews, the ancient of ancients,
Vast desolated cities, the gliding present, all of these and
more are in the pageant-procession.

Geography, the world, is in it,
The Great Sea, the brood of islands, Polynesia, the coast
beyond,
The coast you henceforth are facing – you Libertad! from
your Western golden shores,
The countries there with their populations, the millions
en-masse are curiously here,
The swarming market-places, the temples with idols ranged
along the sides or at the end, bonze, brahmin, and
llama,
Mandarin, farmer, merchant, mechanic, and fisherman,

The singing-girl and the dancing-girl, the ecstatic persons, the secluded emperors,
Confucious himself, the great poets and heroes, the warriors, the castes, all,
Trooping up, crowding from all directions, from the Altay mountains,
From Thibet, from the four winding and far-flowing rivers of China,
From the southern peninsulas and the demi-continental islands, from Malaysia,
These and whatever belongs to them palpable show forth to me, and are seiz'd by me,
And I am seiz'd by them, and friendlily held by them,
Till as here them all I chant, Libertad! for themselves and for you.

For I too raising my voice join the ranks of this pageant,
I am the chanter, I chant aloud over the pageant,
I chant the world on my Western sea,
I chant copious the islands beyond, thick as stars in the sky,
I chant the new empire grander than any before, as in a vision it comes to me,
I chant America the mistress, I chant a greater supremacy,
I chant projected a thousand blooming cities yet in time on those groups of sea-islands,
My sail-ships and steam-ships threading the archipelagoes,
My stars and stripes fluttering in the wind,
Commerce opening, the sleep of ages having done its work, races reborn, refresh'd,

Lives, works resumed – the object I know not – but the old, the Asiatic renew'd as it must be,
Commencing from this day surrounded by the world.

3

And you Libertad of the world!
You shall sit in the middle well-pois'd thousands and thousands of years,
As to-day from one side the nobles of Asia come to you,
As to-morrow from the other side the queen of England sends her eldest son to you.

The sign is reversing, the orb is enclosed,
The ring is circled, the journey is done,
The box-lid is but perceptibly open'd, nevertheless the perfume pours copiously out of the whole box.
Young Libertad! with the venerable Asia, the all-mother,
Be considerate with her now and ever hot Libertad, for you are all,
Bend your proud neck to the long-off mother now sending messages over the archipelagoes to you,
Bend your proud neck low for once, young Libertad.

Were the children straying westward so long? so wide the tramping?
Were the precedent dim ages debouching westward from Paradise so long?
Were the centuries steadily footing it that way, all the while unknown, for you, for reasons?

They are justified, they are accomplish'd, they shall now
be turn'd the other way also, to travel toward you
thence,
They shall now also march obediently eastward for your
sake Libertad.

SEA-DRIFT

Out of the Cradle Endlessly Rocking

Out of the cradle endlessly rocking,
Out of the mocking-bird's throat, the musical shuttle,
Out of the Ninth-month midnight,
Over the sterile sands and the fields beyond, where the child leaving his bed wander'd alone, bareheaded, barefoot,
Down from the shower'd halo,
Up from the mystic play of shadows twining and twisting as if they were alive,
Out from the patches of briers and blackberries,
From the memories of the bird that chanted to me,
From your memories sad brother, from the fitful risings and fallings I heard,
From under that yellow half-moon late-risen and swollen as if with tears,
From those beginning notes of yearning and love there in the mist,
From the thousand responses of my heart never to cease,
From the myriad thence-arous'd words,
From the word stronger and more delicious than any,
From such as now they start the scene revisiting,
As a flock, twittering, rising, or overhead passing,

Borne hither, ere all eludes me, hurriedly,
A man, yet by these tears a little boy again,
Throwing myself on the sand, confronting the waves,
I, chanter of pains and joys, uniter of here and hereafter,
Taking all hints to use them, but swiftly leaping beyond them,
A reminiscence sing.

Once Paumanok,
When the lilac-scent was in the air and Fifth-month grass
    was growing,
Up this seashore in some briers,
Two feather'd guests from Alabama, two together,
And their nest, and four light-green eggs spotted with
    brown,
And every day the he-bird to and fro near at hand,
And every day the she-bird crouch'd on her nest, silent,
    with bright eyes,
And every day I, a curious boy, never too close, never
    disturbing them,
Cautiously peering, absorbing, translating.

Shine! shine! shine!
Pour down your warmth, great sun!
While we bask, we two together.

Two together!
Winds blow south, or winds blow north,
Day come white, or night come black,
Home, or rivers and mountains from home,
Singing all time, minding no time,
While we two keep together.

Till of a sudden,
May-be kill'd, unknown to her mate,
One forenoon the she-bird crouch'd not on the nest,
Nor return'd that afternoon, nor the next,
Nor ever appear'd again.

And thenceforward all summer in the sound of the sea,
And at night under the full of the moon in calmer
  weather,
Over the hoarse surging of the sea,
Or flitting from brier to brier by day,
I saw, I heard at intervals the remaining one, the he-bird,
The solitary guest from Alabama.

Blow! blow! blow!
Blow up sea-winds along Paumanok's shore;
I wait and I wait till you blow my mate to me.

Yes, when the stars glisten'd,
All night long on the prong of a moss-scallop'd stake,
Down almost amid the slapping waves,
Sat the lone singer wonderful causing tears.
He call'd on his mate,
He pour'd forth the meanings which I of all men know.

Yes my brother I know,
The rest might not, but I have treasur'd every note,
For more than once dimly down to the beach gliding,
Silent, avoiding the moonbeams, blending myself with the
  shadows,
Recalling now the obscure shapes, the echoes, the sounds
    and sights after their sorts,

The white arms out in the breakers tirelessly tossing,
I, with bare feet, a child, the wind wafting my hair,
Listen'd long and long.

Listen'd to keep, to sing, now translating the notes,
Following you my brother.

Soothe! soothe! soothe!
Close on its wave soothes the wave behind,
And again another behind embracing and lapping, every one
close,
But my love soothes not me, not me.

Low hangs the moon, it rose late,
It is lagging – O I think it is heavy with love, with love.

O madly the sea pushes upon the land,
With love, with love.

O night! do I not see my love fluttering out among the
breakers?
What is that little black thing I see there in the white?

Loud! loud! loud!
Loud I call to you, my love!
High and clear I shoot my voice over the waves,
Surely you must know who is here, is here,
You must know who I am, my love.
Low-hanging moon!
What is that dusky spot in your brown yellow?
O it is the shape, the shape of my mate!
O moon do not keep her from me any longer.

Land! land! O land!
Whichever way I turn, O I think you could give me my mate back again if you only would,
For I am almost sure I see her dimly whichever way I look.

O rising stars!
Perhaps the one I want so much will rise, will rise with some of you.

O throat! O trembling throat!
Sound clearer through the atmosphere!
Pierce the woods, the earth,
Somewhere listening to catch you must be the one I want.

Shake out carols!
Solitary here, the night's carols!
Carols of lonesome love! death's carols!
Carols under that lagging, yellow, waning moon!
O under that moon where she droops almost down into the sea!
O reckless despairing carols.

But soft! sink low!
Soft! let me just murmur,
And do you wait a moment you husky-nois'd sea,
For somewhere I believe I heard my mate responding to me,
So faint, I must be still, be still to listen,
But not altogether still, for then she might not come immediately to me.

Hither my love!
Here I am! here!
With this just-sustain'd note I announce myself to you,
This gentle call is for you my love, for you.
Do not be decoy'd elsewhere,
That is the whistle of the wind, it is not my voice,
That is the fluttering, the fluttering of the spray,
Those are the shadows of leaves.

O darkness! O in vain!
O I am very sick and sorrowful.

O brown halo in the sky near the moon, drooping upon the sea!
O troubled reflection in the sea!
O throat! O throbbing heart!
And I singing uselessly, uselessly all the night.

O past! O happy life! O songs of joy!
In the air, in the woods, over fields,
Loved! loved! loved! loved! loved!
But my mate no more, no more with me!
We two together no more.

The aria sinking,
All else continuing, the stars shining,
The winds blowing, the notes of the bird continuous
echoing,
With angry moans the fierce old mother incessantly
moaning,
On the sands of Paumanok's shore gray and rustling,
The yellow half-moon enlarged, sagging down, drooping,
the face of the sea almost touching,

The boy ecstatic, with his bare feet the waves, with his hair
 the atmosphere dallying,
The love in the heart long pent, now loose, now at last
 tumultuously bursting,
The aria's meaning, the ears, the soul, swiftly depositing,
The strange tears down the cheeks coursing,
The colloquy there, the trio, each uttering,
The undertone, the savage old mother incessantly crying,
To the boy's soul's questions sullenly timing, some drown'd
 secret hissing,
To the outsetting bard.
Demon or bird! (said the boy's soul,)
Is it indeed toward your mate you sing? or is it really
 to me?
For I, that was a child, my tongue's use sleeping, now I
 have heard you,
Now in a moment I know what I am for, I awake,
And already a thousand singers, a thousand songs, clearer,
 louder and more sorrowful than yours,
A thousand warbling echoes have started to life within me,
 never to die.

O you singer solitary, singing by yourself, projecting me,
O solitary me listening, never more shall I cease
 perpetuating you,
Never more shall I escape, never more the reverberations,
Never more the cries of unsatisfied love be absent from me,
Never again leave me to be the peaceful child I was before
 what there in the night,
By the sea under the yellow and sagging moon,

The messenger there arous'd, the fire, the sweet hell within,
The unknown want, the destiny of me.

O give me the clew! (it lurks in the night here
somewhere,)
O if I am to have so much, let me have more!

A word then, (for I will conquer it,)
The word final, superior to all,
Subtle, sent up – what is it? – I listen;
Are you whispering it, and have been all the time, you
sea-waves?
Is that it from your liquid rims and wet sands?

Whereto answering, the sea,
Delaying not, hurrying not,
Whisper'd me through the night, and very plainly before
daybreak,
Lisp'd to me the low and delicious word death,
And again death, death, death, death,
Hissing melodious, neither like the bird nor like my arous'd
child's heart,
But edging near as privately for me rustling at my feet,
Creeping thence steadily up to my ears and laving me softly
all over,
Death, death, death, death, death.

Which I do not forget,
But fuse the song of my dusky demon and brother,
That he sang to me in the moonlight on Paumanok's gray
beach,
With the thousand responsive songs at random,

My own songs awaked from that hour,
And with them the key, the word up from the waves,
The word of the sweetest song and all songs,
That strong and delicious word which, creeping to my feet,
(Or like some old crone rocking the cradle, swathed in
sweet garments, bending aside,)
The sea whisper'd me.

As I Ebb'd with the Ocean of Life

1

As I ebb'd with the ocean of life,
As I wended the shores I know,
As I walk'd where the ripples continually wash you
Paumanok,
Where they rustle up hoarse and sibilant,
Where the fierce old mother endlessly cries for her
castaways,
I musing late in the autumn day, gazing off southward,
Held by this electric self out of the pride of which I utter
poems,
Was seiz'd by the spirit that trails in the lines underfoot,
The rim, the sediment that stands for all the water and all
the land of the globe.

Fascinated, my eyes reverting from the south, dropt, to
follow those slender windrows,
Chaff, straw, splinters of wood, weeds, and the sea-gluten,
Scum, scales from shining rocks, leaves of salt-lettuce, left
by the tide,
Miles walking, the sound of breaking waves the other side
of me,
Paumanok there and then as I thought the old thought of
likenesses,
These you presented to me you fish-shaped island,

As I wended the shores I know,
As I walk'd with that electric self seeking types.

2

As I wend to the shores I know not,
As I list to the dirge, the voices of men and women wreck'd,
As I inhale the impalpable breezes that set in upon me,
As the ocean so mysterious rolls toward me closer and
closer,
I too but signify at the utmost a little wash'd-up drift,
A few sands and dead leaves to gather,
Gather, and merge myself as part of the sands and drift.

O baffled, balk'd, bent to the very earth,
Oppress'd with myself that I have dared to open my
mouth,
Aware now that amid all that blab whose echoes recoil
upon me I have not once had the least idea who or
what I am,
But that before all my arrogant poems the real Me stands
yet untouch'd, untold, altogether unreach'd,
Withdrawn far, mocking me with mock-congratulatory
signs and bows,
With peals of distant ironical laughter at every word I have
written,
Pointing in silence to these songs, and then to the sand
beneath.

I perceive I have not really understood any thing, not a
single object, and that no man ever can,
Nature here in sight of the sea taking advantage of me to
dart upon me and sting me,
Because I have dared to open my mouth to sing at all.

3

You oceans both, I close with you,
We murmur alike reproachfully rolling sands and drift,
knowing not why,
These little shreds indeed standing for you and me and all.

You friable shore with trails of debris,
You fish-shaped island, I take what is underfoot,
What is yours is mine my father.

I too Paumanok,
I too have bubbled up, floated the measureless float, and
been wash'd on your shores,
I too am but a trail of drift and debris,
I too leave little wrecks upon you, you fish-shaped island.

I throw myself upon your breast my father,
I cling to you so that you cannot unloose me,
I hold you so firm till you answer me something.

Kiss me my father,
Touch me with your lips as I touch those I love,
Breathe to me while I hold you close the secret of the
murmuring I envy.

4

Ebb, ocean of life, (the flow will return,)
Cease not your moaning you fierce old mother,
Endlessly cry for your castaways, but fear not, deny
not me,
Rustle not up so hoarse and angry against my feet as I
touch you or gather from you.

I mean tenderly by you and all,
I gather for myself and for this phantom looking down
where we lead, and following me and mine.

Me and mine, loose windrows, little corpses,
Froth, snowy white, and bubbles,
(See, from my dead lips the ooze exuding at last,
See, the prismatic colors glistening and rolling,)
Tufts of straw, sands, fragments,
Buoy'd hither from many moods, one contradicting
another,
From the storm, the long calm, the darkness, the swell,
Musing, pondering, a breath, a briny tear, a dab of liquid
or soil,
Up just as much out of fathomless workings fermented and
thrown,
A limp blossom or two, torn, just as much over waves
floating, drifted at random,
Just as much for us that sobbing dirge of Nature,
Just as much whence we come that blare of the
cloud-trumpets,

We, capricious, brought hither we know not whence,
    spread out before you,
You up there walking or sitting,
Whoever you are, we too lie in drifts at your feet.

Tears

Tears! tears! tears!
In the night, in solitude, tears,
On the white shore dripping, dripping, suck'd in by the sand,
Tears, not a star shining, all dark and desolate,
Moist tears from the eyes of a muffled head;
O who is that ghost? that form in the dark, with tears?
What shapeless lump is that, bent, crouch'd there on the sand?
Streaming tears, sobbing tears, throes, choked with wild cries;
O storm, embodied, rising, careering with swift steps along the beach!
O wild and dismal night storm, with wind – O belching and desperate!
O shade so sedate and decorous by day, with calm countenance and regulated pace,
But away at night as you fly, none looking – O then the unloosen'd ocean,
Of tears! tears! tears!

To the Man-of-War Bird

Thou who hast slept all night upon the storm,
Waking renew'd on thy prodigious pinions,
(Burst the wild storm? above it thou ascended'st,
And rested on the sky, thy slave that cradled thee,)
Now a blue point, far, far, in heaven floating,
As to the light emerging here on deck I watch thee,
(Myself a speck, a point on the world's floating vast.)

Far, far at sea,
After the night's fierce drifts have strewn the shore with
wrecks,
With re-appearing day as now so happy and serene,
The rosy and elastic dawn, the flashing sun,
The limpid spread of air cerulean,
Thou also re-appearest.
Thou born to match the gale, (thou art all wings,)
To cope with heaven and earth and sea and hurricane,
Thou ship of air that never furl'st thy sails,
Days, even weeks untired and onward, through spaces,
realms gyrating,
At dusk that look'st on Senegal, at morn America,
That sport'st amid the lightning-flash and thunder-cloud,
In them, in thy experiences, had'st thou my soul,
What joys! what joys were thine!

Aboard at a Ship's Helm

Aboard at a ship's helm,
A young steersman steering with care.

Through fog on a sea-coast dolefully ringing,
An ocean-bell – O a warning bell, rock'd by the waves.

O you give good notice indeed, you bell by the sea-reefs ringing,
Ringing, ringing, to warn the ship from its wreck-place.

For as on the alert O steersman, you mind the loud admonition,
The bows turn, the freighted ship tacking speeds away under her gray sails,
The beautiful and noble ship with all her precious wealth speeds away gayly and safe.

But O the ship, the immortal ship! O ship aboard the ship!
Ship of the body, ship of the soul, voyaging, voyaging, voyaging.

On the Beach at Night

On the beach at night,
Stands a child with her father,
Watching the east, the autumn sky.

Up through the darkness,
While ravening clouds, the burial clouds, in black masses
spreading,
Lower sullen and fast athwart and down the sky,
Amid a transparent clear belt of ether yet left in the east,
Ascends large and calm the lord-star Jupiter,
And nigh at hand, only a very little above,
Swim the delicate sisters the Pleiades.
From the beach the child holding the hand of her father,
Those burial-clouds that lower victorious soon to
devour all,
Watching, silently weeps.

Weep not, child,
Weep not, my darling,
With these kisses let me remove your tears,
The ravening clouds shall not long be victorious,
They shall not long possess the sky, they devour the stars
only in apparition,
Jupiter shall emerge, be patient, watch again another night,
the Pleiades shall emerge,
They are immortal, all those stars both silvery and golden
shall shine out again,

The great stars and the little ones shall shine out again, they
endure,
The vast immortal suns and the long-enduring pensive
moons shall again shine.

Then dearest child mournest thou only for Jupiter?
Considerest thou alone the burial of the stars?

Something there is,
(With my lips soothing thee, adding I whisper,
I give thee the first suggestion, the problem and
indirection,)
Something there is more immortal even than the stars,
(Many the burials, many the days and nights, passing
away,)
Something that shall endure longer even than lustrous
Jupiter,
Longer than sun or any revolving satellite,
Or the radiant sisters the Pleiades.

The World Below the Brine

The world below the brine,
Forests at the bottom of the sea, the branches and leaves,
Sea-lettuce, vast lichens, strange flowers and seeds, the
    thick tangle, openings, and pink turf,
Different colors, pale gray and green, purple, white, and
    gold, the play of light through the water,
Dumb swimmers there among the rocks, coral, gluten,
    grass, rushes, and the aliment of the swimmers,
Sluggish existences grazing there suspended, or slowly
    crawling close to the bottom,
The sperm-whale at the surface blowing air and spray, or
    disporting with his flukes,
The leaden-eyed shark, the walrus, the turtle, the hairy
    sea-leopard, and the sting-ray,
Passions there, wars, pursuits, tribes, sight in those
    ocean-depths, breathing that thick-breathing air, as so
    many do,
The change thence to the sight here, and to the subtle air
    breathed by beings like us who walk this sphere,
The change onward from ours to that of beings who walk
    other spheres.

On the Beach at Night Alone

On the beach at night alone,
As the old mother sways her to and fro singing her husky
    song,
As I watch the bright stars shining, I think a thought of the
    clef of the universes and of the future.

A vast similitude interlocks all,
All spheres, grown, ungrown, small, large, suns, moons,
    planets,
All distances of place however wide,
All distances of time, all inanimate forms,
All souls, all living bodies though they be ever so different,
    or in different worlds,
All gaseous, watery, vegetable, mineral processes, the
    fishes, the brutes,
All nations, colors, barbarisms, civilizations, languages,
All identities that have existed or may exist on this globe,
    or any globe,
All lives and deaths, all of the past, present, future,
This vast similitude spans them, and always has spann'd,
And shall forever span them and compactly hold and
    enclose them.

Song for All Seas, All Ships

1

To-day a rude brief recitative,
Of ships sailing the seas, each with its special flag or
ship-signal,
Of unnamed heroes in the ships – of waves spreading and
spreading far as the eye can reach,
Of dashing spray, and the winds piping and blowing,
And out of these a chant for the sailors of all nations,
Fitful, like a surge.

Of sea-captains young or old, and the mates, and of all
intrepid sailors,
Of the few, very choice, taciturn, whom fate can never
surprise nor death dismay,
Pick'd sparingly without noise by thee old ocean, chosen by
thee,
Thou sea that pickest and cullest the race in time, and
unitest nations,
Suckled by thee, old husky nurse, embodying thee,
Indomitable, untamed as thee.

(Ever the heroes on water or on land, by ones or twos
appearing,
Ever the stock preserv'd and never lost, though rare,
enough for seed preserv'd.)

2

Flaunt out O sea your separate flags of nations!
Flaunt out visible as ever the various ship-signals!
But do you reserve especially for yourself and for the soul of man one flag above all the rest,
A spiritual woven signal for all nations, emblem of man elate above death,
Token of all brave captains and all intrepid sailors and mates,
And all that went down doing their duty,
Reminiscent of them, twined from all intrepid captains young or old,
A pennant universal, subtly waving all time, o'er all brave sailors,
All seas, all ships.

Patroling Barnegat

Wild, wild the storm, and the sea high running,
Steady the roar of the gale, with incessant undertone
  muttering,
Shouts of demoniac laughter fitfully piercing and pealing,
Waves, air, midnight, their savagest trinity lashing,
Out in the shadows there milk-white combs careering,
On beachy slush and sand spirts of snow fierce slanting,
Where through the murk the easterly death-wind breasting,
Through cutting swirl and spray watchful and firm
  advancing,
(That in the distance! is that a wreck? is the red signal
  flaring?)
Slush and sand of the beach tireless till daylight wending,
Steadily, slowly, through hoarse roar never remitting,
Along the midnight edge by those milk-white combs
  careering,
A group of dim, weird forms, struggling, the night
  confronting,
That savage trinity warily watching.

After the Sea-Ship

After the sea-ship, after the whistling winds,
After the white-gray sails taut to their spars and ropes,
Below, a myriad myriad waves hastening, lifting up their
    necks,
Tending in ceaseless flow toward the track of the ship,
Waves of the ocean bubbling and gurgling, blithely prying,
Waves, undulating waves, liquid, uneven, emulous waves,
Toward that whirling current, laughing and buoyant, with
    curves,
Where the great vessel sailing and tacking displaces the
    surface,
Larger and smaller waves in the spread of the ocean
    yearnfully flowing,
The wake of the sea-ship after she passes, flashing and
        frolicsome under the sun,
A motley procession with many a fleck of foam and many
    fragments,
Following the stately and rapid ship, in the wake following.

PENGUIN

LITTLE BLACK

CLASSICS

PENGUIN

LITTLE BLACK

CLASSICS

PENGUIN

LITTLE BLACK

CLASSICS

“它来了——

毫不迟延的造物……”

PENGUIN

LITTLE BLACK

CLASSICS

* 关于本书中破折号的使用说明：因狄金森习惯在句末用英文短破折号“—”来表达诗歌的节奏感，中文译本保留了这一用法，但因汉语标点符号的使用规则，统一改为中文长破折号“——”。

我的生命是一杆上实弹的枪

My life had stood a loaded gun

［美］艾米莉·狄金森　著
周琰　译

中信出版集团 | 北京

图书在版编目（CIP）数据

企鹅经典：小黑书．第三辑：汉、英 /（英）简·奥斯汀等著；夏星等译．-- 北京：中信出版社，2019.6

书名原文：Penguin Little Black Classics

ISBN 978-7-5217-0407-5

Ⅰ．①企… Ⅱ．①简… ②夏… Ⅲ．①世界文学－作品综合集－汉、英 Ⅳ．①I11

中国版本图书馆 CIP 数据核字 (2019) 第 072172 号

My life had stood a loaded gun

This selection is taken from *Complete Poems*, Martin Secker, 1933. This selection first published in Penguin Classics 2016.

企鹅经典：小黑书　第三辑

我的生命是一杆上实弹的枪

著　　者：[美] 艾米莉·狄金森

译　　者：周琰

出版发行：中信出版集团股份有限公司

（北京市朝阳区惠新东街甲 4 号富盛大厦 2 座 邮编 100029）

承 印 者：北京楠萍印刷有限公司

开　　本：787mm × 1092mm　1/32　　印　　张：45.75　　字　　数：756 千字

版　　次：2019 年 6 月第 1 版　　印　　次：2019 年 6 月第 1 次印刷

京权图字：01－2018－6477　　广告经营许可证：京朝工商广字第 8087 号

书　　号：ISBN 978－7－5217－0407－5

定　　价：149.00 元（全 10 册）

服务热线：400－600－8099

投稿邮箱：author@citicpub.com

目录

[1]

一只受伤的鹿跳得最高，
我听那猎人讲：
那不过是死的惊恐，
然后矮树丛寂然不动。

被重击的岩石迸涌，
被践踏的钢铁涌流：
面颊总是骤然绯红
当一阵潮热激刺！

欢乐是苦痛的铠甲，
在内里它小心武装，
以免任何人察觉血迹
而惊呼“你受伤了”！

1. 狄金森原诗均无标题，为查阅方便，目录取每首诗首句为标题。——编者注

❧

那是一种珍贵，粉碎成尘的愉悦，
与一本古老的书相遇，
他恰恰穿着他的世纪的衣裳；
一种特权，我想，

握着他可敬的手，
在我们的手里温暖他，
一段，或者两段回程，抵达
他年轻时候的岁月。

检视他古雅的看法，
打开他的知识，
关于我们的心灵共同关注的
过去的文学。

学者最感兴趣的，
竞争追逐的，
当柏拉图是一种确然，

索福克勒斯[1]是个人；

当萨福[2]是个活生生的女孩，
贝阿特丽切穿着
被但丁神话了的长袍。
事实，多少世纪前，

他寻常般遍历，
就像有人会来到城里
告诉你你所有的梦都会成真：
他住在梦诞生的地方。

他的出现是魅惑，
你祈求他不要走；
老卷本摇摇他们羊皮纸的头
吊人胃口，就这样。

1. 索福克勒斯（Sopocëls，约公元前 496—前 406），古希腊悲剧家之一。——编者注
2. 萨福（Sappho，约公元前 7—前 6 世纪），古希腊女诗人，出身贵族。——编者注

响亮地战斗很勇敢，
可是勇士，据我所知，
胸中满怀
骑士的悲痛。

他赢了，王国看不见，
他失败，无人察觉，
没有哪个国以对爱国者的爱
瞩目他垂死的双眼。

我们相信，为这样的人
天使们身披羽翅列队，
按等级依序前行，甚至脚
和制服都是白雪。

大脑在它的沟槽中

均衡并且真实地运动;

可要是让一个碎片骤然偏转,

对你来说那样

更易让水回流;

当洪水已裂开山峦,

并为自己挖出一道迂回之路,

还毁掉了磨坊!

我谁都不是！你是谁？
难道你也寂寂无名？
那我们俩就是一对——别吭声！
他们会驱逐我们，你知道。

做个有头脸的人物多无趣！
多风光，像只青蛙
一整天对着一片爱慕的泥沼
宣扬自己的名字！

我能涉水蹚过，
整池的悲伤，——
我习惯了。
可是快乐微微一推
就折断了我的脚，
我歪倒——醉了。
别让哪颗石子笑，
那是新酒，——
那是一切！

力量只是痛苦，
通过自律，拧成股，
直到沉重都挂起。
把没药[1]给巨人们
他们会萎靡，就像常人。
给他们喜马拉雅山，——
他们会扛着他！

1. 没药，中药名，为橄榄科植物地丁树的干燥树脂。——编者注

[1]

我喜欢看它折叠里程，
并舔过山谷，
然后停下来在水槽那儿补给；
之后，令人惊愕，绕过

一叠群山，
盛气凌人，窥探
路边的棚屋；
然后修剪一副残骸

好和它的半边毛皮合体，再蜿蜒穿过，*
用可怕，呜呜的音节
一路抱怨；
之后追赶自己跑下山

像半尼其[2]一样嘶鸣；

---

1. 这首诗是写火车的。19 世纪时，人们对火车有许多好奇和想象。诗文中常见，绘画、摄影也一样。（说明：书中脚注除特别标明之外，均为译者注。）
2. 半尼其，出自《马可福音》3:17：“还有西庇太的儿子雅各和雅各的兄弟约翰，又给这两个人起名叫半尼其，就是雷子的意思。”

然后，像一颗星星般准时，
停在它自己的马厩门口
温顺而全能——

*这句是关于火车运动对风景裁剪的形象描述。火车行过，穿过风景，如同撕裂一个完整的身体，同时遮挡了一半风景。“quarry”是被捕获的鹿的一部分骨架，扔给猎狗吃的。“pare”是剥皮修剪。诗中第一节让人联想到猫儿、马儿，而到第二节，对火车代表的工业革命这个庞然大物，心理上感觉可怕，还不明所以，狄金森对感受到的它潜在的全能和毁灭性做了隐喻。这两句的力量，体现了一个诗人捕捉集体心理、预言时代的能力。文德勒谈这首诗，问诗中可能暗示了哪些动物，其实它既暗示某些动物，又暗示了上帝，科技来临相当于上帝重现。狄金森的父亲曾致力于把火车引入艾摩斯特市，火车站后来就设在离狄金森家不远的地方。文德勒说诗中的火车是狄金森自己的戏仿，表面上看知书达礼，温文尔雅，实际上却像那个庞大的机器一般，充满兽性和全能。

老天是个医生吗?

　　他们说他能治病;

可是死后的药

　　不可得。

老天是座金库吗?

　　他们谈论我们所拥有的;

可是那种磋商

　　我不是加入其中的一员。

[1]

我手中紧握我的力量
和世界作对；
没有大卫拥有的那么多力量，
可我双倍勇敢。

我的石子投中了，可我自己
是那唯一栽倒的人。
难道歌利亚太巨大，
还是我太小？

1. 本诗可参见圣经故事：大卫与歌利亚之战。

在我把我的眼睛弄瞎前，
我不妨也像其他
有眼睛的生命一样看，
不晓得还有其他办法。

可要是告诉我，就今天，
我也许能自个儿拥有
整个天空，我告诉你我的心
就我的那么大小，会裂开。

草地是我的，山脉是我的，——
所有的森林，无止尽的星星，
在我有限的双眼之间
我所能尽取的正午。

点水的鸟儿的动作，
闪电连接的道路，
要喜欢尽由我的眼睛去看，——
这消息会让我呆若木鸡！

那么，安全点，仅以我搁在
窗台上的灵魂猜想
其他生命的眼睛也看着那儿，
而对太阳毫无戒备。

不像我的心那般沉重的心，
悠然晚归，
它经过我的窗口
给自己吹着一个小曲儿，——

漫不经心的一段，一支谣曲，
一首街头小调；
可是对我恼怒的耳朵来说
却是多么甜美的抚慰，

就好像一只食米鸟，
闲逛到这边，
一边欢歌一边沉思接着又欢歌，
歌声婉转缓缓消逝。

那就好像一条潺湲的小溪
流过艰辛的路程
让流血的双脚跳起小步舞
却不知为何。

明日，夜会再度来临，

疲惫，也许，酸痛。

啊，号角，在我窗边，

恳求你再来溜达。

我知道他存在
在某处，在沉默中。
从我们粗俗的眼前
他藏起了他珍稀的生命。

这片刻间的游戏，
这愚蠢的埋伏，
只是为了让喜乐
自己赢得惊讶！

可倘若这游戏
证实刺穿了最诚挚的心，
倘若欢喜在死亡
僵硬的凝视中呆滞，

难道那乐子
不是看来太过奢侈？
难道那玩笑
不是伸得太远？

我可以为珍珠操点心
　　它拥有广袤的大海；
或领针，当皇帝
　　把红宝石骤雨般朝我猛扔；

或者金子，他是矿山的王公；
　　或钻石，当我看见
可以配上一个穹顶的王冠
　　持续为我加冕。

我感觉我的心神中有一道裂缝
　　好像我的大脑已经裂开；
我试图拼起它，严丝合缝，
　　却不能让它们对齐。

我努力让后面的念头接上
　　前面的念头，
可是次序散开无法控制
　　就像地板上的线球。

❧

缄默的火山藏着
　　他永不休眠的计划；
不向任何靠不住的人
　　吐露他粉色的规划。

如果自然不讲
　　耶和华告诉她的故事，
难道没有一个倾听者
　　人性就不能够幸存？

被她紧扣的双唇告诫
　　让多嘴的人随便。
人所藏着的唯一秘密
　　是不朽。

没能把我们全都触摸的米达斯[1]，
摸过的东西中的一个，
是那倾心相诉的浪子，
乐而无忧的金莺。

这般沉醉，他用
戏谑的占卜[2]否认它；
这般炫目，我们错把他
当成一座降落的藏宝窟[3]。

花言巧语的家伙，骗子，
贪图享欲的人，一个贼，——

---

1. 米达斯，希腊神话中弗里吉亚国王，“点石成金”的出处来自他的故事。他解救了酒神狄俄尼索斯的老师西勒诺斯，酒神允他实现他的愿望，他希望触手所碰一切成金。愿望实现，最终他的女儿也被他变成了一座金子雕像。他悔恨不已，再求酒神解救。酒神让他去帕克托罗斯河洗澡，洗去了点石成金的魔力。米达斯后舍弃王位，追随酒神。“米达斯的触摸”因此成为一个隐喻。
2. “占卜”（divine），参见《创世记》44:15：约瑟对他们说：你们做的是什么事呢？你们岂不知像我这样的人必能占卜吗？
3. “藏宝窟”（mine），一词双关，既是“藏宝库”，也暗指“我的宝贝”“我的珍宝”。

偶尔也是一个演说家，
销魂首领；

果园的耶稣，
一边欺骗一边诱走
全部的玫瑰精油
为他的潜逃之需。

金丝雀的光芒，
鸟中的流星，
谣曲和歌手
露天表演般的华丽道别。

我从没想过伊阿宋
是为了寻求什么金羊毛；
可那时我是个乡下人，
想法只为图个安宁。

可要是真有个伊阿宋，
传统容忍我
看苹果树上
他失去的报偿。

我如此畏惧那第一只知更鸟，
但是现在他已经驯服，
我习惯了他成长，——
尽管，他有些伤人。

我想要是我能只活到
那第一声鸣叫过去，
不是所有林中的钢琴
都有力量撕碎我——

我不敢与水仙花相见，
因为害怕她们黄色的长袍
会以完全相异于
我自己的风尚刺穿我。

我希望青草快点长，
这样当去看的时候，
他就会太高，最高的一个
能够伸展到看着我。

我受不了蜜蜂要来，
我希望他们远远待在
他们所去的那些幽暗国度：
他们有什么话对我说？

可是，他们在这儿；没一个生命爽约，
没有一朵花避开
温柔地顺从我，
髑髅地的女王。

在他走时每一个都向我致敬，
而我是我孩子气的羽毛
在哀恸中明白
他们无情地鼓鸣时，飘举。

一条隐没的路；
有一只旋转的轮子；
绿宝石的振鸣，
胭脂虫的急奔；
树丛上的每一朵花
调整乱转的头，——
突尼斯来的信，或许，
早晨一趟轻松的出行。

谁劫掠了树林，
不知提防的树林？
毫无疑心的树木
拿出他们的荚壳和青苔
取悦他的幻想。
他好奇，浏览他们的小饰物，
他抓取，他夺走。
一本正经的铁杉，
还有枞树会说什么？

树叶，像女人，交换
　　精明的私语；
有点头称赞，也有
　　暗示的推断。

两种情形下的对话者
　　享受秘密，——
对曝光泄露
　　达成绝不违背的约定。

听起来街道在奔跑，
然后街道又静静站立。
日食是我们在窗口能看到的一切，
敬畏是我们能感受到的一切。

渐渐地，最勇敢的人偷偷溜出他的隐蔽所，
去看看时间是不是还在那儿。
自然戴着它绿玉色的花冠，
搅动着更新鲜的空气。

老鼠是最节俭的房客。
他不付房租，——
否认义务，
蓄意如此。

让我们的聪明受挫、
探测或绕行，

恨无法伤害
这般悄悄的敌人。

法令
也不禁止他，
合法得
如同公正。

紫色的船只轻轻摇荡
在黄水仙的大海之上，
奇妙的水手融入其中，
而后——码头寂然。

熠然铄金，熄灭于紫色，
猎豹般跃向天空，
而后在古老的地平线
俯下她斑驳的脸，去死；

倾身低俯与厨房窗户般高，
触摸屋顶，微染谷仓，
对着草地飞吻她的女帽，——
白日的魔术师走了！

有一个词

它带着一把剑

能刺穿一个全副武装的人。

它掷出它带刺的音节，——

马上又变得沉默。

可在它落下的地方

被拯救的人

会在爱国日告诉，

某个佩戴肩章的兄弟

尽情呼吸。

不管那气喘吁吁的太阳在哪儿奔跑，

不管白天在哪儿浪游，

有它无声的进攻，

有它的胜利！

看那最精准的神枪手！

最成功的射击！

时间最崇高的目标

是一个灵魂“被忘记”！

他笨拙地触弄你的精神，
　　就像演奏者触弄琴键，
在他们奏出完整的音乐前；
　　他让你一点一点地惊叹，

让你脆弱不堪的心性准备
　　迎接那飘然出尘的打击，
以那轻柔的音槌，在很远处听到，
　　然后近了，变得那么缓慢。

你的呼吸有时间得以舒展，
　　你的大脑浮想联翩，——
发出唯一庄严的雷击
　　它剥去你赤裸灵魂的头皮。

因为我不能为死亡而停步,
他亲切地为我止步;
马车只载着我们自己
还有不朽。

我们驾马缓行,他不疾不徐,
而我也放下
我的劳作,还有我的悠闲,
因为他殷勤有礼。

我们经过一个学校,孩子们在玩耍,
围成一圈扭打,
我们经过谷物凝视着的田野,
我们经过落日。

我们在一所房子面前稍歇
它像是地上隆起的肿块;
屋顶几乎看不见,
飞檐不过是个土堆。

从那时起已是许多世纪；可每个世纪
都感觉比那一天短暂；
我初猜那天马儿的头
是朝向永生。

精油被榨出:

玫瑰中的花油

不只是被太阳榨取,

它也是技艺的礼物。

寻常的玫瑰衰败;

可这朵,在女子的抽屉里,

创造了夏天,当那女子

躺在无尽的玫瑰经颂祷中。

死亡像那虫子
　　威胁着树，
足能杀死它，
　　但可能被引诱。

用香脂诱惑它，
　　用刀子寻找它，
思量，它是否让你付出
　　生命中的一切。

如果它已经钻出
　　技艺所及之处，
敲响大树并离开它，——
　　这是害虫的意愿。

丧失了一切，我出国远游，
　　并未减少丧失感
在一座新的半岛上，——
　　坟墓先我而行，

很快我也找到我的寄居处，
　　而当我寻找我的床，
它却是一座坟墓，在枕头上
　　安放下我的头。

我醒来，发现它比我先醒，
　　我起来，——它跟着我；
我想把它扔在人群中，
　　把它丢进大海，

在一杯杯人工安眠剂中
　　把它的形影睡去，——
坟墓消失了，可是铲子
　　还保留在记忆中。

我感觉大脑里有一场葬礼，
　　送葬者，来来去去，
不停地踩踏，踩踏，直到似乎
　　感知挣脱而出。

当他们都坐下来，
　　一场仪式像一面鼓
不停地敲啊敲，直到我以为
　　我的意识变得麻木。

然后我听到他们举起一个棺材，
　　又一次，踩着那铅做的靴子，
嘎吱嘎吱穿过我的灵魂，
　　而后空间开始鸣响，

仿佛整个天穹是一口钟，
　　而存在只是一只耳朵，
我和沉默是某种奇怪的种类，
　　遇难，孤独，就在这儿。

声名是浮浪不定的食物
在一个飘移的盘子上,
它的桌子曾为一个客人摆好，可是
不会再摆第二次。

乌鸦检视它的碎屑,
以嘲弄的聒聒
飞过它去找农夫的谷物;
人们吃了它而死去。

我的轮子在黑暗中，——
我看不到一根轮辐，
可是知道它嘀嗒嗒的脚
绕了一圈又一圈。

我的脚踩在浪涛上——
一条人迹罕至的路，
可是所有的路
尽头都有一块空地。

有些人放弃了织布机，
有些在忙碌的坟墓
找到稀奇的消遣，
有些用崭新、庄重的脚步
尊贵地经过大门，
把问题又抛回给你和我。

夏天开始有了样子，
迷人大书的穷究者
不情愿，可的确察觉——
姗姗来迟的树叶上新的收获。

秋天开始得以暗示
从云朵的女帽那儿，
或是萦绕永在的山峦的
那条披肩上深沉的颜色。

眼睛开始贪得无厌，
冥想精练了言辞，
一株远树的染匠
重拾他绚艳的活计。

结束是一切的归程，
几乎是终年常在，
然后逃脱了稳定，
召回到不朽。

今天或这个正午,
她待得这么近,
我几乎都摸到了她;
今夜她卧着
经过街邻——
还有树干和尖塔——
此刻越过了猜想。

圣经是一部古老的书
由消逝的人们写成，
应圣灵的建议——
主题——伯利恒——
伊甸园——那古老的家园——
撒旦——敌将，
犹大——伟大的失职者，
大卫——游吟诗人。
罪恶——一个著名的绝境
其他人必须抵制，
“虔信的”男孩子们
非常孤独——
别的男孩已经“迷失”。
若故事有个巧言讲述者
所有的男孩都会来——
俄耳甫斯的布道惑人，
它并不谴责。

真挚，我不温不火的朋友，
别来和我戏耍！
心灵的没药和穆哈
是它的有失平衡。

我的火山上长了青草，——
一个沉思的地点，
一只鸟儿会去挑选的地方
将是通常的想法。

火在下面熏烧得多红，
草皮多不安全——
我透露了吗，我的孤独
将充满敬畏。

颜色，地位，教派——
这些是时间的事儿，
死亡的分类划分
不知道它们是什么。

就像在睡眠中——这儿的一切都被遗忘，
教义丢在脑后，
死亡硕大的民主的手指
抹去了名号。

假若是茧蛹——他才不操心——
假若他收起
金色或红棕的蝶蛹，
都同样是蝴蝶

从死亡一清二楚的
他的昏冥中，它们浮现；
我们最细微的直觉
注定不可信。

厄运是没有大门的房子——
它从太阳那儿进来，
然后梯子被扔掉
因为逃跑没戏。

外面它们都在干什么
在梦里情景各异，
当松鼠玩耍，野莓死掉——
万物向上帝躬身致意。

我栖居于可能性中，
比散文更漂亮的一座房子，
有更多窗户，
比门高级。

房间，是雪松木的——
眼睛不能穿透；
而经久的房顶
是天空的复折屋顶[1]。

让最漂亮的客人——
拥有——这个——
我窄小的双手展开的广阔
好收集乐园。

1. 这个版本中第二节第四行的“gambels”（三角墙）是1933年版本中手稿辨识中辨认为错误的词语，严重影响这首诗的准确和人们的理解。正确的词语应当是“gambrels”（复折屋顶）。

要阻挡他黄色的计划，
太阳不允许
大气的反复无常；
甚至当雪

像恶作剧的男孩扔起雪球
到他的眼睛里，
他也不过是转过头；
正忙于崇高的事业！

催动大地
磁吸大海是他的事儿，
并让天象各安其所——
可每个过客

都认为我们更繁忙，
就像一只飘荡的微不足道的蜜蜂
支持一道闪电，
理应是颗炸弹！

（用一朵花）
所有我能写的信
都没有这一封漂亮，
丝绒的音节，
长毛绒的句子，
红宝石的深度，深不见底，
藏起，轻诉，为你——
是一只蜂鸟演唱它
它刚刚啜饮了我！

它来了——毫不迟延的造物，
它获得街区现在又获得了大门，
从所有其他的栓扣中挑选了它的门闩，
进来，说——“你认识我吗，先生？”
简单的问候和确然相认，
要是敌人便无畏——要是朋友便简洁，
用薄饼和冰溜装扮每座房子，
并且拿出去一座送给上帝。

我的生命是一杆上实弹的枪
立在角落，直到一天
主人经过——验明正身，
带走我。

一时我们游荡在绝美的树林，
一时我们猎取母鹿——
而每次我代他而言
群山径自回应。

若我微笑，热忱的光
便闪耀山谷——
就像一张维苏威的脸，[1]
让它的喜悦由衷焕发。

而在夜晚，当我们美好的白日结束，
我守护着我主人的头，
那比曾经共享的

1. 维苏威是意大利那不勒斯的著名火山。

厚厚的鸭绒枕头要好。

对他的仇敌我无比仇恨，
不用第二次刺激
我便投以怒黄之眼
或是按下断然的拇指。

尽管可能是我而不是他活得更久，
他却必须比我活得更久，
因为我只有杀戮的技艺——
却没有去死的力量。

早上好，午夜！
我就回家，
白天厌倦了我——
可我怎能厌倦他？

阳光照耀之处是可爱的地方，
我喜欢逗留——
可是现在——早晨不想要我——
那么晚安，白天！

我能看，不能吗？
当东方变红的时候？
那时，山峦有它们的办法，
让心游历海外。

你没有那么美，午夜——
我选择白天，
可接受一个小女孩吧
他却转过身去！

渴望就像种子
在地里努力，
相信如果它求情
最终会被发现。

时辰和区域
每个情境都不清楚，
必须达到何种恒心，
在它终见太阳之前！

一只癞蛤蟆会见光而死！
　　死亡是癞蛤蟆和人
　共同的权利，——
也是伯爵和蠓虫的

特权。
　　还要妄自尊大吗？
小蚋虫的霸权
和你的一样大。

狄金森诗集版本概要

/

狄金森生前的诗歌作品主要在朋友和家人之间流传。在 1850 年至 1866 年间，共有 10 首诗由她的朋友交给报纸匿名发表。1878 年，诗人海伦·亨特·杰克逊（Helen Hunt Jackson）哄诱狄金森在《诗人的面具》（*A Masque of Poets*）中发表了一些诗歌，这是一本作者完全匿名的诗集。

1886 年狄金森去世后，她的妹妹拉维尼亚发现了数百首之前狄金森从未示人的诗歌手稿。狄金森总共留下了大约 1800 首诗歌。拉维尼亚认为狄金森的诗歌理应得到出版。在她的努力下，梅布尔·卢米斯·托德（Mabel Loomis Todd）和托马斯·温特沃斯·希金森（Thomas Wentworth Higginson）于 1890 年编辑出版了第一本狄金森诗集《狄金森诗歌》(*Poems of Emily Dickinson*)。两位编辑对狄金森的诗歌按照当时的诗歌阅读传统和他们自己对诗歌的认识做了大量修改，包括规范标点、增加标题、按照韵律需要修改用词等等。第一版诗集取得了很大成功，一年后，他们又出版了《狄金森诗歌第二卷》(*Poems of Emily Dickinson, Second Series*)。其后，托德又分别于1894年编辑出版了《狄金森书信集》(*Dickinson's Letters*)和1896年的《狄金森诗歌第三卷》(*Poems of Emily Dickinson, Third Series*)。

狄金森的外甥女玛莎·狄金森·比安奇(Martha Dickinson Bianchi)不赞同托德和希金森对狄金森诗歌的过度编辑，根据她从拉维尼亚和狄金森的嫂嫂苏珊·狄金森(Susan Dickinson)那儿继承的狄金森手稿，先后编辑出版了六卷狄金森诗歌。她采取了与托德截然不同的编辑方式，不改变原诗的韵律，不添加标题。1945年，托德的女儿完成了托德生前未完成的对所保留的全部狄金森手稿的编辑，出版了《旋律霹雳》(*Bolts of Melody*)。这样，在几个不同的版本中，狄金森的大多数诗歌均得以出版，但是并没有一个完整收录所有诗歌的选集。

1955年托马斯·H. 约翰逊(Thomas H. Johnson)的《狄金森诗歌》出版。约翰逊的版本基本完整收录了狄金森的诗歌。他依据狄金森手稿，忠实于狄金森的原文。此外，他对狄金森的诗歌按照年代进行了排列。这是一个划时代的文学事件，对诗歌界和读者重新认识评价狄金森起到了决定性作用。

拉尔夫·W. 富兰克林在约翰逊的成就之上，进一步关注手稿和诗人的书写过程。1981 年，他出版了带有狄金森手稿复印件的版本《狄金森手稿集》（*The Manuscript Books of Emily Dickinson*）。之后，1998 年他又出版了《狄金森诗歌全集》（*The Poems of Emily Dickinson*）。2016 年克蕾斯坦纳·米勒（Cristanne Miller）编辑出版了一个全新版本《狄金森诗歌：如她所保留》（*Emily Dickinson's Poems: As She Preserved Them*），声称最忠实地保留了狄金森诗歌原作的状态。

2016 年重印的《企鹅经典：小黑书》系列中的这本狄金森诗选，是 1933 年马丁·塞克尔（Martin Secker）从玛莎·狄金森·比安奇 1924 年编选出版的《狄金森诗全集》（*The Complete Poems of Emily Dickinson*）中摘选的。这个版本目前已经非常少见了。自从 1955 年约翰逊版本出版以来，通行的英文版本和各种翻译版本都是以约翰逊、富兰克林等人的版本为基础编辑翻译的。这个早期版本的再版，对读者和研究者了解早期狄金森诗歌出版和认知状况非常有益，可以和大家熟悉的通行版本对照阅读。

周琰

2018 年 7 月

PENGUIN

LITTLE BLACK

CLASSICS

‘It’s coming–
the postponeless
Creature . . .’

EMILY DICKINSON

My life had stood a loaded gun

Contents

A wounded deer leaps highest,
I've heard the hunter tell;
'Tis but the ecstasy of death,
And then the brake is still.

The smitten rock that gushes,
The trampled steel that springs:
A cheek is always redder
Just where the hectic stings!

Mirth is the mail of anguish,
In which it caution arm,
Lest anybody spy the blood
And 'You're hurt' exclaim!

A precious, mouldering pleasure 'tis
To meet an antique book,
In just the dress his century wore;
A privilege, I think,

His venerable hand to take,
And warming in our own,
A passage back, or two, to make
To times when he was young.

His quaint opinions to inspect,
His knowledge to unfold
On what concerns our mutual mind,
The literature of old;

What interested scholars most,
What competitions ran
When Plato was a certainty,
And Sophocles a man;

When Sappho was a living girl,
And Beatrice wore
The gown that Dante deified.
Facts, centuries before,

He traverses familiar,
As one should come to town
And tell you all your dreams were true:
He lived where dreams were born.

His presence is enchantment,
You beg him not to go;
Old volumes shake their vellum heads
And tantalize, just so.

To fight aloud is very brave,
But gallanter, I know,
Who charge within the bosom,
The cavalry of woe.

Who win, and nations do not see,
Who fall, and none observe,
Whose dying eyes no country
Regards with patriot love.

We trust, in plumed procession,
For such the angels go,
Rank after rank, with even feet
And uniforms of snow.

The brain within its groove
Runs evenly and true;
But let a splinter swerve,
'Twere easier for you
To put the water back
When floods have slit the hills,
And scooped a turnpike for themselves,
And blotted out the mills!

I'm nobody! Who are you?
Are you nobody, too?
Then there's a pair of us — don't tell!
They'd banish us, you know.

How dreary to be somebody!
How public, like a frog
To tell your name the livelong day
To an admiring bog!

I can wade grief,
Whole pools of it, –
I'm used to that.
But the least push of joy
Breaks up my feet,
And I tip – drunken.
Let no pebble smile,
'Twas the new liquor, –
That was all!

Power is only pain,
Stranded, through discipline,
Till weights will hang.
Give balm to giants,
And they'll wilt, like men.
Give Himmaleh, –
They'll carry him!

I like to see it lap the miles,
And lick the valleys up,
And stop to feed itself at tanks;
And then, prodigious, step

Around a pile of mountains,
And, supercilious, peer
In shanties by the sides of roads;
And then a quarry pare

To fit its sides, and crawl between,
Complaining all the while
In horrid, hooting stanza;
Then chase itself down hill

And neigh like Boanerges;
Then, punctual as a star,
Stop – docile and omnipotent –
At its own stable door.

Is Heaven a physician?
  They say that He can heal;
But medicine posthumous
  Is unavailable.

Is Heaven an exchequer?
  They speak of what we owe;
But that negotiation
  I'm not a party to.

I took my power in my hand
And went against the world;
'Twas not so much as David had,
But I was twice as bold.

I aimed my pebble, but myself
Was all the one that fell.
Was it Goliath was too large,
Or only I too small?

Before I got my eye put out,
I liked as well to see
As other creatures that have eyes,
And know no other way.

But were it told to me, to-day,
That I might have the sky
For mine, I tell you that my heart
Would split, for size of me.

The meadows mine, the mountains mine, –
All forests, stintless stars,
As much of noon as I could take
Between my finite eyes.

The motions of the dipping birds,
The lightning's jointed road,
For mine to look at when I liked, –
The news would strike me dead!

So, safer, guess, with just my soul
Upon the window-pane
Where other creatures put their eyes,
Incautious of the sun.

Heart not so heavy as mine,
Wending late home,
As it passed my window
Whistled itself a tune, –

A careless snatch, a ballad,
A ditty of the street;
Yet to my irritated ear
An anodyne so sweet,

It was as if a bobolink,
Sauntering this way,
Carolled and mused and carolled,
Then bubbled slow away.

It was as if a chirping brook
Upon a toilsome way
Set bleeding feet to minuets
Without the knowing why.

To-morrow, night will come again,
Weary, perhaps, and sore.
Ah, bugle, by my window,
I pray you stroll once more!

I know that he exists
Somewhere, in silence.
He has hid his rare life
From our gross eyes.

'Tis in instant's play,
'Tis a fond ambush,
Just to make bliss
Earn her own surprise!

But should the play
Prove piercing earnest,
Should the glee glaze
In death's stiff stare,

Would not the fun
Look too expensive?
Would not the jest
Have crawled too far?

'Tis little I could care for pearls
  Who own the ample sea;
Or brooches, when the Emperor
  With rubies pelteth me;

Or gold, who am the Prince of Mines;
  Or diamonds, when I see
A diadem to fit a dome
  Continual crowning me.

I felt a cleavage in my mind
  As if my brain had split;
I tried to match it, seam by seam,
  But could not make them fit.

The thought behind I strove to join
  Unto the thought before,
But sequence ravelled out of reach
  Like balls upon a floor.

The reticent volcano keeps
  His never slumbering plan;
Confided are his projects pink
  To no precarious man.

If nature will not tell the tale
  Jehovah told to her,
Can human nature not survive
  Without a listener?

Admonished by her buckled lips
  Let every babbler be.
The only secret people keep
  Is Immortality.

One of the ones that Midas touched,
Who failed to touch us all,
Was that confiding prodigal,
The blissful oriole.

So drunk, he disavows it
With badinage divine;
So dazzling, we mistake him
For an alighting mine.

A pleader, a dissembler,
An epicure, a thief, —
Betimes an oratorio,
An ecstasy in chief;

The Jesuit of orchards,
He cheats as he enchants
Of an entire attar
For his decamping wants.

The splendor of a Burmah,
The meteor of birds,
Departing like a pageant
Of ballads and of bards.

I never thought that Jason sought
For any golden fleece;
But then I am a rural man,
With thoughts that make for peace.

But if there were a Jason,
Tradition suffer me
Behold his lost emolument
Upon the apple-tree.

I dreaded that first robin so,
But he is mastered now,
And I'm accustomed to him grown, —
He hurts a little, though.

I thought if I could only live
Till that first shout got by,
Not all pianos in the woods
Had power to mangle me.

I dared not meet the daffodils,
For fear their yellow gown
Would pierce me with a fashion
So foreign to my own.

I wished the grass would hurry,
So when 'twas time to see,
He'd be too tall, the tallest one
Could stretch to look at me.

I could not bear the bees should come,
I wished they'd stay away
In those dim countries where they go:
What word had they for me?

They're here, though; not a creature failed,
No blossom stayed away
In gentle deference to me,
The Queen of Calvary.

Each one salutes me as he goes,
And I my childish plumes
Lift, in bereaved acknowledgment
Of their unthinking drums.

A route of evanescence
With a revolving wheel;
A resonance of emerald,
A rush of cochineal;
And every blossom on the bush
Adjusts its tumbled head, —
The mail from Tunis, probably,
An easy morning's ride.

Who robbed the woods,
The trusting woods?
The unsuspecting trees
Brought out their burrs and mosses
His fantasy to please.
He scanned their trinkets, curious,
He grasped, he bore away.
What will the solemn hemlock,
What will the fir-tree say?

The leaves, like women, interchange
  Sagacious confidence;
Somewhat of nods, and somewhat of
  Portentous inference,

The parties in both cases
  Enjoining secrecy, —
Inviolable compact
  To notoriety.

It sounded as if the streets were running,
And then the streets stood still.
Eclipse was all we could see at the window,
And awe was all we could feel.

By and by the boldest stole out of his covert,
To see if time was there.
Nature was in her beryl apron,
Mixing fresher air.

The rat is the concisest tenant.
He pays no rent, —
Repudiates the obligation,
On schemes intent.

Balking our wit
To sound or circumvent,
Hate cannot harm
A foe so reticent.

Neither decree
Prohibits him,
Lawful as
Equilibrium.

Where ships of purple gently toss
On seas of daffodil,
Fantastic sailors mingle,
And then — the wharf is still.

Blazing in gold and quenching in purple,
Leaping like leopards to the sky,
Then at the feet of the old horizon
Laying her spotted face, to die;

Stooping as low as the kitchen window,
Touching the roof and tinting the barn,
Kissing her bonnet to the meadow, –
And the juggler of day is gone!

There is a word
        Which bears a sword
      Can pierce an armed man.
It hurls its barbed syllables, —
    At once is mute again.

But where it fell
The saved will tell
    On patriotic day,
Some epauletted brother
    Gave his breath away.

Wherever runs the breathless sun,
    Wherever roams the day,
There is its noiseless onset,
    There is its victory!
Behold the keenest marksman!
    The most accomplished shot!
Time's sublimest target
    Is a soul 'forgot'!

He fumbles at your spirit
  As players at the keys
Before they drop full music on;
  He stuns you by degrees,

Prepares your brittle substance
  For the ethereal blow,
By fainter hammers, further heard,
  Then nearer, then so slow

Your breath has time to straighten,
  Your brain to bubble cool, —
Deals one imperial thunderbolt
  That scalps your naked soul.

Because I could not stop for Death,
He kindly stopped for me;
The carriage held but just ourselves
And Immortality.

We slowly drove, he knew no haste,
And I had put away
My labor, and my leisure too,
For his civility.

We passed the school where children played
At wrestling in a ring;
We passed the fields of gazing grain,
We passed the setting sun.

We paused before a house that seemed
A swelling of the ground;
The roof was scarcely visible,
The cornice but a mound.

Since then 'tis centuries; but each
Feels shorter than the day
I first surmised the horses' heads
Were toward eternity.

Essential oils are wrung:
The attar from the rose
Is not expressed by suns alone,
It is the gift of screws.

The general rose decays;
But this, in lady's drawer,
Makes summer when the lady lies
In ceaseless rosemary.

Death is like the insect
  Menacing the tree,
Competent to kill it,
  But decoyed may be.

Bait it with the balsam,
  Seek it with the knife,
Baffle, if it cost you
  Everything in life.

Then, if it have burrowed
  Out of reach of skill,
Ring the tree and leave it, —
  'Tis the vermin's will.

Bereaved of all, I went abroad,
  No less bereaved to be
Upon a new peninsula, –
  The grave preceded me,

Obtained my lodgings ere myself,
  And when I sought my bed,
The grave it was, reposed upon
  The pillow for my head.

I waked, to find it first awake,
  I rose, – it followed me;
I tried to drop it in the crowd,
  To lose it in the sea,

In cups of artificial drowse
  To sleep its shape away, –
The grave was finished, but the spade
  Remained in memory.

I felt a funeral in my brain,
  And mourners, to and fro,
Kept treading, treading, till it seemed
  That sense was breaking through.

And when they all were seated,
  A service like a drum
Kept beating, beating, till I thought
  My mind was going numb.

And then I heard them lift a box,
  And creak across my soul
With those same boots of lead, again,
  Then space began to toll

As all the heavens were a bell,
  And Being but an ear,
And I and silence some strange race,
  Wrecked, solitary, here.

Fame is a fickle food
Upon a shifting plate,
Whose table once a Guest, but not
The second time, is set.

Whose crumbs the crows inspect,
And with ironic caw
Flap past it to the Farmer's corn;
Men eat of it and die.

My Wheel is in the dark, –
I cannot see a spoke,
Yet know its dripping feet
Go round and round.

My foot is on the tide –
An unfrequented road,
Yet have all roads
A 'clearing' at the end.

Some have resigned the loom,
Some in the busy tomb
Find quaint employ,
Some with new, stately feet
Pass royal through the gate,
Flinging the problem back at you and me.

Summer begins to have the look,
Peruser of enchanting Book
Reluctantly, but sure, perceives —
A gain upon the backward leaves.

Autumn begins to be inferred
By millinery of the cloud,
Or deeper color in the shawl
That wraps the everlasting hill.

The eye begins its avarice,
A meditation chastens speech,
Some Dyer of a distant tree
Resumes his gaudy industry.

Conclusion is the course of all,
Almost to be perennial,
And then elude stability
Recalls to immortality.

To-day or this noon
She dwelt so close,
I almost touched her;
Tonight she lies
Past neighborhood –
And bough and steeple –
Now past surmise.

The Bible is an antique volume
Written by faded men,
At the suggestion of Holy Spectres –
Subjects – Bethlehem –
Eden – the ancient Homestead –
Satan – the Brigadier,
Judas – the great Defaulter,
David – the Troubadour.
Sin – a distinguished Precipice
Others must resist,
Boys that 'believe'
Are very lonesome –
Other boys are 'lost'.
Had but the tale a warbling Teller
All the boys would come –
Orpheus' sermon captivated,
It did not condemn.

Candor, my tepid Friend,
Come not to play with me!
The Myrrhs and Mochas of the Mind
Are its Iniquity.

On my volcano grows the grass, –
A meditative spot,
An area for a bird to choose
Would be the general thought.

How red the fire reeks below,
How insecure the sod –
Did I disclose, would populate
With awe my solitude.

Color, Caste, Denomination –
These are Time's affair,
Death's division classifying
Does not know they are.

As in sleep – all here forgotten,
Tenets put behind,
Death's large democratic fingers
Rub away the brand.

If Circassian – He is careless –
If He put away
Chrysalis of Blonde or Umber,
Equal butterfly

They emerge from His obscuring;
What Death knows so well,
Our minuter intuitions
Deem incredible.

Doom is the House Without the Door —
'Tis entered from the sun,
And then the ladder's thrown away
Because escape is done.

'Tis varied by the dream
Of what they do outside,
When squirrels play and berries die —
And hundreds bow to God.

I dwell in Possibility,
A fairer house than Prose,
More numerous of windows,
Superior of doors.

Of chambers, as the cedars –
Impregnable of eye;
And for an everlasting roof
The gables of the sky.

Of visitors – the fairest –
For occupation – this –
The spreading wide my narrow hands
To gather Paradise.

To intercept his yellow plan
The sun does not allow
Caprices of the atmosphere;
And even when the snow

Heaves balls of specks like vicious boy
Directly in his eye,
Does not so much as turn his head —
Busy with majesty!

'Tis his to stimulate the earth,
And magnetize the sea,
And bind astronomy in place —
Yet any passer-by

Would deem Ourselves the busier,
As the minutest bee
That rides supports a thunder,
A bomb to justify!

(*With a flower*)

All the letters I can write
Are not fair as this,
Syllables of velvet,
Sentences of plush,
Depths of ruby, undrained,
Hid, lip, for thee —
Play it were a humming bird
And just sipped me!

It's coming — the postponeless Creature,
It gains the block and now it gains the door,
Chooses its latch from all the other fastenings,
Enters with a — 'You know me, Sir?'
Simple salute and certain recognition,
Bold — were it enemy — brief were it friend,
Dresses each house in crêpe and icicle,
And carries one out of it to God.

My life had stood a loaded gun
In corners, till a day
The owner passed – identified,
And carried me away.

And now we roam the sov'reign woods,
And now we hunt the doe –
And every time I speak for him
The mountains straight reply.

And do I smile, such cordial light
Upon the valley glow –
It is as a Vesuvian face
Had let its pleasure through.

And when at night, our good day done,
I guard my master's head,
'Tis better than the eider duck's
Deep pillow to have shared.

To foe of his I'm deadly foe,
None stir the second time
On whom I lay a yellow eye
Or an emphatic thumb.

Though I than he may longer live,
He longer must than I,
For I have but the art to kill –
Without the power to die.

Good morning, Midnight!
I'm coming home,
Day got tired of me –
How could I of him?

Sunshine was a sweet place,
I liked to stay –
But Morn didn't want me – now –
So good night, Day!

I can look, can't I?
When the East is red?
The hills have a way, then,
That puts the heart abroad.

You are not so fair, Midnight –
I chose Day,
But please take a little Girl
He turned away!

Longing is like the seed
That wrestles in the ground,
Believing if it intercede
It shall at length be found.

The hour and the zone
Each circumstance unknown,
What constancy must be achieved
Before it see the sun!

A toad can die of light!
        Deaths is the common right
    Of toads and men, –
Of earl and midge

The privilege.
        Why swagger then?
The gnat's supremacy
Is large as thine.

Penguin Little Black Classics Vol. III

21. JANE AUSTEN
The Beautifull Cassandra

22. FYODOR DOSTOYEVSKY
The Meek One

23. AESOP
The Cat and Venus

24. CHARLES DICKENS
To Be Read at Dusk

25. JOHANN PETER HEBEL
How a Ghastly Story Was Brought to Light by a Common or Garden Butcher's Dog

26. OSCAR WILDE
Lord Arthur Savile's Crime

27. LEO TOLSTOY
The Death of Ivan Ilyich

28. MICHEL DE MONTAIGNE
How We Weep and Laugh at the Same Thing

29. EMILY DICKINSON
My life had stood a loaded gun

30. WALT WHITMAN
On the Beach at Night Alone

企鹅经典：小黑书　第三辑

“没有一种品质
只配我们拥有，
而且永远拥有。”

PENGUIN

LITTLE BLACK

CLASSICS

* 本文译自法国伽利玛出版社（Gallimard）1962 年出版的古法语版《蒙田全集》（*Les Essais*），并参考了之后收录于同一出版社“七星文库”（*Bibliothèque de la Pléiade*）中的《蒙田全集》。

我们为何为同一件事哭和笑

How We Weep and Laugh at the Same Thing

［法］蒙田　著
马振聘　译

中信出版集团 | 北京

图书在版编目（C I P）数据

企鹅经典：小黑书．第三辑：汉、英 /（英）简·奥斯汀等著；夏星等译．-- 北京：中信出版社，2019.6

书名原文：Penguin Little Black Classics

ISBN 978-7-5217-0407-5

Ⅰ．①企… Ⅱ．①简… ②夏… Ⅲ．①世界文学－作品综合集－汉、英 Ⅳ．① I11

中国版本图书馆 CIP 数据核字 (2019) 第 072172 号

企鹅经典：小黑书　第三辑

我们为何为同一件事哭和笑

著　　者：[法] 蒙田
译　　者：马振骋
出版发行：中信出版集团股份有限公司
（北京市朝阳区惠新东街甲 4 号富盛大厦 2 座 邮编 100029）
承 印 者：北京楠萍印刷有限公司

开　　本：787mm × 1092mm　1/32　　印　　张：45.75　　字　　数：756 千字
版　　次：2019 年 6 月第 1 版　　印　　次：2019 年 6 月第 1 次印刷
京权图字：01-2018-6477　　广告经营许可证：京朝工商广字第 8087 号
书　　号：ISBN 978-7-5217-0407-5
定　　价：149.00 元（全 10 册）

服务热线：400-600-8099
投稿邮箱：author@citicpub.com

目录

我们为何为同一件事哭和笑

／

［理解矛盾情感的复杂性，能够使我们避免片面解读伟人及其悲痛。］[1]

我们在史书中读到，安提柯对儿子非常不满，因为他刚才在一场争斗中把他的敌人皮洛士国王杀了，提了头颅来献给他；他看到头颅却号啕大哭起来。还有洛林的勒内公爵打败勃艮第的查理公爵后不久也为他的死亡惋惜，还在他的葬礼上服丧。在奥雷战役中，蒙福尔伯爵战胜查理·德·布卢瓦，赢得了他的布列塔尼公爵封

1. 每篇散文前的附加内容均为英文版译者 M.A. 斯克里奇（M.A.Screech）单独添加，由谢万容单独翻译。——编者注

邑，战胜者看到敌人的尸体，深表哀悼。但是读了这些不应该立刻惊叫：

> 普天之下，人的心灵
> 都隐藏这些不同的感情，
> 脸上表现时而喜悦时而阴郁。
>
> ——彼特拉克

有人把庞培的首级献给恺撒时，史书记载说他转过头去，仿佛看到了丑恶、惨不忍睹的情景。他们两人长期一起商量国家大计，同舟共济，相互协助，建立联盟，所以不应该认为这个举动完全是装腔作势，像这位说的：

> 他想这回可以安心当岳丈了。
> 眼泪是挤出来的，
> 呻吟发自欢愉的心。
>
> ——卢卡努

因为，虽然我们大部分行为实际上只是门面与装饰，有时也可能是真心的：

继承人当面哭，背后笑。

——普布利流斯·西鲁斯

然而在评判这些事时，必须考虑我们的心灵怎样经常受各种情欲的冲击。就像我们的躯体内是各种体液[1]的大汇合，根据我们的性情使其中一种占主导地位；同样，我们的心灵内也有各种不同的活动冲击它，必然也有一个活动统率全局。但是这种优势并不会一直保持下去，我们的心灵变化不定，那些原本较弱的活动也会趁势反扑，收复失地。从这里看出，不但孩子一切都天真地从本性出发，经常为同一件事哭和笑，我们中间也有人虽然很想出外旅行，在跟家人和朋友道别时，却也不能吹嘘，否则会感到勇气受挫；眼泪若没有完全流出来，至少踏上马镫时会黯然神伤。不管好人家的女儿心里燃着怎样的热情，还是要把她们从母亲的脖子上拉下来，送

1. 古希腊有“体液学说”，认为机体的生命取决于四种体液：血液、黏液、黄胆汁和黑胆汁。每一种液体与一定的“气质”相适应，每个人的气质则取决于他体内占优势的那种液体。例如，在蒙田那个时代，人们认为忧郁症是体液不平衡、黑色胆汁分泌过多所致。——编者注

到夫婿家，不管这位好心的同伴怎么说：

> 维纳斯是不是跟新娘有冤仇，
> 还是为了哄骗快活的爹娘，
> 在房前床边流几滴眼泪？
> 眼泪也可能不是真的！上帝帮帮我吧！
> ——卡图鲁斯

一个人人皆曰可杀的人死了，还是有人悼念，也是不奇怪的。

当我斥责仆人时，真的是火冒三丈，不是装模作样骂几声；但是怒气发过以后，他若对我有所要求，我还是乐意帮他忙；我立即把这一页翻了过去。当我骂他笨蛋蠢驴，不是要他一辈子背这个名声，也不想收回这句话立即再称他是正人君子。没有一种品质只配我们拥有，而且永远拥有。如果自言自语算不上是疯子行为，没一天我不听到心里在骂自己："大笨蛋！"这绝不是在说我自己真是这样的人。

如果谁看到我在妻子面前一会儿冷若冰霜，一会儿春风满面，就认为这都是装的，他就是个傻子。尼禄下令淹死自己的母亲，跟她分手时突然动了情，对这次母子诀别感到厌恶与怜悯。

有人说太阳放光不是连续不断的，它是不停地让一束束新光照射着我们，以至我们辨别不出而以为是连续的了：

太阳，不歇的以太之源，火的洪流，
使天空永远白昼如新，
光明接着光明。

——卢克莱修

我们的心灵也是巧思纷呈，细流无声。

阿尔塔巴努斯无意中看到他的侄子泽尔士，问他为什么刚才神色大异。泽尔士正在考虑他的军队无比强大，要通过赫勒斯旁海峡去进攻希腊。起初看到有成千上万人归他指挥，踌躇满志，面露欣喜之情。但是继而就在同时想到那么多的生命至迟在本世纪内就要消失，不由得皱起眉头，伤心得落下了眼泪。

我们曾经坚定不移地报仇雪耻，为胜利而欢天喜地，可是也因而落眼泪。我们不是为了胜利而落泪，事情没有丝毫变化，只是我们不是怀着同一颗心去看待它，看到的就是另一副面目。因为每件事都有不同的侧面、不同的光线。心头想起血缘之亲、昔日的情谊，根据不同情况会激动一时，但是轮廓的闪现那么突然，我们无法把握。

> 说到速度，什么也比不上
> 思想的闪动，要来就来，
> 思想灵活多变，超过任何
> 置于目光下、落入感觉中的物体。
>
> ——卢克莱修

由于这个原因，要用这一系列断断续续的闪念构筑一个物体，必然会出差错。蒂莫利昂经过深思熟虑大义灭亲以后，他哭了，他哭的不是祖国恢复了自由，他哭的不是暴君，他哭的是他的兄弟。当他的一部分职责完成后，另一部分职责又要他履行了。

论良心

/

［良心最初指纵容默许。良心的概念深深吸引着蒙田，即我们个人的是非观，抑或是我们的负罪感与正义感。宗教战争期间，蒙田目睹了种种残忍行径、诬告栽赃，见惯了对犯人的严刑拷打，由此开始重点反思良心。他发现，非常奇怪的是，“拷问”（刑讯逼供）所依凭的道德准则似乎正是出于人们对良心力量的尊重——一个人内心是负罪还是无辜，都体现在他忍受苦痛的能力是削弱还是增强上。蒙田此篇主要受圣·奥古斯丁和璜·路易斯·斐微斯的启发。关于奥古斯丁的《上帝之城》，斐微斯

曾经写下一篇激情洋溢的笔记，谈论要减少人们对酷刑的过度信任。]

内战时期，我的兄弟拉勃鲁斯领主和我有一次在旅途中，遇见一位风度翩翩的贵族，他属于我们的敌对派别，但是我并不知道，因为他掩饰得很巧妙。这类战争中最糟的是局势错综复杂，从外表、语言和穿戴来说，敌人和你无法得以区分，双方接受同样的法律，遵守同样的习俗，呼吸同样的空气，难免混淆不清。我害怕在一个陌生地方遇见我们的军队，不得不说出自己的名字，这时真是生死难卜。我以前遇到过这样的事，在那次不幸的遭遇中，我人马俱损，不但如此，他们还残忍地杀害了一名意大利宫廷侍从贵族，我精心培育过他，一个有着光明前程的年轻的生命就这样消失了。

但是那位贵族非常容易惊慌失措，我看他每次遇见骑马的人过来，穿越效忠于国王的城市，都吓得要死，我终于猜到他的恐惧是由于他的良心而来的。这名青年觉得，人家通过他的面具和大氅上的十字架可以看到他内心的秘密意图。良心的力量竟是那么奇妙！良心使我们背叛，使我们控诉，使我们战斗；在没有外界证人的情况下，良心会追逐我们，反对我们：

用无形的鞭子抽打，充当刽子手。

——朱维纳利斯

这已是妇孺皆知的故事：一个名叫贝苏斯的帕奥尼人，被人指责说他故意打下一个鸟窝，把里面的小鸟统统杀光，他说自己做得有理，因为这些小鸟不停地无端指责他害死了自己的父亲。这桩弑父罪进行得滴水不漏，直到那时也没有人知晓；但是良心提出了申冤，使这个背上沉重赎罪包袱的人无法自制。

柏拉图认为，惩罚紧紧跟在罪恶的后面，赫西俄德纠正了柏拉图的说法，他说惩罚是与罪恶同时开始的。谁在等待惩罚，就在受惩罚；谁该受惩罚，就在等待惩罚。恶意给怀恶意的人带来痛苦：

做坏事的人最受做坏事的苦！

——拉丁谚语

胡蜂刺伤了人，但是自己受害更深，因为它从此失去了自己的刺和力量。

> 它们把自己的生命留在了伤疤里。
>
> ——维吉尔

由于自然界的矛盾对立规律，斑蝥身上分泌一种自身毒液的解毒素。所以，即使人在作恶时感受到乐趣，良心上却会适得其反，产生一种憎恶感，引起许多痛苦和联想，不论睡时醒时都折磨着自己。

> 这样的罪人不在少数，
> 在睡梦或谵妄中自怨自艾，
> 泄露了长期隐藏的罪过。
>
> ——卢克莱修

暴君阿波罗多罗斯在梦中见到自己被斯基泰人剥掉了皮，放在一口锅里煮，他的心喃喃地对他说：“你的所有痛苦都是我引起的。”伊壁鸠鲁说：“坏人无处藏身，因为他们躲在哪儿都不安宁，良心会暴露他们。”

没有一名罪人在自我判决中得到赦免，

这才是主要的惩罚。

——朱维纳利斯

良心可使我们恐惧，也可使我们坚定和自信。我敢于说人生道路上经过许多险阻而步伐始终不乱，就是因为我对自己的意图深有了解，自己的计划光明正大。

人的内心充满恐惧还是希望，

全凭良心的判断。

——奥维德

这类例子成千上万，这里只需举出同一个人物的三个例子。

西庇阿有一次在罗马人民面前被指控犯了一桩大罪，他不但不要求宽恕或向法官讨情，还对他们说："好哇，你们还不是靠了我才有权力审判每个人，如今竟要起我的脑袋来了。"

又有一次，人民法庭对他起诉，他决不声辩，只是侃侃而谈："来吧，我的公民们，去向神祇拜谢，也是在今天这样的日子，让我战胜了迦太基人。”说罢，他大踏步向神庙走去，只见所有人跟在他后面，其中还有他的起诉人。

又是人民法庭应加图的要求，传讯西庇阿，要他对安蒂奥克省的一切开支做出汇报。西庇阿为此事来到元老院，从袍子下抽出账册，说这本账册把一切收支原原本本记了下来；但是他没有同意把它转交给法院档案室保存，说他不愿意自取其辱，便在元老院当着众人的面亲手把账册撕成碎片。我不相信这个饱经沧桑的灵魂会弄虚作假。李维说他天性慷慨豪爽，一向气度恢宏，他决不会当个罪人，低三下四去声辩自己是无辜的。

苦刑是一项危险的发明，这像是在检验人的耐性而不是检验人的真情。能够忍受苦刑的人会隐瞒真情，不能够忍受苦刑的人也会隐瞒真情。痛苦能够使我供认事实，为什么就不能使我供认非事实呢？另一方面，如果那个受到无理指责的人有耐性忍受这些折磨，罪有应得的人难道就没有耐性忍受这些折磨，去获得美好的生命报偿吗？

我相信这项发明的理论基础是建立在良心力量的想法上。因为对有罪的人，似乎利用苦刑可以使他软弱，说出他的错误；然而无罪的人则会更加坚强，不畏苦刑。说实在的，这个方法充满不确定性和危险。

为了躲过难忍的痛苦，什么话不会说，什么事不会做呢？

痛苦会迫使无辜的人撒谎。

——普布利流斯·西鲁斯

审判者折磨人是为了不让他清白死去，而结果是让那个人受尽折磨后清白死去。成千上万的受刑者脑袋里装满了假忏悔。我想到亚历山大审判菲罗塔斯的情景，以及他受折磨的过程。我尤其要以菲罗塔斯作为例子。

然而有人却说，揭示人类弱点的许多发明中，苦刑还是痛苦最少的一项发明。

依我看来也是最不人道、最无意义的发明！有许多被希腊和罗马称为野蛮的国家，在这方面却不及希腊和罗马野蛮，它们认为折磨和杀害一个人们对其错误还只是心存怀疑的人，是可怕的残酷行为。你不知道实情，他又能怎么样呢？你不想无缘无故地杀他，对他做的事却比杀他还糟糕，你没有不公正吗？事情就是如此：多少次他宁愿无缘无故地死去，也不愿接受审讯，这种审讯往往比死刑还痛苦，这等于在执行死刑以前已把人处决了。

我不知道从哪儿听来这个故事，但是它如实地代表了我们良心的公正。一名村妇在一位军队司令兼大法官面前控诉一名士兵，说他抢去了她仅剩下的喂几个小孩的一点点面糊，这支军队已把四周村庄掠夺一空。然而没有证据。这位将军首先告诫妇女要对自己说的话仔细想一想，若是诬告就要判罪，她坚持不改口，将军下令割开士兵的肚子验证事实真相。妇女说的话是对的。罪证确凿。

命运与理智经常相遇在一条道上

［罗马的审查官对蒙田有关命运（区别于天意）的言论甚是不满——这很奇怪，因为几个世纪以来，变幻莫测的命运以及命运之轮早已是老生常谈。（“命运”一词在蒙田散文中出现多达三百五十次。）］

命运变幻无常，在我们面前展现的面貌也就千变万化。这不也是在明白无误地伸张正义吗？瓦朗蒂努瓦公爵恺撒·波齐亚决心要毒死科尔内托的红衣主教阿德里安，他的父亲亚历山大六世教皇偕同他到梵蒂冈吃晚饭。公爵事先差人送了一瓶毒酒交给司膳总管，嘱他好好看管。教皇在儿子之前到，要求喝酒，司膳总管以为这是瓶好酒，交给他就是给教皇喝的，就倒了一杯敬教皇；公爵本人恰在上点心时赶到，以为他自己的那瓶酒还没开过，也就拿来喝了；这样父亲立即暴死，儿子长期受病痛折磨，命运更加悲惨。

有时候命运好像有意跟我们作对。德斯特雷领主是旺多姆殿下的军旗手，里克领主是阿尔斯霍特公爵的随从副官，虽分属对立的部队，但都在追求封凯泽尔领主的妹妹（在前线相邻的两支部队常有这样的事）。里克领主求婚成功；但是在婚礼那天，不幸的是新郎在上床之前，要去逞能来取悦新娘，离家到了圣奥梅尔附近跟人交了手，却让德斯特雷领主占了上风，把他捉了当俘虏。

> 离开年轻郎君的怀抱，
> 让一个冬天，又一个冬天，
> 在漫漫长夜中烧尽了他们的烈火。
>
> ——卡图鲁斯

为了摆足威风，德斯特雷迫使那位夫人亲自来向他求情，把他的俘虏客客气气还给她；人也确实放了，法国贵族从不拒绝夫人的要求。

君士坦丁（一世），海伦娜的儿子，创立了君士坦丁帝国；多少世纪以后，又是一个君士坦丁（十一世），也是海伦娜的儿子，断送了君士坦丁帝国。这不像是巧妙的命运安排吗？

有时候，命运喜欢跟奇迹争高低。我们知道克洛维斯国王围困昂古莱姆时，城墙自个儿坍塌，如有神助。布歇援引某位作者的话，虔诚者罗伯特二世国王在围城时，偷偷离开前线溜回奥尔良庆祝圣埃尼昂节，正当他弥撒做到中途顶礼膜拜时，围城的城墙不攻自破了。这跟我们在米兰战争中发生的事恰恰相反。朗佐统帅在为我们包围阿罗纳城时，命人在一堵大墙下埋炸药。这堵墙突然被炸离地面，又直挺挺落下竖在地基上，被困的人还是安然无恙。

有时候，命运还会治病。费雷斯的亚逊胸口长了个脓疮，医生都已束手无策，他一心要摆脱折磨，即使死了也甘心。在一次战役中他奋不顾身冲进敌阵，被刺穿身子，恰巧伤在病患处，脓疮破裂，这下子治愈了。

命运在艺术技艺方面不是还超过了画家普罗托盖纳斯吗？画家画了一条疲劳的狗，全身什么部位都感到很称心，但就是狗嘴里的口水画得不中意，他对自己的画发起了脾气，拿起一块蘸满各种颜料的海绵朝它扔了过去，要把它都擦掉；命运让那块海绵恰好扔在狗嘴上，在上面留下的正是艺术家想画而画不出的艺术效果。

有时，命运不是在指导我们、改正我们吗？英格兰伊莎贝尔女王率领一支军队去支援儿子反对她的丈夫，要从泽兰回到王国内；她若按原计划抵达港口必然完了，敌人都在那里等着她，但是命运却不顾她的意愿让她在一个安全地点登了陆。那位古人，拿起石头要砸狗，却砸死了自己的老娘，不是很有理由念一念这句诗吗？

> 命运比我们更有主意。
>
> ——米南德

蒂莫利昂在西西里岛阿德拉诺暂住，伊塞特召了两名士兵要杀他。他们决定在他献祭时动手。他们混在人群中，正在相互发信号趁机会下手时，突然来了第三个人，在其中一位头上狠狠砍了一剑，待他死在地上后，自己拔腿就跑。那位同伴以为自己被人识破，脱不了身，奔到祭台，答应把一切都招供出来，要求宽恕。

正当他在交代阴谋过程时，那第三个人被大家当作谋杀犯抓住了，推推搡搡穿过人群到了蒂莫利昂和在场的显贵面前。这时那个人大叫饶命，说他杀死的只是杀他父亲的凶手。他运气来得正好，当场有人证明他的父亲确是在利恩泰奈人的城里被那个他杀死报仇的人杀的。他由于这件巧事得到了一大笔赏金，既报了父亲的仇，又救了西西里父母官的命。这样的命运在讨回公道方面，是任何人精心制定的法律也难以达到的。

最后一个例子。这件事还不能清楚说明命运总是倾向于善良与赤诚之心吗？伊格纳蒂乌斯父子被罗马三世执政放逐，决定做出惊人之举，互相结束对方的生命，不让暴政者得逞施加酷刑。他们手握宝剑朝着对方奔去。命运指挥着他们的剑头，两剑都立即夺去他们的生命，为了表彰这么美好的父子情，还让他们有力气从洞穿的身子里抽出鲜血淋漓的手臂与宝剑，相互紧紧拥抱，再也一动不动。刽子手无法把他们分离，只得一下子割下两人的头颅，让两具尸体始终有尊严地贴在一起，伤口对着伤口深情地吮吸着对方的血与残留的生命。

论对懦夫行为的惩罚

［文艺复兴时期的法律学者，如安德烈·蒂亚居伊想要通过研究人的动机与局限，从而缓和社会的严刑峻法。在这里，蒙田效仿前者，对战争年代的男士们表达了深切担忧。］

曾听到一位亲王、杰出的将领说过，一名士兵不能因丧失勇气而被处死。他在用餐时听到德·韦尔万领主一案，后者因献出布洛涅而被判处死刑。

因软弱造成的错误与因恶意造成的错误，中间有巨大的差别，这样说实在是有道理的。恶意是我们有心鼓动自己违背天性形成的理智规则。至于软弱，不妨也拿天性来自我辩护，说是它造成了我们这样的不完美和缺陷，以至不少人想到，只有违背自己良心做事才可以加以责备。这条规则，使一部分人形成这样的看法，反对对异教徒和无信仰者使用极刑，同样认为律师和法官不必承担无知渎职的责任。

但是，说到懦夫行为，最常见的惩罚是当众羞辱。据说这条规则最早是由法学家夏隆达斯提出的，在他以前，希腊法律以死刑处分临阵脱逃的人。夏隆达斯只是罚那些人穿上妇女服装在广场中央坐三天，指望他们羞愧后恢复勇气，还能入伍打仗。“与其让男人血流在地上，还不如让他血涌到脸上。”（德尔图良）

从前，罗马法律对逃兵也是判死罪。据安米阿努斯·马西利纳斯的叙述，在帕提亚战役中，有十名士兵冲锋时转身往回跑，朱利安皇帝先把他们逐出军队，后来据说依古法处死。然而另一次，有人犯了相似的罪过，他只是处分他们跟囚徒一起待在辎重部队。罗马人对在卡尼战役中逃跑的士兵，还有在同一场战争中随同执政官法尔维乌斯吃败仗的士兵，惩罚再严也不至把他们处死。

然而有一事必须提防，羞辱使他们失去颜面，不但会使他们冷漠无情，还会将他们变为敌人。

在我们祖辈那个时代，弗朗杰领主当过德·夏蒂永元帅的副官，受德·夏巴纳元帅派遣，取代杜·吕德大人当富恩塔拉比亚总督。他把富恩塔拉比亚拱手让与西班牙人，因此被废除贵族称号，他与他的后代都被贬为平民，要缴人头税，不准入伍当兵。这一严厉的判决是在里昂执行的。后来纳索伯爵带军队开进吉兹时，城里的全体贵族都遭到类似的惩罚；后来其他类似的事也复如此处理。

然而，如果无知与懦夫行为过于恶劣或明显，超出了一般的程度，那时就有理由把它看成是确凿的证据，说明当事人的狡猾和恶意，并以此定罪。

论言过其实

/

［尽管蒙田对语言的运用已炉火纯青，他本人却鄙视文字，崇尚行动或“实事”。早在开始散文创作之前，他就曾在雷蒙德·塞朋德《自然神学》一书译作的开篇献词——“给父亲的一封信”中表达了该观点。对“行动胜于雄辩”的尊重，正是他景仰古代斯巴达王国的原因，同时也是当世所欠缺的品质。］

从前一位修辞学家说，他的职业是把小事物说得大，显得大。这就像鞋匠给一对小脚丫做上一双大鞋子。在斯巴达靠吹牛说谎为职业就会挨鞭子。我相信阿基达默斯国王听到修昔底德的回答不会不表示惊讶。国王问他与伯里克利角斗谁更强，他回答说:“这不好验证，因为我在角斗中把他摔倒在地，他却说服在场观看的人说他没有倒地，于是他赢了。”

有人让女人戴上面纱，涂脂抹粉，这为害不大，因为不能看到她们处在自然状态，不是大不了的损失；而其他人要欺骗的不是我们的眼睛，而是我们的判断，要歪曲和败坏的是事物的本质。像克里特、斯巴达这样的城邦，局势稳定，治理有方，并不重视雄辩家。

阿里斯托给修辞学下了个聪明的定义：说服老百姓的技术。苏格拉底、柏拉图则说是骗人和拍马的艺术。有人从大道理上否定它，却在自己的训诫中到处使用。

伊斯兰教禁止向孩子传授修辞学，因为它无用。

雅典人发现修辞学的使用在都城里有上升趋势，这是很有害的，下令把煽动情绪的主要篇章，连同前言和结论部分一齐删去。

修辞学的发明，是为了操纵和煽动一群乌合之众和暴徒。这个工具专门用于病态政体，就像是药。在那些庸人、无知的人或任何人独占一切的地方，如雅典、罗德岛和罗马，在那些局势纷争不已的地方，演说家才应运而生。的确，在这些政体里，很少有人是不靠口才而平步青云的；庞培、恺撒、克拉苏、卢库卢斯、兰图卢斯，都是慷慨陈词以后得到极大的支持，最后登上权柄的高位，他们依仗口才更甚于军队，这与太平盛世的看法是相悖的。

L. 沃卢姆努斯当众演说，支持 Q. 法比乌斯和 P. 德基乌斯当选为执政官，他说：“这些人是为战争而生的，建功立业的大人物，打嘴仗也毫不示弱，是真正的执政人才；头脑精明，说话服众和博学多才，可以管理城市，执政主持民事裁判工作。”

当政局一片混乱，内战的风暴搅得人心惶惶时，罗马城内的雄辩家如沐春风，就像一块没有开垦的荒地上野草丛生。这样看来，由单独君主控制的政府不像其他政府那样需要这种东西；因为百姓愚昧轻信，耳边听了甜言蜜语，很容易受到操纵和误导，不会用理智的力量去审察和认识事物的真相；对这种轻信态度，我要说，在君主个人身上是不容易存在的，良好教育与好言规劝也较为容易使他免受这种毒药的危害。在马其顿和波斯就没出过一个有名气的雄辩家。

我刚才跟一位意大利人谈过话，才引起我说了上面一番话。他曾给已故的红衣主教加拉法当过司膳总管，直至主教过世。我请他谈谈他的差使。他神色严肃，把这门讲究口腹之欲的学问，一本正经地说了一通，仿佛在跟我讲神学的大道理。他向我细分不同的胃口：饥饿时的胃口，上了两三道菜后的胃口；什么方法吃了只不过使胃舒服，什么方法引得胃口大开；调料使用方法，一般的，特殊的，针对菜肴的特点和作用；不同季节的沙拉也不同，有需要加热的，也有需要冷食的，如何搭配花色使它们赏心悦目。在这之后，又说到上菜的顺序，其中的微妙大有讲究。

怎样切兔肉，如何斩鸡块，
当然都大有学问。

——朱维纳利斯

言辞里充满崇论闳议，就像在发表治国大略。这使我想起我的朋友：

太咸啦！烧煳啦！淡啦！恰到好处！
下次就照这样做！我教他们，

以我浅薄的学识尽心尽力。
总之，德梅亚，我要他们
拿锅子当镜子，教他们毫不留一手。

——泰伦提乌斯

埃米利乌斯·波勒斯从马其顿回来，宴请希腊人；希腊人对他宴会的组织安排大加赞赏；但是我这里说的不是他们做了什么，而是他们说了什么。

我不知道别人听了是不是与我有同感。当我听到我们的建筑师踌躇满志，大谈壁柱、下楣、挑檐、科林斯和陶立克柱型，还有他们类似的行话，我不由自主地想到阿波里东宫；实际上，我发现那是指我家厨房上那几条质地单薄的横档。

当你听到有人说替代、隐喻、讽喻这类语法词汇，那不是像在指某个罕见冷僻的语言现象吗？其实是涉及你的女仆唠叨的用语。

还有一种与此相近的花招，就是用罗马人的显赫官衔来称呼我们的官吏，然而他们在职务上没有丝毫相似之处，更没有那样的权威与权力。这种做法我相信，总有一天会说明我们这个世纪的荒谬绝伦，把古代荣耀了几个世纪的一两位人物的最光辉称号，不恰当地加到我们中意的人身上。称柏拉图是神，这是举世公认的，谁也不会嫉妒。然而意大利人，他们自诩整体上跟他们那个时代的其他民族相比，更为隽智和明白事理，这话有点道理，但是不久前却把那个尊号安到了阿雷蒂诺头上，这一位除了说话诙谐刻薄，确有高明之处，只是经常牵强附会，莫名其妙。就算他口才高明，我也看不出他有什么才能超越他同一世纪的大多数作家，更不用说跟古人的神号相去甚远了。

“伟大”这个词，我们却动辄加在并不比群众伟大的亲王身上。

探讨哲学就是学习死亡

/

[蒙田一直以来安于愁思，如今却是轻描淡写。他被死亡的恐惧所困扰，这种恐惧通常源于行将就木时所遭受的折磨——以前人们往往难逃临死的苦痛。对此，蒙田的处理可谓言辞雄辩，却并不客观冷漠，而是努力找寻普通人身上的美好品质。]

西塞罗说，探讨哲学不是别的，只是准备死亡。尤因探讨与静观可以说是让我们的灵魂脱离肉体而独自行动，有点像在学习与模拟死亡；或者也可以说，人类的一切智慧与推理归根结底，就是要我们学习不怕死亡。

说实在的，理智不是在冷嘲热讽，而是把目标定在使我们满足上。理智的工作，总的是要人活得好，要我们如《圣经》所说的“终身喜乐行善”。世上人人都是这种看法，尽管表达形式各有不同，快乐是我们的目标；与此不同的看法一出笼就被排斥，若有人说什么他的目的是让我们受苦受难，那谁会去听呢？

在这方面，哲学宗派之间的分歧只表现在口头上。“别去听那些美妙的妖言。”（塞涅卡）在这么一个神圣的学科中不应该有那么多的顽固与恶言。某人不论扮演什么角色，扮演的总是他自己。他们不论说什么，即使谈到美德，瞄准的最终目标也是感官享乐。他们听到这个词那么反感，而我偏要在他们耳边说个不休。如果这个词意味着最强的欢乐与极度的满足，那时美德的介入才胜过其他东西的介入。这种感官享乐不论如何纵情胡闹，粗野强健，也只是更加享乐而已。我们还不如称为欢乐，更容易接受，更温和自然，而不是曾用的“精力”一词。

另一种感官享乐——若也可用这个好名词的话——较为庸俗，也是应该相提并论的，但并不更占优势。我觉得它不像美德那样不包含放肆与邪念。除了感受更短暂、更流动、毫无新鲜感，它还有熬夜、挨饿、辛苦和血与汗；此外还有各种各样的情感折磨，然后再有这种沉重的满足，这无异于一种受罪了。

我们还大错特错地认为，这些磨难可以成为温情的刺激物与调味品，好像大自然中的万物相生相克；也不要说当我们转向美德时，同样的障碍与困难会压倒它，使它变得严峻、不可接近；而在美德介入的情况下，会使这种神圣完美的欢乐更高尚、更兴奋、更昂扬，要胜过低级的享乐许多。

一个人权衡他的所失与所得，不知道美德的温馨与作用，当然是不配认识这种欢乐的。有人劝导我们说美德的追求艰辛曲折，美德的享受则是愉快的，这岂不是在对我们说它不会令人快乐吗？因为哪个人曾有法子获得过它呢？最成功的人也只是做到向往它，接近它，而没有获得过它。

但是那些人错了，要知道追求我们所认识的任何乐趣，这本身就是乐趣；行动包含的乐趣，存在于我们眼前的美好目标，因为这是与大部分激情共生共灭的。在美德中闪闪发光的愉悦福乐，自有千百条渠道小路，引导你进入第一个入口，直至最后一道墙。那时美德的主要好处是对死亡的蔑视，这样使人的一生过得恬然安逸，让我们专注于愉悦的享受，不如此，其他一切享乐都会黯然无光。

这说明为什么一切规则都集中和会合在这个主题上。虽则那些规则也一致认为要蔑视痛苦、贫困和其他隶属于人生的遭遇，这在关心的程度上不一样，因为有的遭遇不是必然发生的（许多人一生中没有经历过贫困，有的还不曾有过疼痛的病患，如音乐师色诺菲吕斯，他活了一百零六岁，身体一直良好），还可以在万不得已时轻生，把烦恼一了百了。但是死亡本身则是不可避免的。

人人都被推向同一个方向，

我们的命运在缸里转动，

迟早会从里面跃出，

上了船，

带往不归路。

——贺拉斯

因而，要是死亡使我们害怕，这就成了一个说不完的痛苦话题，而又不能使心情纾解一丝一毫。死亡从哪儿都可以向我们袭击；我们就会不停地左右窥视，像进了一座疑阵以防不测："这就像永世悬在坦塔罗斯头上的岩石。"[1]（西塞罗）我们的法院经常把罪犯送到案发地点处决，一路上押着他们经过漂亮的房子，让他们拣好吃的吃个痛快：

> ……西西里岛的盛宴
> 也引不起他的馋涎。
> 鸟语与琴声
> 都不能使他入眠。
>
> ——贺拉斯

不妨想一想，他们能够高兴起来吗？游街的最终意图昭然若揭，难道不会败坏他们领受这一切恩典的兴致？

> 他打听道路，他掐算日子，

1. 据希腊神话，坦塔罗斯把儿子剁成碎块祭神，触怒主神宙斯，将他永世置于随时会砸落的岩石下。（说明：书中脚注除特别标明的之外，均为译者注。）

走了多少还剩下多少，

想到眼前的极刑痛不欲生。

——克洛迪安

我们生涯的终点是死亡，我们必须注视的是这个结局；假若它使我们害怕，怎么可能走前一步而又不发愁呢？凡人的药方是把它置之脑后。只是愚蠢透顶才会这么懵然无知！真是把马笼头套在了驴子尾巴上。

因为他决定了往回走。

——卢克莱修

他经常跌入陷阱也就不足为奇了。这让我们这些人一说到死亡就害怕，大多数人像听到魔鬼的名字一样画十字。由于遗嘱中必然提到这件事，就别指望在医生给他们宣读终审判决以前，他们会动手立遗嘱。在痛苦与惊慌之间，他们会以怎样清晰的判断力，给你凑合出一份遗嘱，只有天知道了。

由于这个词听在他们的耳朵里太刺激，这个声音对他们又像不吉利，罗马人学会了用婉转的说法来减弱或冲淡它的含意。不说：他死了，他停止了生命；只说：他活过了。只要是“活”，即使过去式也感到安慰。我们的“故人某某”就是从他们那里借来的。

说到这里，是不是像俗语说的，时间就是金钱？我生于一五三三年二月的最后一天，是按现行的以正月为一年之始的年历来说的[1]。恰好十五天前刚过了三十九岁，至少还可以活那么久；可是急着去考虑那么远的事不是发疯吗？但怎么说呢，年轻人与老年人同样都会抛下生命。刚刚进来的人照样可以随即离去。再衰老的人，只要还看到玛土撒拉[2]走在前面，都相信自己的身子还可以撑上二十年。

再说，你这个可怜的傻瓜，谁给你规定了寿限啦？你这是根据医生的胡说八道。还不如瞧一瞧事实与经验吧。按照事物的常规，你活到今天已是鸿运高照了。你已超过了常人的寿数。为了证明这一点，算一算你的朋友中间有多少人在你这个年龄以前已经谢世，肯定比达到你的年龄的人要多。再来列一张表，记上一生中名声显赫的人，我敢打赌在三十五岁前死的要比在这以后死

1. 原先以复活节为一年之始。

2.《圣经·旧约》中的人物，据说活了九百六十九岁。

的多。把耶稣基督作为人类的楷模，也是十分理智与虔诚的，因为耶稣在三十三岁就结束了人生。亚历山大是最伟大的凡人，也是在这岁数去世的。

死亡又有多少种袭击方式？

> 时时刻刻需要提防危险，
> 人是难以预料的。
>
> ——贺拉斯

且不说发高烧和胸膜炎病人。谁想到一位布列塔尼公爵会在人群中挤死？我的邻居克莱芒五世教皇进入里昂也是这样。你没看到我们的一位国王在比武游戏中被误伤丧了命吗？他的一位祖先竟会被一头公猪撞死？埃斯库罗斯眼看一幢房子要坍塌，徒然躲到空地上，有一只苍鹰飞过空中，从爪子里丢下一块乌龟壳，把他砸死了。还有人被一颗葡萄核梗死；一位皇帝在梳头时被梳子划破头皮而死；埃米利乌斯·李必达脚绊在门槛上，奥菲迪乌斯进议院时撞上了大门。还有死于女人大腿间的教士科内利乌斯·加吕，罗马巡逻队长蒂日利努斯，曼图亚侯爵吉·德·贡萨格的儿子吕多维可。

更糟糕的例子是柏拉图派哲学家斯珀西普斯和我们的一位教皇。可怜的伯比乌斯法官给诉讼一方八天期限，自己却突然得病，没有活到那个时候。凯乌斯·朱利乌斯是医生，在给病人上眼药膏时，死神来给他闭上了眼睛。我还该说一说我自己的弟弟，圣马丁步兵司令，年二十三岁，早已显出大胆勇敢，打网球时球击中他左耳上方，表面看不出挫伤和破裂，他甚至没有坐下来休息，但是五六小时后，他死于这次球击引起的中风。

这些都是发生在我们眼前的例子，稀松平常，怎么还能够不去想到死亡呢？怎么能够不觉得死神每时每刻在掐我们的脖子呢？

你们或许会对我说，既然不管怎样总是要来的，大家就不用去操这份心了吧？我同意这个看法；若有什么方法可以躲过死亡的袭击，即使是藏在一张牛皮底下，我也不是个会退缩回避的人。因为我只要过得自在就够了；我自己尽量往最好的方面去做，至于荣耀与表率则不在我的考虑之内。

我宁可被人看成傻子与呆子，

只要我的古怪令我痛快，叫我开心，

也不去当个聪明人愤愤不平。

——贺拉斯

以为这样就能做到了，这也是妄想。他们来了，他们去了，他们骑马，他们跳舞，闭口不谈死亡。这一切多么美好。毫不注意，毫不防范，当死亡降临到他们身上，或者他们的妻儿朋友身上时，则悲痛欲绝，呼天抢地，愤怒失望！你们几曾见过如此萎靡、恍惚、混乱！我们必须及早防范。一个头脑明白的人，对待死亡却像动物似的混混沌沌，我认为这是要不得的，也会让我们付出沉重的代价。如果死亡是个可以躲开的敌人，我建议大家不妨拿起胆小鬼的武器。但是既然它是不可避免的，既然退缩求饶和勇敢面对，它都是要把你抓走的：

他对逃跑中的壮汉穷追不舍，
也不放过胆怯的后生
露出的腿弯与背脊。

——贺拉斯

既然没有铁甲保护你：

躲在盔甲下也是枉然，

死神会让他露出后缩的脑袋。

——普罗佩提乌斯

我们必须学习挺身而出，面对它进行斗争。为了打落它的气势，我们必须采取逆常规而行的办法。不要把死亡看成是一件意外事，要看成是一件常事，习惯它，脑子里常常想到它。时时刻刻让它以各种各样的面目出现在我们的想象中。马匹惊跳，瓦片坠落，针轻轻一刺，立即想到:“要是这就是死亡呢？”这时候我们要坚强，要努力。

欢天喜地的时候，总是想到我们的生存状态，不要纵情而忘乎所以，记得多少回乐极会生悲，死亡会骤然而至。埃及人设宴，席间在上好菜时，叫人抬上一具干尸，作为对宴客的警告。

照亮你的每一天都当作最后一天，

赞美它带来的恩惠与意外的时间。

——贺拉斯

死亡在哪里等着我们是很不确定的，那就随时恭候它。事前考虑死亡也是事前考虑自由。谁学习了死亡，谁也就学习了不被奴役。死亡的学问使我们超越任何束缚与强制。一个人明白了失去生命不是坏事，那么生命对他也就不存在坏事了。可怜的马其顿国王当了波勒斯·伊米利厄斯的俘虏，差人求他不要把他带到凯旋仪式上，伊米利厄斯答复说："让他向自己求情吧。"

其实，在一切事情上，天公若不助一臂之力，手段与心计都很难施展。我本性并不忧郁，但爱好空想。从小对什么事都没像对死亡想得那么多，即使在放荡的岁月也是这样。

年少风流，青春欢悦。

——卡图鲁斯

在女人堆里寻欢作乐时，有人以为我站在一旁醋性大发，或者抱着希望拿不定主意，其实我在想着今已不知是谁的那个人，他就在几天前突然发高烧一命呜呼了；当他离开这样一次盛会时，满脑子是闲情、爱欲和好时光，像我一样，耳边也响着同样的话：

> 好时光即将消逝，消逝后再不回来。
>
> ——卢克莱修

这个想法不会比其他事情更叫我皱眉头。最初想到这类事不可能没有感触。但是日子一久，翻来覆去想多了，无疑也就习以为常了，否则我会终日提心吊胆；因为从来没有人会那么舍弃生命，没有人会那么不计较寿命的长短。直到今天为止，我一直精力充沛，极少生病，健康既没有使我对生命的期望增大，疾病也没有使我对生命的期望减少。我觉得自己每分钟都在逃过一劫。我不停地对自己唱：“另一天会发生的事，今天也会发生。”

说真的，意外与危险并不使我们更靠近死亡。如果我们想到，即使没有这桩好像威胁着我们的最大事件，还有成千上万桩其他事件悬在我们头上，我们就会明白，不论精力充沛还是高烧难退，在海上还是在家里，战场上还是休息中，死亡离我们都一样近。“谁都不比谁更脆弱，也不比谁对明天更有把握。”（塞涅卡）

去世前我有事要做，即使只需一小时就可完成，我也不敢说一定有时间去做完。日前有人翻阅我的记事册，发现一份备忘录，列上我在死前要做的事。我实实在在地对他说，那时我离家才一里地，还精神十足，心情愉快，但还是匆匆把这些事记了下来，因为没把握一定能够回到家。我这个人脑子随时随地在想东西，随即把它们记在心里，时刻做好充分准备；当死亡突然降临，对我也不算是突如其来的新鲜事。

应该随时穿好鞋子，准备上路，尤其要注意和做到的是这事只与自己有关。

短短的一生内何必计划成堆？

——贺拉斯

不算上这件事我们已经够忙碌的了。有一个人抱怨死亡，只是因为死亡使他功亏一篑，没有打完一场漂亮的胜仗；另一个人自思自叹，没把女儿嫁出去或把孩子教育安排好就会撒手人寰；这人舍不得抛下妻子，那人离不开儿子，这都是人生的主要乐趣。

我现在——感谢上帝——处于这样的状态下，可以应召离开，对什么事都毫无牵挂，虽然对人生尚有依恋，失去它会感到哀伤。我正在给自己松绑，已跟大家告别了一半，除了对自己。没有人对离开世界做了那么干脆与充分的准备，那么彻底摆脱一切，如同我正在做的一样。

> 可怜啊可怜，他们说，只要一个凶日
> 就会掳走我在世上的全部财富！
>
> ——卢克莱修

而建筑师说：

> 工程未完成，前功尽弃，
> 墙头砌到一半，摇摇欲坠。
>
> ——维吉尔

凡事不必筹备过于长期的规划，至少对于看不到其完成的事也保持热诚。我们生来是为了行动：

> 当我死时，但愿正在工作。
>
> ——奥维德

我愿意大家行动，尽量延长生命的功能，死神来时我若正在园子里种菜，不在乎它，更不在乎园子还没种完。我看见过一个人死去，他到了人生最后关头，不停地埋怨命运割断了他手中的历史之线，他还只写到我们的第十五或第十六位国王。

谁也不能说，对财物的留恋
不会也存在于你的残骸中。

——卢克莱修

应该摆脱这些庸俗有害的心态。正因为如此，坟墓盖在教堂附近，在城市里人来人往最多的地方，据利库尔戈斯说，这是为让男女老少不要看到死人而发毛，不断看见骸骨、坟墓和送灵，提醒着我们什么是人的处境：

古代用杀人给宴会助兴，
让武士相互残杀，
身子跌倒在酒杯上，

鲜血洒满宴席。

——西流斯·伊塔利库斯

埃及人在宴会结束后，给宾客展示一张死神的巨像，举像的人对着他们大叫：“喝吧，玩吧，死后你就是这个样。”因而我也养成了习惯，不但心里老惦念着死，嘴边也念叨着死，干什么都没那么乐意地去打听人的死亡，他们那时说过些什么，脸上表情怎么样，神态如何；读史书时也最注意这方面的章节。

我的书里充斥着这些例子，也可看出我对这些材料情有独钟。如果我编书，就要出一部集子，评论形形色色的死亡。教人如何死亡，也是在教人如何生活。

狄凯阿科斯编了一部题目类似的书，但内容不同，不很实用。

有人跟我说，事实远远超出想象，当人到了那个地步，剑法再高明也有失手时。让他们去说吧，事前考虑必定大有裨益。再说，脸不变色心不动，从容前赴，难道不算本领吗？

况且，大自然会伸出援助之手，给我们勇气。如果是暴卒，我们来不及害怕。若情况相反，我发觉随着病情的进展，也自然而然对生命日益蔑视。我发现身体有病时比身体健康时更易下决心去死。尤其我并不眷恋人生的欢乐，理由是我已开始失去享受的乐趣，对死亡也看得不如以前那么害怕。这使我希望做到离生愈远，离死愈近，也愈容易实行生与死的交替。

我在许多情况下试验过恺撒的说法：事物远看时常比近看显得大。我发觉自己健康时要比生病时更怕死亡。当我高高兴兴时，欢乐与力量使我把生与死的状态看得明显不成比例，成倍夸大烦恼以及它们造成的心理压力，我真的有病缠身时从来不至于如此。

我希望死亡来时我也有这样好的心态。体验变化与衰退很正常：这好比是大自然悄悄让我们在不知不觉中衰败凋零。往日青春年少的活力，在一位老人身上还留下多少？

唉，老人身上还剩下多少生命。

——马克西米努斯

恺撒有一名卫兵，神情憔悴，在街上向他走来，要求他批准自己去寻死。恺撒看他失魂落魄的样子，风趣地回答:“你居然以为自己在活着。”谁要是猝然消失，我相信我们谁都难以忍受。但是我们被它牵着手，从一条感觉不出的斜坡上，慢慢地一步步滑入这种惨境，再与之相适应。所以当青春在我们身上消逝时我们不觉得震动。虽然从本质与实情来说，青春消逝也是一种死亡，要比郁郁而死及寿终正寝更加严酷的死亡。尤其从恶活到不活这个跳跃不是很沉重，还比不得从青春欢乐的人生跌入痛苦艰难的境地。

佝偻的身躯背不起重担，心灵也是如此。必须让心灵开朗飞扬才能顶住这个死敌的压力。因为心灵害怕时就永远不会安宁。一旦心灵安宁了，它就可以自豪地说，焦虑、恐惧甚至微不足道的烦恼不足以干扰它。这差不多超越了我们人类的处境。

坚如磐石的心动摇不了，
无论是暴君威逼的目光，
亚得里亚海上肆虐的风暴，
还是朱庇特的霹雳掌。

——贺拉斯

心灵就成了情欲与贪婪的主宰，匮乏、羞耻、贫困和其他一切厄运的主宰。谁能够主宰谁就应去获得这种心灵优势。这才是至高无上的自由，让我们养成浩气去取笑武力与不公，嘲弄监牢与铁链：

我叫你戴上手铐脚镣，
交给一个恶吏看管——神会来救我的。
——你是说：我会死的，以死来一了百了？

——贺拉斯

在我们的宗教中，人最可靠的基础就是蔑视生命。不光是理智的推理要我们这样去做：有一件东西失去后不可能后悔，我们又为什么害怕失去呢？而且既然我们受到那么多死亡方式的威胁，害怕一切方式还不如忍受一种方式而少受些痛苦吧？既然死亡是不可避免的，什么时候来也就不管它了吧？当苏格拉底听人说："三十僭主已经判了你死刑。"他回答："自然法则也会轮到他们的。"

走在摆脱一切苦难的旅程上难过起来，这是何等的愚蠢！

一切事物随我们诞生而诞生，同样，一切事物随我们死亡而死亡。为一百年后我们不会活着的一切哭泣，犹如为一百年前我们不曾活过的一切哭泣，都是一样傻。死亡是另一种生命的开始，正如我们当年哭闹着到来，正如我们艰难地走进这个生命，正如我们进去时换下了以前的面纱。

凡事仅有一次也就无所谓痛苦。有什么理由为瞬息的事去担那么长久的忧？活得短与活得长在死亡面前都一样。对于不复存在的东西，长与短也不存在。亚里士多德说，希帕尼斯河上有些小动物只能活上一天。上午八点钟死的属于青春夭折，下午五点钟死的属于寿终正寝。对这段时间的幸与不幸斤斤计较，我们中间谁见了不会嘲笑？我们最长与最短的生命，若与永恒相比，或者跟山川、星辰、树木甚至某些动物相比，也是同样可笑。

但是大自然逼迫我们走上这条路。它说：你们怎么来到也就怎么走出这个世界。从死到生这条路你们走时不热情也不害怕，从生到死你们也这样去走。你们的死亡是宇宙秩序的一个组成部分，地球生命中的一刹那——

世人之间传递生命，

就像赛跑手交接火炬。

——卢克莱修

事物这样紧密安排，我能为你做出任何改变吗？这是你诞生的条件，死亡也是你的一部分；你这是在躲避自己。你享受的人生对生与对死均是有份的。你诞生的第一天引导你走向死，也同样引导你走向生。

第一时刻提供生命，同时也侵蚀生命。

——塞涅卡

诞生时开始了死亡，根源中包含了终结。

——马尼利乌斯

你生活的一切，是从生命那里窃取的；你活着是对生命的侵害。你一生中不断营造的是死亡。当你在生命中，你也是在死亡中。当你不再活着时，你的死亡也过去了。

因此，你若更喜欢如此，在活过了以后再死吧。可是在生活中你是个垂死的人，垂死的人要比已死的人遭受死亡的冲击更严酷，更强烈，更本质。

你若得到过人生的好处，享尽了欢乐，那就心满意足地走吧。

为何不像酒足饭饱的宾客一样离开人生宴席？

——卢克莱修

你若不曾欢度人生，它对你没有用处，失去它又有什么要紧的呢？你留下又做什么用呢？

必然要失去的时间，一事无成的时间，

又何必苦苦去延长呢？

——卢克莱修

生命本身既不好也不坏：按照你给它什么位子才会有好坏之分。你若生活了一天，也就一切都看见了。一天与天天是相同的。没有其他的光，也没有其他的暗。这个太阳，这个月亮，这些星星，这样的排列，跟你的祖先欣赏到的一样，也将让你的后代同样欣赏。

你的祖先看到的不是别的，

你的后代也不会看到其他。

——马尼利乌斯

再差的话，我的喜剧里每一幕的演员搭配与剧情变化也都在一年内轮转一遍。如果你注意到我的四季更替，这四季包含了尘世的童年、青年、壮年和老年。它完成它的工作，没有其他奥妙，只是周而复始，永无止境。

我们绕着我们永远待着的圈子在转。

——卢克莱修

一年四季环绕着自己的足迹转动。

——维吉尔

我决不会故意给你设计其他的新消遣。

我不能给你有什么创新，

新的游戏同老的游戏一样。

——卢克莱修

你给别人让出位子，犹如别人曾给你让出位子。

平等是公正的主要组成部分。人人逃脱不了的地方你也逃脱不了，这能怨谁吗？不管你活着还是不活，你不能把你死的时间减少一二。这一切都是徒劳的，你在你害怕的这个状态里依然待得这么长，犹如你在吃奶的婴儿时期死去一样——

你就是称心如意活了几世纪，
死亡还是千秋万代存在下去。

——卢克莱修

我将妥善安排你，不让你有任何怨言——

你知道吧，死亡不会让
另一个你活下来，站在
你的尸体前哭泣。

——卢克莱修

也不让你留恋你那么难舍的生命——

无人会想起他一己的生命，
我们也不会悼念自身伤心。

——卢克莱修

死比无还不值得害怕，还有什么比无更少的吗？
在我们看来死亡代表失去，
但已经是无，还能失去什么呢？

——卢克莱修

这跟你在生时与死时都无关。生时，因为你还存在；死时，因为你不再存在。

谁都不会在寿数已尽前去世。你死后留下的时间，正如你生前过去的时间，都不是你的，跟你无关。

从前天长地久的时间，
对我们已了无影踪。

——卢克莱修

你的生命不论在何地结束，总是整个留在了那里。生命的价值不在于岁月长短，而在于如何度过。有的人寿命很长，但内容很少；当你活着的时候要提防这一点。你活得是否有意义，这取决于你的意愿，不是岁数多少。你不停往那儿走的地方，你可曾想过会走不到吗？何况条条道路都是有尽头的。

如果有人相伴可以给你安慰，世界不正是跟你并肩而行吗？

你的生命结束，万物跟随你死亡。

——卢克莱修

不是一切都随着你摇晃而摇晃吗？哪有什么不跟着你一起衰老的呢？成千上万的人、动物、其他生灵都在你死亡的一刻死亡：

白天接着黑夜，黑夜接着白天，

不会听不到

葬礼上的哭丧声

与婴儿的呱呱声响成一片。

——卢克莱修

既然身后无路，倒退又有什么用？你见过不少人很乐意死去，借此结束了莫大的苦难。但是不乐意死去的，你曾经见过吗？有的事你没亲自经历过，也没通过别人体验过，就加以谴责，岂不是太天真了吗？你为什么要抱怨我和命运？我们错待你了吗？是你控制我们，还是我们控制你？你虽说年纪还不大，生命却已经到了尽头。人无论大小都是一个完整的人。人及其生命都不是以尺子来丈量的。萨图恩是掌管时间与生命的神，儿子喀戎听了他介绍不死的条件后，断然拒绝永生。

“你可以想象对于人来说永生永世不死，实在比我给他规定的有限人生更难忍受，更艰苦。如果你不会死，你会不停地咒骂我没给你准备死亡。我有意在死亡中增添了一些悲情，免得你看到死亡来得方便，过于迫切和随便地去拥抱它。为了让你把节制铭记在心，既不逃避生，也不逃避死——这是我对你的要求——我把生与死调节在苦与乐之间。

“你们七贤中的第一人泰勒斯，我教导他说生与死并

无区别；因而，有人问他为什么不去死，他非常聪明地回答：‘因为这并无区别。’

“水、土、火以及我们这个球体建筑的其他组件，既构成你的生命，也构成你的死亡。你为什么担心最后一天？它并不比其他的每一天更促成你的死亡。劳累不是最后一步走出来的，只是在最后一步表现出来了。每天都走向死亡，最后一天走到了。”

以上是我们大自然母亲的忠告。我经常思忖怎么会这样，就是战争期间，我们在自己和别人身上见到死亡的面目，不像在家里见到的那么狰狞，无从相比，要不又是一大群医生与哭哭啼啼的人。同样是死，村民与老百姓心里要比其他阶层的人泰然得多。

我相信实际上还是我们围绕死者露出可怕的神情，制造阴沉的气氛，比死亡本身更加吓人。生活完全变了样，老母妻儿号啕大哭，惊慌发呆的亲友前来吊丧，脸色苍白、两眼垂泪的一大群仆人四处张罗，不见日光的一个房间里点着蜡烛，床头围着医生与教士；总之，我们四周惊恐万状。在那时候，我们未死的人也被埋葬在土里了。孩子看到自己的小朋友戴了面具会害怕，我们也是这样。人的面具与事物的面具同样应该摘掉。摘掉以后，我们发现罩在面具之下的这个死亡，跟不久前一名仆人或丫鬟平平静静的死亡并无两样。

铲除了这一切繁文缛节，死亡是幸福的！

企鹅经典：小黑书　第三辑

21.　漂亮的卡桑德拉

[英] 简 · 奥斯汀

22.　温顺的女人

[俄] 陀思妥耶夫斯基

23.　猫与维纳斯

[古希腊] 伊索

24.　黄昏之读

[英] 查尔斯 · 狄更斯

25.　一个可怕的故事是如何被一条普通的屠夫的狗公之于众的

[德] 约翰 · 彼得 · 黑贝尔

26.　亚瑟 · 萨维尔勋爵的罪行

[英] 奥斯卡 · 王尔德

27.　伊凡 · 伊里奇之死

[俄] 列夫 · 托尔斯泰

28.　我们为何为同一件事哭和笑

[法] 蒙田

29.　我的生命是一杆上实弹的枪

[美] 艾米莉 · 狄金森

30.　独自在黑夜的海滩上

[美] 沃尔特 · 惠特曼

Penguin Little Black Classics Vol. III

21. JANE AUSTEN

    The Beautifull Cassandra

22. FYODOR DOSTOYEVSKY

    The Meek One

23. AESOP

    The Cat and Venus

24. CHARLES DICKENS

    To Be Read at Dusk

25. JOHANN PETER HEBEL

    How a Ghastly Story Was Brought to Light by a Common or Garden Butcher's Dog

26. OSCAR WILDE

    Lord Arthur Savile's Crime

27. LEO TOLSTOY

    The Death of Ivan Ilyich

28. MICHEL DE MONTAIGNE

    How We Weep and Laugh at the Same Thing

29. EMILY DICKINSON

    My life had stood a loaded gun

30. WALT WHITMAN

    On the Beach at Night Alone

目录

伊凡·伊里奇之死

一

在法院大厦里，当梅尔文斯基案审讯暂停时，法官和检察官都聚集在伊凡·叶果罗维奇·谢贝克的办公室里，谈论着闹得满城风雨的克拉索夫案件。费多尔·瓦西里耶维奇情绪激动，认为此案不属本院审理范围；伊凡·叶果罗维奇坚持相反意见；彼得·伊凡内奇一开始就没加入争论，始终不过问此事，而是翻阅着刚送来的《公报》。

“诸位！”他说，“伊凡·伊里奇死了。”

“真的吗？”

“喏，您看吧！”他对费多尔·瓦西里耶维奇说，同时把那份散发出油墨味的刚出版的《公报》递给他。

公报上印着一则带黑框的讣告:“普拉斯柯菲雅·费多罗夫娜·高洛文娜沉痛哀告亲友,先夫伊凡·伊里奇·高洛文法官于1882年2月4日逝世。兹定于礼拜五下午一时出殡。”

伊凡·伊里奇是在座几位先生的同事,大家都喜欢他。他病了几个礼拜,据说患的是不治之症。他生病以来职位还给他保留着,但大家早就推测过,他死后将由阿历克谢耶夫接替,而阿历克谢耶夫的位置则将由文尼科夫或施塔别尔接替。因此,一听到伊凡·伊里奇的死讯,办公室里在座的人首先想到的就是,他一死对他们本人和亲友在职位调动和升迁上会有什么影响。

“这下子我很可能弄到施塔别尔或文尼科夫的位置,”费多尔·瓦西里耶维奇想,“这个位置早就说好给我了,而这样一提升,我就可以在车马费之外每年净增加八百卢布收入。”

“这下子我可以申请把内弟从卡卢加调来。”彼得·伊凡内奇想,“妻子一定会很高兴的。如今她可不能再说我不关心她家的人了。”

“我早就想到,他这一病恐怕起不来了,”彼得·伊凡内奇说，“真可怜！”

“他究竟害的是什么病啊？”

“几个医生都说不准。或者说，各有各的说法。我最后一次看见他，还以为他会好起来呢。”

“自从过节以来我就没有去看过他，去是一直想去的。”

“那么，他有财产吗？”

“他妻子手里大概有一点，但很有限。”

“是啊，应该去看看她。他们住得太远。”

“从您那儿去是很远。您到什么地方去都很远。”

“嘿，我住在河对岸，他总是有意见。”彼得·伊凡内奇笑眯眯地瞧着谢贝克说道。大家又说了一通城市太大、市内各区距离太远之类的话，然后回到法庭上。

伊凡·伊里奇的死讯使每个人不由得推测，人事上会因此发生什么变动，同时照例使认识他的人都暗自庆幸：“还好，死的是他，不是我。”

“嘿，他死了，可我没有死。”人人都这样想，或者有这样的感觉。伊凡·伊里奇的知交，他的所谓朋友，都同时不由自主地想，这下子他们得遵循习俗，参加丧礼，慰问遗孀了。

费多尔·瓦西里耶维奇和彼得·伊凡内奇是伊凡·伊

里奇最知心的朋友。

彼得·伊凡内奇跟伊凡·伊里奇在法学院时是同学，自认为受过伊凡·伊里奇的恩惠。

午饭时，彼得·伊凡内奇把伊凡·伊里奇的死讯告诉了妻子，同时讲了争取把内弟调到本区的想法。饭后他没休息，就穿上礼服，乘车到伊凡·伊里奇家里去了。

伊凡·伊里奇家门口停着一辆自备轿车和两辆出租马车。在前厅衣帽架旁的墙上，靠着带穗子和擦得闪闪发亮的金银饰带的棺盖。两位穿黑衣的太太在这里脱去皮外套。其中一位是伊凡·伊里奇的姐姐，彼得·伊凡内奇认识她；另一位没有见过面。彼得·伊凡内奇的同事施瓦尔茨从楼上下来，一看见他进门，就站住向他使了个眼色，仿佛在说："伊凡·伊里奇真没出息，咱们可不至于如此。"

施瓦尔茨脸上留着英国式络腮胡子，瘦长的身体穿着礼服，照例表现出一种典雅庄重的气派，但这同他天生的顽皮性格不协调，因此显得很滑稽。彼得·伊凡内奇心里有这样的感觉。

彼得·伊凡内奇让太太们先走，自己则慢吞吞地跟着她们上楼。施瓦尔茨在楼梯顶上站住，没有下来。彼得·伊凡内奇懂得施瓦尔茨的用意：他想跟他约定，今晚到什么地方去打桥牌。太太们上楼向孀妇屋里走去；施瓦尔茨却一本正经地抿着厚嘴唇，眼睛里露出戏谑的神气，挤挤眉向彼得·伊凡内奇示意，死人在右边房间。

彼得·伊凡内奇进去时照例有点困惑，不知做什么好。但有一点他很清楚，凡是到这种场合，画十字总是不会错的。至于要不要同时鞠躬，他可没有把握，因此选择了个折中的办法：他走进屋里，动手画十字，同时微微点头，好像在鞠躬。在画十字和点头时，他向屋子里偷偷环顾了一下。有两个青年和一个中学生，大概是伊凡·伊里奇的侄儿们，正一面画十字，一面从屋子里出来。一个老妇人一动不动地站在那里。一个眉毛弯得出奇的女人在对她低声说话。诵经士身穿法衣，精神饱满，神态严峻，大声念着什么，脸上表现出神圣不可侵犯的样子，充当餐室侍仆的庄稼汉盖拉西姆蹑手蹑脚地从彼得·伊凡内奇面前走过，把什么东西撒在地板上。彼得·伊凡内奇一看见这情景，立刻闻到淡淡的腐尸臭。他上次探望伊凡·伊里奇时，在书房里看到过这个庄稼汉。当时他在护理伊凡·伊里奇，伊凡·伊里奇特别喜爱他。彼得·伊凡内奇一直画着十字，向棺材、诵经士和屋角桌上的圣像微微鞠躬。后来，他觉得十字已画得够了，就停下来打量死人。

死人躺在那里，也像一般死人那样，显得特别沉重，僵硬的四肢陷在棺材衬垫里，脑袋高高地靠在枕头上，蜡黄的前额高高隆起，半秃的两鬓凹进去，高耸的鼻子仿佛压迫着上唇。同彼得·伊凡内奇上次看见他时相比，他的模样大变了，身体更瘦了，但他的脸也像一般死人那样，比生前好看，显得端庄。脸上的神态似乎表示，他已尽了责任，而且尽得很周到。此外，那神态还好像在责备活人或者提醒他们什么事。彼得·伊凡内奇却觉得没有什么事需要提醒他，至少没有事跟他有关系。他心里有点不快，就又匆匆画了个十字——他自己也觉得这个十字画得太快，未免有点失礼——转身往门口走去。施瓦尔茨宽宽地叉开两腿站在穿堂里等他，双手在背后玩弄着大礼帽。彼得·伊凡内奇瞧了瞧服饰雅致、模样顽皮可笑的施瓦尔茨，顿时精神振作起来。他知道施瓦尔茨性格开朗，不会受这里哀伤气氛的影响。他那副神气仿佛表示：伊凡·伊里奇的丧事绝没有理由破坏他们的例会，也就是说不能妨碍他们今天晚上就拆开一副新牌，在仆人点亮的四支新蜡烛照耀下打牌。总之，这次丧事不能影响他们今晚快乐的聚会。他就把这个想法低声告诉从旁边走过的彼得·伊凡内奇，并建议今晚到费多尔·瓦西里耶维奇家打牌。不过，彼得·伊凡内奇今天显然没有打牌的运气。普拉斯柯菲雅·费多罗夫娜同几位太太从内室出来了。她身材矮胖，尽管千方百计要自己消瘦，可是肩膀以下的部分却一个劲儿向横里发展。她穿一身黑衣，头上包一块花边头巾，眉毛像站在棺材旁那个女人一样弯得出奇。她把她们送到灵堂门口，说："马上要做丧事礼拜了，你们请进。"

施瓦尔茨微微点头站住，显得犹豫不决，是不是接受这个邀请。普拉斯柯菲雅·费多罗夫娜认出彼得·伊凡内奇，叹了一口气，走到他跟前，握住他的手说："我知道您是伊凡·伊里奇的知心朋友……"她说到这里对他瞧瞧，等待他听了这话后做出相应的反应。彼得·伊凡内奇知道，既然刚才应该画十字，那么这会儿就得握手，叹气，说一句："真是想不到！"他就这样做了。做了以后，他发觉达到了预期的效果：他感动了，她也感动了。

"现在那边还没有开始，您来一下，我有话要跟您说，"孀妇说，"您扶着我。"

彼得·伊凡内奇伸出手臂挽住她，他们向内室走去。经过施瓦尔茨身边时，施瓦尔茨失望地向彼得·伊凡内奇使了个眼色。“唉，牌打不成了！要是我们另外找到搭档，您可别怪我们。要是您能脱身，五人一起玩也行。”他那淘气的目光仿佛在这么说。

彼得·伊凡内奇更深沉更悲伤地叹了口气，普拉斯柯菲雅·费多罗夫娜便感激地捏了捏他的手臂。他们走进灯光暗淡、挂着玫瑰红花布窗帘的客厅，在桌旁坐下来：她坐在沙发上，彼得·伊凡内奇坐在弹簧损坏、凳面凹陷的矮沙发凳上。普拉斯柯菲雅·费多罗夫娜想叫他换一把椅子坐，可是觉得此刻说这些话不得体，就作罢了。彼得·伊凡内奇坐到沙发凳上时，想起伊凡·伊里奇当年装饰这客厅时曾同他商量，最后决定用这种带绿叶的玫瑰红花布做窗帘和沙发套。客厅里摆满家具杂物，孀妇走过时，她那件黑斗篷的黑花边在雕花桌上挂住了。彼得·伊凡内奇欠起身，想帮她解开斗篷，沙发凳一摆脱负担，里面的弹簧立刻蹦起来，往他身上弹。孀妇自己解开斗篷，彼得·伊凡内奇又坐下来，把跳动的弹簧重新压下去。但孀妇没有把斗篷完全解开，彼得·伊凡内奇又欠起身，弹簧又往上蹦，还噔地响了一声。等这一切都过去了，她拿出一块洁净的麻纱手绢，哭起来。斗篷钩住和沙发凳的弹簧蹦跳这些插曲使彼得·伊凡内奇冷静下来，他皱紧眉头坐着。这当儿，伊凡·伊里奇的男仆索科洛夫走进来，把这种尴尬局面打破了。他报告普拉斯柯菲雅·费多罗夫娜，她指定的那块坟地要价两百卢布。普拉斯柯菲雅·费多罗夫娜止住哭，可怜巴巴地瞟了一眼彼得·伊凡内奇，用法语说她的日子很难过。彼得·伊凡内奇默默地做了个手势，表示他深信她说的是实话。

“您请抽烟。”她用宽宏大量而又极其悲痛的语气说，然后同索科洛夫谈坟地的价钱。彼得·伊凡内奇一面吸烟，一面听她怎样详细询问坟地的价格，最后决定买哪一块。谈完坟地，她又吩咐索科洛夫去请唱诗班。索科洛夫走了。

“什么事都是我自己料理。”她对彼得·伊凡内奇说，把桌上的照相簿挪到一边。接着发现烟灰快掉到桌上，连忙把烟灰碟推到彼得·伊凡内奇面前，嘴里说：“要是说我悲伤得不能做事，那未免有点做作。相反，现在只有为他的后事多操点心，我才感到安慰……至少可以排遣点悲伤。”她掏出手绢，又要哭，但突然勉强忍住，打起精神，镇静地说：“我有点事要跟您谈谈。”

彼得·伊凡内奇点点头，不让他身下蠢蠢欲动的沙发弹簧再蹦起来。

“最后几天他真是难受。”

“非常难受吗？”彼得·伊凡内奇问。

“唉，太可怕了！他不停地叫嚷，不是一连几分钟，而是一连几个钟头。三天三夜嚷个不停。实在叫人受不了。我真不懂我这是怎么熬过来的。隔着三道门都听得见他的叫声。唉，我这是怎么熬过来的哟！”

“当时他神志清醒吗？”彼得·伊凡内奇问。

“清醒，”她喃喃地说，“直到最后一分钟都清醒。他在临终前一刻钟跟我们告了别，还叫我们把伏洛嘉带开。”

彼得·伊凡内奇想到，他那么熟识的这个人，原先是个快乐的孩子，小学生，后来成了他的同事，最后竟受到这样的折磨。尽管他觉得自己和这个女人都有点做作，但想到这一点，心里却十分恐惧。他又看见那个前额和那个压住嘴唇的鼻子，不禁感到不寒而栗。

“三天三夜极度的痛苦，然后死去。这种情况也可能随时落到我的头上。”他想，刹那间感到毛骨悚然。但是，他自己也不知怎的，一种常有的想法很快就使他镇静下来：“这种事只有伊凡·伊里奇会碰上，我可绝不会碰上。这种事不应该也不可能落到我的头上。”他想到这些，心情忧郁，但施瓦尔茨分明向他做过暗示，他不该有这种心情。彼得·伊凡内奇思考了一下，镇静下来，详细询问伊凡·伊里奇临终前的情况，仿佛这种事故只会发生在伊凡·伊里奇身上，可绝不会发生在他身上。

在谈了一通伊凡·伊里奇肉体上所受非人痛苦的情况以后（这种痛苦，彼得·伊凡内奇是从普拉斯柯菲雅·费多罗夫娜神经所受的影响上领会的），孀妇显然认为该转到正题上了。

“唉，彼得·伊凡内奇，真是难受，真是太难受了，太难受了。”她又哭起来。

彼得·伊凡内奇叹着气，等她擦去鼻涕眼泪，才说：“真是想不到……”

接着她又说起来，说到了显然是她找他来的主要问题。她问他，丈夫去世后要怎样向政府申请抚恤金。她装作向彼得·伊凡内奇请教，怎样领取赡养费，不过他看得出，因丈夫去世她可以向政府弄到多少钱，这事她已经了解得清清楚楚，比他知道得还清楚。她不过是想知道，可不可以通过什么办法弄到更多的钱。彼得·伊凡内奇竭力思索，想到几种办法，但最后只是出于礼节骂了一通政府的吝啬，说不可能弄到更多的钱了。于是她叹了一口气，显然是要摆脱这位来客。他理会了，就摁灭香烟，站起身，同孀妇握了握手，走到前厅。

餐厅里摆着伊凡·伊里奇十分得意地从旧货店买来的大钟。彼得·伊凡内奇在那里遇见神父和几个来参加丧事礼拜的客人，还看见一位熟识的美丽小姐，就是伊凡·伊里奇的女儿。她穿一身黑衣，腰身本来很苗条，如今似乎变得更苗条了。她的神态忧郁、冷淡，甚至还有点愤慨。她向彼得·伊凡内奇鞠躬，但那副神气显出仿佛他有什么过错似的。女儿后面站着一个同样面带愠色的青年。彼得·伊凡内奇认识他是法院侦讯官，家里很有几个钱，而且听说是她的未婚夫。彼得·伊凡内奇沮丧地向他们点点头，正要往死人房间走去，这时楼梯下出现了逝者在中学念书的儿子。这孩子活脱就是年轻时的伊凡·伊里奇。彼得·伊凡内奇记得伊凡·伊里奇在法学院念书时就是这个模样。这孩子眼睛里含着泪水，神态也像那些十三四岁的愣小子。他一看见彼得·伊凡内奇，就忧郁而害臊地皱起眉头。彼得·伊凡内奇向他点点头，走进灵堂。丧事礼拜开始了：又是蜡烛，又是呻吟，又是神香，又是眼泪，又是啜泣。彼得·伊凡内奇皱紧眉头站着，眼睛瞅着自己的双脚。他一眼也不看死人，直到礼拜结束他的心情都没有受悲伤气氛的影响，并且第一个走出灵堂。前厅里一个人也没有。充任餐厅侍仆的庄稼汉盖拉西姆从灵堂奔出来，用他那双强壮的手臂努力地在一排外套中间翻寻着，终于把彼得 · 伊凡内奇的外套找出来，递给他。

“嗯，盖拉西姆老弟，你说呢？”彼得 · 伊凡内奇想说句话应酬一下，“可怜不可怜哪？”

“这是上帝的意思！我们都要到那里去的。”盖拉西姆露出一排洁白整齐的庄稼汉的牙齿，说完就像在紧张地干活那样猛地推开门，大声呼喊马车夫，把彼得 · 伊凡内奇送上车，又奔回台阶上，仿佛在考虑还有些什么事要做。

在闻过神香、尸体和石碳酸的臭味以后，彼得 · 伊凡内奇特别爽快地吸了一大口新鲜空气。

“上哪儿，老爷？”马车夫问。

“不晚。还可以到费多尔 · 瓦西里耶维奇家去一下。”

彼得 · 伊凡内奇就去了。果然，他到的时候，第一局牌刚结束，因此他就顺当地成了第五名赌客。

二

伊凡 · 伊里奇的身世极其普通、极其简单而又极其可怕。

他是个法官，去世时才四十五岁。他父亲是彼得堡一名官员，曾在好几个政府机关任职，虽不能胜任某些要职，但凭着他的资格和身份，从没被逐出官场，因此总能弄到一些有名无实的官职和六千到一万卢布的有名有实的年俸，并一直享受到晚年。

伊里亚·叶斐莫维奇·高洛文就是这样一个多余机关里的多余的三等文官。

他有三个儿子。伊凡·伊里奇排行第二。老大像他父亲一样官运亨通，不过在另一个机关，也快到领干薪的年龄。老三没有出息。他在几个地方都败坏了名声，眼下在铁路上供职。父亲也好，两位哥哥也好，特别是两位嫂子，不仅不愿同他见面，而且非万不得已从不会想到有他这样一个兄弟。姐姐嫁给了格列夫男爵，他同他岳父一样是彼得堡的官员。伊凡·伊里奇是家里所谓的佼佼者[1]。他不像老大那样冷淡古板，也不像老三那样放荡不羁。他介于他们之间：聪明，活泼，乐观，文雅。他跟弟弟一起在法学院念过书。老三没有毕业，念到五

1. 原文为法语。（说明：书中脚注均为编者注。）

年级就被学校开除了；伊凡 · 伊里奇则毕了业，而且成绩优良。他在法学院里就显示了后来终生具备的特点：能干，乐观，厚道，随和，但又能严格履行自认为应尽的责任，而他心目中的责任就是达官贵人所公认的职责。他从小不会巴结拍马，成年后还是不善于阿谀奉承，但从青年时代起就像飞蛾扑火那样追随上层人士，模仿他们的一举一动，接受他们的人生观，并同他们交朋友。童年时代和少年时代的热情在他身上消失得干干净净。他开始迷恋声色，追逐功名，最后发展到了自由放纵的地步。不过，他的本性还能使他保持一定分寸，不至于过分逾越常规。

在法学院里，他认为自己的有些行为很卑劣，因此很嫌恶自己。但后来看到地位比他高的人都在那样干，而且并不认为卑劣，他也就不以为意，不再把它们放在心上，即使想到也无动于衷。伊凡 · 伊里奇在法学院毕业，获得十等文官官衔，从父亲手里领到治装费，在著名的沙尔玛裁缝铺里定制了服装，表坠上挂一块刻着“高瞻远瞩”[1]的纪念章，向导师和任校董的亲王辞了

1. 原文为法语。

行，跟同学们在唐农大饭店欢宴话别，带着从最高级商店买来的时式手提箱、衬衣、西服、剃刀、梳妆用品和旅行毛毯，走马上任，当了省长特派员。这个官职是他父亲替他谋得的。伊凡·伊里奇到了外省，很快就像在法学院那样过得称心如意。他奉公守法，兢兢业业，生活得欢快而又不失体统。他有时奉命到各县视察，待人接物稳重得体，对上待下恰如其分，不贪赃枉法，而且总能圆满完成上司交下的差事，主要是处理好分裂派教徒事件。他虽然年轻放荡，但处理公务却异常审慎，甚至可以说是铁面无私；在社交场中，他活泼风趣而又和蔼有礼，正像他的上司和上司太太——他是他们家的常客——称赞他的那样，是个好小子[1]。他同省里一位死缠住他这个风流法学家的太太有暧昧关系；还同一个女裁缝私通；有时同巡察的副官们狂饮欢宴，饭后还去花街柳巷寻欢作乐。他奉承上级长官，甚至长官夫人，手法高明，无懈可击，从未引起非议，人家至多说一句法国谚语：年轻时放荡在所难免。这一切他都干得体体面面，嘴里说的又是法国话，主要则是因为他跻身在最上层，

1. 原文为法语。

容易博得达官显贵的青睐。伊凡·伊里奇就这样干了五年。接着他的工作调动了，因为成立了新的司法机关，需要新的官员。

于是伊凡·伊里奇就调任了这样的新职。

伊凡·伊里奇被推荐任法院侦讯官的职务，他接受了，虽然这位置在另一个省里，因此他得放弃原有的各种关系，另起炉灶，重新结交朋友。朋友们给伊凡·伊里奇饯行，同他一起拍照，还赠给他一个银烟盒留念。那之后，他便走马上任去了。

伊凡·伊里奇当法院侦讯官同样循规蹈矩[1]，公私分明，并且像做特派员一样受到普遍尊敬。对伊凡·伊里奇来说，侦讯官的工作比原来的工作有趣得多，迷人得多。以前让他感到扬扬得意的是，身穿精工缝制的文官制服，昂首阔步地经过战战兢兢等待接见的来访者和对他羡慕不已的官员们面前，一直走进长官办公室，并且跟长官一起喝茶吸烟；但那时直接听命于他的人，只有县警察局的局长和分裂派教徒，而且还是要在他奉命出差的时候。他对待他们总是客客气气，使他们感到，他

1. 原文为法语。

尽管操着生杀大权，却平易近人，毫无架子。那个时候，这样直接听命于他的人不多。如今伊凡·伊里奇当上法院侦讯官，他懂得就连达官贵人的命运也都操在他手里，他只要在公文上批几句，随便哪个要人都会成为被告或证人来到他面前，并且得站着回答他的问题，如果他不请他坐下的话。伊凡·伊里奇从不滥用权力，相反总是不露锋芒，而这种权力的意识和适当用权的技术，就成了他担任新职后最感兴趣的事。从事这项新职，也就是说审查工作，伊凡·伊里奇很快就掌握了一种本领，能排除一切与本案无关的情节，使各种错综复杂的案情在公文上表现得简单明了，不带丝毫个人意见，完全符合公文要求。这是一项新的工作，而伊凡·伊里奇则属于第一批执行1864年新法典的人。

自从在新地方就任法院侦讯官以来，伊凡·伊里奇结交了一批新朋友，建立了一些新关系，获得了新的社会地位，并多少采取了新作风。他在省里同政府保持一定距离，却周旋于司法界头面人物和豪门巨富之间，对当局稍表不满，发表温和的自由主义言论和开明观点。此外，伊凡·伊里奇就任新职后仍旧讲究服饰，注意仪表，只是不再刮去下巴颏上的胡子而任其自然生长。

伊凡·伊里奇在新地方过得很愉快。他跟一批反对省长的人关系很好；薪俸比以前优厚；他逢场作戏，打打纸牌，以增添乐趣。他头脑聪敏，很会打牌，因此常常赢钱。

伊凡·伊里奇在新地方任职两年后遇见了后来成为他妻子的普拉斯柯菲雅·费多罗夫娜·米海尔。她是伊凡·伊里奇出入的圈子里最迷人最伶俐最出色的姑娘。伊凡·伊里奇在办公之余，找点消遣，其中就包括同普拉斯柯菲雅·费多罗夫娜戏谑调情。

伊凡·伊里奇任特派员时常常跳舞，但当上侦讯官后就难得跳了。如今他跳舞只是为了要显示，尽管他身为侦讯官和五等文官，跳舞水平可绝不比别人差。有时晚会将近结束，他就请普拉斯柯菲雅·费多罗夫娜一起跳舞，主要借这种机会去征服普拉斯柯菲雅·费多罗夫娜的心。她爱上了他。伊凡·伊里奇并没有明确想到要结婚，但既然人家姑娘爱上了他，他就问自己："是啊，那么何不就结婚呢？"

普拉斯柯菲雅·费多罗夫娜出身望族，长得不错，而且小有家产。伊凡·伊里奇可以指望找到一个更出色的配偶，但这个配偶也不错。

伊凡·伊里奇自己有薪俸收入，他希望她也有同样多的进款。她出身名门，又生得温柔美丽，很有教养。说伊凡·伊里奇同她结婚，是因为爱上这位小姐，并且发觉她的人生观同他一致，那不符合事实。说他结婚，是因为在他的圈子里大家都赞成这门婚事，那同样不符合事实。伊凡·伊里奇结婚是出于双重考虑：娶这样一位妻子是幸福的，而达官贵人们又都赞成这门亲事。

伊凡·伊里奇就这样结了婚。

在准备结婚和婚后初期，夫妻恩爱，妻子尚未怀孕，再加上崭新的家具，崭新的餐具，崭新的衣服，日子过得很美满。伊凡·伊里奇认为他原来的生活轻松愉快而又高尚体面，并且受到上流社会的赞许，如今结婚不仅不会损害这种生活，而且使它更加美满。但在妻子怀孕几个月后，出现了一种痛苦难堪而有失体统的新局面，那是他万万没有料到的，而且怎么也无法摆脱。

伊凡·伊里奇认为妻子完全是出于任性[1]，破坏了快乐体面的生活，莫名其妙地动辄猜疑，要求他更加体贴她。不论什么事她都横加挑剔，动不动就对他大吵大闹。

1. 原文为法语。

起初伊凡·伊里奇想继续用快乐体面的人生态度来排除烦恼。他不管妻子的情绪，照旧高高兴兴地过日子：请朋友到家里来打牌，自己上俱乐部或者到朋友家串门子。可是有一次妻子气势汹汹地对他破口大骂。这以后只要他稍不顺她的意，她就把他臭骂一顿，显然非把他制服不可，也就是说要他安守在家里，并且像她一样唉声叹气，无病呻吟，这使伊凡·伊里奇感到心惊胆战。他懂得了，夫妇生活，至少是他同妻子的生活，并不能始终维持快乐和体面，相反，这样的气氛常常会被损害，因此必须设法防范。伊凡·伊里奇借口公务繁忙，来对付普拉斯柯菲雅·费多罗夫娜。他发现这种办法很有效，因此常用它来保卫自己的独立天地。

孩子出生后，喂养很费事，常常发生这样那样的麻烦，不是婴儿害病就是做母亲的害病，有时是真病，有时是假病。不管怎样，伊凡·伊里奇都得照顾，尽管他对这些事一窍不通。伊凡·伊里奇保卫自己独立天地、不受家庭干扰的欲望越来越强烈。

妻子的脾气越来越暴躁，要求越来越苛刻，伊凡·伊里奇也越来越把生活的重心转移到公务上。他更加喜爱官职，醉心功名。

不久，在结婚一年后，伊凡·伊里奇懂得了，夫妇生活虽然也有一些好处，但却是一件很复杂很痛苦的事。而要尽到自己的责任，过一种受社会赞许的体面生活，必须像做官一样建立适当的关系。

伊凡·伊里奇就给自己建立了这样的夫妇关系。他对家庭生活的要求，只是能吃到家常便饭，生活上有照料和过床笫生活，而这些都是她能向他提供的。他主要的要求是维持社会所公认的体面的夫妇关系。此外，他就自寻欢乐，获得了欢乐也就心满意足。要是家里遇到不愉快，他就立刻逃到公务活动的独立天地里去，并在那里自得其乐。

伊凡·伊里奇当侦讯官，声誉显赫，三年后就升任副检察官。新的官职、重要的地位、控诉和拘捕任何人的权力、当众的演说、辉煌的功绩——这一切使伊凡·伊里奇更加官迷心窍。

孩子一个个生下来。妻子变得越来越乖戾，越来越易怒，但伊凡·伊里奇确立的家庭关系几乎不受妻子脾气的影响。

伊凡·伊里奇在这个城市里任职七年，接着被调到另一个省里当检察官。他们搬了家，手头的钱不多，妻子又不喜欢新地方。薪俸尽管比原来多，但生活成本也高了，再说又死了两个孩子，因此伊凡·伊里奇就感到家庭生活比以前更乏味了。

普拉斯柯菲雅·费多罗夫娜搬到新地方后，不论遇到什么麻烦，总要责怪丈夫。夫妇间不论谈什么事，尤其是谈教育孩子的问题，总会联想到以前的不和，引起新的争吵。夫妇俩如今难得有恩爱的时刻，即使有，也是很短暂的。他们在爱情的小岛上临时停泊一下，不久又会掉进互相敌视的汪洋大海，彼此冷若冰霜。要是伊凡·伊里奇认为家庭生活不该如此，他准会对这种冷漠感到伤心，不过他不仅认为这样的局面是正常的，而且正是他所企求的。他的目标就是要尽量摆脱家庭生活的烦恼，而表面上又要装得若无其事，保持体面。为了达到这一目的，他尽量少同家人待在一起，如果不得已必须这样做，也总是竭力找有旁人在场的机会。不过，伊凡·伊里奇这样过日子，主要靠的是他有公务。他把全部生活乐趣都集中在官场的天地里。而这种乐趣支配了他的整个身心。意识到自己的权力，对任何人都操有生杀大权，每次走进法庭和遇到下属时那种威风凛凛的气派（即使只是表面的），在上司与下属之间周旋的本领，尤其是自觉高明的办事能力——这一切都使他扬扬得意，再加上跟同事们谈天、宴会和打牌，他的生活就显得很充实。总之，伊凡·伊里奇的生活过得合乎他的愿望：快乐而体面。

就这样他又过了七年。大女儿已经十六岁，另外又死了一个孩子，只剩下一个男孩在中学念书。这个孩子是引起夫妇争吵的一大因素。伊凡·伊里奇要送他读法学院，而普拉斯柯菲雅·费多罗夫娜却偏把他送进普通中学。女儿在家里学习，成绩良好；儿子学得也不错。

三

伊凡·伊里奇婚后就这样过了十七年的光阴。现在他已是一个老检察官了。他推辞了几次工作上的调动，一心想找个更称心的职司，不料出了一件不愉快的事，把他生活的安宁给破坏了。伊凡·伊里奇想谋取大学城首席法官的位置，但被戈佩捷足先得。伊凡·伊里奇十分生气，提出责问，同戈佩吵嘴，又冒犯顶头上司；他从此受冷遇，下一次任命也没有他的份儿。

这是 1880 年，也是伊凡·伊里奇一生中最倒霉的年头。他一方面入不敷出，另一方面又被人家遗忘。他觉得人家待他极不公平，人家却认为对他已仁至义尽。就连父亲都认为无须再帮助他了。他觉得大家都把他抛弃了，并认为他有三千五百卢布年俸已很不错，甚至可说是十分幸福了。人家待他这么不公平，妻子经常责骂他，家里入不敷出，开始负债。这种情况当然谈不上正常，而且只有他一个人知道。

今年夏天，伊凡·伊里奇为了节省开支，同妻子一起到内弟乡下度假。

在乡下不做事，伊凡·伊里奇第一次不仅感到无聊，而且十分愁闷。他认定无法这样过活，必须断然采取措施。

伊凡·伊里奇不能入睡，在露台上踱了个通宵，决定上彼得堡奔走一番，争取调到其他部门工作，以惩罚他们，惩罚那些不会赏识他才能的人。

第二天早晨，他不顾妻子和内弟的劝阻，乘车上彼得堡。

他唯一的目的就是弄到一个年俸五千卢布的位置。他不再计较是哪个机关，是哪个派别和哪种工作。他只要一个位置，年俸五千卢布的位置，不论政府机关、银行、铁路、玛丽皇后御用机关，甚至海关都行，但一定要有五千卢布收入，一定要离开那个不会赏识他才能的机关。

伊凡·伊里奇此行取得了意外收获。在库尔斯克火车站，头等车厢里上来一个熟人，名叫伊林。伊林告诉他库尔斯克省刚接到电报，部里最近人事上有重大变动，彼得·伊凡内奇的位置将由伊凡·谢苗内奇接任。

这次调动，除了对国家有一定影响外，对伊凡·伊里奇具有特殊意义，因为起用了新人彼得·彼得罗维奇和他的朋友扎哈尔·伊凡内奇。这对他伊凡·伊里奇极其有利，因为扎哈尔·伊凡内奇是伊凡·伊里奇的同学，又是他的好朋友。

在莫斯科，这个消息得到了证实。伊凡·伊里奇来到彼得堡，找到了扎哈尔·伊凡内奇，后者答应给他在原来的司法部里谋一个好差事。

一个星期后，他给妻子发了一封电报。

“扎哈尔接替米勒，我申请后即可提升。”

伊凡·伊里奇通过这次人事调动在他的旧部里获得意外任命：比同事高两级，年俸五千，再加调差费三千五百。伊凡·伊里奇消除了对原来对头和整个机关的怨气，感到十分得意。

伊凡·伊里奇回到乡下，兴高采烈。他好久没有这样快活了。普拉斯柯菲雅·费多罗夫娜也很高兴，夫妇俩和好了。伊凡·伊里奇讲到他在彼得堡怎样受祝贺，原来的对头怎样厚着脸皮巴结他，怎样羡慕他的地位，特别讲到他在彼得堡怎样受人尊敬。

普拉斯柯菲雅·费多罗夫娜听着他讲，装出相信的样子，也不打岔，心里却盘算着怎样到新地方去重新安排生活。伊凡·伊里奇高兴地看到，她的想法同他的想法不谋而合，他们一度坎坷的生活重又变得快乐而体面了。

伊凡·伊里奇只回家几天。九月十日他就得走马上任。此外，他还得在新地方安顿下来，把家具什物从省里运去，再要添置和定做许多新东西。总之，要根据他同普拉斯柯菲雅·费多罗夫娜几乎一致的想法把新居布置好。

现在，一切都进行得称心如意，他同妻子又意气相投。他们俩一起生活的时间很少像现在这样投契，除了婚后头几年，还不曾有过。伊凡·伊里奇本想举家搬走，可他的嫂子和姐夫对伊凡·伊里奇一家忽然十分亲热，弄得伊凡·伊里奇只好独自先走。伊凡·伊里奇走了，事业上一帆风顺，同妻子言归于好，这两件事互为因果，使他心情愉快。他找到一座精美的住宅，恰合夫妇俩的心意，高大宽敞的老式客厅、豪华舒适的书房、妻子的房间、女儿的房间、儿子的书房，一切像是为他们特意设计的。伊凡·伊里奇亲自布置房间，选择墙纸，添置家具——从旧货店买来的，式样特别古雅，定制了沙发套和窗帘。房子布置得越来越漂亮，符合他的理想。他布置到一半，发觉比他希望的更美。他相信，等全部完工，将更加富丽堂皇，而绝不会流于庸俗。临睡前，他想象他的前厅将是什么样子。他瞧着没有布置好的客厅，仿佛看到壁炉、屏风、古董架、散放着的小椅子、墙上的挂盘和铜器都已安放得井井有条。他想到妻子和女儿在这方面跟他有同样的爱好，看到这种排场，准会大吃一惊，不禁暗暗高兴。她们一定想不到会有这样的气派。他特别得意的是买到一些价廉物美的古董，使整座房子显得格外豪华。他在信里故意把情况说得差一些，这样她们一看到就会更加惊讶。他热衷于装饰新居，就连对心爱的公务都不那么感兴趣了。有时法院开庭，他也心不在焉：他在考虑究竟用什么样的窗帘顶檐，直的还是拱的。他对这事兴致勃勃，亲自动手安放家具，重新挂上窗帘。有一次他爬到梯子上，指点愚笨的沙发裁缝怎样挂窗帘，一不留神失足掉下来，但他是个强壮而灵活的汉子，立刻站住了，只是腰部撞在窗框上。伤处痛了一阵，不久就好了。

这一时期，伊凡 · 伊里奇觉得自己特别快乐和健康。他写信说：“我感到自己仿佛年轻了十五岁。”他原想到九月底把房子布置好，结果拖到十月半。不过，房子布置得十分雅致——不仅他自己这么认为，凡是看到的人都这么说。

其实，房子里的摆设无非是那种不太富裕却一味模仿富裕人家的小康之家的气派，千篇一律地尽是花缎、红木家具、盆花、地毯、古铜器、发亮铜器等等。一定阶级的人总是拿这些东西来表示他们一定的身份。伊凡 · 伊里奇家里的摆设同人家没有什么两样，因此引不起人家的注意，但他却扬扬自得，以为与众不同。他到车站去接家眷，把他们带到装修一新的寓所里，系白领带的男仆打开摆满鲜花的前厅，他们走进客厅、书房，高兴得欢呼起来。他领他们到各处观看，得意扬扬地听着他们的称赞，容光焕发，感到十分幸福。当天晚上喝茶的时候，普拉斯柯菲雅 · 费多罗夫娜随便问到他是怎么摔跤的，他就笑着做给他们看，他怎样从梯子上掉下来，把沙发裁缝吓坏了。

“幸亏我练过体操。要是换了别人，准会摔坏的，可我只在这儿撞了一下，摸摸有点疼，但已经好多了，只是有点青肿。”

就这样他们在新居开始生活，并且也像一般人移居到新地方那样，觉得还少一个房间，收入虽然增加，但还嫌钱少——少这么五百卢布。不过总的来说，他们感到称心如意了。最初他们过得特别愉快，房子还没有完全布置好，需要再买些什么，定制些什么，有些东西需要搬动，有些东西需要调整。尽管夫妇之间有时意见分歧，但两人对新的生活都很满意，而且有许多事要做，因此没有发生大的争吵。等一切都安排完毕，他们开始感到有点空虚，但当时还需要结交一批新朋友，培养新习惯，因此生活还是很充实。

伊凡·伊里奇上午在法院办公，下午回家吃饭，起初那段时光情绪很好，虽然为房子的事有时也有点烦恼（例如，他发现桌布或沙发罩子上有污点，窗帘系带断了，就会发脾气，因为看到他煞费苦心置办的东西被损坏，心里难过）。不过，伊凡·伊里奇的生活还是过得合乎他的理想：轻松、愉快而体面。他每天早晨九时起床，喝咖啡，看报，然后穿上制服去法院。那儿已为他准备好“轭”，让他一到就套到身上：接见来访者，处理与诉讼有关的问题，主持诉讼案件，出席公开庭和预备庭。他必须排除各种外来干预，免得妨碍诉讼程序，同时严禁徇私枉法，严格依法办事。要是有人想探听什么事，而这事不属伊凡·伊里奇主管，他就不能同这人发生任何关系，但要是这人有正式公文，上面写明事由，那么伊凡·伊里奇就会根据法律许可的范围尽力去办，并且办得不违反人情，也就是说面子上过得去。但只要公事一结束，其他关系也就结束了。分清法律和人情这种本领伊凡·伊里奇已达到登峰造极的地步，而且凭着天赋的才能和长期的经验，他有时还会故意把法律和人情混淆起来。他之所以敢于这样做，那是因为他自信总有能力划清两者的界限，如果需要的话。伊凡·伊里奇办这种事不仅轻松、愉快和体面，简直可以说是得心应手。在休庭时，他吸烟、喝茶，随便谈谈政治、社会新闻和纸牌，而谈得最多的还是官场中的任命。然后，他好像第一小提琴手，出色地演奏完毕，疲劳地乘车回家。回到家里，发现母女俩出去了，有时在接待客人，儿子上学了，有时在跟补课教师复习功课。一切都井井有条。饭后要是没有客人来，伊凡·伊里奇就看些当时流行的书籍。晚上，他坐下来处理公事：批阅文件，查看法典，核对证词。他干这些，既不感到无聊，也不觉得有趣。要是有机会打牌，那么处理公事就感到无聊；要是没有机会打牌，那么处理公事总比独自闲坐或者跟妻子面面相对要好得多。伊凡·伊里奇喜欢举行便宴，邀请有权有势的先生夫人参加。这种消遣跟其他同样身份的人没有差别，犹如他的客厅跟人家的客厅没有差别一样。

他们家里还举行过一次舞会。舞会办得很好，伊凡·伊里奇心情愉快，可惜最后为蛋糕糖果的事同妻子大闹了一场。普拉斯柯菲雅·费多罗夫娜有她的打算，但伊凡·伊里奇坚持要到最高级的糖果铺去买糕点，结果买了许多蛋糕。争吵就是由于蛋糕太多吃不完，而糖果铺的账却高达四十五卢布引起的。争吵很激烈，闹得很不愉快。普拉斯柯菲雅·费多罗夫娜骂他："傻瓜，低能。"伊凡·伊里奇气得双手抱住脑袋，恨恨地说出离婚之类的话来。不过，晚会本身还是很快活的，前来参加的都是社会名流。伊凡·伊里奇同特鲁峰诺娃公爵夫人跳舞。特鲁峰诺娃公爵夫人的姐姐就是著名的"消灭苦难会"的创办人。身居要职的乐趣在于自尊心的满足，社会活动的乐趣在于虚荣心的满足，但伊凡·伊里奇的真正乐趣却在于打牌。他认为，不管生活上遇到什么烦恼，那像蜡烛一样驱除黑暗的最大乐趣，就是同几个规规矩矩的好搭档坐下来一起打牌，而且一定要四人一起

（五人一起打就很难有结果，虽然得装出很感兴趣的样子），认认真真地打（要是顺手的话），然后吃点夜宵，喝一大杯葡萄酒。打过牌以后睡觉，尤其是稍微赢一点钱（赢得太多也不好），伊凡·伊里奇觉得特别愉快。

他们就这样过着日子。他们家的来客都是达官贵人，有的地位显赫，有的年少英俊。

夫妻和女儿待人的态度完全一致。凡是满脸堆笑、投奔到他们那间墙上装饰着日本盘子的客厅来的潦倒亲友，他们都加以排斥。不久，这些寒酸的亲友便不再上门，高洛文家的来客就限于达官贵人。年轻人纷纷追求丽莎，其中包括彼特利歇夫。那是德米特里·伊凡内奇·彼特利歇夫的儿子，又是他财产的唯一继承人，现任法院侦讯官。他也在热烈地追求丽莎，弄得伊凡·伊里奇已在跟普拉斯柯菲雅·费多罗夫娜商量：要不要让他们一起坐三驾马车，或者举办一次堂会看看表演。他们就这样过着日子，一切都称心如意，没有任何变化。

四

家里人个个身体健康。只有伊凡·伊里奇有时说，他嘴里有一种怪味，左腹有点不舒服，但不能说有病。

这种不舒服的感觉逐渐增长，虽还没有转变为疼痛，但他经常感到腰部发胀，情绪恶劣。他的心情越来越坏，影响了全家快乐而体面的生活。夫妇吵嘴的事越来越多，轻松愉快的气氛消失了，体面也很难维持。争吵更加频繁，夫妇之间相安无事的日子少得就像汪洋大海里的小岛。

如今普拉斯柯菲雅·费多罗夫娜说丈夫脾气难弄，那倒不是没有理由的。她说话喜欢夸张，往往夸张地说，他的脾气一直很坏，要不是她心地善良，这二十年可真没法忍受。的确，现在的争吵总是由伊凡·伊里奇引起的。他吃饭总要发脾气，往往从吃汤开始。他一会儿发现碗碟有裂痕，一会儿批评饭菜烧得不好吃，一会儿责备儿子吃饭把臂肘搁在桌上，一会儿批评女儿的发式不正派。而罪魁祸首总是普拉斯柯菲雅·费多罗夫娜。普拉斯柯菲雅·费多罗夫娜起初向他回敬，也对他说了一些难听的话，但有两三次他一开始吃饭就勃然大怒。她明白了，这是一种由进食而引起的病态，就克制自己，不再还嘴，只是催他快吃。普拉斯柯菲雅·费多罗夫娜认为自己的忍让是一种值得称道的美德。她认定丈夫脾气极坏，给她的生活带来不幸。她开始可怜自己。她越是可怜自己，就越是憎恨丈夫。她巴不得他早点死，但又觉得不能这样想，因为他一死就没有薪俸了。而这一点却使她更加恨他。她认为自己不幸极了，因为就连他的死都不能拯救她。她变得很容易发脾气，但又强忍着，而她这样勉强忍住脾气，却使他的脾气变得更坏。

有一次夫妻争吵，伊凡·伊里奇特别不讲理。事后他解释说，他确实脾气暴躁，但这是由于病的缘故。普拉斯柯菲雅·费多罗夫娜就对他说，既然有病，就得治疗，要他去请教一位名医。

他乘车去了。一切都不出他所料，一切都照章办理。又是等待，又是医生装出一副煞有介事的样子——这种样子他是很熟悉的，就跟他自己在法庭上一样，——又是叩诊，又是听诊，又是各种不问也知道的多余问题，又是那种威风凛凛的神气，仿佛在说："你一旦落到我手里，就得听我摆布。我知道该怎么办，对付每个病人都是这样的。"一切都同法庭上一样。医生对待他的神气，就如他在法庭上对待被告那样。

医生说，如此这般的症状表明您有如此这般的病，但要是化验不能证明如此这般的病，那就得假定您有如此这般的病。要是假定有如此这般的病，那么……对伊凡·伊里奇来说，只有一个问题是重要的：他的病有没有危险？但医生对这个不合时宜的问题置之不理。从医生的观点来说，这问题没有意思，不值得讨论；存在的问题只是估计一下可能性：是游走肾，还是慢性盲肠炎。这里不存在伊凡·伊里奇的生死问题，只存在游走肾和盲肠炎之间的争执。在伊凡·伊里奇看来，医生已明确认定是盲肠炎，但又保留说，等小便化验后可以得到新的资料，到那时再做进一步诊断。这一切，就跟伊凡·伊里奇上千次振振有词地对被告宣布罪状一模一样。医生也是那么得意扬扬，甚至从眼镜上方瞧了一眼“被告”，振振有词地做了结论。从医生的结论中伊凡·伊里奇断定，情况严重，对医生或其他人都无所谓，可是对他却非同小可。这结论对伊凡·伊里奇是个沉重的打击，使他十分怜悯自己，同时十分憎恨那遇到如此严重问题却无动于衷的医生。

不过他什么也没有说，就站起来，把钱往桌上一放，叹了一口气。“也许我们病人常向您提些不该问的问题，”他说，“一般说来，这病是不是有危险？”

医生用一只眼睛从眼镜上方狠狠地瞪了他一下，仿佛在说：被告，你说话要是越出规定的范围，我将不得不命令把你带出法庭。

“我已把该说的话都对您说了，”医生说，“别的，等化验结果出来了再说。”医生结束道。

伊凡·伊里奇慢吞吞地走出诊所，垂头丧气地坐上雪橇回家。一路上他反复分析医生的话，竭力把难懂的医学用语翻译成普通的话，想从中找出问题的答案：“我的病严重？十分严重？或者还不要紧？”他觉得医生所有的话，都表示病情严重。伊凡·伊里奇觉得街上的一切都是阴郁的：马车夫是阴郁的，房子是阴郁的，路上行人是阴郁的，小铺子是阴郁的。他身上的疼痛一秒钟也没有停止，听了医生模棱两可的话后就觉得越发厉害。伊凡·伊里奇如今更加心情沉重地忍受着身上的疼痛。

他回到家里，给妻子讲了看病的经过。妻子听着。他讲到一半，女儿戴着帽子进来，准备同母亲一起出去。女儿勉强坐下来听他讲这无聊的事，但她听得不耐烦了，母亲也没有听完他的话。

“哦，我很高兴，”妻子说，“今后你一定要准时吃药。把药方给我，我叫盖拉西姆到药房去抓药。”说完她就去换衣服。

妻子在屋子里时，他不敢大声喘气，等她走了，他才深深地叹了一口气。

“好吧，”伊凡·伊里奇说，“也许真的还不要紧……”

他听医生的话，服药，养病。验过小便后，医生又改了药方。不过，小便化验结果和临床症状之间有矛盾。不知怎的，医生说的与实际情况不符。也许是医生疏忽了，也许是撒谎，也许有什么事瞒着他。

不过伊凡·伊里奇还是照医生的话养病，最初心里感到安慰。

伊凡·伊里奇看过病后，努力执行医生的指示，讲卫生，服药，注意疼痛和大小便。现在他最关心的是疾病和健康。人家一谈到病人、死亡、复原，特别是谈到跟他相似的病，他表面上装作镇定，其实全神贯注地听着，有时提些问题，把听到的情况同自己的病做着比较。

疼痛没有减轻，但伊凡·伊里奇强迫自己认为好一点了。没有事惹他生气，他还能欺骗自己。要是同妻子发生争吵，公务上不顺利，打牌输钱，他立刻感到病情严重。以前遇到挫折他总是希望时来运转，打牌顺手，获得大满贯，因此还能忍受。可是现在每次遇到挫折，他都会悲观绝望，丧失信心。他对自己说：“唉，我刚刚有点好转，药物刚刚见效，就遇到这倒霉的事……”于是他恨那种倒霉事，恨给他带来不幸并要置他于死命的人。他明白这种愤怒在危害他的生命，但他无法自制。照理他应该明白，他这样怨天尤人只会使病情加重，因此遇到不愉快的事，不应该放在心上，可是他的行为正好相反。他说，他需要安宁，并且特别警惕破坏安宁的事。只要他的安宁稍稍遇到破坏，他就大发雷霆。他读医书，向医生请教，结果有害无益。情况是逐渐恶化的，因此拿今天同昨天比较，差别似乎并不大，他还能聊以自慰，但同医生一商量，就觉得病情在不断恶化，而且发展得很快。尽管如此，他还是经常请教医生。

这个月里他又找了一位名医。这位名医的话，简直同原来那位一模一样，但问题的提法不同。请教这位名医，只增加伊凡·伊里奇的疑虑和恐惧。另外有位医生，是他朋友的朋友，也很出名。这位医生对他的病做了完全不同的诊断。尽管保证他能康复，但提出的问题和假设却使伊凡·伊里奇更加疑虑。一个提倡顺势疗法的医生又做了另一种诊断，给了不同的药，伊凡·伊里奇偷偷地服了一个礼拜。可是，一个礼拜后并没有见效，伊凡·伊里奇对原来的疗法丧失了信心，对这种新疗法也丧失了信心，于是越发沮丧了。有一次，一位熟识的太太给他介绍圣像疗法。伊凡·伊里奇勉强听着，并相信她的话。但这事使他不寒而栗。“难道我真的那样神经衰弱吗？”他自言自语。“废话！真是荒唐，这样神经过敏要不得，应该选定一个医生，听他的话好好疗养。就这么办，这下子主意定了。我不再胡思乱想，我要严格遵照这种疗法，坚持到夏天。到那时会见效的。别再犹豫不决了！”这话说说容易，实行起来可难了。腰痛在折磨他，越来越厉害，一刻也不停。他觉得嘴里的味道越来越难受，还有一股恶臭从嘴里出来，胃口越来越差，体力越来越弱。他不能欺骗自己：他身上出现了一种空前严重的情况。这一点只有他自己明白，周围的人谁也不知道，或者不想知道。他们总以为天下太平，一切如旧。这一点使伊凡·伊里奇觉得格外难受。家里人，尤其是妻子和女儿，热衷于社交活动。他看到，她们什么也不明白，还埋怨他情绪不好，难以伺候，仿佛还是他不对似的。他看出，尽管她们嘴里没说，他已成了她们的累赘，妻子对他的病已有定见，不管他说什么或做什么，她的态度都不会变。

“不瞒您说，”她对熟人说，“伊凡·伊里奇也像一切老实人那样，不能认真遵照医生的话养病。今天他听医生的话服药，吃东西；明天我一疏忽，他就忘记吃药，还吃鳇鱼（那是医生禁止的），而且坐下来打牌，一打就打到深夜一点钟。”

“哼，几时有过这种事？”伊凡·伊里奇恼怒地说，“总共在彼得·伊凡内奇家打过一次。”

“昨天不是跟谢贝克一起打过吗？”

“反正我痛得睡不着……”

“不管怎么说，你这样就永远好不了，还要折磨我们。”

普拉斯柯菲雅·费多罗夫娜向人家也向伊凡·伊里奇本人说，他生病主要是他自己不好，给她这个做妻子的带来痛苦。伊凡·伊里奇觉得她有这样的看法是很自然的，但心里总感到难受。

在法院里，伊凡·伊里奇发现或者心里感到人家对他抱着奇怪的态度：一会儿，人家把他看作一个不久将把位置空出来的人；一会儿，朋友们不怀恶意地嘲笑他神经过敏，因为他自认为有一种神秘可怕的东西，在不断吮吸他的精神，硬把他往那儿拉。朋友们觉得这事挺好玩，就拿来取笑他。尤其是施瓦尔茨说话诙谐生动而又装得彬彬有礼，使伊凡·伊里奇想起十年前他自己的模样，因而格外生气。

来了几个朋友，坐下来打牌。他拿出一副新牌，洗了洗，发了牌。他把红方块跟红方块叠在一起，总共七张。他的搭档说：没有王牌，给了他两张红方块。还指望什么呢？快乐，兴奋，得了大满贯。伊凡·伊里奇突然又感到那种抽痛，嘴里又有那股味道。他在这种情况下还能为赢得大满贯而高兴，未免太荒唐了。

他瞧着他的搭档米哈伊尔·米哈伊洛维奇，看他怎样用厚实的手掌拍着桌子，客客气气地不去抓一墩牌，却把它推给伊凡·伊里奇，使他一举手就能享受赢牌的乐趣。“他是不是以为我身子虚得手都伸不出去了？”伊凡·伊里奇想，忘记了王牌，却用更大的王牌去压搭档的牌，结果少了三墩牌，失去了大满贯。最可怕的是他看见米哈伊尔·米哈伊洛维奇脸色十分痛苦，却表现得若无其事。他怎么能若无其事，这一点想想也可怕。

大家看出他很痛苦，对他说：“要是您累了，我们就不打了。您休息一会儿吧。”休息？不，他一点也不累，可以把一圈牌打完。大家闷闷不乐，谁也不开口。伊凡·伊里奇觉得是他害得大家这样闷闷不乐，但又无法改变这种气氛。客人们吃过晚饭，各自走散了。伊凡·伊里奇独自留在家里，意识到他的生命遭到了毒害，还毒害了别人的生命，这种毒不仅没有减轻，而且越来越深地渗透到他的全身。

他常常带着这样的思想，再加上肉体上的疼痛和恐惧躺到床上，疼得大半夜不能合眼。可是天一亮又得起来，穿好衣服，乘车上法院，说话，批公文，要是不上班待在家里，那么一天二十四小时，每个小时都得活受罪。而且，在这样的生死边缘上，他只能独自默默地忍受，没有一个人了解他，也没有一个人可怜他。

五

就这样过了两个月光景。新年前夕，他的内弟来到他们城里，住在他们家。那天，伊凡·伊里奇上法院尚未回家。普拉斯柯菲雅·费多罗夫娜上街买东西去了。伊凡·伊里奇回到家里，走进书房，看见内弟体格强壮，脸色红润，正在打开手提箱。他听见伊凡·伊里奇的脚步声，抬起头，默默地对他瞧了一会儿。他的眼神向伊凡·伊里奇说明了问题。内弟张大嘴，正要喔唷一声叫出来，但立刻忍住了。这个动作证实了一切。

“怎么，我的样子变了吗？”

“是的……有点变。”

接着，不管伊凡·伊里奇怎样想使内弟再谈谈他的模样，内弟却绝口不提。普拉斯柯菲雅·费多罗夫娜一回来，内弟就到她屋里去了。伊凡·伊里奇锁上房门，去照镜子，先照正面，再照侧面。他拿起同妻子合拍的照片，拿它同镜子里的自己做着比较。变化很大。然后他把双臂露到肘部，打量了一番，才放下袖子，在软榻上坐下来，脸色变得漆黑。

“别这样，别这样。”他对自己说，霍地站起来，走到写字台边，打开卷宗，他开始批阅公文，可是脑子里什么也进不去。他打开门，走到前厅，客厅的门关着。他踮着脚走到门边，侧着耳朵听。

“不，你说得过分了。”普拉斯柯菲雅·费多罗夫娜说。

“怎么过分？你没发觉，他已经像个死人了。你看看他的眼睛，没有一点光。他这是怎么搞的？”

“谁也不知道。尼古拉耶夫（一位医生）说如此这般，可我不知道。列谢季茨基（名医）说的正好相反……”

伊凡·伊里奇回到自己屋里，躺下来想：“肾，游走肾。”他回忆起医生们对他说过的话，肾脏怎样离开原位而游走。他竭力在想象中捕捉这个肾脏，不让它游走，把它固定下来。这事看上去轻而易举。“不，我还是去找找彼得·伊凡内奇（那个有医生朋友的朋友）。”他打了铃，吩咐套车，准备出去。

“你上哪儿去，约翰？”妻子露出异常忧愁和矫揉造作的贤惠神情问。

这种矫揉造作的贤惠使他生气。他阴沉着脸对她瞅了一眼。

“我去找彼得·伊凡内奇。”

他去找这个有医生朋友的朋友。然后跟他一起到医生家去。他遇见医生，跟他谈了好半天。

医生根据解剖学和生理学对他的病做了分析，他全听懂了。

盲肠里有点毛病，有点小毛病。全会好的。只要加强一个器官的功能，减少另一个器官的活动，多吸收一点，就会好的。吃饭时，他晚到了一点。吃过饭，他兴致勃勃地谈了一通，但好一阵不能定下心来做事。最后他回到书房，立刻动手工作。他批阅公文，处理公事，但心里念念不忘有一件要事被耽误了。等公事完毕，他才记起那件事就是盲肠的毛病。但他故作镇定，走到客厅喝茶。那里有几个客人，正在说话，弹琴，唱歌。他得意的未来女婿——法院侦讯官也在座。据普拉斯柯菲雅·费多罗夫娜说，伊凡·伊里奇那天晚上过得比谁都快活，其实他一分钟也没有忘记盲肠的毛病被耽误了。十一点钟他向大家告辞，回自己屋里去。自从生病以来，他就独自睡在书房里。他走进屋里，脱去衣服，拿起一本左拉的小说，但没有看，却想着心事。他想象盲肠被治愈了。通过吸收，排泄，功能恢复正常。“对了，就是那么一回事，”他自言自语，“只要补养补养身体就好了。”他想到了药，支起身来，服了药，又仰天躺下，仔细体味药物怎样在治病，怎样在制止疼痛。“只要按时服药，避免不良影响就行；我现在已觉得好一点了，好多了。”他按按腰部，按上去不疼了。“是的，不疼了，真的好多了。”他灭了蜡烛，侧身躺下……盲肠在逐渐恢复，逐渐吸收。突然他又感觉到那种熟悉的隐痛，痛得一刻不停，而且很厉害。嘴里又是那种恶臭。他顿时心头发凉，头脑发晕。“天哪！天哪！”他喃喃地说。“又来了，又来了，再也好不了啦！”突然他觉得完全不是那么一回事。“哼，盲肠！肾脏！”他自言自语，“问题根本不在盲肠，不在肾脏，而在生和……死。是啊，有过生命，可现在它在溜走，在走，而我又留不住它。是啊！何必欺骗自己呢？除了我自己，不是人人都很清楚我快死了吗？问题只在于还有几个礼拜、几天，还是现在就死。原来有过光明，现在却变成一片黑暗。我此刻在这个世界，但不久就要离开！到哪儿去？”他觉得浑身发凉，呼吸停止，只听见心脏在扑扑跳动。

“等我没有了，那还有什么呢？什么也没有了。等我没有了，我将在哪儿？难道真的要死了吗？不，我不愿死。”他霍地跳起来，想点燃蜡烛，用颤动的双手摸索着。蜡烛和烛台被碰翻，落到地上。他又仰天倒在枕头上。“何必呢？反正都一样。”他在黑暗中瞪着一双眼睛，自言自语。“死。是的，死。他们谁也不知道，谁也不想知道，谁也不可怜我。他们玩得可快乐了（他听见远处传来喧闹和伴奏声）。他们若无其事，可他们有朝一日也要死的。都是傻瓜！我先死，他们后死，他们也免不了一死。可他们还乐呢。畜生！”他愤怒得喘不过气来。他痛苦得受不了。难道谁都得受这样的罪吗！他坐起来。

“总有什么地方不对头，我得定下心，从头至尾好好想一想。”他开始思索。“对了，病是这样开始的。先是腰部撞了一下，但过了一两天我还是好好的。稍微有点疼，后来疼得厉害了，后来请医生，后来泄气了，发愁了，后来又请医生，但越来越接近深渊。体力越来越差，越来越接近……越来越接近……我的身子虚透了，我的眼睛没有光。我要死了，可我还以为是盲肠有病。我想治好盲肠，其实是死神临头了。难道真的要死吗？”他又感到魂飞魄散，呼吸急促。他侧身摸索火柴，用臂肘撑住床几。臂肘撑得发痛，他恼火了，撑得更加使劲，结果把床几推倒了。他绝望得喘不过气来，又仰天倒下，恨不得立刻死去。

这当儿，客人们纷纷走散。普拉斯柯菲·费多罗夫娜送他们走。她听见什么东西倒下，走进来。

“你怎么了？”

“没什么，不留神把它撞倒了。”

她走出去，拿着一支蜡烛进来。他躺着，喘息得又重又急，好像刚跑完了几里路，眼睛停滞地瞧着她。

“你怎么了，约翰？”

“没……什么。撞……倒了。”他回答，心里却想，“有什么可说的。她不会明白的。”

她确实不明白。她扶起床几，给他点上蜡烛，又匆匆走掉了：她还得送客。

等她回来，他仍旧仰天躺着，眼睛瞪着天花板。

“你怎么了，更加不舒服吗？”

“是的。”

她摇摇头，坐下来。

“我说，约翰，我们把列谢季茨基请到家里来好吗？”

这就是说，不惜金钱，请那位名医来出诊。他冷笑了一声说：“不用了。”她坐了一会儿，走到他旁边，吻了吻他的前额。

她吻他的时候，他从心底里憎恨她，好容易才忍住不把她推开。

“再见。上帝保佑你好好睡一觉。”

“嗯。”

六

伊凡 · 伊里奇看到自己快要死了，经常处于绝望中。

他心里明白，他快要死了，但他对这个念头很不习惯，他实在不理解，怎么也不能理解。

他在基捷韦帖尔的逻辑学里读到这样一种三段论法：盖尤斯是人，凡人都要死，因此盖尤斯也要死。他始终认为这个例子只适用于盖尤斯，绝对不适用于他。盖尤斯是人，是个普通人，这个道理完全正确；但他不是盖尤斯，不是个普通人，他永远是个与众不同的特殊人物。

他原来是小伊凡，有妈妈，有爸爸，有两个兄弟——米嘉和伏洛嘉，有许多玩具，有马车夫，有保姆，后来又有了妹妹卡嘉，还有儿童时代、少年时代和青年时代的喜怒哀乐。难道盖尤斯也闻到过他小伊凡所喜爱的那种花皮球的气味吗？难道盖尤斯也那么吻过妈妈的手，听到过妈妈绸衣褶裥的声吗？难道盖尤斯也曾在法学院里因点心不好吃而闹过事吗？难道盖尤斯也那么谈过恋爱吗？难道盖尤斯能像他那样主持审讯吗？

盖尤斯的确是要死的，要他死是正常的，但我是小伊凡，是伊凡·伊里奇，我有我的思想感情，跟他截然不同。我不该死，要不真是太可怕了。

这就是他的心情。

“我要是像盖尤斯那样也要死，那我一定会知道，一定会听到内心的声音，可是我心里没有这样的声音。我和我的朋友们都明白，我跟盖尤斯完全不同。可是如今呢！”他自言自语，“这是不可能的，不可能发生的，可是偏偏发生了。这是怎么搞的？这事该怎么理解？”

他无法理解，就竭力驱除这个想法，把这个想法看成是虚假、错误和病态的，并且用正确健康的想法来挤掉它。但这不只是思想，而是现实，它出现了，摆在他面前。

他故意想想别的事来排挤这个想法，希望从中找到精神上的支持。他试图用原来的一套思路来对抗死的念头。但奇怪得很，以前用这种办法可以抵挡和驱除死的念头，如今却不行。近来，伊凡·伊里奇常常想恢复原来的思绪，以驱除死的念头。有时他对自己说："我还是去办公吧，我一向靠工作过活。"他摆脱心头的种种疑虑，到法院去。他跟同事们谈话，在法庭上坐下来，照例漫不经心地扫一眼人群，两条干瘦的胳膊搁在麻栎椅扶手上，照例侧身凑近旁边的法官，挪过卷宗，同他耳语几句，然后猛地抬起眼睛，挺直身子，说几句老套，宣布开庭。但审讯到一半，腰部不顾正在开庭，突然又抽痛起来。伊凡·伊里奇定下神，竭力不去想它，可是没有用。它又来了，站在他面前，打量着他。他吓得呆若木鸡，眼睛里的光也熄灭了。他又自言自语："难道只有它是真的吗？"同事和下属惊奇而痛心地看到，像他这样一位精明能干的法官竟然说话颠三倒四，在审讯中出差错。他竭力振作精神，定下心来，勉强坚持到庭审结束，闷闷不乐地回家去。他明白，法院开庭也不再能回避他想回避的事，他在审讯时也不能摆脱它。最最糟糕的是，它吸引他，并非要他有什么行动，而只是要他瞧着它，面对面地瞧着它，什么事也不做，难堪地忍受着折磨。

为了摆脱这种痛苦，伊凡·伊里奇寻找另一种屏风来自卫，但另一种屏风也只能暂时保护他，不久又破裂了，或者变得透明了，仿佛它能穿透一切，什么东西也挡不住它。

有一次他走进精心布置的客厅——他摔跤的地方，他嘲弄地想，正是为了布置它而献出了生命，因为他知道他的病是由跌伤引起的——他发现油漆一新的桌上有被什么东西划过的痕迹。他研究原因，发现那是被照相簿上弯卷的青铜饰边划破的。他拿起他深情地贴上照片的照相簿，对女儿和她那些朋友的粗野很恼火——有的地方撕破了，有的照片被颠倒了。他把照片仔细整理好，把照相簿饰边扳平。

然后他想重新布置，把照相簿改放到盆花旁的角落里。他吩咐仆人请女儿或者妻子来帮忙，可是她们不同意他的想法，反对搬动。他同她们争吵、生气。但这样倒好，因为他可以不再想到它，不再看见它。

不过，当他亲自动手挪动东西的时候，妻子对他说："啊，让仆人搬吧，你又要糟蹋自己了。"这当儿，它突然又从屏风后面出现，他又看见了它。它的影子一闪，他还希望它能再消失，可是他又注意到自己的腰。腰还是在抽痛。他再也无法把它忘记，它明明在盆花后面瞧着他。“这是干什么呀？”

“真的，我为了这窗帘就像冲锋陷阵一样送了命。难道真是这样吗？多么可怕而又多么愚蠢哪！这不可能！不可能！但这是事实。”

他回到书房里躺下，又同它单独相处。他同它又面面相对，但对它束手无策。他只能瞧着它，浑身发抖。

七

伊凡·伊里奇生病的第三个月的情况怎样，很难说，因为病情是逐步发展的，不易察觉。但妻子也好，女儿也好，儿子也好，用人也好，朋友也好，医生也好，主要是他自己，都知道，大家唯一关心的事是，他的位置是不是快空出来，活着的人能不能解除由于他存在而招惹的麻烦，他自己是不是快摆脱痛苦。

他的睡眠越来越少；医生给他服鸦片，注射吗啡，但都不能减轻他的痛苦。他在昏昏沉沉中所感到的麻木，起初使他稍微好过些，但不久又感到同样痛苦，甚至比清醒时更不好受。

家里人遵照医生的指示给他做了特殊的饭菜，但他觉得这种饭菜越来越没有滋味，越来越倒胃口。

他大便这件事也被做了特殊的安排。每次大便他都觉得很痛苦，因为不清洁，不体面，有臭味，还得麻烦别人帮忙。

不过，在这件不愉快的事上，伊凡·伊里奇倒也得到一种安慰。每次大便总是由男仆盖拉西姆伺候。

盖拉西姆是个年轻的庄稼汉，衣着整洁，容光焕发，因为长期吃城里伙食长得格外强壮。他性格开朗，总是乐呵呵的。这个整洁的小伙子身穿俄罗斯民族服，做着这种不体面的事，总使伊凡·伊里奇感到困窘。

有一次，他从便盆上起来，无力拉上裤子，就倒在沙发上。他看见自己皮包骨头的大腿，不禁心惊胆战。

盖拉西姆脚蹬散发着柏油味的大皮靴，身上系着干净的麻布围裙，穿着干净的印花布衬衫，卷起袖子，露出年轻强壮的胳膊，带着清新的冬天空气走进来。他目光避开伊凡·伊里奇，竭力抑制着从焕发的容光中表现出来的生的欢乐，免得病人见了不高兴，走到便盆旁。

“盖拉西姆。”伊凡·伊里奇有气无力地叫道。

盖拉西姆打了个哆嗦，显然害怕自己什么地方做得不对，慌忙把他那张刚开始长胡子的纯朴善良而又青春洋溢的脸转过来对着病人。

“老爷，您有什么吩咐？”

“我想，你做这事一定很不好受。你要原谅我，我是没有办法。”

“哦，老爷，好说。”盖拉西姆闪亮着眼睛，露出一排洁白健康的牙齿。“那算得了什么？您有病嘛，老爷。”

他用他那双强壮的手熟练地做着做惯的事，轻悄地走了出去。过了五分钟，又那么轻悄地走回来。

伊凡·伊里奇一直那么坐在沙发上。

“盖拉西姆，”当盖拉西姆把洗干净的便盆放回原处时，伊凡·伊里奇说，“请你帮帮我，你过来。”盖拉西姆走过去。“你搀我一把。我自己爬不起来，德米特里被我派出去了。”

盖拉西姆走过去。他用他那双强壮的手，也像走路一样轻松、利索而温柔地把主人抱起来，一只手扶住他，另一只手给他拉上裤子，想让他坐下。但伊凡·伊里奇要求把他扶到长沙发上。盖拉西姆一点也不费劲，稳稳当当地把他抱到长沙发上坐下。

“谢谢。你真行，干得真轻巧。”

盖拉西姆又微微一笑，想走。可是伊凡·伊里奇同他一起觉得很愉快，不肯放他走。

“还有，请你把那把椅子给我推过来。不，是那一把，让我搁腿。腿搁得高，好过些。”

盖拉西姆端过椅子，轻轻地把它放在长沙发前，然后抬起伊凡·伊里奇的双腿放在上面。当盖拉西姆把他的腿高高抬起时，他觉得舒服些。

“腿抬得高，我觉得舒服些，”伊凡·伊里奇说，“你把这个枕头给我垫在下面。”

盖拉西姆照他的吩咐做了。他又把他的腿抬起来放好。盖拉西姆抬起他的双腿，他觉得确实好过些。双腿一放下，他又觉得不舒服。

“盖拉西姆，”伊凡·伊里奇对他说，“你现在有事吗？”

“没有，老爷。”盖拉西姆说，他已学会像城里仆人那样同老爷说话。

“你还有什么活要干？”

“我还有什么活要干？什么都干好了，只要再劈点木柴留着明天用。”

“那你把我的腿这么高高抬着，行吗？”

“有什么不行的？行！”盖拉西姆把主人的腿抬起来，伊凡·伊里奇觉得这样一点也不疼了。

“那么劈柴怎么办？”

“不用老爷您操心。这我来得及的。”

伊凡·伊里奇叫盖拉西姆坐下抬着他的腿，并同他谈话。真奇怪，盖拉西姆抬着他的腿，他觉得好过多了。

从此以后伊凡·伊里奇就常常把盖拉西姆唤来，要他用肩膀扛着他的腿，并喜欢同他谈天。盖拉西姆做这事轻松愉快，态度诚恳，使伊凡·伊里奇很感动。别人身上的健康、力量和生气往往使伊凡·伊里奇感到屈辱；只有盖拉西姆的力量和生气不仅没有使他觉得伤心，反而使他感到安慰。

伊凡·伊里奇觉得最痛苦的事就是听谎言，听大家出于某种原因都相信的那个谎言，他只是病了，并不会死，只要安心治疗，一定会好的。可是他知道，不论采取什么办法，他都不会好了，痛苦只会越来越厉害，直到死去。这个谎言折磨着他。他感到痛苦的是，大家都知道，他自己也知道他的病很严重，但大家都讳言真相而撒谎，还要迫使他自己一起撒谎。谎言，在他临死前夕散布的谎言，把他不久于人世这样严肃可怕的大事，缩小到访问、挂窗帘和晚餐吃鳇鱼等小事，这使他感到极其痛苦。说也奇怪，好多次当他们就他的情况编造谎言时，他差一点大声叫出来："别再撒谎了，我快要死了。这事你们知道，我也知道，所以大家别再撒谎了。"但他从来没有勇气这样做。他看到，他不久于人世这样严肃可怕的事，被周围的人看成只是一件不愉快或者不体面的事（就像一个人走进会客室从身上散发出臭气一样），还要勉强维持他一辈子苦苦撑住的"体面"。他看到，谁也不可怜他，谁也不想了解他的真实情况。只有盖拉西姆一人了解他，并且可怜他。因此只有同盖拉西姆在一起他才觉得好过些。盖拉西姆有时通宵扛着他的腿，不去睡觉，还说："您可不用操心，老爷，我回头会睡个够的。"这时他感到安慰。或者当盖拉西姆脱口而出亲热地说："要是您没病就好了，我这样伺候伺候您算得了什么？"他也感到安慰。只有盖拉西姆一人不撒谎，显然也只有他一人明白真实情况，并且认为无须隐讳，但他怜悯日益消瘦的老爷。有一次伊凡·伊里奇打发他走，他直截了当地说："我们大家都要死的。我为什么不能伺候您呢？"他说这话的意思就是，现在他不辞辛劳，因为伺候的是个垂死的人，希望将来有朝一日轮到他的时候也有人伺候他。

除了这个谎言，或者正是由于这个谎言，伊凡·伊里奇觉得特别痛苦的是，没有一个人像他所希望的那样可怜他。伊凡·伊里奇长时期受尽折磨，有时特别希望——尽管他不好意思承认——有人像疼爱有病的孩子那样疼爱他。他真希望有人疼他，吻他，对着他哭，就像人家疼爱孩子那样。他知道，他是个显赫的大官，已经胡子花白，因此这是不可能的，但他还是抱着这样的希望。他同盖拉西姆的关系近似这种关系，因此跟盖拉西姆在一起，他感到安慰。伊凡·伊里奇想哭，要人家疼他，对着他哭，不料这时他的法院同事谢贝克走来了，伊凡·伊里奇不仅没有哭，没有表示亲热，反而板起脸，现出严肃和沉思的神气，习惯成自然地说了他对复审的意见，并且坚持自己的看法。他周围的这种谎言和他自己所做的谎言，比什么都厉害地毒害了他生命的最后日子。

八

有一天早晨，伊凡·伊里奇知道这是早晨，因为每天早晨都是盖拉西姆从书房里出去，男仆彼得进来吹灭蜡烛，拉开一扇窗帘，悄悄地收拾房间。早晨也好，晚上也好，礼拜五也好，礼拜天也好，反正都一样，反正没有区别：永远是一刻不停的令人难堪的疼痛；他意识到生命正在无可奈何地消逝，但还没有完全消逝；那愈益逼近的可怕而又可恨的死，只有它才是真实的，其他一切都是谎言。在这种情况下，几天、几个礼拜和几小时有什么区别？

“老爷，您要不要用茶？”

“他还是老一套，知道老爷太太每天早晨都要喝茶。”他想，接着回答说，“不用了。”

“您要不要坐到沙发上去？”

“他得把屋子收拾干净，可我在这里碍事。我太邋遢，太不整齐了，”他想了想回答说，“不，不用管我。”

男仆继续收拾屋子。伊凡·伊里奇伸出一只手。彼得殷勤地走过去。

“老爷，您要什么？”

“我的表。”

彼得拿起手边的表，递给他。

“八点半了。她们还没有起来吗？”

“还没有，老爷。瓦西里·伊凡内奇（这是儿子）上学去了，普拉斯柯菲雅·费多罗夫娜关照过，要是您问起，就去叫醒她。要去叫她吗？”

“不，不用了。”他回答，接着想，“要不要喝点茶呢？”于是就对彼得说：“对了，你拿点茶来吧。”

彼得走到门口。伊凡·伊里奇独自留着觉得害怕。“怎么把他留住呢？有了，吃药。”他想了想，说：“彼得，给我拿药来。”接着又想：“是啊，说不定吃药还有用呢。”他拿起匙子，把药吃下去。“不，没有用。一切都是胡闹，都是欺骗，”他一尝到那种熟悉的甜腻腻的怪味，就想，“不，我再也不能相信了。可是那个疼，那个疼，要是能停止一会儿就好了。”他呻吟起来。彼得向他回过头来。“不，你去吧，拿茶来。”

彼得走了，剩下伊凡·伊里奇一个人。他又呻吟起来。他疼得很厉害，可呻吟主要不是由于疼痛，而是由于悲伤。“老是那个样子，老是那样的白天和黑夜。但愿快一点。什么快一点？死，黑暗。不，不！好死不如赖活！”

彼得托着茶盘进来，伊凡·伊里奇茫然看了他好一阵，认不出他是谁，不知道他是来干什么的。他这种目光弄得彼得很狼狈。彼得现出尴尬的神色，伊凡·伊里奇才醒悟过来。

“噢，茶……”他说，“好的，放着。你帮我洗洗脸，拿一件干净衬衫来。”

伊凡·伊里奇开始梳洗。他断断续续地洗手，洗脸，刷牙，梳头，然后照照镜子。他感到害怕，特别是看到他的头发怎样贴着苍白的前额。

彼得给他换衬衫。他知道他要是看到自己的身体，一定会更加吃惊，因此不往身上看。梳洗完毕了，他穿上晨衣，身上盖了一条方格毛毯，坐到扶手椅上喝茶。有那么一会儿他觉得神清气爽，但一喝茶，立刻又感到那种味道、那种疼痛。他勉强喝完茶，伸直腿躺下来。他躺下，让彼得走。

还是那个样子。一会儿出现了一线希望，一会儿又掉进绝望的海洋。老是疼，老是疼，老是悲怆凄凉，一切都是老样子。独个儿待着格外悲伤，想叫个人来，但他知道同人家待在一起更难受。“最好再来点儿吗啡，把什么都忘记。我要请求医生，叫他想点别的办法。这样可真受不了，真受不了！”

一小时、两小时就这样过去了。忽然前厅里响起了铃声。会不会是医生？果然是医生。他走进来，精神饱满，容光焕发，喜气洋洋。那副神气仿佛表示：你们何必这样大惊小怪，我这就来给你们解决问题。医生知道，这样的表情是不得体的，但他已经习惯了，改不掉，好像一个人一早穿上大礼服，就这样穿着一家家去拜客，没有办法改变了。

医生生气勃勃而又使人宽慰地搓搓手。

“啊，真冷，可把我冻坏了。让我暖和暖和身子。”他说这话时的神气仿佛表示，只要稍微等一下，等他身子一暖和，就什么问题都解决了。

“嗯，怎么样？”

伊凡·伊里奇觉得，医生想说：“情况怎么样？”但他觉得不该那么问，就说：“晚上睡得怎么样？”

伊凡·伊里奇望着医生的那副神气表示：“您老是撒谎，怎么不害臊？”但医生不理会他的表情。

伊凡·伊里奇就说：“还是那么糟。疼痛没有消除，也没有减轻。您能不能想点办法……”

“啊，你们病人总是这样。嗯，这会儿我可暖和了，就连普拉斯柯菲雅·费多罗夫娜那么仔细，也不会对我的体温有意见了。嗯，您好。”医生说着握了握病人的手。

接着医生收起戏谑的口吻，现出严肃的神色给病人看病：把脉，量体温，叩诊，听诊。

伊凡·伊里奇清清楚楚地知道，这一切都毫无意思，全是骗人的，但医生跪在他面前，身子凑近他，用一只耳朵忽上忽下地细听，脸上显出极其认真的神气，像体操运动员一般做着各种姿势。伊凡·伊里奇面对这种场面，屈服了，就像他在法庭上听辩护律师发言一样，尽管他明明知道他们都在撒谎以及为什么撒谎。

医生跪在沙发上，还在他身上敲着。这当儿门口传来普拉斯柯菲雅·费多罗夫娜绸衣裳的窸窣声，还听见她在责备彼得没有及时向她报告医生的来到。

她走进来，吻吻大夫，立刻振振有词地说，她早就起来了，只是不知道医生来了才没有及时出来迎接。

伊凡·伊里奇对她望望，打量着她的全身，对她那白净浮肿的双手和脖子、光泽的头发和充满活力的明亮眼睛感到嫌恶。他从心底里憎恨她。她的亲吻更激起他对她的难以克制的憎恨。

她对待他和他的病还是老样子。正像医生对病人的态度都已定型不变那样，她对丈夫的态度也已定型不变：她总是亲昵地责备他没有照规定服药休息，总是怪他自己不好。

“嗳，他这人就是不听话！不肯按时吃药。尤其是他睡的姿势不对，两腿搁得太高，这样睡对他不好。”

她告诉医生他怎样叫盖拉西姆扛着腿睡。

医生鄙夷不屑而又和蔼可亲地微微一笑，仿佛说："有什么办法呢？病人总会做出这样的蠢事来，但情有可原。"

检查完毕，医生看了看表。这时普拉斯柯菲雅·费多罗夫娜向伊凡·伊里奇宣布，不管他是不是愿意，她今天就去请那位名医来，让他同米哈伊尔·达尼洛维奇（平时看病的医生）会诊一下，商量商量。

"请你不要反对。我是为我自己才这样做的。"她嘲讽地说，让他感到这一切都是为她而做的，因此他不该拒绝。他不作声，皱起眉头。他觉得周围是一片谎言，很难判断是非曲直。

她为他做的一切都是为了她自己。她对他说这样做是为了她自己，那倒是真的，不过她的行为叫人很难相信，因此必须从反面来理解。

十一点半，那位名医果然来了。又是听诊，又是当着他的面一本正经地交谈，而到了隔壁房间又是谈肾脏，谈盲肠，又是一本正经地问答，又是避开他现在面临的生死问题，大谈什么肾脏和盲肠有毛病，米哈伊尔·达尼洛维奇和名医又都主张对肾脏和盲肠进行治疗。

名医临别时神态十分严肃，但并没有绝望。伊凡·伊里奇眼睛里露出恐惧和希望的光芒仰望着名医，怯生生地问他，是不是还能恢复健康。名医回答说，不能保证，但可能性还是有的。伊凡·伊里奇用满怀希望的目光送别医生，他的样子显得那么可怜，以至普拉斯柯菲雅·费多罗夫娜走出书房付给医生出诊费时都忍不住哭了。

被医生鼓舞起来的希望并没有持续多久。还是那个房间，还是那些图画，还是那些窗帘，还是那种墙纸，还是那些药瓶，还是他那个疼痛的身子。伊凡·伊里奇呻吟起来，给自己注射了吗啡，便迷迷糊糊睡着了。

他醒来时，天色开始发黑。仆人给他送来晚餐，他勉强吃了一点肉汤。于是一切如旧，黑夜又来临了。

饭后七点钟，普拉斯柯菲雅·费多罗夫娜走进他的房间。她穿着晚礼服，丰满的胸部被衣服绷得隆起，脸上有扑过粉的痕迹。早晨她就提起，今晚她们要去看戏。萨拉·贝娜到这个城里做访问演出，她们订了一个包厢。那也是他的主意。这会儿，他把这事忘记了，她那副打扮使他生气。不过，当他记起是他要她们订包厢去看戏的，认为孩子们看这戏可以获得美的享受，他就把自己的愤怒掩饰起来。

普拉斯柯菲雅·费多罗夫娜进来的时候得意扬扬，

但仿佛又有点负疚。她坐下来，问他身体怎么样，不过他看出，她只是为了应酬几句才问的，并非真的想了解什么，而且知道也问不出什么来。接着她就讲她要讲的话：她本来说什么也不愿去，可是包厢已经订了，爱伦和女儿，还有彼特利歇夫（法院侦讯官，未来的女婿）都要去，总不能让他们自己去，她其实是宁可待在家里陪他的。现在她只希望她不在家时，他能照医生的嘱咐休息。

“对了，费多尔 · 彼得罗维奇（未来的女婿）想进来看看你，行吗？还有丽莎。”

“让他们来好了。”

女儿走进来。她打扮得漂漂亮亮，露出部分年轻的身体。对比之下，他觉得更加难受。她却公然显示她健美的身体。显然她正在谈恋爱，对妨碍她幸福的疾病、痛苦和死亡感到嫌恶。

费多尔 · 彼得罗维奇也进来了。他身穿燕尾服，头发烫出波纹，雪白的硬领夹着青筋毕露的细长脖子，胸前露出一大块白硬衬，瘦长的黑裤紧裹着两条强壮的大腿，手上套着雪白的手套，拿着大礼帽。

一个中学生在他后面悄悄走进来。这个可怜的孩子穿一身崭新的学生装，戴着手套，眼圈发黑——伊凡 · 伊里奇知道为什么会这样。

他总是很怜悯儿子。儿子那种满怀同情的怯生生目光使他心惊胆战。伊凡·伊里奇觉得除了盖拉西姆以外，只有儿子一人了解他、同情他。

大家都坐下来，又问了一下病情。接下来是一片沉默。丽莎问母亲要望远镜。母女俩争吵起来，不知是谁拿了，放在什么地方。这事弄得大家都很不高兴。

费多尔·彼得罗维奇问伊凡·伊里奇有没有看过萨拉·贝娜。伊凡·伊里奇起初没听懂他问什么，后来才说：

“没有，您看过吗？”

“看过了，她演过《阿德里安娜·莱科芙露尔》。”

普拉斯柯菲雅·费多罗夫娜说，她演那种角色特别好。女儿不同意她的看法。大家谈到她的演技又典雅又真挚——那题目已谈过不知多少次了。

谈话中间，费多尔·彼得罗维奇对伊凡·伊里奇瞧了一眼，不作声了。其他人跟着瞧了一眼，也不作声了。伊凡·伊里奇睁大眼睛向前望望，显然对他们很生气。这种尴尬的局面必须改变，可是怎么也无法改变。必须设法打破这种沉默，谁也不敢这样做，大家都害怕，唯恐这种礼貌周到的虚伪做法一旦被揭穿，真相就会大白。

丽莎第一个鼓起勇气，打破了沉默。她想掩饰大家心里都有的感觉，却脱口而出：

“嗯，要是去的话，那么是时候了。”她瞧了瞧父亲送给她的表，说。接着对未婚夫会意地微微一笑，衣服窸窣响着站起来。

大家都站起来，告辞走了。

等他们一走，伊凡·伊里奇觉得好过些，因为虚伪的局面结束了，随着他们一起消失了，但疼痛如旧。依旧是那种疼痛，依旧是那种恐惧，一点也没有缓和，而是每况愈下。

时间还是一分钟又一分钟、一小时又一小时地过去，一切如旧，没完没了，而无法避免的结局却越来越使人不寒而栗。

“好了，你去叫盖拉西姆来。”他对向他提出了问题的彼得给出了这样的回答。

九

妻子深夜才回家。她踮着脚悄悄进来，但他还是听见她的脚步声。他睁开眼睛，连忙又闭上。她想打发盖拉西姆走开，自己陪他坐一会儿。他却睁开眼睛，说：

“不，你去吧。”

“你很难受吗？”

“老样子。”

“服点鸦片吧。”

他同意了，服了点鸦片。她走了。

直到凌晨三时，他一直处在痛苦的迷糊状态中。他仿佛觉得人家硬把他这个病痛的身子往一个又窄又黑又深的口袋里塞，一个劲地往下塞，却怎么也塞不到袋底。这件可怕的事把他折磨得好苦。他又害怕，又想往下沉，不断挣扎，越挣扎越往下沉。他突然跌了下去，随即惊醒过来。依旧是那个盖拉西姆坐在床脚，平静而耐心地打着瞌睡。他却躺在那里，把那双穿着袜子的瘦腿搁在盖拉西姆肩上；依旧是那支有罩的蜡烛，依旧是那种一刻不停的疼痛。

“你去吧，盖拉西姆。”他喃喃地说。

“不要紧，老爷，我坐坐。”

“不，你去吧。”

他放下腿，侧过身子来睡。他开始可怜自己。他等盖拉西姆走到隔壁屋里，再也忍不住，就像孩子般痛哭起来。他哭自己的无依无靠，哭自己的孤独寂寞，哭人们的残酷，哭上帝的残酷和冷漠。

“你为什么要这样做？为什么把我带到这儿来？为什么？为什么这么狠心地折磨我？……”

他知道不会有谁回答，但又因得不到也不可能得到回答而痛哭。疼痛又发作了，但他一动不动，也不呼号。他自言自语：“痛吧，再痛吧！可是为了什么呀？我对你做了什么啦？这是为了什么呀？”后来他安静了，不仅停止哭泣，而且屏住呼吸，提起精神来。他仿佛不是在倾听说话声，而是在倾听灵魂的呼声，倾听自己思潮的翻腾。

“你要什么呀？”这是他听出来的第一句明确的话。“你要什么呀？你要什么呀？”他一再问自己，“要什么？”——“摆脱痛苦，活下去。”他自己回答。

他又全神贯注地倾听，连疼痛都忘记了。

“活下去，怎么活？”心灵里有个声音问他。

“是的，活下去，像我以前那样活得舒畅而快乐。”

“像你以前那样，活得舒畅而快乐吗？”心灵里的声音问。于是他开始回忆自己一生中美好的日子。奇怪的是，所有那些美好的日子现在看来一点也不美好，只有童年的回忆是例外。童年时代确实有过欢乐的日子，要是时光能倒转，那是值得重温的。但享受过当年欢乐的人已经不存在了，存在的似乎只有对别人的回忆。

自从伊凡·伊里奇变成现在这个样子以来，过去的欢乐都在他眼里消失了，或者说，变得不足道了，变得令人讨厌了。

离童年越远，离现在越近，那些欢乐就越显得不足道、越可疑。这是从法学院开始的。在那里还有点真正美好的事：还有欢乐，还有友谊，还有希望。但读到高年级，美好的时光就越来越少。后来开始在官府供职，又出现了美好的时光：那是对一个女人的倾慕。后来生活又浑浑噩噩，美好的时光更少了，越来越少，越来越少。

结婚……是那么意外，那么叫人失望。妻子嘴里的臭味，放纵情欲，装腔作势！死气沉沉地办公，不择手段地捞钱，就这样过了一年，两年，十年，二十年——始终是那么一套。而且越是往后，就越是死气沉沉。我在走下坡路，却还以为在上山。就是这么一回事。大家都说我官运亨通，步步高升，其实生命在我脚下溜掉……如今瞧吧，末日到了！

这究竟是怎么一回事？为什么会这样？生活不该那么无聊，那么讨厌。不该！即使生活确是那么讨厌，那么无聊，那又为什么要死，而且死得那么痛苦？总有点不对头。

“是不是我的生活有些什么地方不对头？”他忽然想到。“但我不论做什么都是循规蹈矩的，怎么会不对头？”他自言自语，顿时找到了唯一的答案：生死之谜是无法解答的。

如今你到底要什么呢？要活命？怎么活？像法庭上听到民事执行吏高呼“开庭了！”时那样活。“开庭了，开庭了！”他一再对自己说。“喏，现在要开庭了！可我又没有罪！”他恨恨地叫道。“为了什么呀？”他停止哭泣，转过脸来对着墙壁，一直思考着那个问题：为什么要忍受这样的恐怖？为什么？

然而，不管他怎样苦苦思索，都找不到答案。他头脑里又出现了那个常常出现的想法：这一切都是由于他生活过得不对头。他重新回顾自己规规矩矩的一生，立刻又把这个古怪的想法驱除掉。

十

又过了两个礼拜。伊凡 · 伊里奇躺在沙发上已经起不来了。他不愿躺在床上，就躺在长沙发上。他几乎一直面对墙壁躺着，孤独地忍受着那难以摆脱的痛苦，孤独地思索着那难以解答的问题：“这是怎么一回事？难道真的要死吗？”心里有个声音回答说：“是的，是要死的。”——“为什么要受这样的罪？”那声音回答说：“不为什么，就是这样。”除此以外就什么也没有了。

自从伊凡·伊里奇开始生病，自从他第一次看医生以来，他的心情就分裂成两种对立的状态，两种状态交替出现着：一会儿是绝望地等待着神秘而恐怖的死亡，一会儿是充满希望和紧张地观察自己身上的器官。一会儿眼前出现了功能暂时停止的肾脏或者盲肠，一会儿又出现了无可避免的神秘而恐怖的死亡。

这两种心情从一开始生病就交替出现；但随着病情的发展，他就觉得肾脏的功能越来越可疑，越来越虚幻，而日益逼近的死亡却越来越现实。

他只要想想三个月前的身体，再看看现在的情况，看看他怎样一步步不停地走着下坡路，任何侥幸的心情就自然而然土崩瓦解了。

近来，他面向沙发背躺着，感到异常孤寂，那是一种身处在闹市和许多亲友中间却没有人理睬他而感到的孤寂，即使跑遍天涯海角都找不到的孤寂。身处在这种可怕的孤寂中，他只能靠回忆往事度日。一幕幕往事像图画般浮现在他眼前。他总是从近期的事开始，一直回忆到遥远的过去，回忆到童年时代，然后停留在那些往事上。譬如他从今天给他端来的李子酱，就会想到童年吃过的干瘪法国李子，觉得别有风味，吃到果核，满口生津。同时他又会想到当年的种种情景：保姆、兄弟、玩具。“那些事别去想了……太痛苦了。”伊凡·伊里奇对自己说，思想又回到现实上来。他瞧着羊皮沙发上的皱纹和沙发背上的纽扣。“山羊皮很贵，又不牢；有一次就为这事争吵过。还记得当年我们撕坏父亲的皮包，因此受罚，但那是另一种山羊皮，是另一次争吵……妈妈还送包子来给我们吃。”他的思想又停留在童年时代，他又感到很难过。他竭力驱散这种回忆，想些别的事。

在对一系列往事的回忆中，他又想到了那件事：他怎样生病和病情怎样恶化。他想到年纪越小，越是充满生气。生命里善的因素越多，生命力也就越充沛。两者互为因果。“病痛越来越厉害，整个生命也就越来越糟，”他想，“生命开始还有一点光明，后来却越来越暗淡，消逝得越来越快，离死越来越近。”他忽然想到，一块石子落下总是不断增加速度，生命也是这样，带着不断增加的痛苦，越来越快地掉落下去，掉进痛苦的深渊。“我在飞逝……”他浑身打了个哆嗦，试图抗拒，但知道这是无法抗拒的。他的眼睛虽已疲劳，却依旧瞪着前面，瞪着沙发背。他等待着，等待着那可怕的坠落、震动和灭亡。“无法抗拒。”他自言自语，“真想知道，为什么会这样？可是无法知道。要是说我生活得不对头，那还有理由解释，可是不能这么说。”他对自己说，想到自己一辈子奉公守法，过着正派而体面的生活。“不能这么说，”他露出冷笑，仿佛人家会看到他这个样子，并且会因此受骗似的，“可是找不到解释！折磨，死亡……为了什么呀？”

十一

这样过了两个礼拜。在这期间发生了伊凡·伊里奇夫妇所希望的那件事：彼特里歇夫正式来求婚。这事发生在一天晚上。第二天，普拉斯柯菲雅·费多罗夫娜走进丈夫房间，考虑着怎样向他宣布彼特里歇夫求婚的事，但就在那天夜里，伊凡·伊里奇的病情又有新的发展。普拉斯柯菲雅·费多罗夫娜发现他又躺在长沙发上，但姿势跟以前不同。他仰天躺着，呻吟着，眼睛呆滞地瞪着前方。

她谈起吃药的事。他把目光转到她身上。她没有把话说完，因为她发现他的目光里充满对她的愤恨。

“看在基督的分儿上，让我安安静静地死吧！”他说。

她正想出去，但这当儿女儿进来向他请安。他也像对妻子那样对女儿望望，而对女儿问候病情的话只冷冷地说，他不久就会让她们解脱的。母女俩默不作声，坐了一会儿走了。

“我们究竟有什么过错呀？”丽莎对母亲说，“仿佛都是我们弄得他这样似的！我可怜爸爸，可他为什么要折磨我们？”

医生按时来给他看病。伊凡·伊里奇对他的问题只回答“是”或者“不是”，并愤怒地盯住医生，最后说：

“您明明知道毫无办法，那就让我去吧！”

“我们可以减轻您的痛苦。”医生说。

“这点您也办不到，让我去吧！”

医生走到客厅，告诉普拉斯柯菲雅·费多罗夫娜情况很严重，只有一样东西可以减轻他的痛苦，就是鸦片。

医生说，他肉体上的痛苦很厉害，这是事实，但精神上的痛苦比肉体上的痛苦更厉害，而这也是让他最难受的事。

他精神上的痛苦就是，那天夜里他瞧着盖拉西姆睡眼惺忪、颧骨突出的善良的脸，忽然想：我这辈子说不定真的过得不对头。

他忽然想，以前说他这辈子生活过得不对头，他是绝对不同意的，但现在看来可能是真的。他忽然想，以前他有过轻微的冲动，反对豪门权贵肯定的好事，这种冲动虽然很快就被他自己克制住，但说不定倒是正确的，而其他一切可能都不对头。他的职务，他所安排的生活，他的家庭，他所献身的公益事业和本职工作，这一切可能都不对头。他试图为这一切辩护，但忽然发现一切都有问题，没有什么可辩护的。

“既然如此，那么现在在我将离开世界的时候，发觉我把天赋予我的一切都糟蹋了，但又无法挽救，那可怎么办？”他自言自语。他仰天躺着，重新回顾自己的一生。早晨他看到仆人，后来看到妻子，后来看到女儿，后来看到医生，他们的一举一动、一言一语，都证实他夜间所发现的可怕真理。他从他们身上看到了自己，看到了他赖以生活的一切，并且明白这一切都不对头，这一切都是掩盖着生死问题的可怕的大骗局。这种思想增加了他肉体上的痛苦，比以前增加了十倍。他不断呻吟，辗转反侧，扯着身上的衣服。他觉得衣服束缚他，使他喘不过气来。他为此憎恨它们。

医生给了他大剂量鸦片，他昏睡过去，但到吃晚饭时又开始折腾。他把所有的人都赶走，不断地翻来覆去。

妻子走过来对他说："约翰，心肝，你就为了我（为了我？）这么办吧。这没有什么害处，常常还有点用。真的，这没什么。健康的人也常常……"

他睁大眼睛，问："什么事？进圣餐吗？干什么呀？不用了！不过……"

她哭了。

"好吗，我的亲人？我去叫我们的神父来，他这人挺好。"

"好，太好了。"他说。

神父来了，听了他的忏悔，他觉得好过些，疑虑似乎减少些，痛苦也减轻了，刹那间心里看到了希望。他又想到了盲肠，觉得还可以治愈。他含着眼泪进了圣餐。

他进了圣餐，又被放到床上，刹那间觉得好过些，并且又出现了生的希望。他想到他们曾建议他动手术。

“活下去，我要活下去！”他自言自语。妻子走来祝贺；她敷衍了几句，又问：“你是不是感到好些？”他眼睛不看她，嘴里说：“是。”她的服装，她的体态，她的神情，她的腔调，全都向他说明一个意思：“不对头。你过去和现在赖以生活的一切都是谎言，都是对你掩盖生死大事的骗局。”他一想到这点，心头就冒起一阵愤恨，随着愤恨又感觉到肉体上的痛苦，同时意识到不可避免的临近的死亡。接着又增加了一种新的感觉：拧痛、刺痛和窒息。

当他说“是”的时候，他的脸色是可怕的。他说了一声“是”，眼睛直盯住她的脸，接着使出全身的力气迅速地把脸转过去，伏在床上嚷道：“都给我走，都给我走，让我一个人待着！”

十二

自从那时起，他连续三天一刻不停地惨叫，叫得那么可怕，就是隔着两道门听了也觉得毛骨悚然。当他回答妻子的时候，他明白他完了，无法挽救了，末日到了，生命的末日到了，可是生死之谜始终没有解决，永远是个谜。

“哎哟！哎哟！哎哟！”他用不同的音调惨叫着。他开始嚷道：“我不要！”接下去又是哎哟哎哟地惨叫。

整整三天，他一刻不停地在那个黑口袋里拼命挣扎，而一个肉眼看不见的力量却无可抗拒地把他往口袋里塞。他好像一个死刑犯，落到刽子手手里，知道没有生路了。他每分钟都感觉到，不管他怎样挣扎，他是越来越接近那恐怖的末日了。他觉得他的痛苦在于他正被人塞到那个黑窟窿里去，而更痛苦的是他不能爽爽快快落进去。他之所以不能爽爽快快落进去，是因为他认为他的生命是有价值的。这种对自己生命的肯定，阻碍了他，不让他走，使他特别痛苦。

突然，他的胸部和腰部受到猛烈的打击，呼吸更加困难，他掉到窟窿里。在窟窿底里有一道亮光。他觉得自己仿佛身处在火车车厢里，你以为火车在前进，其实却在后退。这时他突然辨出了方向。“是的，一切都不对头，”他自言自语，“但没有关系，可以纠正的。可怎样才算‘对头’呢？”他问自己，接着突然沉默了。

第三天傍晚，他临终前两小时，念中学的儿子悄悄地进来，走到父亲床跟前。垂死的人一直在惨叫，挥动双臂。他的一只手落在儿子头上。儿子捉住他的手，把它贴在嘴唇上，哭了起来。

就在这时候，伊凡·伊里奇掉了下去，看见了光。他领悟到他的生活过得不对头，但还可以纠正。他问自己：怎样才“对头”，接着一动不动地留神听着。他感到有人在吻他的手。他睁开眼睛，对儿子瞧了一眼。他可怜起儿子来。妻子走到他跟前。他对她瞧了一眼。她张开嘴，鼻子上和面颊上挂着眼泪，露出绝望的神情瞧着他。他为她难过。“是的，我把他们害苦了，”他想，“他们真可怜，但等我一死，他们就会好过些。”他想把这话说出来，可是没有力气说。“不过，何必说呢，应该行动。”他想。他对着妻子用目光示意说：“带他走……可怜……你也……”他还想说“原谅我”，但却说了“原来我”。他已经没有力气纠正，只摆了摆手，知道谁需要听懂自然会懂的。

他恍然大悟，原来折磨他的东西消失了，从四面八方消失了，从一切方面消失了。他可怜他们，应该使他们不再受罪。应该使他们，也使自己摆脱种种痛苦。“多么简单，多么快乐。”他想。“疼痛呢？”他问自己，“它哪儿去了？嗳，疼痛，你在哪儿啊？”

他留神倾听。“噢，它在这里。好吧，疼就疼吧。”

“那么死呢？它在哪里？”

他寻找着往常折磨他的死的恐惧，可是没有找到。它在哪里？是什么样的死啊？他一点也不觉得恐惧，因为根本没有死。

没有死，只有光。

“原来如此！”他突然说出声来。“多么快乐呀！”

对于他，这一切都只是一刹那的事。

这一刹那的含义没有再变。但旁人看到，临死前他又折腾了两小时。他的胸膛里咯咯发响，皮包骨头的身体不断抽搐。接着咯咯声越来越少，喘息也越来越微弱。

“过去了！”有人在他旁边说。

他听见这话，心里重复了一遍。“死过去了，”他对自己说，“再也不会有死了。”

他吸了一口气，吸到一半停住，两腿一伸就死了。

三死

一

秋天，两辆马车在大道上疾驰。前面的轿车上坐着两个女人。一个是贵夫人，身体消瘦，脸色苍白。另一个是使女，脸色红润，体态丰满。使女干枯的短发老从褪色的帽子里掉下来，她只好用戴破手套的冻红的手不时把头发塞进去。她那高高的胸脯裹着粗披巾，散发出健康的气息。她那双乌溜溜的眼睛时而望望窗外掠过的田野，时而怯生生地瞧瞧太太，时而不安地打量马车的角落。她的鼻子前面晃动着太太那顶挂在网架上的帽子，她的膝盖上躺着一条小狗，她的腿因地上放着一堆匣子而高高地翘着，在车座弹簧的抖动声和车窗玻璃的叮叮声中，可以隐隐听见她的鞋底碰到匣子的声音。

贵夫人双手叠放在膝盖上，闭着眼睛，稍稍皱起眉头，从胸膛里咳嗽着，身子靠在背后的靠垫上微微摇晃。她头上戴着一顶白色睡帽，娇嫩白净的脖子上系着一条浅蓝色头巾。睡帽底下露出笔直的头皮，把她那搽过油的平整的淡褐色头发分开，苍白的头皮显得没有生气，像死人的皮肤一样。她的脸清秀美丽，但皮肤松弛枯黄，两颊和颧骨泛出红潮。她的嘴唇干燥，不断翕动；稀疏的睫毛没有卷起；凹陷的胸脯使她的旅行呢外套现出一条条直褶。她双目紧闭，脸上现出疲倦、烦躁和常有的痛苦神色。

听差双肘支着软椅，在驭座上打瞌睡。驿车夫神气活现地吆喝着，赶着四匹热汗淋漓的高头大马，偶尔回头望望后面篷车上吆喝着的另一名马车夫。宽阔的平行车辙在泥泞的石灰路上均匀而迅速地向前伸展。天空阴沉寒冷，黑雾不断降落到田野和大路上。马车里很闷，散发出花露水和尘土的气味。病人把头往后一靠，慢慢睁开眼睛，她那双眼睛又大又亮，黑得很美。

当使女外套的下摆稍稍触到太太的腿时，她就用消瘦的纤手神经质地把它推开，并且说：“又来了！”她的嘴痛苦地瘪了一下。玛特廖莎双手提起外套，用强壮的腿支起身子，坐得远一点。她那娇嫩的脸上泛起鲜艳的红晕。病人那双美丽的乌黑眼睛紧紧盯着使女的一举一动。太太两手按住座位，也想支起身子坐得高些，但她力不从心。她的嘴瘪了一下，整个脸由于无可奈何的自嘲而变得难看。“你哪怕帮我一把也好啊！唉！不必了！我自己也能，只是对不起，别把你这些麻袋之类的东西都放在我背后！别这么弄，别碰我！”太太闭上眼睛，接着又迅速地抬起眼皮，瞧了使女一眼。玛特廖莎望着她，咬着红红的下唇。病人从胸膛里吐出深沉的叹息，但叹息到一半又变成了咳嗽。她转过脸去，皱起眉头，双手按住胸口。咳嗽完了，她又闭上眼睛，仍旧一动不动地坐着。轿车和篷车驶进了村庄。玛特廖莎从披巾下伸出一只胖鼓鼓的手，画了个十字。

“什么事？”太太问。

“到站了，太太。”

“我问你为什么画十字？”

“有座教堂，太太。”

病人转身对着窗外，睁大眼睛望着马车经过的那座乡村教堂，动手慢慢地画十字。

轿车和篷车同时在驿站前停下。病人的丈夫和医生下车来到轿车跟前。

“您觉得怎么样？”医生把着她的脉问。

“哦，怎么样，亲爱的，不太累吧？”丈夫用法语问，“你不想下车吗？”

玛特廖莎抱起包裹缩在角落里，免得妨碍他们谈话。

“没什么，还是那样，”病人回答，“我不下车。”

丈夫站了一会儿，走进驿站。

玛特廖莎霍地跳下马车，踮着脚跑过泥泞地，也走进驿站大门。

“就算我身体不好，也不能成为您不吃早饭的理由。”

病人含笑对站在车窗旁的医生说。

“他们谁也不来管我。”医生刚轻手轻脚地离开她，跑上驿站台阶，她就这样自言自语，“他们身体好，什么都不在乎。哦！天哪！”

“怎么样，爱德华·伊凡诺维奇？”丈夫遇到医生，快乐地笑着搓搓手说，“我吩咐他们把食盒拿进来，您觉得怎么样？”

“行。”医生回答。

“那么，她怎么样？”丈夫压低声音，扬起眉毛，叹了口气说。

“我说过，她不仅到不了意大利，能到莫斯科就算不错了。特别是碰到这种天气。”

“那怎么办呢？哦，天哪！天哪！”丈夫用手掩住眼睛说。“拿到这儿来！”他对端食盒进来的仆人说。

“本来就该待在家里。”医生耸耸肩膀回答。

“您说，我有什么办法呢？”丈夫反问道，“不瞒您说，我曾想尽办法留住她，我提到费用，提到不得不撇在家里的孩子，提到我的工作，可她什么都不听。她定了在国外生活的计划，仿佛她是个健康人。但如果把她的病情如实告诉她，那就等于要她的命。”

“其实她已经没命了，华西里·德米特里奇，这一点您心里要有数。人没有肺不能活，而肺又不能重新生出来。这确实很让人伤心，难受，但是有什么办法呢？你我所能做到的，只是让她死得尽可能平静些。现在得请神父了。”

“哦，天哪！您要明白我的处境，要问问她有什么遗愿。听天由命吧，我可不能对她说这事。您知道，她这人多么善良……”

“不论怎么说，您还得劝她等路冻硬了再走，”医生意味深长地摇摇头说，“要不路上会出事……”

“阿克秀莎，喂，阿克秀莎！”驿站长的女儿从头上套上一件短袄，在泥泞的后门台阶上跺着脚，尖声喊道，“我们去瞧瞧希尔金家的太太，据说她得了肺病，要到外国去，我还从没见过害痨病的人是什么样子。”

阿克秀莎从门里跳出来，两人手拉着手跑到大门外。她们放慢脚步走过马车，向开着的车窗张望了一下。病人向她们转过头来，发现她们好奇的神色，就皱起眉头转过脸去。

“我的妈呀！”驿站长的女儿连忙转过头来说，“她原来是个多么漂亮的美人，可现在变成什么样了？简直可怕。阿克秀莎，你看见了吗？看见了吗？”

“是啊，真瘦呀！”阿克秀莎附和说，“我们假装到井边去，再去看看。瞧，她转过头去，可我还是看见了。真可怜，玛莎。”

“路上真泥泞啊！”玛莎回答。接着两人都跑回大门里去。

“我的样子一定很可怕，”病人想，“但愿快一点到国外，快一点到国外，到了那边很快就会康复了。”

“你觉得怎么样，我亲爱的？”丈夫走到马车跟前，嘴里还嚼着东西说道。

“问来问去就是这句话，”病人想，“自己还在吃东西！”

“没什么。”她透过牙缝说。

“要知道，亲爱的，我担心这种天气赶路对你更不好。爱德华大夫也这么说。我们还不如回去吧？”

她气呼呼地不吭声。

“天气说不定会好起来，到那时路也就好走了，你的身体也会好些，那时我们再一起去。”

“对不起。要是我早先不听你的话，我现在已到了柏林，身体也完全康复了。”

“有什么办法呢，我的天使，你知道那是办不到的。可现在，你要是肯再等一个月，你的身体就会大大康复，我也可以把事情办完，我们还可以把孩子带去……”

“孩子们身体健康，可是我有病。”

“不过你要明白，亲爱的，在这样的天气里，万一你的病在路上加重……不然至少还在家里。”

“家里，家里怎么样？……叫我死在家里吗？”病人暴躁地说。但死这个字显然使她害怕，她恳求而又询问似的对丈夫瞧瞧。丈夫垂下眼睛没作声。病人的嘴突然像孩子似的瘪了一下，接着眼泪夺眶而出。丈夫用手帕捂住脸，默默地从马车旁走开去。

“不，我要去。”病人抬起眼睛望着天空，抱着双臂，嘴里断断续续地低声说着话。“天哪！这是为什么呀？”她说。泪水流得更多了。她热烈地祈祷了很久，但胸口还是感到疼痛，喘不过气来；天空、田野和道路还是那么阴沉灰暗，秋天的黑雾还是那样不密不稀地落在泥泞的道路上、屋顶上、马车上和车夫们的皮袄上。车夫们热烈而快乐地交谈着，给车轮抹油，套车。

二

轿车套好了，但车夫还在磨蹭。他走进车夫休息的小屋。小屋里又热又闷又暗，充满人气和烤面包、白菜、羊皮袄的气味。正房里有几个车夫，厨娘在炉灶旁忙碌着，炕上躺着一个穿羊皮袄的病人。

“费多尔叔叔！费多尔叔叔！”一个身穿羊皮袄、腰里插着鞭子的年轻车夫走进屋来招呼病人。

“懒鬼，你找费多尔干什么！”一个车夫答应说，“瞧，人家在马车里等你哪。”

“我想问他借双靴子，我这双破了。”小伙子把头发往后一甩，又把手套塞在腰里，回答。“他睡着了？喂，费多尔叔叔！”他走到炕边，又喊道。

“什么事？”一个微弱的声音答应道，接着一张红褐色的瘦脸从炕上探下来。接着，一只毛茸茸的苍白瘦弱的大手拉上一件粗呢大衣，盖住穿着肮脏衬衫的瘦肩膀。“给我点水喝，老弟，你有什么事？”

小伙子递给他一勺水。

“是这么回事，费多尔，”他迟疑不决地说，“你现在大概用不着新靴子了，给我吧，你大概不会到处跑了。”

病人把疲软无力的头俯在光滑的勺子上，稀疏的下垂胡子浸在浑浊的水里，他吃力而贪婪地喝着水。他那蓬乱的胡子很脏，凹陷无神的眼睛勉强抬起来望着小伙子的脸。喝完水，他想举起手来擦擦湿嘴唇，可是没有力气，只能在大衣袖子上蹭一蹭。他没吭声，困难地用鼻子呼吸着，勉强打起精神直盯着小伙子的脸。

“也许你已经答应别人了，”小伙子说，“那就算了。主要是外面地上泥泞，我得出去干活，因此我就想：把费多尔那双靴子借来吧，他大概用不着了。也许你自己要用，那就直说吧……”

病人胸口有什么东西涌上来，咕噜咕噜直响。他佝偻着身子，拼命咳嗽起来。

“他要靴子做什么？”厨娘突然怒气冲冲地嚷起来，嚷得整个屋子都能听见，“他有一个多月没下炕了。嘿，听见他那个咳嗽呀，我连心口都疼了。他要靴子做什么？总不会让他穿着新靴子入土吧。上帝恕我直说，他早该上路了。瞧他那个咳嗽。得把他搬到别的屋子或者什么地方去！听说城里有这种医院，要不他占着整个角落，怎么行。弄得你没有一点儿空地方，还讲究什么干净。”

“喂，谢廖加！快上车，老爷们等着哪！”驿站长向屋里喊道。

谢廖加没等到回答想走，但病人一面咳嗽，一面用目光表示他有话要说。

“谢廖加，你把靴子拿去吧。”他忍住咳嗽，歇了一会儿，“但你听我说，我死后你得给我买块墓碑。”他哑着嗓子加了一句。

“谢谢叔叔，那我拿去了，墓碑我会给你买的。”

“喂，伙计们，听见了没有？”病人还有话要说，但他又佝偻着身子喘不过气来。

“好，听见了，”一个车夫说，“去吧，谢廖加，上车吧，要不站长又要跑来了。你知道，希尔金家的太太正病着呢。”

谢廖加连忙脱下他那双大得出奇的破靴子，把它扔到长凳底下。费多尔叔叔那双新靴子正好合脚，谢廖加端详着那双靴子，向马车走去。

“瞧，多漂亮的靴子！我来给你上点油。”当谢廖加爬上驭座、拿起缰绳时，一个手拿刷子的车夫说，“白白送给你了？”

“你眼红是不是？”谢廖加回答，拉拉粗呢大衣的下摆把腿盖好。“走吧！我的宝贝！”他挥挥鞭子向马吆喝道。于是载着乘客、各种箱子的轿车和篷车就在泥泞的大路上飞驰，渐渐隐没在灰蒙蒙的秋雾里。

生病的车夫留在闷热小屋的炕上，他咳不出痰，好不容易翻了个身，才安静下来。

小屋里，到傍晚一直有人进进出出，来这里吃饭，但谁也不理会病人。晚上，厨娘爬到炕上，伸手从他的腿边拿走羊皮袄。

“你别生我的气，娜斯塔西雅，”病人说，“我很快就会把这地方给你腾出来的。”

“好，好，那有什么，没关系，”娜斯塔西雅含糊地说，“叔叔，你哪儿疼呀？你说吧。”

“五脏六腑都难受。天知道是怎么回事。”

“咳嗽的时候嗓子大概疼吧？”

“哪儿都疼。我快死了，就是那么回事。喔唷，喔唷，喔唷！”病人呻吟道。

“你把腿盖盖好，就这样。”娜斯塔西雅说，顺手替他拉好粗呢大衣，从炕上爬下来。

夜里，小屋里灯光暗淡。娜斯塔西雅和十来个车夫睡在地板上和长凳上，大声打着呼噜。只有病人一人在炕上翻来覆去，微弱地呻吟着，咳嗽着。到早上，他一点声音也没有了。

“昨天晚上我做了一个怪梦，”第二天，厨娘在晨光熹微中伸着懒腰说，“我梦见费多尔叔叔从炕上爬下来，出去劈柴。他说：‘娜斯塔西雅，我来帮你忙。’我就对他说：‘你怎么能劈柴呢？’他却抓起斧头就劈，劈得很有劲，只见木屑飞溅开来。我说：‘你不是有病吗？’他说：‘不，我好了。’他说着抡起斧头猛劈，可把我吓了一跳。我大叫一声就醒了。莫非他死了？喂，费多尔叔叔！叔叔！”

费多尔没有回答。

“可不是，他也许是死了？让我去瞧瞧。”一个刚醒来的车夫说。

一条长满黄褐色茸毛的手臂从炕上垂下来，又白又凉。

“他大概死了，得去告诉驿站长。”车夫说。

费多尔没有亲人，他是个外乡人。第二天，他被埋在小树林后面的新墓地里。娜斯塔西雅一连好几天逢人就说她的梦，并且说是她第一个发现费多尔死了。

三

春天来了。在城里潮湿的街上，湍急的流水潺潺地流过上冻的畜粪；熙来攘往的人群穿着鲜艳的衣衫，热闹地交谈着。在围着篱笆的花园里，树木已经发芽，树枝飒飒地在微风中摇摆。到处都有清澈的水流动着，滴下来……麻雀叽叽喳喳地欢叫，鼓动小翅膀飞来飞去。在向阳的一边，篱笆上、房屋上、树木上，一切都在晃动，一切都闪闪发亮。空中、地上和人们心里都洋溢着青春的欢乐。

大街上一座大公馆门前刚铺上干草；那位急于出国的垂死的女病人就在这个公馆里。

在一间关着的房门口站着病人的丈夫和一个上了

年纪的女人。一位神父坐在沙发上，垂下眼睛，手里拿着一包用长巾包着的东西。一位老太太——病人的母亲——躺在屋角那张高背安乐椅里，伤心地哭着。一个使女拿着一块干净手帕伺候老太太；另一个使女用什么东西揉着老太太的太阳穴，并且吹着她睡帽底下的白发。

“嗯，基督保佑您，我亲爱的。”病人丈夫对站在门口上了年纪的女人说，“她那么信任您。您又那么会同她说话，去吧，您去好好劝劝她。”

他刚要给她开门，但表姐拦住他，几次拿手帕按在自己眼睛上，猛地摇摇头。

“好了，这下子我不像哭过了。”她说，接着自己打开门走进去。

丈夫心里十分焦急，似乎完全手足无措。他向老太太走去，但没走几步又转过身，穿过房间，走到神父跟前。神父对他瞧瞧，扬起眉毛，叹了一口气。他那浓密的花白大胡子也扬起来，接着又垂下。

“天哪！天哪！”丈夫说。

“有什么办法？”神父叹息着说，眉毛和胡子又向上扬起，然后又垂下来。

“她妈妈也在这儿！”丈夫几乎绝望地说，“她可受不了这样的打击。要知道她是多么爱她呀，我没见过谁像她这样爱女儿……神父，您最好想法子安慰安慰她，劝她离开这儿。”

神父站起来，走到老太太跟前。

“是的，做母亲的心是谁也无法估量的，”他说，“不过上帝是仁慈的。”

老太太的整个脸突然抽搐起来，她神经质地打着嗝。

“上帝是仁慈的，”等她稍微平静下来，神父继续说，“我可以告诉您，在我的教区里有一个病人，比玛丽雅·德米特里耶夫娜的病重得多，但有个普通市民用草药很快就把他治好了。而且那个市民现在就在莫斯科。我对华西里·德米特里奇说过，不妨请他来试试。至少对病人是个安慰。上帝是万能的。”

“不，她已经没救了，”老太太说，“上帝不召我去，却要把她带走。”接着，她更厉害地打着神经质的嗝，一会儿就昏过去了。

病人的丈夫双手捂住脸，从屋子里跑出来。

他在走廊里首先遇见他那个六岁的男孩，男孩正一个劲儿地追着妹妹。

“请问，要不要把孩子们带到妈妈那儿去？”保姆问。

“不，她不愿看见他们，这会使她伤心的。”

男孩站了一会儿，凝神瞧瞧父亲的脸，突然撒腿向前跑去，嘴里快乐地嚷嚷着。“爸爸，她好像一匹黑马！”男孩指指妹妹叫道。

这时候在另一个房间里，表姐坐在病人旁边，巧妙地和她谈着话，使她对死有个思想准备。医生在另一扇窗前调药水。

病人穿着宽大的白色睡袍坐在床上，四周围着枕头，默默地望着表姐。

“唉，表姐，”病人突然打断她的话说，“你不用来给我做思想准备。不要把我当孩子。我是个基督徒。我什么都知道。我知道我活不长了。我也知道我的丈夫要是早点听我的话，现在我已经到了意大利，说不定——简直可以肯定——身体已经好了。大家都这么对他说。可是有什么办法呢，看来这是上帝的意思。我们大家都有许多罪孽，这一点我知道，但我相信上帝是仁慈的，人人都会得到宽恕，人人准会得到宽恕。我竭力了解自己。我知道我也有许多罪孽，表姐。因此我受了那么多苦。我一直在努力忍受痛苦……”

“那么，我去叫神父来好吗，表妹？你领了圣餐，一定会好过些。”表姐说。

病人点点头表示同意。

“上帝啊！饶恕我这个罪人吧。”她喃喃地说。

表姐走出去，对神父使了个眼色。

“她是个天使！”她含泪对病人丈夫说。

丈夫哭了，神父走进门去，老太太还是不省人事，第一间屋里鸦雀无声。五分钟后，神父从屋里出来，取下长巾，理理头发。

“感谢上帝，她现在比较安静了，”他说，“她想看看你们。”表姐和丈夫走了进去。病人正望着圣像低声哭泣。

“恭喜你，我亲爱的。”丈夫说。

“谢谢！我现在觉得好多了，我感到说不出的快乐，”病人说，薄薄的嘴唇上露出一丝微笑，“上帝真是仁慈！他是仁慈和万能的，是不是？”她又双眼饱含泪水，目光虔诚地望着圣像。

然后她仿佛突然想起什么事，示意丈夫到她跟前去。“我求你的事，你总是不肯做。”她用微弱的声音不满地说。

丈夫伸长脖子，恭顺地听着。“什么事，我亲爱的？”

“我跟你说过多少次，这些医生什么也不懂，倒是有些郎中能治病……神父说……有一个市民……去把他找来。”

“把谁找来呀，我亲爱的？”

“天哪！你什么也不愿懂！……”病人皱起眉头，闭上眼睛。

医生走到她跟前，拿起她的手。她的脉搏显然越来越弱。他对丈夫使了个眼色。病人发现这眼色，害怕地环顾了一下。表姐转过脸去，哭起来。

“不要哭，不要折磨自己，也不要折磨我，”病人说，“这样你会使我失去最后的安宁。”

“你是个天使！”表姐吻着她的手说。

“不，吻这儿，只有对死人才吻手。天哪！天哪！”

当天晚上，病人已成了一具尸体，尸体入殓后，灵柩停在公馆大厅里。大厅门户紧闭，里面坐着一名诵经士，用鼻音有节奏地念着大卫的诗篇。明亮的烛光从高高的银烛台上投射到死者苍白的额上，投射到那双僵硬的白蜡似的手上，投射到膝盖和脚趾处可怕地凸出的衾衣的挺直皱褶上。诵经士并不懂得所念的诗句，只是有节奏地念着；在肃静的屋子里，诗句古怪地交替响起和静止。从遥远的房间里时而传来孩子们的说话声和脚步声。

“你掩面，他们便惊惶，”诗篇说，“你收回他们的气，他们就死亡，归于尘土。你发出你的灵，他们便受造，你使地面更换为新。愿耶和华的荣耀存到永远。”

死者的脸严峻、平静而庄严。她那冰凉的洁白前额、她那紧闭的嘴都一动不动。她看上去全神贯注。但现在她是否理解这些庄严的诗句呢？

四

一个月后，贵夫人的墓上盖起了一座石头小教堂。车夫的坟上却还没有石碑，坟上长出嫩绿的青草，成为这里埋葬着一个人的仅有标志。

“谢廖加，你真造孽，不给费多尔买块石碑，”驿站的厨娘有一次说，“你说过，冬天买，冬天买，可是到现在还不守信用。你这是当着我的面说的。他来找过你一次了，你再不买，他还会来，会把你掐死的。”

“什么，难道我说话不算数吗？”谢廖加回答，“石碑我会买的，我答应过，我会买的，我会花一个半卢布去买。我没有忘记，但得去把它运回来。哪天进城，我一定去买。”

“你哪怕先去竖个十字架也好，”一个年老的车夫插嘴说，“要不太不像话。靴子倒穿在脚上了。”

“叫我到哪儿去弄十字架呀？总不能用木柴削一个吧？”

“你这算什么话？木柴是削不出来的，你带把斧头一早到小树林去，在那儿做一个不就得了吗？砍一棵白蜡树什么的，不就可以做个十字架吗？要不你还得请护林员喝酒。为这么一根废料请他喝酒可划不来。瞧，前天我弄断一根撬棒，我就去砍了一根新的，挺结实，谁也没说过一句话。”

第二天清早，天色刚亮，谢廖加就拿着斧头到小树林里去。

大地万物盖着一层灰白的寒露，没有照到阳光的露水一滴一滴地滴下来。东方破晓，微弱的曙光映在薄云片片的苍穹上。地上的小草，枝头的树叶，都纹丝不动。只有树丛中鸟雀的扑翼声和地上沙沙的响声偶尔打破树林的寂静。在树林边缘，突然响起一阵与大自然格格不入的响声，然后又沉寂了。接着响声又起，并且在一棵一动不动的树干周围有节奏地重复着。一棵树的树梢异乎寻常地颤动起来，苍翠欲滴的叶子飒飒发响，一只红胸鸲栖在树枝上，叽叽地叫着鼓动翅膀，摇摇尾巴，落到另一棵树上。

斧头低低地发出越来越重浊的响声，湿润的白木片飞落到露珠滚滚的草地上，在砍击声中传出一声轻微的折裂声。整棵树颤动了一下，向一边倾斜，又迅速地挺直，根部恐惧地摇摆着。一瞬间又万籁俱寂，接着那棵树向一边倾斜的树干上又发出折裂声，于是枯枝折断，树枝下垂，一棵树树梢朝下轰隆一声倒在潮湿的地上。斧头声和脚步声都静止了。那只红胸鸲叫了一声，拍拍翅膀往高处飞去。被它的翅膀触动的树枝摇晃了一会儿，又像其他树枝一样一动不动了。树林披着纹丝不动的枝叶，在开阔的新的空地上更加快乐地展示出它们的美丽。

最初的几道阳光穿过透明的云片在空中闪了一下，然后照遍大地和天空。朝雾在谷地里像波浪似的翻腾，草木上露珠滚滚，闪闪发亮，透明的云片在蓝幽幽的空中迅速地飞散开来。鸟儿在树丛中扑腾，兴高采烈地啁啾；苍翠欲滴的叶子在树梢上快乐而宁静地飒飒作响，而那些活着的树木的枝叶也在倒下的死树上面庄严地微微晃动。

图书在版编目（CIP）数据

企鹅经典：小黑书．第三辑：汉、英 /（英）简·奥斯汀等著；夏星等译．-- 北京：中信出版社，2019.6

书名原文：Penguin Little Black Classics

ISBN 978-7-5217-0407-5

Ⅰ．①企… Ⅱ．①简… ②夏… Ⅲ．①世界文学－作品综合集－汉、英 Ⅳ．① I11

中国版本图书馆 CIP 数据核字 (2019) 第 072172 号

企鹅经典：小黑书　第三辑

伊凡·伊里奇之死

著　　者：[俄] 列夫·托尔斯泰

译　　者：草婴

出版发行：中信出版集团股份有限公司

（北京市朝阳区惠新东街甲 4 号富盛大厦 2 座 邮编 100029）

承 印 者：北京楠萍印刷有限公司

开　　本：787mm × 1092mm　1/32　　印　　张：45.75　　字　　数：756 千字

版　　次：2019 年 6 月第 1 版　　印　　次：2019 年 6 月第 1 次印刷

京权图字：01-2018-6477　　广告经营许可证：京朝工商广字第 8087 号

书　　号：ISBN 978-7-5217-0407-5

定　　价：149.00 元（全 10 册）

服务热线：400-600-8099

投稿邮箱：author@citicpub.com

伊凡·伊里奇之死

The Death of Ivan Ilyich

[俄] 列夫·托尔斯泰　著
草婴　译

中信出版集团 | 北京

PENGUIN

LITTLE BLACK

CLASSICS

* 此中文译本译自俄语原文

“只是有点青肿。”

‘No one characteristic clasps us purely and universally in its embrace.’

MICHEL DE MONTAIGNE

How We Weep and Laugh at the Same Thing

Contents

How We Weep and Laugh at the Same Thing

[An understanding of the complexity of conflicting emotions helps us to avoid trivial interpretations of great men and their grief.]

When we read in our history books that Antigonus was severely displeased with his son for having brought him the head of his enemy King Pyrrhus who had just been killed fighting against him and that he burst into copious tears when he saw it; and that Duke René of Lorraine also lamented the death of Duke Charles of Burgundy whom he had just defeated, and wore mourning at his funeral; and that at the battle of Auroy which the Count de Montfort won against Charles de Blois, his rival for the Duchy of Brittany, the victor showed great grief when he happened upon his enemy's corpse: we should not at once exclaim,

> *Et cosi aven che l'animo ciascuna*
> *Sua passion sotto et contrario manto*
> *Ricopre, con la vista hor' chiara hor bruna.*

[Thus does the mind cloak every passion with its opposite, our faces showing now joy, now sadness.]

When they presented Caesar with the head of Pompey our histories say that he turned his gaze away as from a spectacle both ugly and displeasing. There had been such a long understanding and fellowship between them in the management of affairs of State, they had shared the same fortunes and rendered each other so many mutual services as allies, that we should not believe that his behaviour was quite false and counterfeit – as this other poet thinks it was:

tutumque putavit
Jam bonus esse socer; lachrimas non sponte cadentes
Effudit, gemitusque expressit pectore lœto.

[And now he thought it was safe to play the good father-in-law; he poured out tears, but not spontaneous ones, and he forced out groans from his happy breast.]

For while it is true that most of our actions are but mask and cosmetic, and that it is sometimes true that

Hœredis fletus sub persona risus est;

[Behind the mask, the tears of an heir are laughter;]

nevertheless we ought to consider when judging such events how our souls are often shaken by conflicting emotions. Even as there is said to be a variety of humours assembled in our bodies, the dominant one being that which normally prevails according to our complexion, so too in our souls: although diverse emotions may shake them, there is one which must remain in possession of the field; nevertheless its victory is not so complete but that the weaker ones do not sometimes regain lost ground because of the pliancy and mutability of our soul and make a brief sally in their turn. That is why we can see that not only children, who artlessly follow Nature, often weep and laugh at the same thing, but that not one of us either can boast that, no matter how much he may want to set out on a journey, he still does not feel his heart a-tremble when he says goodbye to family and friends: even if he does not actually burst into tears at least he puts foot to stirrup with a sad and gloomy face. And however noble the passion which enflames the heart of a well-born bride, she still has to have her arms prised from her mother's neck before being given to her husband, no matter what that merry fellow may say:

Est ne novis nuptis odio venus, anne parentum
Frustrantur falsis gaudia lachrimulis,
Ubertim thalami quas intra limina fundunt?
Non, ita me divi, vera gemunt, juverint.

[Is Venus really hated by our brides, or do they mock their parents' joy with those false tears which they pour forth in abundance at their chamber-door? No. So help me, gods, their sobs are false ones.]

And so it is not odd to lament the death of a man whom we would by no means wish to be still alive.

When I rail at my manservant I do so sincerely with all my mind: my curses are real not feigned. But once I cease to fume, if he needs help from me I am glad to help him: I turn over the page. When I call him a dolt or a calf I have no intention of stitching such labels on to him for ever: nor do I believe I am contradicting myself when I later call him an honest fellow. No one characteristic clasps us purely and universally in its embrace. If only talking to oneself did not look mad, no day would go by without my being heard growling to myself, against myself, 'You silly shit!' Yet I do not intend that to be a definition of me.

If anyone should think when he sees me sometimes look bleakly at my wife and sometimes lovingly that either emotion is put on, then he is daft. When Nero took leave of his mother whom he was sending to be drowned, he nevertheless felt some emotion at his mother's departure and felt horror and pity.

The sun, they say, does not shed its light in one continuous flow but ceaselessly darts fresh rays so thickly at us, one after another, that we cannot perceive any gap between them:

Largus enim liquidi fons luminis, ætherius sol
Inrigat assidue cælum candore recenti,
Suppeditatque novo confestim lumine lumen.

[That generous source of liquid light, the aethereal sun, assiduously floods thc hcavcns with ncw rays and ceaselessly sheds light upon new light.]

So, too, our soul darts its arrows separately but imperceptibly.

Artabanus happened to take his nephew Xerxes by surprise. He teased him about the sudden change which he saw come over his face. But Xerxes was in fact thinking about the huge size of his army as it was crossing the Hellespont for the expedition against Greece; he first felt a quiver of joy at seeing so many thousands of men devoted to his service and showed this by a happy and festive look on his face; then, all of a sudden his thoughts turned to all those lives which would wither in a hundred years at most: he knit his brow and was saddened to tears.

We have pursued revenge for an injury with a resolute will; we have felt a singular joy at our victory . . . and we weep: yet it is not for that that we weep. Nothing has changed; but our mind contemplates the matter in a different light and sees it from another aspect: for everything has many angles and many different sheens. Thoughts of kinship, old acquaintanceships and affections suddenly seize our minds and stir them each according to their worth: but the change is so sudden that it escapes us:

Nil adeo fieri celeri ratione videtur
Quam si mens fieri proponit et inchoat ipsa.

Ocius ergo animus quam res se perciet ulla,
Ante oculos quarum in promptu natura videtur.

[Nothing can be seen to match the rapidity of the thoughts which the mind produces and initiates. The mind is swifter than anything which the nature of our eyes allows them to see.]

That is why we deceive ourselves if we want to make this never-ending succession into one continuous whole. When Timoleon weeps for the murder which, with noble determination, he committed, he does not weep for the liberty he has restored to his country; he does not weep for the Tyrant: he weeps for his brother. He has done one part of his duty: let us allow him to do the other.

On conscience

[Conscience originally meant connivance. Conscience in the sense of our individual consciousness of right and wrong or of our own guilt or rectitude fascinated Montaigne. It became a vital concern of his during the Wars of Religion with their cruelties, their false accusations and their use of torture on prisoners. Such moral basis as there was for the 'question' (judicial torture) seems, curiously enough, to have been a respect for the power of conscience – of a man's inner sense of his guilt or innocence which would strengthen or weaken his power to withstand pain. A major source of Montaigne's ideas here is St Augustine and a passionate note by Juan Luis Vives in his edition of the City of God *designed to undermine confidence in torture.]*

During our civil wars I was travelling one day with my brother the Sieur de la Brousse when we met a gentleman of good appearance who was on the other side from us; I did not know anything about that since he feigned otherwise. The worst of these wars is that the cards are so mixed up, with your enemy indistinguishable from you by any clear indication of language or deportment, being brought up under the same laws, manners and climate, that it is not easy to avoid confusion and disorder. That made me fear that I myself would come upon our own troops in a place where I was not known, be obliged to state my name and wait for the worst. That did happen to me on another occasion: for, from just such a mishap, I lost men and horses. Among others, they killed one of my pages, pitifully: an Italian of good family whom I was carefully training; in him was extinguished a young life, beautiful and full of great promise.

But that man of mine was so madly afraid! I noticed that he nearly died every time we met any horsemen or passed through towns loyal to the King; I finally guessed that his alarm arose from his conscience. It seemed to that wretched man that you could read right into the very secret thoughts of his mind through his mask and the crosses on his greatcoat. So wondrous is the power of conscience! It makes us betray, accuse and fight against ourselves. In default of an outside testimony it leads us to witness against ourselves:

Occultum quatiens animo tortore flagellum.

[Lashing us with invisible whips, our soul torments us.]

The following story is on the lips of children: a Paeonian called Bessus was rebuked for having deliberately destroyed a nest of swallows, killing them all. He said he was right to do so: those little birds kept falsely accusing him of having murdered his father! Until then this act of parricide had been hidden and unknown; but the avenging Furies of his conscience made him who was to pay the penalty reveal the crime.

Hesiod corrects that saying of Plato's, that the punishment follows hard upon the sin. He says it is born at the same instant, with the sin itself; to expect punishment is to suffer it: to merit it is to expect it. Wickedness forges torments for itself,

Malum consilium consultori pessimum,

[Who counsels evil, suffers evil most,]

just as the wasp harms others when it stings but especially itself, for it loses sting and strength for ever:

Vitasque in vulnere ponunt.

[In that wound they lay down their lives.]

The Spanish blister-fly secretes an antidote to its poison, by some mutual antipathy within nature. So too, just when we take pleasure in vice, there is born in our conscience an opposite displeasure, which tortures us, sleeping and waking, with many painful thoughts.

Quippe ubi se multi, per somnia sœpe loquentes,
Aut morbo delirantes, procraxe ferantur,
Et celata diu in medium peccala dedisse.

[Many indeed, often talking in their sleep or delirious in illness, have proclaimed, it is said, and betrayed long-hidden sins.]

Apollodorus dreamed that he saw himself being flayed by the Scythians then boiled in a pot while his heart kept muttering, 'I am the cause of all these ills.' No hiding-place awaits the wicked, said Epicurus, for they can never be certain of hiding there while their conscience gives them away.

Prima est hæc ultio, quod se
Judice nemo nocens absolvitur.

[This is the principal vengeance: no guilty man is absolved: he is his own judge.]

Conscience can fill us with fear, but she can also fill us with assurance and confidence. And I can say that I have walked more firmly through some dangers by reflecting on the secret knowledge I had of my own will and the innocence of my designs.

Conscia mens ut cuique sua est, ita concipit intra
Pectora pro facto spemque metumque suo.

[A mind conscious of what we have done conceives within our breast either hope or fear, according to our deeds.]

There are hundreds of examples: it will suffice to cite three of them about the same great man.

When Scipio was arraigned one day before the Roman

people on a grave indictment, instead of defending himself and flattering his judges he said: 'Your wishing to judge, on a capital charge, a man through whom you have authority to judge the Roman world, becomes you well!'

Another time his only reply to the accusations made against him by a Tribune of the People was not to plead his cause but to say: 'Come, fellow citizens! Let us go and give thanks to the gods for the victory they gave me over the Carthaginians on just such a day as this!' Then as he started to walk towards the temple all the assembled people could be seen following after him – even his prosecutor.

Again when Petilius, under the instigation of Cato, demanded that Scipio account for the monies that had passed through his hands in the province of Antioch, Scipio came to the Senate for this purpose, took his account-book from under his toga and declared that it contained the truth about his receipts and expenditure; but when he was told to produce it as evidence he refused to do so, saying that he had no wish to act so shamefully towards himself; in the presence of the Senate he tore it up with his own hands. I do not believe that a soul with seared scars could have counterfeited such assurance. He had, says Livy, a mind too great by nature, a mind too elevated by Fortune, even to know how to be a criminal or to condescend to the baseness of defending his innocence.

Torture is a dangerous innovation; it would appear that

it is an assay not of the truth but of a man's endurance. The man who can endure it hides the truth: so does he who cannot. For why should pain make me confess what is true rather than force me to say what is not true? And on the contrary if a man who has not done what he is accused of is able to support such torment, why should a man who has done it be unable to support it, when so beautiful a reward as life itself is offered him?

I think that this innovation is founded on the importance of the power of conscience. It would seem that in the case of the guilty man it would weaken him and assist the torture in making him confess his fault, whereas it strengthens the innocent man against the torture. But to speak the truth, it is a method full of danger and uncertainty. What would you *not* say, what would you *not* do, to avoid such grievous pain?

Etiam innocentes cogit mentiri dolor.

[Pain compels even the innocent to lie.]

This results in a man whom the judge has put to the torture lest he die innocent being condemned to die both innocent and tortured. Thousands upon thousands have falsely confessed to capital charges. Among them, after considering the details of the trial which Alexander made him face and the way he was tortured, I place Philotas.

All the same it is , so they say, the least bad method that human frailty has been able to discover. Very inhumanely, however, and very ineffectually in my opinion. Many peoples less barbarous in this respect than the Greeks and the Romans who call them the Barbarians reckon it horrifying and cruel to torture and smash a man of whose crime you are still in doubt. That ignorant doubt is yours: what has it to do with him? You are the unjust one, are you not? who do worse than kill a man so as not to kill him without due cause! You can prove that by seeing how frequently a man prefers to die for no reason at all rather than to pass through such a questioning which is more painful than the death-penalty itself and which by its harshness often anticipates that penalty by carrying it out.

I do not know where I heard this from, but it exactly represents the conscience of our own Justice: a village woman accused a soldier before his commanding general – a great man for justice – of having wrenched from her little children such sops as she had left to feed them with, the army having laid waste all the surrounding villages. As for proof, there was none. That general first summoned the woman to think carefully what she was saying, especially since she would be guilty of perjury if she were lying; she persisted, so he had the soldier's belly slit open in order to throw the light of truth on to the fact. The woman was found to be right. An investigatory condemnation!

Fortune is often found in Reason's train

[*The Roman censor was not too happy about Montaigne's writing about Fortune (as distinct from Providence) – strangely so, since fickle Fortune and Fortune's Wheel were centuries-old commonplaces. (The word* Fortune *itself occurs some 350 times in the* Essays.*)*]

The changeableness of Fortune's varied dance means that she must inevitably show us every kind of face. Has any of her actions ever been more expressly just than the following? The Duke of Valentinois decided to poison Adrian the Cardinal of Corneto, to whose home in the Vatican he and his father Pope Alexander VI were coming to dine; so he sent ahead a bottle of poisoned wine with instructions to the butler to look after it carefully. The Pope, chancing to arrive before his son, asked for a drink; that butler, who thought that the wine had been entrusted to him merely because of its quality, served it to him; then the Duke himself, arriving just in time for dinner and trusting that nobody would have touched his bottle, drank some too, so that the father died suddenly while the son, after being tormented by a long illness, was reserved for a worse and different fortune.

Sometimes it seems that Fortune is literally playing with us. The Seigneur d'Estrées (who was then ensign to Monseigneur de Vendôme) and the Seigneur de Licques (a lieutenant in the forces of the Duke of Aerschot) were both suitors of the sister of the Sieur de Fouquerolle – despite their being on opposite sides, as often happens with neighbours on the frontier. The Seigneur de Licques was successful. However, on his very wedding-day and, what is worse, before going to bed, the bridegroom desired to break a lance as a tribute to his new bride and went out skirmishing near St Omer; there, he was taken prisoner by the Seigneur d'Estrées who had proved the stronger. To exploit this advantage to the full, d'Estrées compelled the lady –

Conjugis ante coacta novi dimittere collum,
Quam veniens una atque altera rursus hyems
Noctibus in longis avidum saturasset amorem.

[Forced to release her embrace of her young husband before the long nights of a couple of winters had sated her eager love] –

personally to beg him, of his courtesy, to surrender his prisoner to her. Which he did, the French nobility never refusing anything to the ladies . . .

Was the following not Fate apparently playing the artist? The Empire of Constantinople was founded by Constantine son of Helena: many centuries later it was ended by another Constantine son of Helena!

Sometimes it pleases Fortune to rival our Christian miracles. We hold that when King Clovis was besieging Angoulême, by God's favour the walls collapsed of themselves; Bouchet borrows from some other author an account of what happened when King Robert was laying siege to a certain city: he slipped off to Orleans to celebrate the festival of St Aignan; while he was saying his prayers, at a certain point in the Mass the walls of the besieged city collapsed without being attacked. But Fortune produced quite opposite results during our Milanese wars: for after Captain Renzo had mined a great stretch of the wall while besieging the town of Arona for us French it was blown right up in the air, only to fall straight back on to its foundations all in one piece so that the besieged were no worse off.

Sometimes Fortune dabbles in medicine. Jason Phereus was given up by his doctors because of a tumour on the breast; wishing to rid himself of it even by death, he threw himself recklessly into battle where the enemy was thickest; he was struck through the body at precisely the right spot, lancing his tumour and curing him.

Did Fortune not surpass Protogenes the painter in mastery of his art? He had completed a portrait of a tired and exhausted dog; he was pleased with everything else but could not paint its foaming slaver to his own satisfaction; irritated against his work, he grabbed a sponge and threw it at it, intending to blot everything out since the sponge was impregnated with a variety of paints: Fortune guided his throw right to the mouth of the dog and produced the effect which his art had been unable to attain.

Does she not sometimes direct our counsels and correct them? Queen Isabella of England had to cross over to her kingdom from Zealand with her army to come to the aid of her son against her husband; she would have been undone if she had landed at the port she had intended, for her enemies were awaiting her there; but Fortune drove her unwillingly to another place, where she landed in complete safety. And that Ancient who chucked a stone at a dog only to hit his stepmother and kill her could he not have rightly recited this verse:

Ταυτόματον ἡμῶν καλλίω βουλεύεται.

'Fortune has better counsel than we do.' Icetes had bribed two soldiers to murder Tomoleon during his stay in Adrana in Sicily. They chose a time when he was about to make some sacrifice or other; they mingled with the crowd; just as they were signalling to each other that the time was right for their deed, along comes a third soldier who landed a mighty sword-blow on the head of one of them and then ran away. His companion, believing he was discovered and undone, ran to the altar begging for sanctuary and promising to reveal all the truth. Just as he was giving an account of the conspiracy the third man was caught and was being dragged and manhandled through the crowd towards Timoleon and the more notable members of the congregation: he begged for mercy, saying that he had rightly killed his father's murderer, immediately proving by witnesses which good luck had conveniently provided that his father had indeed been murdered in the town of the Leontines by the very man against whom he had taken his revenge. He was granted ten Attic silver-pounds as a reward for his good luck in saving the life of the Father of the Sicilian People while avenging the death of his own father. Such fortune surpasses in rightness the right-rules of human wisdom.

To conclude. Does not the following reveal a most explicit granting of her favour as well as her goodness and singular piety? The two Ignatii, father and son, having been proscribed by the Roman Triumvirate, nobly decided that their duty was to take each other's life and so frustrate the cruelty of those tyrants. Sword in hand they fell on each other. Fortune guided their sword-points, made both blows equally mortal and honoured the beauty of such a loving affection by giving them just enough strength to withdraw their forearms from the wounds, blood-stained and still grasping their weapons, and to clasp each other, there as they lay, in such an embrace that the executioners cut off both their heads at once, allowing their bodies to remain nobly entwined together, wound against wound, lovingly soaking up each other's life-blood.

On punishing cowardice

[Renaissance Jurisconsults such as Tiraquellus were concerned to temper the severity of the Law by examining motives and human limitations. Montaigne does so here in a matter of great concern to gentlemen in time of war.]

I once heard a prince, a very great general, maintain that a soldier should not be condemned to death for cowardice: he was at table, being told about the trial of the Seigneur de Vervins who was sentenced to death for surrendering Boulogne.

In truth it is reasonable that we should make a great difference between defects due to our weakness and those due to our wickedness. In the latter we deliberately brace ourselves against reason's rules, which are imprinted on us by Nature; in the former it seems we can call Nature herself as a defence-witness for having left us so weak and imperfect. That is why a great many people believe that we can only be punished for deeds done against our conscience: on that rule is partly based the opinion of those who condemn the capital punishment of heretics and misbelievers as well as the opinion that a barrister or a judge cannot be arraigned if they fail in their duty merely from ignorance.

Where cowardice is concerned the usual way is, certainly, to punish it by disgrace and ignominy. It is said that this rule was first introduced by Charondas the lawgiver, and that before his time the laws of Greece condemned to death those who had fled from battle, whereas he ordered that they be made merely to sit for three days in the market-place dressed as women: he hoped he could still make use of them once he had restored their courage by this disgrace – '*Suffundere malis hominis sanguinem quam effundere*.' [Make the blood of a bad man blush not gush.]

It seems too that in ancient times the laws of Rome condemned deserters to death: Ammianus Marcellinus tells how the Emperor Julian condemned ten of his soldiers to be stripped of their rank and then suffer death, 'following,' he said, 'our Ancient laws'. Elsewhere however Julian for a similar fault condemned others to remain among the prisoners under the ensign in charge of the baggage. Even the harsh sentences decreed against those who had fled at Cannae and those who in that same war had followed Gnaeus Fulvius in his defeat did not extend to death.

Yet it is to be feared that disgrace, by making men desperate, may make them not merely estranged but hostile.

When our fathers were young the Seigneur de Franget,

formerly a deputy-commander in the Company of My Lord Marshal de Châtillon, was sent by My Lord Marshal de Chabannes to replace the Seigneur Du Lude as Governor of Fuentarabia; he surrendered it to the Spaniards. He was sentenced to be stripped of his nobility, both he and his descendants being pronounced commoners, liable to taxation and unfit to bear arms. That severe sentence was executed at Lyons. Later all the noblemen who were at Guyse when the Count of Nassau entered it suffered a similar punishment; and subsequently others still.

Anyway, wherever there is a case of ignorance so crass and of cowardice so flagrant as to surpass any norm, that should be an adequate reason for accepting them as proof of wickedness and malice, to be punished as such.

On the vanity of words

[Montaigne, despite his own mastery of language, despised words and admired deeds or 'matter'. He showed this before he embarked on the Essays *in the dedicatory letter of his translation of Raymond Sebond's* Natural Theology, *addressed to his father. What Montaigne admired in ancient Sparta – and what he found lacking in his own day – was a genuine respect for action over rhetoric.]*

In former times there was a rhetorician who said his job was to make trivial things seem big and to be accepted as such. He is a cobbler who can make big shoes fit little feet. In Sparta they would have had him flogged for practising the art of lying and deception. And I am sure that Archidamus their king did not hear without amazement the answer given by Thucydides when he asked him whether he was better at wrestling than Pericles: 'That,' Thucydides replied, 'would be hard to prove: for after I have thrown him to the ground in the match he persuades the spectators that he did not have a fall and is declared the winner.' Those who hide women behind a mask of make-up do less harm, since it is not much of a loss not to see them as they are by nature, whereas rhetoricians pride themselves on deceiving not our eyes but our judgement, bastardizing and corrupting things in their very essence. Countries such as Crete and Sparta which maintained themselves in a sound and regulated polity did not rate orators very highly.

Ariston wisely defined rhetoric as the art of persuading the people; Socrates and Plato, as the art of deceiving and flattering; and those who reject this generic description show it to be true by what they teach. The Mahometans will not allow their children to be taught it because of its uselessness. And the Athenians, despite the fact that the practice of it was esteemed in their city, realizing how pernicious it was, ordained that the main part of it which is to work on the emotions should be abolished, together with formal introductions and perorations.

It is a means invented for manipulating and stirring up the mob and a community fallen into lawlessness; it is a means which, like medicine, is used only when states are sick; in states such as Athens, Rhodes and Rome where the populace, or the ignorant, or all men, held all power and where everything was in perpetual turmoil, the orators flooded in. And in truth few great men in those countries managed to thrust themselves into positions of trust without the help of eloquent speech: Pompey, Caesar, Crassus, Lucullus, Lentulus and Metellus all made it their mainstay for scrambling up towards that grandiose authority which they finally achieved, helped more by rhetoric than by arms, contrary to what was thought right in better times. For Lucius Volumnius, making a public address in favour of the candidates Quintus Fabius and Publius Decius during the consular elections, declared, 'These are great men of action, born for war; they have consular minds, uncouth in verbal conflict. Subtle, eloquent, learned minds are good but for Praetors, administering justice in the City.'

Rhetoric flourished in Rome when their affairs were in their worst state and when they were shattered by the storms of civil war, just as a field left untamed bears the most flourishing weeds.

It would seem that polities which rely on a monarch have less use for it than the others: for that animal-stupidity and levity which are found in the masses, making them apt to be manipulated and swayed through the ears by those sweet harmonious sounds without succeeding in weighing the truth of anything by force of reason – such levity, I repeat, is not so readily found in one individual man; and it is easier to protect him by a good education and counsel from being impressed by that poison. No famous orator has ever been seen to come from Macedonia or from Persia.

What I have just said was prompted by my having talked with an Italian who served as chief steward to the late Cardinal Caraffa until his death. I got him to tell me about his job. He harangued me on the art of feeding with a professional gravity and demeanour as though he were explaining some important point of Theology. He listed differences of appetite: the appetite you have when you are hungry, the one you have after the second and third courses; what means there are of simply satisfying it or of sometimes exciting it and stimulating it; how to govern the commonwealth of sauces, first in general then in particular, listing the qualities of every ingredient and its effects; the different green-stuffs in their season, the ones which must be served hot, the ones which must be served cold as well as the ways of decorating them and embellishing them to make them look even more appetizing. After all that he embarked upon how the service should be ordered, full of fine and weighty considerations:

nec minimo sane discrimine refert
Quo gestu lepores, et quo gallina secetur!

[For it is of no small importance to know how to carve a hare or a chicken!]

And all this was inflated with rich and magnificent words, the very ones we use to discuss the government of an empire. I was reminded of that man in the poem:

Hoc salsum est, hoc adustum est, hoc lautum est parum,
Illud recte; iterum sic memento; sedulo
Moneo quæ possum pro mea sapientia.

Postremo, tanquam in speculum, in patinas, Demea,
Inspicere jubeo, et moneo quid facto usus sit.

['This is too salty; this has been burned; this needs to be properly washed; this is excellent – remember that next time.' I advise them carefully as far as my wisdom allows; finally I tell them, Demea, to polish the dishes until they can see their faces in them as in a mirror. I tell them the lot.]

Even the Greeks after all highly praised the order and arrangement which were observed in the banquet which Paulus Aemilius threw for them on his return from Macedonia; but I am not talking here of deeds but of words.

I cannot tell if others feel as I do, but when I hear our architects inflating their importance with big words such as pilasters, architraves, cornices, Corinthian style or Doric style, I cannot stop my thoughts from suddenly dwelling on the magic palaces of Apollidon: yet their deeds concern the wretched parts of my kitchen-door!

When you hear grammatical terms such as metonymy, metaphor and allegory do they not seem to refer to some rare, exotic tongue? Yet they are categories which apply to the chatter of your chambermaid.

It is a similar act of deception to use for our offices of state the same grandiloquent titles as the Romans did, even though they have no similarity of function and even less authority and power. Similar too – and a practice which will, in my judgement, bear witness one day to the singular ineptitude of our century – is our unworthily employing for anybody we like those glorious cognomens with which Antiquity honoured one or two great men every few hundred years. By universal acclaim Plato bore the name *divine*, and nobody thought to dispute it with him: now the Italians, who rightly boast of having in general more lively minds and saner discourse than other peoples of their time, have made a gift of it to Aretino, in whom (apart from a style of writing stuffed and simmering over with pointed sayings, ingenious it is true but fantastical and far-fetched, and apart from his eloquence – such as it is) I can see nothing beyond the common run of authors of his century, so far is he from even approaching that 'divinity' of the Ancients.

And the title Great we now attach to kings who have nothing beyond routine greatness.

To philosophize is to learn how to die

[Montaigne comes to terms with his melancholy, now somewhat played down. He remains preoccupied with that fear of death – fear that is of the often excruciating act of dying – which in older times seems to have been widespread and acute. His treatment is rhetorical but not impersonal. Montaigne is on the way to discovering admirable qualities in common men and women.

Cicero says that philosophizing is nothing other than getting ready to die. That is because study and contemplation draw our souls somewhat outside ourselves, keeping them occupied away from the body, a state which both resembles death and which forms a kind of apprenticeship for it; or perhaps it is because all the wisdom and argument in the world eventually come down to one conclusion; which is to teach us not to be afraid of dying.

In truth, either reason is joking or her target must be our happiness; all the labour of reason must be to make us live well, and at our ease, as Holy Scripture says. All the opinions in the world reach the same point, that pleasure is our target even though they may get there by different means; otherwise we would throw them out immediately, for who would listen to anyone whose goal was to achieve for us pain and suffering?

In this case the disagreements between the schools of philosophy are a matter of words. '*Transcurramus solertissimas nugas.*' [Let us skip quickly through those most frivolous trivialities.] More stubbornness and prickliness are there than is appropriate for so dedicated a vocation, but then, no matter what role a man may assume, he always plays his own part within it.

Even in virtue our ultimate aim – no matter what they say – is pleasure. I enjoy bashing people's ears with that word which runs so strongly counter to their minds. When pleasure is taken to mean the most profound delight and an exceeding happiness it is a better companion to virtue than anything else; and rightly so. Such pleasure is no less seriously pleasurable for being more lively, taut, robust and virile. We ought to have given virtue the more favourable, noble and natural name of pleasure not (as we have done) a name derived from *vis* (vigour).

There is that lower voluptuous pleasure which can only be said to have a disputed claim to the name not a privileged right to it. I find it less pure of lets and hindrances than virtue. Apart from having a savour which is fleeting, fluid and perishable, it has its vigils, fasts and travails, its blood and its sweat; it also has its own peculiar sufferings, which are sharp in so many different ways and accompanied by a satiety of such weight that it amounts to repentance.

Since we reckon that obstacles serve as a spur to that pleasure and as seasoning to its sweetness (on the grounds that in Nature contraries are enhanced by their contraries) we are quite wrong to say when we turn to virtue that identical obstacles and difficulties overwhelm her, making her austere and inaccessible, whereas (much more appropriately than for voluptuous pleasure) they ennoble, sharpen and enhance that holy, perfect pleasure which virtue procures for us. A man is quite unworthy of an acquaintance with virtue who weighs her fruit against the price she exacts; he knows neither her graces nor her ways. Those who proceed to teach us that the questing after virtue is rugged and wearisome whereas it is delightful to possess her can only mean that she always lacks delight. (For what human means have ever brought anyone to the joy of possessing her?) Even the most perfect of men have been satisfied with aspiring to her – not possessing her but drawing near to her. The contention is wrong, seeing that in every pleasure known to Man the very pursuit of it is pleasurable: the undertaking savours of the quality of the object it has in view; it effectively constitutes a large proportion of it and is consubstantial with it. There is a happiness and blessedness radiating from virtue; they fill all that appertains to her and every approach to her, from the first way in to the very last barrier.

Now one of virtue's main gifts is a contempt for death, which is the means of furnishing our life with easy tranquillity, of giving us a pure and friendly taste for it; without it every other pleasure is snuffed out. That is why all rules meet and concur in this one clause. It is true that they all lead us by common accord to despise pain, poverty and the other misfortunes to which human lives are subject, but they do not do so with the same care. That is partly because such misfortunes are not inevitable. (Most of Mankind spend their lives without tasting poverty; some without even experiencing pain or sickness, like Xenophilus the musician, who lived in good health to a hundred and six.) It is also because, if the worse comes to worse, we can sheer off the bung of our misfortunes whenever we like: death can end them. But, as for death itself, that is inevitable.

Omnes eodem cogimur, omnium
Versatur urna, serius ocius
Sors exitura et nos in æter-
Num exitium impositura cymbæ.

[All of our lots are shaken about in the Urn, destined sooner or later to be cast forth, placing us in everlasting exile via Charon's boat.]

And so if death makes us afraid, that is a subject of continual torment which nothing can assuage. There is no place where death cannot find us – even if we constantly twist our heads about in all directions as in a suspect land: '*Quae quasi saxum Tantalo semper impendet.*' [It is like the rock for ever hanging over the head of Tantalus.] Our assizes often send prisoners to be executed at the scene of their crimes. On the way there, take them past fair mansions and ply them with good cheer as much as you like –

. . . non Siculæ dapes
Dulcem elaborabunt saporem,
Non avium cytharæque cantus
Somnum reducent –

[even Sicilian banquets produce no sweet savours; not even the music of birdsong nor of lyre can bring back sleep] –

do you think they can enjoy it or that having the final purpose of their journey ever before their eyes will not spoil their taste for such entertainment?

Audit iter, numeratque dies, spacioque viarum
Metitur vitam, torquetur peste futura

[He inquires about the way; he counts the days; the length of his life is the length of those roads. He is tortured by future anguish.]

The end of our course is death. It is the objective necessarily within our sights. If death frightens us how can we go one step forward without anguish? For ordinary people the remedy is not to think about it; but what brutish insensitivity can produce so gross a blindness? They lead the donkey by the tail:

Qui capite ipse suo instituit vestigia retro.

[They walk forward with their heads turned backwards.]

No wonder that they often get caught in a trap. You can frighten such people simply by mentioning death (most of them cross themselves as when the Devil is named); and since it is mentioned in wills, never expect them to draw one up before the doctor has pronounced the death-sentence. And then, in the midst of pain and terror, God only knows what shape their good judgement kneads it into!

(That syllable 'death' struck Roman ears too roughly; the very word was thought to bring ill-luck, so they learned to soften and dilute it with periphrases. Instead of saying *He is dead* they said *He has ceased to live* or *He has lived.* They found consolation in living, even in a past tense! Whence our 'late' (*feu*) So-and-So: 'he was' So-and-So.)

Perhaps it is a case of, 'Repayment delayed means money in hand', as they say; I was born between eleven and noon on the last day of February, one thousand five hundred and thirty-three (as we date things nowadays, beginning the year in January); it is exactly a fortnight since I became thirty-nine: 'I ought to live at least as long again; meanwhile it would be mad to think of something so far off'. – Yes, but all leave life in the same circumstances, young and old alike. Everybody goes out as though he had just come in. Moreover, however decrepit a man may be, he thinks he still has another twenty years to go in the body, so long as he has Methuselah ahead of him. Silly fool, you! Where your life is concerned, who has decided the term? You are relying on doctors' tales; look at facts and experience instead. As things usually go, you have been living for some time now by favour extraordinary. You have already exceeded the usual term of life; to prove it, just count how many more of your acquaintances have died younger than you are compared with those who have reached your age. Just make a list of people who have ennobled their lives by fame: I wager that we shall find more who died before thirty-five than after. It is full of reason and piety to take as our example the manhood of Jesus Christ: his life ended at thirty-three. The same term applies to Alexander, the greatest man who was simply man.

Death can surprise us in so many ways:

> *Quid quisque vitet, nunquam homini satis*
> *Cautum est in horas.*

[No man knows what dangers he should avoid from one hour to another.]

Leaving aside fevers and pleurisies, who would ever have thought that a Duke of Brittany was to be crushed to death in a crowd, as one was during the state entry into Lyons of Pope Clement, who came from my part of the world! Have you not seen one of our kings killed at sport? And was not one of his ancestors killed by a bump from a pig? Aeschylus was warned against a falling house; he was always on the alert, but in vain: he was killed by the shell of a tortoise which slipped from the talons of an eagle in flight. Another choked to death on a pip from a grape; an Emperor died from a scratch when combing his hair; Aemilius Lepidus, from knocking his foot on his own doorstep; Aufidius from bumping into a door of his Council chamber. Those who died between a woman's thighs include Cornelius Gallus, a praetor; Tigillinus, a captain of the Roman Guard; Ludovico, the son of Guy di Gonzaga, the Marquis of Mantua; and – providing even worse examples – Speucippus the Platonic philosopher, and one of our Popes.

Then there was that wretched judge Bebius; he was just granting a week's extra time to a litigant when he died of a seizure: his own time had run out. Caius Julius, a doctor, was putting ointment on the eyes of a patient when death closed his. And if I may include a personal example, Captain Saint-Martin, my brother, died at the age of twenty-three while playing tennis; he was felled by a blow from a tennis-ball just above the right ear. There was no sign of bruising or of a wound. He did not even sit down or take a rest; yet five or six hours later he was dead from an apoplexy caused by that blow.

When there pass before our eyes examples such as these, so frequent and so ordinary, how can we ever rid ourselves of thoughts of death or stop imagining that death has us by the scruff of the neck at every moment?

You might say: 'But what does it matter how you do it, so long as you avoid pain?' I agree with that. If there were any way at all of sheltering from Death's blows – even by crawling under the skin of a calf – I am not the man to recoil from it. It is enough for me to spend my time contentedly. I deal myself the best hand I can, and then accept it. It can be as inglorious or as unexemplary as you please:

> *prœtulerim delirus inersque videri,*
> *Dum mea delectent mala me, vel denique fallant,*
> *Quam sapere et ringi.*

[I would rather be delirious or a dullard if my faults pleased me, or at least deceived me, rather than to be wise and snarling.]

But it is madness to think you can succeed that way. They come and they go and they trot and they dance: and never a word about death. All well and good. Yet when death does come – to them, their wives, their children, their friends – catching them unawares and unprepared, then what storms of passion overwhelm them, what cries, what fury, what despair! Have you ever seen anything brought so low, anything so changed, so confused?

We must start providing for it earlier. Even if such brutish indifference could find lodgings in the head of an intelligent man (which seems quite impossible to me) it sells its wares too dearly. If death were an enemy which could be avoided I would counsel borrowing the arms of cowardice. But it cannot be done. Death can catch you just as easily as a coward on the run or as an honourable man:

Nempe et fugacem persequitur virum,
Nec parcit imbellis juventæ
Poplitibus, timidoque tergo;

[It hounds the man who runs away, and it does not spare the legs fearful backs of unwarlike youth;]

no tempered steel can protect your shoulders;

Ille licet ferro cautus se condat œre,
Mors tamen inclusum protrahet inde caput;

[No use a man hiding prudently behind iron or brass:
Death will know how to make him stick out his
cowering head;]

we must learn to stand firm and to fight it.

To begin depriving death of its greatest advantage over us, let us adopt a way clean contrary to that common one; let us deprive death of its strangeness; let us frequent it, let us get used to it; let us have nothing more often in mind than death. At every instant let us evoke it in our imagination under all its aspects. Whenever a horse stumbles, a tile falls or a pin pricks however slightly, let us at once chew over this thought: 'Supposing that was death itself?' With that, let us brace ourselves and make an effort. In the midst of joy and feasting let our refrain be one which recalls our human condition. Let us never be carried away by pleasure so strongly that we fail to recall occasionally how many are the ways in which that joy of ours is subject to death or how many are the fashions in which death threatens to snatch it away. That is what the Egyptians did: in the midst of all their banquets and good cheer they would bring in a mummified corpse to serve as a warning to the guests:

Omnem crede diem tibi diluxisse supremum.
Grata superveniet, quœ non sperabitur hora.

[Believe that each day was the last to shine on you. If it comes, any unexpected hour will bc welcome indeed.]

We do not know where death awaits us: so let us wait for it everywhere. To practise death is to practise freedom. A man who has learned how to die has unlearned how to be a slave. Knowing how to die gives us freedom from subjection and constraint. Life has no evil for him who has thoroughly understood that loss of life is not an evil. Paulus Aemilius was sent a messenger by that wretched King of Macedonia who was his prisoner, begging not to be led in his triumphant procession. He replied: 'Let him beg that favour from himself.'

It is true that, in all things, if Nature does not lend a hand art and industry do not progress very far. I myself am not so much melancholic as an idle dreamer: from the outset there was no topic I ever concerned myself with more than with thoughts about death – even in the most licentious period of my life.

Jucundum cum aetas florida ver ageret.

[When my blossoming youth rejoiced in spring.]

Among the games and the courting many thought I was standing apart chewing over some jealousy or the uncertainty of my aspirations: meanwhile I was reflecting on someone or other who, on leaving festivities just like these, had been surprised by a burning fever and his end, with his head full of idleness, love and merriment – just like me; and the same could be dogging me now:

Jam fuerit, nec post unquam revocare licebit.

[The present will soon be the past, never to be recalled.]

Thoughts such as these did not furrow my brow any more than others did. At first it does seem impossible not to feel the sting of such ideas, but if you keep handling them and running through them you eventually tame them. No doubt about that. Otherwise I would, for my part, be in continual terror and frenzy: for no man ever had less confidence than I did that he would go on living;

and no man ever counted less on his life proving long. Up till now I have enjoyed robust good health almost uninterruptedly: yet that never extends my hopes for life any more than sickness shortens them. Every moment it seems to me that I am running away from myself. And I ceaselessly chant the refrain, 'Anything you can do another day can be done now.'

In truth risks and dangers do little or nothing to bring us nearer to death. If we think of all the millions of threats which remain hanging over us, apart from the one which happens to appear most menacing just now, we shall realize that death is equally near when we are vigorous or feverish, at sea or at home, in battle or in repose. '*Nemo altero fragilior est: nemo in crastinam sui certior.*' [No man is frailer than another: no man more certain of the morrow.]

If I have only one hour's work to do before I die, I am never sure I have time enough to finish it. The other day someone was going through my notebooks and found a declaration about something I wanted done after my death. I told him straight that, though I was hale and healthy and but a league away from my house, I had hastened to jot it down because I had not been absolutely certain of getting back home. Being a man who broods over his thoughts and stores them up inside him, I am always just about as ready as I can be: when death does suddenly appear, it will bear no new warning for me. As far as we possibly can we must always have our boots on, ready to go; above all we should take care to have no outstanding business with anyone else.

Quid brevi fortes jaculamur ævo
Multa?

[Why, in so brief a span do we find strength to make so many projects?]

We shall have enough to do then without adding to it.

One man complains less of death itself than of its cutting short the course of a fine victory; another, that he has to depart before marrying off his daughter or arranging the education of his children; one laments the company of his wife; another, of his son; as though they were the principal attributes of his being.

I am now ready to leave, thank God, whenever He pleases, regretting nothing except life itself – if its loss should happen to weigh heavy on me. I am untying all the knots. I have already half-said my adieus to everyone but myself. No man has ever prepared to leave the world more simply nor more fully than I have. No one has more completely let go of everything than I try to do.

Miser o miser, aiunt, omnia ademit
Una dies infesta mihi tot præmia vitæ.

['I am wretched, so wretched,' they say: 'One dreadful day has stripped me of all life's rewards.']

And the builder says:

Manent opera interrupta, minaeque
Murorum ingentes.

[My work remains unfinished; huge walls may fall down.]

We ought not to plan anything on so large a scale – at least, not if we are to get all worked up if we cannot see it through to the end.

We are born for action:

Cum moriar, medium solvare inter opus.

[When I die, may I be in the midst of my work.]

I want us to be doing things, prolonging life's duties as much as we can; I want Death to find me planting my cabbages, neither worrying about it nor the unfinished gardening. I once saw a man die who, right to the last, kept lamenting that destiny had cut the thread of the history he was writing when he had only got up to our fifteenth or sixteenth king!

Illud in his rebus non addunt, nec tibi earum
Jam desiderium rerum super insidet una!

[They never add, that desire for such things does not linger on in your remains!]

We must throw off such humours; they are harmful and vulgar.

Our graveyards have been planted next to churches, says Lycurgus, so that women, children and lesser folk should grow accustomed to seeing a dead man without feeling terror, and so that this continual spectacle of bones, tombs and funerals should remind us of our human condition:

> *Quin etiam exhilarare viris convivia cœde*
> *Mos olim, et miscere epulis spectacula dira*
> *Certantum ferro, sæpe et super ipsa cadentum*
> *Pocula respersis non parco sanguine mensis;*

[It was once the custom, moreover, to enliven feasts with human slaughter and to entertain guests with the cruel sight of gladiators fighting: they often fell among the goblets, flooding the tables with their blood;]

so too, after their festivities the Egyptians used to display before their guests a huge portrait of death, held up by a man crying, 'Drink and be merry: once dead you will look like this'; similarly, I have adopted the practice of always having death not only in my mind but on my lips. There is nothing I inquire about more readily than how men have died: what did they say? How did they look? What expression did they have? There are no passages in the history books which I note more attentively. That I have a particular liking for such matters is shown by the examples with which I stuff my book. If I were a scribbler I would produce a compendium with commentaries of the various ways men have died. (Anyone who taught men how to die would teach them how to live.) Dicearchus did write a book with some such title, but for another and less useful purpose.

People will tell me that the reality of death so far exceeds the thought that when we actually get there all our fine fencing amounts to nothing. Let them say so: there is no doubt whatsoever that meditating on it beforehand confers great advantages. Anyway, is it nothing to get even that far without faltering or feverish agitation?

But there is more to it than that: Nature herself lends us a hand and gives us courage. If our death is violent and short we have no time to feel afraid: if it be otherwise, I have noticed that as an illness gets more and more hold on me I naturally slip into a kind of contempt for life. I find that a determination to die is harder to digest when I am in good health than when I am feverish, especially since I no longer hold so firmly to the pleasures of life once I begin to lose the use and enjoyment of them, and can look on death with a far less terrified gaze. That leads me to hope that the further I get from good health and the nearer I approach to death the more easily I will come to terms with exchanging one for the other. Just as I have in several other matters assayed the truth of Caesar's assertion that things often look bigger from afar than close to, I have also found that I was much more terrified of illness when I was well than when I felt ill. Being in a happy state, all pleasure and vigour, leads me to get the other state quite out of proportion, so that I mentally increase all its discomforts by half and imagine them heavier than they prove to be when I have to bear them.

I hope that the same will apply to me when I die. It is normal to experience change and decay: let us note how Nature robs us of our sense of loss and decline. What does an old man still retain of his youthful vigour and of his own past life?

Heu senibus vitae portio quanta manet.

[Alas, what little of life's portion remains with the aged.]

When a soldier of Caesar's guard, broken and worn out, came up to him in the street and begged leave to kill himself, Caesar looked at his decrepit bearing and said with a smile: 'So you think you are still alive, then?'

If any of us were to be plunged into old age all of a sudden I do not think that the change would be bearable. But, almost imperceptibly, Nature leads us by the hand down a gentle slope; little by little, step by step, she engulfs us in that pitiful state and breaks us in, so that we feel no jolt when youth dies in us, although in essence and in truth that is a harsher death than the total extinction of a languishing life as old age dies. For it is not so grievous a leap from a wretched existence to non-existence as it is from a sweet existence in full bloom to one full of travail and pain.

When our bodies are bent and stooping low they have less strength for supporting burdens. So too for our souls:

we must therefore educate and train them for their encounter with that adversary, death; for the soul can find no rest while she remains afraid of him. But once she does find assurance she can boast that it is impossible for anxiety, anguish, fear or even the slightest dissatisfaction to dwell within her. And that almost surpasses our human condition.

Non vultus instantis tyranni
Mente quatit solida, neque Auster
Dux inquieti turbidus Adriæ,
Nec fulminantis magna Jovis manus.

[Nothing can shake such firmness: neither the threatening face of a tyrant, nor the South Wind (that tempestuous Master of the Stormy Adriatic) nor even the mighty hand of thundering Jove.]

She has made herself Mistress of her passions and her lusts, Mistress of destitution, shame, poverty and of all other injuries of Fortune. Let any of us who can gain such a superiority do so: for here is that true and sovereign freedom which enables us to cock a snook at force and injustice and to laugh at manacles and prisons:

in manicis, et
Compedibus, sævo te sub custode tenebo.
Ipse Deus simul atque volam, me solvet: opinor,
Hoc sentit, moriar. Mors ultima linea rerum est.

['I will shackle your hands and feet and keep you under a cruel gaoler.' – 'God himself will set me free as soon as I ask him to.' (He means, I think, 'I will die': for death is the last line of all.)]

Our religion has never had a surer human foundation than contempt for life; rational argument (though not it alone) summons us to such contempt: for why should we fear to lose something which, once lost, cannot be regretted? And since we are threatened by so many kinds of death is it not worse to fear them all than to bear one? Death is inevitable: does it matter when it comes? When Socrates was told that the Thirty Tyrants had condemned him to death, he retorted, 'And nature, them!'

How absurd to anguish over our passing into freedom from all anguish. Just as our birth was the birth of all things for us, so our death will be the death of them all. That is why it is equally mad to weep because we shall not be alive a hundred years from now and to weep because we were not alive a hundred years ago. Death is the origin of another life. We wept like this and it cost us just as dear when we entered into this life, similarly stripping off our former veil as we did so. Nothing can be grievous which occurs but once; is it reasonable to fear for so long a time something which lasts so short a time? Living a long life or a short life are made all one by death: *long* and *short* do not apply to that which is no more. Aristotle says that there are tiny creatures on the river Hypanis whose life lasts one single day: those which die at eight in the morning die in youth; those which die at five in the evening die of senility. Which of us would not laugh if so momentary a span counted as happiness or unhappiness? Yet if we compare our own span against eternity or even against the span of mountains, rivers, stars, trees or, indeed, of some animals, then saying *shorter* or *longer* becomes equally ridiculous.

Nature drives us that way, too: 'Leave this world,' she says, 'just as you entered it. That same journey from death to life, which you once made without suffering or fear, make it again from life to death. Your death is a part of the order of the universe; it is a part of the life of the world:

inter se mortales mutua vivunt . . .
Et quasi cursores vitaï lampada tradunt.

[Mortal creatures live lives dependent on each other; like runners in a relay they pass on the torch of life.]

Shall I change, just for you, this beautiful interwoven structure! Death is one of the attributes you were created with; death is a part of you; you are running away from yourself; this *being* which you enjoy is equally divided between death and life. From the day you were born your path leads to death as well as life:

Prima, quae vitam dedit, hora, carpsit.

[Our first hour gave us life and began to devour it.]

Nascentes morimur, finisque ab origine pendet.

[As we are born we die; the end of our life is attached to its beginning.]

All that you live, you have stolen from life; you live at her expense. Your life's continual task is to build your death. You are *in* death while you are *in* life: when you are no more *in* life you are after death. Or if you prefer it thus: after life you are dead, but during life you are dying: and death touches the dying more harshly than the dead, in more lively a fashion and more essentially.

'If you have profited from life, you have had your fill; go away satisfied:

Cur non ut plenus vitae conviva recedis?

[Why not withdraw from life like a guest replete?]

But if you have never learned how to use life, if life is useless to you, what does it matter if you have lost it? What do you still want it for?

Cur amplius addere quœris
Rursum quod pereat male, et ingratum occidat omne?

[Why seek to add more, just to lose it again, wretchedly, without joy?]

Life itself is neither a good nor an evil: life is where good or evil find a place, depending on how you make it for them.

'If you have lived one day, you have seen everything.

One day equals all days. There is no other light, no other night. The Sun, Moon and Stars, disposed just as they are now, were enjoyed by your grandsires and will entertain your great-grandchildren:

Non alium videre patres: aliumve nepotes
Aspicient.

[Your fathers saw none other: none other shall your progeny discern.]

And at the worst estimate the division and variety of all the acts of my play are complete in one year. If you have observed the vicissitude of my four seasons you know they embrace the childhood, youth, manhood and old age of the World. Its play is done. It knows no other trick but to start all over again. Always it will be the same.

Versamur ibidem, atque insumus usque;

[We turn in the same circle, for ever;]

Atque in se sua per vestigia volvitur annus.

[And the year rolls on again through its own traces.]

I have not the slightest intention of creating new pastimes for you.

Nam tibi præterea quod machiner, inveniamque
Quod placeat, nihil est, eadem sunt omnia semper.

[For there is nothing else I can make or discover to please you: all things are the same for ever.]

Make way for others as others did for you. The first part of equity is equality. Who can complain of being included when all are included?

'It is no good going on living: it will in no wise shorten the time you will stay dead. It is all for nothing: you will be just as long in that state which you fear as though you had died at the breast;

licet, quod vis, vivendo vincere secla,
Mors æterna tamen nihilominus illa manebit.

[Triumph over time and live as long as you please: death eternal will still be waiting for you.]

'And yet I shall arrange that you have no unhappiness:

In vera nescis nullum fore morte alium te,
Qui possit vivus tibi te lugere peremptum,
Stansque jacentem.

[Do you not know that in real death there will be no second You, living to lament your death and standing by your corpse.]

"You" will not desire the life which now you so much lament.

Nec sibi enim quisquam tum se vitamque requirit . . .
Nec desiderium nostri nos afficit ullum.

[Then no one worries about his life or his self; . . . we feel no yearning for our own being.]

Death is less to be feared than nothing – if there be anything less than nothing:

multo mortem minus ad nos esse putandum
Si minus esse potest quam quod nihil esse videmus.

[We should think death to be less – if anything is 'less' than what we can see to be nothing at all.]

'Death does not concern you, dead or alive; alive, because you are: dead, because you are no more.

'No one dies before his time; the time you leave behind you is no more yours than the time which passed before you were born; and does not concern you either:

Respice enim quam nil ad nos ante acta vetustas
Temporis æterní fuerit.

[Look back and see that the aeons of eternity before we were born have been nothing to us.]

'Wherever your life ends, there all of it ends. The usefulness of living lies not in duration but in what you make of it. Some have lived long and lived little. See to it while you are still here. Whether you have lived enough depends not on a count of years but on your will.

'Do you think you will never arrive whither you are ceaselessly heading? Yet every road has its end. And, if it is a relief to have company, is not the whole world proceeding at the same pace as you are?

Omnia te vita perfuncta sequentur.

[All things will follow you when their life is done.]

Does not everything move with the same motion as you do? Is there anything which is not growing old with you? At this same instant that you die hundreds of men, of beasts and of other creatures are dying too.

Nam nox nulla diem, neque noctem aurora sequuta est,
Qua non audierit mistos vagitibus ægris
Ploratus, mortis comites et funeris atri.

[No night has ever followed day, no dawn has ever followed night, without hearing, interspersed among the wails of infants, the cries of pain attending death and sombre funerals.]

'Why do you pull back when retreat is impossible? You have seen cases enough where men were lucky to die, avoiding great misfortunes by doing so: but have you ever seen anyone for whom death turned out badly? And it is very simple-minded of you to condemn something which you have never experienced either yourself or through another. Why do you complain of me or of Destiny? Do we do you wrong? Should you govern us or should we govern you? You may not have finished your stint but you have finished your life. A small man is no less whole than a tall one. Neither men nor their lives are measured by the yard. Chiron refused immortality when he was told of its characteristics by his father Saturn, the god of time and of duration.

'Truly imagine how much less bearable for Man, and how much more painful, would be a life which lasted for ever rather than the life which I have given you. If you did not have death you would curse me, for ever, for depriving you of it.

'Seeing what advantages death holds I have deliberately mixed a little anguish into it to stop you from embracing it too avidly or too injudiciously. To lodge you in that moderation which I require of you, neither fleeing from life nor yet fleeing from death, I have tempered them both between the bitter and the sweet.

'I taught Thales, the foremost of your Sages, that living and dying are things indifferent. So, when asked "why he did not go and die then," he very wisely replied: "Because it *is* indifferent."

'Water, Earth, Air and Fire and the other parts of this my edifice are no more instrumental to your life than to your death. Why are you afraid of your last day? It brings you no closer to your death than any other did. The last step does not make you tired: it shows that you are tired. All days lead to death: the last one gets there.'

Those are the good counsels of Nature, our Mother.

I have often wondered why the face of death, seen in ourselves or in other men, appears incomparably less terrifying to us in war than in our own homes – otherwise armies would consist of doctors and cry-babies – and why, since death is ever the same, there is always more steadfastness among village-folk and the lower orders than among all the rest. I truly believe that what frightens us more than death itself are those terrifying grimaces and preparations with which we surround it – a brand new way of life: mothers, wives and children weeping; visits from people stunned and beside themselves with grief; the presence of a crowd of servants, pale and tear-stained; a bedchamber without daylight; candles lighted; our bedside besieged by doctors and preachers; in short, all about us is horror and terror. We are under the ground, buried in our graves already! Children are frightened of their very friends when they see them masked. So are we. We must rip the masks off things as well as off people. Once we have done that we shall find underneath only that same death which a valet and a chambermaid got through recently, without being afraid. Blessed the death which leaves no time for preparing such gatherings of mourners.

PENGUIN

LITTLE BLACK

CLASSICS

“他并没有无视
那个事实——
谋杀就像是
异教世界的宗教信仰，
除了要有一位祭司，
还需要一名牺牲者。”

PENGUIN

LITTLE BLACK

CLASSICS

亚瑟·萨维尔勋爵的罪行

Lord Arthur Savile's Crime

[英] 奥斯卡·王尔德　著
赵轩　译

中信出版集团 | 北京

图书在版编目（CIP）数据

企鹅经典：小黑书．第三辑：汉、英／（英）简·奥斯汀等著；夏星等译．-- 北京：中信出版社，2019.6

书名原文：Penguin Little Black Classics

ISBN 978-7-5217-0407-5

Ⅰ．①企… Ⅱ．①简… ②夏… Ⅲ．①世界文学－作品综合集－汉、英 Ⅳ．① I11

中国版本图书馆 CIP 数据核字 (2019) 第 072172 号

企鹅经典：小黑书　第三辑

亚瑟·萨维尔勋爵的罪行

著　　者：[英] 奥斯卡·王尔德

译　　者：赵轩

出版发行：中信出版集团股份有限公司

（北京市朝阳区惠新东街甲 4 号富盛大厦 2 座 邮编 100029）

承 印 者：北京楠萍印刷有限公司

开　　本：787mm × 1092mm　1/32　　印　　张：45.75　　字　　数：756 千字

版　　次：2019 年 6 月第 1 版　　印　　次：2019 年 6 月第 1 次印刷

京权图字：01－2018－6477　　广告经营许可证：京朝工商广字第 8087 号

书　　号：ISBN 978－7－5217－0407－5

定　　价：149.00 元（全 10 册）

亚瑟·萨维尔勋爵的罪行

／

一

这是温德米尔夫人在复活节前的最后一场招待会，本廷克山庄比平日里更加热闹。六位内阁大臣直接从议长会议的现场赶来，身上还披挂着星章缎带；所有漂亮女人都穿上了她们最时髦的裙子。在画室尽头站着的，是卡尔斯鲁厄的索菲亚公主。她一副鞑靼人的面相，长着一对黑溜溜的小眼睛，佩戴着华美的翡翠首饰，尖声操着一口蹩脚的法语，无论谁对她说些什么，都报以夸张的大笑作回应。现场云集了各方各派的宾客：漂亮的贵族夫人们与狂热的激进派亲切地交谈，颇有声望的传

教士与大名鼎鼎的无神论者擦肩而过，一群虔诚的主教追随着一位丰腴的歌剧首席女主唱穿堂过室，楼梯上站着几个皇家学院院士，假充成艺术家的样子。据说一时间，晚餐室里高朋满座，佳客云集。事实上，那真是温德米尔夫人最美好的一个夜晚，公主待到了快十一点半才离去。

公主刚一离开，温德米尔夫人就回到了画室，开始和佩斯利公爵夫人攀谈起来。画室里，一位著名的政治经济学家正表情严肃地向一位愤愤不平的匈牙利艺术大师解释音乐的科学原理。温德米尔夫人看上去明艳动人，她那秀颀的脖颈白皙如象牙，大大的眼睛仿佛幽蓝的勿忘我花，一头浓密的卷发闪烁着金色光华——绝不是当今篡夺纯金声名的那种浅淡的麦秸色，而是交织在璀璨阳光里或隐藏在珍稀琥珀中的那种金色。它们为她的脸庞镀上了一圈圣光，全然掩去了她罪人的魅惑。她是一个奇妙的心理学研究课题。年轻的时候，她就发现了一条重要的真理：越是放浪形骸，越是清纯可人。于是经由一系列鲁莽的出格行为——其中多半无伤大雅，她赢得了一位名流所享有的优遇。她换了不止一任丈夫。据《德布雷特英国贵族年鉴》记载，她曾有过三段婚姻。不

过她从来没换过情人，于是坊间早就不再传播她的流言蜚语了。如今她四十年华，无儿女承欢膝下，只对寻欢作乐有着极度的热情，这也是她永葆青春的秘密。

她突然急切地环顾了一下房间，用她清晰而低沉的嗓音问:“我的手相师呢？”

“你的什么，格拉迪斯？”公爵夫人不由自主地高声问道。

“我的手相师，公爵夫人。我现在没他活不下去。”

“亲爱的格拉迪斯，你总是这么别出心裁！”公爵夫人边低声说着，边暗自琢磨手相师到底是什么，心想总不会和手足科医生差不多吧。

“他每周都会来给我看两次手相，”温德米尔夫人继续说道，“有趣极了。”

“我的老天！”公爵夫人自言自语道，“还真是一个手足科医生。太可怕了！我希望他无论如何至少是个外国人，那样的话还不算太糟糕。”

“我一定要把他介绍给您。”

“介绍给我？！”公爵夫人大喊一声，“你的意思是他就在这儿？”她开始四处张望，寻找她的玳瑁小扇子和一件破旧不堪的蕾丝披肩，以便做好准备，即刻离开。

“他当然在这儿。我怎么可能不邀请他来参加我的派对？他说我有一只通灵的手，要是我的拇指再短哪怕一丁点儿，我必定会是一个悲观主义者，会入修道院。”

“哦，我明白了！”公爵夫人如释重负，“他是个占吉卜卦的算命先生？”

“也卜算厄运。”温德米尔夫人答道，“吉凶祸福，前世今生。比如，明年我命里有灾，在陆地或海上都危险，所以我打算住在高空气球上，每天晚上用篮子把吃食拎上来。这些都写在我小手指上，也许是我的掌纹，我记不清是哪个了。”

“但你这必定是在违背天意，格拉迪斯。”

“我亲爱的公爵夫人，我坚信天意是禁得住这一回考验的。我认为每个人每月都应该看一次手相，好知道什么不该做。当然，有的人还是会去做，不过能被提前预警还是好的。现在，如果没有人赶紧去把波杰斯先生找来，我只好自己去了。”

“由我为您效劳吧，温德米尔夫人。”一个高大帅气的年轻男子说道。他一直微笑着站在旁边，饶有兴趣地聆听着她们的对话。

“太感谢了，亚瑟勋爵！可是我怕你不认识他。”

“如果他如您所说的那般出众，温德米尔夫人，我是不会认不出他的。跟我说说他什么样子，我会立刻把他带来。”

“嗯，他一点儿也不像是一个手相师。我的意思是，他并不是一副神秘莫测、深藏不露或不着边际的样子。他是一个矮壮的男人，滑稽的秃头，戴一副大大的金丝眼镜，形貌介于家庭医生和乡村律师之间。实在抱歉，可这并不是我的错——人们太讨厌了，我的钢琴师们都看起来和诗人一模一样，而我的诗人们又仿佛是一群钢琴家。我还记得上一季我邀请了一个曾经炸死过许多人的、极度可怕的阴谋家来吃晚饭，他以前总是穿一件锁子甲，袖子上别着一把匕首。可你知道吗，他来的时候看起来就像是一位和善的老牧师，整晚都在讲笑话。当然了，他非常有趣，可是我失望至极。当我问起他的锁子甲，他只是大笑着说：‘英格兰实在太冷了，没法穿。’啊，波杰斯先生来了！波杰斯先生，我想让你给佩斯利公爵夫人看看手相。公爵夫人，您得把手套脱了。不，不是左手，另一只。”

“亲爱的格拉迪斯，我认为这实在是不妥。”公爵夫人说着，轻轻地脱下了一只脏污的小山羊皮手套。

“但凡有趣的事情都不妥，”温德米尔夫人说，“世事如此。不过，我一定要介绍你们认识。公爵夫人，这是波杰斯先生，我钟爱的手相师。波杰斯先生，这是佩斯利公爵夫人，如果你敢说她手掌上的月亮山[1]比我的大，我就再也不会相信你了。”

“我确信，格拉迪斯，我手上没有那东西。”公爵夫人严肃地说。

“夫人说得没错，”波杰斯先生瞥了一眼那只手指短粗的小胖手，说道，“月亮山没有成形。不过，生命线极好。请您弯一下手腕。谢谢！手腕上三条醒目的主线！您会长命百岁的，公爵夫人，而且非常幸福。志向线——不好不坏。才智线不算突出，情感线——”

“您就直言不讳吧，波杰斯先生！”温德米尔夫人大声说道。

“倘若看出了公爵夫人经历过什么，我自然乐意直言，”波杰斯先生说着，鞠了一躬，“可是很遗憾，我只看到了伟大的情感，伴随着强烈的责任感。”

“请您继续，波杰斯先生。”公爵夫人说道，看上去

1. 西方手相学术语，掌纹名称，被认为与人的想象、创造、本能等相关。（说明：文中脚注均为译者注。）

颇为受用。

“理财是夫人您重要的美德。”波杰斯先生继续说。温德米尔夫人大笑着离开了。

“理财是件极好的事。”公爵夫人自鸣得意地说，“我嫁给佩斯利的时候，他有十一座城堡，可没有一所房子能住人。”

“如今，他有了十二所房子，可一座城堡也没有了。”温德米尔夫人大声说道。

“哦，亲爱的，”公爵夫人说，“我喜欢……”

“舒适，”波杰斯先生说道，“现代化设施，而且每一间卧室里都有热水。夫人您完全正确，舒适是我们的文明带给我们的唯一的东西。”

“你已经准确地讲出了公爵夫人的性格，波杰斯先生，现在你一定要给弗劳拉夫人看看手相。”女主人微笑着点头示意，一位淡褐色头发、削肩膀的高个儿女孩便从沙发后面笨手笨脚地走出来，伸出了一只瘦骨嶙峋的细长的手掌，手指像竹片儿一样。

“哈，一位钢琴师！”波杰斯先生说道，“我看是一位杰出的钢琴师，不过或许还称不上是音乐家。非常矜持，非常坦诚，而且非常爱动物。”

“太对了！”公爵夫人大声说着，转向温德米尔夫人，“完全正确！弗劳拉在麦克洛斯基养了二十四只柯利牧羊犬。如果她父亲允许的话，她会把我们城里的房子变成动物园。”

“哎呀，正巧每个星期四的晚上我也这么对待我的房子。”温德米尔夫人大笑着高声说道，“只不过比起柯利牧羊犬，我更喜欢狮子。”

“这是您的一桩错事，温德米尔夫人。”波杰斯先生说着，浮夸地鞠了一躬。

“如果一个女人不能令她所犯的错事楚楚动人，那她充其量也仅是一位女性罢了。”这是女主人的回答。“不过你一定要给我们多看几个手相。来，托马斯爵士，让波杰斯先生给您看看。”一位身穿白色西装马甲的亲切和蔼的老绅士走上前来，伸出一只厚实粗糙的手，中指尤其长。

“生性爱冒险。以往有过四次长途旅行，即将开启一段新旅程。遭遇过三次船难。不，两次，不过下次旅行会有遭遇海难的风险。一个坚定的保守派，非常守时，酷爱收藏奇珍异宝。在十六岁到十八岁之间生过一场重病，快三十岁的时候继承了一笔财富。对猫和激进派深

恶痛绝。”

“太神奇了！”托马斯爵士惊呼道，“您一定得给我夫人也看看手相！”

“您的第二任夫人，”波杰斯先生依然握着托马斯爵士的手，轻声说道，“您第二任夫人的手。我荣幸之至！”可是马维尔夫人，一个棕色头发、连睫毛都伤感的忧郁女人，完全拒绝将她的过去或未来暴露出来。而温德米尔夫人费尽口舌也没能让俄国大使克洛夫先生脱下他的手套。事实上，似乎许多人都很害怕面对这个满脸一成不变的微笑、戴着金丝眼镜、眼睛贼亮的古怪的小个子男人。而且，当他当着所有人的面，对可怜的弗莫尔夫人说，她其实一点儿都不喜欢音乐，只是非常喜欢音乐家的时候，人们都觉察到，手相学真是一门最危险的科学，不应该受到鼓励，除非是两人私下交流。

然而，亚瑟·萨维尔勋爵全然不知弗莫尔夫人的不幸遭遇，他已经饶有兴致地看了波杰斯先生许久，迫不及待地希望他给自己看看手相，可是又不太好意思主动前去要求。于是他穿过房间走到了温德米尔夫人落座的地方，满脸绯红地询问，是否能请波杰斯先生给他瞧瞧。

“当然了，他会愿意的。”温德米尔夫人说，“那正是

他来这儿的目的。亚瑟勋爵，我所有的狮子都是马戏团演员，无论何时，我一声令下，它们就得跳火圈。不过我得事先警告你，我会把一切都告诉西比尔的。她明天来和我共进午餐，聊聊帽子的事。如果波杰斯先生发现你脾气很坏，或者有痛风的征兆，或是在贝斯沃特金屋藏娇，我必定将一切如实奉告给西比尔。”

亚瑟勋爵微笑着摇了摇头。“我不担心，”他答道，“西比尔对我了如指掌，我对她也一样。”

“啊！你这么说倒令我感到一丝遗憾。婚姻是建立在彼此误解的基石之上的。我可一点儿都不愤世嫉俗，只是有些经验罢了，然而事实正是如此。波杰斯先生，亚瑟·萨维尔勋爵巴不得你快给他看看手相。你可别说出什么‘他和伦敦最漂亮的女孩儿订婚了’之类的话，这消息早在一个月以前就登过《晨报》了。”

“亲爱的温德米尔夫人，”杰德堡侯爵夫人大声说道，“千万让波杰斯先生多留会儿。他刚刚才告诉我，我应该登台表演，我对此颇有兴趣。”

“如果他真是这么说的，杰德堡夫人，我必定得把他带走了。快过来，波杰斯先生，给亚瑟勋爵看看手相。”

“好吧，”杰德堡夫人噘着嘴从沙发上站起身，“就算

我当不成演员，至少能当个听众吧。”

“当然，我们大家都来做听众。”温德米尔夫人说，“现在，波杰斯先生，千万告诉我们点儿好话，亚瑟勋爵可是我特别钟爱的客人之一。”

可是，当波杰斯先生看到亚瑟勋爵的手掌，他竟一言不发，面色变得莫名地苍白。他似乎打了个寒战，粗重的眉毛以一种奇怪又恼人的方式扭曲着，正如每次他困惑不解时的样子。接着他的黄脑门上渗出豆大的汗珠，仿佛有毒的露水，他的粗手指也变得冰冷黏湿。

亚瑟勋爵自然注意到了这些令人不安的奇怪迹象，有生以来第一次，他感觉到了恐惧。他想冲出房间，可是他克制住了自己的冲动。最好能知道最坏的情况，不管是什么，也好过在骇人的未知中惶惶度日。

“愿闻其详，波杰斯先生。”他说道。

“我们都等着呢！”不耐烦的温德米尔夫人急切地大喊道。可是那位手相师偏偏缄口不言。

“我相信亚瑟勋爵也是要登台表演的。”杰德堡夫人说，“只不过刚才被你斥责一番，波杰斯先生就不敢再这样告诉他了。”

突然间，波杰斯先生松开了亚瑟勋爵的右手，抓起

他的左手，低低地俯下身去，仔细查看，眼镜的金边都要蹭到手掌心了。霎时间，他的脸变得惨白，如同一副恐怖的面具，但他很快恢复了镇静。他抬起头看着温德米尔夫人，挤出一个微笑说："这是一个迷人的年轻人的手。"

"当然了！"温德米尔夫人答道，"不过他会是一个可爱的丈夫吗？这才是我想知道的。"

"所有迷人的年轻人都会是可爱的丈夫。"波杰斯先生说道。

"我认为做丈夫的不应该太过迷人，"杰德堡夫人一脸忧思地低声说道，"那太危险了。"

"我亲爱的宝贝，他们永远都不会太过迷人的。"温德米尔夫人大声说，"不过我想知道细节，只有细节才是最有趣的。亚瑟勋爵会发生什么事？"

"哦，未来几个月之内，亚瑟勋爵将外出旅行……"

"没错，当然了，他要去度蜜月。"

"还会失去一位亲戚。"

"但愿可别是他妹妹？"杰德堡夫人用满是怜悯的语气问道。

"当然不是他妹妹，"波杰斯先生做了一个不以为然的手势，"只是个远房亲戚。"

“哦，我真是失望透顶，”温德米尔夫人说，“我明天没有一星半点儿的东西可以透露给西比尔。现如今可没人在乎什么远房亲戚，多少年前就过时了。不过，我想她最好备一块黑丝巾在身边，去教堂总会用得到。好了，我们去吃晚餐吧。他们肯定把什么都吃光了，我们没准儿还能找些热汤喝。弗朗索瓦以前会烹制极美味的鲜汤，可是他现在对政治狂热，我都有些搞不懂他了。我倒是希望布朗热将军能保持安静。公爵夫人，您肯定累了吧？”

“一点儿也不，亲爱的格拉迪斯，”公爵夫人边回答，边蹒跚着走向门口，“我过得非常愉快，那个手足科医生，我是说那个手相师，真是太有意思了。弗劳拉，我的玳瑁扇子在哪儿？哦，谢谢你，托马斯爵士，非常感谢！我的蕾丝披肩呢，弗劳拉？哦，谢谢你，托马斯爵士，你真是个好人！”然后，这位高贵的人物终于走下了楼，途中只把香水瓶弄掉了两次。

这期间，亚瑟·萨维尔勋爵一直站在壁炉旁，挥之不去的恐惧与对厄运将临的胆战心惊笼罩着他。妹妹挽着普利姆代尔勋爵的胳膊从他身边经过，身着粉色织锦，戴着粉色珍珠配饰，楚楚动人，而他只对着妹妹苦笑一

番。他几乎没听到温德米尔夫人在招呼他跟上。他想着西比尔·默顿，想着他们之间可能会产生嫌隙，不禁泪湿了眼眶。

看着他，人们会说，复仇女神涅墨西斯已经偷走了帕拉斯[1]的盾牌，让他看到了蛇发女妖戈耳工的头。他似乎石化了，忧郁阴沉的脸像是大理石一般。他从出生以来就过着富家公子锦衣玉食的生活，无俗事挂心，度过了无忧无虑的美妙的少年时光。此刻，有生以来第一次，他意识到了世事无常、命运捉弄，感受到了在劫难逃的可怕。

这真是疯狂且荒谬至极！这些骇人的秘密罪孽、血红的犯罪征兆，都以一种他自己无法识读的字符，写在他的手掌上，而另一个人却可以破译？没有逃离厄运的可能吗？无论是荣耀还是耻辱，我们难道都如棋子一般，被一股无形的力量左右，如陶工手下的器皿一般任由人搓扁揉圆？他的理智对抗着它，同时他又感到灾难正纠缠着自己，他突然被要求去承担一个难以负荷的重任。演员们太幸运了，他们可以选择演绎悲剧或喜剧，品尝

1. 帕拉斯即为雅典娜，古希腊神话中的战争与智慧女神。

苦涩或欢愉，大笑或哭泣。可现实生活并非如此。大部分男人和女人都被迫扮演一些他们并不能胜任的角色。我们的吉尔登斯吞[1]为我们扮演着哈姆雷特，而我们的哈姆雷特不得不像哈尔王子[2]一样开着玩笑。世界是一个舞台，可是剧里的演员都配错了角色。

波杰斯先生突然走进房间。看到亚瑟勋爵时，他惊了一下，粗鄙肥胖的脸青黄不定。两人目光交错，一时间沉默无言。

“公爵夫人把一只手套落在这里了，亚瑟勋爵，让我给她拿过去。”波杰斯先生终于开口，“啊，在沙发上！晚安！”

“波杰斯先生，我要请教您一个问题，请您务必直言不讳。”

“下次吧，亚瑟勋爵，公爵夫人等着急了，我得赶紧走。”

“先别走，公爵夫人没什么急事。”

“不该让夫人们久等，亚瑟勋爵。”波杰斯先生说着，无力地笑了笑，“女士们很容易不耐烦的。”

亚瑟勋爵任性又轻蔑地撇了撇他轮廓鲜明的嘴唇。

1. 莎士比亚剧作《哈姆雷特》中的角色。

2. 莎士比亚剧作《亨利四世》中的角色。

此刻，那位可怜的公爵夫人对他而言一点儿都不重要。他穿过房间，来到波杰斯先生身旁，伸出他的手。

“告诉我您看到了什么，”他说，“实话实说。我必须知道真相。我不是个小孩儿。”

金丝眼镜后面，波杰斯先生的眼睛眨了眨。他不安地交错着步子，手指紧张地把弄着一条闪闪发光的表链。

“您为什么会认为除了我告诉您的那些，我还在您手上看到了更多的东西呢，亚瑟勋爵？”

“我就是知道。你不说明白，我是不会罢休的。我可以付钱给你。我会给你一张一百英镑的支票。”

那对绿眼睛闪亮了片刻，紧接着又恢复了暗淡。

“基尼金币[1]？”最终，波杰斯先生低声说道。

“当然。我明天就把支票给您送去。您在哪个俱乐部？”

“我没有俱乐部。也就是说，目前还没有。我的地址是……还是请允许我奉上名片吧。”说着，波杰斯先生从马甲背心口袋里掏出一张镶金边的卡片，递给亚瑟勋爵，并向他深深鞠了一躬。卡片上写着：

1. 英国于 1663 年到 1814 年间铸造并发行的货币名称。

塞普蒂默斯·R.波杰斯 先生

— 职业手相师 —

西月街103a号

“我的工作时间是上午十点到下午四点。”波杰斯先生例行公事地小声说道，“全家一起来有折扣。”

“快点儿吧！”亚瑟勋爵的面色极度苍白，边高声催促，边伸出了他的手。

波杰斯先生紧张地环顾四周，拉上了厚重的门帘。

“要花点儿时间，亚瑟勋爵，您最好先坐下。”

“长话短说，先生！”亚瑟勋爵再次大声催促，在光可鉴人的地板上愤怒地跺着脚。

波杰斯先生笑了笑，从他胸前的口袋里掏出一面小放大镜，用手帕小心地擦拭着。

“我准备好了。”他说。

二

十分钟以后，大惊失色、悲痛欲绝的亚瑟勋爵从大

条纹雨篷周遭站着的一群穿毛皮大衣的男仆们中间挤过去，冲出了本廷克山庄，似乎对一切视而不见、充耳不闻。那天晚上天寒地冻，广场四周的煤气灯闪烁在凛冽的寒风中。可是他的双手却热得发烫，他的额头如火烧火燎一般。他迈着醉汉似的步伐，走了又走。他经过一个警察的身边，警察好奇地打量他；一个乞丐懒散地从拱廊中走出来，乞求施舍，看眼前人的痛苦更甚于自己，反倒害怕起来。他一度在路灯下驻足，看看自己的双手。他仿佛能觉察到上面已沾满血污，颤抖的双唇间迸出一声微弱的呜咽。

谋杀！那手相师看出来的竟是一场谋杀！此刻的夜晚似乎也洞悉了一切，荒凉的风在他耳畔呼啸，漆黑的街角也满是这秘密，这秘密在房顶上对他咧着嘴笑。

他先是来到公园，那里阴暗的树林似乎对他有强烈的吸引力。精疲力竭的他倚靠在栏杆上，额头抵着湿冷的金属降温。他倾听着林木间令人战栗的寂静。“谋杀！谋杀！”他不断地重复着，仿佛反复的诉说可以减弱这个词的恐怖。他自己的声音令他胆战心惊，然而他又希望回声女神或许能听到他，把这座酣睡的城市从梦境中唤醒。他感到一种强烈的欲望，想要拦住随便哪个过往

的行人，将一切说与他听。

而后，他游荡过牛津街，来到逼仄腌臜的小巷子。他经过的时候，两个浓妆艳抹的女人逗弄他。一个漆黑的院子里传来打骂声，紧接着是尖叫声，然后他看到了弯腰驼背挤成一团的穷人和老者，都蜷缩在门前潮湿的台阶上。一种莫名的怜悯之情涌上心头。罪恶与苦难注定是这些人的结局吗？就像他也有命定的归宿一样？难道他们也和他一样，仅仅是一场大秀中的提线木偶吗？

然而击溃他的不是个中谜题，而是受难的喜剧性。它的全然无用，它荒谬至极得毫无意义。一切看起来是多么不合逻辑！毫无和谐可言！他惊诧于白日浅薄的乐观主义与真实存在的事实之间的不协调。他还非常年轻。

片刻之后，他发现自己来到了马里波恩教堂前。安静的车道看起来像是一条长长的亮闪闪的银缎带，斑驳错落的光影仿佛深色的蔓藤花纹。远处弯弯曲曲一排明灭不定的煤气灯，一座带围墙的小房子外面孤零零地停放着一辆双轮马车，车夫正在里面睡觉。他急匆匆地向着波特兰广场的方向走去，还不时地四处张望，似乎在担心被人跟踪。在里奇街的街角站着两个男人，他们正读着公告牌上的一张小布告。一股莫名的好奇心驱使他

凑上前去。他刚一走近，那两个黑字——“谋杀”就映入他的眼帘。他吓了一跳，两颊变得通红。那是一张悬赏公告，为了抓捕一个中等身材、年龄在三十岁到四十岁之间、头戴圆顶毡帽、身穿黑色大衣和格子裤子、右脸上有道疤的男人。他读了一遍又一遍，想着那个可怜的男人会不会被抓住，猜想他脸上的疤是怎么来的。或许，某一天，他自己的名字也会出现在伦敦街墙的布告栏上。或许，某一天，人们也会给他的人头开个悬赏捉拿价。

这想法令他毛骨悚然。他猛然转身，快步没入夜色之中。

他不清楚自己身在何处。他模模糊糊地记得自己游荡过一片迷宫一样的脏房子，在一大片纵横交错的幽暗的街道中迷了路。最后他发现自己走到了皮卡迪利广场，此时已是曙光初照，黎明破晓。他溜达着回家，向贝尔格雷夫广场走去，路上遇见了驶向科芬园的四轮运货大马车。马车夫们身穿白色罩衫，留着粗糙的卷发，晒伤的脸上满是欢愉。他们稳坐在马车上，马鞭子挥得噼啪作响，彼此间时不时地高喊几声。这支嘈杂的队伍中为首的是一匹大灰马，马背上坐着一个胖嘟嘟的男孩，他破旧的帽子里有一束报春花。他一路笑着，小手紧紧地

抓着马鬃毛。堆得高高的蔬菜看上去就像是许多块翡翠直冲云霄，又像是美艳玫瑰的粉红花瓣上镶嵌的碧玉。亚瑟勋爵被莫名地感动，说不清是为什么。黎明时分的柔和美妙中有些东西似乎于他而言是无以言表的可悲，他想起所有那些初时晴好、晚时暴风雨侵袭的日子。还有这些庄稼人，他们粗粝又欢快的声音，他们满不在乎的举止，他们眼中的伦敦是多么不寻常啊！没有夜晚的罪行，没有白天的烟雾，伦敦，一个毫无生气的鬼魅般的城市，一座荒冢之城！他好奇他们如何看待它，他们是否了解它的壮丽与耻辱，它热烈的色彩斑斓的欢乐，它恐怖的饥荒，它从早到晚的创造与破坏。也许对他们而言，它只不过是一个可以卖水果的集市，是他们至多逗留几个小时的地方——他们离开时街道依然安静，房屋依然沉睡未醒。观察这些过往的行人成为他的一件乐事。粗野的人们穿着笨重的大头鞋，迈着笨拙的步子，散发着几分超然世外的感觉。他觉得这些人与大自然共生，而自然教会了他们平和。他羡慕他们对许多事都不知晓。

他走到贝尔格雷夫广场的时候，天空泛着微蓝，花园中的鸟儿开始叽叽喳喳。

三

亚瑟勋爵醒来的时候是十二点，正午的阳光透过象牙色丝绸窗帘照进他的房间。他起身望向窗外。这座伟大的城市被笼罩在热气蒸腾的朦胧的雾中，一所所房子的屋顶是暗银色。下面广场上一闪一闪的绿色中，一些孩子正像白色的蝴蝶一般飞舞着，人行道上满是去往公园的人。在他眼中，生命从未如此美妙，邪祟从未离他如此遥远。

他的贴身男仆用托盘给他送来一杯巧克力。他喝完巧克力，拨开厚重的桃红色长丝绒门帘，走进浴室。柔和的光从上方倾泻下来，穿过透明的缟玛瑙薄板，大理石水池里的水像块月长石一样闪闪发光。他急切地跳了进去，直到清凉的水波触到了脖子、头发，然后他把头沉下去，仿佛这样可以洗刷掉一些可耻的斑驳记忆。他迈步出来的时候，感到几乎平静了。此刻他敏锐的身体状况支配了他，正如许多本质精纯的事物一样，心智就像是烈火，既可用于提纯，亦可用于毁灭。

早餐之后，他瘫坐在沙发床上，点了根烟。壁炉架上，精致的旧织锦相框中，立着一幅西比尔·默顿的大

照片。照片中的人一如他在诺埃尔夫人的舞会上初见时的模样。形状精致的小脑袋微微垂向一侧，就好像那个细长如芦苇似的脖子没法承担如此的美貌一般；双唇微启，仿佛专为甜美的音乐而生；一双满是好奇的梦幻的眼睛透出少女的清纯。她穿着柔软贴身的中国绉纱的裙子，手持大大的叶形团扇，看上去就像是一尊人们在塔纳格拉[1]附近的橄榄树丛中找到的那种精美的小陶俑。而她的仪态风度中确有些希腊风范。尽管她个子并不娇小，但她比例匀称完美——在那个大多数女人要么太魁梧，要么太微不足道的年纪，这可是件难得的事。

此刻亚瑟勋爵看着她，心中由爱而生出万般怜悯。他感到自己头上悬着谋杀的宿命，娶她为妻是一种堪比犹大的背叛，是连波吉亚家族[2]做梦也想不出的更恶劣的罪行。他可能在任何时刻受到感召，去实践那个写在他手上的罪大恶极的预言。如此，他们两个还有什么幸福可言呢？当命运依然掌握着这个可怕的天平，他们的生

1. 古希腊维奥蒂亚城邦中雅典以北的一个城镇和自治区，距离底比斯不远，在古代因为以此地名命名的女像小陶俑而闻名。

2.15 世纪和 16 世纪欧洲极具影响力的西班牙裔意大利贵族，因为犯罪、通奸、贿赂、乱伦、谋杀等一系列丑闻而臭名昭著。

活会如何呢？无论如何，婚礼必须要推迟，对此他毅然决然。尽管他深爱着那个女孩，当他们坐在一起时，哪怕是手指轻触，也会令他全身上下每一个神经因无比的欢愉而震颤，然而他清楚地意识到自己的责任所在，也完全明白那个事实——在他完成这桩谋杀之前，他没有权利结婚。完成之后，他可以和西比尔·默顿站在圣坛前，把自己的一生交付于她的手上，不再惧怕有恶事发生；完成之后，他可以拥她入怀，知道她再也不用因为他而脸红，再也不用羞愧得抬不起头。可是，完成这桩谋杀必须是第一要务，对他们两个人而言，越快越好。

许多男人如果处于他的境遇，会优先选择寻欢作乐的鲜花小径，而非承担责任的悬崖峭壁。可亚瑟勋爵太过认真尽责，以至于无法将快乐建立在原则之上。他的爱可不是一时意乱情迷，西比尔对他来说就是一切美好高贵的象征。有那么一瞬间，他对于自己要去做的事情本能地产生强烈的厌恶，不过那感觉转瞬即逝。他的内心告诉他这不是罪行，而是牺牲；他的理智提醒他，没有其他出路。他必须在为自己而活还是为他人而活之间做出选择。尽管毫无疑问，加之于他身上的责任非常糟糕，可他知道不能让自私战胜爱。早晚我们都会面临同

样的抉择，我们所有人都会被问同样的问题。亚瑟勋爵的问题来得早一些，他的本性还没有被中年斤斤计较的愤世嫉俗而腐坏，他的心还没有被我们这个时代流行的浅薄的自负而侵蚀，他毫不犹豫地选择承担自己的责任。对他而言同样幸运的是，他既不是空想家，也不是懒散的不学无术之徒。他如果是那样的人，就会犹豫踌躇，会像哈姆雷特一样，让优柔寡断毁了他的目标。可他本质上是一个务实主义者。对他来说，生命意味着行动，而非思考。他拥有最难能可贵的东西——直觉决断力。

前一晚狂乱混沌的感觉此刻已经完全褪去，回想自己走街串巷地疯狂游荡，回想起自己情感上经历的剧烈的苦痛挣扎，他甚至觉得有些羞愧。他那些锥心刻骨的痛苦现在似乎变得很不真实。他很纳闷，自己怎么会傻到对无可避免之事埋天怨地。唯一令他苦恼的问题是，他要杀死谁？他并没有无视那个事实——谋杀就像是异教世界的宗教信仰，除了要有一位祭司，还需要一名牺牲者。他不是天才，没有敌人，而且他确实感觉到，这次不是意气用事或满足个人好恶的时机，他卷入的任务是一件最重大、最严肃的事件。于是，他在一页纸上列出了他的亲友名单，经过一番深思熟虑，他最终选择了

自己的远房表亲克莱门蒂娜·比彻姆夫人，一位住在可胜街的可爱的老妇人。他一直非常喜欢克莱姆[1]夫人——每个人都这么称呼她，而且他法定年龄一到就继承了拉格比勋爵的所有财产，自己非常富有，并不会从她的离世中获得什么钱物的好处。事实上，他越琢磨就越觉得她是最合适的人选，任何拖延都是对西比尔的不公，他决意即刻安排行事。

首先要搞定的当然是手相师。于是他在窗边的谢拉顿[2]小书桌前坐下来，开了一张一百零五英镑的支票，受款人为塞普蒂默斯·波杰斯先生。接着，他将支票装进信封，令他的贴身男仆送去西月街。而后他打电话给马厩，叫了一辆马车，自己穿戴好就出了门。离开房间之前，他回头看了看西比尔·默顿的照片，发誓无论如何，他绝不会让她知道自己为她做了什么，他要将自我牺牲的秘密永远深埋在心中。

在去往白金汉宫俱乐部的路上，他去了一趟花店，为西比尔递送了一篮水仙，俏丽的白色花瓣，鲜艳夺目

1. 克莱门蒂娜的简称。

2. 托马斯·谢拉顿（Thomas Sheraton，1751—1806）是18世纪英国最著名的家具设计师与家具生产商之一，此处指谢拉顿风格的家具。

的花蕊副冠，漂亮极了。他一到俱乐部，就径直走向图书馆，摇响服务铃，向侍者要一杯柠檬苏打水和一本毒物学的书。他心意已决，毒药是解决这件麻烦事的最佳方式。人与人之间任何形式的暴力行为都令他反感，况且，他非常担心杀死克莱姆夫人可能会引起大众关注。他很讨厌成为人们在温德米尔夫人家嘲讽戏弄的谈资，更不愿看到自己的名字出现在恶俗的社会新闻报道中。他还要考虑西比尔的父母，他们是非常传统守旧的人，倘若牵涉任何丑闻，他们很可能会反对这桩婚姻。尽管他也确信无疑，如果他将这件事情的来龙去脉告诉他们，他们会是最理解他行事动机的人。因此，无论怎么看，毒药都是最佳选择。安全、安静、万无一失，能避免出现任何痛苦的场面——像大多数英国人一样，他从骨子里拒绝一切痛苦的场面。

然而，他对毒物学一无所知，而且除了《拉夫入门指南》和《贝利杂志》，侍者在图书馆中也实在找不出什么东西。他亲自查看了书架，终于发现一册装帧精美的《药典》，还有一本由皇家医师学院院长马修·里德爵士编纂的厄斯金的《毒物学》。马修·里德爵士是白金汉宫最古老的成员之一，曾因为其他人被误选，那次令人

窘困的意外事件大大激怒了委员会，以至于当真人出现的时候，他们全体一致投票反对他。亚瑟勋爵读不懂两本书中的专业术语，已经开始后悔当初在牛津大学没认真上古典文学课程了。不过他在《毒物学》第二卷中发现一个非常有趣的关于乌头碱性能的详细记录，是用简单易读的英文记述的，看起来正是他想要的毒药。毒发快——几乎是即刻生效，完全无痛，而且据马修爵士的建议，如果以胶囊的形态服用，丝毫不会难以下咽。他在衬衫袖口上记下足以致命的药剂量，将书放回原位，然后漫步到圣詹姆斯街的帕索-亨贝大药房。帕索先生常与贵族阶层打交道，对于亚瑟勋爵的需求，他感到十分惊讶，极其毕恭毕敬地低声说道，买这些药品必须要有诊断书的。亚瑟勋爵解释说是为了解决一只挪威巨獒，因为它出现了早期的狂犬病症状，已经咬了马车夫小腿肚子两次。帕索先生对这个理由非常满意，还恭维了亚瑟勋爵丰富的毒物学知识，并立刻配好了药。

亚瑟勋爵在邦德街一家商店的橱窗里发现一个漂亮的银质小糖果盒。他将胶囊装进糖果盒中，丢掉帕索-亨贝大药房的丑陋的药盒，然后立刻动身前往克莱姆夫人家。

“好啊，坏小子，”他一进屋，老夫人就大声说道，

“怎么这么长时间没来看我？”

“我亲爱的克莱姆夫人，我实在无暇抽身。”亚瑟勋爵笑着说。

“我猜你的意思是你整日间都陪在西比尔·默顿小姐身边，买衣服、聊废话？我真是不理解人们为何对结婚这样小题大做。在我那个年代，我们从没想过在公共场合喁喁私语、卿卿我我，甚至私下也不曾。”

“向您保证，克莱姆夫人，我已经二十个小时没见过西比尔了。依我看，她是完全属于她的女帽商的。”

“当然了，要不是这样，你也不会来看望我这个丑老太婆。我很纳闷，你们男人怎么不引以为戒？我年轻的时候也有人为我痴狂，现如今变成一个风湿病缠身的可怜的老东西，一副假牙外加一副臭脾气。要不是亲爱的詹森夫人四处搜罗些蹩脚的法国小说给我送来，我估计都熬不过这一天。医生真是百无一用，就会向我收钱。他们连我烧心的毛病都治不好。”

“我给您带来了治疗烧心的药，克莱姆夫人，”亚瑟勋爵一脸严肃地说，“美国人研制的，药效奇佳。”

“我可不喜欢美国人的发明创造，亚瑟。我一点儿也不喜欢。我最近读了几部美国小说，全都不知所云。”

“哦，我这个可不是不知所云的东西，克莱姆夫人！我向您保证，药到病除。您一定要答应我试试看。”说着，亚瑟勋爵从口袋里拿出那个小盒子，递给她。

“嗯，这个盒子还挺精致的，亚瑟。真是给我的礼物吗？你真是太贴心了。这是那个灵丹妙药吗？看上去像一颗糖果。我现在就吃。”

“我的天啊！克莱门蒂娜夫人，”亚瑟勋爵大喊一声，抓住她的手，“现在可不行，它是顺势疗法[1]的药，如果在不烧心的时候吃，可能会后患无穷呢。等您难受的时候再吃，您会被药效吓一跳的。”

“那我现在就该吃。”克莱姆夫人说着，将小小的透明胶囊举到灯前，里面流动着液态乌头碱的泡沫。“我相信它一定很好吃。事实上，我虽然讨厌医生，却很喜欢药。不过，我还是等下次犯病时再吃吧。”

“那会是什么时候呢？”亚瑟勋爵急切地问道，“会很快吗？”

1. 顺势疗法是德国医生塞缪尔·哈内曼（Samuel Hahnemann，1755—1843）于1796年创立的替代治疗方法，声称如果某些物质能够引发健康人身体的某种症状，那么这些物质就可以治疗产生同样症状的病人的疾病，类似我们俗称的“以毒攻毒”。

"但愿一个星期内不要再犯了。我昨天早上烧心，难受极了。不过，谁知道呢？"

"那么，克莱姆夫人，您肯定在这个月底之前还会再犯病？"

"怕是如此。不过，亚瑟，你今天真是有心啊！真的，西比尔让你变得更好了。你现在得离开了，我一会儿要和几个非常无聊的人吃晚饭，他们从来不聊八卦丑闻，我如果现在不睡一会儿，晚饭的时候是没法保持清醒的。再见，亚瑟！代我问候西比尔，还有谢谢你带来的美国药。"

"您可别忘了吃啊，克莱姆夫人。"亚瑟勋爵从座位上起身说道。

"我当然不会忘啊，傻孩子。你这样为我着想，真是太贴心了！我如果需要更多，会写信告诉你的。"

亚瑟勋爵兴高采烈地离开了，感到如释重负。

那天晚上他和西比尔·默顿碰了面。他告诉她，他突然被置于一个极其困难的境地，无论出于尊严还是责任，他都无法退缩；他告诉她婚礼必须推迟，因为直到他摆脱那个可怕的纠缠物，他才能恢复自由之身；他恳求她相信自己，请她对未来不要有任何怀疑，一切都会

走上正轨，但必须要忍耐。

这场景发生在帕克巷默顿先生家的花房里，亚瑟勋爵平日里常来这儿吃晚饭。今夜的西比尔处于莫大的幸福之中，有那么一刻，亚瑟勋爵险些向心中懦弱的部分屈服，打算写信向克莱门蒂娜夫人要回药丸，让婚礼照常进行，假装这世上根本没有波杰斯先生这个人。然而，他良善的本性很快占了上风，甚至当西比尔埋在他怀中痛哭流涕时，他也没有犹疑。令他心旌荡漾的美丽也触动了他的良心。他觉得为了几个月的快乐而毁掉如此美好的一生，是大错特错的。

直到临近午夜，他一直陪着西比尔，两人彼此慰藉。第二天一早，他给默顿先生写了一封充满男子气概的意志坚决的信，言明婚礼不得不推迟，然后就动身前往威尼斯了。

四

在威尼斯，他见到了他的弟弟瑟比顿勋爵。瑟比顿正巧乘着他的游艇从科孚岛来，两个年轻人一起度过了愉快的两周。早上，他们在利多岛上骑马，或是乘着狭

长的黑色贡多拉在绿色的水道中滑行；下午，他们通常在游艇上招待访客；晚上，他们在佛罗莱恩餐厅吃饭，在皮亚扎广场上没完没了地抽烟。但不知怎的，亚瑟勋爵并不开心。他每天都要读《泰晤士报》的讣告栏，希望能看到克莱门蒂娜夫人去世的消息，可每天都是失望。他开始担心是不是发生了什么意外。他经常后悔，当初她迫切地希望尝试药效的时候，自己阻止了她服下那枚乌头碱。尽管西比尔的信满是爱与信任以及温柔，却也总是语带哀伤。他常常在某些时候觉得自己与她永别了。

两周之后，瑟比顿勋爵厌倦了威尼斯，决定沿海岸南下，到拉文那去，因为他听说那里的松树园里有一些重要的射猎活动。一开始，亚瑟勋爵坚决拒绝同往，不过，他钟爱的瑟比顿最终说服了他，说他如果自己待在达涅利酒店，会闷死的。15 号的早上，他们借着一阵强劲的东北风，在惊涛骇浪中出发了。那项运动十分精彩，而自由的户外生活也让亚瑟勋爵的脸上又焕发了生机。可是到了 22 号，他又开始担忧起克莱门蒂娜夫人的事，于是不顾瑟比顿的反对，乘坐火车回到了威尼斯。

他刚刚从贡多拉中迈步出来，踏上酒店的台阶，酒店老板就拿着一沓电报迎了上来。亚瑟勋爵从他手中一

把夺过电报，把它们撕开。大功告成！克莱门蒂娜夫人于 17 号夜里突然离世！

他首先想到的是西比尔，于是发了一封电报告诉她自己即刻赶回伦敦。接着他让贴身男仆收拾行李，连夜赶车。他支付了贡多拉船夫五倍的船费，终于怀着轻松的心情、迈着轻快的步伐回到了家，直奔起居室。起居室里有三封给他的信。一封来自西比尔，满是同情与哀悼。另外两封分别来自他的母亲和克莱门蒂娜夫人的律师。似乎那天晚上老夫人先和公爵夫人吃了饭，席间相谈甚欢，可是因为烧心难受，提早离开了。第二天早上，她被发现死在了床上，很显然走得安详，没遭罪受苦。马修·里德爵士立刻被请来，当然也是于事无补，回天乏术。她将于 22 号被安葬在比彻姆-查克特。她去世前几天刚刚立了遗嘱，除了将袖珍画收藏品都留给了自己的姐妹玛格丽特·拉福德夫人，紫水晶项链留给了西比尔·默顿之外，她将自己可胜街的小房子、所有的家具、个人财物、藏画等等悉数留给了亚瑟勋爵。遗产倒是不值什么，可律师曼斯菲尔德先生急切地要亚瑟勋爵尽早赶回来，因为有许多账单要支付，克莱门蒂娜夫人生前从没有理财记账的习惯。

克莱门蒂娜夫人对亚瑟勋爵的善念让他动容，他觉得波杰斯先生要为此事负很大的责任。然而他对西比尔的爱支配了其他所有情感，他认为自己履行了应尽的职责，这让他平静安宁。当他抵达查令十字街时，他感到全然的幸福。

默顿一家亲切地招待了他，西比尔让他发誓再也不会有什么东西挡在两人之间。婚礼定在6月7日。他的生活又变得光明美好起来，往日的欢乐再次回到他身边。

这天，他在克莱门蒂娜夫人的律师和西比尔的陪同下，来到可胜街的那间房子。他们烧掉了一包包褪色的信件，收拾出一抽屉一抽屉的垃圾。突然，那个年轻的女孩兴奋地叫出了声。

“你发现了什么，西比尔？”亚瑟勋爵停下手中的活儿，抬起头微笑着问道。

“这个可爱的银质小糖果盒，亚瑟。你不觉得它古雅别致、有几分荷兰风格吗？把它给我吧！我知道八十岁以前我都用不上那条紫水晶项链的。”

是那个装了乌头碱的盒子。

亚瑟勋爵吓了一跳，两颊泛红。他几乎全然忘记了自己的所作所为。对他来说，这真是奇怪的巧合：西

比尔，这个让他经历那一切烦忧的人，也最先让他想起了它。

“你当然可以拥有它，西比尔。本就是我送给可怜的克莱姆夫人的。”

“哦！谢谢你，亚瑟。这颗糖也给我吗？我都不知道克莱门蒂娜夫人喜欢吃糖。我原以为她是理性行事的人。”

亚瑟勋爵面色惨白如纸，一个可怕的念头闪过他的脑海。

“糖？西比尔，你什么意思？”他用沙哑的声音缓慢地说。

“里面有一颗糖果，只有一颗，看上去很旧，沾满了灰尘，我可一点儿也不想吃它。怎么了，亚瑟？你脸色怎么这么差？”

亚瑟勋爵快步穿过房间，抓过那个盒子。里面正是带有毒性泡沫的琥珀色胶囊。原来克莱门蒂娜夫人是寿终正寝！

这个发现令他震惊不已！他将胶囊扔进火里，一屁股坐在沙发上，发出绝望的悲声。

五

第二次推迟婚礼让默顿先生忧心忡忡，而茱莉亚夫人已经订好了参加婚礼的礼服，因此她竭力劝说西比尔断了这段姻缘。西比尔虽深爱着自己的母亲，也同样将终身托付给了亚瑟勋爵，无论茱莉亚夫人说什么都动摇不了她的信念。亚瑟勋爵自己则用了好多天才平复了巨大的沮丧，有一段时间，他处于神经衰弱的状态。然而，他绝佳的直觉决断力很快占了上风，他强健务实的大脑并没有让他陷于长久的迟疑之中。毒药计划彻底失败了，炸药或爆炸物显然值得一试。

他再次检视了一遍亲友名单，经过一番慎重考虑，他决定炸死他的舅舅，奇切斯特教长。这位学识渊博的教长酷爱钟表，收藏了一批从十五世纪到当代的精美钟表。在亚瑟勋爵看来，这位好教长的这个嗜好恰恰为他实施计划提供了绝佳的机会。当然，去哪儿搞来一套爆炸装置，那得再做打算了。《伦敦通讯簿》在这方面没有提供任何信息，而且他觉得就算去苏格兰场[1]也探听不到

1. 伦敦地区警察机关的名称，多用于代指伦敦警察厅。

什么，因为在爆炸之前，他们似乎从来也搞不清楚炸药的来龙去脉，甚至炸过之后，依然一无所知。

他突然想起了他的朋友鲁沃洛夫，一个极具革命主义倾向的年轻俄国人，冬天的时候，他们曾经在温德米尔夫人家碰过面。据说鲁沃洛夫伯爵正在撰写彼得大帝的传记，来到英国是为了调研这位沙皇在此当造船工人时期的相关资料。不过人们普遍怀疑他是一名虚无主义特工。毫无疑问，俄国大使馆十分不愿意看到他出现在伦敦。亚瑟勋爵觉得他正是那个能助自己一臂之力的人。于是，亚瑟在一天早上驱车前往鲁沃洛夫位于布鲁姆斯伯里的寓所，去寻求意见和协助。

“所以您当真要投身政治？”当亚瑟勋爵道出此行目的时，鲁沃洛夫伯爵如此问道。可亚瑟勋爵讨厌任何形式的招摇，觉得有必要承认自己对社会问题没有一星半点儿的兴趣，仅仅是需要一个爆炸装置来处理一件纯粹的家务事，而这件事只牵涉他自己，无关任何其他人。

鲁沃洛夫伯爵惊诧地看了他一会儿，发觉他十分认真，于是在纸上写下一个地址，签了名，递给桌子对面的他。

“苏格兰场可是不惜代价想得到这个地址，我亲爱的

朋友。”

“他们不会知道的。”亚瑟勋爵大笑着高声说道。和这个年轻的俄国人热情地握手之后，他跑下楼，看了一眼纸条，让马车夫带他去苏荷广场。

到了那儿，他让马车夫先回去，自己则步行到希腊街，最终来到一个叫贝尔庭院的地方。他穿过拱廊，走进一个奇怪的死胡同。这里显然是一家法国洗衣店，晾衣绳在房屋之间纵横交错成一张完美的大网，亚麻布在清晨的空气中飘动着。他径直走到头儿，敲了敲一所绿色小房子的门。在等人应门的空当，院子里的每一扇窗户都映出一张张模糊的窥探的脸。开门的是一个长相极其粗鄙的外国人，用一口蹩脚的英语问他有什么事。亚瑟勋爵递上鲁沃洛夫伯爵写给他的纸条。那个男人看到纸条后，鞠了一躬，将亚瑟勋爵请进了房屋底层一间破败不堪的前厅。没多久，温克尔科夫先生——在英格兰人们都这样称呼他——急匆匆地走进房间，脖子上围着沾了红酒渍的餐巾，左手还拿着一把餐叉。

“鲁沃洛夫伯爵介绍我来找您。”亚瑟勋爵鞠躬说道，“我急需和您简单聊聊，谈笔买卖。我叫史密斯，罗伯特·史密斯先生，我希望您卖给我一只能爆炸的钟表。”

“很高兴见到您，亚瑟勋爵！”和蔼可亲的小个子德国人大笑着说道，“别紧张，我的职责就是认识每一个人，我记得某个夜晚在温德米尔夫人家见过您。我希望夫人她万安！您介意坐下来陪我吃完早餐吗？有一盘上乘的美味佳肴，我那些好心的朋友们都说我的莱茵葡萄酒比他们在德国大使馆喝到的还要好。”亚瑟勋爵还没从被认出的惊讶中缓过来，发现自己已经在里屋落座了。手持铭刻着皇家纹饰的浅黄色大酒杯，小口品着最美味的莱茵白葡萄酒，亚瑟勋爵十分友好地和这位著名的阴谋家交谈起来。

“爆炸钟表，”温克尔科夫先生说道，“可不是什么海外出口的好东西，就算成功通过了海关，可火车运输太不规律，经常还没运到目的地就爆炸了。不过，如果您是想家用，我倒是可以给您提供一件绝佳的物件，效果包您满意。我能问您是要给谁用吗？如果是针对警察，或者任何与苏格兰场有关的人，我恐怕没法帮您。英国警探们真是我们的好朋友，我发现仰仗他们的愚蠢，我们可以为所欲为。我可不想让他们任何一个遭殃。”

“我向您保证，”亚瑟勋爵说，“这件事和警察绝无半点牵连。其实，这钟表是给奇切斯特教长的。”

“哎呀！亚瑟勋爵，我都不知道您对宗教有如此强烈的态度。如今已经鲜少有年轻人如此了。”

“恐怕您抬举我了，温克尔科夫先生。”亚瑟勋爵红着脸说，“事实上，我对神学一无所知。”

“那么就是一件纯粹的私人恩怨了？”

“纯粹私事。”

温克尔科夫先生耸了耸肩，离开了房间。几分钟后回来的时候，他手里多了一小块一分钱硬币大小的圆形炸药，一只精美的法式钟表，顶端是一尊镀金的自由神像，脚踏象征独裁专政的九头蛇。

亚瑟勋爵一见到它不禁面露喜色。“正是我想要的。”他大喊道，“快告诉我怎么让它爆炸。”

“啊！那是我的秘密。”温克尔科夫先生回答道，他注视着自己的发明创造，满脸是无可厚非的自豪。“告诉我您希望它什么时间爆炸，我会把这个装置设定到那个时间。”

“那么，今天是星期二，如果您能马上把它送去……”

“那可不行。我现在要为莫斯科那边的朋友处理一些重要的事情。不过，我明天倒是可以送出去。”

“哦，那时间足够了！”亚瑟勋爵礼貌地说，“如果

明晚或周四一早抵达。爆炸时间，定在周五正午时分如何？那时候，教长通常会在家里。”

“星期五，正午时分。”温克尔科夫先生重复着，在壁炉旁衣柜上放着的大账本上做了大致记录。

“那么现在，”亚瑟勋爵从座位上起身说道，“请告诉我该支付您多少钱。”

“小事一桩，亚瑟勋爵，我可没打算从中牟利。那个炸药七先令六便士，钟表三镑十先令，马车费大约五先令。能为鲁沃洛夫伯爵的朋友服务，我感到万分荣幸。”

“可是劳您费了工夫，温克尔科夫先生。”

“哦，那没什么！我很乐意效劳。我工作可不是为了钱，我完全是为了我的艺术而活。”

亚瑟勋爵在桌上放了四英镑二先令六便士，向友善的小个子德国人道了谢，拒绝了下周六在某个茶会上见一些无政府主义者的邀请，然后离开了那所房子，前往帕克巷。

接下来的两天，他都处于极度兴奋的状态中。周五中午十二点，他驱车前往白金汉宫等待消息。整个下午，呆头呆脑的门厅侍者贴出来自全国各地的电报，公布赛马结果、离婚案的陪审团裁决、天气报告，诸如此类；

电报机上打出下议院整晚会议的乏味细节，以及证券交易所的一小场恐慌。四点钟，各类晚报来了。亚瑟勋爵拿着《帕摩尔街报》《圣詹姆斯报》《环球报》《回声报》一头扎进了图书馆。古德柴尔德上校对此义愤填膺，他想要阅读关于他上午在伦敦市长官邸发表的一篇演讲的报道，演讲主题是南非传教以及在各省设立黑人主教的建议。而出于种种原因，他对《晚间新闻报》抱有强烈的偏见。然而，所有报纸上都没有奇切斯特的任何消息，亚瑟勋爵猜想这次尝试肯定又失败了。这对他是一次沉重的打击，他一度感到万念俱灰。第二天他去见了温克尔科夫先生。温克尔科夫先生万分诚恳地道歉，主动提出为他免费提供另一块钟表，或者以成本价卖给他一套硝化甘油炸药装置。不过亚瑟勋爵已经对爆炸彻底死心，温克尔科夫先生自己也承认，现如今什么事都掺假，连炸药都不纯。这个小个子德国人承认那个装置一定是出了什么问题，可是那个钟表还是可能会爆炸的。他举例子说，他曾经给敖德萨的军政长官送去一个气压计装置，预设在十天之后爆炸，可是三个月过去了都没动静。后来它果真爆炸了，仅仅把女仆炸得粉碎，军政长官早在六个星期以前就出城了。不过这至少证明了，虽然时间

总是不准，可一旦奏效，炸药的杀伤力还是威力无穷的。亚瑟勋爵听了这些才感到一丝丝欣慰，可是这点儿希望也最终破灭了，因为两天之后，他正准备上楼时，公爵夫人把他叫到自己的房间，给他看了一封她刚刚收到的从教区发来的信。

“简的信向来写得生动。”公爵夫人说道，“你一定要读一读最近这一封，完全像穆迪送来的那些小说一样好看。”

亚瑟勋爵从她手中接过信件。内容如下：

教区，奇切斯特

5 月 27 日

我最亲爱的姑妈：

十分感谢您为多加会[1]送来法兰绒和方格布。我非常赞同您的观点，她们想要穿漂亮衣服，这真是太荒唐了。可现如今，每一个人都如此激进，如此反宗教，很难让她们明白她们不该穿得像上流社会。我不确定我们的未来将

1. 由基督教教会发起的慈善团体，目的是向穷人提供衣物援助。

如何。正如爸爸经常在布道时所说的，我们生活在一个没有信仰的年代。

我们这儿最近发生了一件趣事。上周四，某个匿名仰慕者给爸爸送来一只钟表。它被装在一个木头盒子里，邮资已付，寄件地址是伦敦。爸爸认为一定是某个人读了他杰出的布道文《放纵即为自由吗？》，然后送来了这东西，因为在钟表的上面是一尊女像，爸爸说她头上的帽子代表自由。我觉得它并不好看，可是爸爸说它有年头了，所以我猜想它应该还不错。帕克拆开了盒子，爸爸把钟表放在了图书室的壁炉架上。星期五早上我们都坐在那里，当钟表指针指向十二点的时候，我们听到嗡嗡的一声，人像底座冒出一小股烟，自由女神掉了下来，撞上壁炉挡板，撞坏了鼻子！玛丽亚吓了一大跳，可是当时太可笑了，詹姆斯和我不禁大笑起来，甚至连爸爸都被逗乐了。我们上前检查，才发现它其实是一只闹钟，如果你把它设定在某一时刻，然后在一个小锤子下面放些火药和一个小火帽，它可以在你预设的时刻爆

炸。爸爸说它会产生噪声，不能放在图书室，因此雷吉把它带去了讲堂。它一点儿用处都没有，就是成天到晚地小规模爆炸。你觉得亚瑟会想要一个作为结婚礼物吗？我觉得它们在伦敦算是时鲜的玩意儿。爸爸说它们其实寓意深远，表明自由不能长久，最终会坠落。爸爸还说自由是在法国大革命时期被发明出来的。真是糟透了！

我现在得去多加会了，去给她们朗读您启迪心灵的书信。亲爱的姑妈，您说得太对了，她们这个阶层就应该穿一些简朴的衣服。我必须说，她们愁穿戴这件事真是太荒唐了，毕竟在这个世界上，在未来的日子里，还有那么多更加重要的事情。我很高兴您那件印花底绸效果很好，蕾丝花边都没坏。我打算在星期三的主教学校穿您送给我的那件黄缎子，我想看上去一定很不错。您会佩戴蝴蝶结吗？詹宁斯说如今每个人都佩戴蝴蝶结，而且衬裙要有荷叶边。雷吉那边又爆炸了，爸爸命令他把钟表送去马厩。我觉得爸爸不像刚开始那么喜欢它了，

尽管有人送来这么一件漂亮精巧的玩具还是令他颇为受用的，至少说明人们读了他的布道文，并从中受益。

爸爸让我问候您，还有詹姆斯、雷吉和玛丽亚都问您好。希望塞西尔姑父痛风的毛病好些了。相信我，亲爱的姑妈，永远爱您的侄女。

简·佩尔西

又及，记得回答我蝴蝶结的问题，詹宁斯非说这是现在的时尚。

公爵夫人因为这封信大笑不已，亚瑟勋爵对着它却面色凝重，十分不快。

“我亲爱的亚瑟，”她大声说道，“我再也不会给你看年轻女士的信了！可是对于那只钟表我真是无话可说。我想它是一件伟大的发明，我自己也应该拥有一只。”

“我可没什么兴趣。”亚瑟勋爵苦笑着说道。他亲吻了母亲，然后离开了房间。

上楼以后，他瘫坐在沙发上，满眼噙泪。他殚精竭虑地去完成这桩谋杀，可两次都失败了，而且错都不在他。他已经努力去履行自己的责任了，可命运女神似乎

背叛了他。他因为良愿无法达成而烦忧，因为徒劳无功而烦忧。或许，彻底取消这场婚姻更好一些。西比尔会痛苦，没错，可是这痛苦并不会真的毁掉她高洁的本质。至于他自己，有什么关系呢？人终有一死，既然生无可恋，死亦无惧。就让命运主宰厄运吧，他也不费力去帮命运女神了。

七点半，他穿好衣服去俱乐部。瑟比顿正在那儿和年轻的人们开派对。他被迫留下来和他们共进晚餐。他们琐碎的闲谈和无聊的笑话实在提不起他的兴趣，上咖啡的时候，他谎称自己还有约会，先行离开了。他刚一走出俱乐部，侍者就递给他一封信。信来自温克尔科夫先生，邀请他第二天晚上屈尊前去看一个只要一打开就会爆炸的雨伞。这是最新的发明，刚刚从日内瓦运来。他把信撕得粉碎。他已经下定决心不再做任何尝试。然后他游逛到泰晤士河堤岸，在河边坐了几个小时。月亮从鬃毛一般的黄褐色的云团间透出头，仿佛是一只狮子的眼睛；空洞无边的苍穹中数不清的星光闪烁，仿佛在紫色的穹顶上撒满了金粉；偶尔，一只驳船摇荡着进入混浊的水流，随着起落的潮水漂远；铁路信号灯由绿变红，火车呼啸着驶过大桥。过了一会儿，威斯敏斯特高

塔上发出十二点的低沉的钟声，每一声洪亮的钟声都仿佛让黑夜震颤。接着，火车信号灯熄灭了，一盏孤零零的路灯发出柔弱的光，就像是一根巨大的船桅杆上镶嵌着一颗硕大的红宝石。喧嚣的城市渐渐沉寂。

凌晨两点，他站起身，漫步去黑衣修士桥。一切看起来多么不真实！多像是一场奇怪的梦！河对岸的房子似乎建在黑暗中。人们会说银光黑影重新装点了这个世界。圣保罗教堂的大屋顶若隐若现，就像是朦胧天空中的一个气泡。

他走到克利奥帕特拉方尖碑[1]的附近，见一个男人正靠在矮墙上。等他再走近一些，那个男人抬起了头，煤气灯光照亮了他的整张脸。

是波杰斯先生，那个手相师！谁都不会认错那张松弛的胖脸，那副金丝眼镜，那个苍白无力的微笑，那张魅惑的巧嘴。

亚瑟勋爵停下脚步。一个机智的念头闪过他的脑海，他悄无声息地来到他的身后。说时迟，那时快，他一把抓住波杰斯先生的双腿，把他丢进了泰晤士河。一声粗

1. 位于伦敦地区威斯敏斯特市的方尖大石碑。1819 年，埃及统治者为了纪念尼罗河战役和亚历山大战役的胜利，将其赠予英国。

俗的咒骂和一片重重的水花飞溅之后，一切归于平静。亚瑟勋爵紧张地观望，看不到那个手相师的踪迹，只有一顶高帽在月光照耀下的河水中随漩涡旋转着。过了一会儿，高帽也沉了，再寻不到波杰斯先生的任何踪迹。他一度以为大桥楼梯上一个身形高大的怪异的人看到了他，一股挫败的恐怖感笼罩了他。不过后来他发现那只是一个倒影，当月亮从云后面出来，它就消失不见了。终于，他似乎完成了命运的裁决。他长长地舒了一口气，如释重负，嘴边呢喃着西比尔的名字。

“您丢了什么东西吗，先生？”一个声音突然出现在他身后。

他转过身，看到一个手持牛眼灯的警察。

“没什么重要的，警察先生。”他微笑着回答。他招呼了一辆路过的马车，跳上去，让车夫驶往贝尔格雷夫广场。

接下来的几天，他在希望与恐惧之间煎熬。有时候，他期待波杰斯先生走进房间；有时候，他又觉得命运不该对他如此不公。他去了两次西月街手相师的住处，可是没勇气按响门铃。他希望得到确信，又害怕它。

它终于来了。他正坐在俱乐部的吸烟室喝茶，心不

在焉地听着瑟比顿描述狂欢会上最后一首滑稽歌曲，侍者拿着晚报走进来。他拿起《圣詹姆斯报》，百无聊赖地翻看，一个奇怪的标题引起了他的注意：

一名手相师的自杀

他赶紧读起来，脸色因为兴奋而变得苍白。文章是这样写的：

> 昨天早上七点钟，著名手相师塞普蒂默斯·R. 波杰斯先生的尸体被冲刷上了船坞酒店前的格林威治河岸。这位不幸的先生已经失踪数日，手相圈已经开始担心他的安危。据推测，他由于劳累过度，引发暂时性精神错乱，进而选择了自杀，今天下午验尸陪审团也证实了这一推断。波杰斯先生刚刚完成了一篇主题为"人类手相"的优秀论文，将于不久后发表，届时必将引发广泛关注。逝者六十五岁，似乎没有任何亲眷在世。

亚瑟勋爵拿着报纸冲出俱乐部，门厅侍者惊诧万分，企图拦住他，却是徒劳。他立刻乘车赶往帕克巷。西比尔透过窗户看到了他，感觉到他似乎带来了什么好消息。她跑下楼去迎接他，当她看到他的脸，她知道云开雾散了。

“我亲爱的西比尔，”亚瑟勋爵人喊道，“我们明天就结婚吧！”

“你这个傻瓜！急什么？蛋糕都没订呢！”西比尔说着，眼眶含泪，笑逐颜开。

六

大约三个星期之后，他们举行了婚礼，圣彼得教堂挤满了身着锦衣华服的人。奇切斯特教长极其郑重庄严地主持了婚礼仪式，所有人都承认他们从没见过比这对新人更漂亮的夫妻。然而，不只是漂亮，他们还非常幸福。亚瑟勋爵从未曾有一时半刻后悔他为西比尔所承受的一切苦楚，而她也给予了他一个女人可以给予男人的最好的东西——崇拜、温柔，还有爱。对于他们而言，现实没有扼杀情爱。他们一直感到年轻。

几年之后，他们有了两个漂亮的孩子。温德米尔夫

人来到奥尔顿修道院探望他们。奥尔顿修道院是个可爱的老房子，是公爵送给儿子的结婚礼物。一天下午，她正和亚瑟夫人坐在花园里的酸橙树下，看着小男孩和小女孩像是跃动的阳光一般在玫瑰小径上蹦蹦跳跳。她突然握住女主人的手，问道："你幸福吗，西比尔？"

"亲爱的温德米尔夫人，我当然幸福。您呢？"

"我没时间幸福，西比尔。我总会喜欢新结识的人。我一旦和谁变得熟识，就会对他们厌烦。"

"您的狮子们也无法取悦您吗，温德米尔夫人？"

"哦，当然不能！狮子的趣味超不过一季。一旦它们的狮鬃被剪掉，它们就变成了世界上最无聊的东西。而且，如果你对它们非常好，它们就得寸进尺起来。你记得那个讨人厌的波杰斯先生吗？他是个大骗子。当然，我全然不在意，甚至当他想向我借钱的时候，我都原谅了他，但我无法忍受他向我求爱。他让我打心底里厌恶手相学。我现在相信传心术。那可好玩儿多了！"

"您可别在这儿说任何手相学的不好，温德米尔夫人。这是唯一一个亚瑟不喜欢别人打趣的话题。我向您保证，他是很认真的。"

"你不会告诉我他信手相学吧，西比尔？"

“您自己问他，温德米尔夫人，他来了。”亚瑟勋爵手捧着一大束黄玫瑰出现在花园中，他的两个孩子绕着他嬉闹。

“亚瑟勋爵？”

“什么事，温德米尔夫人？”

“别告诉我你相信手相学？”

“我当然相信啊。”那个年轻的男子微笑着说。

“可是，为什么呢？”

“因为我毕生的幸福都多亏了手相学。”他低声说着，坐到柳条椅上。

“我亲爱的亚瑟勋爵，它给了你什么？”

“西比尔。”他边回答，边将那束玫瑰献给妻子，并深深凝望着她紫色的眼睛。

“胡说八道！”温德米尔夫人大声说道，“我这辈子都没听过这种胡话！”

企鹅经典：小黑书　第三辑

21. 漂亮的卡桑德拉

　　[英] 简·奥斯汀

22. 温顺的女人

　　[俄] 陀思妥耶夫斯基

23. 猫与维纳斯

　　[古希腊] 伊索

24. 黄昏之读

　　[英] 查尔斯·狄更斯

25. 一个可怕的故事是如何被一条普通的屠夫的狗公之于众的

　　[德] 约翰·彼得·黑贝尔

26. 亚瑟·萨维尔勋爵的罪行

　　[英] 奥斯卡·王尔德

27. 伊凡·伊里奇之死

　　[俄] 列夫·托尔斯泰

28. 我们为何为同一件事哭和笑

　　[法] 蒙田

29. 我的生命是一杆上实弹的枪

　　[美] 艾米莉·狄金森

30. 独自在黑夜的海滩上

　　[美] 沃尔特·惠特曼

Penguin Little Black Classics Vol. III

21. JANE AUSTEN
The Beautifull Cassandra

22. FYODOR DOSTOYEVSKY
The Meek One

23. AESOP
The Cat and Venus

24. CHARLES DICKENS
To Be Read at Dusk

25. JOHANN PETER HEBEL
How a Ghastly Story Was Brought to Light by a Common or Garden Butcher's Dog

26. OSCAR WILDE
Lord Arthur Savile's Crime

27. LEO TOLSTOY
The Death of Ivan Ilyich

28. MICHEL DE MONTAIGNE
How We Weep and Laugh at the Same Thing

29. EMILY DICKINSON
My life had stood a loaded gun

30. WALT WHITMAN
On the Beach at Night Alone

PENGUIN

LITTLE BLACK

CLASSICS

PENGUIN

LITTLE BLACK

CLASSICS

‘It is only a bruise.’

LEO TOLSTOY

The Death of Ivan Ilyich

Contents

The Death of Ivan Ilyich

1

In the large law court building, during an adjournment of the Melvinsky trial, the members of the Bench and the public prosecutor had come together in the office of Ivan Yegorovich Shebek, and the conversation touched on the celebrated Krasovsky case. Fyodor Vasilyevich argued vehemently that it was beyond their jurisdiction, Ivan Yegorovich had his own view and was sticking to it, while Pyotr Ivanovich, who had kept out of the discussion at the outset and was still not contributing, was perusing a copy of the *Gazette* which had just been delivered.

'Gentlemen!' he said. 'Ivan Ilyich is dead.'

'Is he really?'

'Here you are. Read it yourself,' he said to Fyodor Vasilyevich, handing him the paper, fresh off the press and still smelling.

There was an announcement within a black border: 'It is with profound sorrow that Praskovya Fyodorovna Golovina informs family and friends that her beloved husband, Ivan Ilyich Golovin, Member of the Court of

Justice, passed away on the 4th of February this year, 1882. The funeral will take place on Friday at 1 p.m.'

Ivan Ilyich had been a colleague of the gentlemen assembled there, and they had all liked him. He had been ill for several weeks, and the word was that his illness was incurable. His post had been kept open for him, but there was an understanding that in the event of his death Alexeyev would step into his place, and Alexeyev's place would be taken by either Vinnikov or Shtabel. So, the first thought that occurred to each of the assembled gentlemen on hearing the news of his death was how this death might affect his own prospects, and those of their acquaintances, for transfer or promotion.

'I'm sure to get Shtabel's job now, or Vinnikov's,' thought Fyodor Vasilyevich. 'They promised me ages ago, and a promotion like that would give me another eight hundred roubles a year, plus expenses.'

'I must apply to have my brother-in-law transferred from Kaluga,' thought Pyotr Ivanovich. 'My wife will be delighted. She won't be able to tell me I never do anything for her people.'

'I had a feeling he wasn't going to get better,' said Pyotr Ivanovich. 'It's sad.'

'What was actually wrong with him?'

'The doctors couldn't decide. Well, they could, but they all decided differently. The last time I saw him I thought he was going to come through it.'

'And I haven't been to see him since Christmas. I kept meaning to go.'

'Was he all right financially?'

'His wife had a bit of money, I think. Nothing very much.'

'Well, we'll have to go and see her. They live an awfully long way away.'

'For you they do. Where you live, everywhere's a long way away.'

'Look at that. He can't forgive me for living across the river,' said Pyotr Ivanovich, smiling at Shebek. The conversation turned to the long distances between the different parts of the city, and then they walked back into session.

Apart from the speculations aroused in each of them by this death, concerning the transfers and possible changes that this death might bring about, the very fact of the death of someone close to them aroused in all who heard about it, as always, a feeling of delight that he had died and they hadn't.

'There you have it. He's dead, and I'm not' was what everyone thought or felt. But his closest acquaintances, Ivan Ilyich's so-called friends, couldn't help thinking that they would now have to fulfil some tedious social obligations such as attending the funeral and calling on the widow to express their condolences.

Closest of all were Fyodor Vasilyevich and Pyotr Ivanovich.

Pyotr Ivanovich was an old friend from law school, and he felt indebted to Ivan Ilyich.

Over dinner he told his wife about the death of Ivan Ilyich and the mooted possibility of her brother being transferred to their district, and then, dispensing with his usual nap, he put on a dress-coat and set off for Ivan Ilyich's house.

At the entrance stood a carriage and two cabs. Downstairs in the entrance hall, next to the coat stand, a coffin lid with silk brocade, tassels and gold braid that had been powdered and polished stood propped against a wall. Two ladies in black were taking off their fur cloaks. He knew one of them, Ivan Ilyich's sister, but not the other. His colleague Schwartz was at the top of the stairs about to come down, but when he saw Pyotr Ivanovich he stopped and gave him a wink that seemed to say, 'Ivan Ilyich has messed things up – not what you or I would have done.'

Schwartz's face, with its English sidewhiskers and his lean figure in formal dress, exuded, as always, an air of elegant solemnity and, although the solemnity belied his playful personality, it was particularly poignant here, or so it seemed to Pyotr Ivanovich.

Pyotr Ivanovich allowed the ladies to pass on ahead, and slowly followed them upstairs. Instead of coming down, Schwartz stood waiting at the top. Pyotr Ivanovich knew why; he clearly wanted to arrange a game of whist somewhere that evening. The ladies proceeded upstairs to see the widow, but Schwartz pursed his lips tightly with all seriousness, though his eyes had a mischievous look as he twitched his eyebrows, directing Pyotr Ivanovich off to the right and into the room where the dead man lay.

Pyotr Ivanovich entered the room, and hesitated, as people always do on these occasions, not knowing precisely what to do. The only thing he was certain of was that in this situation you couldn't go wrong if you made the sign of the cross. Whether or not you should bow at the same time he wasn't sure, so he went for a compromise, crossing himself as he walked in and giving a bit of a bow as he did so. At the same time, as far as hand and head movements permitted, he glanced round the room. Two young persons, nephews apparently, one of them a schoolboy, were crossing themselves as they left the room. A little old woman was standing there motionless. And a lady with curiously arched eyebrows was whispering to her. A church reader in a frock-coat – a hearty character of considerable spirit – was reading something out in a loud voice and a tone that brooked no contradiction. Gerasim, the peasant who waited at table, darted ahead of Pyotr Ivanovich, sprinkling something on the floor. Seeing this, Pyotr Ivanovich instantly recognized a slight smell of decaying flesh. When he had visited Ivan Ilyich for the last time he had seen this peasant in Ivan Ilyich's room, acting as a sick nurse, and Ivan Ilyich had had a special fondness for him.

Pyotr Ivanovich kept on crossing himself, and aimed a slight bow midway between the reader, the coffin and the icons on the corner table. Then, when the business of crossing himself seemed to be going on too long, he paused and took a close look at the dead man.

The dead man lay as all dead men lie, unusually heavy with his dead weight, with rigid limbs sinking into the soft lining of the coffin and his head bowed for eternity on the pillow, and he displayed what dead people always display, a waxen yellow forehead (with bald patches over his hollow temples) and a protruding nose that seemed to be pressing down hard on his upper lip. He had changed a good deal; he was even thinner than he had been when Pyotr Ivanovich had last seen him, but, as with all dead bodies, his face had acquired greater beauty, or, more to the point, greater significance, than it had had in life. Its expression seemed to say that what needed to be done had been done, and done properly. More than that, the expression contained a reproach, or at least a reminder, to the living. The reminder seemed out of place to Pyotr Ivanovich, or at least he felt it didn't apply to him personally. But an unpleasant feeling came over him, and he crossed himself again, hurriedly – too hurriedly, he thought, the haste was almost indecent – before turning and heading for the door.

Schwartz was waiting for him in the next room with his feet planted wide apart and both hands fiddling with the top hat held behind his back. One glance at his mischievous, immaculately elegant figure and Pyotr Ivanovich felt restored. He could see that Schwartz was above all this, and would be impervious to anything that might have been depressing. His very appearance spoke volumes: in no way would the occasion of Ivan Ilyich's funeral serve as a reason for cancelling their usual session; in other words, nothing would prevent them from breaking open a new pack and riffling through the cards that evening while a servant set up four new candles. There was, in fact, no reason to think that this occasion should stop them having a good time that very evening. He said so in a low voice to Pyotr Ivanovich as he walked past, proposing that they meet for a game at Fyodor Vasilyevich's.

But Pyotr Ivanovich was clearly not destined to play whist that evening. Praskovya Fyodorovna, a short, plump woman whose body expanded from the shoulders down despite her best efforts to the contrary, done out in black, with a lace shawl over her head and the same curiously arched eyebrows as the lady facing the coffin, emerged from her chambers with some other ladies, showed them to the door of the dead man's room, and said, 'The service is about to begin. Do go in.'

Schwartz made an indeterminate bow, and stood there without accepting or rejecting this invitation. Praskovya, recognizing Pyotr Ivanovich, gave a sigh, went straight up to him, took him by the hand, and said, 'I know you were a good friend to Ivan Ilyich . . .' And she looked at him, anticipating a suitable response. Pyotr Ivanovich knew that just as he had had to cross himself in there, out here it was necessary to squeeze her hand and say with a sigh, 'Believe me . . .' And that's what he did. Having done it, he felt that the desired effect had been achieved – he had been touched, and she had been touched.

'Let's go in before they get started. I must have a word with you,' said the widow. 'Give me your arm.'

Pyotr Ivanovich offered an arm and they made their way into the inner rooms, walking past Schwartz, who gave Pyotr Ivanovich a gloomy wink. 'No whist for you, then. You won't mind if we find another partner. We might make up a fivesome when you can get free,' said his mischievous glance.

Pyotr Ivanovich sighed even more deeply and plaintively, and Praskovya showed her gratitude by squeezing his hand. Proceeding into her drawing-room, which was done out in pink cretonne and lit by one dismal lamp, they sat down near to a table, she on a sofa, he on a low pouffe with broken springs that wobbled unevenly as he sat on it. Praskovya had wanted to warn him off into another chair, but a warning like that did not seem appropriate in the circumstances, so she thought better of it. As he sat down on his pouffe, Pyotr Ivanovich remembered the time when Ivan Ilyich had been decorating this room and had asked his advice about this pink cretonne with the green leaves. On her way past the table to sit down on the sofa – the room was crammed with furniture and knick-knacks – Praskovya snagged the black lace of her black shawl on the carved edge of the table. Pyotr Ivanovich rose slightly to disentangle it, thus releasing the pouffe, which quivered and pushed up at him. The widow began disentangling the lace herself, so Pyotr Ivanovich sat down again, crushing the rebellious pouffe back into submission. But the widow had not finished disentangling herself, so Pyotr Ivanovich rose again, and so did the pouffe, rebellious and even creaking. When this was all over, she took out a clean cambric handkerchief and burst into tears. But Pyotr Ivanovich had cooled somewhat after the episode with the lace and the battle with the pouffe, and he sat there with a scowl on his face. The embarrassment was broken when Sokolov, Ivan Ilyich's footman, came in to report that the plot which Praskovya had chosen in the cemetery was going to cost two hundred roubles. She had stopped weeping, and she looked at Pyotr Ivanovich with a victimized air as she told him in French how hard things were for her. Pyotr Ivanovich made a silent gesture to acknowledge his absolute conviction that it could not be otherwise.

'Do smoke if you would like to,' she said in a tone of voice that was magnanimous yet flat with defeat, and she went on to discuss the cost of the plot with Sokolov. As he lit his cigarette, Pyotr Ivanovich heard that she had made detailed enquiries about the cost of various plots of land before settling on the one she wanted. That was not all: once the plot had been ordered, she went on to make arrangements for the choir. Then Sokolov left.

'I'm doing everything myself,' she told Pyotr Ivanovich, pushing aside some albums on the table. Noticing that the table was under threat from the cigarette, she swiftly moved an ashtray across and spoke again. 'I think it would be hypocritical to claim that I cannot manage practicalities because of my grief. On the contrary, if anything can . . . I won't say console me, but . . . take my mind off things, it's seeing to what has to be done about him.' She took out her handkerchief again as if on the verge of tears, but suddenly she seemed to get a grip on her feelings, snapped out of it and spoke calmly. 'But there is one thing I would like to discuss with you.'

Pyotr Ivanovich bowed his head. The springs shifted under him, but he did not let them have their way.

'He suffered terribly those last few days.'

'Did he really?' asked Pyotr Ivanovich.

'Oh yes, terribly. The last few minutes, no, hours really, he never stopped screaming. He screamed for three solid days without stopping for breath. It was unbearable. I don't know how I got through it. You could hear him three rooms away. Oh, I've been through it all right!'

'And was he conscious?' asked Pyotr Ivanovich.

'Yes,' she whispered. 'To the very end. He said goodbye a quarter of an hour before he died, and he was still asking us to take Volodya away.'

For all the disagreeable awareness of hypocrisy, his

own and hers, the thought of the suffering endured by a man he had known so well, first as a happy young lad, then as a schoolboy, then as an adult colleague, left Pyotr Ivanovich with a feeling of horror. Once again he could see that forehead, the nose pressing down on the upper lip, and he felt a pang of fear for himself.

'Three days and three nights of horrible suffering, and then death. Just think, it could happen to me any time, now,' he thought, and he felt that momentary pang of fear. But immediately he was saved, without knowing how, by the old familiar idea that this had happened to Ivan Ilyich, not him, and it could not and would not happen to him, and that kind of thinking would put him in a gloomy mood, for which there was no need, as Schwartz's face had clearly demonstrated. Pursuing this line of thought, Pyotr Ivanovich calmed down and began to show a close interest in the details of Ivan Ilyich's death, as if death was a chance experience that may have applied to Ivan Ilyich but certainly didn't apply to him.

After giving a detailed account of the truly horrendous physical agony that Ivan Ilyich had endured (details that Pyotr Ivanovich learned only in terms of the distressing effect they had had on Praskovya), the widow clearly saw that it was now necessary to get down to business.

'Oh, Pyotr Ivanovich, it's dreadful, absolutely dreadful.' She burst into tears again.

Pyotr Ivanovich gave a sigh, and waited for her to blow her nose. When she had blown her nose, he said, 'Believe me . . .' Then she spoke out again, and told him what must have been the main reason for consulting him: it was all a matter of using the death of her husband to get some money from the Treasury. She made it seem as if she was asking Pyotr Ivanovich's advice about getting a pension, but he could see that here she knew more than he did, she knew the finest details of this subject down to the last penny that could be screwed out of the Treasury in terms of death benefits. What she wanted to know was whether there might be some way of screwing a bit more out of them. Pyotr Ivanovich tried to think of some way of doing this but, having given it some thought and doing the decent thing by cursing the government for being so stingy, he said he thought there was no more to be had. Upon which she gave a sigh, and made no bones about getting rid of her visitor. He got the message, stubbed his cigarette out, stood up, shook hands, and went out into the hall.

In the dining-room with the clock that Ivan Ilyich had prided himself on having acquired in an antique shop, Pyotr Ivanovich came across a priest and a number of people that he knew, here for the funeral, and he saw a pretty young lady whom he also knew, Ivan Ilyich's daughter. She was all in black. Her tiny waist looked tinier than ever. She looked gloomy, assertive, almost truculent. She bowed to Pyotr Ivanovich in a way that suggested he was to blame for something. Behind the daughter stood a wealthy young man, also known to

Pyotr Ivanovich, who looked no less offended – he was an examining magistrate, her fiancé by all accounts. Pyotr Ivanovich gave a gloomy bow in their direction and was about to walk through into the dead man's room when Ivan Ilyich's schoolboy son, the image of his father, appeared from behind the stairwell. This was the little Ivan Ilyich that Pyotr Ivanovich remembered from law school. His tear-filled eyes were those of a twelve- or thirteen-year-old boy who has lost his innocence. Seeing Pyotr Ivanovich, he looked embarrassed and scowled morosely. Pyotr Ivanovich gave him a nod and walked into the dead man's room. The funeral service was soon under way – candles, moaning, incense, tears, sobbing. Pyotr Ivanovich stood there with a frown on his face, staring at the legs of those in front of him. Not once did he look at the dead man or succumb to any feelings of weakness; he was one of the first to leave. There was no one in the hall. Gerasim, the servant of peasant stock, darted out of the dead man's room, and sorted through all the fur coats with his big strong hands before finding Pyotr Ivanovich's coat and handing it over.

'Gerasim. How are you feeling, my boy?' said Pyotr Ivanovich, who had to say something. 'A bit sad?'

''Tis God's will, sir. 'Twill come to us all,' said Gerasim, displaying an even white row of peasant's teeth, and then, with the air of a man with a lot of work to do, he wrenched the door open, called the driver up and sprang back to the porch steps, wondering what else needed to be done.

Pyotr Ivanovich found it particularly pleasant to inhale the fresh air after the incense, the corpse and carbolic.

'Where to, sir?' asked the coachman.

'It's still quite early. I think I'll drop in on Fyodor Vasilyevich.'

And that's where he went. And there they were, sure enough, finishing the first rubber. He was just in time to make up a fifth.

2

The past history of Ivan Ilyich's life had been straightforward, ordinary and dreadful in the extreme.

Ivan Ilyich had died at forty-five, a member of the Court of Justice. He was the son of an official who had worked his way through various ministries and departments in Petersburg, carving out the kind of career which brings people to a position from which, despite their obvious incapacity for doing anything remotely useful, they cannot be sacked because of their status and long years of service, so they end up being given wholly false and fictitious jobs to do for which they receive salaries that are anything but fictitious, anything from six to ten thousand a year, and this enables them to live on to a ripe old age.

Such a man was Ilya Yefimovich Golovin, Privy Councillor, superfluous member of various superfluous institutions.

He had three sons. Ivan Ilyich was the second son. The eldest had carved out the same career as his father but in a different ministry, and was now near to achieving the kind of seniority that confers sinecure status. The third son was a failure. He had gone through a series of jobs, ruining his prospects in all of them, and he now worked for the railways. His father, his brothers and especially their wives not only hated meeting him but forgot his existence unless compelled to do otherwise. Their sister had married Baron Greff, a Petersburg official cut from the same cloth as his father-in-law. Ivan Ilyich was what they called *le phénix de la famille*. He was neither as cold and starchy as the elder brother nor as profligate as the younger. He was halfway between – an intelligent, lively, personable and decent man. He had attended law school along with his younger brother. The younger brother didn't finish the course; he was expelled in the fifth grade, whereas Ivan Ilyich passed with honours. As a student he was already the kind of person he remained for the rest of his life, a capable man, cheerful and kind, sociable and convinced of the need to follow the path of duty – duty being anything so designated by higher authority. Boy and man he had avoided toadyism, but from his earliest years he was like a moth to the flame in being drawn towards people in authority, he assumed their mannerisms along with their philosophy of life, and he was on good terms with them. All the distractions of childhood and youth had passed him by leaving scarcely a trace; he had succumbed to both sensuality and vanity, and then in the top classes to liberal thinking, but always within limits unerringly set by his own instinctive feelings.

In his student days he had done things that at first he thought of as utterly revolting, things that made him feel disgusted with himself even as he was doing them, but in later life, noticing that the same things were being done by people of high standing without a qualm, although he couldn't quite bring himself to think they were good, he did manage to dismiss them, and he felt no pangs of remorse when he recalled them.

When he graduated from law school, qualifying for the tenth grade of the civil service, and received enough money from his father to buy his basic necessities, Ivan Ilyich ordered a new set of clothes from Scharmer's, hung a medallion on his watch chain inscribed with the words *Respice finem*, said goodbye to the prince and principal, dined at Donon's with his friends, and set off for one of the provinces with his fashionable luggage, linen, clothes, shaving tackle, toiletries and travelling rug, all ordered and purchased from the very best shops, to take up a position arranged for him by his father as special assistant to the governor.

In the provinces it did not take Ivan Ilyich long to

arrange a lifestyle that was as easy and agreeable as the one he had enjoyed at law school. He did his work, pursued his career and at the same time discreetly enjoyed himself. He went off now and then on official visits to country districts, cutting a dignified figure with superiors and inferiors alike, and he prided himself on carrying out his duties, especially in matters concerning religious dissidents, with scrupulous fairness and incorruptibility.

In his official duties, despite his youth and an attitude of some frivolity, he was exceedingly conservative, bureaucratic and even forbidding, but on the social side he was often amusing and witty, and always pleasantly polite – what the governor and the governor's wife called a *bon enfant*, and with them he was like one of the family.

In the provinces he had an affair with a lady only too keen to liaise with a smart young lawyer. There was also a milliner, and there were drinking sessions with visiting aides-de-camp, as well as after-dinner excursions to a certain street on the outskirts. There was a need to work on the governor and even the governor's wife in order to win them over. But all of this bore the stamp of high respectability to such an extent that no one could have called it by a bad name; all of it was catered for by what the French describe as 'youth having its fling'. All of it was conducted with clean hands, in clean linen, in French phrases, and – what mattered most – at the highest level of society, which meant with approval from those in authority.

Ivan Ilyich spent five years in this kind of service, but the time came for a career change. New legal institutions were opening up; new men were needed.

Ivan Ilyich became one of the new men.

Ivan Ilyich was offered the post of examining magistrate, and he took it, even though it meant moving to a new province, dropping all his old contacts and establishing new ones. Ivan Ilyich was given a send-off by his friends, who presented him with a silver cigarette case; they had a group photograph taken, and off he went to his new job.

As an examining magistrate Ivan Ilyich was just as *comme il faut* and respectable, just as capable of separating official duty from private life and earning respect as he had been when working as a special assistant to the governor. The new work itself struck Ivan Ilyich as far more interesting and rewarding than his earlier job. Before, he had quite liked strutting about in his Scharmer uniform, sauntering past anxious petitioners and envious officials and walking straight into the governor's office, where he would sit down for a cup of tea and a smoke. But not many people had been under his authority – only the rural police chiefs and the religious dissidents that he came across on his assignments – and he loved to treat these dependent people with a courteous, almost comradely spirit, he loved to let them feel that although he had the power to crush them he was being straight with them, treating them like friends. There had not been many of them then, but now that Ivan Ilyich was an examining magistrate he felt that everyone without exception was in his power, even the most important and self-satisfied of people; at a stroke from his pen on headed notepaper any important or self-satisfied person could be brought before him as a defendant or witness to answer questions and be kept on his feet if Ivan Ilyich chose not to let him sit down. Far from abusing this power, he did his best to play it down, but his consciousness of that power and the very chance to play it down were what gave his new job its interest and appeal. In the work itself, the process of investigation, Ivan Ilyich soon mastered the technique of distancing himself from all irrelevancies and reducing the most complicated cases to a version that could be set down on paper in objective outline, excluding any personal opinion on his part, while observing all the necessary formalities, which was what mattered most. This was the new way of working, and he was one of the first men to implement the reformed Legal Code of 1864.

Ivan Ilyich's transfer to a new town and the post of examining magistrate meant meeting new people and making new contacts; he also struck a new attitude, and slightly changed his tone. The new attitude involved distancing himself somewhat from the provincial authorities while cultivating the best circles among the judiciary and the wealthy gentry of the town, and the new tone entailed mild dissatisfaction with the government, a degree of liberalism and a civilized man's sense of public duty. At the same time, without compromising the fastidiousness of his dress sense, in his new situation he left his chin unshaven, allowing his beard to grow as and where it wanted.

In his new town, too, Ivan Ilyich set himself up very nicely. The section of society opposed to the governor was friendly and agreeable, his pay had gone up, and one thing that made his life particularly pleasurable was the playing of whist, which he now took to with the enjoyment of a skilled card-player, astute, quick-thinking and almost invariably a winner.

After two years working in the new town Ivan Ilyich met his future wife. Praskovya Fyodorovna Mikhel was the most attractive, intelligent and colourful young lady in the social circle frequented by Ivan Ilyich. To the list of other distractions and relaxations from his work as an examining magistrate Ivan Ilyich added a mild flirtation with Praskovya.

When he had been an assistant on special commissions Ivan Ilyich had been quite a dancer, but now he was an examining magistrate he took to the floor much less frequently. When he danced it was only as if to say, 'Look, I may be part of the reformed system, and I've got as far as Grade 5, but if you want to see me on the floor I can show you that even in dancing I can be the best.' So, just occasionally, he would take to the floor with Praskovya at the end of an evening, and it was actually while dancing like this that he won her heart. She fell in love with him. Ivan Ilyich had no clear and definite plans for marriage, but once the girl fell in love with him he began to wonder. 'When all's said and done, why shouldn't I get married?' he asked himself.

This young woman, Praskovya Fyodorovna, belonged to a good family, and she was quite attractive. She also came with a little money. Ivan Ilyich might have held out for a more brilliant partner, but she was herself a decent catch. Ivan was earning good money, and he could count on something similar from her. It would be a good match – she was a nice girl, quite pretty and a thoroughly decent young woman. To claim that Ivan Ilyich got married because he was in love with his bride, and saw in her someone who shared his outlook on life, would have been no more justifiable than to say that he married because the match met with the approval of the society that he moved in. Ivan Ilyich married for both reasons. He was pleasing himself by acquiring such a wife, but at the same time he was appealing to his superiors and their sense of propriety.

So, Ivan Ilyich got married.

The process of getting married, and the early days of married life, with conjugal caresses, new furniture, new crockery, new linen, everything up to his wife's pregnancy, went very smoothly, to the extent that Ivan Ilyich was beginning to think that marriage would not disrupt his easy, agreeable and enjoyable lifestyle, which was decency itself, approved of by society and something that Ivan Ilyich considered to be part of life itself – and it might even improve it. But it was at this stage, during the first months of his wife's pregnancy, that something happened, something new, unexpected, unpleasant, difficult and disgusting, something that could not have been anticipated and could not in any way be got rid of.

For no reason that Ivan Ilyich could fathom, other than what he called *gaîté de coeur*, his wife did begin to disrupt the pleasant and decent run of his life. She became jealous of him for no apparent cause, demanded his closest attention, laid into him and started arguments that were unpleasantly vulgar.

At first Ivan Ilyich hoped to escape the unpleasantness of his new situation by relapsing into the same carefree but respectable way of life that had stood him in good stead before – he tried to ignore his wife's moodiness and carry on in the easy, agreeable way that he had formerly enjoyed, inviting friends round for a game of cards and trying to get out and drive round to the club or visit people close to him. But there came a time when his wife started shouting at him so furiously, using such foul language, determined to keep on yelling at him when he failed to do what she wanted, obviously with every intention of keeping it up until he came to heel, stayed in and went through the same anguish that she felt, that Ivan

Ilyich was horrified. He realized that married life – at least with his wife – didn't always mean enjoyment and decency, but, on the contrary, it often disrupted them, and it was therefore necessary to guard against such disruptions. And Ivan Ilyich began to seek ways of doing this. His work was the one thing that impressed Praskovya, and it was through work and the commitments associated with it that he took on his wife and asserted his own independence.

When the baby was born, with the various difficulties with feeding, the real and imaginary illnesses of mother and child, which demanded his sympathetic involvement even though he understood nothing about them, the need for Ivan Ilyich to safeguard his independence became even more urgent.

As his wife grew more and more irritable and demanding, Ivan Ilyich gradually shifted his life's centre of gravity on to his work. He loved his work more and more, and became more ambitious than he had been.

It didn't take him long – no more than a year after his wedding – to realize that although married life did provide some conveniences, it was actually rather a complex and difficult business, and the path of duty, which meant leading a decent life approved of by society, called for a clearly defined attitude, as at work.

And Ivan Ilyich managed to establish such an attitude towards his married life. He required of it whatever domestic conveniences it could provide in terms of meals on the table, a good household and a bed and, most important, the outward show of respectability that society required. Beyond this, he required some enjoyment and pleasure, and if he found this he was very thankful, but if he was met with rejection and crabbiness he immediately took himself off into his own separate, carefully guarded world, the world of work which gave him pleasure.

Ivan Ilyich was considered a good colleague, and within three years he was promoted to assistant chief prosecutor. His new responsibilities, the importance that they entailed, the opportunity of bringing people before the court and sending them to prison, the publicity given to his speeches, and the success enjoyed by Ivan Ilyich in these matters – all of this made his work seem even more enjoyable.

Other children were born. His wife was becoming more and more bad-tempered and crabby, but the new attitude established by Ivan Ilyich towards his home life made him all but impervious to her crabbiness.

After serving for seven years in the same town Ivan Ilyich was transferred to another province, as public prosecutor. They moved, they were short of money, and his wife didn't like the town they had moved to. His salary had gone up, but so had their living expenses. On top of that, two of their children died, and family life became even more unpleasant for Ivan Ilyich.

Praskovya blamed her husband for all the setbacks they

were suffering in their new place of residence. Most of the topics of conversation between husband and wife, especially about bringing up the children, led to questions that reminded them of past arguments, and new arguments were liable to flare up at any moment. They were left with a few short periods of amorousness that came over them as husband and wife, but these did not last long. These were nothing more than little islands where they could anchor for a while, only to plunge back into a sea of hidden hostility as they grew further and further apart. This growing apart might have upset Ivan Ilyich if he had thought there was anything wrong with it, but now not only did he consider this state of affairs to be quite normal, he saw it as the whole point of his role in the family. His role was to distance himself increasingly from all the unpleasantness and give it an air of harmless respectability; this he achieved by spending less and less time with the family, and when he was forced to be with them he sought to safeguard his own position by ensuring the presence of others. But the main thing was that Ivan Ilyich did have his work. It was in the world of his work that the whole interest of his life came into focus. And this interest absorbed him totally. The knowledge of the power that he wielded, the possibility of ruining anyone that he fancied ruining, the gravitas (even if it was all outward show) which could be sensed as he walked into court or dealt with his subordinates, the success that he was enjoying with his superiors and subordinates alike, and, above all, his masterly handling of the cases – all of this gave him pleasure, and, along with chit-chat with colleagues, dinners and whist, filled his life to the full. And so, life in general proceeded for Ivan Ilyich just as he thought it should proceed – pleasantly and respectably.

He lived like this for about seven years. Their daughter, the eldest child, was now sixteen, another child had died and their one remaining son was the subject of strong disagreement. Ivan Ilyich wanted to send him to law school, but Praskovya had defied him by putting him down for the high school. The daughter was being educated at home, and was developing nicely; the boy too was doing quite well at his studies.

3

This was the course that Ivan Ilyich's life had taken during the seventeen years that followed his wedding. He was now a senior public prosecutor who had turned down several transfers in the hope of securing an even more desirable position, but then suddenly an unpleasant circumstance arose which looked like completely disrupting the peaceful progress of his life. Ivan Ilyich was expecting an appointment as presiding judge in a university town, but Hoppe pipped him at the post and got the job. Ivan Ilyich was livid, and he made some insinuations, taking issue with Hoppe himself and his immediate superiors. He was met with a chill rebuff, and was overlooked again when the next appointment came up.

This was in 1880. That year was the hardest he ever lived through. It was a year in which it transpired, for one thing, that they couldn't make ends meet financially, and, for another, that he was a forgotten man and, whereas he saw himself as the victim of an outrageously cruel injustice, everyone else thought it was just the way things went. Even his father saw it as no duty of his to help out. He felt deserted by everyone; they all thought that his situation, with a salary of three thousand five hundred roubles, was perfectly normal, even fortunate. He was the only person who knew that, with all the injustices that had been visited upon him, with nothing but nagging from his wife, and the debts that were now mounting up because he was living beyond his means – he was the only one who knew that his position was anything but normal.

That summer, in order to cut costs, he took leave of absence and went with his wife for a country holiday at her brother's place. In the country, with no work to occupy him, Ivan Ilyich had his first experience of not just boredom but unbearable anguish. He decided he couldn't go on like this – definite steps must be taken.

During a sleepless night, the whole of which he spent pacing the terrace, he decided he would go to Petersburg and make representations; he would get his own back on *those men* who had underestimated him, by changing ministries. Next morning he defied all the remonstrations from his wife and brother-in-law, and left for Petersburg.

He went with one aim in mind: to get himself a position that would bring in five thousand a year. By now he had no allegiance to any particular ministry, faction or function. All he needed was a job, a job that would bring in five thousand a year, in administration, in one of the banks, with the railways, in one of the charitable institutions set up by the Dowager Empress Maria, even in the customs service; all that mattered was five thousand a year and an immediate transfer from the ministry where he was so undervalued.

And his trip was crowned with unexpected, unbelievable success. At Kursk, an acquaintance of his, F. S. Ilyin, got into his first-class carriage, sat down and told him that the governor of the province had just received a telegram informing him of a reshuffle in the ministry – Pyotr Ivanovich was being replaced by Ivan Semyonovich.

The proposed reshuffle, whatever its impact on Russia at large, meant something special to Ivan Ilyich: the emergence of Pyotr Petrovich, and also apparently his friend, Zakhar Ivanovich, was very good news for him. Zakhar Ivanovich was a colleague and friend.

The new development had been confirmed in Moscow; now, arriving in Petersburg, Ivan Ilyich looked up

Zakhar, who promised him a definite position in his former department, the Ministry of Justice.

Within a week he was able to send the following telegram to his wife: *Zakhar replaces Miller. Appointment mine with first report.*

Because of this change of staff Ivan Ilyich had suddenly achieved a position in his former ministry which put him two grades higher than his colleagues, with five thousand a year plus three thousand five hundred roubles removal expenses. All the acrimony that he had felt towards his enemies and the ministry in general was forgotten, and Ivan Ilyich was a happy man.

He returned to the country feeling in high spirits, more contented than he had been for a long time. Praskovya's spirits had also picked up, and a truce was declared between the two of them. Ivan Ilyich described how honoured he had been in Petersburg, how his former enemies had been put to shame and were now licking his boots, how people envied him his new position, and, most of all, how popular he had been in Petersburg.

Praskovya listened to all of this, pretending to believe it and not querying anything, but her real interest was only in sketching out the new way of life that they would lead in the city to which they were moving. And Ivan Ilyich was delighted to see that her plans were his plans, they were together as one, and that his life, having hit a bad patch, was now getting back to its old way, its true path of happy enjoyment and respectability.

Ivan Ilyich had not come back for long. He had to take up his duties on the 10th of September, and before that he had to settle into new surroundings, have all his things brought in from the provinces, buy in and order up many more items – in other words he had set up home just as he had worked things out in his own mind, which was almost exactly as Praskovya had worked things out in her own heart.

And now that everything had been set up so successfully, and he and his wife were agreed in their aims, having lived together so little of late, they came together more closely than at any time since they were first married. Ivan Ilyich had intended to move his family in straightaway, but at the insistence of his sister-in-law and brother-in-law, who were suddenly all over Ivan Ilyich and his family, it was arranged for him to go on alone.

Ivan Ilyich set out on his journey. The happy feelings brought on by his success and a rapprochement with his wife, each intensifying the other, never left him. He found a delightful place, a dream apartment for him and his wife. The spacious, high-ceilinged reception rooms with their old-fashioned décor, the gracefully appointed and comfortable study, the rooms for his wife and daughter, the classroom for his son – all of it seemed to have been designed with them in mind. Ivan Ilyich took it upon himself to organize the fittings and furnishings; he chose the wallpaper, purchased furniture, predominantly of the old-fashioned style which he considered to be *comme il faut*, the upholstery . . . and the whole thing grew and grew, approaching the ideal that he had set himself. Even halfway through the refurbishment, the whole thing exceeded his expectations. He could see how elegant it would all be, quite *comme il faut* and devoid of vulgarity, when it was completed. As he went to sleep he would imagine what the large reception room was going to look like. When he glanced into the half-finished drawing-room he could envisage the fireplace, the screen, the whatnot and the little chairs dotted about the room, the plates and dishes on the walls and the bronze pieces, everything in its proper place. He enjoyed the thought of surprising Pasha and Lizanka, who were not without taste themselves. This was beyond their expectations. He had been particularly successful in tracking down antiques and buying them at bargain prices; they now gave the whole place an air of distinction. He deliberately understated everything in his letters home so that they would be surprised. He was so taken up with all of this that the work he loved so dearly interested him less than he had thought it would. In court he found his mind wandering; he would be miles away, wondering whether to have plain or moulded cornices with his curtains. He became so involved that he often did the work himself, rearranging the furniture and rehanging the curtains. On one occasion, climbing a stepladder to show a dull-witted upholsterer how to hang the draperies, he slipped and fell, though he was strong and agile enough to hold on, and all he did was bump his side on a window-frame knob. The bruised place hurt for a while but it soon passed off. And all this time Ivan Ilyich felt particularly well and in the best of spirits. 'I seem to have shed fifteen years,' he wrote home. He had hoped to get it all finished by the end of September, but things dragged on until mid-October. Still, it was magnificent, and he wasn't the only one to say so – everybody did.

But these were essentially the accoutrements that appeal to all people who are not actually rich but who want to look rich, though all they manage to do is look like each other: damasks, ebony, plants, rugs and bronzes, anything dark and gleaming – everything that all people of a certain class affect so as to be like all other people of a certain class. And his arrangements looked so much like everyone else's that they were unremarkable, though he saw them as something truly distinctive. When he met his family at the railway station, brought them home and ushered them into his well-lit furnished apartment and a footman wearing a white tie opened the door into the entrance hall decorated with flowers, and then they went into the drawing-room and the study, ooh-ing and ah-ing with delight, he was a very happy man, showing them around everywhere, revelling in their praise and beaming with delight. That evening, as they took tea, when Praskovya asked him casually about his fall he gave a laugh and demonstrated how he had gone flying and given the upholsterer a scare.

'It's a good job I'm athletic. Any other man would have killed himself, but all I did was bruise myself a bit here. It hurts when you touch it, but it's getting better. It is only a bruise.'

And so they began life in their new abode, where, as always happens with people who have recently settled in, they found themselves just one room short, and their new income wouldn't quite run to it, though it was only a matter of five hundred roubles or so. Still, they were very nicely off, especially during the early days when not everything was finished and work was still to be done – things had to be bought, ordered, rearranged, adjusted. There were one or two disagreements between husband and wife, but both of them were so satisfied and so busy that everything resolved itself without serious arguments. When there was nothing more to be finished off they developed a feeling of dullness and a sense of something missing, but by this time they had got to know new people and formed new habits. Their lives had filled out.

Ivan Ilyich would return for lunch after a morning in court and in those early days he tended to be in a good mood; any slight distress that he suffered came from the apartment itself. (The slightest stain on a tablecloth or upholstery, or a loose cord on the draperies annoyed him; he had put so much effort into the furnishings that the slightest disturbance upset him.) But, all things considered, Ivan Ilyich's life went along, as he saw it, just as life ought to go – easily, pleasantly, decently. He rose at nine, drank some coffee, read the newspaper, then put on his uniform and went to court. There, the collar that he worked in had been worn into shape and he soon found that it fitted him well – the petitioners, the enquiries received, the office, the public sessions and the administrative meetings. In all of this the trick was to eliminate the element of crude everyday life that always disrupts the smooth flow of official business; no relationships should be entered into beyond the official ones, the reason behind any relationship had to be strictly official and the relationship itself had to be strictly official. Say, for example, a person arrives wanting to know something. This is not the responsibility of Ivan Ilyich; he can have no relationship with such a person. But if this person were to approach him in his capacity as a member of the judiciary and in a relationship that can be set down on letterhead paper, within the terms of that relationship Ivan Ilyich will do anything he can, and do it decisively, while maintaining a semblance of friendly human relations – nothing more than common courtesy. At the point where an official relationship breaks off, everything else breaks off, too. The skill of compartmentalizing the official side of things and keeping that apart from his own real life was one that Ivan Ilyich possessed in the highest degree; long practice and natural talent had enabled him to refine it to such a degree that now he could act like a virtuoso performer, occasionally allowing himself to mix human and official relationships by way of a joke. He allowed himself this liberty because he felt strong enough whenever necessary to reinstate the distinction between the official and the human by discarding the latter. This was more than just an easy, pleasant and decent thing for Ivan Ilyich to do – he was acting like a virtuoso performer. During his breaks he would have a smoke, drink tea and chat, exchange a word or two about politics, current affairs and cards, and a whole lot more about who was in and who was out. And he would go home tired, but feeling like a virtuoso performer, a first violin in the orchestra, who has given of his best. At home his daughter and his wife would either have been out visiting or would have entertained someone at home, while his son, back from school, would have had a session with his private tutors and gone on to cram whatever it is they teach in schools. Everything was fine. After dinner, if there were no guests, Ivan Ilyich sometimes read a book that people were talking about, and later in the evening he sat down to do some work, reading through papers, studying the law, comparing depositions and sorting them by statute. This neither bored nor amused him. He found it boring when he might have been playing whist, but if whist was off it was better than just sitting there on his own or with his wife. What gave Ivan Ilyich real pleasure, though, was having little dinner parties to which he would invite ladies and gentlemen of good social standing and passing the time with them precisely as such people invariably do pass the time, in the way that his drawing-room was exactly like all the others.

One day they held an evening party with dancing. Ivan Ilyich enjoyed it and everything went swimmingly, except for a big row between him and his wife over the cakes and sweets. Praskovya had had her own ideas, but Ivan Ilyich had insisted on bringing in an expensive caterer who had provided too many cakes; the leftovers had caused the row when the caterer's bill came to forty-five roubles. The row was a big one, very nasty, and it ended with Praskovya calling him a stupid fool while he clutched his head and muttered something about divorce. But he still enjoyed the party. The best people were there and Ivan Ilyich danced with Princess Trufonova, whose sister had famously founded the charity known as 'Take Away My Sorrow'. Pleasure derived from work was self-indulgence, pleasure derived from socializing tickled his vanity, but real pleasure came to Ivan Ilyich only from playing cards. He was prepared to admit that, at the end of the day, with any amount of unpleasantness behind him, the one pleasure that outshone all others like a beacon was to sit down and play whist with quiet-mannered partners, good players, always in a foursome (sitting out was such a bore when there were five, and you had to pretend not to mind), and playing seriously and playing well (when you got a decent hand) before going on to supper with a glass of wine. And after a game of cards, especially if he had won a small amount (big winnings were not nice), Ivan Ilyich would go to bed in the very best of spirits.

This was how they lived. They moved in the best of circles, receiving people of quality, and the younger set.

In their attitude towards the circle of their acquaintances husband, wife and daughter were of one mind. Without collusion, each of them in the same way shrugged off and discarded all the shabby friends and relatives who flocked around fawning on them in the drawing-room with the Japanese plates on the walls. It wasn't long before the shabby friends stopped flocking around and left the Golovin family to the best people in society and no one else. Young men were attracted to their little Liza and one examining magistrate by the name of Petrishchev, the son of Dmitriy Ivanovich Petrishchev and his sole heir, became so attentive towards her that Ivan Ilyich mentioned this once or twice to Praskovya and wondered whether they ought perhaps to take them out for a ride in a troika or set up some private theatricals. This was how they lived. This was how things went, nothing changed, and everything was fine.

4

They were all in good health. The fact that Ivan Ilyich sometimes complained of a strange taste in his mouth and a funny feeling in his left side didn't count as ill health. But as it happened this funny feeling began to get worse and turned into, if not pain exactly, a constant dragging sensation in his side, which put him in a bad mood. And this bad mood, which got worse and worse, began to spoil the pleasant, easy-going and respectable way of life that the Golovins had just set up for themselves. There were more and more quarrels between husband and wife, the pleasant, easy-going way of life lapsed, and they were hard put to keep up an appearance of decency. Once again scenes became more and more frequent. They were left once again with nothing more than those little islands, all too few of them, on which husband and wife could come together without an explosion.

And now Praskovya began to say, not without justification, that her husband was a hard man. With her usual capacity for exaggeration she claimed that he had always been horrible like that and only her good nature had enabled her to put up with it for twenty years. It was true that all the arguments now began on his side. His jibes always started just as they sat down to dinner, often over the soup. There was always something – if it wasn't chipped crockery or something wrong with the food, he would go on about his son putting his elbow on the table or his daughter's hair. And it was always Praskovya's fault. To begin with, Praskovya would take issue with him and say something nasty, but on a couple of occasions he flew into such a rage at the beginning of dinner that she realized this was a pathological condition brought on by consuming food, so she bit it all back, stopped objecting and got on with her dinner as fast as she could. Praskovya took great pride in biting things back. Convinced that her husband was a horrible man who had made her life a misery, she was now sorry for herself. And the sorrier she became, the more she hated her husband. She began to wish he was dead, and then not to, because without him there would be no income. All of which made her even more exasperated with him. She felt thoroughly miserable at the thought that not even his death could rescue her. She was exasperated, though she hid it, but her hidden exasperation served only to strengthen his exasperation.

After one scene during which Ivan Ilyich had been particularly unfair and after which, by way of explanation, he had admitted being exasperating but claimed he was ill, she told him that if he was ill he needed treatment and insisted that he must go and see a famous doctor.

He did. The whole thing turned out just as he had expected, and as it always does. He was made to wait, the doctor was full of his own importance – an attitude he was familiar with because it was one that he himself assumed in court – then came all the tapping and listening, the questions with predetermined and obviously superfluous answers, the knowing look that seemed to say, 'Just place yourself in our hands and we'll sort it out, we know what we're doing, there's no doubt about it, we can sort things out the same way as we would for anyone you care to name.' It was just like being in court. The way he looked at the accused in court was exactly the way he was being looked at now by the famous doctor.

The doctor was holding forth. Such-and-such demonstrates that in your insides there is such-and-such, but if this is not confirmed by our tests on this-and-that then you will need to go on to such-and-such. And if you go on to such-and-such, then . . . and so on. As far as Ivan Ilyich was concerned there was only one question that mattered: is this condition life-threatening or not? But the doctor treated this question as irrelevant, and ignored it. From the doctor's point of view it was a pointless question not worthy of discussion; the only thing was a balancing of probabilities – floating kidney, chronic colitis, problem with the blind gut. The question of Ivan Ilyich living or dying didn't arise; there was just this conflict between the floating kidney and the blind gut. And before his very eyes the doctor resolved the conflict at a brilliant stroke in favour of the floating kidney, with the sole proviso that new evidence might emerge from the urine test, and if that happened the case would have to be reviewed. All of it from start to finish was precisely what Ivan Ilyich himself had done to the accused a thousand times and with no less brilliance. Brilliant indeed was the doctor's summing-up of the situation as he looked in triumph bordering on delight over his glasses at his own prisoner in the dock. From the summary Ivan Ilyich drew only one conclusion: he was in a bad way and the doctor didn't care, nobody cared probably, but he was in a bad way. And this conclusion left Ivan Ilyich with a sickly feeling, filling him with self-pity and great animosity towards the doctor who showed so much indifference to such an important question.

But he said nothing about it. He got up, laid his money on the table and said, with a sigh, 'I'm sure that when we're ill we ask a lot of pointless questions. But, er, is it life-threatening or not . . . ?'

The doctor glared at him through one eye over his glasses as if to say, 'Prisoner in the dock, if you will not confine yourself to answering the questions put to you I shall have to arrange for you to be removed from the courtroom.'

'I have already told you what I consider necessary and appropriate. Anything further will be determined by the tests.' The doctor bowed.

Ivan Ilyich walked out slowly, climbed gloomily into his sledge and drove home. All the way back he kept going over in his mind everything the doctor had said, trying to translate his confusingly complex technicalities into everyday speech and find in them an answer to one question: am I in a bad way, a really bad way, or is it nothing to worry about just now? And it seemed to him that the message from all that the doctor had said was yes, you're in a very bad way. Ivan Ilyich thought the streets looked dismal. The drivers looked dismal, the houses looked dismal, and so did the pedestrians and the shops. And in the light of the doctor's confusing pronouncements the pain, that dull, nagging pain that never went away, was taking on a new and more serious significance. It was with a new feeling of dejection that Ivan Ilyich focused on it.

He reached home and started to tell his wife. His wife listened closely, but halfway through his account their daughter came in wearing a little hat – she and her mother were on their way out. She made an effort to sit down and listen to his boring story, but she couldn't contain herself for long and her mother gave up listening.

'Well, I'm very pleased,' said his wife. 'And now, you listen to me. Make sure you take your medicine properly. Give me the prescription and I'll send Gerasim to the chemist's.' And she went off to get dressed.

He had hardly paused for breath while she was in the room, and when she went out he gave a deep sigh.

'Oh well,' he said. 'Maybe that's right. Nothing to worry about just now . . .'

He started taking his medicine and following the doctor's instructions, though these were changed once the urine test results were in. But at this point it turned out that there was some confusion over the test itself and what was supposed to follow it. Without getting at the doctor, it was becoming clear that what was going on was not what the doctor had said. He must have overlooked something, or he had been telling lies, or he was hiding something.

Nevertheless, Ivan Ilyich started to follow his instructions, and from the process of doing so he derived some comfort for a while. Since his visit to the doctor Ivan Ilyich had made it his main preoccupation to follow all instructions to the letter in matters of hygiene, the taking of medicine, focusing on his pain and monitoring all his bodily functions. His main interests were in human sickness and human health. When he overheard anyone talking about people who had fallen ill, died or recovered, especially if the illness sounded like his own, he tried to hide his agitation but he listened closely, asked lots of questions and applied what he heard to his own illness.

The pain was not getting any less, but Ivan Ilyich made every effort to make himself believe he was feeling better. And he was able to delude himself as long as nothing upset him. But the moment he fell out with his wife, or something went wrong at work or he got a bad hand at whist, he felt the full force of his illness. Before this he had been able to withstand setbacks like these, expecting to put things right before long, to win through, succeed again, come out with a grand slam. But now the slightest setback cut the ground from under him and left him in despair. He would say to himself, 'Look at that. I was just starting to get better and the medicine was just beginning to work, and now this damn thing comes up, this rotten luck . . .' And he raged against his misfortune or against those people who were causing his problems and killing him off; he sensed that it was his own rage that was killing him and he couldn't control it. It ought to have been obvious to him that raging against his situation and the people around him was only feeding his illness and, because of that, he ought to ignore any unpleasant developments, but he thought the exact opposite: he told himself he needed peace of mind so he had to get on to anything that disrupted his peace of mind, and the slightest disruption left him exasperated. His situation was made worse by the fact that he had taken to reading medical books and consulting doctors. The decline was so gradual that he was able to delude himself by comparing one day with another and seeing little difference. But the moment he consulted a doctor he thought he was going downhill, and fast. Yet, despite this, he kept on consulting the doctors.

That month he went to see another celebrity. This celebrity told him more or less the same as the first one, but put things differently. And the consultation with this celebrity served only to reinforce Ivan Ilyich's doubts and fears. A friend of a friend – a very good doctor – diagnosed something entirely different and, even though he swore he would get better, his questions and assumptions confused Ivan Ilyich even more and deepened his suspicions. A homeopath produced yet another diagnosis and gave him some medicine, which Ivan Ilyich took for a week or so without telling anyone. But by the end of the week, feeling no better and losing faith in every treatment that had been prescribed so far including that one, he felt more despondent than ever. One day a lady of his acquaintance talked to him about the curative powers of icons. Ivan Ilyich caught himself listening closely to what she was saying, and beginning to accept it as fact. This scared him. 'Am I really going weak in the head?' he wondered. 'Nonsense. It's all rubbish! I'm not falling for stupid ideas like that. I'd rather pick one doctor and stick to what he says. That's what I'm going to do. That's it. I'm going to stop thinking about it, and follow the treatment to the letter until the summer. Then we'll see. No more shilly-shallying.' This was easy to say but impossible to do. The pain in his side went on wearing him down and seemed to be getting worse, nagging incessantly, while the taste in his mouth got more and more peculiar and he began to think that his breath smelt awful, and his appetite and strength fell away. The time for fooling himself was over: something new and dreadful was going on inside Ivan Ilyich, something significant, more significant than anything in his whole life. And he was the only one who knew it; the people around him didn't know, or didn't want to know – they thought that everything in the world was going on as before. This was what tormented Ivan Ilyich more than anything. He could see that his family – especially his wife and daughter, whose visiting season was in full swing – had no inkling; it annoyed them that he was not much fun and asked so much of them – as if he was to blame. Despite their best efforts to hide it, he could see that he was in their way. His wife had developed an attitude to his illness and she was sticking to it whatever he might say or do. Her attitude went like this: 'You know what it's like,' she would say to her friends. 'Ivan Ilyich can't be like other people. He won't stick to his treatment. One moment he takes his drops and eats what he's supposed to, and goes to bed when he should; the next day, if I'm not watching him, he doesn't take his medicine, he eats sturgeon – which he's not allowed – and he stays up playing whist until one in the morning.'

'Oh, come on,' says Ivan Ilyich. 'I did that once, with Pyotr Ivanovich.'

'What about yesterday, with Shebek?'

'It made no difference. I couldn't sleep with all that pain . . .'

'Well, it doesn't matter why. Only you'll never get better like that, and it's getting us down.'

Praskovya's attitude towards Ivan Ilyich's illness, of which she made no secret to other people or to him, was that it was all his fault; he was making his wife's life a misery yet again. Ivan Ilyich felt she was doing this unconsciously, but that didn't make things any easier for him.

In court Ivan Ilyich noticed, or thought he noticed,

the same strange attitude towards him. There were times when he thought people were watching him closely like a man who was about to give up his job; at other times his associates would make friendly little jokes about the way he worried over his health, as if this ghastly, fearful, unheard-of thing that had got going inside him and was now incessantly gnawing at him and inexorably taking him away was a good subject and a laughing matter. The one who infuriated him most was Schwartz, with his playfulness, *joie de vivre* and all-round respectability which recalled the Ivan Ilyich of ten years before.

His friends have come round for a game of cards. They take their places and deal, softening the new cards. He sorts his diamonds – seven of them. His partner bids no trumps and supports him with two diamonds. Couldn't be better. This should be a wonderful, joyous moment – a grand slam is on. But suddenly he feels that gnawing pain, that taste in his mouth, and he is struck by the barbarity of rejoicing in a grand slam.

He glances across at his partner, Mikhail Mikhaylovich, who is tapping the table with an eager hand, politely and graciously holding back from grabbing the tricks and pushing them towards Ivan Ilyich so that he can enjoy the pleasure of raking them in without having to make any effort or reaching very far. 'Does he think I'm too weak to reach out?' thinks Ivan Ilyich, forgetting what are trumps and overtrumping his partner with his own, which leaves them three tricks short of a grand slam. And worst of all, he can see how upset Mikhail Mikhaylovich is, and he doesn't care. And it is awful to think why he doesn't care.

They can all see that he is distraught, and they say to him, 'We can stop if you're feeling tired. Why don't you have a rest?' Rest? No, he's *not tired*. They finish the rubber. They are all gloomy and silent. Ivan Ilyich senses that he has caused the gloom, and he cannot dispel it. They have supper and go home, and Ivan Ilyich is left there alone with the knowledge that his life has been poisoned and is poisoning other people's lives, and the poison is not wearing off, it is working its way deeper and deeper into his very being.

And he has to take this knowledge to bed with him, along with the physical pain and the terror, often to spend a near-sleepless night because of the pain. And next morning he has to get up again, put on his clothes, go to court, talk, write or, if he doesn't go out, stay in with every one of those twenty-four hours that make up a day and a night, each one of them an agony. And he has to live like this on the edge of destruction, alone, with nobody at all to understand and pity him.

5

One month passed like this, then another. His brother-in-law came to their town to stay with them for the New Year celebrations. Ivan Ilyich was in court when he arrived. Praskovya was out shopping. On his return Ivan Ilyich walked into his study and found his brother-in-law already there, a strong, fit young man, busy unpacking his own suitcase. He looked up when he heard Ivan Ilyich approaching and stared at him in silence for a moment. That stare told Ivan Ilyich everything. His brother-in-law opened his mouth to exclaim, but managed to restrain himself. That movement confirmed everything.

'I've changed, haven't I?'

'Well . . . you have rather.'

And after this, however hard Ivan Ilyich tried to raise the subject of his appearance, his brother-in-law wouldn't say a word. Praskovya arrived home and her brother went to see her. Ivan Ilyich locked the door and went to have a good look at himself in the mirror, full face, then in profile. He picked up a photograph of himself with his wife and compared his likeness with what he now saw in the mirror. The difference was enormous. Then he pulled his sleeves up, looked at his arms, pulled his sleeves back down and sat down on an ottoman, looking blacker than night.

'No, no. I mustn't,' he told himself. He jumped up and went to his desk, where he opened a file and began to read, but he couldn't go on. He opened the door and went out into the hallway. The door into the drawing-room was shut. He tiptoed over to it and started to listen.

'No, you're exaggerating,' Praskovya was saying.

'What do you mean, exaggerating? You can't see it. He's a dead man. Look at his eyes – there's no light in them. What is it he's got exactly?'

'Nobody knows. Nikolayev [yet another doctor] said something, but I don't know what it was. Leshchetitsky [the celebrity] said the exact opposite . . .'

Ivan Ilyich walked away back into his room, lay down and started to think things over. 'Kidney, a floating kidney . . .' He could remember everything the doctors had told him about it becoming detached and starting to wander. With an effort of his imagination he tried to catch the kidney, stop it moving and fix it strongly. It seemed to take so little effort. 'No, I'm going back to Pyotr Ivanovich [the friend who was the doctor's friend].' He rang the bell, ordered the carriage and prepared to go out.

'*Jean*, where are you going?' asked his wife, looking very gloomy but uncharacteristically kind.

The uncharacteristic kindness infuriated him. He gave her a dark look. 'I've got to go and see Pyotr Ivanovich.'

He went to see the friend with the friend who was the doctor, and on with him to the doctor himself, who was in. They had a long talk.

Going through the details of anatomy and physiology in terms of what the doctor considered to be happening in his insides made everything quite clear to him.

There was a little bit of something, a tiny little thing,

in his blind gut. It could all be put right. By raising the energy level in one organ and lowering the activity of another, absorption could be achieved and everything would be all right. He was a little late for dinner. He talked cheerfully after dinner, but for some time he couldn't bring himself to go to his room and work. Eventually he did go off to his study and he got straight down to it. He worked at the files for a while, but he couldn't shrug off the awareness that he had some important unfinished personal business that would have to be attended to in the end. When he had finished the files he remembered that this personal business meant thinking about his gut. But instead of giving in to this he went to take tea in the drawing-room. They had guests – there was conversation, piano-playing and singing – and among them was the examining magistrate who was such a good match for his daughter. As Praskovya remarked, he enjoyed the evening more than usual, but never for a minute did he forget that he had some important unfinished thinking to do, about his gut. At eleven o'clock he said goodnight and went to his room. He had been sleeping alone since his illness began, in a tiny little room next to his study. He went in, undressed and took up a Zola novel, but instead of reading it he lapsed into thought. And in his imagination the longed-for healing of his blind gut took place; absorption was followed by evacuation and its proper function was restored. 'Yes, that's how it goes,' he said to himself. 'All you have to do is give nature a helping hand.' He remembered his medicine, eased himself up and took it, then lay on his back focusing on the good that the medicine was doing and the way it was getting rid of the pain. 'Keep taking it regularly and avoid anything harmful. I feel a bit better already, a lot better.' He felt his side – no pain to the touch. 'No, there's no feeling there. It really is getting a lot better.' He put out the candle and lay on his side . . .

Absorption; the blind gut was curing itself. Then suddenly he could feel the same old dull gnawing pain, quiet, serious, unrelenting. The same nasty taste in his mouth. His heart sank and his head swam. 'O God! O God!' he muttered. 'It's here again, and it's not going away.' And suddenly he saw things from a completely different angle. 'The blind gut! The kidney!' he said to himself. 'It's got nothing to do with the blind gut or the kidney. It's a matter of living or . . . dying. Yes, I have been alive, and now my life is steadily going away and I can't stop it. No. There's no point in fooling myself. Can't they all see – everybody but me – that I'm dying? It's only a matter of weeks, or days – maybe any minute now. There has been daylight; now there is darkness. I have been *here*; now I'm going *there*. Where?' A cold shiver ran over him; he stopped breathing. He could hear nothing but the beating of his heart.

'When I'm dead, what happens then? Nothing happens. So where shall I be when I'm no longer here? Is this really death? No, I won't have it!' He jumped up, tried to light the candle, fumbling with trembling hands, dropped the candle and the stick on the floor and flopped back down on to his pillow. 'Why bother? It doesn't make any difference,' he said to himself, staring into the darkness with his eyes wide open. 'Death. Yes, it's death. And not one of them knows, or wants to know. They have no pity for me. Too busy playing.' (Through the door he could hear the distant sounds of a singing voice and the accompaniment.) 'They don't care, but they're going to die, too. Fools! Me first, then them, but they've got it coming to them. And they're enjoying themselves! Animals!' He was choking with spite. And he felt a wave of agonizing, unbearable misery. It surely wasn't possible that everybody everywhere should be condemned to this awful horror. He sat up.

'Something's not right. I've got to calm down and think it through from the beginning.' And he began to think. 'Yes, the beginning of the illness. I banged my side, but I felt just the same that day and the next. A bit of discomfort, then a bit more, then doctors, depression, worry, more doctors, and all the time I was getting nearer and nearer to the edge. Less and less strength. Nearer and nearer. And I've been wasting away. No light in my eyes. Death is here, and I've been worrying about my gut. Worrying about getting my gut better, and this is death. Is it really death?'

Horror swept over him again, he gasped for breath, bent over and groped for the matches, leaning with one elbow on the bedside table. It was in his way, hurting him; he lost his temper with it, pressing down on it even harder in exasperation, and knocked it over. Breathless and in despair, he flopped down on to his back, expecting to die at any moment.

By this time the guests were leaving. Praskovya was seeing them out. She heard something fall, and came in.

'What's the matter?'

'Nothing. I just dropped something.'

She went out and came back with a candle. He lay there, puffing and panting heavily like a man who has just run a mile. His eyes settled on her.

'What's the matter, *Jean*?'

'No-thing. I . . . dropped it.' ('No use talking to her. She won't understand,' he thought.)

And she didn't. She picked up the candle and lit it for him, then she hurried out of the room to say goodnight to another guest.

When she came back he was still lying there on his back, staring upwards.

'What's wrong? Are you feeling worse?'

'Yes.'

She shook her head and sat down.

'Listen, *Jean*. I think perhaps we ought to ask Leshchetitsky to visit you at home.'

This meant asking the celebrated doctor to come to them, whatever the expense. He gave her a vitriolic smile and said no. She sat there for a while, then came over and kissed him on the forehead.

He hated her with every fibre of his being while she was kissing him, and it took all his strength not to push her away.

'Goodnight. God willing, you'll soon go to sleep.'

'Yes.'

6

Ivan Ilyich could see that he was dying, and he was in constant despair.

In the depths of his soul Ivan Ilyich knew he was dying but, not only could he not get used to the idea, he didn't understand it, couldn't understand it at all.

All his life the syllogism he had learned from Kiesewetter's logic – Julius Caesar is a man, men are mortal, therefore Caesar is mortal – had always seemed to him to be true only when it applied to Caesar, certainly not to him. There was Caesar the man, and man in general, and it was fair enough for them, but he wasn't Caesar the man and he wasn't man in general, he had always been a special being, totally different from all others, he had been Vanya with his mama and his papa, with Vitya and Volodya, with his toys, and the carriage-driver, then little Katya, with all the delights, sorrows and rapture of childhood, boyhood and youth. Did Caesar have anything to do with the smell of that little striped leather ball that Vanya had loved so much? Was it Caesar who had kissed his mother's hand like that, and was it for Caesar that the silken folds of his mother's dress had rustled the way they did? Was he the one who had rebelled at law school over the provision of snacks? Had Caesar been in love like him? Could Caesar chair a session like him?

Yes, Caesar is mortal and it's all right for him to die, but not me, Vanya, Ivan Ilyich, with all my feelings and thoughts – it's different for me. It can't be me having to die. That would be too horrible.

These were the feelings that came to him.

'If I had to be like Caesar and die, I would have been aware of it, an inner voice would have told me, but there hasn't been anything like that on the inside. I've always thought – and all my friends have, too – that we're not the same as Caesar. And now look what's happened!' he said to himself. 'It can't be. It can't be, but it is. How can it be? What's it all about?'

He couldn't understand, and he tried to banish the idea – it was false, wrong and morbid – and replace it with proper, healthy thinking. But the same thought – it wasn't just a thought but something that seemed like reality – kept coming back and facing him.

And in order to dispel these thoughts he started calling up different thoughts one after another, hoping to get support from them. He tried to get back to his earlier ways of thinking which had once protected him from thinking about death. But, strange to say, everything that once had protected him by hiding and eliminating any awareness of death was unable to perform that function now. In these latter days Ivan Ilyich spent most of his time trying to get back to the earlier ways of feeling that had protected him from death. He would say to himself, 'I must get down to some work. When all's said and done it's what I've been living for.' And he would go off to court banishing all his doubts, get into conversation with his colleagues and casually take his seat as he had done so many times before, contemplating the crowd before him with a pensive air and resting his wasted hands on the oaken arms of his chair, leaning over in his usual way to exchange whispered words with a colleague while toying with a file before raising his eyes suddenly and sitting up straight in order to go through the familiar words and begin the proceedings. But then suddenly there it was, the pain in his side, irrespective of where they had got to in the proceedings, and it was beginning to gnaw at him. Ivan Ilyich focused on it, drove the thought of it away, but it continued to make itself felt. *It* kept coming back, facing him and looking at him, while he sat there rigid, the fire went out of his eyes and he began to wonder whether *It* was the only truth. And his colleagues and subordinates looked on in distress, amazed that he, a man of such brilliant and subtle judgement, was getting confused and making mistakes. He would pull himself together, try to bring himself round and somehow bring the session to a conclusion, only to return home sadly aware that his judicial work could no longer hide him, as it once had done, from what he wanted to conceal, that he could not use his judicial work to rid himself of *It*. And the worst thing was that *It* was distracting him not in order to make him do something but only to get him to look *It* straight in the eye, just look at *It* and do nothing but suffer beyond words.

And in order to escape from this situation Ivan Ilyich sought other forms of consolation, other ways of screening it off; other screens appeared and for a while they seemed to be the saving of him, but immediately they were not so much destroyed as shone right through; it was as if *It* could penetrate anything, no defence being any good.

Sometimes in these latter days he would go into the drawing-room that he had furnished – the very room where he had had his fall, the room which (it was bitterly amusing to reflect) he had given his life to furnish, because he knew his illness had started with that bruise – he would go in and notice a scratch on a lacquered table top left behind by something sharp. Looking for the cause he would find it in the decorative bronzework on an album with one edge bent up. He would pick up the album, an expensive one which he had compiled with loving care, annoyed at the carelessness shown by his daughter and her friends – it was torn in places and some of the photographs were upside down. He would go to a lot of trouble sorting it out and bending the bronzework back into place.

Then it would occur to him to move this entire

établissement of albums over into a corner near the flowers. He would call the footman. Either his wife or his daughter would come to help. They wouldn't agree, they would take issue with him, he would argue and lose his temper – but none of this mattered because he had stopped remembering *It*. *It* was nowhere to be seen.

But once, when he was moving something himself, his wife said, 'Let the servants do that. You'll hurt yourself again,' and suddenly *It* flashed through the screen – he saw *It*. *It* flashed at him and, even as he longed for *It* to disappear, he couldn't help focusing on his side – still there, the same ache that would not be ignored, and *It* was staring straight at him from behind the flowers. What was it all about?

'And that's the truth of it – I've lost my life here on this curtain, my battleground. Have I really? How horrible and how stupid! It can't be! It can't be, but it is.'

He would go into his study, lie down and find himself alone again with *It*. Face to face with *It*. Nothing to be done about *It*. Only stare at *It* and go cold.

7

How it came about in the third month of Ivan Ilyich's illness no one could have said, because it came on imperceptibly, by stages, but it happened that all of them – his wife, and daughter, and son, and the servants, and their friends, and the doctors, and most importantly he himself – everybody knew that the only interesting thing about him now was whether it would take him a long time to give up his place, finally release the living from the oppression caused by his presence, and himself be released from his suffering.

He slept less and less. He was given opium and injected with morphine, but this brought no relief. To begin with, the dull feeling of anguish which he experienced in his semi-conscious state gave him a sense of relief simply by being something new, but then it became just as agonizing as the raw pain, perhaps more so.

They gave him special food cooked from recipes provided by the doctors, but the food became more and more tasteless, more and more repulsive.

For the call of nature he also had special arrangements, and each time it was agonizing. The agony came from the dirtiness, the unseemliness, the smell and also the knowledge that someone else had to be involved in it.

But this most unpleasant business brought one consolation to Ivan Ilyich. The person who came to take things away was Gerasim, the peasant servant who waited on them at table.

Gerasim was a clean, fresh peasant lad, always bright and cheerful, who had fattened up on city food. To begin with, Ivan Ilyich was embarrassed to watch him, always so neatly dressed in his Russian costume, performing such a distasteful service.

One day as he got up from the chamber pot not strong enough to pull up his own trousers he collapsed into a soft armchair and looked down in horror at his bared puny thighs with their starkly protruding muscles.

Who should come in but Gerasim, wearing his thick boots and exuding both their nice tarry smell and that of the fresh winter air, Gerasim with his light but firm tread, sporting a clean hessian apron and a clean cotton shirt, with his sleeves rolled up his bare strong young arms, and without a glance at Ivan Ilyich – to spare the sick man's feelings he was clearly suppressing the joyful vitality that shone from his face – he walked over to the pot.

'Gerasim,' said Ivan Ilyich feebly.

Gerasim started, clearly worried that he might have done something wrong, and in one swift movement he presented to the sick man his fresh, kind, open young face which was showing the first traces of a beard.

'Yes, sir?'

'This is not very nice for you, is it? You'll have to forgive me. I can't help it.'

'Please don't worry, sir.' And Gerasim's eyes flashed as he bared his young white teeth. 'It's no trouble. You're a sick man.'

And with his quick strong hands he did his usual thing and walked out with a light step. And five minutes later with the same light step he came back in.

Ivan Ilyich was still sitting there in his armchair.

'Gerasim,' he said, when the lad had replaced the clean, freshly washed chamber pot, 'would you mind helping me? Over here.' Gerasim came across. 'Lift me up, please. I can't manage it on my own, and I've sent Dmitriy away.'

Gerasim came over. In one movement that was as easy as his way of walking, he put his strong arms gently round Ivan Ilyich, lifted him up and held him with one hand, pulled up his trousers with the other, and tried to settle him down. But Ivan Ilyich asked to be taken across to the sofa. Effortlessly and apparently without tightening his grip, Gerasim took him, almost carried him, to the sofa and settled him down there.

'Thank you. You do everything so . . . nicely. So well.'

Gerasim gave another smile and made as if to leave the room. But Ivan Ilyich felt so comfortable with him that he didn't feel like letting him go.

'That's better . . . Would you mind moving that chair over here? No, that one. Under my legs. It feels easier when my legs are up high.'

Gerasim brought the chair over, set it squarely on the floor without banging it down, and lifted Ivan Ilyich's legs up on to it. Ivan Ilyich felt an easing of the pain as Gerasim raised his legs.

'I feel better when my legs are up,' said Ivan Ilyich. 'Would you put that cushion under me?'

Gerasim did so. He raised his legs again and put the cushion under them. Again Ivan Ilyich felt better when

Gerasim was holding his legs. When he lowered them he felt worse.

'Gerasim,' he asked, 'are you busy just now?'

'Not in the slightest, sir,' said Gerasim, who had learned from the townspeople how to speak to the masters.

'What do you have on at the moment?'

'What do I have on? I've done everything there is to do – except chop the firewood for tomorrow.'

'Well, I'd like you to hold my legs up. Would you mind?'

'Of course not. I don't mind.' Gerasim held his legs up, and Ivan Ilyich could have sworn that in this position he couldn't feel any pain.

'But what about the firewood?'

'Don't you worry about that, sir. We'll manage.'

Ivan Ilyich told Gerasim to sit down and hold his legs up. He struck up a conversation and, strangely enough, he seemed to feel better with Gerasim holding his legs.

After that Ivan Ilyich would send for Gerasim now and then and have his legs held up on his shoulders. He liked it when they talked to each other. Gerasim did all of this easily, willingly and with a kindliness that Ivan Ilyich found moving. Health, strength and vitality in all other people were offensive to Ivan Ilyich; only Gerasim's strength and vitality gave him comfort rather than distressed him.

Ivan Ilyich's worst torment was the lying – the lie, which was somehow maintained by them all, that he wasn't dying, he was only ill, and all he had to do was keep calm and follow doctor's orders and then something good would emerge. Whereas he knew that, whatever was done to him, nothing would emerge but more and more agony, suffering and death. And this lie was torture for him – he was tortured by their unwillingness to acknowledge what they all knew and he knew; they wanted to lie to him about his terrible situation, and they wanted him – they were compelling him – to be a party to this lie. All this lying to him, lie upon lie, on the eve of his death, lying that was inexorably reducing the solemn act of his death to the same level as their social calls, their draperies, the sturgeon for dinner . . . it was all a terrible torment for Ivan Ilyich. And strangely enough, on many occasions when they were acting out this farce in front of him, he was within a hair's breadth of screaming at them, 'Stop all this lying! You know and I know that I'm dying, so the least you can do is stop lying to me.' But he never quite had the nerve to do it. He could see that the awful, terrible act of his dying had been reduced by those around him to the level of an unpleasant incident, something rather indecent (as if they were dealing with someone who had come into the drawing-room and let off a bad smell), and this was done by exploiting the very sense of 'decency' that he had been observing all his life. He could see that no one had any pity for him because no one had the slightest desire to understand his situation. Gerasim was the only one who did understand his situation, and he was sorry for him. This was why Ivan Ilyich felt comfortable only with Gerasim. It was a comfort to him when Gerasim, sometimes for nights on end, held his legs up and refused to go to bed, saying, 'Please don't worry about it, Ivan Ilyich. I'll catch up on my sleep.' Or else he would suddenly address him in familiar language and add, 'It'd be different if you weren't ill, but with things the way they are why shouldn't I help you out?' Gerasim was the only one who didn't lie to him; everything showed that he was the only one who understood what was going on and saw no need to hide it. He just felt sorry for his weak and emaciated master. Once, when Ivan Ilyich was dismissing him, he put it quite bluntly: 'We've all got to die one day. Why shouldn't I give you a hand?' This was to say there was a good reason for not making a fuss about helping out: he was doing it for a dying man and he hoped that when his time came someone would help him out in the same way.

Apart from all this lying, or perhaps because of it, the most tormenting thing of all for Ivan Ilyich was the fact that no one showed him any pity in the way that he wanted them to. There were some moments, after long periods of suffering, when what Ivan Ilyich wanted more than anything else – however embarrassed he would have been to admit it – what he wanted was for someone to take pity on him as if he were a sick child. He wanted to be kissed and cuddled and have a few tears shed over him in the way that children are cuddled and comforted. He knew he was a big man and something of a greybeard, which made this impossible, but nevertheless that is what he wanted. And his relationship with Gerasim offered something close to this, which was why the relationship with Gerasim gave him comfort.

Here is Ivan Ilyich wanting to weep, wanting to be cuddled and have tears shed over him, when in comes his colleague Shebek and, instead of weeping and getting some tenderness, Ivan Ilyich puts on a solemn and serious face, looks thoughtful and from sheer habit not only comments on the significance of a decision handed down by the Court of Cassation, but goes on to defend it strongly.

It was this living a lie, all around him and within him, that did most to poison the last days in the life of Ivan Ilyich.

8

It was morning. It was morning only because Gerasim had gone and Pyotr the servant was there, putting out the candles, opening one curtain and quietly tidying up. Morning or evening, Friday or Sunday – it didn't matter, it was all the same – grinding, agonizing pain, never for a moment relenting; an awareness of life hopelessly slipping away but not yet gone; the same terrible, relentless approach of hateful death, the only reality; and still all that lying. With all of this, what did the days, weeks and hours matter?

'Can I get you some tea, sir?'

'He likes good order. The masters must have their tea in the morning,' he thought, but all he said was, 'No.'

'Would you care to move over to the sofa, sir?'

'He wants to tidy the room, and I'm in the way. I am dirt and disorder,' he thought, but all he said was, 'No. Leave me alone.'

The servant went about his work again. Ivan Ilyich stretched out one hand. Pyotr came over ready to help.

'What can I do for you, sir?'

'My watch.'

Pyotr took the watch, which was lying nearby, and handed it over.

'Half-past eight. Are they still in bed?'

'No, sir, they're not. Master Vasily [his son] has gone to school and madam asked me to wake her if you wanted her. Shall I do that?'

'No. Don't brother.' Ivan Ilyich wondered whether to try some tea. Yes. 'Bring me some tea.'

Pyotr moved towards the door. Ivan Ilyich felt terrified at the thought of being left alone. How could he stop him leaving? Oh yes, medicine. 'Pyotr, would you give me my medicine?' Well, why not? The medicine might help. He took a spoonful and swallowed it. No, it wouldn't help. It was all rubbish. Just pretending. He felt sure of this as the old familiar taste returned, sickly and beyond hope.

No, his faith was gone. And the pain, the pain, why couldn't it ease up just for a minute? He gave a groan. Pyotr came back in.

'No, carry on. Get me some tea.'

Pyotr left the room. Ivan Ilyich groaned, not really from the pain, however terrible that was, but from anguish. It was the same thing all the time, day and night, with no end to it. Make it soon. Make *what* soon? Death, darkness. No, no. Anything was better than death!

When Pyotr came back in with the tea tray Ivan Ilyich looked at him distractedly for some time, unable to work out who he was or what he was doing there. Pyotr was embarrassed by the long look. The embarrassment brought Ivan Ilyich to his senses.

'Yes,' he said. 'Tea . . . Good. Leave it there. But I'd like you to help me get washed and put a clean shirt on.'

And Ivan Ilyich began to wash himself. With pauses for rest he washed his hands and face, cleaned his teeth, combed his hair and then took a look in the mirror. He was horrified. The most horrible thing was the limp way his hair stuck to his pallid forehead.

As he had his shirt changed he knew it would be more horrible still to glance down at his body, so he looked away. At last it was done. He put on his dressing-gown, wrapped a rug around himself and sat down in the armchair with his tea. For one moment he felt refreshed, but at the first drink of tea there it was again, the same taste, the same pain. He forced the tea down, then lay back and stretched out his legs. He lay down and told Pyotr he could go.

The same thing again. One glittering drop of hope followed by a raging sea of despair, and nothing but pain, more pain, more anguish, always the same thing. It was depressing to be left alone, and he felt like calling somebody in, but he knew in advance that to have other people there would be even worse. Oh, for another dose of morphine – he might lose himself in that. He must tell that doctor to think of something else. 'I can't go on like this. I can't.'

An hour goes by like this, then another. The bell rings in the hall – could it be the doctor? Yes, it is the doctor, fresh and cheerful, fleshy and hearty, with a look on his face that seems to say, 'Well now, you seem to have had a bit of a fright, but we'll soon sort you out.' The doctor knows that this look is out of place here, but he has assumed it once and for all and he can't get rid of it any more than a man who has gone out visiting can get rid of the frock-coat he put on that morning.

The doctor rubs his hands cheerfully, reassuringly.

'Chilly out there. Thick frost. Give me a minute to get warmed up.' His manner of speaking implies that he won't take long, he just needs to warm up and once he is warmed up he'll put everything right.

'Right then. How are you feeling?'

Ivan Ilyich senses that the doctor feels like saying, 'How's tricks?' but even he can see that this won't do, so he says, 'What sort of night did you have?'

Ivan Ilyich fixes the doctor with a look that seems to ask whether anything would ever make him feel too ashamed to go on lying. The doctor does not wish to understand.

So Ivan Ilyich says, 'No change. Terrible. The pain won't go. It's there all the time. There must be something you can do!'

'Yes, it's normal for patients like you to say that sort of thing. Right then. I think I'm warm enough now. Your good lady is a stickler for these things, but even she wouldn't say I was too cold. So. Good morning to you . . .' And the doctor shakes him by the hand.

And now, dropping all the banter, the doctor adopts a serious attitude and begins to examine the patient – pulse, temperature, tapping and listening.

Ivan Ilyich knows full well – it is beyond doubt – that this is all nonsense, an empty sham, but when the doctor goes down on his knees, reaches across him, applies his ear higher up and lower down, and then with the gravest look on his face performs a selection of gymnastic contortions, Ivan Ilyich accedes to this just as he once acceded to speeches from lawyers even when he was well aware that they were lying, and why they were lying.

The doctor is still kneeling on the sofa, busily tapping away, when from the doorway comes the rustling of a silk dress and Praskovya can be heard reproaching Pyotr for not letting her know the doctor has arrived.

She comes in, kisses her husband and immediately

begins to make it clear that she has been up for some time and only a little misunderstanding has prevented her from being there when the doctor arrived.

Ivan Ilyich looks at her searchingly, resenting everything about her, the whiteness, fullness and cleanliness of her arms and neck, the sheen of her hair and the light in her eyes that are so full of life. He loathes her with every fibre of his being. Physical contact with her is agony for him because it brings on a surge of loathing.

Her attitude towards him and his illness is still the same. Just as the doctor has worked out an attitude towards his patients which he cannot now get rid of, she has worked out a particular attitude towards him – he is failing to do something he ought to do, and it's his fault, and she lovingly reproaches him for it – and she has not been able to rid herself of this attitude towards him.

'He just won't do as he's told! He forgets to take his medicine. And the worst thing is he will lie there in a position that must be bad for him – with his legs up.'

She described how he got Gerasim to hold his legs up for him.

The doctor gave a sweetly condescending smile. 'Can't be helped,' he seemed to be saying. 'These sick people do sometimes have silly ideas. We can't blame them.'

When the examination was over the doctor consulted his watch and then Praskovya informed Ivan Ilyich that, like it or not, she had invited a celebrated specialist to visit them that day and, along with Mikhail Danilovich (the name of the regular doctor), he would conduct an examination and consultation.

'Now please don't argue with me. I'm doing this for myself,' she said sarcastically, implying that she was doing it all for him and this alone deprived him of any right to refuse. He scowled and said nothing. He felt that the lies that enveloped him were now so messy that he could hardly make sense of anything.

Everything she did for him she was doing for herself, and she told him she was doing for herself what she was actually doing for herself, but she made it sound so implausible that he was forced to assume the opposite.

Sure enough, at half-past eleven, the celebrated specialist arrived. More soundings and grave consultations both in his presence and in the next room concerning the kidney and the blind gut, with questions and answers expressed with such an air of gravity that, instead of the real life-and-death question which was the only one staring him in the face, up came the question of his kidney and blind gut, which were not doing quite what they should and which would shortly be set upon by Mikhail Danilovich and made to work properly.

The celebrated specialist took his leave looking serious but not hopeless. And in answer to the question put to him diffidently by Ivan Ilyich, whose eyes were glistening with fear and hope, as to whether there was any possibility of recovery, he replied that nothing could be guaranteed but there was a possibility. The look of hope on Ivan Ilyich's face as he watched the doctor leave was so pathetic that when she saw it Praskovya actually burst into tears as she walked out of the study to give the celebrated specialist his fee.

The lifting of his spirits induced by the doctor's words of encouragement was short-lived. It was still the same room, the same pictures, curtains, wallpaper, medicine bottles, and the same body, his body, still suffering, racked with pain. And Ivan Ilyich began to moan, so they gave him an injection and he lapsed into unconsciousness.

When he came to, it was getting dark. They brought him his dinner. He forced down a little thin soup, then it was the same again, with another night coming on.

When dinner was over, at seven o'clock, Praskovya came in dressed for going out, with her ample breasts well supported and traces of powder on her face. That morning she had reminded him that they were going to the theatre. Sarah Bernhardt was in town, and they had a box which they had taken at his insistence. By now he had forgotten this, and he was offended to see her dressed up. But he hid his feelings when he remembered having insisted that they reserve the box and go, this being an aesthetic experience of educational value for the children.

As she came in Praskovya had looked pleased with herself, if rather guilty. She sat down on the edge of a chair and asked how he was feeling, though he could see that she was asking for the sake of asking rather than to find out, since she knew there was nothing to find out, and then she launched into what she felt she had to say, that nothing would have induced her to go out tonight, but the box had been reserved, Hélène and her daughter were going and so was Petrishchev (their daughter's fiancé, the examining magistrate), and they couldn't be allowed to go alone. But for that, she would have preferred to stay in with him. And he must be sure to follow the doctor's orders while she was out.

'Oh yes, and Fyodor [the fiancé] would like to come in. Do you mind? And Liza.'

'Let them come in.'

In came his daughter, dressed up to the nines, an exposed young body – while his body was causing him so much suffering. And she was flaunting it. Healthy and strong, obviously in love, she had no time for the illness, suffering and death that were marring her happiness.

In came Fyodor Petrovich, also in evening dress and sporting an *à la Capoul* hairstyle. The veins stood out on his long neck which was squeezed into its tight collar over a vast expanse of white shirtfront, and his narrow black trousers were tightly stretched over his strong thighs. One of his hands wore a close-fitting white glove and he carried an opera hat.

Creeping in unobtrusively behind him came the schoolboy, wearing a new uniform and gloves, poor chap, with terrible dark blue rings under his eyes, the meaning of which was not lost on Ivan Ilyich.

He had always felt sorry for his son. And his frightened, compassionate look was dreadful to behold. Apart from Gerasim, Ivan Ilyich thought, Vasya was the only one who understood and felt sorry for him.

They all sat down and asked how he was feeling. Then for a while no one spoke. Liza asked her mother whether she had the opera glasses. Mother and daughter had a little argument about who had put them where. It ended nastily.

Fyodor asked Ivan Ilyich whether he had ever seen Sarah Bernhardt. At first Ivan Ilyich didn't quite catch what the question was, but then he said, 'No. Have you?'

'Yes. In *Adrienne Lecouvreur*.'

Praskovya mentioned something she had been particularly good in. Her daughter demurred. They were off into a conversation about her charm and naturalism as an actress, the same old conversation that everybody else has.

In the midst of it Fyodor looked across at Ivan Ilyich and suddenly broke off. The others looked, and they stopped, too. Ivan Ilyich was staring straight ahead, his eyes glittering, and he was obviously furious with them. Things had to be put right, but there was absolutely no way of putting things right. Somehow the silence had to be broken. No one made a move, and everyone was becoming terrified that the living lie demanded by propriety would somehow be shattered and seen by everyone for what it was. It was Liza who made the first move. She broke the silence. She wanted to cover up what everyone was feeling, but by speaking out she revealed it.

'Oh well, if we're *going* it's time we got started,' she said, glancing at her watch, a present from her father, and she smiled almost imperceptibly at her young man to convey something known only to the two of them as she got up, rustling her skirts.

They all got up, took their leave and drove off.

When they had gone Ivan Ilyich seemed to feel easier; the lie had gone, gone away with them – but the pain was still there. That same pain, that same feeling of dread made sure that nothing was harder, nothing easier. Everything was worse.

Once again the minutes passed one after another, then the hours one after another; it was always the same, endlessly, and the inevitable end itself was all the more horrible.

'Yes, send Gerasim in,' he said in reply to a question from Pyotr.

9

It was late at night when his wife returned. She tiptoed into the room, but he heard her; he opened his eyes and rapidly closed them again. She wanted to dismiss Gerasim and sit with him herself. He opened his eyes and said, 'No. You go.'

'Are you in a lot of pain?'

'It doesn't matter.'

'Take some opium.'

He consented, and drank some. She went away.

Until about three in the morning he was in a state of excruciating pain and delirium. He dreamt that somehow he was being forced, along with his pain, into the depths of a narrow black sack, being forced further and further in and not quite getting there. It was a harrowing, agonizing process. And he was scared, he wanted to get through and out, he was struggling, trying to help. Then suddenly he lost his hold and fell, and woke up. Gerasim was still there, sitting at the foot of the bed, dozing quietly, patiently. And he himself was lying there with his withered stockinged legs raised up on Gerasim's shoulders. The same candle was there, with its shade, and the same unremitting pain.

'Go away, Gerasim,' he whispered.

'I don't mind, sir. I'll just sit here for a bit longer.'

'No, you go away.'

He lowered his legs, turned sideways on to one arm and felt sorry for himself. He waited only for Gerasim to go out into the next room, and then he could restrain himself no longer: he burst into tears like a child. He was weeping because of his own helpless state, and his loneliness, and other people's cruelty, and God's cruelty, and God's non-existence.

'Why hast Thou done all of this? Why hast Thou

brought me to this point? Why oh why dost Thou torture me like this? . . .'

He was not expecting any answers; he was weeping because there were not and could not be any answers. The pain struck him again, but he didn't move and didn't call out. He said to himself, 'Here it comes again. Hit me then! But what's it for? What have I done to Thee? What is it for?'

Then he fell silent, and not only stopped crying, he stopped breathing. Suddenly he was all ears; he seemed to be listening not to a voice speaking in words but to the voice of his soul, the thoughts welling up in his mind.

'What do you want?' was the first expressible concept that came to him. 'What do you want? What do you want?' he repeated to himself. 'What is it?'

'No more pain. Staying alive,' came the answer.

And once again his concentration became so intense that not even the pain could distract him.

'Staying alive? How?' asked the voice of his soul.

'Oh, life like it used to be. Happy and good.'

'Life like it used to be? Happy and good?' came the voice.

And in his imagination he started to run through the best times of his happy life. But what was strange was that all the best times of his happy life no longer seemed anything like what they had been before. Nothing did – except the first recollections of his childhood. There, in his childhood, there was something truly happy that he could have lived with if it returned. But the person living out that happiness no longer existed; it was like remembering someone quite different.

At the point where he, today's Ivan Ilyich, began to emerge, all the pleasures that had seemed so real melted away now before his eyes and turned into something trivial and often disgusting.

And the further he was from childhood, the nearer he got to the present day, the more trivial and dubious his pleasures appeared. It started with law school. That had retained a little something that was still really good: there was fun, there was friendship, there was hope. But in the last years the good times had become more exceptional. Then, at the beginning of his service with the governor, some good times came again: memories of making love to a woman. Then it became all confused, and the good times were not so many. After that there were fewer still; the further he went the fewer there were.

Marriage . . . an accident and such a disappointment, and his wife's bad breath, and all that sensuality and hypocrisy! And the deadliness of his working life, and those money worries, going on for a year, two years, ten, twenty – always the same old story. And the longer it went on the deadlier it became.

'It's as if I had been going downhill when I thought I was going uphill. That's how it was. In society's opinion I was heading uphill, but in equal measure life was slipping away from me . . . And now it's all over. Nothing left but to die!

'So what's it all about? What's it for? It's not possible. It's not possible that life could have been as senseless and sickening as this. And if it has really been as sickening and senseless as this, why do I have to die, and die in agony? There's something wrong. Maybe I didn't live as I should have done?' came the sudden thought. 'But how can that be when I did everything properly?' he wondered, instantly dismissing as a total impossibility the one and only solution to the mystery of life and death.

'So, what *do* you want now? To live? Live how? To live as you do in court when the usher yells out, "The Court is in session!"' 'Court in session, sessions in court,' he repeated to himself. 'Here comes judgement! But I'm not guilty,' he cried out angrily. 'What is this for?'

And he stopped crying, turned to face the wall and let his mind dwell on one single question: 'Why all this horror? What's the reason for it?'

But, for all his dwelling on it, he could find no answer. And whenever the thought occurred to him – which it often did – that all this was happening to him because he had been living the wrong kind of life, he would instantly remember how proper his life had been and dismiss such a bizarre notion.

10

Another two weeks went by. Ivan Ilyich no longer rose from his sofa. He didn't care to lie in bed, so he lay on the sofa. And lying there, almost invariably facing the wall, he endured all the inexplicable agony in solitude, and in solitude he brooded on the same inexplicable question: 'What is this? Can it really be death?' And an inner voice would reply, 'Yes, that's what it is.' 'What is this torture for?' And the voice would reply, 'It's just there. It's not for anything.' Above and beyond this there was nothing.

From the very onset of his illness, since the first time he had driven round to see the doctor, his life had divided itself into two opposite and alternating moods: either despair and the anticipation of a horribly incomprehensible death, or hope accompanied by an obsessive fascination for the workings of his body. He had eyes for only two things: either a kidney or blind gut that had temporarily stopped doing what it should do, or a horribly incomprehensible death, which there was no way to avoid.

These two moods alternated in him from the very outset of his illness, but the further the illness progressed the more dubious and preposterous his notions of a kidney became, and the more realistic was his awareness of impending death.

All he had to do was remember what he had been like three months before and what he was now, remember how steadily he had gone downhill, and any possibility of hope was shattered.

In his last days of solitude, when he found himself lying there facing the back of the sofa, solitude in the midst of a populous city and his own friends and family – a solitude more complete than anything anywhere, at the bottom of the sea or in the bowels of the earth – in these last days of terrible solitude Ivan Ilyich lived only by recreating the past. Images of his past life came back to him one after another. This process always began with the most recent ones and proceeded back to the most remote, to childhood, and there it lingered. If Ivan Ilyich remembered the stewed prunes he had been offered for dinner that day he would remember the raw and wrinkly French prunes of his childhood, their special taste and how his mouth watered when he got down to the stone, and along with the memory of that taste would come a whole series of further memories of that time: his nurse, his brother, his toys. 'No, don't, not that. It's too painful,' Ivan Ilyich would say to himself, transporting himself back to the present: there it was – a button of the back of the sofa, creases in the morocco. 'Morocco is expensive, and it doesn't wear well. It started an argument. But that was different morocco and a different argument – when we tore father's briefcase and got punished, and mother brought us some tarts.' Once again his thoughts were settling on his childhood, and again they were too painful for Ivan Ilyich, so he tried to drive them away and think of something else.

And once again, along with this train of recollections, another train of recollections troubled his spirit – the way in which his illness had grown and got worse. Here, too, the further back he went the more life there was. More goodness in life, more of life itself. The two things were merging. 'It's like the pain getting worse and worse – all of my life has been getting worse and worse,' he thought. There was one point of light back there at the beginning of life, but after that everything had been getting blacker and blacker. 'In inverse proportion to the square of the distance from death,' he thought. And this image of a stone accelerating as it flies down imprinted itself on his soul. Life, a series of increasing sufferings, flies ever faster towards its end, the most terrible suffering. 'I'm flying somewhere . . .' He would shiver and shudder, trying to resist, but he knew by now that resistance was impossible, and he would turn his eyes to the back of the sofa, eyes that were weary of looking, but couldn't stop looking, at what lay ahead. And he was waiting, waiting for that terrible fall, shock and annihilation. 'Resistance is impossible,' he would say to himself. 'But if only I could see what it's all about! No, that's impossible, too. There would be an explanation if I could say I've been wrong in the way I've lived my life. But you couldn't say that. It's not possible,' he would tell himself, recalling how fastidious he had been about the propriety and respectability of his life. 'You can't say that. It's not possible,' he would tell himself, twisting his lips into a smile as if someone might see it and be taken in by it. 'There is no explanation. Agony and death . . . What for?'

11

Two weeks went by like this. During those two weeks an event took place that Ivan Ilyich and his wife had been hoping for: Petrishchev made a formal proposal. It happened one evening. The next morning Praskovya came in to see her husband, wondering how best to break the news of Fyodor's proposal, but during that night Ivan Ilyich's condition had taken another turn for the worse. Praskovya found him on the same sofa, but in a different position. He was lying flat on his back, moaning and staring ahead with a fixed look.

She started talking about his medicine. He transferred his gaze to her. She didn't finish what she had started to say; there was so much enmity in that gaze, and it was levelled straight at her.

'For Christ's sake, let me die in peace!' he said.

She made as if to leave the room, but at that moment in walked their daughter, who came over to say good morning. He gave her the same look he had directed at his wife, and in response to her enquiries about his health he said drily that soon he would no longer be a burden to them. Both of them sat on for a while, saying nothing, and then they left.

'What have we done wrong?' Liza asked her mother. 'Anyone would think it was our fault. I'm sorry for Papa, but why do we have to suffer?'

The doctor arrived at his usual time. Ivan Ilyich responded to him with a yes and no, fixing him with a malevolent look, and finally he said, 'Look, you know you can't help me. Just leave me alone.'

'We can ease the pain,' said the doctor.

'You can't. Leave me alone.'

The doctor went out into the drawing-room and told Praskovya that things were very bad. Only one thing could help – opium. That might ease the pain, which must be dreadful.

The doctor said that the physical pain must be dreadful, which was true. But more dreadful than the physical pain was the suffering in spirit, his greatest agony.

His spiritual suffering took the form of a thought that had suddenly struck him that night as he looked at Gerasim's sleepy-eyed, good-natured face with its high cheekbones. 'What if I really have been *wrong* in the way I've lived my whole life, my conscious life?'

It occurred to him that what had once seemed a total impossibility – that he had not lived his life as he should have done – might actually be true. It occurred to him that the slight stirrings of doubt he had experienced about what was considered good by those in the highest positions, slight stirrings that he had immediately repudiated – that these misgivings might have been true and everything else might have been wrong. His career, the ordering of his life, his family, the things that preoccupied people in society and at work – all of this might have been wrong. He made an attempt at defending these things for himself. And suddenly he sensed the feebleness of what he was defending. There was nothing to defend.

'But if it's like that,' he said to himself, 'and I am leaving this life knowing I have ruined everything I was given, and it can't be put right, what then?' He lay on his back and started to go through his whole life again in a different way. Next morning, when he saw his servant, then his wife, then his daughter, then the doctor – their every movement and every word bore out the terrible truth that had been revealed to him during the night. In them he saw himself and all he had lived by, and he could clearly see that it was all wrong; it was all a gross deception obscuring life and death. This knowledge exacerbated his physical suffering, making it ten times worse. He moaned and writhed, and clutched at his clothing, which seemed to be choking and stifling him. And he hated them for it.

After being given a heavy dose of opium he lost consciousness, but by dinner time it had all begun again. He sent everyone away and lay there tossing and turning.

His wife came to him and said, '*Jean*, darling, please

do this for my sake.' (For *her* sake?) 'It can't do any harm, and it often helps. Look, it's nothing much. Even healthy people . . .'

He opened his eyes wide.

'What? Take communion? What for? I'm not doing that . . . Oh, I don't know . . .'

She burst into tears.

'All right, my dear? I'll send for our priest. He's such a nice man.'

'All right. That's fine,' he said.

When the priest came and heard his confession, Ivan Ilyich relaxed, feeling some relief from his doubts and therefore from his suffering, and he experienced a moment of hope. His mind turned again to his blind gut and the possibility of a cure for it. When he took communion there were tears in his eyes.

When he was laid down after taking communion he felt better for a while; there was hope that he might live on. His thoughts turned to the operation that he had been offered. 'I want to live. I do want to live,' he said to himself. His wife came in to greet him after communion. She said the usual things, and then added: 'You really do feel better, don't you?'

'Yes,' he said, looking away.

Her clothes, her figure, the look on her face, the sound of her voice – all said the same thing to him: 'This is wrong. Everything you have lived by, and still do, is a lie, a deception that hides life and death away from you.'

And the moment this thought occurred to him, his hatred welled up, and along with the hatred came physical suffering and agony, and along with the agony came awareness of the inevitable destruction that was now so close. There was something different about it: a twisting, shooting pain, and constricted breathing.

The look on his face as he said 'Yes' had been dreadful. When he had got the word out, looking straight at her, he wrenched himself over face down remarkably quickly for one so weak, and roared at her: 'Get out! Go away! Leave me alone!'

12

From that moment on the screaming began. It went on unbroken for three days, so terrible that people two rooms away were horrified to hear it. At the moment when he had answered his wife he had realized he was done for, there was no way back, the end was here, the absolute end, and his unresolved doubts would remain as doubts.

'Oh! Oh! Oh!' he cried, varying the tone. He began by crying out, 'Oh no!' and went on screaming the letter 'o'. Throughout the three days, during which time had ceased to exist for him, he struggled with the black sack into which he was being crammed by an invisible, unstoppable force. He resisted like a condemned man resisting his executioner, knowing that he is not going to be spared, and with every minute that passed he sensed that, despite all his fighting and struggling, he was getting nearer and nearer to the thing that terrified him. He sensed that the pain came from being thrust into that black hole and, what was worse, not being able to get through. What was preventing him from getting through was his insistence that his life had been a good one. This vindication of his lifestyle was holding him down, preventing him from moving on, and causing him the greatest suffering.

Suddenly he felt a strong jolt in his chest and side, and a further constriction of his breathing. He was into the hole, and there at the end of the hole a kind of light was shining. What was happening to him was like when he had been in a railway carriage and you think you are going forwards but you are really going backwards, and suddenly you know what the right direction is.

'Yes, it's all been wrong,' he told himself, 'but that doesn't matter. It's possible to do the right thing. But what is the right thing?' he wondered, and suddenly he was calm.

It was nearing the end of the third day, an hour before his death. At that very moment his schoolboy son crept in to see his father and came over to his bed. The dying man was still screaming desperately and waving his arms about. His hand happened to catch the boy's head. The boy took hold of it, pressed it to his lips and burst into tears.

This was the very moment when Ivan Ilyich had fallen through and seen a light, and it was revealed to him that his life had not been what it should have been, but that it could still be put right. He was wondering what the right thing was, and he had calmed down, listening. Now he could feel someone kissing his hand. He opened his eyes and looked at his son. He felt sorry for him. His wife came over. He looked at her. With her mouth open and the tears not wiped away from her nose and cheek she was looking at him in despair. He felt sorry for her.

'Yes, I'm hurting them,' he thought. 'They feel sorry for me, but they'll be all right when I'm dead.' He wanted to tell them this, but he wasn't strong enough to get the words out. 'Anyway . . . no good talking. Must *do* something.' He looked at his wife, motioned to their son and said: 'Take him away . . . sorry for him . . . and you . . .' He tried to say, 'Forgive me,' but it came out as, 'For goodness . . .' Too weak to correct himself, he waved his hand knowing that he who needed to would understand.

And suddenly everything was clear to him: what had been oppressing him and would not go away *was* now going away, all at once, on two sides, ten sides, all sides. He felt sorry for them, and he must do something to stop hurting them. Set them free, and free himself from all this suffering. 'So nice, and so simple,' he thought. 'But what about the pain?' he wondered. 'Where's it gone? Hey, pain, where are you?'

He listened and waited.

'Oh, here it comes. So what? Bring on the pain.'

'What about death? Where is it?'

He was looking for his earlier, accustomed fear of death, but he couldn't find it. Where was death? What death? There was no fear whatsoever, because there was no death.

Instead of death there was light.

'So that's it!' he said suddenly, out loud. 'Oh, bliss!'

All of this happened to him in a single moment, and the meaning of that moment was not going to change. For those present, his agony went on for another two hours. There was a rattling in his chest. His wasted body shook. Then the rattling and the wheezing dwindled away.

'He's gone!' said someone over him.

He caught these words and repeated them in spirit. 'Death has gone,' he told himself.

'It's gone.'

He took in some air, stopped halfway through a deep breath, stretched out, and died.

Three Deaths

1

It was autumn. Two carriages were bowling along the highway at a fast trot. In the first carriage there were two women. One was a lady, thin and pale. The other was her maid, with a shiny red face and a stout figure; her short, dry hair kept straggling out from under her faded bonnet, and she pushed it back fitfully with a red hand in a torn glove. Her full bosom, covered by a thick cloth of carpet material, exuded good health, and her black eyes were busy; one moment they were peering through the window at the fields flashing by, then they would glance across diffidently at the mistress, or watch the corners of the carriage with some concern. In front of the maid's nose dangled her mistress's bonnet, hanging from the rack, and on her knees lay a puppy. Her feet, raised up on boxes standing on the floor, could just about be heard drumming along with the creaking springs and the rattling of the window-panes.

With her hands folded on her lap and her eyes shut the lady rocked feebly against the cushions placed behind her back, frowned slightly and gave a little cough from time to time. She wore a white nightcap on her head, and a light blue scarf was wound round her delicate white neck. A straight parting disappeared under her nightcap, dividing her remarkably sleek, pomaded, light brown hair, and there was something deathly and desiccated in the white skin that formed the parting. The withered, yellowing skin hung loosely over the thin but beautiful contours of her face, with crimson on her prominent cheekbones. Her lips were dry and restless, her thinning eyelashes had no curl in them, and a cloth travelling cloak lay in straight folds across her sunken chest. Even though her eyes were shut, the lady's face gave an impression of weariness, irritation and continual suffering.

A footman, wedged into his seat with his elbows on the sides, was dozing on the box. The coach driver drove his four big, sweating horses, yelling them on and glancing back now and then at another driver calling to him from a little open carriage behind them. Broad tyre tracks spread themselves evenly in speeding parallel lines along the limy, muddy road. The sky was grey and cold, and a damp mist was settling on the fields. Inside the carriage it was stuffy, smelling of eau-de-Cologne and dust. The invalid lady put her head back and opened her eyes. Her eyes were splendidly dark, and glittering.

'Again,' she said, and her beautiful thin hand nervously pushed away the hem of her maid's cloak which was brushing lightly against her leg, and her mouth was contorted with pain. Matryosha gathered up her cloak with both hands, half-rose on her strong legs and shifted away. Her fresh face was flushed bright red. The splendidly dark eyes of the invalid lady followed the maid's every movement. Her mistress gripped the seat with both hands and also tried to lift herself and sit up higher, but she couldn't manage it. Her mouth contracted and her whole face twisted itself into an expression of impotent, malevolent irony. 'A fat lot of help you are! Oh, don't bother! I can do it myself, and you needn't shove all your bags behind me. Please don't! No, don't touch me. You've no idea!' The lady closed her eyes, then raised her eyelids again sharply and glared at her maid. Matryosha looked back at her, biting her red lower lip. A heavy sigh arose in the invalid's bosom, but it was a sigh that cut itself short as it turned into a cough. She looked away, scowling, and clutched at her chest with both hands. When the coughing spasm was over she closed her eyes again and sat there without moving. The two carriages, one large and one small, drove into the village. Matryosha reached out from under her cover and made the sign of the cross.

'What is it?' asked her mistress.

'A post station, madam.'

'Why are you crossing yourself? That's what I'm asking you.'

'There's a church, madam.'

The invalid turned towards the window and began

crossing herself slowly, her eyes widening at the sight of the country church that her carriage was driving past.

The two carriages stopped together by the church. From the small one two men emerged: the invalid lady's husband and a doctor. They walked over to the large carriage.

'How are you feeling?' asked the doctor, taking her pulse.

'How are you, darling? Not too tired?' asked her husband, in French. 'Would you like to get out?'

Matryosha had scraped up her belongings and was squeezing back into the corner so as not to interfere with their conversation.

'Not too bad. Just the same,' the sick woman replied. 'I'm not getting out.'

The husband stood there for a short while, then went into the station building.

Matryosha skipped down from the carriage and ran tiptoeing in through the gateway.

'If I feel bad, that's no reason for you to miss lunch.' The sick lady gave a feeble smile as she spoke to the doctor, who was standing by her window.

'They're not bothered about me, any of them,' she added, talking to herself, as soon as the doctor had walked gently away and trotted up the steps into the station house. 'They're all right, and that's all that matters. Oh! My God!'

'Well then, Edward Ivanovich,' said the husband,

rubbing his hands with a cheerful smile as he welcomed the doctor in. 'I've told them to bring the lunch basket in. How does that strike you?'

'Not a bad idea,' replied the doctor.

'How is she doing, then?' the husband asked with a sigh, lowering his voice and raising his eyebrows.

'I've told you. She won't make it, not to Italy. She'll need God's grace to get to Moscow. Especially in this weather.'

'What can we do, then? Oh, my God! My God!' The husband buried his face in one hand. 'Put it down here,' he said to the man who was bringing in the lunch basket.

'She should have stayed put,' answered the doctor with a shrug.

'Oh yes, but what could I have done?' the husband protested. 'Look, I did all I could to stop her. I told her how about the money involved, leaving the children behind, my work. She just wouldn't listen. She was planning her life abroad as if she was well again. And telling her about her condition – well, that would have been the same as killing her off.'

'She's already been killed off. That's what you must realize, Vasily Dmitrich. A person cannot live without lungs, and lungs won't grow back. It's sad, it's hard to bear, but what can you do? Only one thing matters for you and me – to give her the most peaceful ending we can. And for that we need a priest.'

'Oh, my God! You can imagine my situation, having to remind her about her last wishes. Whatever happens, I'm not going to talk to her about that. You know how good she is . . .'

'Well, try and persuade her to wait until the roads are frozen over,' said the doctor, with a meaningful shake of his head. 'Otherwise something nasty might happen out on the road . . .'

'Aksyusha! Hey, Aksyusha!' yelled the stationmaster's daughter, throwing a jacket over her head and stamping on the dirty back porch. 'Let's go and have a look at that Shirkin lady. She's supposed to be goin' abroad with that disease in her chest. I ain't never seen how it is with them consumptives.'

Aksyusha skipped out on to the threshold, and both girls ran out through the gate, linking hands. They slowed down, walked past the carriage and took a look in through the lowered window. The sick lady turned to face them, but when she saw their curiosity she scowled and looked away.

'Gosh!' said the stationmaster's daughter, whirling her head round. 'She must have been a real beauty – and now look what's happened to her. It's horrible. Did you see her, Aksyusha? Did you see her?'

'Yes, all thin, wasn't she?' said Aksyusha, eager to back her up. 'Let's go and have another look, as if we're going to the well. She looked away, see, and I never got a good look. It's such a pity, Masha.'

'Yes, but look at all this mud!' said Masha, and they both ran back in through the gate.

'I must be a terrible sight,' thought the invalid lady. 'Must get going, as soon as we can, go abroad. I'll soon get better there.'

'Now then, how are you feeling, my dear?' said her husband, coming over to the carriage and chewing as he came.

'Always the same question,' thought the sick woman, 'but he's eating.'

'So-so,' she managed to get out, through clenched teeth.

'Do you know what, my dear, I'm afraid you're going to feel worse out on the road in this weather, and Edward says the same. Don't you think we should go back home?'

Furious with him, she said nothing.

'The weather might improve, the road could harden up, and you might feel better. Then we could all travel together.'

'I'm sorry. If I had stopped listening to you ages ago I'd be in Berlin by now, and I'd be better again.'

'We can't help it, my angel. It just wasn't possible, as you know. And now, if you would just stay on for another month, you'd feel so much better, I could get my business finished and we could bring the children . . .'

'The children are well. I'm not.'

'Darling, you must understand. In this kind of weather, if you take a turn for the worse out on the road . . . I mean, when you're at home, at least . . .'

'What? What could I do at home? . . . Die there?' The sick woman's response was venomous. But the word 'die' had clearly shaken her; she looked at her husband imploringly, her eyes questioning. He looked down, saying nothing. The woman's mouth crumpled like a child's, and tears streamed from her eyes. The husband buried his face in a handkerchief, and he walked away from the carriage without a word.

'No, I'm going on,' she said, raising her eyes to the heavens and folding her arms. She began to whisper incoherently. 'Oh my God, what's it all for?' she said, her tears flowing faster than ever. For some time she prayed, fervently, but her chest felt so painful and tight, the sky, the fields and the road looked so steeped in their gloomy grey, and the autumn mist never thickened and never thinned as it drizzled down in the same old way on to the muddy road, the roofs, the carriage and the thick coats of the drivers chatting to each other in ringing, cheerful voices while they greased the wheels and got the horses ready for the carriage.

2

The carriage was ready, but the driver was in no hurry. He had disappeared into the drivers' cabin. Inside it was hot and stuffy, dark and oppressive, smelling of people, newly baked bread, cabbage and sheepskins. There were one or two drivers there, a cook was fussing over the stove, and on the stove-top itself a sick man lay stretched out on some sheepskins.

'Uncle Fedya! Hey, Uncle Fedya!' said the young driver, still wearing his top-coat and a whip in his belt, as he came in and spoke to the sick man.

'What'm you doin' hangin' about here askin' after Fedya?' responded another driver. 'Look, they'm waitin' for you out in the carriage.'

'I want to ask him about his boots. Mine are worn out,' answered the young man, tossing his hair back and straightening the mittens in his belt. 'Maybe he's asleep. Hey, Uncle Fedya!' he repeated, walking over to the stove.

'You what?' came a feeble voice, and a thin, ruddy face bent down from the stove-top. A broad, skinny, pale and hairy arm jerked a coat up over a bony shoulder in a dirty shirt. 'Give us something to drink, me lad. What was you saying?'

The lad offered him some water in a dipper.

'Well, Fedya, it's . . . er . . . like this,' he said, shifting from one foot to the other. 'I don't imagine you needs new boots now. You could let me 'ave 'em. Seems as if you won't be doing no walking.'

The sick man brought his weary head down to the shiny dipper, wetting his thin, straggling whiskers in the dark water as he drank feebly but thirstily. His matted beard was dirty, and his sunken clouded eyes didn't find it easy to look up at the young man's face. Finishing with the water, he tried to lift one hand to wipe his wet lips, but he couldn't manage it and he wiped himself on the coat sleeve. Saying nothing, he breathed in heavily through his nose and looked the young man straight in the eye, getting his strength up.

'Maybe they're already spoken for,' said the young man. 'If they are, it doesn't matter. The thing is – it's wet out there, and I've got my work to do, and I just thought I'd ask old Fedya about his boots – maybe he don't need them any more. Perhaps you do need them. Just tell me . . .'

There was a rumbling and a gurgling in the sick man's chest. He bent double and started choking on a throaty cough that never really got going.

'How can he need them?' the cook snapped unexpectedly, speaking angrily to the whole cabin. 'He ain't been down off that stove for a couple of months. You can hear him. Gives you a pain inside just to listen to him. Can't be needing no boots, can he? They're not going to bury him with new boots on. His time's up, God forgive me, I'm a sinner. You can see he's cracking up. He ought be taken away into another hut or somewhere else. What I'm saying is, there's hospitals in town. And what right has he got taking up all that corner? No two ways about it. Some of us don't have no room at all. And they keeps telling you to keep the place clean.'

'Hey, Sergey! Get yourself on board. The master and mistress is waiting,' called the post-controller from outside.

Sergey made as if to go, without waiting for a response, but the sick man's eyes signalled while he was coughing that he wanted to give him an answer.

'You can have my boots, Sergey,' he said, stifling his cough. 'But listen,' he added wheezily, 'you buy me a stone when I'm dead.'

'Thanks, Uncle. All right, I'll take them. And I really will get you a stone.'

'That's it, then. You heard that, lads.' The sick man was finding it hard to speak, and he bent double again, choking.

'Sure, we heard,' said one of the drivers. 'Get going, Sergey, or the boss'll be back. That Shirkin lady's not well, you know.'

Sergey slipped off his worn-out boots – they were too big for him – and chucked them under the bench. Uncle Fyodor's new boots fitted him nicely, and Sergey looked down at them as he walked out to the carriage.

'Nice pair of boots! Let me grease them for you,' said a driver with a handful of axle grease as Sergey got up on his box and gathered the reins. 'Got 'em for nothing?'

'Not jealous, are you?' Sergey replied, half-rising and tucking the bottom of his coat round his legs. 'Forget it! Come on, me beauties!' he cried to the horses, cracking the whip, and the two carriages – one large and one small, with their drivers, bags and baggage – disappeared into the grey autumn mist, rocking as they sped away down the wet road.

The sick driver was left behind on his stove in the stuffy hut. Unable to stifle his coughing, he made a big effort, turned on to his other side and lay there still and quiet.

The hut was busy until late in the day with people coming and going and having their supper. Not a sound came from the sick man. As night drew on, the cook climbed up on to the stove and reached across his legs to get at her long coat.

'Don't moan at me, Nastasya,' said the sick man. 'I'll soon make room for you in this corner.'

'All right. All right. Don't go on about it. 'Taint nothing,' muttered Nastasya. 'Where's it hurt, Uncle? You can tell me.'

'It's me insides. All gone wrong. God knows what.'

'Throat giving you trouble, with all that coughing?'

'It all hurts. Time for me to die – and that's it. Oh, oh, oh . . .' moaned the sick man.

'Cover your feet up. 'Ere, like this,' said Natasha, clambering down and pulling his coat over him as she did so.

A night light burned feebly in the hut. Nastasya and a dozen drivers were asleep on the floor or on benches, snoring loudly. Only the sick man could be heard wheezing and coughing as he tossed and turned on the stove. When morning came he was completely quiet.

'I've had a fantastic dream,' said the cook, stretching herself in the half-light of a new morning. 'Uncle Fyodor got down from the stove and went out to chop some wood. "Come on, Nastasya," he says. "Let me give you some help." And I says to him, "How can you go out chopping wood?" but off he goes with the axe, chopping away like mad and the chips flying everywhere. "What's all this?" I says. "I thought you was ill." He says, "No, I'm all right now", and he swings that axe round – scared me stiff, he did. I shouted out and woke up. He's not dead, is he? Uncle Fyodor. Hey, Uncle!'

Fyodor didn't answer.

'I wonder if he has died. Ought to go and have a look,' said one of the drivers, who had just woken up.

The scrawny arm dangling down from the stove, covered in reddish hair, was cold and pale.

'Go and tell the boss it looks like he's dead,' said the driver.

Fyodor didn't have any relatives – he came from miles away. They buried him the next day in the new cemetery beyond the wood, and for several days Nastasya went around telling everybody about her dream and how she had been the first to find out Uncle Fyodor was dead.

3

It was now spring. Gurgling rivulets of water ran down the wet city streets, scurrying between frozen chunks of manure; people bustled about in a bright display of colour and sound given off by their clothing and their chatter. In little fenced-off gardens the buds had begun to swell on the trees, and you could just catch the murmur of branches rocking in the breeze. Limpid droplets dripped and trickled everywhere . . . Sparrows squawked and twittered amidst a fluttering of tiny wings. On the sunny side, on fences, houses and trees, everything shimmered and shone. Joy and youth shone in the sky, and on earth and in the heart of man.

One of the main streets, outside a large house belonging to a member of the gentry, had been strewn with fresh straw; inside, the lady who had been rushing to travel abroad lay dying.

The sick lady's husband and an elderly woman stood by the closed doors of her room. On the sofa sat a priest with downcast eyes, holding on to something wrapped in his stole. In one corner an old woman reclined in a high-backed armchair – the sick lady's mother – weeping bitter tears. At her side, holding a clean handkerchief, stood a maid waiting to be called; another maid was using some sort of cloth to massage the old woman's temples while she blew upon her grey head under her cap.

'Christ be with you, my dear,' said the husband of an elderly lady standing with him by the door. 'She has so much faith in you, and you know exactly how to talk to her. Try and persuade her, as nicely as you can. Go in and see her.'

He was about to open the door for her, but she, a cousin of the invalid, stopped him, pressed a handkerchief to her eyes several times, and shook her head.

'Now I don't look as if I've been crying,' she said, opening the door herself and walking through.

The husband was in a state of extreme agitation; he looked distraught. He set off towards the old woman, but within a few strides he turned away and headed for the priest. The priest looked at him, raised his eyebrows to Heaven and sighed. His thick beard, shot through with grey, also raised and lowered itself.

'My God, my God!' said the husband.

'What can we do?' said the priest with another sigh, and once again his eyebrows and his short beard were raised and lowered.

'And her mother's here!' said the husband, on the verge of despair. 'That will finish her off. So much love, so much love for her, and she . . . oh, I don't know. Maybe you could comfort her, Father, and get her to go away.'

The priest got up and went to the old lady.

'Quite so,' he said. 'No one can appreciate a mother's heart. But God is merciful.'

The old lady's face suddenly started to twitch all over, and she was retching with hysteria.

'God is merciful,' continued the priest once she was a little calmer. 'I can tell you this. In my parish there was a man who was ill – much worse than Marya Dmitrievna – and – do you know what? – he was cured in no time by a tradesman with some herbs. And you'll find that tradesman alive in Moscow today. I was just saying to Vasily Dmitrievich that we might give him a try. At least it would bring some comfort to the poor woman. For God, all things are possible.'

'No, she's not going to live,' put in the old woman. 'It should be me, but God's taking her.' And her hysterical retching came on so strongly that she fell into a faint.

The invalid's husband buried his face in his hands and rushed out of the room.

Out in the passage the first person he ran into was a six-year-old boy chasing a younger girl as fast as his legs would carry him.

'What would you like me to do? Should I take the children in to see their mother?' asked the nanny.

'No, she doesn't want to see them. It will upset her.'

The boy stopped for a moment, looked his father straight in the face, lashed out with his foot and ran off again yelling with delight.

'She's being a black horse, Daddy!' cried the little boy, pointing to his sister.

Meanwhile, in the next room the invalid's cousin was sitting at her side, conducting a forced conversation in which she was trying to prepare her for death. The doctor stood by another window, stirring his drink.

The sick woman was sitting up in bed, clad in a white dressing-gown and beset with pillows on every side, watching her cousin in silence.

'Oh, my dear friend,' she said, suddenly interrupting, 'don't prepare me. Don't treat me like a child. I'm a Christian. I know it all. I know I haven't got long to live, and

I know that if only my husband had listened to me I'd have been in Italy by now, and I might have been better – I probably *would* have been. Everybody told him. But there's nothing we can do. It seems to have been God's will. We all bear many sins, I know that, but I trust in God's mercy that all will be forgiven. It must surely be that all will be forgiven. I am trying to come to terms with myself. I too have borne many sins, my dear. But think how much I have suffered. I've tried to bear my sufferings with patience . . .'

'So, should I tell the priest to come in? You'll feel better when you've taken communion,' said her cousin.

The invalid inclined her head in agreement.

'God forgive me, sinner that I am,' she whispered.

Her cousin went out and winked at the holy father.

'She's an angel!' she said to the husband with tears in her eyes.

The husband burst into tears, the priest walked in through the door, the old woman was still lost to the world, and in the room itself all was completely quiet. Five minutes later the priest emerged from the room, took off his stole and ran a hand through his hair.

'Thank God she's calmer now,' he said. 'She wants to see you.'

The cousin and the husband went in. The invalid was weeping softly, looking at an icon.

'Well done, my darling,' said her husband.

'Thank you! I feel so well now. I feel a kind of

sweetness,' said the invalid, a gentle smile playing on her thin lips. 'God is so merciful! Isn't that right? So merciful, and omnipotent.' And she looked at the icon again, her eyes brimming with tears and eager with supplication.

Then suddenly she seemed to remember something. She beckoned her husband closer. 'You never want to do what I ask,' she said in a feeble and petulant voice.

Her husband craned his neck, listening submissively. 'What's that, darling?'

'How many times have I told you the doctors are ignorant? There are folk healers, and they can cure people . . . The priest was telling me just now . . . about a tradesman . . . Send for him.'

'Who?'

'Oh God! You're determined not to understand! . . .' The invalid scowled and closed her eyes.

The doctor came over and took her hand. Her pulse was getting noticeably weaker and weaker. He winked at the husband. The invalid noticed the gesture and looked round in alarm.

'Don't cry, and torment yourself or me,' said the patient. 'You're taking away my last consolation.'

'You're an angel!' said her cousin, kissing her hand.

'No. Kiss me here. Only dead people get kissed on the hand. Oh God! Oh God!'

By that evening the patient had become a body, and the body lay in its coffin in the biggest room in the large house. A deacon sat alone in that great room with the doors wide open, intoning the Psalms in a nasal voice. A bright waxy light fell from the tall silver candlesticks on to the pallid face of the dead lady, the heavy waxen hands and the frozen folds of her pall, which stuck up horribly at her knees and toes. The deacon droned on, with no understanding of his words – words which rang out and died away horribly. Now and then the sounds of children's voices and their rumpus floated in from a distant room.

'Thou hidest Thy face, they are troubled,' ran the psalter. 'Thou takest away their breath, they die and return to their dust. Thou sendest forth Thy spirit, they are created, and Thou renewest the face of the earth. The glory of the Lord shall endure for ever.'

The face of the dead lady was stern, tranquil and majestic. Neither on her clear cold brow nor on her tightly closed lips was there any movement. She was all ears. But was she even now understanding those solemn words?

4

A month later a stone chapel had been erected above the dead lady's grave. Above the driver's grave the stone had yet to appear; nothing more than bright green grass came up from the mound that served as the only indication of the past existence of a man.

'It'll be a sin on your conscience,' said the cook one day at the post station, 'if you don't buy a stone for Fyodor. You kept on saying, "It's winter. It's winter," but now it's different – why don't you keep your promise? You know I witnessed it. He's been back once to ask why you haven't bought it. Next time he'll throttle you.'

'What are you on about? Have I gone back on my word?' Sergey answered. 'I'm going to buy him a stone, like I said, and I will. I'll shell out one and a half roubles. I haven't forgotten, but it's got to be fetched. When I'm in town I'll go and buy it.'

'At least you ought to stick a cross up, that's what I says,' put in an old driver. "Tis just plain wrong if you don't. You'm wearing his boots.'

'Where am I going to get a cross from? I can't chop one out of a log.'

'Can't chop one out of a log – what are you talking about? Take your axe, get yourself out in the forest first thing, and you can cut one there. Go on, cut a little ash tree down . . . and there's your cross. Either that or buy the forester a few drinks. Doesn't mean you've got to treat him for any old bit of rubbish. Couple of days ago when I broke me splinter bar I cut meself a smashing new one, and nobody said nothing about it.'

Early next morning at the crack of dawn Sergey took his axe and went into the woods.

Everything was covered with a cold blanket of dew that was still settling, untouched by the sun. The east was getting imperceptibly brighter, reflecting its feeble light on the vault of heaven that was still thinly veiled with clouds. Not a blade of grass below, not a leaf on the topmost branches stirred. Only now and then the disturbing sounds of wings flapping in the brushwood or a rustling on the ground intruded on the silence of the forest. Then suddenly a strange noise, alien to the world of nature, rang out and died away on the edge of the forest. But the noise came again and repeated itself rhythmically at the bottom of the trunk of one of the motionless trees. One of the treetops gave an unusual shudder, its sappy leaves whispering, and a little robin who had been sitting on one of its branches gave a chirrup and flitted about a couple of times before cocking its tail and transferring to another tree.

Down below, the ring of the axe sounded more and more muffled, sappy white splinters flew down on to the dewy grass, and through the chopping came a slight creaking sound. The tree shook throughout its whole body, lurched over and quickly straightened up, wobbling with alarm upon its roots. Everything was quiet for a moment, but then the tree lurched again, another creak came from its trunk, and with its branches snapping and its boughs dangling it crashed down crown first on to the damp ground. The sounds of chopping and the footsteps stopped. The robin gave a chirrup and fluttered up higher. Its wings snagged against a twig, which shook for a moment or two before settling its leaves like all the others. The trees revelled in the beauty of their branches all the more joyously in the newly created space.

The first rays of the sun found their way through the thinning clouds, shone out against the sky and ran across the ground and sky together. Mist rolled down the valleys in waves, the dew glittered as it toyed with the greenery, and limpid whitening cloudlets sped across the azure firmament. Birds stirred in the thickets, twittering their happy song for all they were worth. On high, the succulent leaves whispered in peace and joy, and the boughs of the living trees slowly stirred themselves, looking down in majesty on the dead tree that lay flat out on the ground.

‘He was not blind to the fact that murder, like the religions of the Pagan world, requires a victim as well as a priest.’

OSCAR WILDE

Lord Arthur Savile's Crime

Lord Arthur Savile's Crime

I

It was Lady Windermere's last reception before Easter, and Bentinck House was even more crowded than usual. Six Cabinet Ministers had come on from the Speaker's Levée in their stars and ribands, all the pretty women wore their smartest dresses, and at the end of the picture-gallery stood the Princess Sophia of Carlsrühe, a heavy Tartar-looking lady, with tiny black eyes and wonderful emeralds, talking bad French at the top of her voice, and laughing immoderately at everything that was said to her. It was certainly a wonderful medley of people. Gorgeous peeresses chatted affably to violent Radicals, popular preachers brushed coat-tails with eminent sceptics, a perfect bevy of bishops kept following a stout prima-donna from room to room, on the staircase stood several Royal Academicians, disguised as artists, and it was said that at one time the supper-room was absolutely crammed with geniuses. In fact, it was one of Lady

Windermere's best nights, and the Princess stayed till nearly half-past eleven.

As soon as she had gone, Lady Windermere returned to the picture-gallery, where a celebrated political economist was solemnly explaining the scientific theory of music to an indignant virtuoso from Hungary, and began to talk to the Duchess of Paisley. She looked wonderfully beautiful with her grand ivory throat, her large blue forget-me-not eyes, and her heavy coils of golden hair. *Or pur* they were – not that pale straw colour that nowadays usurps the gracious name of gold, but such gold as is woven into sunbeams or hidden in strange amber; and they gave to her face something of the frame of a saint, with not a little of the fascination of a sinner. She was a curious psychological study. Early in life she had discovered the important truth that nothing looks so like innocence as an indiscretion; and by a series of reckless escapades, half of them quite harmless, she had acquired all the privileges of a personality. She had more than once changed her husband; indeed, Debrett credits her with three marriages; but as she had never changed her lover, the world had long ago ceased to talk scandal about her. She was now forty years of age, childless, and with that inordinate passion for pleasure which is the secret of remaining young.

Suddenly she looked eagerly round the room, and said, in her clear contralto voice, 'Where is my cheiromantist?'

'Your what, Gladys?' exclaimed the Duchess, giving an involuntary start.

'My cheiromantist, Duchess; I can't live without him at present.'

'Dear Gladys! you are always so original,' murmured the Duchess, trying to remember what a cheiromantist really was, and hoping it was not the same as a cheiropodist.

'He comes to see my hand twice a week regularly,' continued Lady Windermere, 'and is most interesting about it.'

'Good heavens!' said the Duchess to herself, 'he is a sort of cheiropodist after all. How very dreadful. I hope he is a foreigner at any rate. It wouldn't be quite so bad then.'

'I must certainly introduce him to you.'

'Introduce him!' cried the Duchess; 'you don't mean to say he is here?' and she began looking about for a small tortoise-shell fan and a very tattered lace shawl, so as to be ready to go at a moment's notice.

'Of course he is here, I would not dream of giving a party without him. He tells me I have a pure psychic hand, and that if my thumb had been the least little bit shorter, I should have been a confirmed pessimist, and gone into a convent.'

'Oh, I see!' said the Duchess, feeling very much relieved; 'he tells fortunes, I suppose?'

'And misfortunes, too,' answered Lady Windermere, 'any amount of them. Next year, for instance, I am in great danger, both by land and sea, so I am going to live in a balloon, and draw up my dinner in a basket every evening. It is all written down on my little finger, or on the palm of my hand, I forget which.'

'But surely that is tempting Providence, Gladys.'

'My dear Duchess, surely Providence can resist temptation by this time. I think every one should have their hands told once a month, so as to know what not to do. Of course, one does it all the same, but it is so pleasant to be warned. Now, if some one doesn't go and fetch Mr Podgers at once, I shall have to go myself.'

'Let me go, Lady Windermere,' said a tall handsome young man, who was standing by, listening to the conversation with an amused smile.

'Thanks so much, Lord Arthur; but I am afraid you wouldn't recognise him.'

'If he is as wonderful as you say, Lady Windermere, I couldn't well miss him. Tell me what he is like, and I'll bring him to you at once.'

'Well, he is not a bit like a cheiromantist. I mean he is not mysterious, or esoteric, or romantic-looking. He is a little, stout man, with a funny, bald head, and great gold-rimmed spectacles; something between a family doctor and a country attorney. I'm really very sorry, but it is not my fault. People are so annoying. All my pianists look exactly like poets, and all my poets look exactly like

pianists; and I remember last season asking a most dreadful conspirator to dinner, a man who had blown up ever so many people, and always wore a coat of mail, and carried a dagger up his shirt-sleeve; and do you know that when he came he looked just like a nice old clergyman, and cracked jokes all the evening? Of course, he was very amusing, and all that, but I was awfully disappointed; and when I asked him about the coat of mail, he only laughed, and said it was far too cold to wear in England. Ah, here is Mr Podgers! Now, Mr Podgers, I want you to tell the Duchess of Paisley's hand. Duchess, you must take your glove off. No, not the left hand, the other.'

'Dear Gladys, I really don't think it is quite right,' said the Duchess, feebly unbuttoning a rather soiled kid glove.

'Nothing interesting ever is,' said Lady Windermere: '*on a fait le monde ainsi*. But I must introduce you. Duchess, this is Mr Podgers, my pet cheiromantist. Mr Podgers, this is the Duchess of Paisley, and if you say that she has a larger mountain of the moon than I have, I will never believe in you again.'

'I am sure, Gladys, there is nothing of the kind in my hand,' said the Duchess gravely.

'Your Grace is quite right,' said Mr Podgers, glancing at the little fat hand with its short square fingers, 'the mountain of the moon is not developed. The line of life, however, is excellent. Kindly bend the wrist. Thank you. Three distinct lines on the *rascette*! You will live to a great

age, Duchess, and be extremely happy. Ambition – very moderate, line of intellect not exaggerated, line of heart –'

'Now, do be indiscreet, Mr Podgers,' cried Lady Windermere.

'Nothing would give me greater pleasure,' said Mr Podgers, bowing, 'if the Duchess ever had been, but I am sorry to say that I see great permanence of affection, combined with a strong sense of duty.'

'Pray go on, Mr Podgers,' said the Duchess, looking quite pleased.

'Economy is not the least of your Grace's virtues,' continued Mr Podgers, and Lady Windermere went off into fits of laughter.

'Economy is a very good thing,' remarked the Duchess complacently; 'when I married Paisley he had eleven castles, and not a single house fit to live in.'

'And now he has twelve houses, and not a single castle,' cried Lady Windermere.

'Well, my dear,' said the Duchess, 'I like –'

'Comfort,' said Mr Podgers, 'and modern improvements, and hot water laid on in every bedroom. Your Grace is quite right. Comfort is the only thing our civilisation can give us.'

'You have told the Duchess's character admirably, Mr Podgers, and now you must tell Lady Flora's;' and in answer to a nod from the smiling hostess, a tall girl, with sandy Scotch hair, and high shoulder-blades, stepped

awkwardly from behind the sofa, and held out a long, bony hand with spatulate fingers.

'Ah, a pianist! I see,' said Mr Podgers, 'an excellent pianist, but perhaps hardly a musician. Very reserved, very honest, and with a great love of animals.'

'Quite true!' exclaimed the Duchess, turning to Lady Windermere, 'absolutely true! Flora keeps two dozen collie dogs at Macloskie, and would turn our town house into a menagerie if her father would let her.'

'Well, that is just what I do with my house every Thursday evening,' cried Lady Windermere, laughing, 'only I like lions better than collie dogs.'

'Your one mistake, Lady Windermere,' said Mr Podgers, with a pompous bow.

'If a woman can't make her mistakes charming, she is only a female,' was the answer. 'But you must read some more hands for us. Come, Sir Thomas, show Mr Podgers yours;' and a genial-looking old gentleman, in a white waistcoat, came forward, and held out a thick rugged hand, with a very long third finger.

'An adventurous nature; four long voyages in the past, and one to come. Been shipwrecked three times. No, only twice, but in danger of a shipwreck your next journey. A strong Conservative, very punctual, and with a passion for collecting curiosities. Had a severe illness between the ages of sixteen and eighteen. Was left a fortune when about thirty. Great aversion to cats and Radicals.'

'Extraordinary!' exclaimed Sir Thomas; 'you must really tell my wife's hand, too.'

'Your second wife's,' said Mr Podgers quietly, still keeping Sir Thomas's hand in his. 'Your second wife's. I shall be charmed;' but Lady Marvel, a melancholy-looking woman, with brown hair and sentimental eyelashes, entirely declined to have her past or her future exposed; and nothing that Lady Windermere could do would induce Monsieur de Koloff, the Russian Ambassador, even to take his gloves off. In fact, many people seemed afraid to face the odd little man with his stereotyped smile, his gold spectacles, and his bright, beady eyes; and when he told poor Lady Fermor, right out before every one, that she did not care a bit for music, but was extremely fond of musicians, it was generally felt that cheiromancy was a most dangerous science, and one that ought not to be encouraged, except in a *tête-à-tête*.

Lord Arthur Savile, however, who did not know anything about Lady Fermor's unfortunate story, and who had been watching Mr Podgers with a great deal of interest, was filled with an immense curiosity to have his own hand read, and feeling somewhat shy about putting himself forward, crossed over the room to where Lady Windermere was sitting, and, with a charming blush, asked her if she thought Mr Podgers would mind.

'Of course, he won't mind,' said Lady Windermere, 'that is what he is here for. All my lions, Lord Arthur, are performing lions, and jump through hoops whenever I

ask them. But I must warn you beforehand that I shall tell Sybil everything. She is coming to lunch with me to-morrow, to talk about bonnets, and if Mr Podgers finds out that you have a bad temper, or a tendency to gout, or a wife living in Bayswater, I shall certainly let her know all about it.'

Lord Arthur smiled, and shook his head. 'I am not afraid,' he answered. 'Sybil knows me as well as I know her.'

'Ah! I am a little sorry to hear you say that. The proper basis for marriage is a mutual misunderstanding. No, I am not at all cynical, I have merely got experience, which, however, is very much the same thing. Mr Podgers, Lord Arthur Savile is dying to have his hand read. Don't tell him that he is engaged to one of the most beautiful girls in London, because that appeared in the *Morning Post* a month ago.

'Dear Lady Windermere,' cried the Marchioness of Jedburgh, 'do let Mr Podgers stay here a little longer. He has just told me I should go on the stage, and I am so interested.'

'If he has told you that, Lady Jedburgh, I shall certainly take him away. Come over at once, Mr Podgers, and read Lord Arthur's hand.'

'Well,' said Lady Jedburgh, making a little *moue* as she rose from the sofa, 'if I am not to be allowed to go on the stage, I must be allowed to be part of the audience at any rate.'

'Of course; we are all going to be part of the audience,' said Lady Windermere; 'and now, Mr Podgers, be sure and tell us something nice. Lord Arthur is one of my special favourites.'

But when Mr Podgers saw Lord Arthur's hand he grew curiously pale, and said nothing. A shudder seemed to pass through him, and his great bushy eyebrows twitched convulsively, in an odd, irritating way they had when he was puzzled. Then some huge beads of perspiration broke out on his yellow forehead, like a poisonous dew, and his fat fingers grew cold and clammy.

Lord Arthur did not fail to notice these strange signs of agitation, and, for the first time in his life, he himself felt fear. His impulse was to rush from the room, but he restrained himself. It was better to know the worst, whatever it was, than to be left in this hideous uncertainty.

'I am waiting, Mr Podgers,' he said.

'We are all waiting,' cried Lady Windermere, in her quick, impatient manner, but the cheiromantist made no reply.

'I believe Arthur is going on the stage,' said Lady Jedburgh, 'and that, after your scolding, Mr Podgers is afraid to tell him so.'

Suddenly Mr Podgers dropped Lord Arthur's right hand, and seized hold of his left, bending down so low to examine it that the gold rims of his spectacles seemed almost to touch the palm. For a moment his face became

a white mask of horror, but he soon recovered his *sang-froid*, and looking up at Lady Windermere, said with a forced smile, 'It is the hand of a charming young man.'

'Of course it is!' answered Lady Windermere, 'but will he be a charming husband? That is what I want to know.'

'All charming young men are,' said Mr Podgers.

'I don't think a husband should be too fascinating,' murmured Lady Jedburgh pensively, 'it is so dangerous.'

'My dear child, they never are too fascinating,' cried Lady Windermere. 'But what I want are details. Details are the only things that interest. What is going to happen to Lord Arthur?'

'Well, within the next few months Lord Arthur will go on a voyage –'

'Oh yes, his honeymoon, of course!'

'And lose a relative.'

'Not his sister, I hope?' said Lady Jedburgh, in a piteous tone of voice.

'Certainly not his sister,' answered Mr Podgers, with a deprecating wave of the hand, 'a distant relative merely.'

'Well, I am dreadfully disappointed,' said Lady Windermere. 'I have absolutely nothing to tell Sybil to-morrow. No one cares about distant relatives nowadays. They went out of fashion years ago. However, I suppose she had better have a black silk by her; it always does for church, you know. And now let us go to supper. They are sure to have eaten everything up, but we may find some hot soup.

François used to make excellent soup once, but he is so agitated about politics at present, that I never feel quite certain about him. I do wish General Boulanger would keep quiet. Duchess, I am sure you are tired?'

'Not at all, dear Gladys,' answered the Duchess, waddling towards the door. 'I have enjoyed myself immensely, and the cheiropodist, I mean the cheiromantist, is most interesting. Flora, where can my tortoise-shell fan be? Oh, thank you, Sir Thomas, so much. And my lace shawl, Flora? Oh, thank you, Sir Thomas, very kind, I'm sure;' and the worthy creature finally managed to get downstairs without dropping her scent-bottle more than twice.

All this time Lord Arthur Savile had remained standing by the fireplace, with the same feeling of dread over him, the same sickening sense of coming evil. He smiled sadly at his sister, as she swept past him on Lord Plymdale's arm, looking lovely in her pink brocade and pearls, and he hardly heard Lady Windermere when she called to him to follow her. He thought of Sybil Merton, and the idea that anything could come between them made his eyes dim with tears.

Looking at him, one would have said that Nemesis had stolen the shield of Pallas, and shown him the Gorgon's head. He seemed turned to stone, and his face was like marble in its melancholy. He had lived the delicate and luxurious life of a young man of birth and fortune, a life exquisite in its freedom from sordid care, its beautiful boyish insouciance; and now for the first time he became

conscious of the terrible mystery of Destiny, of the awful meaning of Doom.

How mad and monstrous it all seemed! Could it be that written on his hand, in characters that he could not read himself, but that another could decipher, was some fearful secret of sin, some blood-red sign of crime? Was there no escape possible? Were we no better than chessmen, moved by an unseen power, vessels the potter fashions at his fancy, for honour or for shame? His reason revolted against it, and yet he felt that some tragedy was hanging over him, and that he had been suddenly called upon to bear an intolerable burden. Actors are so fortunate. They can choose whether they will appear in tragedy or in comedy, whether they will suffer or make merry, laugh or shed tears. But in real life it is different. Most men and women are forced to perform parts for which they have no qualifications. Our Guildensterns play Hamlet for us, and our Hamlets have to jest like Prince Hal. The world is a stage, but the play is badly cast.

Suddenly Mr Podgers entered the room. When he saw Lord Arthur he started, and his coarse, fat face became a sort of greenish-yellow colour. The two men's eyes met, and for a moment there was silence.

'The Duchess has left one of her gloves here, Lord Arthur, and has asked me to bring it to her,' said Mr Podgers finally. 'Ah, I see it on the sofa! Good evening.'

'Mr Podgers, I must insist on your giving me a straightforward answer to a question I am going to put to you.'

'Another time, Lord Arthur, but the Duchess is anxious. I am afraid I must go.'

'You shall not go. The Duchess is in no hurry.'

'Ladies should not be kept waiting, Lord Arthur,' said Mr Podgers, with his sickly smile.

'The fair sex is apt to be impatient.'

Lord Arthur's finely-chiselled lips curled in petulant disdain. The poor Duchess seemed to him of very little importance at that moment. He walked across the room to where Mr Podgers was standing, and held his hand out.

'Tell me what you saw there,' he said. 'Tell me the truth. I must know it. I am not a child.'

Mr Podgers's eyes blinked behind his gold-rimmed spectacles, and he moved uneasily from one foot to the other, while his fingers played nervously with a flash watch-chain.

'What makes you think that I saw anything in your hand, Lord Arthur, more than I told you?'

'I know you did, and I insist on your telling me what it was. I will pay you. I will give you a cheque for a hundred pounds.'

The green eyes flashed for a moment, and then became dull again.

'Guineas?' said Mr Podgers at last, in a low voice.

'Certainly. I will send you a cheque to-morrow. What is your club?'

'I have no club. That is to say, not just at present. My address is –, but allow me to give you my card;' and producing a bit of gilt-edged pasteboard from his waistcoat pocket, Mr Podgers handed it, with a low bow, to Lord Arthur, who read on it,

MR SEPTIMUS R. PODGERS
Professional Cheiromantist
103a West Moon Street

'My hours are from ten to four,' murmured Mr Podgers mechanically, 'and I make a reduction for families.'

'Be quick,' cried Lord Arthur, looking very pale, and holding his hand out.

Mr Podgers glanced nervously round, and drew the heavy *portière* across the door.

'It will take a little time, Lord Arthur, you had better sit down.'

'Be quick, sir,' cried Lord Arthur again, stamping his foot angrily on the polished floor.

Mr Podgers smiled, drew from his breast-pocket a small magnifying glass, and wiped it carefully with his handkerchief.

'I am quite ready,' he said.

II

Ten minutes later, with face blanched by terror, and eyes wild with grief, Lord Arthur Savile rushed from Bentinck House, crushing his way through the crowd of fur-coated footmen that stood round the large striped awning, and seeming not to see or hear anything. The night was bitter cold, and the gas-lamps round the square flared and flickered in the keen wind; but his hands were hot with fever, and his forehead burned like fire. On and on he went, almost with the gait of a drunken man. A policeman looked curiously at him as he passed, and a beggar, who slouched from an archway to ask for alms, grew frightened, seeing misery greater than his own. Once he stopped under a lamp, and looked at his hands. He thought he could detect the stain of blood already upon them, and a faint cry broke from his trembling lips.

Murder! that is what the cheiromantist had seen there. Murder! The very night seemed to know it, and the desolate wind to howl it in his ear. The dark corners of the streets were full of it. It grinned at him from the roofs of the houses.

First he came to the Park, whose sombre woodland seemed to fascinate him. He leaned wearily up against the railings, cooling his brow against the wet metal, and listening to the tremulous silence of the trees. 'Murder! murder!' he kept repeating, as though iteration could

dim the horror of the word. The sound of his own voice made him shudder, yet he almost hoped that Echo might hear him, and wake the slumbering city from its dreams. He felt a mad desire to stop the casual passer-by, and tell him everything.

Then he wandered across Oxford Street into narrow, shameful alleys. Two women with painted faces mocked at him as he went by. From a dark courtyard came a sound of oaths and blows, followed by shrill screams, and, huddled upon a damp doorstep, he saw the crook-backed forms of poverty and eld. A strange pity came over him. Were these children of sin and misery predestined to their end, as he to his? Were they, like him, merely the puppets of a monstrous show?

And yet it was not the mystery, but the comedy of suffering that struck him; its absolute uselessness, its grotesque want of meaning. How incoherent everything seemed! How lacking in all harmony! He was amazed at the discord between the shallow optimism of the day, and the real facts of existence. He was still very young.

After a time he found himself in front of Marylebone Church. The silent roadway looked like a long riband of polished silver, flecked here and there by the dark arabesques of waving shadows. Far into the distance curved the line of flickering gas-lamps, and outside a little walled-in house stood a solitary hansom, the driver asleep inside. He walked hastily in the direction of Portland Place, now and then looking round, as though he feared

that he was being followed. At the corner of Rich Street stood two men, reading a small bill upon a hoarding. An odd feeling of curiosity stirred him, and he crossed over. As he came near, the word 'Murder,' printed in black letters, met his eye. He started, and a deep flush came into his cheek. It was an advertisement offering a reward for any information leading to the arrest of a man of medium height, between thirty and forty years of age, wearing a billy-cock hat, a black coat, and check trousers, and with a scar upon his right cheek. He read it over and over again, and wondered if the wretched man would be caught, and how he had been scarred. Perhaps, some day, his own name might be placarded on the walls of London. Some day, perhaps, a price would be set on his head also.

The thought made him sick with horror. He turned on his heel, and hurried on into the night.

Where he went he hardly knew. He had a dim memory of wandering through a labyrinth of sordid houses, of being lost in a giant web of sombre streets, and it was bright dawn when he found himself at last in Piccadilly Circus. As he strolled home towards Belgrave Square, he met the great waggons on their way to Covent Garden. The white-smocked carters, with their pleasant sunburnt faces and coarse curly hair, strode sturdily on, cracking their whips, and calling out now and then to each other; on the back of a huge grey horse, the leader of a jangling team, sat a chubby boy, with a bunch of primroses in his

battered hat, keeping tight hold of the mane with his little hands, and laughing; and the great piles of vegetables looked like masses of jade against the morning sky, like masses of green jade against the pink petals of some marvellous rose. Lord Arthur felt curiously affected, he could not tell why. There was something in the dawn's delicate loveliness that seemed to him inexpressibly pathetic, and he thought of all the days that break in beauty, and that set in storm. These rustics, too, with their rough, good-humoured voices, and their nonchalant ways, what a strange London they saw! A London free from the sin of night and the smoke of day, a pallid, ghost-like city, a desolate town of tombs! He wondered what they thought of it, and whether they knew anything of its splendour and its shame, of its fierce, fiery-coloured joys, and its horrible hunger, of all it makes and mars from morn to eve. Probably it was to them merely a mart where they brought their fruits to sell, and where they tarried for a few hours at most, leaving the streets still silent, the houses still asleep. It gave him pleasure to watch them as they went by. Rude as they were, with their heavy, hob-nailed shoes, and their awkward gait, they brought a little of Arcady with them. He felt that they had lived with Nature, and that she had taught them peace. He envied them all that they did not know.

By the time he had reached Belgrave Square the sky was a faint blue, and the birds were beginning to twitter in the gardens.

III

When Lord Arthur woke it was twelve o'clock, and the mid-day sun was streaming through the ivory-silk curtains of his room. He got up and looked out of the window. A dim haze of heat was hanging over the great city, and the roofs of the houses were like dull silver. In the flickering green of the square below some children were flitting about like white butterflies, and the pavement was crowded with people on their way to the Park. Never had life seemed lovelier to him, never had the things of evil seemed more remote.

Then his valet brought him a cup of chocolate on a tray. After he had drunk it, he drew aside a heavy *portière* of peach-coloured plush, and passed into the bathroom. The light stole softly from above, through thin slabs of transparent onyx, and the water in the marble tank glimmered like a moonstone. He plunged hastily in, till the cool ripples touched throat and hair, and then dipped his head right under, as though he would have wiped away the stain of some shameful memory. When he stepped out he felt almost at peace. The exquisite physical conditions of the moment had dominated him, as indeed often happens in the case of very finely-wrought natures, for the senses, like fire, can purify as well as destroy.

After breakfast, he flung himself down on a divan, and lit a cigarette. On the mantel-shelf, framed in dainty old

brocade, stood a large photograph of Sybil Merton, as he had seen her first at Lady Noel's ball. The small, exquisitely-shaped head drooped slightly to one side, as though the thin, reed-like throat could hardly bear the burden of so much beauty; the lips were slightly parted, and seemed made for sweet music; and all the tender purity of girlhood looked out in wonder from the dreaming eyes. With her soft, clinging dress of *crêpe-de-chine*, and her large leaf-shaped fan, she looked like one of those delicate little figures men find in the olive-woods near Tanagra; and there was a touch of Greek grace in her pose and attitude. Yet she was not *petite*. Yet she was simply perfectly proportioned – a rare thing in an age when so many women are either over life-size or insignificant.

Now as Lord Arthur looked at her, he was filled with the terrible pity that is born of love. He felt that to marry her, with the doom of murder hanging over his head, would be a betrayal like that of Judas, a sin worse than any the Borgia had ever dreamed of. What happiness could there be for them, when at any moment he might be called upon to carry out the awful prophecy written in his hand? What manner of life would be theirs while Fate still held this fearful fortune in the scales? The marriage must be postponed, at all costs. Of this he was quite resolved. Ardently though he loved the girl, and the mere touch of her fingers, when they sat together, made each nerve of his body thrill with exquisite joy, he recognised none the less clearly where his duty lay, and was fully

conscious of the fact that he had no right to marry until he had committed the murder. This done, he could stand before the altar with Sybil Merton, and give his life into her hands without terror of wrongdoing. This done, he could take her to his arms, knowing that she would never have to blush for him, never have to hang her head in shame. But done it must be first; and the sooner the better for both.

Many men in his position would have preferred the primrose path of dalliance to the steep heights of duty; but Lord Arthur was too conscientious to set pleasure above principle. There was more than mere passion in his love; and Sybil was to him a symbol of all that is good and noble. For a moment he had a natural repugnance against what he was asked to do, but it soon passed away. His heart told him that it was not a sin, but a sacrifice; his reason reminded him that there was no other course open. He had to choose between living for himself and living for others, and terrible though the task laid upon him undoubtedly was, yet he knew that he must not suffer selfishness to triumph over love. Sooner or later we are all called upon to decide on the same issue – of us all, the same question is asked. To Lord Arthur it came early in life – before his nature had been spoiled by the calculating cynicism of middle-age, or his heart corroded by the shallow, fashionable egotism of our day, and he felt no hesitation about doing his duty. Fortunately also, for him, he was no mere dreamer, or idle dilettante. Had he

been so, he would have hesitated, like Hamlet, and let irresolution mar his purpose. But he was essentially practical. Life to him meant action, rather than thought. He had that rarest of all things, common sense.

The wild, turbid feelings of the previous night had by this time completely passed away, and it was almost with a sense of shame that he looked back upon his mad wanderings from street to street, his fierce emotional agony. The very sincerity of his sufferings made them seem unreal to him now. He wondered how he could have been so foolish as to rant and rave about the inevitable. The only question that seemed to trouble him was, whom to make away with; for he was not blind to the fact that murder, like the religions of the Pagan world, requires a victim as well as a priest. Not being a genius, he had no enemies, and indeed he felt that this was not the time for the gratification of any personal pique or dislike, the mission in which he was engaged being one of great and grave solemnity. He accordingly made out a list of his friends and relatives on a sheet of notepaper, and after careful consideration, decided in favour of Lady Clementina Beauchamp, a dear old lady who lived in Curzon Street, and was his own second cousin by his mother's side. He had always been very fond of Lady Clem, as every one called her, and as he was very wealthy himself, having come into all Lord Rugby's property when he came of age, there was no possibility of his deriving any vulgar monetary advantage by her death. In fact, the more he

thought over the matter, the more she seemed to him to be just the right person, and, feeling that any delay would be unfair to Sybil, he determined to make his arrangements at once.

The first thing to be done was, of course, to settle with the cheiromantist; so he sat down at a small Sheraton writing-table that stood near the window, drew a cheque for £105, payable to the order of Mr Septimus Podgers, and, enclosing it in an envelope, told his valet to take it to West Moon Street. He then telephoned to the stables for his hansom, and dressed to go out. As he was leaving the room, he looked back at Sybil Merton's photograph, and swore that, come what may, he would never let her know what he was doing for her sake, but would keep the secret of his self-sacrifice hidden always in his heart.

On his way to the Buckingham, he stopped at a florist's, and sent Sybil a beautiful basket of narcissi, with lovely white petals and staring pheasants' eyes, and on arriving at the club, went straight to the library, rang the bell, and ordered the waiter to bring him a lemon-and-soda, and a book on Toxicology. He had fully decided that poison was the best means to adopt in this troublesome business. Anything like personal violence was extremely distasteful to him, and besides, he was very anxious not to murder Lady Clementina in any way that might attract public attention, as he hated the idea of being lionised at Lady Windermere's, or seeing his name figuring in the paragraphs of vulgar society-newspapers. He had also to think

of Sybil's father and mother, who were rather old-fashioned people, and might possibly object to the marriage if there was anything like a scandal, though he felt certain that if he told them the whole facts of the case they would be the very first to appreciate the motives that had actuated him. He had every reason, then, to decide in favour of poison. It was safe, sure, and quiet, and did away with any necessity for painful scenes, to which, like most Englishmen, he had a rooted objection.

Of the science of poisons, however, he knew absolutely nothing, and as the waiter seemed quite unable to find anything in the library but Ruff's *Guide* and Bailey's *Magazine*, he examined the book-shelves himself, and finally came across a handsomely-bound edition of the *Pharmacopoeia*, and a copy of Erskine's *Toxicology*, edited by Sir Mathew Reid, the President of the Royal College of Physicians, and one of the oldest members of the Buckingham, having been elected in mistake for somebody else; a *contretemps* that so enraged the Committee, that when the real man came up they black-balled him unanimously. Lord Arthur was a good deal puzzled at the technical terms used in both books, and had begun to regret that he had not paid more attention to his classics at Oxford, when in the second volume of Erskine, he found a very interesting and complete account of the properties of aconitine, written in fairly clear English. It seemed to him to be exactly the poison he wanted. It was swift – indeed, almost immediate, in its effect – perfectly

painless, and when taken in the form of a gelatine capsule, the mode recommended by Sir Mathew, not by any means unpalatable. He accordingly made a note, upon his shirt-cuff, of the amount necessary for a fatal dose, put the books back in their places, and strolled up St James's Street, to Pestle and Humbey's, the great chemists. Mr Pestle, who always attended personally on the aristocracy, was a good deal surprised at the order, and in a very deferential manner murmured something about a medical certificate being necessary. However, as soon as Lord Arthur explained to him that it was for a large Norwegian mastiff that he was obliged to get rid of, as it showed signs of incipient rabies, and had already bitten the coachman twice in the calf of the leg, he expressed himself as being perfectly satisfied, complimented Lord Arthur on his wonderful knowledge of Toxicology, and had the prescription made up immediately.

Lord Arthur put the capsule into a pretty little silver *bonbonnière* that he saw in a shop-window in Bond Street, threw away Pestle and Humbey's ugly pill-box, and drove off at once to Lady Clementina's.

'Well, *monsieur le mauvais sujet*,' cried the old lady, as he entered the room, 'why haven't you been to see me all this time?'

'My dear Lady Clem, I never have a moment to myself,' said Lord Arthur, smiling.

'I suppose you mean that you go about all day long with Miss Sybil Merton, buying *chiffons* and talking

nonsense? I cannot understand why people make such a fuss about being married. In my day we never dreamed of billing and cooing in public, or in private for that matter.'

'I assure you I have not seen Sybil for twenty-four hours, Lady Clem. As far as I can make out, she belongs entirely to her milliners.'

'Of course; that is the only reason you come to see an ugly old woman like myself. I wonder you men don't take warning. *On a fait des folies pour moi*, and here I am, a poor, rheumatic creature, with a false front and a bad temper. Why, if it were not for dear Lady Jansen, who sends me all the worst French novels she can find, I don't think I could get through the day. Doctors are no use at all, except to get fees out of one. They can't even cure my heartburn.'

'I have brought you a cure for that, Lady Clem,' said Lord Arthur gravely. 'It is a wonderful thing, invented by an American.'

'I don't think I like American inventions, Arthur. I am quite sure I don't. I read some American novels lately, and they were quite nonsensical.'

'Oh, but there is no nonsense at all about this, Lady Clem! I assure you it is a perfect cure. You must promise to try it;' and Lord Arthur brought the little box out of his pocket, and handed it to her.

'Well, the box is charming, Arthur. Is it really a present? That is very sweet of you. And is this the wonderful medicine? It looks like a *bonbon*. I'll take it at once.'

'Good heavens! Lady Clem,' cried Lord Arthur, catching hold of her hand, 'you mustn't do anything of the kind. It is a homoeopathic medicine, and if you take it without having heartburn, it might do you no end of harm. Wait till you have an attack, and take it then. You will be astonished at the result.'

'I should like to take it now,' said Lady Clementina, holding up to the light the little transparent capsule, with its floating bubble of liquid aconitine. 'I am sure it is delicious. The fact is that, though I hate doctors, I love medicines. However, I'll keep it till my next attack.'

'And when will that be?' asked Lord Arthur eagerly. 'Will it be soon?'

'I hope not for a week. I had a very bad time yesterday morning with it. But one never knows.'

'You are sure to have one before the end of the month then, Lady Clem?'

'I am afraid so. But how sympathetic you are to-day, Arthur! Really, Sybil has done you a great deal of good. And now you must run away, for I am dining with some very dull people, who won't talk scandal, and I know that if I don't get my sleep now I shall never be able to keep awake during dinner. Good-bye, Arthur, give my love to Sybil, and thank you so much for the American medicine.'

'You won't forget to take it, Lady Clem, will you?' said Lord Arthur, rising from his seat.

'Of course I won't, you silly boy. I think it is most kind

of you to think of me, and I shall write and tell you if I want any more.'

Lord Arthur left the house in high spirits, and with a feeling of immense relief.

That night he had an interview with Sybil Merton. He told her how he had been suddenly placed in a position of terrible difficulty, from which neither honour nor duty would allow him to recede. He told her that the marriage must be put off for the present, as until he had got rid of his fearful entanglements, he was not a free man. He implored her to trust him, and not to have any doubts about the future. Everything would come right, but patience was necessary.

The scene took place in the conservatory of Mr Merton's house, in Park Lane, where Lord Arthur had dined as usual. Sybil had never seemed more happy, and for a moment Lord Arthur had been tempted to play the coward's part, to write to Lady Clementina for the pill, and to let the marriage go on as if there was no such person as Mr Podgers in the world. His better nature, however, soon asserted itself, and even when Sybil flung herself weeping into his arms, he did not falter. The beauty that stirred his senses had touched his conscience also. He felt that to wreck so fair a life for the sake of a few months' pleasure would be a wrong thing to do.

He stayed with Sybil till nearly midnight, comforting her and being comforted in turn, and early the next morning he left for Venice, after writing a manly, firm letter to

Mr Merton about the necessary postponement of the marriage.

IV

In Venice he met his brother, Lord Surbiton, who happened to have come over from Corfu in his yacht. The two young men spent a delightful fortnight together. In the morning they rode on the Lido, or glided up and down the green canals in their long black gondola; in the afternoon they usually entertained visitors on the yacht; and in the evening they dined at Florian's, and smoked innumerable cigarettes on the Piazza. Yet somehow Lord Arthur was not happy. Every day he studied the obituary column in the *Times*, expecting to see a notice of Lady Clementina's death, but every day he was disappointed. He began to be afraid that some accident had happened to her, and often regretted that he had prevented her taking the aconitine when she had been so anxious to try its effect. Sybil's letters, too, though full of love, and trust, and tenderness, were often very sad in their tone, and sometimes he used to think that he was parted from her for ever.

After a fortnight Lord Surbiton got bored with Venice, and determined to run down the coast to Ravenna, as he heard that there was some capital cock-shooting in the Pinetum. Lord Arthur, at first, refused absolutely to come,

but Surbiton, of whom he was extremely fond, finally persuaded him that if he stayed at Danielli's by himself he would be moped to death, and on the morning of the 15th they started, with a strong nor'-east wind blowing, and a rather sloppy sea. The sport was excellent, and the free, open-air life brought the colour back to Lord Arthur's cheeks, but about the 22nd he became anxious about Lady Clementina, and, in spite of Surbiton's remonstrances, came back to Venice by train.

As he stepped out of his gondola on to the hotel steps, the proprietor came forward to meet him with a sheaf of telegrams. Lord Arthur snatched them out of his hand, and tore them open. Everything had been successful. Lady Clementina had died quite suddenly on the night of the 17th!

His first thought was for Sybil, and he sent her off a telegram announcing his immediate return to London. He then ordered his valet to pack his things for the night mail, sent his gondoliers about five times their proper fare, and ran up to his sitting-room with a light step and a buoyant heart. There he found three letters waiting for him. One was from Sybil herself, full of sympathy and condolence. The others were from his mother, and from Lady Clementina's solicitor. It seemed that the old lady had dined with the Duchess that very night, had delighted every one by her wit and *esprit*, but had gone home somewhat early, complaining of heartburn. In the morning she was found dead in her bed, having apparently

suffered no pain. Sir Mathew Reid had been sent for at once, but, of course, there was nothing to be done, and she was to be buried on the 22nd at Beauchamp Chalcote. A few days before she died she had made her will, and left Lord Arthur her little house in Curzon Street, and all her furniture, personal effects, and pictures, with the exception of her collection of miniatures, which was to go to her sister, Lady Margaret Rufford, and her amethyst necklace, which Sybil Merton was to have. The property was not of much value; but Mr Mansfield the solicitor was extremely anxious for Lord Arthur to return at once, if possible, as there were a great many bills to be paid, and Lady Clementina had never kept any regular accounts.

Lord Arthur was very much touched by Lady Clementina's kind remembrance of him, and felt that Mr Podgers had a great deal to answer for. His love of Sybil, however, dominated every other emotion, and the consciousness that he had done his duty gave him peace and comfort. When he arrived at Charing Cross, he felt perfectly happy.

The Mertons received him very kindly, Sybil made him promise that he would never again allow anything to come between them, and the marriage was fixed for the 7th June. Life seemed to him once more bright and beautiful, and all his old gladness came back to him again.

One day, however, as he was going over the house in Curzon Street, in company with Lady Clementina's

solicitor and Sybil herself, burning packages of faded letters, and turning out drawers of odd rubbish, the young girl suddenly gave a little cry of delight.

'What have you found, Sybil?' said Lord Arthur, looking up from his work, and smiling.

'This lovely little silver *bonbonnière*, Arthur. Isn't it quaint and Dutch? Do give it to me! I know amethysts won't become me till I am over eighty.'

It was the box that had held the aconitine.

Lord Arthur started, and a faint blush came into his cheek. He had almost entirely forgotten what he had done, and it seemed to him a curious coincidence that Sybil, for whose sake he had gone through all that terrible anxiety, should have been the first to remind him of it.

'Of course you can have it, Sybil. I gave it to poor Lady Clem myself.'

'Oh! thank you, Arthur; and may I have the *bonbon* too? I had no notion that Lady Clementina liked sweets. I thought she was far too intellectual.'

Lord Arthur grew deadly pale, and a horrible idea crossed his mind.

'*Bonbon*, Sybil? What do you mean?' he said, in a slow, hoarse voice.

'There is one in it, that is all. It looks quite old and dusty, and I have not the slightest intention of eating it. What is the matter, Arthur? How white you look!'

Lord Arthur rushed across the room, and seized the

box. Inside it was the amber-coloured capsule, with its poison-bubble. Lady Clementina had died a natural death after all!

The shock of the discovery was almost too much for him. He flung the capsule into the fire, and sank on the sofa with a cry of despair.

V

Mr Merton was a good deal distressed at the second postponement of the marriage, and Lady Julia, who had already ordered her dress for the wedding, did all in her power to make Sybil break off the match. Dearly, however, as Sybil loved her mother, she had given her whole life into Lord Arthur's hands, and nothing that Lady Julia could say could make her waver in her faith. As for Lord Arthur himself, it took him days to get over his terrible disappointment, and for a time his nerves were completely unstrung. His excellent common sense, however, soon asserted itself, and his sound, practical mind did not leave him long in doubt about what to do. Poison having proved a complete failure, dynamite, or some other form of explosive, was obviously the proper thing to try.

He accordingly looked again over the list of his friends and relatives, and, after careful consideration, determined to blow up his uncle, the Dean of Chichester. The Dean, who was a man of great culture and learning, was

extremely fond of clocks, and had a wonderful collection of timepieces, ranging from the fifteenth century to the present day, and it seemed to Lord Arthur that this hobby of the good Dean's offered him an excellent opportunity for carrying out his scheme. Where to procure an explosive machine was, of course, quite another matter. The London Directory gave him no information on the point, and he felt that there was very little use in going to Scotland Yard about it, as they never seemed to know anything about the movements of the dynamite faction till after an explosion had taken place, and not much even then.

Suddenly he thought of his friend Rouvaloff, a young Russian of very revolutionary tendencies, whom he had met at Lady Windermere's in the winter. Count Rouvaloff was supposed to be writing a life of Peter the Great, and to have come over to England for the purpose of studying the documents relating to that Tsar's residence in this country as a ship carpenter; but it was generally suspected that he was a Nihilist agent, and there was no doubt that the Russian Embassy did not look with any favour upon his presence in London. Lord Arthur felt that he was just the man for his purpose, and drove down one morning to his lodgings in Bloomsbury, to ask his advice and assistance.

'So you are taking up politics seriously?' said Count Rouvaloff, when Lord Arthur had told him the object of his mission; but Lord Arthur, who hated swagger of any kind, felt bound to admit to him that he had not the

slightest interest in social questions, and simply wanted the explosive machine for a purely family matter, in which no one was concerned but himself.

Count Rouvaloff looked at him for some moments in amazement, and then seeing that he was quite serious, wrote an address on a piece of paper, initialled it, and handed it to him across the table.

'Scotland Yard would give a good deal to know this address, my dear fellow.'

'They shan't have it,' cried Lord Arthur, laughing; and after shaking the young Russian warmly by the hand he ran downstairs, examined the paper, and told the coachman to drive to Soho Square.

There he dismissed him, and strolled down Greek Street, till he came to a place called Bayle's Court. He passed under the archway, and found himself in a curious cul-de-sac, that was apparently occupied by a French Laundry, as a perfect network of clothes-lines was stretched across from house to house, and there was a flutter of white linen in the morning air. He walked right to the end, and knocked at a little green house. After some delay, during which every window in the court became a blurred mass of peering faces, the door was opened by a rather rough-looking foreigner, who asked him in very bad English what his business was. Lord Arthur handed him the paper Count Rouvaloff had given him. When the man saw it he bowed, and invited Lord Arthur into a very shabby front parlour on the ground-floor, and in a few

moments Herr Winckelkopf, as he was called in England, bustled into the room, with a very wine-stained napkin round his neck, and a fork in his left hand.

'Count Rouvaloff has given me an introduction to you,' said Lord Arthur, bowing, 'and I am anxious to have a short interview with you on a matter of business. My name is Smith, Mr Robert Smith, and I want you to supply me with an explosive clock.'

'Charmed to meet you, Lord Arthur,' said the genial little German, laughing. 'Don't look so alarmed, it is my duty to know everybody, and I remember seeing you one evening at Lady Windermere's. I hope her ladyship is quite well. Do you mind sitting with me while I finish my breakfast? There is an excellent *pâté*, and my friends are kind enough to say that my Rhine wine is better than any they get at the German Embassy,' and before Lord Arthur had got over his surprise at being recognised, he found himself seated in the back-room, sipping the most delicious Marcobrünner out of a pale yellow hock-glass marked with the Imperial monogram, and chatting in the friendliest manner possible to the famous conspirator.

'Explosive clocks,' said Herr Winckelkopf, 'are not very good things for foreign exportation, as, even if they succeed in passing the Custom House, the train service is so irregular, that they usually go off before they have reached their proper destination. If, however, you want one for home use, I can supply you with an excellent article, and guarantee that you will be satisfied with the result. May

I ask for whom it is intended? If it is for the police, or for any one connected with Scotland Yard, I'm afraid I cannot do anything for you. The English detectives are really our best friends, and I have always found that by relying on their stupidity, we can do exactly what we like. I could not spare one of them.'

'I assure you,' said Lord Arthur, 'that it has nothing to do with the police at all. In fact, the clock is intended for the Dean of Chichester.'

'Dear me! I had no idea that you felt so strongly about religion, Lord Arthur. Few young men do nowadays.'

'I am afraid you overrate me, Herr Winckelkopf,' said Lord Arthur, blushing. 'The fact is, I really know nothing about theology.'

'It is a purely private matter then?'

'Purely private.'

Herr Winckelkopf shrugged his shoulders, and left the room, returning in a few minutes with a round cake of dynamite about the size of a penny, and a pretty little French clock, surmounted by an ormolu figure of Liberty trampling on the hydra of Despotism.

Lord Arthur's face brightened up when he saw it. 'That is just what I want,' he cried, 'and now tell me how it goes off.'

'Ah! there is my secret,' answered Herr Winckelkopf, contemplating his invention with a justifiable look of pride; 'let me know when you wish it to explode, and I will set the machine to the moment.'

'Well, to-day is Tuesday, and if you could send it off at once –'

'That is impossible; I have a great deal of important work on hand for some friends of mine in Moscow. Still, I might send it off to-morrow.'

'Oh, it will be quite time enough!' said Lord Arthur politely, 'if it is delivered to-morrow night or Thursday morning. For the moment of the explosion, say Friday at noon exactly. The Dean is always at home at that hour.'

'Friday, at noon,' repeated Herr Winckelkopf, and he made a note to that effect in a large ledger that was lying on a bureau near the fireplace.

'And now,' said Lord Arthur, rising from his seat, 'pray let me know how much I am in your debt.'

'It is such a small matter, Lord Arthur, that I do not care to make any charge. The dynamite comes to seven and sixpence, the clock will be three pounds ten, and the carriage about five shillings. I am only too pleased to oblige any friend of Count Rouvaloff's.'

'But your trouble, Herr Winckelkopf?'

'Oh, that is nothing! It is a pleasure to me. I do not work for money; I live entirely for my art.'

Lord Arthur laid down £4:2:6 on the table, thanked the little German for his kindness, and, having succeeded in declining an invitation to meet some Anarchists at a meat-tea on the following Saturday, left the house and went off to the Park.

For the next two days he was in a state of the greatest

excitement, and on Friday at twelve o'clock he drove down to the Buckingham to wait for news. All the afternoon the stolid hall-porter kept posting up telegrams from various parts of the country giving the results of horse-races, the verdicts in divorce suits, the state of the weather, and the like, while the tape ticked out wearisome details about an all-night sitting in the House of Commons, and a small panic on the Stock Exchange. At four o'clock the evening papers came in, and Lord Arthur disappeared into the library with the *Pall Mall*, the *St James's*, the *Globe*, and the *Echo*, to the immense indignation of Colonel Goodchild, who wanted to read the reports of a speech he had delivered that morning at the Mansion House, on the subject of South African Missions, and the advisability of having black Bishops in every province, and for some reason or other had a strong prejudice against the *Evening News*. None of the papers, however, contained even the slightest allusion to Chichester, and Lord Arthur felt that the attempt must have failed. It was a terrible blow to him, and for a time he was quite unnerved. Herr Winckelkopf, whom he went to see the next day, was full of elaborate apologies, and offered to supply him with another clock free of charge, or with a case of nitro-glycerine bombs at cost price. But he had lost all faith in explosives, and Herr Winckelkopf himself acknowledged that everything is so adulterated nowadays, that even dynamite can hardly be got in a pure condition. The little German, however, while admitting

that something must have gone wrong with the machinery, was not without hope that the clock might still go off, and instanced the case of a barometer that he had once sent to the military Governor at Odessa, which, though timed to explode in ten days, had not done so for something like three months. It was quite true that when it did go off, it merely succeeded in blowing a housemaid to atoms, the Governor having gone out of town six weeks before, but at least it showed that dynamite, as a destructive force, was, when under the control of machinery, a powerful, though a somewhat unpunctual agent. Lord Arthur was a little consoled by this reflection, but even here he was destined to disappointment, for two days afterwards, as he was going upstairs, the Duchess called him into her boudoir, and showed him a letter she had just received from the Deanery.

'Jane writes charming letters,' said the Duchess; 'you must really read her last. It is quite as good as the novels Mudie sends us.'

Lord Arthur seized the letter from her hand. It ran as follows: –

'The Deanery, Chichester,
'27th May.

'My Dearest Aunt,

'Thank you so much for the flannel for the Dorcas Society, and also for the gingham. I quite agree with you that it is nonsense their wanting to wear pretty things, but

everybody is so Radical and irreligious nowadays, that it is difficult to make them see that they should not try and dress like the upper classes. I am sure I don't know what we are coming to. As papa has often said in his sermons, we live in an age of unbelief.

'We have had great fun over a clock that an unknown admirer sent papa last Thursday. It arrived in a wooden box from London, carriage paid; and papa feels it must have been sent by some one who had read his remarkable sermon, "Is Licence Liberty?" for on the top of the clock was a figure of a woman, with what papa said was the cap of Liberty on her head. I didn't think it very becoming myself, but papa said it was historical, so I suppose it is all right. Parker unpacked it, and papa put it on the mantelpiece in the library, and we were all sitting there on Friday morning, when just as the clock struck twelve, we heard a whirring noise, a little puff of smoke came from the pedestal of the figure, and the goddess of Liberty fell off, and broke her nose on the fender! Maria was quite alarmed, but it looked so ridiculous, that James and I went off into fits of laughter, and even papa was amused. When we examined it, we found it was a sort of alarum clock, and that, if you set it to a particular hour, and put some gunpowder and a cap under a little hammer, it went off whenever you wanted. Papa said it must not remain in the library, as it made a noise, so Reggie carried it away to the schoolroom, and does nothing but have small explosions all day long. Do you think Arthur would like one for a wedding present? I

suppose they are quite fashionable in London. Papa says they should do a great deal of good, as they show that Liberty can't last, but must fall down. Papa says Liberty was invented at the time of the French Revolution. How awful it seems!

'I have now to go to the Dorcas, where I will read them your most instructive letter. How true, dear aunt, your idea is, that in their rank of life they should wear what is unbecoming. I must say it is absurd, their anxiety about dress, when there are so many more important things in this world, and in the next. I am so glad your flowered poplin turned out so well, and that your lace was not torn. I am wearing my yellow satin, that you so kindly gave me, at the Bishop's on Wednesday, and think it will look all right. Would you have bows or not? Jennings says that every one wears bows now, and that the underskirt should be frilled. Reggie has just had another explosion, and papa has ordered the clock to be sent to the stables. I don't think papa likes it so much as he did at first, though he is very flattered at being sent such a pretty and ingenious toy. It shows that people read his sermons, and profit by them.

'Papa sends his love, in which James, and Reggie, and Maria all unite, and, hoping that Uncle Cecil's gout is better, believe me, dear aunt, ever your affectionate niece,

'Jane Percy

'P. S. – Do tell me about the bows. Jennings insists they are the fashion.'

Lord Arthur looked so serious and unhappy over the letter, that the Duchess went into fits of laughter.

'My dear Arthur,' she cried, 'I shall never show you a young lady's letter again! But what shall I say about the clock? I think it is a capital invention, and I should like to have one myself.'

'I don't think much of them,' said Lord Arthur, with a sad smile, and, after kissing his mother, he left the room.

When he got upstairs, he flung himself on a sofa, and his eyes filled with tears. He had done his best to commit this murder, but on both occasions he had failed, and through no fault of his own. He had tried to do his duty, but it seemed as if Destiny herself had turned traitor. He was oppressed with the sense of the barrenness of good intentions, of the futility of trying to be fine. Perhaps, it would be better to break off the marriage altogether. Sybil would suffer, it is true, but suffering could not really mar a nature so noble as hers. As for himself, what did it matter? There is always some war in which a man can die, some cause to which a man can give his life, and as life had no pleasure for him, so death had no terror. Let Destiny work out his doom. He would not stir to help her.

At half-past seven he dressed, and went down to the club. Surbiton was there with a party of young men, and he was obliged to dine with them. Their trivial conversation and idle jests did not interest him, and as soon as coffee was brought he left them, inventing some engagement in order to get away. As he was going out of the

club, the hall porter handed him a letter. It was from Herr Winckelkopf, asking him to call down the next evening, and look at an explosive umbrella, that went off as soon as it was opened. It was the very latest invention, and had just arrived from Geneva. He tore the letter up into fragments. He had made up his mind not to try any more experiments. Then he wandered down to the Thames Embankment, and sat for hours by the river. The moon peered through a mane of tawny clouds, as if it were a lion's eye, and innumerable stars spangled the hollow vault, like gold dust powdered on a purple dome. Now and then a barge swung out into the turbid stream, and floated away with the tide, and the railway signals changed from green to scarlet as the trains ran shrieking across the bridge. After some time, twelve o'clock boomed from the tall tower at Westminster, and at each stroke of the sonorous bell the night seemed to tremble. Then the railway lights went out, one solitary lamp left gleaming like a large ruby on a giant mast, and the roar of the city became fainter.

At two o'clock he got up, and strolled towards Blackfriars. How unreal everything looked! How like a strange dream! The houses on the other side of the river seemed built out of darkness. One would have said that silver and shadow had fashioned the world anew. The huge dome of St Paul's loomed like a bubble through the dusky air.

As he approached Cleopatra's Needle he saw a man

leaning over the parapet, and as he came nearer the man looked up, the gas-light falling full upon his face.

It was Mr Podgers, the cheiromantist! No one could mistake the fat, flabby face, the gold-rimmed spectacles, the sickly feeble smile, the sensual mouth.

Lord Arthur stopped. A brilliant idea flashed across him, and he stole softly up behind. In a moment he had seized Mr Podgers by the legs, and flung him into the Thames. There was a coarse oath, a heavy splash, and all was still. Lord Arthur looked anxiously over, but could see nothing of the cheiromantist but a tall hat, pirouetting in an eddy of moonlit water. After a time it also sank, and no trace of Mr Podgers was visible. Once he thought that he caught sight of the bulky misshapen figure striking out for the staircase by the bridge, and a horrible feeling of failure came over him, but it turned out to be merely a reflection, and when the moon shone out from behind a cloud it passed away. At last he seemed to have realised the decree of destiny. He heaved a deep sigh of relief, and Sybil's name came to his lips.

'Have you dropped anything, sir?' said a voice behind him suddenly.

He turned round, and saw a policeman with a bull's-eye lantern.

'Nothing of importance, sergeant,' he answered, smiling, and hailing a passing hansom, he jumped in, and told the man to drive to Belgrave Square.

For the next few days he alternated between hope and

fear. There were moments when he almost expected Mr Podgers to walk into the room, and yet at other times he felt that Fate could not be so unjust to him. Twice he went to the cheiromantist's address in West Moon Street, but he could not bring himself to ring the bell. He longed for certainty, and was afraid of it.

Finally it came. He was sitting in the smoking-room of the club having tea, and listening rather wearily to Surbiton's account of the last comic song at the Gaiety, when the waiter came in with the evening papers. He took up the *St James's*, and was listlessly turning over its pages, when this strange heading caught his eye:

SUICIDE OF A CHEIROMANTIST.

He turned pale with excitement, and began to read. The paragraph ran as follows: –

> Yesterday morning, at seven o'clock, the body of Mr Septimus R. Podgers, the eminent cheiromantist, was washed on shore at Greenwich, just in front of the Ship Hotel. The unfortunate gentleman had been missing for some days, and considerable anxiety for his safety had been felt in cheiromantic circles. It is supposed that he committed suicide under the influence of a temporary mental derangement, caused by overwork, and a verdict to that effect was returned this afternoon by the coroner's jury. Mr Podgers had just completed an elaborate treatise on the subject of

the Human Hand, that will shortly be published, when it will no doubt attract much attention. The deceased was sixty-five years of age, and does not seem to have left any relations.

Lord Arthur rushed out of the club with the paper still in his hand, to the immense amazement of the hall-porter, who tried in vain to stop him, and drove at once to Park Lane. Sybil saw him from the window, and something told her that he was the bearer of good news. She ran down to meet him, and, when she saw his face, she knew that all was well.

'My dear Sybil,' cried Lord Arthur, 'let us be married tomorrow!'

'You foolish boy! Why the cake is not even ordered!' said Sybil, laughing through her tears.

VI

When the wedding took place, some three weeks later, St Peter's was crowded with a perfect mob of smart people. The service was read in a most impressive manner by the Dean of Chichester, and everybody agreed that they had never seen a handsomer couple than the bride and bridegroom. They were more than handsome, however – they were happy. Never for a single moment did Lord Arthur regret all that he had suffered for Sybil's sake, while she,

on her side, gave him the best things a woman can give to any man – worship, tenderness, and love. For them romance was not killed by reality. They always felt young.

Some years afterwards, when two beautiful children had been born to them, Lady Windermere came down on a visit to Alton Priory, a lovely old place, that had been the Duke's wedding present to his son; and one afternoon as she was sitting with Lady Arthur under a lime-tree in the garden, watching the little boy and girl as they played up and down the rose-walk, like fitful sunbeams, she suddenly took her hostess's hand in hers, and said, 'Are you happy, Sybil?'

'Dear Lady Windermere, of course I am happy. Aren't you?'

'I have no time to be happy, Sybil. I always like the last person who is introduced to me; but, as a rule, as soon as I know people I get tired of them.'

'Don't your lions satisfy you, Lady Windermere?'

'Oh dear, no! lions are only good for one season. As soon as their manes are cut, they are the dullest creatures going. Besides, they behave very badly, if you are really nice to them. Do you remember that horrid Mr Podgers? He was a dreadful impostor. Of course, I didn't mind that at all, and even when he wanted to borrow money I forgave him, but I could not stand his making love to me. He has really made me hate cheiromancy. I go in for telepathy now. It is much more amusing.'

'You mustn't say anything against cheiromancy here,

Lady Windermere; it is the only subject that Arthur does not like people to chaff about. I assure you he is quite serious over it.'

'You don't mean to say that he believes in it, Sybil?'

'Ask him, Lady Windermere, here he is;' and Lord Arthur came up the garden with a large bunch of yellow roses in his hand, and his two children dancing round him.

'Lord Arthur?'

'Yes, Lady Windermere.'

'You don't mean to say that you believe in cheiromancy?'

'Of course I do,' said the young man, smiling.

'But why?'

'Because I owe to it all the happiness of my life,' he murmured, throwing himself into a wicker chair.

'My dear Lord Arthur, what do you owe to it?'

'Sybil,' he answered, handing his wife the roses, and looking into her violet eyes.

'What nonsense!' cried Lady Windermere. 'I never heard such nonsense in all my life.'

企鹅经典：小黑书　第三辑

21. 漂亮的卡桑德拉

[英] 简・奥斯汀

22. 温顺的女人

[俄] 陀思妥耶夫斯基

23. 猫与维纳斯

[古希腊] 伊索

24. 黄昏之读

[英] 查尔斯・狄更斯

25. 一个可怕的故事是如何被一条普通的屠夫的狗公之于众的

[德] 约翰・彼得・黑贝尔

26. 亚瑟・萨维尔勋爵的罪行

[英] 奥斯卡・王尔德

27. 伊凡・伊里奇之死

[俄] 列夫・托尔斯泰

28. 我们为何为同一件事哭和笑

[法] 蒙田

29. 我的生命是一杆上实弹的枪

[美] 艾米莉・狄金森

30. 独自在黑夜的海滩上

[美] 沃尔特・惠特曼

Penguin Little Black Classics Vol. III

21. JANE AUSTEN
The Beautifull Cassandra

22. FYODOR DOSTOYEVSKY
The Meek One

23. AESOP
The Cat and Venus

24. CHARLES DICKENS
To Be Read at Dusk

25. JOHANN PETER HEBEL
How a Ghastly Story Was Brought to Light by a Common or Garden Butcher's Dog

26. OSCAR WILDE
Lord Arthur Savile's Crime

27. LEO TOLSTOY
The Death of Ivan Ilyich

28. MICHEL DE MONTAIGNE
How We Weep and Laugh at the Same Thing

29. EMILY DICKINSON
My life had stood a loaded gun

30. WALT WHITMAN
On the Beach at Night Alone

“这时候魔鬼推了一下
这个女人的胳膊：
‘看上去这个屠夫
好像在他的围裙下面
藏着一大笔钱！’”

PENGUIN

LITTLE BLACK

CLASSICS

*此中文译本译自德语原文

一个可怕的故事是如何被一条普通的屠夫的狗公之于众的

How a Ghastly Story Was Brought to Light by a Common or Garden Butcher's Dog

[德] 约翰·彼得·黑贝尔 著

杜旻 译

中信出版集团 | 北京

图书在版编目（CIP）数据

企鹅经典：小黑书．第三辑：汉、英 /（英）简·奥斯汀等著；夏星等译．-- 北京：中信出版社，2019.6

书名原文：Penguin Little Black Classics
ISBN 978-7-5217-0407-5

Ⅰ．①企… Ⅱ．①简… ②夏… Ⅲ．①世界文学－作品综合集－汉、英 Ⅳ．① I11

中国版本图书馆 CIP 数据核字 (2019) 第 072172 号

企鹅经典：小黑书　第三辑
一个可怕的故事是如何被一条普通的屠夫的狗公之于众的

著　　者：[德] 约翰·彼得·黑贝尔
译　　者：杜旻
出版发行：中信出版集团股份有限公司
（北京市朝阳区惠新东街甲 4 号富盛大厦 2 座 邮编 100029）
承 印 者：北京楠萍印刷有限公司

开　　本：787mm × 1092mm　1/32　　印　　张：45.75　　字　　数：756 千字
版　　次：2019 年 6 月第 1 版　　印　　次：2019 年 6 月第 1 次印刷
京权图字：01-2018-6477　　广告经营许可证：京朝工商广字第 8087 号
书　　号：ISBN 978-7-5217-0407-5
定　　价：149.00 元（全 10 册）

目录

银勺

／

在维也纳有一位军官，他盘算着：“我怎么着也得去红牛[1]吃顿午饭。”

如同其他地方一样，酒店里充斥着各色人等：既有熟客，也有生人；既有社会名流，也有无名鼠辈；既有坦荡君子，也有江湖骗子。人们在这里吃吃喝喝，有人吃得多，有人吃得少。人们在这里聊天闲扯，从摩拉维亚[2]最近为什么会天降陨石雨，一直聊到法国有个叫玛钦的家伙打败了大恶狼。总有某人向自己的听众们吹嘘：

1. 红牛酒店（Gasthaus Roter Ochsen）是维也纳一家历史悠久的豪华酒店。（说明：书中脚注均为译者注。）

2. 今捷克共和国东南部地区的旧称，当时属于奥地利帝国领土。

自己比其他人提前一年从相好的那里洞悉了不可告人的天机。

在午餐快要结束的时候，总有一两个家伙举着还剩下半升匈牙利葡萄酒的杯子开怀畅饮，另一个家伙就像药剂师生产药丸那样把软面包搓成一个个的球，第三个家伙则耍起了刀子、叉子或者银勺子。军官注意到：一个穿着绿色上衣的家伙正玩着银勺子，忽然勺子滑进了他的衣袖里，再也没有出现。

如果换作别人，可能会想："这关我什么事儿？"然后就视而不见，或者干脆跟着一块儿胡闹。军官却想："我不知道那个偷勺子的绿衣服家伙是谁，这可能会引起误会。所以在老板过来结账之前，我得保持沉默。"

当老板过来结账的时候，军官拿起一把银勺子，插进了自己上衣的两个扣眼之间——一个扣眼进，另一个扣眼出，就像士兵们在战场上携带勺子那样，只是没有汤。在军官买单的时候，老板盯着他的外套，心中暗想："这位先生佩戴的勋章真是别具一格啊，莫非他是曾经与一碗龙虾汤英勇战斗，因此才获得了一把银勺子？或者这把勺子就是属于我的？"

在买完单之后，军官故意板着脸说："这把勺子是送的，对不对？账单已经够贵的了。”老板回答：“我们这儿可没这规矩！如果您家里没有勺子使，我可以送您一把钢的，但我这把还请您留下！”

这时候军官站了起来，拍着老板的肩膀笑了。“我和那边那位穿绿色外套的先生，我们俩这是跟您开玩笑呢，”他说，“那位绿衣服的先生，如果您能把您的勺子从袖子里拿出来，我也把我的勺子交出来。”偷勺子的贼人意识到：他双手不诚实的举动已经落入了一双诚实的眼睛里。他想：最好还是假装开玩笑，把勺子还给店主吧。

就这样，老板的财产终于物归原主，偷勺子的贼也笑了——然而他并没能得意多久。目睹了事件经过的其他顾客们齐心协力追打辱骂着行径暴露的贼人，将他轰出了酒店。老板也让佣人在贼人身后撒上了满满一把没有燃尽的炉灰[1]。这位好样儿的军官因为他正直的行为获得了一瓶匈牙利葡萄酒作为奖赏。

注意：不应该偷银勺子！

注意：正义从来不会缺席！

（1810 年）

1. 基督教风俗，有让罪人悔改之意。

廉价午餐

有一句古老的谚语：自己挖坑埋自己。在某个小镇有家狮子客栈，这里发生的故事，恰好就说明了这句话的含义。

有一位衣冠楚楚的客人，他声称要点一份上等的肉汤、一块牛排和一份蔬菜。

客栈老板小心翼翼地问他："您是否还想来一杯葡萄酒？"

"当然了，"客人回答，"只要对得起我兜里这钱。"

在把这些食物都一扫而光之后，客人掏出一枚磨损的五芬尼[1]硬币放到桌上，对客栈老板说："老板先生，这

1. 芬尼（Pfennig）是德国历史上最小的货币单位之一。

是我的钱。”

客栈老板大怒：“这叫什么玩意儿？难道这顿饭不值一塔勒[1]吗？”

客人回答道：“我可没有说要点一顿价值一塔勒的饭菜，我说的是要点一顿对得起我兜里这钱的饭菜。我的钱就搁在这儿了，再多也没有了。是您饭菜给多了，这是您的错儿。”

很显然，客栈老板因为自己的傲慢和大意被顾客耍弄了，事情本应该到此为止的。然而，故事到这里并没有结束。

“您是个狡猾的流氓，”客栈老板说，“我本该好好收拾您一顿，然而这顿午饭算我白请，我再送给您二十四枚十字币[2]，请您再去到隔壁的大熊客栈，对他们重复一遍刚才的把戏。”

客栈老板之所以这么说，是因为他和隔壁大熊客栈的同行一直是竞争关系，双方彼此仇视，经常赌咒发誓，

---

1. 塔勒（Taler）是德国及中欧地区古代通行的大银币，每枚价值相当于 360 芬尼。

2. 十字币（Kreuzerstück）是德国南部及奥地利古代通行的银质辅币，因钱币上有十字架图案而得名，每枚价值相当于 4 芬尼。

不共戴天。然而狡猾的客人一把攥紧了客栈老板给的钱币，小心地看了一眼门外，对客栈老板道了一声晚安，最后笑着说：“我之前已经去过隔壁的大熊客栈了，是他们家老板让我上您这儿来的。”

鹬蚌相争，渔翁得利。然而如果这两位客栈老板能够有所领悟，并且彼此和解的话，他们还是应该好好感谢这位狡猾的客人。所谓和则两利，斗则两伤。

（1804 年）

户外午餐

人们常常抱怨：与某些人打交道是多么不容易。这么说当然没问题。然而在这些难打交道的人当中，很多人并不是坏人，只是脾气古怪而已。一旦别人正确理解了他们的思想和行为，并且用适当的方法对待他们，既不固持己见，也不一味附和，就会发现和他们相处其实是非常轻松愉快的。

从前有一位仆人对他的主人就是这么做的。这位仆人时常做错事，有时候也因为不是自己犯下的错误而受到责难。有一天，主人怒气冲冲地回到家里，坐下开始吃午餐。可能是因为汤太烫了，太凉了，或者不冷不热了，总而言之，主人怒了。他抄起盛汤的碗，从敞开的窗户将碗连同里面的汤汤水水一起扔到了外面的庭院里。

这时候仆人是怎么做的呢？他毫不犹豫地拿起本来要上到餐桌上的肉，将它像汤那样扔到了庭院里，随后他又把面包、葡萄酒以及包括桌布在内桌上的所有东西一股脑儿都扔了出去。

“你这冒失鬼想要干吗？”主人从沙发上暴跳起来，怒气冲冲地问道。仆人不慌不忙地回答：“如果我错误理解了您的意思的话，还请您原谅我。我没想别的，只是以为您今天想去庭院里吃饭。空气是多么新鲜，天空是多么湛蓝，开花的苹果树是多么可爱，蜜蜂都在花间愉快地享用它们的午餐。”

——这一次汤被扔出了窗外，但以后再也不会了。主人认识到了自己的错误，他欣赏着窗外美妙的春光，为仆人机智的反应会心一笑，并且在心中暗自感谢仆人给他上的这一课。

（1805 年）

机智的法官

我们曾经听说过：并不是所有在东方国家发生的事情都是不公平的。下面这件事情就发生在那里。

有一位财主因为疏忽大意遗失了被他缝在布袋里的一大笔钱。当他发现把钱弄丢了以后，他顺理成章地悬赏一百塔勒来奖励那个找到钱的诚实的发现者。

不久就来了一个诚实的好人。“您的钱我找到了。分文不少！如数奉还！”当好人说这番话的时候，他坦荡的目光中透着诚实和善良，真是好样儿的。可是财主只在财产失而复得的瞬间露出了笑容。他不诚实的品性很快就会展现在我们面前。财主一边数着钱，一边暗中盘算：按照我之前的承诺，我将要付给这位发现者一大笔赏金。

“好伙计，”财主说，“布袋里原来一共有八百塔勒，但是现在只剩七百了，我猜您一定从缝隙里拿走了一百塔勒作为赏金，谢谢您。”

这真是太坏了。然而我们的故事并没有结束。诚实永垂不朽，而制造不公平的人却总是搬起石头砸自己的脚。这位诚实的发现者努力捍卫自己的清白正直，他保证自己将捡到的布袋原封不动还给了失主。

最后他们一起来到了法官面前。这两人各执一词，一位声称布袋里原本就有八百塔勒，另一位则坚持自己并没有从布袋里拿走一分一毫。两人唇枪舌剑好一番。

然而这位机智的法官早已看出了这两人一个胸怀磊落，一个心怀鬼胎，于是他眉头一皱，计上心来。他表示相信当事双方的陈述都是真实可靠的，并且做出了如下的判决：“照这么说，你们两人一个遗失了有八百塔勒的布袋，另一个捡到了有七百塔勒的布袋，所以你捡到的这个布袋很显然不是他遗失的那个。你，诚实的发现者，把你捡到的这笔钱先拿回去，直到遗失了七百塔勒的那人过来找你。至于你嘛，我也没有什么好说的，你应该耐心等着那个捡到八百塔勒的人来找你。”这就是法官的判决，并且是终审判决。

（1805 年）

狡猾的轻骑兵

有一位参加最后一战[1]的轻骑兵，在街道上遇到向他迎面走来的一位庄稼汉。他得知这位庄稼汉刚刚由于出售干草而获得了一百古尔登[2]，正打算带着这笔钱回家。因此他打算向庄稼汉要点儿钱去买烟打酒。谁知道他会不会因为讨到几个子儿而满足呢？

---

1. 指 19 世纪初由欧洲各国封建君主组成的“反法同盟”围攻拿破仑指挥下的法国军队的战争。
2. 原文中的 Florin 在当代西方语言中通常指代英国自 1849 年开始通行的面值 2 先令银币，但作者成书距此尚有近半个世纪之久。经译者考据，Florin 另有一个含义是 17 世纪至 19 世纪德意志神圣罗马帝国境内通行的古尔登（Gulden）银币，其价值约为 1/2 塔勒，即 180 芬尼，此译法也与下面原文中将要提到的古尔登相吻合。

然而那位庄稼汉却指天咒地地说：他的最后一枚十字币已经在隔壁的村庄花光了，现在他已经是一文不名。

“这地方离我们驻地不远，”轻骑兵说，“所以我们应该都能找到一些援助；但因为你啥都没有，我也啥都没有，所以我们得先走到圣阿方索[1]面前，如果他今天给咱俩恩赐的话，咱俩就像兄弟一样平分。”

所谓的圣阿方索，其实不过是立在乡村小路旁一座古老而人迹罕至的小教堂里的石头雕像。

起初，庄稼汉对徒步朝圣并没有什么兴趣，然而轻骑兵却不由分说，生拉硬拽着他一块儿上了路，还向他强调：圣阿方索从没有让他陷入过困境。这让农夫心中也燃起了一丝希望。

或许在小教堂里有一位轻骑兵的战友或者伙伴在等着他们？才没有呢！那儿只有一座圣阿方索的雕像，他俩在雕像前跪了下来，轻骑兵开始假装虔诚地祈祷。

“现在，”轻骑兵对他的伙伴耳语，“圣人在召唤我了。”他站起身，将自己的耳朵贴在石像的嘴唇上，然后面露喜色地回到他的同伴那里。

---

1. 圣阿方索（St. Alphonsus，1696—1787），出生于意大利那不勒斯，著名天主教神父，著有多部神学著作，死后由教皇庇护九世册封为圣人。

“圣人送给我一枚古尔登，就在我的衣兜里。”轻骑兵当着庄稼汉的面从衣兜里掏出一枚他事先藏好的古尔登，然后他俩就如同事先所约定的那样，像兄弟般平分了这笔钱。

庄稼汉觉得这很合理，他催促轻骑兵如法炮制再试一次。轻骑兵依样画葫芦又表演了一通，然后又欣喜若狂地从圣人那里回来了。“这一次好心的圣阿方索给了咱们一百古尔登，就在你的衣兜里。”

当庄稼汉听到这番话的时候，他的面色变得惨白起来，他再三保证，自己连一枚十字币都没剩下。然而轻骑兵告诉庄稼汉：他应该相信圣人，圣阿方索是不会骗他的。无论结果如何，他都应该把衣兜翻出来清空。

当一百枚古尔登出现在两人面前的时候，庄稼汉也只有打落门牙肚里吞，像轻骑兵之前和他平分自己的一枚古尔登那样，和轻骑兵平分了他这一百枚古尔登。

这件事儿办得机智而巧妙，然而这么做是不对的，尤其是在教堂里。

（1807 年）

牙医

╱

有两个懒汉，在一起东游西荡已经有些日子了。他俩懒得去赚那点儿打工的小钱，又身无长技，找不到快速致富的门道，最后变得穷困潦倒，走投无路。

于是他俩想到一个主意：挨家挨户去乞讨，不是为了填饱肚子，而是为了坑蒙拐骗。他俩把讨来的面包又揉又捏，做成小药片和药丸的形状，再混上被虫蛀过的烂木头的碎屑，看起来和药剂师那里的黄色药丸一模一样。

随后他俩从书籍装订商那里花几个巴岑[1]买来了一些

1. 巴岑（Batzen），瑞士古代通行的银质辅币，价值相当于 1/15 古尔登。

红色的纸张（漂亮的颜色对每一种骗局都有所帮助）。他们把纸裁开，每张包上六到八颗“药丸”。

现在其中一人来到了镇上的年集，走进了一家红狮酒馆，希望能多招徕一些客人。他要了一杯葡萄酒，然而并不喝，而是坐在角落里，双手托腮露出一副痛苦的表情，不断发出低声的呻吟。

酒馆里纯朴的农民和镇上的人，都认定这个可怜人应该是患上了严重的牙疼。然而怎么办呢？人们同情他，安慰他说这一切很快就会过去，喝完了杯中的葡萄酒，又回到各自的工作中去了。

这时候另一个懒汉出现了。这两个混蛋看起来就好像这辈子从来不认识对方一样。他们并没有彼此注视对方，直到第二个家伙好像被坐在角落里的第一个家伙的呻吟声所吸引。“好伙计，”他说，“您看上去好像犯了牙疼？”然后他缓缓迈着大步走到了对方跟前。

“我是特拉法尔加[1]的施瑙齐乌斯·拉朋齐乌斯医生。”他接着说。这样一个奇特而响亮的名字就如同醒目的颜色一样，有助于实施诈骗。“如果您服下我的牙疼药

1. 西班牙西南部的海角地区。

丸的话，”他接着说，“即使是如此严重的症状，只需要一颗，最多两颗就可以药到病除。”

“看在上帝的分儿上。”另一个骗子回答。于是这位冒牌的拉朋齐乌斯医生从口袋里掏出红色的纸包，从里面取出一颗药丸，命令病人把药丸放在那颗坏牙上，完全嚼碎。顾客们一个接一个从桌边探过头来，围观这奇迹般的治愈。

接下来发生的事情您可想而知。病人不想从第一颗药丸开始就吹嘘它神奇的功效，于是他发出了一声尖利的号叫。这让医生感到非常满意。“您的疼痛，”他说，“已经开始被打破了。”说着他迅速拿出了第二颗药丸，用同样的方式让病人服下。

所有的疼痛立刻消失了。病人欢快地一跃而起，擦去额头上由于紧张而冒出的汗珠，尽管他手中其实空空如也，他还是假装对救命恩人千恩万谢，并掏出一笔貌似可观的报酬放到对方手中表示感谢。

这种伎俩看起来非常高明，而且的确行之有效。每一个在场的人现在都想要拥有这种神奇的药丸。“医生”对每包药丸开价二十四个十字币，在几分钟之内药丸就被一抢而空。

这两个骗子一前一后分别离开了，当他俩再次相聚的时候，他们为人们的单纯以及他们因此骗来的钱财而放声大笑。

这些“面包”可真是价值不菲啊。损失二十四枚十字币这笔小钱并不能让人陷入贫困，然而这对受骗的人们来说还不是最糟糕的。软面包球随着时间的流逝会变得像石子儿一样坚硬。在一年半载之后，当一位可怜的受骗者牙疼发作，他自信满满地一颗接一颗用他的坏牙咬碎坚硬的药丸，然而并没有被治愈，而是感到撕心裂肺的疼痛。而这种疼痛就是用他当初从自己兜里掏出去的那二十四枚十字币换来的！

由此我们可以看到，人们是多么容易被四处游荡的流浪汉的伪装所欺骗，这些骗子他们今生前所未见，今后也不会再见。有些读者看到这里可能会想：“我是如此的单纯，曾经也上过类似的当。”

记住：那些知道如何从其他地方骗钱的家伙，当他们来到村庄或者年集上的时候，可不会穿着有破洞的袜子，或者在右脚和左脚的鞋上分别安上白色和黄色的鞋扣。

（1807 年）

小站

一位驿站站长对一位驾着两匹马正向他的驿站驶来的犹太人说："从这儿开始您必须得有三匹马！因为前面是上坡路，而且路面柔软，这样的话，您得花三小时才能赶到那儿。"

犹太人问："如果我驾着四匹马，多长时间能赶到那儿？"

——"两小时。"

"驾着六匹马呢？"

——"一小时。"

"您知道的，"犹太人最后说，"给我套上八匹马吧，这样我不用赶路就直接到了！"

（1813 年）

一份特殊的酒馆账单

一个恶作剧的念头有时候会成功，有时候却需要付出外套甚至是皮肤作为代价。这一次仅仅是外套。

从前有三个浪荡的大学生，他们在旅途中一路风流快活，衣兜里连一个赫勒[1]都没剩下。像往常那样，他们又走进了一家小酒馆，盘算着白吃白喝一顿然后悄悄从后门溜走。

天遂人愿，当时酒馆里只有年轻柔弱的老板娘一个人。他们仨一边胡吃海喝，一边高深莫测地对话，诸如：这个世界已经存在了几千年之久，将来还会存在这么久，

1. 赫勒（Heller）是德国古代通行的铜质辅币，1 赫勒价值相当于 1/2 芬尼。

直到某一天的某一个时辰，每一年、每一天、每一小时都会像六千年前那样从头开始。

“是的。”他们中的一位终于发声了，他对坐在窗户旁，手里一边做着针线活儿，一边认真倾听的老板娘说道，“这是我们从学过的书籍里知道的。”

另一位则厚颜无耻地声称：他依稀记得他们在六千年前曾经来过这个地方，他还能清楚地认出老板娘那张美丽而友善的脸庞。

这样的对话持续了好长一段时间，老板娘看起来越是相信他们说的一切，这几个年轻的浪荡子弟越是卖力地享用着葡萄酒、烤肉和纽结面包。最后他们账单上的数字一路攀升到了五古尔登外加十六枚十字币。当他们吃饱喝足之后，哥仨打算按照之前计划的那样逃之夭夭。

“老板娘女士，”其中一位说，“这回哥几个手头有点儿紧。这条街上有很多酒馆，我们有幸找到了您这位聪明的女士，我们希望这次您作为老朋友能让我们赊账。如果您不介意的话，当六千年后哥几个再回来的时候，咱们新账旧账一块儿算。”

聪明的老板娘并没有面露愠色，而是显得十分愉快。她表示：几位先生如此满意，这让她也十分高兴。随后她不声不响地站在了酒馆的门口，要求这几位先生立刻把六千年前欠下的五古尔登外加十六枚十字币的账付了。因为按照他们所说，今天所发生的一切，从前已经原封不动地发生过一遍了。

不幸的是，这时村里的警长正领着几个精壮的汉子，走进酒馆想要为他们的荣誉喝上一杯。这对这几位瓮中之鳖来说可不是什么好事儿。很快警长就做出了判决："欠账六千年可不是件光荣的事情，这几位先生要么立刻把债还清，要么就把身上崭新的上衣脱下来抵债。"

哥仨不得不选择了第二个选项，而老板娘也保证：如果六千年后他们几个带着钱回来的话，她会把衣服一件一件全部还给他们。

这个故事就发生在1805年4月17日泽灵根[1]的酒馆里。

（1808年）

1. 泽灵根（Segringen），今德国南部巴符州一小镇。

意外的重逢

五十多年前，在瑞典的法伦有一位年轻的矿工，他亲吻着美丽的未婚妻，对她说："在圣露西亚节[1]我们的爱情将会在牧师手中得到祝福，我们将成为夫妻，共同建筑爱巢。"

"那里面将充满了宁静和爱，"美丽的未婚妻带着甜蜜的微笑说，"你是我的唯一和全部，离开你，我除了坟墓哪里也不想去。"

然而，他俩还没来得及站在圣露西亚面前，牧师还

1. 圣露西亚节（Sankt Luciä）是北欧国家通行的基督教节日，为纪念罗马帝国时期的女圣人圣露西亚（Sankt Luciä，283—304）而设立，时间通常在每年的 12 月 13 日。

没有机会说:“如果有谁反对这两位新人结成婚姻的，请站出来陈述理由。”——死亡就站出来了。

有一天早上，小伙子穿着他乌黑的矿工制服从姑娘的房前经过——矿工总是穿着他自己的寿衣——他又一次敲响了她的窗户，对她说早安，然而他却没能对她说晚安。他再也没能从矿井里回来。

那天早上，姑娘因为无聊系上了她为婚礼准备的带着红边的黑色围巾。当得知未婚夫的噩耗之后，她把围巾扯了下来，为他哭泣，念念不忘。

与此同时，葡萄牙的里斯本城被地震摧毁[1]，七年战争[2]结束了，弗兰茨一世皇帝[3]去世了，耶稣会[4]被解散，

1. 1755 年 11 月 1 日，里斯本发生了迄今为止欧洲发生过的最大地震，地震引发了 30 米高的海啸，整个城市被摧毁，6~10 万人遇难，占当时里斯本人口的 1/4 至 1/5。
2. 1756 年至 1763 年欧洲各国之间围绕着王位继承权和殖民地利益而爆发的一系列战争，最后以英国、普鲁士等一方胜利，法国、奥地利、俄罗斯等一方失败告终。
3. 欧洲历史上有多位名叫弗兰茨一世（Franz der Erste）的君主，此处应为哈布斯堡王朝的弗兰茨 · 史蒂芬（Franz I. Stephan，1708—1765）。
4. 1534 年成立于法国的天主教修会，1773 年被教皇敕令解散。

波兰被瓜分[1]，玛丽亚·特利莎女皇[2]去世，施特林泽[3]被处决，美国宣告独立，法国和西班牙联军没能攻破直布罗陀[4]。土耳其人将斯坦因将军关进了匈牙利的“老兵山洞”[5]，约瑟夫皇帝[6]也去世了。瑞典的古斯塔夫国王[7]从俄罗斯手里夺取了芬兰，法国大革命引发了长期的战争，利奥波德二世皇帝[8]也进了坟墓。拿破仑征服了普鲁士[9]，

1. 1795 年波兰被俄、普、奥三国最终瓜分。
2. 玛丽亚·特利莎（Maria Theresia），奥地利女君主（1717—1780）。
3. 约翰·弗里德里希·施特林泽（Johann Friedrich Struensee，1737—1772），德国人，丹麦和挪威国王克里斯蒂安七世（Christian Ⅶ，1749—1808）的御医，因篡夺权位以及与王后私通被斩首分尸。
4. 直布罗陀（Gibraltar），西班牙伊比利亚半岛最南端的海岬，1704 年在西班牙王位继承战争中被英军占领，此后西班牙多次设法收复，至今未果。
5. 此事应发生在 1787 年至 1792 年第六次俄土战争期间，当时奥地利帝国参与了俄罗斯一方。
6. 约瑟夫二世（Joseph Ⅱ，1741—1790），奥地利帝国皇帝，特利莎女皇之子。
7. 此处应为古斯塔夫三世（Gustav Ⅲ，1746—1792）。
8. 利奥波德二世［Leopold Ⅱ.（HRR），1747—1792］，神圣罗马帝国皇帝，波西米亚、克罗地亚及匈牙利国王。
9. 1806 年普鲁士军队在第四次反法同盟中被法军彻底击败，被迫于次年签订了割地赔款的季利济特条约。

英国人炮轰哥本哈根[1]。农民们播种又收割，磨坊主磨面，铁匠们敲打，矿工们在地下工场中挖掘金属矿脉。

然而，在 1809 年圣约翰节[2]前后，法伦的矿工们想要在两条竖井之间打开一条通道，在距离地面三百多腕尺[3]的碎石和酸水中，他们挖出了一具年轻男子的尸体。他在绿矾水的保护下，毫发未损，栩栩如生。人们可以清晰地辨认出他的容貌和年龄，仿佛他在一小时之前刚刚死去，或者正在工作间隙打盹儿。

当人们把尸体抬出矿井的那天，他的父母双亲、好友故知都早已离世，没有人能够认出这个长眠的小伙子，或者述说他不幸的遭遇。直到矿工的未婚妻认出了那张某一天从她面前消逝、一去不返的面庞。

她苍白的脸上已布满皱纹，拄着一根拐棍来到广场上辨认她的未婚夫。她跪倒在爱人的尸体前，心中的喜悦胜过了忧伤。她内心波澜起伏，久久才平静下来。“他

---

1. 1807 年，由于害怕中立国丹麦–挪威王国与拿破仑领导下的法国结盟，英国军队在不宣而战的情况下对该国首都哥本哈根进行了为期三天的炮击，造成了大量人员财产伤亡损失。
2. 圣约翰节（Johannistag），基督教节日，为纪念施洗者约翰——为耶稣洗礼的基督教先知而设立，时间通常在每年 6 月 24 日。
3. 腕尺（Ellen），德国古代长度单位，1 腕尺相当于现代公制的 45~56 厘米。

是我的未婚夫，”她终于说道，“五十年来我一直牵挂着他，如今在上帝的安排之下，我终于在离世之前再次见到了他。在我们婚礼之前八天他下了矿井，从此一去不返。”

那位昔日的未婚妻，无情的时光已经在她脸上刻满了皱纹，而她的未婚夫，面容却依然像年轻时候那样英俊。好像在五十年后，她胸中年轻时爱的火焰又被重新点燃了，然而他却再也不能发出笑声，眼睛再也不能睁开了。围观的人们都被这悲伤的情景感动得热泪盈眶。

最后她让矿工们把他的尸体抬进了她的小屋，就仿佛她是他所拥有的唯一东西，而他也拥有这样的权利，直到在教堂墓地里他的墓穴被挖好。

第二天，墓穴已经挖好了，矿工们抬着尸体走向教堂墓地。她从一个小箱子里拿出那条带着红边的黑色围巾系上，穿上她最好的衣服，陪伴着他走上她每周日去教堂的必经之路，就仿佛这是他俩的婚礼，而不是他的葬礼。

当人们把他的尸体放进教堂墓地的墓穴，她说：“安息吧，在冰冷的婚床上再待上几天，不要感到时光漫长。我还有一点儿事情要处理，重逢的日子不远了。——大地已经将你还给了我，它不会再次将你夺走的。”她一步三回头地离开了。

（1811 年）

狡猾的朝圣者

几年前，有一个四处游荡的流浪汉，他把自己打扮成虔诚的朝圣者的样子，声称自己来自帕德伯恩[1]，正走在朝拜耶路撒冷神圣墓地[2]的路上。

在米尔海姆[3]的驿站，他曾经向人打听："这儿离耶路撒冷还有多远？"

别人告诉他："需要七百个小时，但如果你从毛兴[4]的

1. 帕德博恩（Paderborn），德国中西部城市。

2. 此处指位于耶路撒冷的耶稣墓地。

3. 米尔海姆（Müllheim），德国西南部城市。

4. 毛兴（Mauchen），米尔海姆附近一小镇。

小路走的话，就可以省下一刻钟的时间[1]。”

这听上去还不赖，所谓不积跬步，无以至千里嘛。毕竟节省或者赚到一个巴岑的机会，要比获得一个古尔登的机会多得多。

然而十五个巴岑毕竟就相当于一个古尔登。所以在七百个小时的旅程中，每五小时里就能省下一刻钟的话，谁知道一共能够省下多少时间呢。

但是这位冒牌的朝圣者可不是这么想的，他就是一门心思东游西荡，蹭吃蹭喝。

一个乞丐永远不应该忘记一句古老的谚语：不要去一个贫穷的村庄乞讨，因为讨来的东西还抵不上一路上鞋底的磨损，尤其是光着脚的时候更不要去。朝圣者也是这么想的，所以他很快就回到了大路上，这里有富人们的房屋和丰盛的食物。

这个无赖并不满足于作为一个普通朝圣者从一双双

1. 考虑到作者成书的年代距今已有两个世纪，德语原文中的“七百小时”其实是路人的信口开河，只是大概虚数；而“一巴岑”与“一刻钟”则分别是流浪汉作为缺乏教育的社会底层人物所能理解的最小货币和时间单位，因此用二者来做类比，虽然与“一古尔登”和“五小时”在比例上并不准确，但非常符合其思维逻辑。

充满同情而虔诚的手中获取的寻常食物，他除了“营养丰富”的卵石汤[1]以外，什么都不想喝。

只要在路旁看到上好的酒馆，比如说克罗琴根[2]的驿站，或者施林根[3]的巴塞尔酒吧，他就装出一副极其谦卑和饥饿的样子，向别人乞讨一碗由清水和卵石煮成的汤，看在上帝的份儿上，钱自然是不付的。

当好心的老板娘对他说“虔诚的朝圣者，鹅卵石太硬了，在胃里没法儿消化！”的时候，他回答道：“所以我才要吃它！去耶路撒冷的路这么远，这玩意儿吃下去比面包顶饿！当然如果您能送我一杯葡萄酒的话，肯定会有助于我的消化。”

这时候老板娘会说：“然而，虔诚的朝圣者，这样的一碗汤没法儿给您提供足够的能量啊。”

朝圣者这样回答：“如果您能把清水换成肉汁的话，肯定会更有营养的。”

---

1. 卵石汤（Kieselstein suppen）源自一个古老的欧洲民间传说：一群饥饿的旅人谎称用清水煮石头可以做出人间美味，以此骗村民们将自己的食物投入锅中与其分享，也被称为“斧头汤”或者“纽扣汤”，其含义与中文的“空手套白狼”有相似之处。
2. 克罗琴根（Krotzingen），德国西南部小城。
3. 施林根（Schliengen），德国西南部小城。

现在老板娘给他端来了这样一碗汤，并且说：“底料还没煮得那么软。”朝圣者回答道：“是啊，而且肉汁看上去也太稀了。您能不能往汤里再添上满满几勺蔬菜或者一块肉，或者二者都添上？”

当好心的老板娘把蔬菜和肉加进汤碗里之后，朝圣者说道：“上帝保佑您！现在请把面包给我，我要喝汤了。”

于是朝圣者扔下他的手杖，挽起衣袖，坐下了。他满心欢喜地端起他的杰作，将最后一粒面包屑，最后一根肉丝，最后一滴葡萄酒和肉汁都吃喝得干干净净。然后用餐巾或者袖口擦了擦嘴，或者根本不擦嘴，说道：“老板娘女士，您的汤把我撑得太饱了，所以我无法勉为其难吃下这些美丽的鹅卵石了。太可惜了！但还是请您把它们收好。当我回来的时候，我会送给您一枚来自亚实基伦[1]的神圣贝壳或者一朵来自杰里科[2]的玫瑰。”

（1808年）

1. 亚实基伦（Ashkelon），以色列南部古城，临近地中海东岸。

2. 杰里科（Jericho），以色列中部古城，位于死海北岸河谷中，因盛产玫瑰而著称。

司令官和轻装步兵在赫斯菲尔德

在上一次与普鲁士–俄罗斯联军的战役中[1]，法国军队和一大部分联盟[2]军队都驻扎在波兰和普鲁士境内，其中有一支来自巴登[3]的轻装步兵队伍在黑森[4]的赫斯菲尔德[5]担任警戒任务。此地在战端初起之时，就已经被皇帝[6]派

1. 此处应指1806年至1807年的第四次反法同盟。
2. 此处指1806年至1813年由法国扶植德意志地区众邦国组建的“莱茵联盟”（Rheinbund）。
3. 巴登（Baden），当时为“莱茵联盟”境内公国，领土包括今日德国西南部巴符州南部地区。
4. 黑森（Hessen），当时亦为“莱茵联盟”境内公国，领土包括今日德国中部黑森州大部分地区。
5. 赫斯菲尔德（Hersfeld），黑森公国境内城市。
6. 此处指拿破仑一世。

兵占领，据为己有了。

相比旧的统治者而言，经常为非作歹的占领军显然不受当地居民的待见，因此他们在赫斯菲尔德也遇到了许多反抗，其中一起是一位法国军官被杀害了。

法国皇帝正在前线与不计其数的敌军鏖战，他可不允许敌人在他身后捣乱，造成这样的事情发生，因为即使是一点星星之火，也可能卷起燎原的烈焰。

赫斯菲尔德可怜的居民们，很快就被要求为自己鲁莽的行为承担后果。按照法国皇帝的命令，赫斯菲尔德市必须遭到劫掠，然后四处纵火，被烧成灰烬。

赫斯菲尔德是一个居民富足，有着许多工厂和美丽建筑的地方。当这样一个坏消息传来的时候，这些可怜的父老乡亲是一种什么样的心情，大家可想而知。穷人们仅有的身家将被人一把夺走，而富人们的财产则将被人用一辆辆马车运走。广场旁的豪宅和角落里的寒舍将化成同样的灰烬，就如同教堂墓地也是富人和穷人共同的归宿。

然而，最坏的情况并没有发生。在法国驻卡塞尔[1]和

1. 卡塞尔（Kassel），德国中部城市，当时为黑森公国首都。

赫斯菲尔德司令官的求情下，惩罚明显减轻了：只有四座房屋被烧毁，损失有限；然而劫掠还将照旧执行，这依然是非常严厉的惩罚。

当不幸的居民们听到最终判决的时候，他们恐惧万分，魂飞魄散。他们对在仁慈的司令官面前进行徒劳无益的抱怨和请求已经不抱任何希望，只想争分夺秒在劫掠开始前将自己最重要的财物抢救出来。

恐怖的时刻终于来临了，鼓声在不幸的人们的号啕大哭声中响起。士兵们匆匆忙忙穿过恐惧、奔逃、绝望的人群，来到了他们的集合点。

于是这位正直的司令官站在他的轻装步兵队列前面，他首先声情并茂地向他们描述了居民们的悲惨遭遇，随后说道："士兵们！劫掠的许可从现在开始生效。谁有兴趣参加的，请出列。"

没有人站出来，一个都没有！司令官又重复了一遍命令，依然没有人迈步。司令官表示：如果没有人想要参与劫掠，那他就只好自己去了。然而依然没有人愿意服从。于是显而易见，这次任务就被放弃了。

当居民们知道这件事情的时候，他们的心情就仿佛刚刚从一场噩梦中醒来一样。他们的快乐简直无法形容。

他们立刻派出一位代表去见司令官，向他的宽宏大量表示感谢，并且送给他一份丰厚的礼物作为报答。谁知道如果没有他将会发生什么！

然而司令官却拒绝了礼物，他说，自己做好事不是为了钱财。

这个故事于 1807 年发生在赫斯菲尔德，这座小城至今依然屹立。

（1808 年）

坏的奖赏

在上一次与普鲁士的战争中，法国人攻入了普鲁士国王[1]所在的城市柏林[2]，许多属于王室的财产被夺走，它们被人占有，或者被变卖。因为战争从不会带来任何东西，它只会掠夺东西。

人们发现了许多精心藏匿的财宝，作为战利品的一部分，但王室财产并没有全都被找到。有大量属于王室的木质建材尚未被发现，保存完好。

1. 此处指腓特烈 · 威廉三世（Frederick William Ⅲ，1770—1840）。
2. 1806 年 10 月，法军在与第四次反法同盟的战争中大败普军，占领了包括柏林在内的普鲁士大部分地区，腓特烈 · 威廉三世被迫逃亡到位于东部的柯尼希堡（Königsberg）。

在国王的侍从中有一个无赖，他想着借此好好赚上一笔。他跑到法国司令官那里，挤眉弄眼地告诉他：在某某地方有一批质量上乘的橡木和杉木，价值数千古尔登。

然而这位正直的司令官婉言谢绝了这种背叛行为，他说："就让那些上乘的木料待在它们原来的地方吧，不应该对敌人赶尽杀绝。"

当国王回国之后，他命令用这些木材给这位"忠诚"的侍从建起了一座崭新的绞刑架，以此作为对他"忠诚"的报答。

在莱茵兰[1]的朋友如果欣赏这个故事的话，可以试着在自家的森林里挖一挖，或许能找到一些当时被遗忘的木材呢。

（1809 年）

---

1. 莱茵兰（Rhineland），今属德国西部的莱法州，当时为普鲁士王国领土。

奇怪的鬼故事

去年秋天，有一位陌生的绅士来到了施林根这个美好的地方。在登山的时候，他放弃骑马，选择了步行。在途中，他向一位克罗伊茨纳赫[1]人讲述了一个他亲身经历的故事。

半年前，这位绅士在丹麦旅行，一天深夜他来到了一座村庄，村庄不远处的山丘上有一座整洁的小城堡，他决定就在村里过夜了。

客栈老板告诉他，当天晚上已经没有足够的床位了，而明天早上将有一场行刑，他将和三个刽子手一起过夜。

1. 克罗伊茨纳赫（Krenzach），德国西部莱法州城市。

于是这位绅士回答说："我要去那座小城堡，那里的领主或者主人会让我进去，并且给我提供一张空床铺。"

老板说："那里有许多挂着丝绸床幔的美丽的床，就在居高临下的房间里，而我负责保管城堡的钥匙。然而我不建议您去那里。三个月之前，城堡仁慈的主人和他的妻子儿女一起出了远门，打那以后，这座小城堡就被鬼魂占据了。城堡的看守和仆人们都待不下去了，其他去过小城堡的人就没有再去第二次的。"

这位陌生的绅士笑了。他是一个勇敢的人，对鬼魂毫不惧怕。他说："我想去试试。"

尽管客栈老板对此表示反对，他还是从老板手里拿到了钥匙。随后他准备好了拜访鬼魂所需要的物品，与一直跟随他的仆人一起走进了城堡。

在城堡里，他衣不解带，睡意全无，一心等待着将要发生的事情。他把两盏点亮的灯放在桌上，旁边摆上两把上好膛的手枪，看着用细细的红丝带悬挂在镜框下面的金色纸片，欣赏着美丽的图画，回想着与莱茵兰发小儿共度的往日时光。很长时间过去了，可什么都没有发生。

然而到了午夜时分，教堂的屋顶开始闪烁，大钟敲响了十二点，一片乌云飘过来遮住了城堡，巨大的雨滴敲打着窗户，发出比敲打大门大三倍的响声。一个有着漆黑而空洞的眼睛、半肘长的鼻子、突出的牙齿和山羊胡子、全身长满了乱蓬蓬的毛发的身影开始在房间里游荡，并且发出可怕的鼻音:“我是梅菲斯特[1]，欢迎来到我的宫殿。你们要和你们的老婆孩子永别了！”

陌生的绅士感到一股冷气从大脚趾上升起，顺着后背一直蹿到了睡帽上。至于他可怜的仆人，就更不用想了。

然而有着恐怖鬼脸的梅菲斯特正向他走来，膝盖抬得高高的，就好像在火焰上漫步一样。可怜的绅士想:以上帝的名义，在此一举了。他勇敢地站起身，用枪指着那个鬼魂，喊道:“不许动！不然我就开枪了！”

在这种情况下，没有任何鬼怪会感到害怕，因为尽管人们想开枪，但要么枪打不响，要么子弹对鬼怪毫发无损，反而飞回来击中开枪自卫的那个人。

然而梅菲斯特却高高地举起他的大脚趾，慢慢转过身，像他来的时候那样迈着缓慢的步伐离开了。

---

1. 梅菲斯特（Mephistopheles）是当时德国文学中常见的魔鬼形象，在同时代歌德的《浮士德》中亦有出现。

当陌生人看到魔鬼在火药面前心生畏惧的时候，他想：现在没有危险了。他用另一只手拿起灯，蹑手蹑脚地慢慢跟在鬼魂的身后。而这位仆人，他用最快的速度蹿出城堡，回到了客栈，他宁可跟刽子手在一起过夜，也不要和鬼魂待在一起。

然而，在过道里，鬼魂忽然从大胆的跟踪者的眼前消失了，看起来就仿佛沉入了地底一样。

当绅士想要再往前走几步一探究竟的时候，他脚下的地板忽然消失了，他掉进了一个地洞里。他看到迎面而来的火光，相信自己马上就要一命归西了。然而当他的十个脚趾终于安全落地的时候，他才发现自己身在一个有着穹顶的地窖里，毫发无损地躺在一堆干草上。有六个外形奇特的家伙围着火堆站着，梅菲斯特也在其中。在他们周围摆放着各种各样稀奇古怪的装备，在两张桌子上堆满了闪闪发光的伪造塔勒，一张比一张更迷人。

这时候陌生人终于恍然大悟：原来他们是一个伪造钱币的秘密团伙，所有人都是有血有肉的活人。他们利用城堡主人不在的时机，将造币设备秘密运进了城堡，有一些熟悉城堡情况的内部人员或许也参与其中。为了保证他们的秘密行动不被打扰和发现，他们开始装神弄鬼，每个来到城堡里的人都惊恐万状，以至于下次再也不来了。

然而现在旅行者开始为他没有听从村里客栈老板的劝告而感到后悔了。因为他被塞进一个狭窄的洞穴里一处阴森的小屋，并且听到他们的“战争法庭”在讨论对自己的处治方案。

“最好还是把他宰了，然后把尸体埋起来。”有人说。

然而另一个人却说：“我们应该先审问一下他，他是谁，他叫什么名字，他从哪儿来。”

当他们听到他是一位贵族绅士，并且要去哥本哈根觐见国王的时候，他们面面相觑，瞪大了眼睛。在把他扔回阴森的储藏室之后，他们说：“这下大事不好了，一旦他失踪了，人们就会从客栈老板那里知道他进了城堡再也没有出来的事情。轻骑兵一夜之间就会来到这里，把我们揪出来。我们长期的苦心经营，就要毁于一旦了。”

他们表示愿意放过这位俘虏，前提是他发誓不把他们的秘密泄露出去。此外他们还威胁说，他们会在哥本哈根派人监视他。他们还要求他在誓词里把自己的住处说出来。

他说："在野人左手附近有着绿色百叶窗的大房子。"

然后他们送给他一杯勃艮第葡萄酒作为起床饮料。在天亮之前他整晚看着他们如何铸造假塔勒。

当阳光穿过缝隙照进了地窖的时候，街上传来了啪啪的鞭子声和哞哞的牛叫声。陌生人告别了阴暗的地窖，向主人们的"友好招待"表示了感谢，带着欢快的神情回到了客栈，全然不顾他的怀表、烟斗和手枪还留在城堡里。

老板说："谢天谢地，终于再见到您了，我整个晚上都没睡着。您那边怎么样？"

然而旅人却想："一诺千金。虽然是为了保命而许下的誓言，然而也不应该将它泄露出来，否则就是对上帝的亵渎。"

所以他一言不发。这时钟声又敲响了，那些可怜的罪犯已经把现场清理干净，一切就这样过去了。

在哥本哈根，他也对这件事情守口如瓶，几乎都快想不起来了。

然而，在几个星期后，邮局给他送来了一个小箱子，里边装着一对儿崭新的带着银饰价值不菲的手枪，一块崭新的镶嵌着昂贵宝石的金质怀表，一个带着金链子和金线刺绣烟袋的土耳其烟斗，还有一封短信。

短信上写着:“我们给您送上这份礼物，以此表达对给您带来惊吓的补偿，以及对您站在我们一边、保持沉默的感谢。现在一切都过去了，如果您愿意的话，可以把这个故事讲出来了。”

这就是那位绅士之所以把这个故事讲给克罗伊茨纳赫人听的原因。当他在登山途中听到赫廷根正午时分的钟声，掏出来对时的，就是他说的那块金表。后来在巴塞尔的仙鹤旅馆[1]，有一位法国将军出价七十五枚崭新的杜布伦[2]。然而他没有答应。

（1809 年）

1. 仙鹤旅馆（Gasthof zum Storchen）是巴塞尔一家历史悠久的豪华酒店。

2. 杜布伦（Dublone），古代欧洲通行的金币，西班牙、法国、瑞士等均有铸造，1 杜布伦价值约相当于 3 古尔登。

废话连篇

有一位富裕的施瓦本[1]绅士将他的儿子送到巴黎去学习法语和礼仪。过了一年多，这位父亲的仆人也来到了巴黎。

当年轻的绅士看到仆人的时候，他充满惊喜和友善地叫出了声："嗨，汉斯！哪阵风把你吹来的？家里怎么样？有什么消息吗？"

"没啥消息，威廉先生，只是一年前牧场工人送给您的那只美丽的乌鸦在十天前死了。"

"可怜的动物，"这位威廉先生回答，"它怎么

1. 施瓦本（Schwabenland），今德国巴伐利亚州西南部地区，当时为公国。

死的？”

“唉，您知道，当咱家美丽的马一匹接一匹地死去之后，它可能吞吃了太多的尸体。我就知道会这样。”

“什么？我父亲那四匹美丽的摩尔马[1]都死了？”威廉先生问道，“这是怎么回事？”

“当咱家的房子和农场着火的时候，它们因为运水而劳累过度，我们对此也无能为力。”

“天哪！”威廉先生惊叫，“咱家的房子烧了？这是什么时候的事儿？”

“那天晚上我们正在火化您父亲的尸体，有人一不留神，一颗小火星就把房子点着了。”

“多么不幸的消息！”威廉先生哀号着，“那我的妹妹还好吧？”

“您还没出嫁的妹妹生了个没有父亲的孩子，是个男孩。这就是令尊大人被活活气死的原因。除此以外就没有什么消息了。”他补充道。

（1809 年）

1. 摩尔马（Mohren schimmel）指肤色类似摩尔人的棕黑色马种。

赔本买卖

在大都市伦敦及其周围地区，有许多极其愚蠢的傻瓜，他们对别人的金钱、怀表或者昂贵的戒指有着孩子般的喜好，不弄到一模一样的，誓不罢休。

他们常常通过诡计或者欺骗来达到自己的目的，更多时候则是通过明火执仗的抢劫，这样的抢劫有时就发生在光天化日之下开阔的公路上。其中有的成功了，有的则失败了。伦敦的狱卒或者刽子手可以讲述很多这样的故事。

有一天，一个奇特的故事就发生在一位高贵而富有的先生身上。

一个美丽的夏日，国王和许多贵族仕女聚集在一座巨大的王家花园中，那里有一条幽长曲折的道路，一直通往森林的深处。

有许多其他人等也聚集在那里，他们并没有兴趣花几个小时去小路上一探究竟，只要看到他们热爱的国王和王室成员就感到非常愉快和幸运了。

人们又吃又喝，歌舞嬉戏，成双成对或者独自一人在美丽的小路上或者茂密的玫瑰花丛中漫步。

一个衣冠楚楚的人，打扮得就好像众人中的一员，在外套下面掖着一把手枪，藏身在花园与森林交界处的一棵树后，等着有人路过。

说曹操，曹操就到。有一位绅士戴着闪闪发光的戒指、叮当作响的表链、钻石镶嵌的带扣、宽阔的绶带和金星，心无杂念地走进了凉爽的树荫里。

正在他心无杂念的时候，那个家伙从他面前的树林里走出来，给了这位好先生一个“谦卑的欢迎”。他从外套下面的马甲里掏出手枪，将枪口指着绅士的胸口，并且礼貌地要求他不要作声，因为他不想让别人听到他们之间的谈话。

当人站在枪口前面的时候，难免会感到恐惧，因为你也不知道枪里装着什么。

这位绅士理智地思考了一下：身体比钱财更有价值，而失去戒指总比失去手指要强。于是他同意保持沉默。

“尊贵的老爷，”这家伙开口了，“您能不能把您的两块金表出一个好价钱卖了呢？我们的校长每天都要找别人对表，而日晷上的刻度又非常模糊，我们总是不清楚准确的时间。”

不管这位富有的绅士是否情愿，他不得不以几个斯蒂博[1]的价格将怀表卖给了这个无赖，这点儿钱甚至都不够去喝上一杯四分之一升的酒。

就这样，这个无赖右手举着枪，左手拿着几个小钱，一件一件地从绅士那里买来了戒指、带扣和金星。

到最后绅士想：“终于完事儿了，谢天谢地！”可这时无赖却耍起了新的花招：“尊贵的老爷，鉴于咱俩之间相处得还是挺融洽的，您想不想从我这儿买点儿东西呢？”

绅士思考了一下这句话，觉得面对这桩糟糕买卖，还是应该有个好的表情，于是说道：“让我瞧瞧吧！”

于是无赖就从口袋里掏出了各种各样的小玩意儿，

1. 斯蒂博（Stüber）是古代荷兰发行的辅币，每枚价值相当于 4 芬尼。

这些都是他从“件件两巴岑”的杂货店里买来的，现在可算是找到一位不还价的买主了。那位好绅士不得不把所有的东西以高昂的价格一件一件从他手里买过来。

到最后，除了手枪无赖把所有东西都卖光了，而绅士的绿色丝绸钱包里还剩下一些迷人的杜布伦。无赖还在说着：“尊贵的老爷，您难道不想用手里剩下的钱，买下我这把手枪吗？它是由伦敦最好的工匠打造的，看在咱哥俩的情面上，两个杜布伦卖给你。”

绅士惊讶地想：“你这个蠢贼！”然后买下了手枪。

当他把手枪买下之后，他立刻掉转枪口喊道：“不许动，坏家伙，立刻给我往前走，我叫你去哪儿你就去哪儿，否则我就一枪毙了你。”

无赖一下蹿进了树林，嘴里喊着：“尽管开枪吧，尊贵的老爷，枪没上膛！”

绅士扣动了扳机，枪果然没有响。他把通条插进了枪管，里面一粒火药都没有。

这时那个贼人已经逃进了树林深处，这位高贵的英国人只好面红耳赤地回去了。今天这段可怕的经历，够他好好回味一阵子的。

（1809 年）

秘密斩首

/

我不知道，在某一年6月17日的早晨，兰道[1]的刽子手是否曾经再三向我们在天上的父虔诚地祈祷。

但在他的祈祷中，他肯定没有祈求一封来自南锡[2]的短信在那一天到来。

在这封信上写着："兰道的邻居！您必须带上砍头用的大剑，立刻到南锡来。在这儿您将被告知要执行的任务，并且得到丰厚的报酬。"—— 一辆旅行马车已经停在了他家门前。

1. 在德国和奥地利有多处以兰道（Landau）为名的城镇，根据上下文推断，此处应为今日德国西部莱法州境内的兰道（Landau in der Pfalz）。
2. 南锡（Nanzig），今法国东部洛林省首府，历史上曾数次在法德之间易主。

刽子手想:“这是我的工作。”于是就坐进了马车。

在离南锡还有一小时车程的时候，太阳已经和血红色的晚霞一起落下，夜幕降临了。车夫悄悄把车停下，说了声:“明天又是个好天气。”

这时候路边来了三个全副武装的壮汉，上车坐在刽子手的身旁，他们向他保证不会伤害他，但他必须让他们把他的眼睛蒙住。当把刽子手的眼睛蒙好以后，他们说道:“车夫，走吧。”

车夫驾车继续向前。刽子手感觉足足过去了十二个小时，但却不知道自己身处何方。一路上他听到了午夜猫头鹰的叫声，听到了公鸡的打鸣声，听到了早晨的钟声。

马车终于再次停了下来，有人把刽子手带进了一所房子，给了他一杯饮料和一根上好的香肠。

当食物和饮料让他恢复了体力之后，有人领着他在房子里继续前行，进进出出穿过一道道门，上上下下走过一级级台阶，当他的蒙眼布被解开的时候，他发现自己身处一座巨大的大厅之中。大厅的四周被黑布遮蔽，桌上点着蜡烛。

在大厅中央的椅子上坐着一个人，她的脖子裸露着，脸上戴着面具，她的嘴好像被什么东西堵住了，因此不能说话，只能发出呜咽声。

在四周的墙边站着许多穿着黑色外衣，脸部蒙着黑色面纱的绅士，这样下次当他再遇见他们的时候，就完全认不出他们来了。其中的一个人命令刽子手举起剑，把坐在椅子上的那个人的头颅砍下来。

可怜的刽子手感觉心脏里好像被冰凉的水灌满了，他表示：他的剑是为了执行法律而铸造的，他不能用谋杀去亵渎它。

这时候其中一位绅士掏出一把手枪，从远处指着刽子手说："您选吧！如果您不执行命令的话，那您再也见不到兰道的教堂钟楼了。"

刽子手想起了家中的老婆孩子。"既然别无选择的话，"他说，"愿我剑下这无辜之人的鲜血，流到你们的脖子上。"他一刀砍下去，那个可怜的人顿时身首异处。

行刑结束之后，这些绅士给了刽子手一个钱袋，里面装着二百杜布伦。有人把他的眼睛又蒙上了，领着他坐上了同一辆马车，还是同样那几个人陪着他一起返程。

当马车最后又停下来的时候，他被允许离开马车。解开蒙眼布，他发现自己又回到了那天晚上他遇见三个男人时距离南锡一小时车程的地方。然而这一次，马车匆匆掉头回去了。

这就是兰道的刽子手所经历的故事。这位好朋友非常遗憾自己无法说出是怎样一个可怜的灵魂通过这条血腥的道路去了天堂。

是啊，没有人知道她是谁，她犯了什么罪，也没有人知道她的坟墓在哪里。

（1810 年）

假宝石

在斯特拉斯堡[1]的梅齐格门[2]前有一座美丽的花园，任何人只要有钱就可以进去参加一些有趣而公平的娱乐活动。这其中就有一个衣冠楚楚的男人，像别人一样，端着个小啤酒杯坐在那里。他的手指上还戴着一枚戒指，戒指上镶嵌着一枚价值昂贵的宝石，闪闪发光。

这时候来了一个犹太人。他说道："我没有恶意，先生。您戒指上的宝石真漂亮。它闪闪发光的样子，难道

1. 斯特拉斯堡（Straßburg），今法国东部阿尔萨斯省首府，历史上曾多次在法德之间易主。

2. 梅齐格门（Metzgertor），斯特拉斯堡地标性建筑之一，位于市中心的奥斯特里茨广场。

不像祭司亚伦[1]胸牌上的乌灵与土明[2]吗？”

这个衣冠楚楚的陌生人简短而生硬地说：“这块宝石是假的。如果它是真的，可能就已经戴在别人的手指，而不是我的手指上了。”

犹太人请求陌生人把戒指给他看看。他把戒指拿在手里，翻来覆去，左看右看。“这块宝石难道不是真的吗？”他想着。随后他向陌生人出价两枚崭新的杜布伦购买这枚戒指。

那个陌生人不情愿地说：“我骗您干吗？您已经听到了，这块宝石是假的。”

犹太人请求把宝石给一位行家鉴定一下。这时候旁边坐着的一位开口了：“我可以为这个以色列人担保，这块宝石或许真像他所说的那样值点儿钱。”

陌生人说：“我不需要什么担保，这块宝石不是真的。”

在这座花园的另一张桌子上，有一位此间的常客正和他的狐朋狗友们一起进行着有趣而公平的金钱游戏。

---

1. 亚伦（Aaron），《圣经》中犹太人领袖摩西（Moses）的兄长。
2. 乌灵与土明（Urim und Thummim），古代犹太教祭司置于胸牌中，用于占卜神意的两件法器，通常被认为是黑白两色的两枚宝石。

其中一个人是精于此道的金匠。他曾经为一位在奥斯特利茨之战[1]失去了鼻子的士兵用银子打造了一个假鼻子，涂上肌肤的颜色，这个鼻子除了不能用来呼吸以外，看上去和真的毫无二致。

犹太人向那位金匠走过去。“先生，”他说，“这块宝石究竟是不是真的呢？所罗门王[2]的王冠上能不能有一块比它更漂亮的呢？”

那位金匠，也算是半个宝石专家，说道：“它就像天空中的毕宿五[3]一样闪亮，我愿意出九十杜布伦向您收购这枚戒指。如果您能够花言巧语把它买过来的话，那您就赚到了。”

犹太人转身回到陌生人跟前说：“不管真的假的，我给您六个杜布伦。”说着，他数出几枚崭新的钱币放在桌上。

陌生人把戒指又戴回了手指上，并且说：“这玩意儿

---

1. 在 1805 年 12 月，法国军队与奥地利–俄罗斯联军在当时奥地利帝国境内的奥斯特利茨（Austerlitz，今属捷克）进行决战，史称奥斯特利茨之战（Schlacht von Austerlitz）或“三皇会战”（Dritter Koalitionskrieg），此役以法军完胜告终，第三次反法同盟也随之瓦解。

2. 所罗门王（König Salomon，公元前 971—前 931），以色列国王，以其财富和智慧而著称。

3. 毕宿五（Aldebaran）是位于金牛座中的双星，是天空中最闪亮的星星之一。

我不卖。这块假宝石的做工太逼真了，如果您把它当成真的买了，我心里会过意不去的。”说着，他把手插进了口袋里，这样贪心的以色列人就看不见那块宝石了。

“八杜布伦。”

“不行。”

“十杜布伦。”

“不行。”

“十二——十四——十五杜布伦。”

“这样的话，”陌生人终于说道，“如果您不肯让我安静一下，坚持要买的话，当着在场所有先生的面，我得跟您说好了：这块宝石是假的，我从来没有说过它是真的。我不想引起任何误会。这枚戒指现在是您的了。”

犹太人欢天喜地地把这枚戒指拿到金匠面前，说：“明天我来找您拿钱吧。”

然而这位从未被人蒙骗过的金匠，却吃惊地瞪大了双眼说道：“好伙计，这不是您两分钟以前拿给我看的那枚戒指。看在咱哥们儿的情面上，这块宝石最多就值二十枚十字币。它是圣布拉辛[1]的玻璃工厂制造的。”

1. 圣布拉辛（Sankt Blasien）是德国西南部莱法州小城。

原来这个陌生人早就把一枚和在他手指上闪闪发光的真戒指看上去一模一样的假戒指藏在了口袋里，当犹太人和他交易的时候，他把手插进口袋里，用拇指把真戒指从手指上撸下来，再戴上假戒指，拿出来交给了犹太人。

受骗者怒气冲天地回到了陌生人那里，喊着："天哪，天哪！我上当了！我真倒霉！这块宝石是假的！"

然而这个陌生人却十分沉着冷静地回答道："我卖给您的就是假的，在场的先生们都能见证。"

（1810 年）

一个可怕的故事是如何被一条普通的屠夫的狗公之于众的

两个屠夫一同来到郊外的一个村庄，他们在天鹅客栈门前分手，一个向左走，一个向右走，说：“我们在天鹅客栈里再见。”然而他俩再也没能重逢。

他们中的一人随着一位农夫走进了畜栏，农夫的妻子尽管正在厨房洗碗，也跟着一同走了进去，农夫的孩子也在后面跟着。

这时候魔鬼推了一下这个女人的胳膊：“看上去这个屠夫好像在他的围裙下面藏着一大笔钱！”

女人对她的男人使了个眼色，男人也给她回了个眼色。他俩一起砸死了那个可怜的屠夫，然后迅速把他的尸体用稻草掩盖了起来。

魔鬼又推了一下女人的胳膊:“瞧,谁正在看着。”

女人环顾四周,看到了自己的孩子。

于是他们一行人惊魂未定地回到了家中,紧锁房门,如临大敌。

这个心如蛇蝎的女人说道:“孩子,看看你把自己弄成什么样了,到厨房来,我给你洗洗。”

在厨房里,她把孩子的脑袋按进滚烫的肥皂水里,活活烫死了。

现在她感觉一切终于清静了,然而她却没有想到被谋杀的屠夫的那只狗。

被谋杀的屠夫的狗,和它的同伴们在一起旅行已经有些日子了。在孩子被烫死,并被迅速扔进火炉的时候,它就已经嗅到了味道。它顺着畜栏门外主人熟悉的味道一路嗅了过来,它扒着农舍的门,意识到这里发生了一些非同寻常的事情。它猛然蹿回村庄,寻找它的同伴。很快,它拉扯着另一个屠夫的上衣,呜咽哀号着,那个屠夫也意识到了什么。所以他和狗一同回到了农舍,他立刻判断出这里曾经发生过一些可怕的事情,于是挥手招来了两个从远处路过的男人。

当那两个杀人凶手听到了狗的哀鸣声和屠夫的呼喊声，他们的眼前仿佛出现了刑场的情景，心脏也仿佛掉进了地狱。

那个男人想要从后窗跳出去逃跑，女人却拉住他的外套说："留下来吧！"

男人说："跟我走吧！"

女人回答："我走不动，我的双脚好像灌了铅一样。你没看见窗前那个可怕的身影吗？它有着闪亮的眼神和炽热的呼吸。"

这时候房门被撞开了，人们很快找到了被谋杀者的尸体。这两名罪犯被双手反绑送到了法官面前。

六个星期之后，他俩被执行了车轮刑[1]。他们丑陋的尸体支离破碎地挂在车轮上，这时候乌鸦们说道："这堆肉的味道不错！"

（1810 年）

1. 车轮刑（Rädern 或 Radebrechen）是古代欧洲通行的一种酷刑，因使用车轮作为行刑工具而得名。具体执行方式为将犯人绑在车轮侧面用铁棒打断四肢然后任其自然死亡，或直接将犯人用车轮砸死或者碾压致死。

狡猾的施泰尔马克人

在“最后一战”期间，在施泰尔马克[1]有一位富有的农夫，他思考着：在这样艰难的世道里，我怎么能保住我的皇冠塔勒[2]和杜卡特[3]呢？

“我经历过玛丽亚·特利莎女王的时代，愿上帝保佑她；约瑟夫皇帝的时代，愿上帝保佑他；以及弗兰茨皇帝的时代，愿上帝保佑他健康长寿，到现在依然安然无恙。

“如果有人认为在这些仁慈的君主统治下，还是比

1. 施泰尔马克（Steiermark），今奥地利东南部格拉茨州首府。
2. 皇冠塔勒（Kronentaler），18 世纪中期奥地利属尼德兰地区发行的大银币，因上有皇冠图案而得名，其质量较通常塔勒更重，每枚价值约合 2⅔ 古尔登。
3. 杜卡特（Ducat），古代欧洲各国通行的金币，每枚价值约合 4 古尔登。

较容易将自己的钱财藏匿或者转移的话，那么现在敌人[1]的鼻子已经伸进了村庄，很有可能把他抓进洛林[2]或者香槟[3]的监狱里去。这样的话，这位可怜的臣民的心就要为爱国主义而流血了。”

“我明白了，”他说，“说干就干。”于是在一个伸手不见五指的黑夜里，他把钱埋进了菜园里。“天上的七星不会出卖我的。”他说。

在菜园里，他把钱埋在了甘蓝菜与甜豌豆之间的地方。然后他在旁边与糖萝卜之间的小径上又挖了一个坑，并且把挖出来的泥土全部堆在了埋钱的地方，再在四周插满美丽的花茎和菜梗，看上去就像为了制作混合泡菜而种植的那样。

星期一已经开始有轻骑兵在整个地区四处巡逻，星期二有一支新来的队伍开进了村里的磨坊，他们用白色的胳膊肘[4]推搡着农民们。“把钱交出来，老乡，”一个松德高[5]人挥舞着明晃晃的马刀喊道，“否则就准备向天父

1. 指当时与奥地利交战的法国。

2. 洛林（Lothringen），法国东部省份，历史上曾多次在德法之间易主。

3. 香槟（Champagne），法国东北部省份，因作为香槟酒的产地而闻名。

4. 当时的法军制服上衣为白色红边。

5. 松德高（Sundgau），今法国东部阿尔萨斯省境内与德国接壤地区。

做临终祈祷吧。”

农夫表示：看在上帝的分儿上，他们可以把能找到的东西都拿走，他所有的钱在昨天和前天已经全部被抢走了。“在你们面前没有人能把东西藏起来，”他说，“你们就是法律。”

果然，他们除了几枚铜质的十字币，一枚带着玛丽亚·特利莎女皇头像的镀金五芬尼硬币，以及一枚小戒指以外，一无所获。

“老乡，”那个松德高人说道，“你肯定是把钱藏起来了，把你藏钱的地方指出来吧，否则你可以不用做临终祈祷，直接去见天父了。”

“我没法儿向您指出那个地方，”农夫说，“那帮匪徒是如此的凶恶，所以我不得不把他们带到菜园里。我可以向您指出我曾经藏钱的那个地方，并且告诉您曾经发生的事情。那帮坏人在昨天和前天已经来过这里，并且把找到的全部钱财都带走了。”

轻骑兵们立刻把目光转向了菜园，在那里他们看到的景象与农夫所描述的毫无二致。他们中没有人想到钱就藏在土堆下面，而是看着空空如也的地洞想：“我要是早点儿来就好了。”

“要是他们没有伤害这些美丽的甘蓝菜和香罗兰就好了！”农夫说道。这就是他成功骗过了眼下这位以及之前包括弗兰茨皇帝、约瑟夫皇帝、玛丽亚·特利莎女皇以及至高无上的利奥波德一世大公在内所有接踵而至的王公贵族，成功保住埋藏在地下的钱财的方法。

（1811 年）

土耳其故事

在土耳其有正义。

有一位商人的仆人，他在夜间赶路时感到十分疲惫，于是就把他驮着昂贵货物的马系在距护林人小屋不远的树上，自己在树荫下睡着了。

当他在晨风中被鹌鹑的拍打声惊醒的时候，发现当自己熟睡时，马儿已经不见了。

他立刻跑到这个行省的总督，也就是正驻扎在附近的卡洛斯曼·奥格鲁王子那里，在他的审判席前诉说了自己的困境。

王子倾听了一会儿，说道："你离护林人的小屋如此之近，为什么不再向前走五十步，以确保自己的安全呢？这是由你的大意造成的过失。”

于是商人的仆人说道:“尊贵的王子，在您统治的土地下，难道我应该为在露天睡觉而感到恐惧吗？”

这番话让卡洛斯曼王子感到非常高兴，同时也感觉受了刺激。“今晚喝下这杯土耳其烈酒,”王子说，“然后回到树下再睡上一觉。”

仆人照办了。

第二天早晨，当他又好好睡了一觉，在晨风中被鹌鹑的拍打声惊醒的时候，他发现自己的马儿驮着所有珍贵的货物又被系在了他身旁，而树上吊着一个死人。那个贼，他再也见不到日出了。

在许多地方还有很多树，或大或小。

（1811 年）

最轻的死刑判决

有人可能认为这是断头台，然而并不是！[1]

有个男人，尽管他为祖国做出了许多贡献，并且受到了亲王的明文表彰，但还是因为一次由激情驱使的犯罪行为，被判处了死刑。

常言道："如果乞求得不到的，祈祷也得不到。"然而由于他曾经受过亲王的明文表彰，他还是被获准选择自己最喜欢的死法，这意味着他可以选择用任意一种方式死去。

于是高等书记官来塔楼[2]拜访他，说道："公爵想要向

1. 在古代欧洲有许多类似于前文中车轮刑的酷刑，斩首和绞刑被认为是死刑中最轻的刑罚。

2. 古代欧洲统治者常常将塔楼用作囚禁贵族囚犯的监狱，例如著名的伦敦塔。

您展现他的仁慈。如果您想要被执行车轮刑，那么您将被执行车轮刑。如果您想要被执行绞刑，那么您将被执行绞刑。绞刑架上已经挂着两个人了，然而众所周知还有第三个位置。如果您想要吞耗子药的话，药剂师那儿有的是。公爵说了，无论您选择哪一种死法，都悉听尊便。然而您必须死，这您应该明白。”

于是这位罪犯说道:“如果我必须去死的话，车轮刑是一种非常憋屈的死法。而绞刑呢，尤其是在有风的时候，晃来晃去太难受了。然而您可能没有正确理解这个判决。依我来说，我一直相信，由于衰老而导致的死亡是最温和的。既然公爵让我选择死法，这就是我的选择，没人能够改变。”于是他就活了下来，没有被处决。

因此，这个男人得以重获自由，并且继续活着直到老死。公爵说:“一言既出，驷马难追。”

这个小故事来自我的岳母，如果她能够救别人的生命，她绝不会袖手旁观。

（1811 年）

被欺骗的杂货商

在俄罗斯，一卢布就是一枚银质硬币，价值相当于二十七巴岑；而一帝国币[1]则是一枚价值十卢布的金币。

人们当然可以用一帝国币换来一卢布，比方说在牌桌上输了九卢布的时候，然而却不可能用一卢布换来一帝国币。

然而在莫斯科有一个狡猾的士兵却说："明天我要去年集上，用一卢布做诱饵，赚上两帝国币。"

第二天，年集上的货摊已经排成了一条长龙，在每个摊位前都站着人，人们或夸耀或贬损着商品，讨价还

1. 帝国币（Imperial），18 世纪至 19 世纪俄罗斯发行的金质硬币。

价。人群忽而聚集忽而散开，小伙子们向姑娘们打着招呼。这时候士兵手拿一卢布来到了这里。

“这枚印着皇帝头像的卢布是谁的？是您的吗？”他向每一个摊位前站着的每一位摊主询问。

其中有位摊主其实并没有丢钱，他观察了一阵，最后想：要是你觉得这钱在你手里烧得慌，还不如拿过来给我呢。他喊道：“这边来，步兵！这个卢布是我的。”

步兵说：“如果您不喊我的话，我在人群中还真不容易找到您呢。”说着就把卢布给了摊主。

这位商人拿着这枚卢布左看右看，想从声音上确定它是否是真的。直到确定是真的之后，才把它放进了口袋。

“要是没问题的话，现在请把我的帝国币还给我。”那位步兵说道。

商人回答：“我没有拿过您的帝国币，所以我也不欠您的钱。如果您只是想开个玩笑的话，您可以把您的那一枚卢布拿回去。”

然而步兵却说：“我的一枚两帝国币已经给您了，我不是在跟您开玩笑，我要去找市场保安和警察了。”

于是他俩你一言我一语地争吵了起来，从宽容说到固执，从固执说到卑鄙，在摊位前聚集的人越来越多，就好像蜂箱上聚集的一群蜜蜂一样。

突然，有个身影像鼹鼠一样穿过了人群。

“这儿发生什么事情了？”这位警官带着手下一边穿过人群，一边问道。

“发生什么了？问我吗？”这位杂货商不善言辞，偏偏步兵却是个能言善辩的家伙。

步兵声称，在一刻钟之前，他在杂货商那里买了价值一卢布的商品，然而当他付钱的时候，翻遍了所有的口袋，只找到爷爷临终之前留给他的一枚价值两帝国币的金币。所以他只好把帝国币作为押金留下，去取卢布。当他拿着一卢布回来的时候，却找不到刚才那个货摊了，他只好在所有的摊位前询问：“我欠谁一卢布？”眼前这位商人承认自己就是刚才卖货给他的那一位，并且收下了那一卢布，然而他却拒绝承认关于帝国币的事情。

警官询问摊位周围的人，他们说道：“这位步兵确实曾经向每个货摊询问过这枚卢布是属于谁的，当这位杂货商听到步兵的声音，他承认这枚卢布是属于他的。他收下了卢布，并且通过听声音辨别了真伪。”

当警长听到这里，他立刻做出了裁决：“既然您已经收下了那枚卢布，那么就把士兵的帝国币还给他，否则我就让人用长钉子把您的摊位封起来，您将在属于自己的木板之间过上与世隔绝的生活，于是您将长时间忍饥挨饿，这样您就可以健康长寿了。”

这就是警察局长所说的。于是商人就这样以一帝国币的代价从步兵手里换来了一卢布。[1]

注意：就像新雪会使旧雪融化一样。贪恋陌生人的财物，难免殃及自身。

（1811 年）

1. 此处与上文中提到“两帝国币”似有冲突，疑为泛指，同时与本文开头呼应。

好耐性

一个法国人骑马路过一座桥梁，这座位于河流之上的桥非常狭窄，以至于两名骑马的人都无法同时通过。

一个英国人也从另一端骑马上了桥，他俩在桥的中间狭路相逢了，双方谁都不愿意给对方让路。

“一个英格兰人是不会给一个法国人让路的。”那个英格兰人说道。

“上帝啊”[1]，法国人回答，“我的马也是英格兰马[2]，所以您如果想要我掉头，给您看看它的秃尾巴的话，门儿

1. 此处原文为法语 Par Dieu。

2. 原文中的“英格兰人”和“英格兰马”都是德语“Engländer”，此处法国人显然有羞辱英格兰人之意。

都没有。要不还是让您骑着的这匹英格兰马给我骑着的这匹英格兰马让路吧。您这匹看起来比我这匹要年轻一些，我这匹可是在路易十四[1]时代的公元1702年就参加过卡法奥泽战役[2]的。”

英格兰人自然对这种冒犯感到些许不快，然而他说道：“我可以等。我现在有了一个绝好的机会来读读今天的报纸。我可以一直等到您愿意给我让路为止。”说着，他就像英格兰人通常那样，非常冷漠地从口袋里掏出一张报纸，像叠手绢那样把它折了起来，骑着马在桥上看了整整一小时。

然而太阳却并不愿意长时间地注视这两个笨蛋，它飞快地朝着山头落了下去。

一小时之后，英格兰人终于看完了报纸，他把报纸重新收好，盯着法国人，说道：“好了吧？”[3]

---

1. 路易十四（Louis XIV，1638—1715），法国国王，自称“太阳王”（le Roi Solei），在位七十二年间曾发动多次对外战争，法国的版图及国际影响力均有所扩大。
2. 在1702年期间英法两国的确为西班牙王位继承战争的交战双方，但历史文献中从未有“卡法奥泽”（Käferolse）这一地名出现，更遑论相关战役。此处显然系法国人信口开河。
3. 此处原文为法语“Eh bien”。

然而法国人却不肯点头，他回答道:“英格兰人，把您的报纸给我看一会儿吧，我可以看看它，直到您愿意让路为止。”

当英格兰人终于见识到了对手的耐性的时候，他说道:“你猜怎么着，法国人？过来吧，我给你让路。”

于是英格兰人给法国人让了路。

（1812 年）

伟大的游泳者

在漫长的战争爆发之前[1]，人们还可以不受阻碍地从法国前往英国旅行，在多佛尔[2]喝上一小杯酒，或者买块儿衣料缝制马甲。每周有两班大型邮轮从加莱[3]穿过海峡开往多佛尔，然后返回。因为两国之间的海洋只有几英里宽而已[4]。

当然，人们如果想搭船的话，必须在开船之前到达

1. 开始于 1793 年的法国与反法同盟各国之间的战争，至作者写作此文时已经持续了 20 年，给欧洲人民带来了巨大的痛苦。
2. 多佛尔（Dover），英格兰东南部海港城市，英伦三岛最靠近欧洲大陆的地点。
3. 加莱（Calais），法国北部海港城市，欧洲大陆最靠近英国的地点。
4. 多佛尔与加莱之间距离 34 公里，合 21 英里。

船所在的地点。有一位来自加斯科涅[1]的法国人似乎不明白这个道理，他迟到了一刻钟，这时从加莱出发的邮轮船舱已经关闭，天空中只有云彩在飘荡。

“难道我就束手无策地在这儿坐上几天，直到下一班船过来吗？不行，”他想，“要不然，我就花十二苏[2]找个船夫，让他驾船跟在邮轮的后面。小船速度比大邮轮快，这样就能赶上邮轮了。”

然而当他坐进一艘敞篷的船只里的时候，船夫对他说道：“要是我想到会这样，我就带上一块遮雨布了！现在已经开始下雨了，不是吗？一会儿高高的夜空中就将降下倾盆大雨，就像天上有一座海洋将要倾泻到地上的海洋中那样。”

然而那个加斯科涅人却想：“这真有趣。”

“上帝保佑，”船夫终于说道，“我看见邮轮了。”

他们终于赶上了邮轮。当加斯科涅人于午夜时分在海中央登船，穿过客舱的小门走进船里的时候，每个人都十分好奇他从哪里来，为什么这么晚，一个人，而且浑身湿透。

---

1. 加斯科涅（Gascogne），法国西南部地区，与西班牙接壤。

2. 苏（Sou），法国古代小额铜币，价值 5 生丁，约相当于德国的 6 芬尼。

这样的一次海上航行，就像坐在地窖里一样。除了船舱内的谈话、海员们的呼喊、船发出的噪声、海鸥的鸣叫以及海浪声以外，他们听不到外界的其他声音，也没有人意识到外面正在下雨。

“您看起来，”其中一个人说道，“就好像刚刚被龙骨拖曳[1]过，我的意思是说，被绑在船底下拖来拖去。”

“是吗？”加斯科涅人说，“您觉得有人能在游泳的时候身体保持干燥吗？如果您能找到一个这样的人，我也很想见识一下。我是来自奥莱龙[2]的信使，每个星期一我都要带着信件和公文游泳去大陆，因为这样速度比较快。”

“我现在要去英格兰办一些事情。如果你们允许的话，”他继续说道，“我现在想和你们一起搭个船，遇到你们真是太幸运了。从星星判断，离多佛尔已经不远了。”

“同胞，”其中一人说道，他嘴里的烟斗冒出一团烟雾（其实他并不是同胞，而是一个英格兰人），“既然您

---

1. 龙骨拖曳（Kielholen）是古代欧洲船只上经常采取的一种体罚方式，将受刑人捆绑后，将其从船的侧舷投入水中，利用船的动力进行拖曳，因此时受刑人的身体常常位于船龙骨下方，故得名。

2. 奥莱龙岛（Oleron），位于法国西部比斯开湾中的岛屿。

从加莱远跨重洋游到了这里，那您肯定比伦敦的那位黑人游泳者还要厉害。”

“那当然没错儿。”加斯科涅人说。

“如果您想要跟他比试比试的话，”英格兰人回答，“我下注一百金路易[1]赌您赢。”

加斯科涅人说：“我来！”

英格兰的富人们有在体育竞技项目上一掷千金进行赌博的传统，因此船上那位英格兰人按照他开出的价格将加斯科涅人带到了伦敦，好吃好喝地招待着，为的是让他保持良好的体力。

“阁下，”他对伦敦的一位好朋友说，“我从海上花一百基尼[2]找来了一个游泳者，让他跟你的摩尔人比一比怎么样？”

那位好朋友说：“行啊！”

于是第二天这两位都带着自己的游泳者来到了泰晤士河边约定的地方，这时候已经有数百人聚集在了那里，

---

1. 金路易（Louisdor），法国古代金币，每枚价值 60 苏，约相当于德国的 $1\frac{1}{2}$ 古尔登。

2. 基尼（Guinee），英国古代金币，每枚价值 21 先令又 6 便士，约合德国的 9 古尔登，此处显然是英格兰人在夸海口。

他们之间也相互下注。这个人赌摩尔人赢，那个人赌加斯科涅人赢，一先令[1]、六先令、一基尼、二基尼、五基尼、十基尼、二十基尼。摩尔人看上去跟加斯科涅人旗鼓相当。

当两人都脱去衣服之后，加斯科涅人用一根皮带将一个小盒子绑在了腰间，他并没有说明缘由，仿佛这就是理所当然的那样。

摩尔人说:“您这是搞什么名堂？莫非您是想要向伟大的潜水员学习，在脚上绑个铅球，以免自己在逮兔子的时候跳得比兔子还高？”

加斯科涅人打开那个小盒子，说道:“这里面只有一小瓶葡萄酒、几根干香肠以及一小块面包。我正想问问您，把食物放在哪儿了。我现在要沿着泰晤士河一直游到北海，再穿过海峡进入大西洋，最后抵达加的斯[2]。按照我的估计，直到16号我从奥莱龙岛返回之前，我们在路上不会再见面了。然而我早上会在加的斯的小马酒店订上一桌上好的午饭，等我吃完饭的时候，您应该就随

---

1. 先令（Schilling），英国及多个英联邦国家发行的辅币，当时1先令相当于1/2英镑或12便士，约合德国的1/3古尔登。

2. 加的斯（Cadix），西班牙西南部海港城市。

后赶到了。”

聪明的读者们或许很难相信这种夸夸其谈，然而那位摩尔人却被吓得头晕目眩。

“在这只公鸭子面前，”他对他的主人说，“我肯定游不过他。您看着办吧。”说着他又重新穿上了衣服。

于是这场赌局就此宣告结束。加斯科涅人从他为英格兰人赢得的赌注当中分得了一大笔奖赏，而摩尔人则受到了每个人的耻笑。

无论大家是否发觉法国人的所作所为不过是一场骗局，每个人在从这个滑稽的故事及其出人意料的结局中得到乐趣之余，都应该认识到：此人打那以后在所有的客栈和啤酒馆里已经畅通无阻地赌了四个星期之久，而他其实一生中从来没有下过水。

（1813 年）

天气操纵者

/

就如同一位筛子工匠或者一位补锅工匠那样，作为手艺人，当他居住在一个小地方的时候，他的同乡们不能给他提供全年的工作以及给养，所以他就需要在周边地区四处奔走，打工赚钱。

这位五金工匠像其他手艺人那样勤奋地在周边地区奔走，只不过他兜售的不是五金小玩意儿，而是欺骗和谎言。他就靠着蛊惑人心在客栈里骗吃骗喝。

有一天他来到了上埃欣根[1]，径直去了镇长那儿。

“镇长先生，”他说道，“您难道不想换个天气吗？刚

1. 上埃欣根（Obernehingen），今德国西南部巴符州境内小镇。

才我从您的田地上经过，土地深处已经吸收了太多雨水，这对庄稼的生长可不好。”

镇长表示，说起来倒是轻巧，要做起来可就需要本事了。

“嗯，”这位“五金工匠”回答，“在这一趟旅行中我就做到了。在意大利波隆纳改变天气的人不就是我吗？那里种着酸橙和柠檬，所有的天气都按照安排好的那样出现了。这方面你们德国人已经落后了。”

这位镇长是个正直的好人，他属于那种想快速致富，而不是缓慢积累的人。所以他接受了这位“五金工匠”的提议，然而还是希望保持一些谨慎。

“明天早上就给我来个晴天试试吧，”他说，“天空中还要有一些淡淡的白云，这样一整天一缕缕闪亮的阳光就可以从其间温和地投射下来。在中午时分您可以放飞第一只黄色的蝴蝶，在傍晚时分天气又重新变得凉爽。”

“五金工匠”回答：“我可不接只有一天的活儿，镇长先生。这对我来说不合算。我从来都只接为期一年的活儿，到那时候您就要为找不到足够的地方存放您的粮食和新酿的葡萄酒而发愁了。”

关于镇长先生提出的关于操纵一年天气所需要的费用问题，他表示：一切准备就绪至少需要三天时间，在此期间他除了每天一枚古尔登以及免费的酒水以外，别无所求。

“打那以后，您在每一桶[1]葡萄酒上都能收获更多，”他说道，“比最好的年份还要多四分之一。每一马尔脱[2]粮食都能多收一赛斯特[3]。”

“这好像不多啊。”镇长说。

在当地，人们说“多”的时候，通常是用“veil”，而不是“viel”。为了表示对“五金工匠”的尊敬，镇长特地用了标准德语。

正当他从柜子里取出纸笔，想要让“五金工匠”把未来的天气按月份写下来的时候，“五金工匠”提出了新的意见：“这可不行，镇长先生！如果这样的话，您就得听听公民们的意见。毕竟天气是一件公共事务，您不能指望所有人都赞同您对天气的安排。”

---

1. 原文的量词“Saum”是奥地利南部及瑞士德语区方言，意思是容量为130~180公升的大酒桶。
2. 马尔脱（Malter），德国古代计量单位，1马尔脱约相当于110公升。
3. 赛斯特（Sester），德国古代谷物计量单位，1赛斯特相当于15~17公升。

镇长说道:“您说得对！您真是个明白事理的人。”

聪明的读者可能已经识破了“五金工匠”的伎俩，正如同他之前估计的那样，公民们不可能就这个问题达成一致。第一次镇民大会没有任何结果，第七次也没有。在第八次大会上，在经过一系列严肃的演讲之后，有位聪明的律师提出的意见终于获得了镇民们的一致认可:最好把钱付给这位天气操纵者，把他送走。

于是镇长告诉天气操纵者:“这是您的九古尔登，麻烦制造者，请您务必要离开，把谋杀和凶杀从镇上带走。”

“五金工匠”并不需要第二遍催促。他拿上这笔钱，留下了大约二十大壶[1]葡萄酒的酒馆账单，天气也一如既往没有发生任何改变。

总之，这位“五金工匠”真是一位有教育意义的人物啊。

注意:迄今为止，那位至高的统治者已经按照他自己的意志将天气安排妥当。即使我们的日历制定者、日月星辰和各界贤达[2]，也不会轻易去问及这方面的问题，

1. 原文的量词“Maß”在奥地利南部及瑞士德语区方言中意为装酒的大壶。

2. 此处德语原文“Landstànde”意为中世纪时期由社会各界贤达人士组成的地方仪会代表。

更遑论改变岁月静好的日子了。所以如果有人提起这事儿，还是洗洗睡吧。

（1819 年）

最安全的路[1]

有些时候即使是一个醉汉也会思考，或者突然冒出一个好主意，比如不走平时熟悉的道路从城里回家，而是从水里抄个近道。

他遇到了一位充满爱心、非常乐意向落难之人或者醉汉伸出援手的绅士。

“好伙计，”绅士说，“您没有注意到您正在水里走着吗？道路在这边哪！”

醉汉回答：尽管他觉得在干燥的道路上走着也很舒服，但这一次他还是想往另一边走走。

1. 本书作者黑贝尔去世于 1826 年，本篇是他生前未能完成的作品，具体写作年代不详。

“话虽如此，”绅士说道，“还是让我帮您从溪水里出来吧。”

“话虽如此，”醉汉回答，“还是让我待在水里吧。要是我在小溪里摔倒了，那么我还在路上。可如果我在路上摔倒了，我就得掉进小溪里了。”

他一边这么说着，一边用食指敲打着额头，仿佛那里面除了醉意之外，还有别人意想不到的其他什么东西。

（遗作）

PENGUIN

LITTLE BLACK

CLASSICS

PENGUIN

LITTLE BLACK

CLASSICS

“我打量着他
一直盯着我的眼睛
和有点阴郁的脸，
脑海中产生了一个
可怕的念头，
这是一个灵魂，
不是人类。”

‘The devil gave the woman a nudge: “Look at that belt full of money peeping out from under the butcher’s shirt!” ’

JOHANN PETER HEBEL

How a Ghastly Story was Brought to Light by a Common or Garden Butcher's Dog

Contents

The Silver Spoon

An officer in Vienna was thinking, 'Just for once I'll dine at the Red Ox,' and into the Red Ox he went. There were regulars there and strangers, important and unimportant people, honest men and rascals such as you'll find anywhere. They were eating and drinking, some a great deal, others little. They talked and argued about this and that, about how it had rained rocks at Stannern in Moravia, for instance, or about Machin who fought the great wolf in France. When the meal was almost over one or two were drinking a small jug of Tokay to round things off, one man was making little balls from bread crumbs as if he were an apothecary making pills, another was fiddling with his knife or his fork or his silver spoon. It was then the officer happened to notice how a fellow in a green huntsman's coat was playing with a silver spoon when it suddenly disappeared up his sleeve and stayed there.

Someone else might have thought, 'It's no business of mine,' and said nothing, or have made a great fuss. The officer thought, 'I don't know who this green spoon-hunter is and what I might let myself in for,' and he kept as quiet as a mouse, until the landlord came to collect his money. But when the landlord came to collect his money the officer, too, picked up a silver spoon, and tucked it through two button holes in his coat, in one and out the other as soldiers sometimes do in war when they take their spoons with them, but no soup. As the officer was paying his bill the landlord was looking at his coat and thinking, 'That's a funny medal this gentleman's wearing! He must have distinguished himself battling with a bowl of crayfish soup to have got a silver spoon as a medal! Or could it just be one of mine?' But when the officer had paid the landlord he said, without a sign of a smile on his face, 'The spoon's included, I take it? The bill seems enough to cover it.' The landlord said, 'Nobody's tried that one on me before! If you don't have a spoon at home I'll give you a tin one, but you can't have one of my silver spoons!' Then the officer stood up, slapped the landlord on the shoulder and laughed. 'It was only a joke we were having,' he said, 'that gentleman over there in the green jacket and me! – My green friend, if you give back that spoon you have up your sleeve I'll give mine back too.' When the spoon-hunter saw that he had been caught in the act and that an honest eye had observed his dishonest hand, he thought, 'Better pretend it was a joke,' and gave back his spoon. So the landlord got his property back, and the spoon thief smiled too – but not for long. For when the other customers saw what had happened they set about him with curses and hounded him out of the Holy of Holies and the landlord sent the boots after him with a big stick. But he stood the worthy officer a bottle of Tokay to toast the health of all honest men.

Remember: You must not steal silver spoons!

Remember: Someone will always stand up for what is right.

The Cheap Meal

There is an old saying: The biter is sometimes bit. But the landlord at the Lion in a certain little town was bitten first. He received a well-dressed customer who curtly demanded a good bowl of broth, the best his money would buy. Then he ordered beef and vegetables too for his money. The landlord asked him, all politeness, if he wouldn't like a glass of wine with it. 'Indeed I would,' his guest replied, 'if I can have a good one for my money.' When he had finished, and he enjoyed it all, he took a worn six-kreuzer piece from his pocket and said, 'Here you are, landlord, there's my money!' The landlord said, 'What's this? You owe me a thaler!' The customer answered, 'I didn't ask for a meal for a thaler, but for my money. Here it is. It's all I have. If you gave me too much for it then that's your fault!' It wasn't really such a clever trick. It called only for cheek and a devil-may-care view of the consequences. But the best is yet to come.

'You're an utter villain,' said the landlord, 'and don't

deserve this. But you can have the meal for nothing and take this twenty-four kreuzer bit as well. Just keep quiet about it and go over to my neighbour who keeps the Bear and try the same trick on him!' He said this because he had had a quarrel with his neighbour and resented his success and each was keen to do the other down.

But the artful customer smiled as he took the money he was offered in his one hand and reached carefully for the door with the other, wished the innkeeper good afternoon, and said, 'I went to the Bear first, it was the landlord there who sent me over here!'

So really both of the innkeepers had been tricked; the cunning customer took advantage of their quarrel. Yet he might have also earned a further reward, grateful thanks from both of them, if they had learnt the right lesson from it and had made things up between them. For peace pays, whereas quarrels have to be paid for.

Dinner Outside

We often complain how difficult or impossible it is to get on with certain people. That may of course be true. But many such people are not bad but only strange, and if you got to know them well with all their ins and outs and learnt to deal with them properly, neither too wilfully nor too indulgently, then many of them might easily be brought to their senses. After all, one servant did manage to do that with his master. Sometimes he could do nothing right by him and, as often happens in such situations, was blamed for many things that were not his fault. Thus one day his master came home in a very bad mood and sat down to dinner. The soup was too hot or too cold for him, or neither; no matter, he was in a bad mood! So he picked up the dish and threw it and its contents out of the open window into the yard below. So what do you think the servant did? He didn't hesitate, he threw the meat he was bringing to table down into the yard after the soup, then the bread, the wine, and finally the tablecloth and everything on it, all down into the yard too. 'What the devil do you think you're doing?' said his master angrily and rose threateningly to his feet. But the servant replied quietly and calmly, 'Pardon me if I misunderstood your wishes. I thought you wanted to eat outside today. The air's warm, the sky's blue, and look how lovely the apple blossom is and how happy the bees are sipping at the flowers!' Never again would the soup go out through the window! His master saw he was wrong, cheered up at the sight of the beautiful spring day, smiled to himself at his man's quick thinking, and in his heart he was grateful to him for teaching him a lesson.

The Clever Judge

Not everything that happens in the East is so wrong. We are told the following event took place there. A rich man had been careless and lost a large sum of money sewn up in a cloth. He made his loss known, and in the usual way offered a reward for its return, in this case a hundred thalers. Soon a good honest man came to see him. 'I have found your money,' he said. 'This must be yours.' He had the open look of an upright fellow with a clear conscience, and that was good. The rich man looked happy too, but only at seeing his precious money again. As for his honesty, that we shall see! He counted the money and worked out quickly how he could cheat this man of the promised reward. 'My friend,' he said, 'there were in fact eight hundred thalers sewn up in this cloth. But I can find only seven hundred. So I take it you must have cut open a corner and taken your one hundred thalers' reward. You acted quite properly. I thank you!' That was not good. But we haven't got to the end yet. Honesty is the best policy, and wrongdoing never proves right. The honest man who had found the money and who was less concerned for his reward than for his blameless name protested that he had found the packet just as he handed it over, and had handed over exactly what he had found. In the end they appeared in court. Both of them stuck to their stories, one that eight hundred thalers were sewn up in the cloth, the other that he had left the packet just as he found it and had taken nothing from it. It was hard to know what to do. But the clever judge, who seemed from the outset to recognize the honesty of the one and the bad faith of the other, approached the problem as follows. He had both swear their statements on solemn oath, and then passed the following judgement: 'Since one of you lost eight hundred thalers and the other found a packet containing only seven hundred, the package found by that second party cannot be the one to which the first party has just claim. You, my honest friend, take back the money you found and put it into safe keeping until the person who lost only seven hundred thalers makes himself known. And you I can only advise to be patient until someone says he has found your eight hundred thalers.' That was his judgement, and that was final.

The Artful Hussar

A hussar in the last war knew that the farmer he met on the road had just sold his hay for a hundred guilders and was on his way home with the money. So he asked him for something to buy tobacco and brandy. Who knows, he might have been happy with a few coppers. But the farmer swore black and blue he had spent his last kreuzer in the nearby village and had nothing left. 'If we weren't so far from my quarters,' said the hussar, 'we could both be helped out of this difficulty; but you have nothing, and neither have I; so we'll just have to go to Saint Alphonsus! We'll share what he gives us like brothers.' This Saint Alphonsus stood carved from stone in an old, little frequented chapel in the fields. At first the farmer was not too keen to make the pilgrimage. But the hussar allowed no objection, and on the way he was so vigorous in his assurances that Saint Alphonsus had never let him down when in need that the farmer began to cherish hopes himself. So you think the hussar's comrade and accomplice was hiding in the deserted chapel, do you? Not a bit of it! No one was there, only the stone figure of Alphonsus, and they knelt before him, and the hussar appeared to be praying fervently. 'This is it!' he whispered to the farmer, 'the saint has just beckoned to me.' He got to his feet and went to put his ear to the lips of stone and came back delighted. 'He's given me a guilder, he says it's in my purse!' And indeed to the other's amazement the hussar took out a guilder, but one that he had had there all the time, and shared it like a brother as promised. That made sense to the farmer and he agreed that the hussar should try again. All went just as before. This time the hussar was even happier when he came back to the farmer. 'Now Saint Alphonsus has given us a hundred guilders all in one go! They're in your purse.' The farmer turned deadly white when he heard this and repeated his protests that he had no money at all. But the hussar persuaded him he must trust Saint Alphonsus and just take a look; Alphonsus had never deceived him! So whether he liked it or not he had to turn his pockets inside out and empty them. Then the hundred guilders appeared all right, and since he had taken half of the hussar's guilder it was no use pleading and imploring, he had to share his hundred.

That was all very artful and cunning, but that doesn't make it right, especially in a chapel.

The Dentist

Two loafers who had been roaming around the country together for some time because they were too lazy to work or had learnt no trade finally got into a tight corner because they had no money left, and they saw no quick way of getting any. Then they had this idea: they went begging at doors for bread which they intended to use, not to fill their stomachs, but to stage a trick. For they kneaded and rolled it into little balls and coated them with the dust from old, rotten worm-eaten wood so that they looked just like yellow pills from the chemist. Then for a couple of pence they bought some sheets of red paper at the bookbinder's (for a pretty colour often helps take people in). Next they cut up the paper and wrapped the pills in it, six or eight to a little packet. Then one of them went on ahead to a village where there was a fair and into the Red Lion where he hoped to find a good crowd. He ordered a glass of wine, but he didn't drink it but sat sadly in a corner holding his face in his hand, moaning under his breath and fidgeting and turning this way and that. The good farmers and townsfolk in the inn thought the poor fellow must have terrible toothache. Yet what could they do? They pitied him, they consoled him, saying it would soon go away, then went back to their drinks and their market-day affairs. Meanwhile the other idler came in. The two scoundrels pretended they had never seen each other in their lives before. They didn't look at each other until the one seemed to react to the other's moans in the corner. 'My friend,' he said, 'have you got toothache?' and he strode slowly over to him. 'I am Dr Schnauzius Rapunzius from Trafalgar,' he continued. Such resounding foreign names help take people in too, you know, like pretty colours. 'If you take my tooth pills,' he went on, 'I can easily get rid of the pain, one of them will do the trick, at most two.' 'Please God you're right!' said the other rogue. So now the fine doctor Rapunzius took one of the red packets from his pocket and prescribed one pill, to be placed on the tongue and bitten on firmly. The customers at the other tables now craned their necks and one by one they came over to observe the miracle cure. You can imagine what happened! But no, the first bite seemed to do the patient no good at all, he gave a terrible scream. The doctor was pleased! They had, he said, got the better of the pain, and quickly he gave him the second pill to be taken likewise. Now suddenly the pain had all gone. The patient jumped for joy, wiped the sweat from his brow, though there was none there, and pretended to show his thanks by pressing more than a trifling sum into his saviour's hand. The trick was artfully done and had its desired effect. For all those present now wanted some of these excellent pills too. The doctor offered them at twenty-four kreuzers a packet, and they were all sold in a few minutes. Of course the two scoundrels now left separately one after the other, met up to laugh at the people's stupidity, and had a good time on their money.

The fools had paid dear for a few crumbs of bread! Even in times of famine you never got so little for twenty-four kreuzers. But the waste of money was not the worst part of it. For in time the pellets of breadcrumbs naturally became as hard as stone. So when a year later a poor dupe had toothache and confidently bit on a pill with the offending tooth, once and then again, just imagine the awful pain that he had got himself for twenty-four kreuzers instead of a cure!

From this we can learn how easy it is to be tricked if you believe what is told you by any vagrant whom you meet for the first time in your life, have never seen before and will never see again. Some of you who read this will perhaps be thinking: 'I was once silly like that too and brought suffering on myself!'

Remember: Those who can, earn their money elsewhere

and don't go around villages and fairs with holes in their stockings, or a white buckle on one shoe and a yellow one on the other.

A Short Stage

The postmaster told a Jew who drove up to his relay station with two horses, 'From here on you'll have to take three! It's a hard pull uphill and the surface is still soft. But that way you'll be there in three hours.' The Jew asked, 'When will I get there if I take four?' 'In two hours.' 'And if I take six?' 'In one hour.' 'I'll tell you what,' said the Jew after a while, 'Harness up eight. That way I shan't have to set off at all!'

Strange Reckoning at the Inn

Sometimes a cheeky trick comes off, sometimes it costs you your coat, often your skin as well. But in this case it was only coats. One day, you see, three merry students on their travels didn't have a brass farthing left between them, they had spent everything on a good time, but nevertheless they went into another inn intending to leave without sneaking out by the back door, and it suited them fine that they found only the landlord's nice young wife inside. They ate and drank merrily and talked very learnedly about the world being many thousands of years old and how it would last as long again, and how each year, to the day and the hour, everything that happened came to pass as it had done on that day and at that hour six thousand years before. Eventually one of them turned to the landlady, who was sitting on one side by the window knitting and listening attentively, and said, 'That's how it is, ma'am, we've had to learn that from our learned tomes.' And one had the impudence to assert that he just about remembered their being there six thousand years ago, and he remembered the landlady's pretty friendly face very well indeed. They carried on talking for some time, and the more the landlady seemed to believe everything they said the more the young gadabouts tucked into the wine and the meat and a fistful of pretzels, and in the end their bill stood chalked up at five guilders and sixteen kreuzers. They had eaten and drunk their fill, and now they came out with the trick they had planned.

'Ma'am,' said one, 'this time we are short of money, for there are so many inns on the road. But since we know you're a clever woman we hope that as old friends we can have credit here, and if you agree, in six thousand years' time when we come again we'll pay our old bill together with the new one.' The sensible landlady was not upset by that, it was fine by her, she was delighted that the young gentlemen were well served. But before they had noticed her move she was standing in front of the door and was asking the gentlemen kindly just to settle now the bill of five guilders and sixteen kreuzers that they owed from six thousand years ago, since, as they said, everything that happened now was an exact repetition of what had taken place before. Unfortunately just at that moment the village mayor came in with a couple of sturdy men to enjoy a glass of wine together. That didn't suit our gay young dogs at all! For now the official verdict was pronounced and carried out: you had to give it to someone who had allowed credit for six thousand years! The gentlemen were therefore to pay their old debt immediately or leave their newish overcoats as a pledge. They were obliged to take the second option, and the landlady promised to return their coats in six thousand years' time when they came again with a bit more money.

This took place in 1805 on the 17th of April in the inn at Segringen.

Unexpected Reunion

At Falun in Sweden, a good fifty years ago, a young miner kissed his pretty young bride-to-be and said, 'On the feast of Saint Lucia the parson will bless our love and we shall be man and wife and start a home of our own.' 'And may peace and love dwell there with us,' said his lovely bride, and smiled sweetly, 'for you are everything to me, and without you I'd sooner be in the grave than anywhere else.' When however, before the feast of Saint Lucia, the parson had called out their names in church for the second time: 'If any of you know cause, or just hindrance, why these two persons should not be joined together in holy Matrimony' – Death paid a call. For the next day when the young man passed her house in his black miner's suit (a miner is always dressed ready for his own funeral), he tapped at the window as usual and wished her good morning all right, but he did not wish her good evening. He did not return from the mine, and in vain that same morning she sewed a red border on a black neckerchief for him to wear on their wedding day, and when he did not come back she put it away, and she wept for him, and never forgot him.

In the meantime the city of Lisbon in Portugal was destroyed by an earthquake, the Seven Years War came and went, the Emperor Francis I died, the Jesuits were dissolved, Poland was partitioned, the Empress Maria Theresa died, and Struensee was executed, and America became independent, and the combined French and Spanish force failed to take Gibraltar. The Turks cooped up General Stein in the Veterane Cave in Hungary, and the Emperor Joseph died too. King Gustavus of Sweden conquered Russian Finland, the French Revolution came and the long war began, and the Emperor Leopold II too was buried. Napoleon defeated Prussia, the English bombarded Copenhagen, and the farmers sowed and reaped.

The millers ground the corn, the blacksmiths wielded their hammers, and the miners dug for seams of metal in their workplace under the ground.

But in 1809, within a day or two of the feast of Saint John, when the miners at Falun were trying to open up a passage between two shafts, they dug out from the rubble and the vitriol water, a good three hundred yards below ground, the body of a young man soaked in ferrous vitriol but otherwise untouched by decay and unchanged, so that all his features and his age were still clearly recognizable, as if he had died only an hour before or had just nodded off at work. Yet when they brought him to the surface his father and mother and friends and acquaintances were all long since dead, and no one claimed to know the sleeping youth or to remember his misadventure, until the woman came who had once been promised to the miner who one day had gone below and had not returned. Grey and bent, she hobbled up on a crutch to where he lay and recognized her bridegroom; and, more in joyous rapture than in grief, she sank down over the beloved corpse, and it was some time before she had recovered from her fervent emotion. 'It is my betrothed,' she said at last, 'whom I have mourned these past fifty years, and now God grants that I see him once more before I die. A week before our wedding he went under ground and never came up again.' The hearts of all those there were moved to sadness and tears when they saw the former bride-to-be as an old woman whose beauty and strength had left her, and the groom still in the flower of his youth; and how the flame of young love was rekindled in her breast after fifty years, yet he did not open his mouth to smile, nor his eyes to recognize her; and how finally she, as the sole relative and the only person who had claim to him, had the miners carry him into her house until his grave was made ready for him in the churchyard.

The next day when the grave lay ready in the churchyard and the miners came to fetch him she opened a casket and put the black silk neckerchief with the red stripes on him, and then she went with him in her best Sunday dress, as if it were her wedding day, not the day of his burial. You see, as they lowered him into his grave in the churchyard she said, 'Sleep well for another day or a week or so longer in your cold wedding bed, and don't let time weigh heavy on you! I have only a few things left to do, and I shall join you soon, and soon the day will dawn.

'What the earth has given back once it will not withhold again at the final call', she said as she went away and looked back over her shoulder once more.

The Sly Pilgrim

A few years ago an idler roamed around the countryside pretending to be a pious pilgrim, saying he came from Paderborn and was making for the Holy Sepulchre in

Jerusalem, and already at the Coach and Horses in Mülheim he was asking, 'How far is it to Jerusalem now?' They told him, 'Seven hundred hours. But you'll save a quarter of an hour if you take the path to Mauchen.' So he went by way of Mauchen to save himself a quarter of an hour on his long journey. That wasn't such a bad idea. You must not scorn a small gain or a bigger one won't come your way. You more often get a chance to save or make threepence than a florin. But eight threepennies make a florin, and if on a journey of seven hundred hours you can save a quarter of an hour every five hours, over the whole journey you will save – now, who can work that out? How many hours? But that wasn't how our supposed pilgrim saw it! Since he was only after an easy life and a good meal he didn't care which way he went. As the old saying goes, a beggar can never take the wrong turning, it's a poor village indeed where he can't collect more than the cost of the shoe leather he has worn out on the road, especially if he goes barefoot. Yet our pilgrim intended to get back as soon as he could to the main road where he'd find rich people's houses and good cooking. For this rascal wasn't content, as a true pilgrim should be, with common food given in compassion by a pious hand, he wanted nothing but nourishing pebble soup! You see, whenever he saw a nice inn by the road, for instance the Post House at Krozingen or the Basel Arms at Schliengen, he would go in and very humbly and hungrily ask for a nice soup made of pebbles and water, in God's name, he had no money. And when the innkeeper's wife took pity on him and said, 'Pious pilgrim, pebbles are not easy to digest!', he said, 'That's just it! Pebbles last longer than bread and it's a long way to Jerusalem. But if you were to give me a little glass of wine too, in God's name, it would help me digest them.' Now if she said, 'But good pilgrim, a soup like that won't give you any strength at all!' then he replied, 'Well, if you use broth instead of water then of course it would be more nourishing.' And when she brought him his broth and said, 'The bits at the bottom are still a bit hard, I'm afraid,' then he'd say, 'You're right, and the broth looks a little thin. Would you have a couple of spoonfuls of vegetables to add to it, or a scrap of meat, or maybe both?' If now the innkeeper's wife still felt sorry for him and put some meat and vegetables in the bowl, he said, 'God bless you! Now just hand me a piece of bread and I'll tuck into your soup!' Then he would push back the sleeves of his pilgrim's habit, sit down and set to work with relish, and when he had eaten the last crumb of bread, drained the wine, and finished the last morsel of meat and vegetables and the last drop of broth, he would wipe his mouth on the tablecloth or his sleeve, or perhaps he wouldn't bother, and he'd say, 'Missus, your soup has strengthened me as a good soup should, what a shame I can't find room for the nice pebbles now! But put them by, and when I come back I'll bring you a holy conch from the seashore at Ascalon or a Jericho rose.'

The Commandant and the Light Infantry in Hersfeld

In the last campaign in Prussia and Russia when the French Army and a large part of the allied troops were in Poland and Prussia, a contingent of the Baden Light Infantry was in Hessen and stationed at Hersfeld. For the Emperor had taken that state at the beginning of the campaign and stationed troops there. The inhabitants who preferred the way things had been before defied the new order and there were several acts of lawlessness, particularly in the town of Hersfeld. In one incident a French officer was killed. The French Emperor was engaged face to face with great numbers of the enemy and couldn't allow hostilities behind his back or let a spark spread into a great fire. The unfortunate people of Hersfeld thus had cause to regret their rashness. For the Emperor ordered the town to be looted, set alight at each corner and burnt to the ground.

This town of Hersfeld has many factories and thus many rich inhabitants and fine buildings; and all of us with a heart can understand how its unfortunate people, those fathers and mothers with families, felt when they heard the dreadful news. The poor whose possessions could be carried off in one pair of arms were just as much affected as the rich whose goods couldn't all be loaded on a train of wagons. Great houses on the town square and small dwellings in the alleyways are all the same when burnt to the ground, just like rich and poor in the graveyard.

But the worst didn't happen. The French Commandant in Kassel and Hersfeld interceded and the punishment was reduced. Only four houses were to be burnt down, and that was lenient. But the plundering was to take place as ordered, and that was hard enough. The wretched townsfolk, hearing this latest decision, were so cowed and robbed of all presence of mind that the benevolent Commandant himself had to urge them, instead of weeping and pleading in vain, to remove their most precious possessions in the short time that was left. The dreadful hour arrived, the drums sounded over the wails of anguish. The soldiers hurried to their place of assembly through the crowds fleeing in despair. Then the stalwart Commandant of Hersfeld stood before the ranks of the infantry, and first he painted a vivid picture of the sad fate of the townspeople, then he said, 'Men, you now have permission to loot! Those who wish to take part, fall out!' Not one man moved. Not a single one! The order was repeated. Not one pair of boots stirred, and if the Commandant had intended the town to be plundered he would have had to do it himself. But no one was more pleased than he was that things turned out as they did, that is easy to tell. When the townsfolk learnt this, it was as if they woke from a bad dream. No one can describe their joy. They sent a delegation to the Commandant to thank him for his kindness and magnanimity, and offered him a handsome gift to mark their gratitude. Who knows what they might not have done! But the Commandant refused and said he wouldn't be paid for a good deed.

This happened in Hersfeld in the year 1807, and the town is still standing.

A Poor Reward

When in the last Prussian war the French came to Berlin where the King of Prussia resides, a great deal of the royal property as well as other people's was taken and carried off or sold. For war brings nothing, it only takes. Much was claimed as booty, however well it was hidden they found it, but not everything. A large store of royal building timber remained undiscovered and untouched for some time. But eventually a rascal among the king's own subjects thought, there's a fair penny to be made here, and with a smirk and a wink he went to tell the French commandant what a lovely stack of oak and pine logs was still at such and such a place, and it was worth a few thousand guilders. But the French commandant paid him badly for this betrayal and said, 'Just you leave those fine logs where they are! There's no call to deprive the enemy of his most basic needs. For when your king returns he will need timber for new gallows for trusty subjects like you!'

Your Family Friend can only applaud that, and he would make a present of a few logs from his own coppice if they were needed.

A Curious Ghost Story

Last autumn a gentleman was travelling through Schliengen, a nice little place. And as he was walking up the hill to spare the horses he told a man from Grenzach the following story of what had happened to him.

Six months earlier this gentleman was on his way to Denmark, and late one evening he arrived in a village with a fine mansion on a hill outside, and he wanted to stay the night. But the innkeeper said he had no room, there was a hanging the next day and three hangmen were staying with him. So the gentleman replied, 'Then I'll ask up there in the big house. The owner, the governor or whoever he is, will take me in and find a spare bed for me.' The innkeeper said, 'There are plenty of fine beds with silk hangings up there all ready made up, and I'm in charge of the keys. But I wouldn't advise you to go there! Three months ago the lord and the lady and the young master went away on a long journey, and since then the mansion house has been haunted by ghosts. The steward and the servants had to leave, and all the others who have been to the house never went back a second time.' Our stranger smiled. For he was a plucky man who wasn't afraid of ghosts, and he said, 'I'll risk it!' Despite all the innkeeper's objections he had to hand over the key, and after the traveller had put together what was needed to pay a visit on ghosts he went to the mansion with his servant who was travelling with him.

Once inside he didn't undress or get ready for bed, but waited to see what happened. He put two lights to burn on the table and a pair of loaded pistols next to them, and to pass away the time he picked up the Rhinelanders' Family Friend, bound in gold paper, which was hanging by a red silk ribbon under the mirror in its frame on the wall, and looked at the nice pictures. For a long time nothing happened. But when midnight stirred in the church tower and the clock struck twelve, and a rainstorm was passing over the house and large drops were beating against the window, there were three loud knocks on the door and a ghastly apparition with black squinting eyes, a nose half a yard long, gnashing teeth, a beard like a goat and hair all over its body came into the room and said in a horrible growl: 'I am the lord Mephistopheles. Welcome to my palace! Have you said your goodbyes to your wife and children?' The visitor felt a cold shiver run up from his big toes over his back and up under his night-cap, and his poor servant was in a worse state still. But when this Mephistopheles came towards him, scowling dreadfully and stepping high as if he was crossing a floor of flames, the unfortunate gentleman thought: in God's name, this is the test! And he stood up boldly and pointed his pistol at the monster and said, 'Halt, or I'll shoot!' Not every ghost can be stopped like that, for even if you pull the trigger it doesn't go off, or the bullet flies back and hits you instead of the target. But Mephistopheles raised his first finger in warning, turned slowly on his heels and strode away just as he had come. Now when our traveller saw that this devil had respect for gunpowder, he thought, 'There's no danger now!', picked up a light in his free hand and followed the ghost cautiously along the passage; and his servant who was standing behind him ran for all he was worth out of this blessed place and down to the village, thinking he'd sooner spend the night with the hangmen than with spooks.

But suddenly in the passage the ghost disappeared from under the eyes of its plucky pursuer just as if it had gone through the floor. And when the gentleman went on another few paces to see where it had gone, all at once there was no floor under his feet and he fell down through a hole towards a flaming fire, and he himself thought he was on the way to hell. But after dropping about ten feet he found himself lying unharmed on a heap of hay in a cellar. And six weird fellows were standing around the fire, that Mephistopheles with them. All sorts of strange implements were piled up around them, and two tables stood heaped with shining thalers, each one more lovely than the other.

Now the stranger knew what was going on. For this was a secret band of forgers, all with blood running in their veins. They had taken advantage of the owner's absence and set up their mint in his mansion, and some of them were probably servants of the house who knew their way about; and to make sure they were not disturbed and discovered they wailed like ghosts, and anyone who came to the house was so frightened he never came back to take a second look. Yet the plucky traveller now had cause to regret his lack of prudence in not listening to the innkeeper's warnings. For he was pushed through a narrow opening into a small dark room and could hear them deciding his fate: 'The best thing is to kill him!' said one. But another said, 'First we must question him, find out who he is and where he's from.' When they then learnt he was a man of consequence and on his way to Copenhagen to see the king they looked at each other wide-eyed. And when he was back in the dark storeroom they said, 'This is a bad business. For if he's missed and they find out from the innkeeper that he came here and didn't leave, the hussars will come overnight and fetch us out, and there's plenty of hemp in the fields this year, so hangmen's nooses come cheap.' So they told their prisoner they would let him go if he swore an oath not to betray them, threatening they would have him watched in Copenhagen. And he had to tell them on oath where he lived. He told them, 'Next to the Green Man, on the left in the big house with green shutters.' Then they poured him some Burgundy wine and he watched them coining their thalers until it was light.

When the morning light shone down through the gratings, and they heard the sound of whips on the road and the cowherd blowing his horn, the traveller took leave of his night-time companions, thanked them for having him and went gaily back to the inn, quite forgetting that he had left his watch and pipe and the pistols behind in the mansion. The innkeeper said, 'Thank God you're back, I didn't get a wink of sleep! How did you get on?' But the traveller thought, an oath is an oath, and you mustn't take God's name in vain to save your life. So he said nothing, and as the bell was ringing and the wretched malefactor was being led out everyone ran off to watch. He said nothing in Copenhagen either, and almost forgot the incident himself.

A few weeks later, however, he received a parcel by the post, and in it were a pair of expensive new pistols inlaid with silver, a new gold watch set with diamonds, a Turkish pipe with a gold chain and a silk tobacco-pouch embroidered with gold, and in the pouch was a note. It said, 'We are sending you this to make up for the fright we gave you and to thank you for keeping quiet. It's all over now, and you can tell anyone you like.' So the traveller told the man from Grenzach, and it was that same gold watch that he took out at the top of the hill to check that the clock at Hertingen was striking noon on time, and later on in the Stork in Basel a French general offered him seventy-five new doubloons for it. But he wouldn't part with it.

One Word Leads to Another

A rich man in Swabia sent his son to Paris to learn French and a few manners. After a year or more his father's farm-hand came to see him. The son was greatly surprised and cried out joyfully, 'Hans, whatever are you doing here? How are things at home, what's the news?'

'Nothing much, Mr William, though your fine raven copped it two weeks ago, the one the gamekeeper gave you.'

'Oh, the poor bird,' replied Mr William. 'What happened to it?'

'Well, you see, he ate too much carrion when our fine horses died one after the other. I said he would.'

'What! My father's four fine greys are dead?' Mr William asked. 'How did that happen?'

'Well, you see, they were worked too hard hauling water when the house and the barns burned down, and it did no good.'

'Oh no!' exclaimed Mr William, horrified. 'Our house burnt down? When was that?'

'Well, you see, nobody thought of a fire when your father lay in his coffin. He was buried at night with torches. A small spark soon spreads.'

'That's terrible news!' exclaimed Mr William in his distress. 'My father dead? And how is my sister?'

'Well, you see, your late father died of grief when the young Miss had a child and no father for it. It's a boy.

'There's nothing much else to tell,' he added.

A Bad Bargain

In the great city of London and round about it there are an extraordinary number of silly fools who take a childish delight in other people's money or fob watches or precious rings and don't rest until they have them for themselves. Sometimes they get them by cunning and trickery, but more often by fearless assault, sometimes in broad daylight on the open road. Some of them do well, others don't. The London jailors and executioners can tell a few tales about that! One day, however, a strange thing happened to a certain rich and distinguished man. The King and many other great lords and their ladies were gathered on a lovely summer's day in a royal park where the winding paths led to a wood in the distance. Crowds of other people were there too, they didn't think their journey or their time wasted if they could see that their beloved King and his family were happy and well. There was food and drink, music and dancing. There were walks to be taken in pairs or alone along the inviting paths and between scented rose bushes. A man, well-dressed so that he appeared to be one of the company, took up his stand with a pistol under his coat by a tree at a secluded spot where the park bordered on the wood, waiting for someone to come his way. And someone did come, a gentleman with a ring sparkling on his finger, a tinkling watch chain, diamonds in his buckles, and a ribbon and a star on his breast. He was strolling in the cool shade and thinking of nothing in particular. And while he was thinking of nothing in particular the fellow behind the tree stepped out, bowed low, pulled his pistol from under his coat, pointed it at the gentleman's breast and asked him politely to keep quiet, no one need know about their conversation! You can't help feeling uneasy when a pistol is aimed at you, you can never be sure what's in it! The gentleman very sensibly thought: better your money than your life, better lose a ring than a finger! and he promised to keep quiet.

'Now, Your Honour,' said this fellow, 'would you part with your two gold watches for a good price? Our schoolmaster adjusts the clock every day, so we can never be sure of the right time, and you can't see the figures on the sundial.' The gentleman had no choice, he was obliged to sell his watches to the scoundrel for a few pence, hardly the price of a glass of wine. In this way the rascal bought his ring and his buckles and the decorations off his breast, one after another and each for a paltry sum, with the pistol in his left hand all the time. When at last the gentleman thought, now he'll let me go, thank God!, the rogue began again.

'Your Honour, since we do business so easily, why don't

you buy some of my things from me?' The gentleman thought, I must grin and bear it, that's the expression, and said, 'Show me what you have!' The fellow took a collection of trinkets from his pocket, things he had bought at a tuppenny stall or filched from somewhere, and the gentleman had to buy them all from him, one after the other, none of them cheap. Eventually the rogue had nothing left but the pistol, but seeing that the gentleman still had a couple of lovely doubloons in his green silk purse he said, 'Sir, won't you buy this pistol of mine with what's left in your purse? It's made by the best gunmaker in London and it's worth two doubloons of anyone's money!' The gentleman was surprised. 'This robber's an idiot!' he thought, and bought the pistol. When he had bought it from the robber he turned the tables on him and said: 'Hands up, my fine friend, and do as I tell you, keep walking in front of me or I'll blow your brains out!' But the rogue darted off into the wood. 'Go ahead and shoot, Your Excellency,' he said, 'it's not loaded!' The gentleman pulled the trigger, and in fact it didn't go off. He pushed the ramrod into the barrel, there was no trace of powder. By now the thief was well away into the wood; and the distinguished Englishman walked back, red in the face at being frightened by an empty threat, and he had something to think about now.

A Secret Beheading

Whether or not on that morning of 17 June that year the executioner at Landau said the Lord's Prayer with proper devotion and its 'Lead us not into temptation but deliver us from evil' – that I don't know. But a delivery came, a note posted from Nancy, and if he hadn't said his prayers, then it arrived on just the right day. The note said: 'Executioner at Landau, come to Nancy straight away and bring your big sword. You will be told what to do and paid well.' A coach was waiting outside. 'It's my job', thought the executioner and got into the coach. When he was still one hour this side of Nancy, it was evening already and the sun was setting among blood-red clouds, the driver drew up, saying, 'It will be fine again tomorrow', when suddenly three strong armed men were standing by the road, climbed in beside the executioner and promised that he wouldn't come to any harm, 'But you must let us blindfold you!' And when they had put the blindfold over his eyes they said, 'Driver, drive on!' The coachman drove on, and it seemed to the executioner that he was taken a good twelve hours further, and he had no way of telling where he was. He heard the midnight owls; he heard the cocks crow; he heard the morning bells. Then without warning the coach stopped again. They took him into a house and gave him something to drink and a nice roll and sausage too. When he was strengthened by food and drink they led him on inside the same building, through several doors and up stairs and down, and then they removed his blindfold and he saw he was in a large room. It was hung all around with black drapes, and wax candles burnt on the tables. In the middle sat a woman on a chair with her neck bared and a mask over her face, and she must have been gagged, for she couldn't speak, only sob. Round the walls stood a number of gentlemen dressed in black and with black crape over their faces so that the executioner could not have recognized them if he had met them again an hour later. And one of them handed him his sword and ordered him to cut off the head of the woman sitting on the chair. The poor executioner's blood ran cold and he said they must excuse him: his sword was dedicated to the service of justice and he could not defile it with murder. But one of the gentlemen by the wall pointed a pistol at him and said, 'Get on with it! Do as we tell you or you'll never set eyes on the church tower at Landau again!' The executioner thought of his wife and children at home. 'If I've no choice,' he said, 'and I must shed innocent blood, then on your head be it!' and with one blow he severed the poor woman's head from her body.

When it was done one of the men gave him a purse with two hundred doubloons. They put the blindfold over his eyes again and took him back to the coach he had come in. The men who had brought him there escorted him again. And when at last the coach drew up and they let him get out and remove the blindfold he was left standing where the three men had joined the coach, one hour this side of Nancy on the Landau road, and it was night. The coach sped off back.

That is what happened to the executioner at Landau, and Your Family Friend is not sorry that he can't say who that poor soul was who had to take such a bloody way to life everlasting. No, nobody found out who she was, what sin she had committed, and nobody knows where she is buried.

The Fake Gem

Outside the Butcher's Gate at Strassburg there is a pleasant garden where anyone can go and spend his money on decent pleasure, and there sat a well-dressed man drinking his wine like everyone else, and he had a ring with a precious stone on his finger and held it so it sparkled. So a Jew came up and said, 'Sir, you have a lovely gem in that ring on your finger, I wouldn't mind that myself! Doesn't it glitter like the Urim and Thummim in the breastplate of Aaron the priest?' The well-dressed stranger answered very curtly, 'The gem is a fake. If it weren't, it would be on someone else's finger, not mine!' The Jew asked to take a closer look at it. He turned it this way and that in his hand and bent his head to look at it from every angle. 'He says this stone is a fake?' he thought, and offered the stranger two new doubloons for the ring. But the stranger said quite angrily, 'Why do you think I'm lying? I told you, it's a fake!' The Jew asked permission to show it to an expert, and someone sitting close by said, 'I'll vouch for the Israelite, he'll know what the jewel is worth!' The stranger said, 'I don't need to consult anyone, the stone's a fake.'

While this was happening Your Family Friend was sitting at another table in the same garden with good friends of his, happily spending money on decent pleasure, and one of the company was a goldsmith who knows all about gems. He fitted a soldier who lost his nose at the battle of Austerlitz with a silver one and painted it skin colour, and it was a good nose. The only thing he couldn't do was breathe the breath of life into it. The Jew came over to this goldsmith. 'Sir,' he said, 'would you say this is a fake stone? Can King Solomon have worn anything more splendid in his crown?' The goldsmith, who was also something of a stargazer, said, 'It shines like Aldebaran in the sky all right. I'll get you ninety doubloons for this ring. If you come by it cheaper the profit is yours.'

The Jew went back to the stranger. 'Fake or not, I'll give you six doubloons!' and he counted them out on the table, sparkling new from the mint. The stranger put the ring back on his finger and said, 'I have no intention of parting with it. If it's such a good fake that you think it's real that doesn't make it worth any less to me,' and he put his hand in his pocket so that the eager Israelite could no longer see the stone. 'Eight doubloons.' 'No.' 'Ten doubloons.' 'No.' 'Twelve – fourteen – fifteen doubloons.' 'Very well,' said the stranger at last, 'if you won't leave me in peace and insist on being deceived at all costs! But I tell you, in front of all these gentlemen here, the stone is a fake, and I'll not say it isn't. For I don't want any trouble. You can have the ring, it's yours.'

Now the Jew took the ring joyfully over to the goldsmith. 'I'll come for the money tomorrow.' But the goldsmith, who had never been taken in by anyone, opened his eyes wide in amazement. 'My friend, this isn't the ring you showed me two minutes ago! This stone is worth twenty kreuzers at most. This is the sort they make in the glass works at Sankt Blasien!' For actually the stranger had in his pocket a fake ring which looked as good as the one that had first sparkled on his finger, and while the Jew was bargaining with him and his hand was in his pocket, he pushed the genuine ring off his finger with his thumb and slipped his finger into the fake, and that was the one he had given the Jew. At once the dupe shot back to the stranger as if fired on a rocket: 'Oh, woe, woe unto me! I have been tricked, the stone is a fake!' But the stranger said coldly and calmly, 'I sold it to you for a fake. These gentlemen here are witnesses. It's yours now. Did I talk you into buying it or did you talk me into selling it?' All those present had to admit, 'Yes, he told you the stone was a fake when he said you could have it!' So the Jew had to keep the ring and no further fuss was made of the matter.

How a Ghastly Story was Brought to Light by a Common or Garden Butcher's Dog

Two butchers out in their district buying in animals came to a village and split up, one went left past the Swan, the other right, and they said, 'We'll meet up again in the Swan.' But they never did meet up again. For one of them went with a farmer into his cowshed. The farmer's wife went as well, though she was doing the washing in the kitchen, and their child decided to follow too. The devil gave the woman a nudge: 'Look at that belt full of money peeping out from under the butcher's shirt!' The woman gave her husband a wink, he gave her a nod, and they killed the poor butcher in the cowshed and hurriedly hid his body under some straw. The devil nudged the woman again: 'Look who's watching!' She looked round and saw the child. So, driven out of their minds by fear, they went back together into the house and locked the doors as if the enemy were near. Then the woman, whose heart was not just as black as sin but blacker and hotter than hell, said, 'Child, just look at you again! Come into the kitchen,' she said, 'I'll clean you up.' In the kitchen she pushed her child's head into the hot suds and scalded him to death. Now, she thought, there's no one to tell on us – but she didn't think of the murdered butcher's dog.

The murdered butcher's dog had run along a bit with the other butcher, and then, while the child was being boiled and then popped into the bread oven, the dog doubled back and picked up his master's scent, sniffed at the cowshed door, scratched at the door to the house, and knew that something was wrong. Off he ran at once, back into the village, looking for the other butcher. Soon he was whinging and whining and pulling at this butcher's coat, and the butcher, too, knew something was wrong. So he went with the dog back to the house, in no doubt that something dreadful had happened there. He beckoned over two men who were passing nearby. When the murderers heard the dog whining and the butcher shouting, they had nothing but the gallows before their eyes and the fear of hellfire in their hearts. The man tried to escape through the back window but his wife grabbed him by his coat and said, 'Stay here with me!' The man said, 'Come with me!' She answered, 'I can't, my legs won't move! Can't you see that ghastly figure outside the window, with its flaming eyes and fiery breath?' Meanwhile the door had been broken open. They soon found the two corpses. The criminals were taken and brought to court. Six weeks later they were put to death, their villainous corpses bound to the wheel, and even now the crows are still saying, 'That's tasty meat, that is!'

The Cunning Styrian

It was in Styria during the last war and some way off the main road, and a rich farmer was thinking: 'How can I keep my thalers and my dear little ducats safe in these evil times? I'm ever so fond of the Empress Maria Theresa, God bless her, and the Emperor Joseph, God bless him, and the Emperor Francis, God give him long life and health! And just when you think you have these dear sovereigns ever so safe and out of harm's way the enemy gets a whiff of them as soon as he sticks his nose into the village and takes them off prisoner to Lorraine or Champagne! It's enough to make a poor patriotic Austrian's heart bleed!' 'I've got it!' he said, 'I know what I'll do,' and in the dark moonless night he took his money out into the kitchen garden. 'The Seven Sisters will not betray me,' he said. Out in the garden he put the money straight down between the wallflowers and the sweet peas. Next to it he dug a hole in the path between the beds, threw all the soil on top of the coins and trampled on the beautiful flowers and the chard all around like someone treading down sauerkraut. The next Monday the Chasseurs were scouting all round the district, and on the Tuesday a patrol entered the village and went straight to the mill, and then with white elbows from the mill to our farmer. And an Alsatian brandished his sword and bawled at him, 'Out with your money, farmer, or say your last Our Father!' The farmer said they were welcome in God's name to take whatever they could find. He had nothing left, it had all gone yesterday and the day before that. 'You'll not find anything,' he said, 'you fine fellows!' When they found nothing except for a couple of coppers and a gilded threepenny piece with the image of the Empress Maria Theresa on it and a ring to hang it up by, the Alsatian said, 'Farmer, you've buried your money! Show us here and now where you buried your money or you'll leave for the hereafter without saying your last Our Father!' 'I can't show you it here and now,' said the farmer, 'I'm sorry, but you'll have to come with me out into the kitchen garden. I'll show you where it was hidden there and what happened. Our lords and masters, the enemy, were here before you, yesterday and the day before, and they found it and took the lot.' The Chasseurs saw how things looked in the garden, found everything just as the man said, and not one of them thought the money might be lying under the pile of earth, but each of them gazed into the empty hole and thought: 'If only I'd been here earlier!' 'And if only they hadn't ruined the wallflowers, and the chard as well!' said the farmer, and so he fooled them and all those who came after them, and so it was that he saved the whole family of archdukes, the Emperor Francis, the Emperor Joseph, the Empress Maria Theresa, and Leopold the First, the Most Blessed of All, and kept them safe in their own country.

A Report from Turkey

There is justice in Turkey. A merchant's man was overtaken on his journey by night and fatigue, tied his horse laden with precious goods to a tree not far from a guardhouse, lay down under the shelter of the tree and went to sleep. Early next day he was woken by the morning air and the quails calling. He had slept well, but his horse had gone.

So he rushed off to the governor of the province, Prince Carosman Oglu he was called and he was staying nearby, and complained that he had been robbed. The prince cut the hearing short: 'So close to the guardhouse! Why didn't you ride on another fifty yards, then you would have been safe! It's your own stupid fault!' But then the merchant's man said, 'O just prince, should I have feared to sleep in the open in a land where you rule?' That pleased the Prince Carosman, and it annoyed him too. 'Drink a little glass of Turkish brandy tonight,' he said to the merchant's man, 'and sleep under the same tree again.' The man did just as he was told. The next morning when he was woken by the morning air and the quails calling he had slept well again, for the horse was standing there tethered at his side together with all the precious goods, and in the tree hung a dead man, the thief, who never saw the sun rise again.

They do say there are trees enough in most parts, big ones and little ones.

The Lightest Death Sentence

People have said it's the guillotine. But it isn't, you know! A man who had done much for his country and was highly thought of by its ruler was sentenced to death for a crime he'd committed in a fit of passion. Petitions or prayers were no use. But since he was otherwise highly regarded by the ruler, he, the prince, let him choose how he would like to die: he was to die in whatever way he chose. So the chief secretary came to him in prison: 'The prince has determined to show you mercy. If you wish to be put to death on the wheel you shall be put on the wheel; if you wish to be hanged he will have you hanged – there are already two up on the gallows but everybody knows there's room for three at a time. If, however, you would rather take rat poison there is some at the chemist's. For whatever kind of death you choose the prince says it shall be yours. But, as you know, die you must!' The criminal replied, 'If I really must die, then death on the wheel can be bent to suit one's taste, and hanging can be turned to suit one's inclination if the wind lends a hand. But you haven't got the point! For my part I have always thought that death from old age is the easiest way, and since the prince leaves the choice to me I'll choose it and no other!'

And that was his final decision, he wouldn't be talked out of it. So they had to let him go free and live on until he died of old age. For the prince said, 'I gave my word and I'll not break it.'

This little story comes from our mother-in-law who doesn't like to let anyone die if she can possibly help it.

A Stallholder is Duped

A rouble is a silver coin in Russia, worth a bit less than two guilders, whereas an imperial is a gold coin and worth ten roubles. So you can get a rouble for an imperial, for instance if you lose nine roubles at cards, but you can't get an imperial for a rouble. Yet a cunning soldier in Moscow said, 'Want to bet? Tomorrow at the fair I'll get me an imperial for a rouble.' The next day long rows of stalls were set out at the fair, the people were already standing at all the booths, admiring or finding fault, making bids and haggling, the crowd was walking up and down and the boys were saying hello to the girls, when up came the soldier with a rouble in his hand. 'Whose is this rouble? Is it yours?' he asked all the stallkeepers in turn. One of them who wasn't doing much business looked on for some time and then thought: if that money's too hot for you to hold I can warm to it! 'Over here, musketeer, it's my rouble!' The soldier said, 'If you hadn't shouted I would never have found you in the crowd,' and he handed him the rouble. The trader turned it one way and the other and tested its ring; it was a good one all right, and he put it in his purse. 'Now give me back my imperial, please!' said the musketeer. The trader said, 'I don't have any imperial of yours, I owe you nothing. You can have this stupid rouble back if you're playing a trick on me!' But the musketeer said, 'Hand over my imperial, this is no joke, I'm serious and can easily fetch a constable!' One thing led to another, a polite word to a defiant one, defiance to insults, and a crowd gathered around the stall like bees round a honey pot. Then something was burrowing its way through the throng. 'What's going on here?' said the police sergeant who had pushed through the crowd with his men. 'I said, what's all this?' The stallkeeper couldn't say much, but the musketeer had a good story to tell.

Less than a quarter of an hour before, he said, he had bought this and that from this man for one rouble. But when it came to paying he could find only a double imperial, nothing smaller, one his godfather had given him when he was enlisted. So he gave him the imperial until he came back with a rouble. When he came back with the rouble he couldn't find the right stall, so he asked at all the booths, 'Who do I owe a rouble?' And this man said it was him, and it was too, and he took the rouble but pretended he didn't have his imperial. 'Now will you agree to give it back?' The police sergeant questioned those around and they said: Yes, the musketeer asked at all the stalls whose rouble it was and this man said it was his, and took it too, and tested it to see if it was genuine. When the police sergeant heard that, he settled the matter: 'You've got your rouble, so give this soldier his imperial or we'll close down your stall and nail it up with you inside and leave you to starve to death!' Thus the police officer, and the trader it was who had to give the musketeer an imperial for a rouble.

Remember: Other people's property can eat into your own just as fresh snow swallows up the old.

Patience Rewarded

One day a Frenchman rode up on to a bridge over a stream, and it was so narrow there was scarcely room for two horses at once. An Englishman was riding up from the other side, and when they met in the middle neither of them would give way. 'An Englishman does not make way for a Frenchman!' said the Englishman. 'Pardieu,' said the Frenchman, 'My horse has an English pedigree too! It's a pity I can't turn him round and let you have a good look at his backside in retreat! But you could at least let that English fellow you're riding step aside for this English mount of mine. In any case yours seems to be the junior; mine served under Louis XIV in the battle of Kieferholz, 1702!'

But the Englishman was not greatly impressed. 'I have

all the time in the world!' he said. 'This gives me a chance to read today's paper until you are pleased to make way.' So with the coolness the English are famed for he took a newspaper from his pocket and opened it up and sat on his horse on the bridge and read for an hour, and the sun didn't look as if it would shine on this pair of fools for ever, it was going down quickly towards the mountains. An hour later when he had finished reading and was about to fold up the newspaper again he looked at the Frenchman and said, 'Eh bien?' But the Frenchman had kept his head too and replied, 'Englishman, kindly lend me your paper a while, so that I can read it too until you are pleased to make way.' Now, when the Englishman saw that his adversary was a patient man, he said, 'Do you know what, Frenchman? Come on, I'll make way for you!' So the Englishman made way for the Frenchman.

The Champion Swimmer

Before the war and all its afflictions when you could still cross freely from France to England and drink a glass or two in Dover or buy material for a waistcoat, a large mail boat sailed from Calais across the straits to Dover and back again twice a week. For the sea between those two countries is only a few miles wide at that point, you see. But you had to get there before the boat left if you wanted to sail on it. A Frenchman from Gascony seemed not to know that, for he came to Calais a quarter of an hour too late, just as they were shutting up the hens, and the sky was clouding over. 'Must I sit around here for a couple of days twiddling my thumbs? No,' he thought, 'I'd do better to pay a boatman a twelve-sous piece to go after the mail boat.' For a small craft can sail faster than the heavy mail boat, you understand, and will catch up with it. But when he was sitting in the open boat the boatman said, 'If I'd thought I'd have brought a tarpaulin!' For it began to rain, and how! Very soon it poured down from the night sky as if a sea up above was emptying itself into the sea below. But the Gascon thought, 'This is going to be fun!' 'Praise be,' said the boatman at last, 'I can see the mail boat.' And he pulled up alongside and the Gascon climbed aboard, and when he suddenly appeared through the narrow hatchway in the middle of the night and in the middle of the sea and joined the passengers on the ship they all wondered where he had sprung from, all on his own, so late and so wet. For on a ship like that it is like being in a cellar, you can't hear what is going on outside over the talk of the passengers, the sailors' shouts, the noise of the wind, the flapping sails and the crashing waves, and nobody had any idea it was raining. 'You look as if you've been keelhauled,' said one, 'pulled right under the ship from one side to the other, I mean.' 'Is that what you're thinking?' said the Gascon. 'Do you imagine you can go swimming and stay dry? If you can tell me how to do that I'll be glad to hear it, you see I'm the postman from Oléron and every Monday I swim over to the mainland with letters and messages, it's quicker that way. But now I have a message to take to England. With your permission I'll join you, since I was fortunate enough to meet up with you. Judging from the stars it can't be far to Dover now.' 'You're welcome, fellow countryman,' said one (though he wasn't a fellow Frenchman but an Englishman) and blew a cloud of tobacco smoke from his mouth. 'If you have swum this far across the sea from Calais you must be a class above the black swimmer in London!' 'I'm not afraid of competition,' said the Gascon. 'Will you take him on,' replied the Englishman, 'if I place a hundred louis d'or on you?' The Gascon said, 'You can bet I will!' It's the custom of rich Englishmen to bet with each other for large sums placed on men who excel at some physical activity. And so it was that this Englishman on the ship took the Gascon to London with him at his expense and had him eat and drink well so that he stayed fit and strong. 'My lord,' he said to a good friend of his in London, 'I have brought with me a swimmer I found at sea. I bet you a hundred guineas he can beat your Moor!' His friend said, 'You're on!'

The next day they both appeared with their swimmers at an agreed spot on the river Thames, and hundreds of curious people had gathered there and they laid their bets too, some on the Moor, some on the Gascon, one shilling, or six shillings, one, two, five, twenty guineas, and the

Moor didn't give the Gascon much of a chance. But when they had both undressed the Gascon tied a little box to his body with a leather strap without saying why, as if that were quite normal. The Moor said, 'What are you up to? Have you learnt that from the champion jumper who had to tie lead weights to his feet when he was set to catch a hare and was afraid he would jump right over it?' The Gascon opened his box and said, 'I've only got a bottle of wine in here, a couple of saveloys and a small loaf of bread! I was going to ask you where you have your eats. For I shall swim straight down the river Thames into the North Sea and down the Channel into the Atlantic and on to Cadiz, and I suggest we don't call in anywhere on the way, for I have to be back in Oléron by Monday, that's the 16th. But tomorrow morning in Cadiz at the White Horse I'll order a good dinner for you so it will be ready by the time you arrive.' You, good reader, will hardly be imagining that he could escape that way! But the Moor was scared stiff. 'I can't compete against that amphibian!' he told his master. 'You can please yourself what you do!' And he got dressed again.

So the bet was over, the Gascon was given a handsome reward by the Englishman who had brought him there and everyone scoffed at the Moor. For although they must have seen that the Frenchman was only shamming, they were all amused by his bravado and the unexpected outcome, and for a month after that he was treated in the inns and beerhouses by all those who had bet on him, and he admitted he had never been in the water in all his life.

The Weather Man

Just as a sieve-maker or a basket-weaver who lives in a small place cannot earn enough in his village or town to keep himself all year, but has to look for work and practise his craft in the countryside around, so our compasses-maker too does business away from home, and his trade is not in compasses but in knavish tricks that pay for a few drinks at the inn. Thus one day he appeared in Oberehingen and went straight to the mayor. 'Mr Mayor,' he said, 'could you do with different weather? I've seen how things are hereabouts. There's been too much rain on the bottom fields and the crops on the hill are behindhand.' The mayor thought that was easy to say but difficult to put right. 'Just so,' replied the compasses-maker, 'but that's my line of business! Didn't you know I'm the weather man from Bologna?' In Italy, he said, where the oranges and lemons grow, all the weather was made to order. 'You Germans are a bit behind in these matters.' The mayor was a good and trusting fellow and one of those who would like to get rich sooner rather than later. So he was attracted by the offer. But he also thought caution was called for! 'As a test run,' he said, 'make it a clear sky tomorrow with just a few fluffy white clouds, sunshine all day with some streaks of vapour glistening in the air. Let the first yellow butterflies come out round midday, and it can be a nice cool evening!' The compasses-maker replied, 'I can't commit myself just for one day, Mr Mayor! It wouldn't cover my costs. I can only take on the job by the year. But then you'll have problems finding room to store your crops and the new wine!' When the mayor wanted to know how much he would charge for the year he was careful and didn't ask for payment in advance, only a guilder a day and free drinks until the matter was properly in hand, that could take at least three days – 'But after that a pint from each gallon of wine over what you press in your best years, and a peck from every bushel of fruit.' 'That's risnible,' said the mayor. He stood in awe of the compasses-maker and was using refined language, and people in his part of the country think it's refined to say 'risnible' for reasonable. But when he took pen and paper from the cupboard and was drawing up a schedule for the weather month by month the compasses-maker came up with a further complication: 'You can't do that, Mr Mayor! You will have to consult the people. The weather is a community matter. You can't expect everyone to accept your choice of weather.' 'You're right!' said the mayor. 'You're a sensible man.'

You, good reader, will have taken the measure of our compasses-maker and will have foreseen that the people could not agree on the matter. At their first meeting no decision was reached, nor even at the seventh, at the eighth hard words were spoken, and in the end a level-headed lawyer concluded that the best thing to do, to preserve peace and avoid strife in the community, was to pay the weather man off and send him packing. So the mayor summoned the compasses-maker. 'Here are your nine guilders, you mischief-maker, now make sure you leave before there's blood shed in the village!' The compasses-maker didn't have to be told twice. He took the money, left owing for about twelve pints of wine at the inn, and the weather stayed as it was.

Now then, as always the compasses-maker has much to teach us! In this case how good it is that up till now the supreme ruler of the world has always governed the weather according to his will alone. Even we calendar-makers, luminaries and the other estates of the realm are scarcely consulted and need lose no sleep on that score.

The Safest Path

Now and then even someone drunk has the occasional notion or good idea, as a fellow did one day who didn't take his usual path home from town but walked straight into the stream running alongside it instead. There he met a good man ready to offer a hand to a fellow, even a drunk one, in trouble. 'My good friend,' said the man, 'haven't you noticed you're in the water? The footpath's over here.' He too, replied the drinker, generally found it best to use the path, but explained that this time he had had one too many. 'And that's just why I want to help you out of the stream,' said the good man. 'And that's just why I want to stay in it,' replied the drinker. 'Because if I walk in the stream and fall, I fall on to the path, but if I fell when walking on the path, I'd fall into the stream.' And that's what he said, tapping his forehead with his index finger, as if to show that he still knew a thing or two that might not have occurred to anyone else, despite being a bit the worse for wear.

PENGUIN

LITTLE BLACK

CLASSICS

Penguin Little Black Classics Vol. III

21. JANE AUSTEN
The Beautifull Cassandra

22. FYODOR DOSTOYEVSKY
The Meek One

23. AESOP
The Cat and Venus

24. CHARLES DICKENS
To Be Read at Dusk

25. JOHANN PETER HEBEL
How a Ghastly Story Was Brought to Light by a Common or Garden Butcher's Dog

26. OSCAR WILDE
Lord Arthur Savile's Crime

27. LEO TOLSTOY
The Death of Ivan Ilyich

28. MICHEL DE MONTAIGNE
How We Weep and Laugh at the Same Thing

29. EMILY DICKINSON
My life had stood a loaded gun

30. WALT WHITMAN
On the Beach at Night Alone

企鹅经典：小黑书　第三辑

21. 漂亮的卡桑德拉
[英] 简 · 奥斯汀

22. 温顺的女人
[俄] 陀思妥耶夫斯基

23. 猫与维纳斯
[古希腊] 伊索

24. 黄昏之读
[英] 查尔斯 · 狄更斯

25. 一个可怕的故事是如何被一条普通的屠夫的狗公之于众的
[德] 约翰 · 彼得 · 黑贝尔

26. 亚瑟 · 萨维尔勋爵的罪行
[英] 奥斯卡 · 王尔德

27. 伊凡 · 伊里奇之死
[俄] 列夫 · 托尔斯泰

28. 我们为何为同一件事哭和笑
[法] 蒙田

29. 我的生命是一杆上实弹的枪
[美] 艾米莉 · 狄金森

30. 独自在黑夜的海滩上
[美] 沃尔特 · 惠特曼

黄昏之读

To Be Read at Dusk

[英] 查尔斯 · 狄更斯 著

容豆豆 译

中信出版集团 | 北京

图书在版编目（CIP）数据

企鹅经典：小黑书. 第三辑：汉、英 /（英）简·奥斯汀等著；夏星等译. -- 北京：中信出版社，2019.6

书名原文：Penguin Little Black Classics

ISBN 978-7-5217-0407-5

Ⅰ. ①企… Ⅱ. ①简… ②夏… Ⅲ. ①世界文学－作品综合集－汉、英 Ⅳ. ① I11

中国版本图书馆 CIP 数据核字 (2019) 第 072172 号

企鹅经典：小黑书　第三辑

黄昏之读

著　　者：[英] 查尔斯 · 狄更斯
译　　者：容豆豆
出版发行：中信出版集团股份有限公司
（北京市朝阳区惠新东街甲 4 号富盛大厦 2 座 邮编 100029）
承 印 者：北京楠萍印刷有限公司

开　　本：787mm × 1092mm　1/32　　印　　张：45.75　　字　　数：756 千字
版　　次：2019 年 6 月第 1 版　　印　　次：2019 年 6 月第 1 次印刷
京权图字：01－2018－6477　　广告经营许可证：京朝工商广字第 8087 号
书　　号：ISBN 978－7－5217－0407－5
定　　价：149.00 元（全 10 册）

服务热线：400－600－8099
投稿邮箱：author@citicpub.com

目录

黄昏之读

一，二，三，四，五。五个人。

在瑞士大圣伯纳德山口之巅，五个向导坐在修道院门外的长凳上。他们朝远处高山望去，那边巍峨的山峰浸染着落日的颜色，仿佛是谁失手泼洒了大量的红葡萄酒，色彩在山顶表面恣意流淌，好像还没来得及渗入下层白雪似的。

这可不是我的比喻，是那个最壮实的德国向导说的。不过其他向导对这番优美言辞倒没有多在意，就像他们也不在意我一样。此刻，我就坐在修道院门口另一边的长凳上，和他们一样抽着雪茄——也和他们一样——望着远处余晖染红的积雪。我们旁边是一间孤零零的小棚屋，里面放着不少旅行者的尸体，他们因大雪封山被困，从积雪下被挖出来，如今只能躺在地上慢慢干枯萎缩，毕竟这么冷，倒是不会腐烂。

我们就这样看着山顶的红酒一点点渗进雪中，山又恢复了洁白，天空泛着深蓝，风的呼啸声渐大，周遭空气寒冷刺骨。那五个向导扣紧了身上粗毛的大外套。在这里，向导做什么，你就跟着做什么，这样才最安全，于是我也赶忙扣紧了大衣。

先前夕阳映照下的山景打断了五个人的谈话，因为那实在雄伟壮丽，值得静静欣赏。现在太阳落山，他们又继续着之前的谈话。我之前没有听他们说，因为当时还在和一位美国绅士闲聊。他坐在修道院专门接待旅行者的客厅里，面朝壁炉，说要给我讲一个大骗子怎么靠着次次招摇撞骗，混成我们国家首富的故事。

“我的天！”瑞士向导冒出了一句法语。我不敢（像其他作者那样）说这个词可以完全表达出他的本意，但力求用英语写出来不像脏话吧。“如果谈起鬼魂——”

“但我说的不是鬼魂。”德国人说。

“那你要说什么？”瑞士人问。

“我要是知道，”德国人说，“那我懂的可就不止这些了。”

好答案，我心想，一下子就勾起了我的好奇心。因此，我挪到离他们较近的长凳的另一端，背靠着修道院墙，不用参与谈话，也能够听得十分清楚。

“电闪雷鸣！”德国人兴冲冲地说，“当一个人突然想要来看你，而他自己却毫无意识地把这个想法植入你的脑海，整日盘旋，仿佛是遣了某个看不见的信差，你怎么称呼这种现象？当你走在熙熙攘攘的街道——在法兰克福、米兰、伦敦、巴黎——想着身边走过的某个陌生人酷似你的朋友海因里希，另一个擦肩而过的路人也像海因里希，由此产生了一种奇怪的预感——不一会儿你就要见到他了——你还真就见到他了，虽然你一直以为他远在的里雅斯特[1]。你又把这个叫什么呢？”

“这都不是什么稀罕事啊。”瑞士人和其他三个人小声说。

“这很不平常！”德国人说，“平常是什么？平常是黑森林里的樱桃，那不勒斯的通心面。说起那不勒斯倒提醒了我！老侯爵夫人苏珊尼姆在基艾亚[2]的纸牌宴会上尖叫来着——我就在现场，因为当时我服侍的巴伐利亚

1. 的里雅斯特，意大利东北部港口城市。（说明：书中脚注均为编者注。）

2. 基艾亚是那不勒斯的一个区。

一家也去了——哎呀，那侯爵夫人往牌桌前一坐，嘴唇煞白，惊呼道：‘我那在西班牙的妹妹死了！我刚刚感觉到她冰凉的手在摸我的背。’而她的妹妹恰恰就是在那一刻走的，这个你怎么看？”

“还有神职人员祷告后圣热内罗的血液就会溶解[1]——整个世界都知道，每年发生一次，就在我的家乡，”那不勒斯向导停顿了一会儿，带着戏谑的表情说，“您又怎么称呼这个呢？”

“那个！”德国人大声说，“对！我想有个名称可以。”

“神迹？”那不勒斯人依然神色狡黠。

德国人只是抽了口烟，放声大笑，其他人也一起抽烟大笑。

“呸！”过了片刻，德国人啐了一口，“我说的这些都是实在发生的。我要是想看招魂，怎么不找个专业的，钱就值回来了。有些怪事根本和鬼魂无关。说到鬼魂！乔万尼·巴普蒂斯塔，讲讲你那个英国新娘的事吧，里面没有鬼，可就是很诡异。谁来说？”

---

1. 那不勒斯每年有圣热内罗节，举行弥撒仪式，祈祷装在两个小玻璃瓶中的圣热内罗的血溶解。圣热内罗是公元四世纪的殉道者，他的血液至今存放在那不勒斯教堂的一个玻璃瓶中。

一时间大家陷入沉默。我朝旁边瞥了瞥，猜那个重新点了支雪茄的人就是巴普蒂斯塔。果然片刻后他接过了话茬，听口音是热那亚人。

“英国新娘？”他说，“够了！这点小破事谈不上什么故事。不过，也算是吧，是真的。竖起耳朵听好了，各位，绝无半句虚言。发光的不一定都是金子，可我接下来要说的一定是真的。”

接着，他又强调了一遍。

十年前，我带着自己的履历去找一位英国绅士。他住在伦敦邦德街的长龙酒店，正打算旅行一两年。他对我的履历很满意，对我印象也不错。问了价格后，对价钱也相当满意。于是他决定雇我六个月，给我的薪酬待遇也不错。

这位绅士年轻英俊，乐观潇洒，倾心一位貌美的英国富家小姐。他们就要结婚了，接下来的旅行算是度蜜月。为了在炎热的三个月中（当时已是初夏）能够充分休憩，他在里维埃拉[1]租了一栋老宅。从我所在的城市热

1. 意属里维埃拉即利古里亚海岸地区，该海岸以热那亚为中心分界点。

那亚过去，非常方便，前往尼斯也需路过此地。我知不知道那栋宅子？当然。我告诉他，自己很了解那里。老宅带着大花园，有点昏暗阴森，周围树木环绕。不过宅子面积倒是不小，它伫立在海岸边，古老而庄严。他表示自己先前也听人这样讲过，很高兴我能有所了解。虽然里面家具是少了点，但别的地方也都这样。虽然房子阴森了点，但主要是看中了大花园，打算和女主人在树荫下避暑度日。

“所以没问题吧，巴普蒂斯塔？”他问。

“完全没有，先生。非常好。”

我们乘的是崭新的特制双轮马车，无论从哪方面来说都很完美。可以说是万事俱备，别无他求了。之后他们举办了婚礼，非常幸福。我也很高兴，因为生活是如此明快，一切都恰到好处，我又回到了自己长大的城市，还可以胡乱教女仆拉贝拉·卡罗琳娜说一些家乡话。她是一个活泼开朗的年轻女孩，时常被我逗得放声大笑。

时间就这样一天天过去，但我发现——听着，高潮来了！（说到这里向导压低了嗓音）——我发现女主人有的时候会陷入沉思，而且是以非常奇怪、可怕甚至悲伤的方式，脸上愁容惨淡，还有些飘忽不定的惊恐。开始注意到这个，是因为我正走着上坡，跟在马车边，主人早到前面去了。不管怎么说，到法国南部时，那天晚上发生的一些事让我更加确定了。当时女主人唤我把主人叫过来，于是主人又回头，陪着她走了很长的路，一直温柔地安慰她，鼓励她。他把手搭在打开的马车窗边，而女主人坐在车里，把手放在窗户内沿。主人时不时地开怀大笑，仿佛是为了驱散她心中的忧虑。不久之后，她也放声大笑，一切就又好起来了。

这件事有点古怪，我向漂亮的小女仆拉贝拉·卡罗琳娜打听。女主人有哪里不舒服吗？没有。精神不振？没有。担心路况或者强盗土匪？没有。更神秘的是，卡罗琳娜回答问题时不愿意看着我，只是望向远处的风景。

不过，有一天她把秘密告诉了我。

“如果，你真想知道的话，”卡罗琳娜说，“我发现，根据我听到的情况来看，女主人是被鬼缠上了。”

“怎么缠上的？”

“因为一个梦。”

“什么梦？”

“一个有着一张脸的梦。结婚前有三个晚上，她都梦到了一张脸——同一个面孔，只有一个。”

"那张脸恐怖吗？"

"不，是一个相貌非凡、面色黝黑的男人的脸。他一身黑衣，黑头发，还有灰色的小胡子——相当帅气，不过又冷淡又神秘。女主人压根就没见过这张脸，连长得像的都没有。梦里，他只是从黑暗深处静静地凝视着她，什么也不做。"

"后来女主人又做过同样的梦吗？"

"再也没有。但只要想起这个梦境，她心中就充满了不安。"

"为什么会困扰她呢？"

卡罗琳娜摇了摇头。

"这也是主人的疑惑，"卡罗琳娜说，"她不知道，自己也弄不明白。我只听到昨天晚上，她跟主人说如果在意大利的房子里发现那张脸的画像（她担心她会），那就真要崩溃了。"

说实话，这之后我就开始担心（热那亚向导说），等我们到了那座豪华的旧宫殿，真会看到某幅类似的倒霉画像，毕竟那里这种画像还真不少。随着离目的地越来越近，我心中恨不得把整个宅子的画廊都扔到维苏威火山口去。然而好像事情还不够糟一样，偏巧我们到里维埃拉的那晚风狂雨骤，天色阴沉，还打着雷。由于热那亚周围高山环绕，雷声在其间回荡时，显得震耳欲聋。蜥蜴仿佛受了雷鸣的惊吓，在花园颓圮的石墙缝隙间蹿来蹿去。青蛙一直扯着嗓子呱呱大叫。海风咆哮着卷进来，湿透的树木滴着雨水，还有闪电——把圣劳伦斯教堂都照得通亮！

我们都知道一栋热那亚风格的老式宫殿会是什么样——时间和海风会怎样将它玷染，外墙的纹案图饰会怎样像石膏一样片片斑驳脱落，低层的窗框会怎样慢慢生锈发黑，院子里会怎样杂草丛生、日渐荒芜，外围的建筑会怎样颓圮失修，整栋建筑会怎样无人问津、逐渐破败。我们租下的这栋宫殿就是活生生的例子。它大门紧闭已经几个月了。几个月？——不对，应该是好多年！房子里有一种土味，像墓室一样；同时外面露台上的橘子树味，墙边烂熟柠檬的果味，以及破裂的喷泉周围疯长的灌木丛的草味，不知怎的都跑进来，闷在这里面发酵。每个房间都隐约弥漫着一种陈年的腐朽气息，充斥着橱柜和抽屉。到了两个大房间之间用作流通的小间里，这种味道就变得更加令人窒息。如果你想挪动一幅画——说回到画来——是根本就动不了的，因为它们像蝙蝠一样牢牢粘在墙上。

房子里所有的格状百叶窗都紧闭着，只有两个头发灰白的老女仆在照看。其中一人拿着纺锤，站在门口缠卷着，咕哝着，估摸着她随时就能像放进空气一样把坏人放进来。主人、女主人、拉贝拉·卡罗琳娜和我一道穿过宫殿。虽然名字排在最后，但其实我走在最前面，打开了窗玻璃和网格百叶窗，结果自己淋到了几点雨，身上落了些石灰皮，还时不时有打盹的蚊子或热那亚当地带有斑点的大蜘蛛掉下来。

月光照进房间，主人们和拉贝拉·卡罗琳娜才进来。接着，大家查看了四周的画像，我则走进了另一间房。女主人打心底里恐惧，生怕见到和那张脸类似的任何东西——其实我们都怕，不过这没有发生。圣母圣婴、圣弗朗西斯科、圣塞巴斯蒂安、维纳斯、圣卡塔林纳、天使、强盗、修士、落日映照的神殿、战争、白马、森林、使徒和共和国[1]总督，画上尽是平凡无奇的常规题材——确实如此。那个身着黑衣、黑头发灰胡子、带着冷淡神秘气质、从黑暗中凝视女主人的帅气男子则毫无踪影。

1. 这里指（前）威尼斯和热那亚共和国。

最后我们走遍了所有房间，看过了所有画像，来到了花园。这里租给一个园丁后，维护得相当不错，面积很大，树木成荫。其中有一处简陋的露天小剧场，绿草覆盖的斜坡是主舞台：侧面一边三个入口，布景则是缀满叶子、散发着草木清香的绿幕。女主人明亮的大眼睛飞快转动着，即便在这儿，她仍然害怕那张脸会突然冒出来：还好一切正常。

“好了，克拉拉，”主人轻声说，“你看到了，什么都没有，开心点。”

女主人很受鼓舞，之后不久就适应了这个阴沉的宫殿，整天唱歌、弹竖琴，临摹古画，或者和男主人在绿树下或葡萄藤下散步。她光彩照人，他也心情畅快。男主人经常大笑着吩咐我备马，他要在中午热起来前骑马溜达一圈：

“一切都顺利，巴普蒂斯塔！”

“是的先生，谢天谢地，非常好！”

他不需要我陪伴，于是我就带着拉贝拉去看看大教堂、托雷安农齐亚塔[1]、咖啡馆、歌剧院、村庄庆典活动、

---

1. 意大利南部坎帕尼亚大区那不勒斯省的一个城市，坐落于维苏威火山下。

公园、日间剧场、牵线木偶表演。所有这些都能让漂亮的小拉贝拉着迷。她还学会了意大利语——天哪！奇迹啊！我有时会问她，女主人是不是快忘记那个梦了？差不多吧，卡罗琳娜说——基本上是，她在慢慢淡忘。

一天，主人收到了一封信，把我叫过去。

“巴普蒂斯塔！”

“先生。”

“一位别人介绍我认识的绅士说今天要来这里共进晚餐。他叫德尔欧布拉。准备一下，别让我丢脸。”

真是奇怪的名字，我没听说过，不过当时也有很多贵族绅士因为在奥地利受到政治猜忌，然后改名的。可能是其中一位吧。管他呢！德尔欧布拉这个名字对我来说和任何名字一样，没什么不好。

晚餐时间，德尔欧布拉先生来了（说到这里，热那亚向导再一次压低了声音），我把他带到会客室，也就是老宫殿的大厅。主人热情真诚地接待了他，并转身向女主人介绍。而女主人站起身，脸色唰地一变，尖叫一声就晕过去了，直接栽倒在大理石地面上。

接着，我立马看向德尔欧布拉先生，只见他一身黑衣，表情冷淡而神秘，面色黝黑，相貌非凡，还蓄着黑头发和灰色小胡子。

主人把女主人抱回到她的房间，我赶紧让拉贝拉跟过去服侍。后来她告诉我，女主人吓得大半条命没了，整晚脑子里都是之前那个梦。

主人既恼怒又焦躁不安——几近愤怒，心中又很担心。这位德尔欧布拉先生是一位谦和儒雅的绅士，对女主人的病况表示了关心和同情。他说，来自非洲的风已经吹了好些时日（这是他听马耳他十字架酒店的人说的，他住在那里），妖风经常伤人。他还祝愿美丽的夫人能够早日康复。接着便要请辞离开，说自己可以等女主人康复后再行登门。不过主人没有同意，认真挽留他坐下来进餐，最后他们俩一起吃了饭。

德尔欧布拉先生当晚早早走了，第二天又来敲门，骑在马上，问女主人是否安好。一周内他来了那么两三次。

根据我的观察，加上拉贝拉·卡罗琳娜的消息，显然主人正在努力安慰女主人，让她克服胡思乱想的恐惧。他非常温柔体贴，但也理智坚定，慢慢分析给她听，告诉她任何空想都不过是庸人自扰，如果能安定心神，就什么事都没有了。如果她能克服自己奇怪的弱点，成功像英国淑女招待客人那样接纳德尔欧布拉先生，那就永远不会再出事了。最终，德尔欧布拉先生再次到访，女主人招待了他，没有表露出什么明显的痛苦（尽管仍有些局促和忧虑），当晚平静地度过了。主人对这种变化感到十分欣喜，为了急于确认她已好转，于是德尔欧布拉先生成了我们的常客。他的画艺和乐理都十分精湛，还博览群书，这种社交伙伴，在任何沉闷的意大利宫殿，都是相当受欢迎的。

我时常能注意到，女主人并没有真正恢复。在德尔欧布拉先生面前，她会垂下眼睑，低着头，要不就是以害怕又着迷的眼神飞快地瞥他一眼，好像他在这儿就会对她造成什么不好的影响或施加什么邪恶力量。我又看看德尔欧布拉先生，之前在荫蔽的花园或半明半暗的宽敞起居室里，我常常能看到他“从黑暗中凝视着她”，老实说，我并没有忘记拉贝拉·卡罗琳娜对梦中那张脸的描述。

德尔欧布拉先生第二次来访结束后，我听到主人说：

“亲爱的克拉拉，你看，都结束了！德尔欧布拉来了又走，你的忧虑已经完全没有啦。”

“他还——还会再来吗？”女主人问。

“再来？为什么不！当然，他会来很多次的！怎么了，你是不是冷？”（女主人打了个哆嗦。）

“不，亲爱的——但是——我真的害怕他：你确定真的还要他来吗？”

“克拉拉，这是毫无疑问的！”主人愉快地答道。

不过，他对女主人的完全康复倒抱有极大希望，并且这种期冀与日俱增。女主人优雅美丽，他也心情畅快。

“一切都顺利吧，巴普蒂斯塔？”他又对我说一遍。

“是的先生，感谢老天。非常好。”

有一天（热那亚向导微微抬高了嗓门儿），我们都在罗马参加狂欢节。我有个西西里岛的朋友，他也是向导，当时陪同一个英国家庭。我和他出去玩了一整天，晚上回酒店的时候，碰到小卡罗琳娜。她从来不单独离开家，那天却沿着大道狂奔，显得心烦意乱。

“卡罗琳娜！怎么了？”

“哦，巴普蒂斯塔！哦，老天啊！女主人到底去哪儿了？”

“女主人？”

“人家说她不见了。今天早上，因为她前一晚没休息好（太痛苦的缘故），主人出门就没有叫她。本来她应该在床上躺到天黑，再精神抖擞地起来活动。结果现在她不见了，不见了！主人回来了，撞开了门，发现她不见了！美丽大方又善良的女主人！”

娇小漂亮的卡罗琳娜在我面前大喊着，咆哮着，甚至拉扯自己的头发，要不是她最后像中枪一样晕倒在我怀里，我几乎就快控制不住她了。这时主人出现了——我从来没见过他这副模样，仪态、脸色，甚至嗓音都变了。他叫上我（我把小卡罗琳娜抱回她的床上，让内侍女仆陪着她），驾着马车气冲冲地闯进夜色里，横穿荒无人烟的原野。天亮时我们赶到一家破败驿站，可惜所有马匹在十二个小时前已全被租用，分别去往不同的方向。听着！都是德尔欧布拉先生订的，驿站的人说他曾驾车来过这里，还带着一位害怕得蜷缩在角落的英国女士。

打那以后（热那亚向导说着长长地舒了一口气）我再也没有听过她的消息。我所知道的就是，女主人和梦中见过的那张可怖的脸一起消失了，从此湮没在离奇骇人的故事里。

“你怎么解释这种事呢？”德国向导得意扬扬地说，“鬼！那里根本就没有鬼！接下来我要告诉你的事，看看又如何理解呢？鬼嘛！这个故事里也没有鬼！”

我曾经（德国向导继续说道）跟着一位英国绅士干活，他上了年纪，又是单身，当时要去我的祖国德国旅行。这位绅士是做德国进出口贸易的商人，所以懂德语，他在小时候去过德国，但长大成人以后没再去过——据我判断，那大概是六十年前的事了。

他叫詹姆斯，有个双胞胎哥哥叫约翰，也是单身汉。兄弟俩感情深厚，一起在古德曼广场打拼生意，但是并不同住。詹姆斯先生住波兰街，伦敦牛津街的外面，而约翰先生住在埃平森林旁边。

詹姆斯先生和我准备在一周内启程去德国，具体日子看生意安排。约翰先生来到波兰街（当时我就在房子里），准备和詹姆斯先生共度那一周。但是第二天，他却说:“詹姆斯，我有点不舒服。应该问题不大，是痛风的毛病。我想回家，因为老管家很了解我，能好好照顾我。如果好一点了，我就回来，在你走之前看看你。如果我撑不住了回不来，你启程前能不能去看看我呢？”当然，詹姆斯先生答应了。他们握了手——双手交叉互握，一贯如此——然后约翰先生命令双轮马车出发，坐在车里摇摇晃晃地回去了。

第二天晚上——也就是那周的第四天——穿着法兰绒睡袍的詹姆斯先生举着一盏蜡烛走进我的房间，我从熟睡中醒过来。他坐在我床沿，看着我，说：

“威廉，我有理由相信自己得了某种怪病。”

我立即察觉到他的神情非同寻常。

“威廉，”他说，“有些事我不怕告诉你，也不觉得羞耻，但我不愿意告诉其他人。因为你来自一个理智的国度，在那里，这么多年来，疑神疑鬼的事总会有人关心，人们却不会轻易地下结论，也不会不分青红皂白地表示鄙夷。我刚刚看到了哥哥的幽灵。”

我承认（德国向导说）听到这里，我浑身打了个激灵。

“就在刚刚看到的，”詹姆斯先生直视着我重复了一遍，好让我看出他很镇定也很清醒，“哥哥约翰的幽灵。我正坐在床上，毫无困意，突然他就进来了，穿着白袍，严肃地和我打了招呼。然后飘到房间的另一端，扫了眼写字台上的纸，又转过来像刚才一样认真凝望着我，随后出门离去。听着，我根本没有疯，也不想用任何自己以外的客观存在来解释那个幽灵，只是觉得这说明我生病了，现在最好放点血清醒一下。”

我赶紧下床（德国向导说），一边穿衣，一边让他不要慌，我会去请医生过来。正要出门，这时大门外传来巨大的敲门声，有人还按了门铃。我的房间是后院的阁楼，詹姆斯先生的卧室在前院二层，于是我们去到他的房间，打开窗子，看看外面什么情况。

“是詹姆斯先生家吗？”底下一个男人，退回到路对面抬头问。

“是，”詹姆斯先生说，“我认得你，我哥哥的男仆罗伯特。”

“是的先生。很遗憾地告诉您，约翰先生病了，非常严重，可以说是在鬼门关了。他想见您，所以我驾了马车来接您，请不要耽搁了，快跟我走吧。”

詹姆斯先生和我对视了一眼。“威廉，”他说，“太奇怪了。你跟我一起去吧！”我立即服侍他更衣，其实一半衣服都是在车上穿的。马儿跑得飞快，从波兰街到森林这一路不知踩死了多少小草。

这时，听好了！（德国向导说）我和詹姆斯先生一起来到了他哥哥的房间，以下都是我亲眼所见，亲耳所闻。

他哥哥躺在那间狭长卧室里头的床上，老管家站在旁边，还有几个人也在；估计这三四个人从下午就来陪他了。约翰先生一身白色，像幽灵一样，因为他正穿着睡袍。不过他脸色也像幽灵，一看到自己弟弟进来，眼神就直勾勾地盯着他。

不过，当弟弟来到床边时，哥哥支着身子坐起来，眼睛睁得老大，望着他说：“詹姆斯，你见过我的，今晚——你知道的！”

然后就咽气了！

德国向导讲完这个诡异的故事后，我静静等着，还想听他谈谈自己的看法。空气却陷入了沉默。我环顾四周，骇然发现五个向导都不见了：周围如此静谧，仿佛幽幽大山已将他们吞噬，埋入亘古的积雪。此时，寒冷的空气再度侵袭，我一点儿都不想独自待在这可怕的环境中——或者老实说，是压根儿不想一个人。因此，我起身走回修道院的大厅，发现那位美国绅士还很愿意讲那个了不起的骗子的故事，于是我又听了一通。

信号员

“喂！下面的！”

听到有人叫他时，他正站在岗亭前，手里拿着一面卷起的小旗。鉴于我们的相对位置，你可能会觉得他绝不会弄错声音的方向。但是，他不仅没有抬头看上方陡峭岩峰处站着的我，反而转身向铁路远处望去。这一举动里有一些耐人寻味的东西，虽然我可能一辈子也搞不明白到底是什么。但我知道，我已经被吸引了，即使对于站在高处的我来说，他的身影在沟槽底部，显得又矮又暗。而我浑身浸染在晃眼的落日余晖里，只有用手挡住刺眼的光晕才能看清他。

“喂！下面的！”

他把目光从铁路上收回，转过身来抬了抬眼，看到了高处的我。

“这附近有路吗？我可以下去和你说说话。”

他看着我，没有答话，我也低头看了看他，没有再问，不想强迫他回答我无聊的问题。就在这时，地面和四周开始轻微地震颤，并很快演变成了剧烈的震动，一股迎面而来的急流迫使我开始后退，力量之大好像可以把我拖拽下去。从飞驰的火车中涌出的蒸汽升至和我一样的高度，飘过我身旁，渐渐散开。我再次向下望去，看到他正在卷火车经过时挥舞起来的小旗。

我又问了他一遍。他沉默了一阵，似乎是在定睛观察，然后用卷起的小旗指了指和我在同一高度的一个点，距我两三百码[1]远。我冲着下面喊了一句“好的”，随后开始朝着那个点走去。到达后我仔细地环顾了一下四周，发现岩壁上有一条曲曲折折的小道——我就是顺着这条道下去的。

岩壁上的这条路凿得很深，异常的陡峭，开在一块黏湿的巨石上，而且越往下走，石体就愈加湿软。因此，

---

1. 英制长度单位。1 码约等于 91.44 厘米。

我走得十分缓慢，中途还想起了他最初给我指路时表现出的那种奇怪的不情愿，好像被谁胁迫了一样。

当我顺着这条曲折的下坡路走到能看到他的地方时，他正站在火车刚才经过的轨道中间，一副好像正等着我的样子。他的左手扶着下巴，右手则横在胸前托着左肘。他这种期待又警惕的态度让我停下来想了一会儿。

我继续往下走着，来到铁路旁，朝着他的方向走去。眼前的他是一个面色蜡黄的男人，胡须黑森森，眉毛浓密。他工作的地方是我见过的最孤立最凄凉的地方。两旁渗水的粗糙石墙遮蔽了所有的光线，只留下一道缝隙得以窥见天空。往一边望去，这个地牢一般的空间弯弯曲曲不见尽头。而在另一侧，很快就能看到不远处昏暗的红色信号灯和更为昏暗的入口，后者通往一条漆黑的隧道，而这个庞然大物里还弥漫着粗野、压抑和令人生畏的气息。由于能照到这里的阳光少得可怜，四周氤氲着一股令人难以忍受的泥土气息。而且穿堂的冷风一阵接着一阵，吹得我直打颤，我觉得自己已经被冻死了。

在他还纹丝未动时，我就走到了能碰到他的位置。可还没把眼神从我身上移开，他就后退了一步，抬起了手。

这是一个孤独的岗位（我说过），我当时从那边的高处往下看时就完全被它吸引了。我想，来这里的人应该算是稀客了，希望我这个稀客不会让人讨厌。在他眼里，我只是一个终其一生都局限于狭窄的范围内毫无突破的人，一个终获自由后对这些伟大的工作萌发兴趣的人。带着这样的想法，我对他开了口。但是我对自己的用词根本毫无把握，因为除了我本人不喜欢引出话题外，这个人身上有一种令我生畏的东西。

他用一种非常好奇的目光望向隧道口附近的红灯，并仔细地打量了一番，好像那里少了什么东西，然后他才看向我。

那个灯也归他管吗？还是不归？

他低声答道:“你难道不知道它吗？”

我打量着他一直盯着我的眼睛和有点阴郁的脸，脑海中产生了一个可怕的念头，这是一个灵魂，不是人类。此后我就一直怀疑他脑子是不是坏了。

这次轮到我了，我往后退了几步。但在退的时候，我察觉到他眼中有一丝潜在的对我的恐惧。这让那个可怕的念头一扫而空。

“你看我的时候,”我说，强挤出一个笑脸，“感觉你在怕我。”

“我在想，”他答道，“我之前是不是见过你。”

“在哪儿？”

他指了指之前一直看的红灯。

“在那儿吗？”我反问道。

他立刻对我警觉起来，（无声地）说了一声“是”。

“老兄，我去那儿干吗啊？但就算有可能，我也根本没去过，你可以肯定。”

“或许可以，”他接着说道，“是的，我可以。”

他的举止开始放松起来，像我一样。不仅回答爽快利落，用词还很恰当。他的工作很多吗？是的。也就是说，他要承担很多责任。但是他的岗位要求他保持精准和机警，几乎没有什么体力活。变换信号、修理灯具和把这个铁把手拉来推去[1]就是他所有的职责。那些我似乎过于看重的漫长寂寞时光，对他来说，只是被生活中的例行常规填充成现在的模样，他也慢慢习惯了这样的生活。在下边的这段日子他还自学了一门语言——如果看得懂、对发音有一些粗略理解可以算是学会一门语言的话。他还学了分数和小数，以及一点代数。但他还是像小时候一样，算数非

1. 旧铁路线上需要推拉把手以变换铁路路线。

常糟糕。当班的时候他就必须一直待在充斥着潮湿空气的隧道中吗？他永远都不能从那两堵高石墙中走出来感受阳光吗？哎呀，这还要看时机和情境。某些情况下在铁路上的时间确实显得比其他情形下的时间长，在一天之中也有某些时段情况如此。天气晴朗的时候，他确实也会走出阴影，往高处去。但是，由于随时都要注意聆听电铃，而且这种情况下更要加倍小心，他大概并没有我想的那么轻松。

他带我进了岗亭，屋里生着火，桌子上放着一本工作手册——他必须在上边做一些记录，一个带有拨号盘和指针的电报设备，还有他之前提到的小铃铛。他曾说自己受过良好教育——大概是要高于火车站工作人员受教育的水平（希望这么说没有冒犯之意）。我本以为他会对这样的说法感到难为情，但他说大多数人都会撒这样的小谎，并不稀奇。在救济院、警署，甚至是最让人绝望的地方——军队里，他都听过这样的吹嘘。而且他知道不管是干什么的铁路工，或多或少都会这样标榜一下。他年轻的时候曾经（如果说坐在那个小屋里的我还能相信，他自己都不信了）研究过自然哲学[1]，还受过正规的

1. 从前用以指自然科学，特别是物理学。

教育。但当时年少轻狂，不肯好好把握机会，堕落至此，再也没有回头的一天了。他对此倒并无半句怨言，铺好了床，然后躺了上去，看样子也不打算另铺一张了。

所有我现在简洁复述的内容，从他口中说出时都相当平静。那时的他，显得严肃忧郁，一会儿看看我，一会儿又凝视火苗。他时不时会冒出一句“先生”，尤其是在讲述自己年少时光的时候：仿佛是在让我明白，我看到的他就是全部的他。中途有几次谈话被小电铃打断了，他不得不停下来，去读取信息并立即回复。有一次甚至不得不站到门外去，在火车经过的时候挥舞小旗，和司机说几句话。我发现他在履行职责时精准又机敏，一个词都没说完就开始了工作，而且在完成之前会一直保持沉默。

总之，我应该会把这个人列为该岗位上最可靠的人之一，但是他在对我说话时，会突然停下，沉着脸去看并没有发出任何声响的小电铃，而且还会打开小屋的门（之前因为要隔绝有害气体一直关闭着），伸出头去看隧道口附近的红灯。这种情况发生了两次，每次他回到火炉旁，脸上都挂着令人费解的神情，我们当时坐得很远，我说不太清。

起身准备走时，我说了一句：“我差点就以为你活得很惬意。”

（恐怕我必须要承认，我说这话的意思是想让他接的。）

“我觉得我之前是，”他用一开始的低沉嗓音答道，“但是我有麻烦了，先生，我被麻烦缠身了。”

只要愿意，他完全可以收回所说的话。但他还是说了，于是我很快接了上去。

“什么麻烦？你的麻烦是什么？”

“这个很难说清楚，先生。真的很难很难开口。如果你还来的话，我会试着告诉你的。”

“但是我是明确打算再来拜访你的。那么，什么时候呢？”

“我凌晨下班，先生，明天晚上十点再上班。”

“那我十一点过来。”

他谢过我，把我送到了门外。“先生，我会一直亮着白灯的，”他用自己独特的低音说道，“一直到你找到上去的路为止。找到之后，别叫！到了山顶，也别叫！”

他这么说，不禁让我觉得寒意更甚，但我只回了一句：“好的。”

“你明晚下来的时候，不要叫！让我问你最后一个问题。是什么让你今晚喊出那句‘喂！下面的’？”

“谁知道呢，”我说，“我就是喊出那个意思的——”

“别那个意思，先生。它们是具有特殊意义的词。我非常了解它们。”

“我承认它们有特殊意义。我的确那么叫了，因为看到了你就在下面啊。”

“没有其他的原因？”

“还能有什么原因！”

“你没觉得它们是通过某种非自然的方式传递给你的吗？”

“没有。”

他说了声“晚安”后，举起了灯。我沿着下行铁路的边缘走着（有一种火车就要从身后开过来的不适感），最后找到了路。上去要比下来容易些，我非常顺利地回到了自己的旅社。

第二天晚上，我准时赴约，在远方传来十一点钟声的时候，踏上了曲折小路的第一块石板。他在底下等着我，手里的白灯亮着。“我没有喊叫，”靠近后我说了这么一句，“我现在可以说话了吗？”“当然可以，先生。”“那么晚上好。”他伸出了手。“晚上好先生。”我也伸出了我的。随后我们并肩向他的岗亭走去，进来后关上门，在炉火边坐了下来。

“我决定了，先生，”刚一坐下他就探着身子说道，声音只比耳语大一点，“你不用再问我麻烦是什么了。昨晚我把你认作了别人。那就是我的麻烦。”

“认错人吗？”

“不。是那个‘别人’。”

“谁？”

“我不认识。”

“像我吗？”

“不知道。我从来没见过正脸。他的左臂挡在脸前，右臂在挥舞，挥舞得很厉害。就像这样。”

我注视着他的行为，那是一种非常激动与愤怒的姿势——“老天啊，把路让开！”

“那是一个月光皎洁的夜晚，”他说，“我当时正坐在这里，突然听到一声‘喂！下面的！’于是我起身站在门口向外看，那个‘别人’就站在隧道附近的红灯旁，像我刚才那样挥着胳膊。他的声音似乎已经因为喊叫沙哑了，他叫道，‘小心啊！小心！’然后又叫，‘喂！下边的！小心！’我拿起灯，把它调成了红光后向着那个人影边跑边叫，‘怎么了？发生什么事了？在哪里？’他就站在隧道的阴影外。我走到近处时，发现他一直用袖子遮住自己的眼睛，感到非常奇怪。所以我径直走过去，伸出手试图拉掉他的袖子，就在那个时候他消失了。”

“进隧道了。”我说道。

“不。我跑进了隧道，足足跑了五百码。我停下来把灯举过头顶，看到了测距的标记数字，当时潮湿的污渍从壁上缓缓流淌下来，还有些直接从拱顶滴落。我又跑出去，速度比之前还要快（因为我极度厌恶眼前这地方），路上我还用手中的红灯照了照隧道的红信号灯，查看周边情况，并且爬上铁梯去了顶部的走廊，之后又爬下来，跑回了这里。我给两边都拍了电报：‘收到警报，一切可好？’两边的回电都是‘一切正常’。”

我感到一根冰凉的手指正慢慢划过后脊背，我努力克制住自己，告诉他这个人影一定是出现的幻觉，是视觉神经过于脆弱才出了问题，很多病人都曾这样，其中一些已经意识到了这种痛苦的本质，甚至通过医学实验证明了这种认识。“至于那个想象中的喊叫声，”我说，“我们小声说话的时候，你可以听一听这个怪异山谷的风声，听听它们吹过电报线时的诡异尖叫！”

“你说的也有道理。”在我们坐着听了一会儿后，他如是说道。他对大风和电线应该是熟悉的，毕竟他在那里度过了那么多冬夜，经常一个人默默看着这一切。但他跟我说，事情并没有完。

我对打断他的话表示了歉意，于是他慢慢把手搭在我胳膊上，一字一句地说了下面这段话：

“在这个‘现象’出现的六小时后，这条铁路线上最重大的事故发生了，十小时后，伤亡者被抬出隧道，恰好就经过了那个人影曾经站过的地方。”

我竭力克制住浑身的战栗，回答说，这巧合确实是太过出人意料了，仿佛是人为精心设计出来，好叫他永远难忘的。然而，毫无疑问的是，惊人的巧合确实一直都有，谈起类似的话题也必须考虑到这一点。尽管必须承认，我补充道（因为我认为我看出他准备对这番话提出异议），但凡有点常识的人都不会让事故成为日常轨迹的一部分。

他又一次请求继续说下去。

我再次为自己不知不觉打断他的话道了歉。

“这件事，”他说着，再次把手放在我胳膊上，空洞的眼神向后瞟去，“就发生在一年前。六七个月后，我已经从当时的震惊错愕中恢复了过来，有一天破晓时分，我就站在那个门前，朝着红灯的方向看，又看到了那个幽灵。”他停下来，直直地盯着我。

“它叫出声了吗？”

“没有。它很安静。”

“它挥手示警了吗？”

“没有。它倚着灯柱，双手都放在脸前。就像这样。”

我再次看向他。那是哀悼的姿势。我曾在坟墓上的石像上见过这种姿势。

“你过去了吗？”

“我进屋坐了下来，一方面是想理一下思绪，另一方面是因为它让我感到有点晕眩。等我再出门时，太阳已经升得很高了，那个鬼魂也不见了。”

“没有后续了？这之后没有发生什么？”

他一边用食指轻轻戳了我的胳膊两三下，一边极为勉强地点点头：

“就在那一天，当一列火车驶出隧道时，我注意到在我这边的一个车厢窗户边有一些头和手，很混乱，有什么东西在挥舞。我又看到了它，立即给司机示意，停车！司机迅速关火踩刹车，但是火车还是往前走了一百五十码，甚至更多。我在后边追着跑，路上就听到了可怕的尖叫声和哭喊声。一个隔间里的漂亮小姐当场死亡，她被抬进了这里，就放在我们俩中间这片地板上。”

我看着他指的那片地方，不由自主地把自己的椅子向后推了推。

“真的，先生。千真万确。事实就是这样，和我告诉您的一样。”

我不知道该说些什么，也不知道怎么说，我的嘴巴非常干燥。风声和电线共同发出一声长长的哀叹，将故事接了下去。

他继续说道:“现在，先生，记住这个，帮我判断一下我脑子到底怎么了。那个灵魂一周前又回来了。从那之后，它就会时不时地出现在那里，断断续续地。”

“在灯光下？”

“在危险信号灯下。”

“它看上去想要干什么？”

他把之前“老天啊，把路让开”的动作又重复了一遍，似乎是带着更多的激情与愤怒。

然后，他继续说道:“我为了这事日夜不得安宁。它用一种痛苦的语调对我喊道‘下面的！小心！小心啊！’，持续的时间加起来有好几分钟，它就站在那里冲我挥手，敲我的小电铃……”

我突然想到了什么。“昨天晚上我在这里的时候是因为它敲你的铃，你才出门看的吗？”

“两次。”

“哎，你看吧，”我说，“你的想象欺骗了你。我的眼睛是盯着铃铛的，我的耳朵也是听着铃声的，所以如果我是一个活人，我就敢说它在那些时刻并没有响。不，在其他时候也没有响，除非是在火车开过，司机和你交流的时候它响了。”

他摇了摇头：“迄今为止我在那方面从没弄错过，先生。我从来没有把铃声和人声弄混过。鬼魂的铃声是电铃的一种奇怪震动，毫无来由，而且我还没有说，那个电铃就在我的眼前晃动。您没有听到它我并不奇怪。但是我确实听到了。”

“那你往外看时，那个灵魂还在吗？”

“在。”

“两次都是？”

他坚定地重复了一遍：“两次都是。”

“现在你能和我一起到门前去看看它吗？”

他咬了咬自己的下嘴唇，似乎不太情愿，但最终还是站了起来。我打开门，站在台阶上，他则站在门口。向远处望去，那边有危险信号灯，有阴森的隧道口，有凿壁湿漉漉的高墙，有头顶的一片星空。

“你看到它了吗？”我边问边特意看了看他的脸。他的双眼突出，满是紧张的神色，但是当我认真地看向同样的地点时，我的双眼可能更突出，神色更紧张。

“不，”他答道，“它不在那里。”

“同意。”我说道。

我们再次进去，关上了门，坐回原先的位置上。我开始考虑如何才能更好地发挥这个优势——如果他这样肯定的回答能够被称为一种优势的话，他是如此肯定事实的不可争辩，以至于我处在了一个最无力的位置上。

“这次你就彻底明白了吧，先生，”他说，“让我这么抓狂的，是一个问题，那个灵魂到底是什么意思？”

我告诉他，我也不确定，但我充分理解他。

“它让我们警惕什么？”他注视着火苗，沉思着，时不时往我这里看一眼。“危险是什么？危险又在哪里？有危险马上就要来临，就在铁路线上的某处。可怕的灾难就要发生。经历了前两次事故后，这一次不能再犹豫了。但是这对我来说确实太残酷，阴魂不散的。我能做什么呢！”

他扯出自己的手帕，擦了擦热得冒汗的额头。

“如果我发出危险两字，不管是发往其中一边，还是两边都发，我都没办法解释。”他一边继续说着，一边擦拭着手掌心，“我会陷入麻烦，于事无补。他们会觉得我疯了。情况就会是这样——信息：‘危险！当心！’回复：‘什么危险？地点？’信息：‘不知。但务必当心！’他们会辞退我的。要不然还能怎么办呢？”

他的痛苦不禁让人心生怜悯。那是一个意识清醒的人在遭受精神上的折磨，他一直默默背负着某种关乎生命的难以理解的责任，压力已经到了极限。“当它第一次站在危险信号灯下的时候，”他一边继续说着，一边把额前的黑发拢到了脑后，伸手揉着两边的太阳穴，看上去极度悲痛，“为什么不告诉我事故发生的地点——如果它注定要发生？为什么不告诉我规避的方法——如果可以规避？它第二次来的时候遮住了自己的脸，为什么不直接告诉我‘那个女士就要死了，让他们把她留在家里吧’？如果它来的前两次，只是为了告诉我它的警报是正确的，从而让我为第三次做好准备，为什么现在不明白地警告我呢？而且我，老天帮帮我吧！我就是这个冷清车站里一个可怜的信号员而已！为什么不去找一个大家都相信的人呢，或者有能力做出改变的人！”

看到他这样，我意识到为了这个可怜人，也为了公共安全，必须立即平复他的情绪。因此，暂时撇开我们之间所有有关现实和非现实的争论，我告诉他任何一个被赋予职责的人都应该认真履行，虽然他不明白这些莫名其妙的现象到底是什么意思，但至少他明白自己的职责所在，这也是能够让他感到欣慰的地方了。相比于让他放弃自己想法的劝说，我的安慰要成功得多。他镇静了下来，随着夜色越来越深，他的工作对注意力的要求也越来越高。我是在凌晨两点离开的。我提出要过夜，可是他连听都不想听。

我在沿着小路往上走时不止一次地回头看那盏红灯，我并不喜欢那个灯，如果我的床在它下面，我应该已经睡着了，只不过会很不舒服。我没有理由隐瞒这些想法。而且我不喜欢那两场事故和死去的女孩。我也知道没有理由去隐瞒这些。

但是，我想得最多的还是应该怎么做。毕竟我已经知道了这个秘密。我已经证实了这个人聪明、机警、隐忍和严谨。然而他能维持这种状态多久呢？虽然他的职位不高，但做这份工作需要被充分信任，我（举个例子）愿意拿自己的生命做赌注去相信他会一如既往地精准吗？

如果我把他跟我说的这些话告诉公司领导，那就出卖了他。但我实在不愿意背叛他，也不想一开始真诚相待，随后又提出折中方案，于是最终决定陪他（要不然就暂时保守他的秘密）去看这一带最好的医生，照医生说的办。明天晚上就是换班时间，他告诉我，日出后的一两个小时下班，等日落后就赶回来上班。我也相应地做了往返安排。

第二天傍晚天色很好，我早早地就出了门。穿过岩顶凿壁附近的田野小道时太阳还没有下山。我心里盘算再漫步一小时就差不多了，半小时去，半小时回，然后就该去岗亭找信号员了。

继续散步前，我往崖边走了走，机械性地往下看了看，就站在我第一次看见他的地方。这时，我看见一个人影站在隧道口的不远处，左袖遮住了眼睛，正在拼命地挥舞右臂。一种无法形容的恐惧袭上心头。

不过只一瞬间，这种无名恐惧就消失了。我发现那个人影的的确确是一个人，而且不远处还站着另外一小撮人，他似乎正对着这群人排练这个姿势。危险信号灯还没有亮起来。灯柱旁出现了一个我完全没见过的矮小棚屋，由一些木质的支架和防水帆布搭建而成，看上去还没有一张床大。

一种不好的感觉袭上心头——自责带来的恐惧一闪而过，我把那个人留在那里，没让人去注意或纠正他的行为，导致了这一出致命的恶作剧——我以最快的速度从小路冲了下去。

“怎么了？”我问其中一个男人。

“信号员今天早上死了，先生。”

“不是那个岗亭里的人吧？”

“就是他，先生。”

“不是我认识的那个人吧？”

“你会认出他的，先生，如果你认识的话，”那个人说着郑重地脱下帽子，掀起了防水帆布的一角，“因为他的脸非常完好。”

“啊！怎么会这样呢，怎么会这样呢？”随着帆布再次盖上，我挨个问了好几个人。

“他是被火车头撞倒的，先生。在英格兰没有人比他更熟悉这份工作了，但是不知道怎么回事，他没从外轨中出去。当时天已大亮，他打开了信号灯，手里还拿着他的提灯。火车头出隧道的时候，他正背朝着火车，就被撞倒了。那就是开火车的人，正在演示当时的过程。给这位绅士讲一下，汤姆。”

那个穿着粗布深色裙子的男人往后退了几步，站到了之前所在的隧道口：

“当时正在隧道的弯道附近，先生，”他解释道，“我看见了尽头处的他，好像是用望远镜看到的。当时没有时间去检查车速，而且我也知道他会当心的。由于他好像并没有注意到汽笛声，火车冲过去时我就把它关了，靠近的时候拼了命地大声喊他。”

“你喊了什么？”

“我喊的是：‘下面的！小心！小心啊！老天啊，把路让开！’”

我吃了一惊。

“啊！简直是噩梦，先生。我从来都用不着喊他的。这次我只能把胳膊挡在自己眼前，不去看，然后一直挥舞着胳膊，但是都没用。”

我不再继续赘述这几个相较于其他故事来说格外奇特的事件了。在文章结尾，我想说明，火车驾驶员发出警告的巧合，不仅仅是不幸的信号员反复说给我听的那些阴魂不散的话语，而且还有我自己——不是他——看到他模仿的姿势时，只在心里想过的话。

谋杀案审判

/

我发现，即便是智慧超群、学识卓越的人，如果要让他们吐露一下自己奇奇怪怪的心理活动，大家都会变得胆小谨慎。几乎所有人都会担心自己的一番讲述无法引起听众内心世界的共鸣，可能受到质疑或嘲笑。对于一个敢于说实话的旅行者来说，即便是见过（传说中）海蛇怪一般的神奇生物，他也会毫不害怕地说出自己的经历。但是，如果他已有某种奇特的不祥预感、内心冲动、奇思妙想、（所谓的）憧憬展望、梦境，抑或其他特别的心理印象，就会在最终承认前反复犹豫纠结，难以开口。在我看来，大部分以上那些不可言明的因素导致了这种缄默。习惯上，我们不会像谈论客观事物一样去沟通主观的感受。带来的后果就是，这方面的经历常常显得非同寻常，就其不幸与缺憾而言，的确如此。

接下来我要说的，既不是为了讲什么道理，也不是要反驳或声援什么理论。我了解柏林书商[1]的过去，也经戴维·布鲁斯特爵士介绍研究过一位已逝皇家天文学家妻子的案件。此外，我还深入研究过密友们身上发生的鬼魅幻影案。关于最后一点我有必要声明一下，受害人（一位女士）本人和我关系疏远，甚至可以说是毫无瓜葛。那件事的错误假设为我自己的案件提供了部分解释——不过只是部分——因为整件事是完全没有根据的，不能说明我天生就具有某种超能力，况且之前和之后也从没有经历过类似事情。

同时这也没有影射那桩英格兰谋杀案的意思，不记得是很多年还是好几年前了，总之当时那件案子可谓举世关注。这些年我们相继听过不少臭名昭著的谋杀犯，但如果可以，我想彻底埋葬关于那个暴徒的记忆，就像他的身躯被埋进新门监狱[2]地下一样。接下来的讲述中，

1. 柏林书商，指阿道弗斯·亚瑟（1800—1853），当时他的书店是伦敦文人名流聚会之所。

2. 新门监狱，位于伦敦西门的著名监狱。

我会尽量避免透露有关罪犯身份的直接线索。

谋杀案刚发现的时候，还没有人怀疑他——我不能说得太详细，应该说——这名后来入狱的犯人身上还没有任何公开的嫌疑。当时，由于各大报纸并没有对其进行报道，很显然，人们不可能从报纸上读到任何有关他的描述。记住这一点很关键。

我一边吃着早餐，一边翻看晨报，上面对这个谋杀案进行了首次曝光。我饶有兴致地细细读了两三遍。尸体是在卧室发现的，读到这里我放下报纸，突然眼前闪过——划过——流过——不知道应该叫什么，暂时还没找到恰当的词，总之就是我似乎看到那个卧室正穿过自己的房子，就像是画在流水上的一幅画。虽然是一闪而过，但是清晰可见，甚至在我清楚地看到床上没有尸体后，心里还有一丝庆幸。

这种奇妙感觉不是在什么温柔乡产生的，而是在皮卡迪利大街的套间里，紧邻着圣詹姆斯街道的拐角。对此时窝在安乐椅里的我来说，这个案子相当新奇，除了奇妙外还伴有一丝古怪的战栗，让椅子都晃起来。（不过有必要说明椅子下面本来就很滑。）我走到一扇窗旁（房间在二层，有两扇窗），俯视皮卡迪利大街上的车水马龙，放松眼睛。明亮的秋日上午，大街在阳光照耀下熠熠生光，一切都显得愉悦惬意。秋风正劲，从邻近公园裹挟来大量落叶，一阵疾吹之下，只见叶子打着旋儿翻飞上升，形成小圆柱。恍然间，柱子又轰然倒塌，叶片四散。这时我看见马路对面有两个人，一前一后自西向东走去。前面的人时不时扭头往后看，后面的人跟他隔了约三十步，气势汹汹地举着右手。首先，在人来人往的大道上，这持续的怪异举动本身就吸引了我。接着我发现，如此不同寻常的情况，竟然没有任何人注意到。他们在行人间穿梭自如，丝毫不像走在人行道上。目之所及，没有一个人给他们让路、碰到他们或者多看他们一眼。从我窗前走过时，他们还都抬头凝视着我。我也认清了这两张脸，估计到哪儿都不会忘了，他们脸上倒没什么突出特征值得注意，只不过前面那个人一脸苦相，后面那位则面色蜡黄，一脸阴沉。

我是个单身汉，身边只有一名贴身男仆和他妻子跟着。我目前在一所银行分行工作，作为部门主管，我本希望这个职位和人们想的一样轻松。那个秋天，上面安排我待在城里，以防有任何变动。我没有生病，但也不算健康。本篇中，读者将会最大程度地感受到我的厌倦情绪，体会到我对单调乏味生活的失望，甚至还“有点消化不良[1]”。给我看病的那位名医说，我的身体没什么大毛病，在我的要求之下，他写了一份纸质说明给我，我在这里只是引用他的原话。

随着谋杀案的调查逐渐展开，案情日益披露，公众也越来越关心。不过我尽量不去管这些事，不让自己陷入普遍的兴奋情绪。但据我所知，目前已经断定这是一场蓄意谋杀，并且嫌疑犯也已被押送至新门监狱，等候审判。我还知道，由于惯常的偏见和准备辩护所需的时间不够，定于伦敦中央刑事法院的审判被推迟了数个会期。我基本已经猜出，案件会具体推到什么时候开庭，但又觉得自己不知道。

我的客厅、卧室和更衣室都在同一层，更衣室只能从卧室过去。以前更衣室里确实有扇小门通向楼梯，不过多年前浴室重修，就把那里堵上了。当时装修工还顺手把门钉牢，盖上了帆布。

有天深夜，我正站在卧室里，趁仆人睡前吩咐他一些事情。我的脸正对着通向更衣室唯一的那扇门，当时

1. 英文中，单词 dyspeptic 一语双关，既指“消化不良”，也指“（因消化不良而变得）阴郁悲观或暴躁牢骚”。

门紧闭着，仆人背对着听我说话。就在此时，我看见门突然开了，一个男人探头朝这边看，还向我招手，表情严肃而神秘。这个人正是在皮卡迪利大街上后面走着的那位，面色蜡黄，一脸阴沉。

打完招呼后他就退回去，关上了门。我略微怔住，赶紧穿过卧室，打开更衣室房门朝里看。我手上举着点燃的蜡烛，心里倒也不指望真能在更衣室看见那个身形。果然，最后什么也没看到。

想起来仆人还震惊在原地，我转身说："德里克，你相信吗，我刚才十分清醒地看到了一个——"我刚把手放到他胸膛上，他突然猛烈颤抖起来，说："噢，天哪，是的，先生！一个死人在招手！"

此时我意识到，眼前这个忠心耿耿跟了我二十多年的约翰 · 德里克，在我触碰到他之前，其实什么都没有看见，也什么都不知道。他身上的变化实在太过剧烈，我们接触时，我明显感觉到他通过某种神秘的方式，在一瞬间吸取了我的意识，从而得出现在的结论。

我让德里克去取白兰地酒来，给他和自己都倒了点，对于之前发生的事却只字未提。后来我细细回想了一番，可以肯定的是，除了在皮卡迪利大街，自己与这个人从未谋面。对比他在门边招手和在街上抬头凝视时的神情，我明白了：第一次他是要在我脑中留下印象，第二次他是想确认我能够迅速地记住他。

那晚，尽管有一种难以解释的确切预感——知道他不会再回来，我仍然睡得不安稳，天亮时才陷入沉沉睡梦。后来我是被约翰·德里克叫醒的，他来到床边，手里攥着一张纸。

依稀中正是因为这张纸，来者和仆人在门口好一顿争吵。这是一张传票，传唤我去老贝利街参加中央刑事法院的近期开庭。约翰·德里克很清楚我以前从未参加过陪审团，也认为——我不清楚是现在推理得出的还是什么其他方式——陪审团成员的身份通常要比我低，所以一开始婉拒了。传票人却态度倨傲，公事公办，说我去还是不去对他都没有影响，传票就在这里，怎么处理后果自负，与他无关。

一两天过去了，我还没想好到底是回复传票，还是直接无视。我自问心中不存丝毫的奇怪偏见，也没受到什么影响或诱惑，不会偏向于哪一方。说出这样的话，我问心无愧，和自己在这里说的每一句话一样肯定。不过最终我还是决定前去，就当是乏味生活里的一点调剂好了。

约定的那天到来的时候已是十一月，上午出门，天气阴冷。皮卡迪利大街雾气浓重，雾色由棕转黑，在圣殿关[1]附近显得格外压抑。而在法院大楼内，煤气灯照得过道和楼梯灯火通明，整个法院也显得亮堂堂的。我觉得，在我跟着引导官员进入法院见到满堂听众前，我根本不知道那个谋杀犯是今天受审。我觉得，要不是他们费了老大劲才带我挤进这里，估计我也不会知道拿着这张传票到底应该进哪个门。但是我说这话也不十分肯定，因为当时我对大脑所做的这个判断并不是很满意。

我在陪审团的预备席落座，尽力环顾四周，让视线穿过雾气和人们呼出气体的浓密混合物质。我看到巨大窗玻璃外的黑雾像是积满灰尘的窗帘，听到车轮压过稻草发出闷响，又或是鞣料渣洒落街道的窸窣，同时伴有人群逐渐聚拢的嗡嗡声，刺耳的哨音或响亮的歌声、喊声偶尔也会突兀地划过耳畔。不久，两位大法官进来坐下，法庭内原先的嗡嗡耳语迅速消寂，众人目光都集中在被带上来的谋杀犯身上。他出现在被告席栅栏后的一刹那，我就认出来了：他是走在皮卡迪利大街上的前者。

1. 圣殿关，地处商业中心伦敦和政治中心西敏之间的关卡。在狄更斯时代，即1878年之前，这里矗立着克里斯托夫·雷恩设计的石制门坊，即圣殿闩。

如果当时就点名，我可能会惊愕到说不出话。不过好在陪审团里我坐在大概第六、第八的位置，等轮到我时已经缓过来了。“到！”现在，注意了。囚犯之前一直密切却冷漠地注视着每一位陪审员，而就在我踏进陪审席时，他突然变得非常激动，还朝自己的律师打手势，针对我的意思再明显不过了。他强烈反对我就任陪审，闹得不得不暂时休庭。休庭时，辩护律师一只手搭在被告席上与他小声交谈，还不断摇头。后来我向这位绅士打听，他说客户的第一句话就吓到他了。“不惜任何代价，反对那个人！”不过，由于囚犯本人不愿意做任何解释，也承认在我被叫到之前，他从来没有听说过我，所以最终他还是没有如愿以偿。

我不希望唤起任何关于谋杀犯的不快记忆，这一点已经说过，再加上详细说明他的漫长审判过程之于整体叙述而言又并非不可或缺，因此，我准备根据极不寻常的个人经历，谈谈陪审团成员共同度过的十天十夜。这些事估计要比谋杀犯更吸引读者，希望大家关注它们，而不只是《新门记事》[1]上那一纸故事。

1.《新门记事》，18 世纪至 19 世纪英国家喻户晓的通俗月刊，讲述新门监狱里执行死刑的故事。

我被选为陪审团团长。审判的第二天，取证就花了两小时（我亲耳听见教堂的钟敲了两次）。不经意间，我瞥了瞥陪审团的同人们，发现很难数清他们的人数。我来来回回点了好几遍，始终有一种说不清道不明的困难，简而言之，总觉得多了一个人。

我拍拍邻座的同事，悄声说：“帮我点点人数。”听到这个请求他有些惊讶，但是很快扭头开始清点。“为什么，”他突然说，“一共十三——，但是不，不可能。不会，我们一共十二人啊。”

根据我当天的清点，具体到每个人都没有问题，但是总的来看时又显得多了一个。那时还什么都没有发生——也没有任何人物出现——来解答我内心的困惑，但是我有预感，有东西一定会来。

陪审团都住在伦敦酒馆的一间大客房里，有各自的床位，始终受人看护，并且被监视着，尽管那个官员发誓他只是来保障我们安全的。他聪明机警，很有礼貌，乐于助人，同时（我很高兴听说）他在伦敦城也是颇受尊敬的人物，不仅相貌堂堂，眼睛炯炯有神，还有着令人艳羡的黑络腮胡，甚至连嗓音也洪亮悦耳。我觉得这里倒没有必要隐去他的姓名，他叫哈克。

晚上，当我们各自回到床上时，哈克先生的床就会被拉过来横在门口。第二天夜里，我尚无困意，看到哈克先生坐在他的床边，就过去也坐下来，递了一口鼻烟。就在从我手里接过鼻烟盒开始吸烟时，他突然诡异地哆嗦了一下，说：“那是谁！”

我顺着他的目光望去，视线越过房间，看见意料之中的那个人——皮卡迪利大街上的后者。我嗖地站起来，向前跑了好几步，接着停下来，回头看向哈克先生。只见他一脸漫不经心，哈哈大笑，愉快地说：“有一瞬间我还以为出现第十三位没有床的陪审员了，定睛一看只是月光而已呀。”

我没有和哈克先生解释，只是邀请他一起走到房间那头，并且始终注视着眼前的那个身影。他在其他十一位成员床边枕头的位置分别伫立了一会儿，每次都是到床的右边，走到下一张床的床尾时总会闪一下。从他头的位置来看，好像他只是忧郁地看着每个躺下休息的陪审员，根本没注意到我和我的床，尽管我的床离哈克先生最近。接着，他从月光照进来的位置飘然出去，穿过高大的窗玻璃，仿佛踏上了空中步梯一般离开。

次日早餐时，我才知道，昨夜大家好像都不约而同地梦到了被谋杀的死者，除了我和哈克先生。

到此时我已经确信，走在皮卡迪利大街上的第二个人（应该）就是死者，他身体力行的证词已经深深扎根在我的脑海。不过在此之后，还是发生了让我不知所措的一些事。

审判的第五天，当检方陈述接近尾声，一个死者的袖珍画像作为证据被呈上来。这个画像本应在死者的床头，但是在案发现场却不见了踪影，之后它又出现在另一个据目击者称是谋杀犯埋尸的隐秘地点。目击者检查确认后，这项证物上呈给法官，继而交由陪审团。当一位穿着黑袍的官员拿着袖珍像朝我走来时，皮卡迪利大街上第二个人的身影突然自人群中冲出，他从官员手里夺走袖珍像，亲自交到我手上。因为画像在小盒子里，我还没看到画像，就听见他低沉空洞的声音飘来——“我当时还很年轻，脸上也没这么煞白。”这声音在我传给下一个陪审员的时候又出现了，等他传给他身边的另一位时再次响起，就这样每传到下一个人，这话就响起一遍，直到最后，画像又回到了我手里。而其他所有人好像对此都毫无察觉。

陪审团用餐通常都在一处，由哈克先生监管。打第一天开始，我们就会很自然地在饭桌上讨论起当日案情进展。到第五天时，原告方的案情陈述已经结束，陪审团已经从这一角度了解到事件全貌，讨论自然更加热烈，也更为严肃[1]。陪审团中有一位教区代表——我所见过的最愚蠢的白痴——他以非常荒谬的理由否决了最简单确凿的证据，还有两个优柔寡断的教区跟屁虫也支持他。他们三人都是从一个区被选进来的，那个区的治安简直一团糟，我敢说光他们那里的谋杀案审判估计就不下五百起。就在这些笨蛋家伙愈吵愈凶时，我又看到了那个死者，当时已临近午夜，我们中一些人已准备休息了。他阴森森地站在他们身后，朝我挥手。我一走到陪审员中间加入讨论，他就消失了。打那以后，他便时常出现，在我们被关着的这个大房间里来回飘荡。每当同事们把脑袋凑到一起商议时，我就看见他的脑袋也从中间冒出来。每当他们比较分析的内容于他不利时，他就会情不自禁地向我招手，表情一脸严肃。

不过你们要记住，直到审判的第五天，那个袖珍画像出现之前，他可从未在法庭显形。随着案件进入到

1. 英美司法体系中，对于刑事案件，陪审团会分别听取原告被告双方陈述和证据陈列后，再进行封闭式讨论，得出有罪或无罪的判定。

辩护阶段，有三点变化出现了。我先说其中两点吧。首先，死者的身影如今频频出现在法庭上，再也不对着我，而总是向着正在发言的人。比如，死者的喉咙曾被人切断，辩方一开始就指出他很有可能是自己割喉而亡。这时，死者飘到说话人肘边，打开他恐怖的断喉部位（之前藏起来了），任凭支气管在空中交叉晃动，左右手还交替比画，奋力向律师展示，不论哪只手都不可能造成这种伤口。还有一次，有位女性作为品德证人出庭，宣誓说嫌犯是这世上最亲切友善的人。死者立即抵在她的面前，凑上去死命瞪她，还伸出手臂，用手指着犯人阴邪的面孔。

接下来要说的第三点变化给我印象最深刻，也最为震惊。我不想解释分析，只打算准确地描述事实，交由你们来判断。尽管被靠近的对象毫无察觉，但死者的靠近还是会让他们感到些许惊恐与不安。在我看来，好像有一种未知的力量在限制他完全暴露自己，但同时也使得他能够无形无声地侵入别人的大脑。当首席辩护律师提及自杀的假设时，那身形就会闪现在这位博学的绅士旁，扯开自己被割断的喉咙，露出令人毛骨悚然的伤口。不可否认的是，辩护律师在之后的演讲中竟变得结结巴巴，甚至卡顿了几秒钟，忘记了精心准备的说辞，还脸色煞白，不断用手帕擦拭前额。当品德证人面对死者的显形时，我几乎可以肯定她确实按照死者手指的方向看去了，十分犹豫和苦恼地盯着嫌犯。这两个补充例子已经足够说明问题。在审判的第八天，每日午后的照例小憩和茶歇结束，我和陪审员们一起回到法庭，法官还没回来。我站在位子上四处张望，没看见死者，还以为他不在，结果不经意间抬头扫了一眼廊台，发现他身子前倾，正靠在一位优雅的女士身上，似乎是在确定法官们有没有归位。那位女士立即尖叫一声晕了过去，然后被人抬走了。主持审判的大法官是位经验丰富、睿智又耐心的人，他也跟了出去，等到料理好一切，才回来坐好，稳住自己，开始宣读总结陈词。这时死者从法官走进来的门飘入，直接到他桌旁，站在他身后急切地看笔录。法官大人正要翻页，突然脸色陡变，手也僵住，只见熟悉的一阵战栗传遍全身。他结结巴巴地说：“抱歉各位请稍等，不知怎的我被这污浊的空气弄魔怔了。”他端起杯子喝下一整杯水，才缓过来。

没有尽头的十天期限已经挨过了单调枯燥的六天——同样的法官坐在席位上，同一个谋杀犯坐在被告席，同样的律师坐在桌边，同样语气的问答声飘散在法庭上空，同样的沙沙作响声自法官笔下传出，同一批接待员进进出出引导，没有自然光时，同样的灯会在同样的时间亮起，雾天里蒙在巨幅玻璃外窗帘一般的同样的浓雾，雨天里吧嗒吧嗒打下的同样的雨滴，狱吏和囚犯日复一日在同样的地面上留下的同样的脚印，开关重重大门时转动的同样的钥匙——所有这些乏味的反复都让我有一种错觉，好像把这个陪审团团长当到天荒地老了，外面皮卡迪利大街还是当初和巴比伦都城一同繁华起来的。不过那个死者的一举一动我都不曾错过，他太过特别，实在难以忽略。实际上，就我所见，显灵的死者从来没有看向过谋杀犯。我一遍又一遍地想，为什么呢？真的一次都没有。

自打袖珍画像出现直到结案，死者再也没有看我一眼。陪审团在深夜十点还差七分钟的时候，退庭回去商议。由于教区代表和他的两个跟班太过蠢笨，又添了不少麻烦，以至于我们两次回法庭请求重读法官的部分笔录。我们九个人认为这些笔录一点儿问题都没有，随便从法庭上拽一个人估计他都会这么觉得。可那白痴三人组什么都不懂，就知道添乱，一直怀疑反对。我们争论了好久，才说服他们，于是陪审团在十二点十分重返法庭。

此时，死者站在陪审团坐席的正对面，法庭的另一边。待我入座，他十分刻意地盯着我看，然后似乎还比较满意，悠悠地拿起搭在手臂上的灰色大面纱——此前他从来没有戴过——盖住自己的头和整个身子。我宣读裁定时，讲到“判定有罪”，那纱巾一下掉在了地上，里面什么都没有了，他原先所在之处此时空空如也。

依照惯例，法官询问谋杀犯在宣布死刑之前他还有没有话要说，犯人含糊地嘟囔了一番。第二天，各大主要报纸都对此进行了报道，并形容这番话为“有点冗长混乱、不合逻辑、含糊不清的话，显然是为了抱怨自己受到不公，因为觉得陪审团团长早就对他心存偏见”。实际上，他那番不同寻常的说辞如下：“大人，我一看到陪审团团长就座，就知道自己完蛋了。法官阁下，他一定不会放过我的，因为我还没被抓的时候，有一天晚上，他就不知道怎的来到床边，把我叫醒，还要拿绳子勒死我。”

PENGUIN

LITTLE BLACK

CLASSICS

“……在你尽力自助之前，
别祈求别人帮你。
否则，今后你的祈祷
都是徒劳的。”

‘The monstrous thought came into my mind as I perused the fixed eyes and the saturnine face, that this was a spirit, not a man.’

CHARLES DICKENS

To Be Read at Dusk

Contents

To Be Read at Dusk

One, two, three, four, five. There were five of them.

Five couriers, sitting on a bench outside the convent on the summit of the Great St Bernard in Switzerland, looking at the remote heights, stained by the setting sun, as if a mighty quantity of red wine had been broached upon the mountain top, and had not yet had time to sink into the snow.

This is not my simile. It was made for the occasion by the stoutest courier, who was a German. None of the others took any more notice of it than they took of me, sitting on another bench on the other side of the convent door, smoking my cigar, like them, and – also like them – looking at the reddened snow, and at the lonely shed hard by, where the bodies of belated travellers, dug out of it, slowly wither away, knowing no corruption in that cold region.

The wine upon the mountain top soaked in as we looked; the mountain became white; the sky, a very dark blue; the wind rose; and the air turned piercing cold. The five couriers buttoned their rough coats. There being no safer man to imitate in all such proceedings than a courier, I buttoned mine.

The mountain in the sunset had stopped the five couriers in a conversation. It is a sublime sight, likely to stop conversation. The mountain being now out of the sunset, they resumed. Not that I had heard any part of their previous discourse; for, indeed, I had not then broken away from the American gentleman, in the travellers' parlour of the convent, who, sitting with his face to the fire, had undertaken to realize to me the whole progress of events which had led to the accumulation by the Honourable Ananias Dodger of one of the largest acquisitions of dollars ever made in our country.

'My God!' said the Swiss courier, speaking in French, which I do not hold (as some authors appear to do) to be such an all-sufficient excuse for a naughty word, that I have only to write it in that language to make it innocent; 'if you talk of ghosts –'

'But I *don't* talk of ghosts,' said the German.

'Of what then?' asked the Swiss.

'If I knew of what then,' said the German, 'I should probably know a great deal more.'

It was a good answer, I thought, and it made me curious. So, I moved my position to that corner of my bench which was nearest to them, and leaning my back against the convent-wall, heard perfectly, without appearing to attend.

'Thunder and lightning!' said the German, warming, 'when a certain man is coming to see you, unexpectedly; and, without his own knowledge, sends some invisible messenger, to put the idea of him in your head all day, what do you call that? When you walk along a crowded street – at Frankfort, Milan, London, Paris – and think that a passing stranger is like your friend Heinrich, and then that another passing stranger is like your friend Heinrich, and so begin to have a strange foreknowledge that presently you'll meet your friend Heinrich – which you do, though you believed him at Trieste – what do you call *that*?'

'It's not uncommon either,' murmured the Swiss and the other three.

'Uncommon!' said the German. 'It's as common as cherries in the Black Forest. It's as common as maccaroni at Naples. And Naples reminds me! When the old Marchesa Senzanima shrieks at a card party on the Chiaja – as I heard and saw her, for it happened in a Bavarian family of mine, and I was overlooking the service that evening – I say, when the old Marchesa starts up at the card-table, white through her rouge, and cries, "My sister in Spain is dead! I felt her cold touch on my back!" – and when that sister *is* dead at the moment – what do you call that?'

'Or when the blood of San Gennaro liquefies at the request of the clergy – as all the world knows that it does regularly once a-year, in my native city,' said the Neapolitan courier after a pause, with a comical look, 'what do you call that?'

'*That!*' cried the German. 'Well! I think I know a name for that.'

'Miracle?' said the Neapolitan, with the same sly face.

The German merely smoked and laughed; and they all smoked and laughed.

'Bah!' said the German, presently. 'I speak of things that really do happen. When I want to see the conjurer, I pay to see a professed one, and have my money's worth. Very strange things do happen without ghosts. Ghosts! Giovanni Baptista, tell your story of the English bride. There's no ghost in that, but something full as strange. Will any man tell me what?'

As there was a silence among them, I glanced around. He whom I took to be Baptista was lighting a fresh cigar. He presently went on to speak. He was a Genoese, as I judged.

'The story of the English bride?' said he. 'Basta! one ought not to call so slight a thing a story. Well, it's all one. But it's true. Observe me well, gentlemen, it's true. That which glitters is not always gold; but what I am going to tell, is true.'

He repeated this more than once.

Ten years ago, I took my credentials to an English gentleman at Long's Hotel, in Bond Street, London, who was about to travel – it might be for one year, it might be for two. He approved of them; likewise of me. He was pleased to make inquiry. The testimony that he received was favourable. He engaged me by the six months, and my entertainment was generous.

He was young, handsome, very happy. He was enamoured of a fair young English lady, with a sufficient fortune, and they were going to be married. It was the wedding trip, in short, that we were going to take. For three months' rest in the hot weather (it was early summer then) he had hired an old palace on the Riviera, at an easy distance from my city, Genoa, on the road to Nice. Did I know that palace? Yes; I told him I knew it well. It was an old palace, with great gardens. It was a little bare, and it was a little dark and gloomy, being close surrounded by trees; but it was spacious, ancient, grand, and on the sea shore. He said it had been so described to him exactly, and he was well pleased that I knew it. For its being a little bare of furniture, all such places were. For its being a little gloomy, he had hired it principally for the gardens, and he and my mistress would pass the summer weather in their shade.

'So all goes well, Baptista?' said he.

'Indubitably, signor; very well.'

We had a travelling chariot for our journey, newly built for us, and in all respects complete. All we had was complete; we wanted for nothing. The marriage took place. They were happy. *I* was happy, seeing all so bright, being so well situated, going to my own city, teaching my language in the rumble to the maid, la bella Carolina, whose heart was gay with laughter: who was young and rosy.

The time flew. But I observed – listen to this, I pray! (and here the courier dropped his voice) – I observed my mistress sometimes brooding in a manner very strange; in a frightened manner; in an unhappy manner; with a cloudy, uncertain alarm upon her. I think that I began to notice this when I was walking up hills by the carriage side, and master had gone on in front. At any rate, I remember that it impressed itself upon my mind one evening in the South of France, when she called to me to call master back; and when he came back, and walked for a long way, talking encouragingly and affectionately to her, with his hand upon the open window, and hers in it. Now and then, he laughed in a merry way, as if he were bantering her out of something. By and by, she laughed, and then all went well again.

It was curious. I asked la bella Carolina, the pretty little one, Was mistress unwell? – No. Out of spirits? – No. Fearful of bad roads, or brigands? – No. And what made it more mysterious was, the pretty little one would not look at me in giving answer, but *would* look at the view.

But, one day she told me the secret.

'If you must know,' said Carolina, 'I find, from what I have overheard, that mistress is haunted.'

'How haunted?'

'By a dream.'

'What dream?'

'By a dream of a face. For three nights before her marriage, she saw a face in a dream – always the same face, and only One.'

'A terrible face?'

'No. The face of a dark, remarkable-looking man, in black, with black hair and a grey moustache – a handsome man, except for a reserved and secret air. Not a face she ever saw, or at all like a face she ever saw. Doing nothing in the dream but looking at her fixedly, out of darkness.'

'Does the dream come back?'

'Never. The recollection of it, is all her trouble.'

'And why does it trouble her?'

Carolina shook her head.

'That's master's question,' said la bella. 'She don't know. She wonders why, herself. But I heard her tell him, only last night, that if she was to find a picture of that face in our Italian house (which she is afraid she will), she did not know how she could ever bear it.'

Upon my word I was fearful after this (said the Genoese courier) of our coming to the old palazzo, lest some such ill-starred picture should happen to be there. I knew there were many there; and, as we got nearer and nearer to the place, I wished the whole gallery in the crater of Vesuvius. To mend the matter, it was a stormy dismal evening when we, at last, approached that part of the Riviera. It thundered; and the thunder of my city and its environs, rolling among the high hills, is very loud. The lizards ran in and out of the chinks in the broken stone wall of the garden, as if they were frightened; the frogs bubbled and croaked their loudest; the sea-wind moaned, and the wet trees dripped; and the lightning – body of San Lorenzo, how it lightened!

We all know what an old palazzo in or near Genoa is – how time and the sea air have blotted it – how the drapery painted on the outer walls has peeled off in great flakes of plaster – how the lower windows are darkened with rusty bars of iron – how the courtyard is overgrown with grass – how the outer buildings are dilapidated – how the whole pile seems devoted to ruin. Our palazzo was one of the true kind. It had been shut up close for months. Months? – years! It had an earthy smell, like a tomb. The scent of the orange-trees on the broad back terrace, and of the lemons ripening on the wall, and of some shrubs that grew around a broken fountain, had got into the house somehow, and had never been able to get out again. There it was, in every room, an aged smell, grown faint with confinement. It pined in all the cupboards and drawers. In the little rooms of communication between great rooms, it was stifling. If you turned a picture – to come back to the pictures – there it still was, clinging to the wall behind the frame, like a sort of bat.

The lattice-blinds were close shut, all over the house. There were two ugly grey old women in the house, to take care of it; one of them with a spindle, who stood winding and mumbling in the doorway, and who would as soon have let in the devil as the air. Master, mistress, la bella Carolina, and I, went all through the palazzo. I went first, though I have named myself last, opening the windows and the lattice-blinds, and shaking down on myself splashes of rain, and scraps of mortar, and now and then a dozing mosquito, or a monstrous, fat, blotchy, Genoese spider.

When I had let the evening light into a room, master, mistress, and la bella Carolina, entered. Then, we looked round at all the pictures, and I went forward again into another room. Mistress secretly had great fear of meeting with the likeness of that face – we all had; but there was no such thing. The Madonna and Bambino, San Francisco, San Sebastiano, Venus, Santa Caterina, Angels, Brigands, Friars, Temples at Sunset, Battles, White Horses, Forests, Apostles, Doges, all my old acquaintance many times repeated? – yes. Dark handsome man in black, reserved and secret, with black hair and grey moustache, looking fixedly at mistress out of darkness? – no.

At last we got through all the rooms and all the pictures, and came out into the gardens. They were pretty well kept, being rented by a gardener, and were large and shady. In one place, there was a rustic theatre, open to the sky, the stage a green slope: the coulisses, three entrances upon a side, sweet-smelling leafy screens. Mistress moved her bright eyes, even there, as if she looked to see the face come in upon the scene: but all was well.

'Now Clara,' master said, in a low voice, 'you see that it is nothing? You are happy.'

Mistress was much encouraged. She soon accustomed

herself to that grim palazzo, and would sing, and play the harp, and copy the old pictures, and stroll with master under the green trees and vines, all day. She was beautiful. He was happy. He would laugh and say to me, mounting his horse for his morning ride before the heat:

'All goes well, Baptista!'

'Yes, signore, thank God; very well!'

We kept no company. I took la bella to the Duomo and Annunciata, to the Café, to the Opera, to the village Festa, to the Public Garden, to the Day Theatre, to the Marionetti. The pretty little one was charmed with all she saw. She learnt Italian – heavens! miraculously! Was mistress quite forgetful of that dream? I asked Carolina sometimes. Nearly, said la bella – almost. It was wearing out.

One day master received a letter, and called me.

'Baptista!'

'Signore.'

'A gentleman who is presented to me will dine here today. He is called the Signor Dellombra. Let me dine like a prince.'

It was an odd name. I did not know that name. But, there had been many noblemen and gentlemen pursued by Austria on political suspicions, lately, and some names had changed. Perhaps this was one. Altro! Dellombra was as good a name to me as another.

When the Signor Dellombra came to dinner (said the Genoese courier in the low voice, into which he had subsided once before), I showed him into the reception-room, the great sala of the old palazzo. Master received him with cordiality, and presented him to mistress. As she rose, her face changed, she gave a cry, and fell upon the marble floor.

Then, I turned my head to the Signor Dellombra, and saw that he was dressed in black, and had a reserved and secret air, and was a dark remarkable-looking man, with black hair and a grey moustache.

Master raised mistress in his arms, and carried her to her own room, where I sent la bella Carolina straight. La bella told me afterwards that mistress was nearly terrified to death, and that she wandered in her mind about her dream, all night.

Master was vexed and anxious – almost angry, and yet full of solicitude. The Signor Dellombra was a courtly gentleman, and spoke with great respect and sympathy of mistress's being so ill. The African wind had been blowing for some days (they had told him at his Hôtel of the Maltese Cross), and he knew that it was often hurtful. He hoped the beautiful lady would recover soon. He begged permission to retire, and to renew his visit when he should have the happiness of hearing that she was better. Master would not allow of this, and they dined alone.

He withdrew early. Next day he called at the gate, on horseback, to inquire for mistress. He did so two or three times in that week.

What I observed myself, and what la bella Carolina told me, united to explain to me that master had now set his mind on curing mistress of her fanciful terror. He was all kindness, but he was sensible and firm. He reasoned with her, that to encourage such fancies was to invite melancholy, if not madness. That it rested with herself to be herself. That if she once resisted her strange weakness, so successfully as to receive the Signor Dellombra as an English lady would receive any other guest, it was for ever conquered. To make an end, the Signor came again, and mistress received him without marked distress (though with constraint and apprehension still), and the evening passed serenely. Master was so delighted with this change, and so anxious to confirm it, that the Signor Dellombra became a constant guest. He was accomplished in pictures, books, and music; and his society, in any grim palazzo, would have been welcome.

I used to notice, many times, that mistress was not quite recovered. She would cast down her eyes and droop her head, before the Signor Dellombra, or would look at him with a terrified and fascinated glance, as if his presence had some evil influence or power upon her. Turning from her to him, I used to see him in the shaded gardens, or the large half-lighted sala, looking, as I might say, 'fixedly upon her out of darkness'. But, truly, I had not forgotten la bella Carolina's words describing the face in the dream.

After his second visit I heard master say:

'Now see, my dear Clara, it's over! Dellombra has come and gone, and your apprehension is broken like glass.'

'Will he – will he ever come again?' asked mistress.

'Again? Why, surely, over and over again! Are you cold?' (She shivered.)

'No, dear – but – he terrifies me: are you sure that he need come again?'

'The surer for the question, Clara!' replied master, cheerfully.

But, he was very hopeful of her complete recovery now, and grew more and more so every day. She was beautiful. He was happy.

'All goes well, Baptista?' he would say to me again.

'Yes, signore, thank God; very well.'

We were all (said the Genoese courier, constraining himself to speak a little louder), we were all at Rome for the Carnival. I had been out, all day, with a Sicilian, a friend of mine and a courier, who was there with an English family. As I returned at night to our hôtel, I met the little Carolina, who never stirred from home alone, running distractedly along the Corso.

'Carolina! What's the matter?'

'O Baptista! Oh, for the Lord's sake! where is my mistress?'

'Mistress, Carolina?'

'Gone since morning – told me, when master went out on his day's journey, not to call her, for she was tired with not resting in the night (having been in pain), and would lie in bed until the evening; then get up refreshed. She is gone! – she is gone! Master has come back, broken down the door, and she is gone! My beautiful, my good, my innocent mistress!'

The pretty little one so cried, and raved, and tore herself, that I could not have held her, but for her swooning on my arm as if she had been shot. Master came up – in manner, face, or voice, no more the master that I knew, than I was he. He took me (I laid the little one upon her bed in the hôtel, and left her with the chamber-women), in a carriage, furiously through the darkness, across the desolate Campagna. When it was day, and we stopped at a miserable posthouse, all the horses had been hired twelve hours ago, and sent away in different directions. Mark me! – by the Signor Dellombra, who had passed there in a carriage, with a frightened English lady crouching in one corner.

I never heard (said the Genoese courier, drawing a long breath) that she was ever traced beyond that spot. All I know is, that she vanished into infamous oblivion, with the dreaded face beside her that she had seen in her dream.

'What do you call *that*?' said the German courier, triumphantly: 'Ghosts! There are no ghosts *there!* What do you call this, that I am going to tell you? Ghosts! There are no ghosts *here!*'

I took an engagement once (pursued the German courier) with an English gentleman, elderly and a bachelor, to travel through my country, my Fatherland. He was a merchant who traded with my country and knew the language, but who had never been there since he was a boy – as I judge, some sixty years before.

His name was James, and he had a twin-brother John, also a bachelor. Between these brothers there was a great affection. They were in business together, at Goodman's Fields, but they did not live together. Mr James dwelt in Poland Street, turning out of Oxford Street, London. Mr John resided by Epping Forest.

Mr James and I were to start for Germany in about a week. The exact day depended on business. Mr John came to Poland Street (where I was staying in the house), to pass that week with Mr James. But, he said to his brother on the second day, 'I don't feel very well, James. There's not much the matter with me; but I think I am a little gouty. I'll go home and put myself under the care of my old housekeeper, who understands my ways. If I get quite better, I'll come back and see you before you go. If I don't feel well enough to resume my visit where I leave it off, why *you* will come and see *me* before you go.' Mr James, of course, said he would, and they shook hands – both hands, as they always did – and Mr John ordered out his old-fashioned chariot and rumbled home.

It was on the second night after that – that is to say, the fourth in the week – when I was awoke out of my sound sleep by Mr James coming into my bedroom in his flannel-gown, with a lighted candle. He sat upon the side of my bed, and looking at me, said:

'Wilhelm, I have reason to think I have got some strange illness upon me.'

I then perceived that there was a very unusual expression in his face.

'Wilhelm,' said he, 'I am not afraid or ashamed to tell you, what I might be afraid or ashamed to tell another man. You come from a sensible country, where mysterious things are inquired into, and are not settled to have been weighed and measured – or to have been unweighable and unmeasurable – or in either case to have been completely disposed of, for all time – ever so many years ago. I have just now seen the phantom of my brother.'

I confess (said the German courier) that it gave me a little tingling of the blood of hear it.

'I have just now seen,' Mr James repeated, looking full at me, that I might see how collected he was, 'the phantom of my brother John. I was sitting up in bed, unable to sleep, when it came into my room, in a white dress, and, regarding me earnestly, passed up to the end of the room, glanced at some papers on my writing-desk, turned, and, still looking earnestly at me as it passed the bed, went out at the door. Now, I am not in the least mad, and am not in the least disposed to invest that phantom with any external existence out of myself. I think it is a warning to me that I am ill; and I think I had better be bled.'

I got out of bed directly (said the German courier) and

began to get on my clothes, begging him not to be alarmed, and telling him that I would go myself to the doctor. I was just ready, when we heard a loud knocking and ringing at the street door. My room being an attic at the back, and Mr James's being the second-floor room in the front, we went down to his room, and put up the window, to see what was the matter.

'Is that Mr James?' said a man below, falling back to the opposite side of the way to look up.

'It is,' said Mr James; 'and you are my brother's man, Robert.'

'Yes, sir. I am sorry to say, sir, that Mr John is ill. He is very bad, sir. It is even feared that he may be lying at the point of death. He wants to see you, sir. I have a chaise here. Pray come to him. Pray lose no time.'

Mr James and I looked at one another. 'Wilhelm,' said he, 'this is strange. I wish you to come with me!' I helped him to dress, partly there and partly in the chaise; and no grass grew under the horses' iron shoes between Poland Street and the Forest.

Now, mind! (said the German courier). I went with Mr James into his brother's room, and I saw and heard myself what follows.

His brother lay upon his bed, at the upper end of a long bedchamber. His old housekeeper was there, and others were there: I think three others were there, if not four, and they had been with him since early in the afternoon. He was in white, like the figure – necessarily so, because he had his night-dress on. He looked like the figure – necessarily so, because he looked earnestly at his brother when he saw him come into the room.

But, when his brother reached the bedside, he slowly raised himself in bed, and looking full upon him, said these words:

'JAMES, YOU HAVE SEEN ME BEFORE, TO-NIGHT – AND YOU KNOW IT!'

And so died!

I waited, when the German courier ceased, to hear something said of this strange story. The silence was unbroken. I looked round and the five couriers were gone: so noiselessly that the ghostly mountain might have absorbed them into its eternal snows. By this time, I was by no means in a mood to sit alone in that awful scene, with the chill air coming solemnly upon me – or, if I may tell the truth, to sit alone anywhere. So I went back into the convent-parlour, and, finding the American gentleman still disposed to relate the biography of the Honourable Ananias Dodger, heard it all out.

The Signalman

'Halloa! Below there!'

When he heard a voice thus calling to him, he was standing at the door of his box, with a flag in his hand, furled round its short pole. One would have thought, considering the nature of the ground, that he could not have doubted from what quarter the voice came; but, instead of looking up to where I stood on the top of the steep cutting nearly over his head, he turned himself about and looked down the Line. There was something remarkable in his manner of doing so, though I could not have said for my life, what. But, I know it was remarkable enough to attract my notice, even though his figure was foreshortened and shadowed, down in the deep trench, and mine was high above him, so steeped in the glow of an angry sunset that I had shaded my eyes with my hand before I saw him at all.

'Halloa! Below!'

From looking down the Line, he turned himself about again, and, raising his eyes, saw my figure high above him.

'Is there any path by which I can come down and speak to you?'

He looked up at me without replying, and I looked down at him without pressing him too soon with a repetition of my idle question. Just then, there came a vague vibration in the earth and air, quickly changing into a violent pulsation, and an oncoming rush that caused me to start back, as though it had force to draw me down. When such vapour as rose to my height from this rapid train, had passed me and was skimming away over the landscape, I looked down again, and saw him re-furling the flag he had shown while the train went by.

I repeated my inquiry. After a pause, during which he

seemed to regard me with fixed attention, he motioned with his rolled-up flag towards a point on my level, some two or three hundred yards distant. I called down to him, 'All right!' and made for that point. There, by dint of looking closely about me, I found a rough zig-zag descending path notched out: which I followed.

The cutting was extremely deep, and unusually precipitate. It was made through a clammy stone that became oozier and wetter as I went down. For these reasons, I found the way long enough to give me time to recall a singular air of reluctance or compulsion with which he had pointed out the path.

When I came down low enough upon the zig-zag descent, to see him again, I saw that he was standing between the rails on the way by which the train had lately passed, in an attitude as if he were waiting for me to appear. He had his left hand at his chin, and that left elbow rested on his right hand crossed over his breast. His attitude was one of such expectation and watchfulness, that I stopped a moment, wondering at it.

I resumed my downward way, and, stepping out upon the level of the railroad and drawing nearer to him, saw that he was a dark sallow man, with a dark beard and rather heavy eyebrows. His post was in as solitary and dismal a place as ever I saw. On either side, a dripping-wet wall of jagged stone, excluding all view but a strip of sky; the perspective one way, only a crooked prolongation of this great dungeon; the shorter perspective in the other direction, terminating in a gloomy red light, and the gloomier entrance to a black tunnel, in whose massive architecture there was a barbarous, depressing, and forbidding air. So little sunlight ever found its way to this spot, that it had an earthy deadly smell; and so much cold wind rushed through it, that it struck chill to me, as if I had left the natural world.

Before he stirred, I was near enough to him to have touched him. Not even then removing his eyes from mine, he stepped back one step, and lifted his hand.

This was a lonesome post to occupy (I said), and it had riveted my attention when I looked down from up yonder. A visitor was a rarity, I should suppose; not an unwelcome rarity, I hoped? In me, he merely saw a man who had been shut up within narrow limits all his life, and who, being at last set free, had a newly awakened interest in these great works. To such purpose I spoke to him; but I am far from sure of the terms I used, for, besides that I am not happy in opening any conversation, there was something in the man that daunted me.

He directed a most curious look towards the red light near the tunnel's mouth, and looked all about it, as if something were missing from it, and then looked at me.

That light was part of his charge? Was it not?

He answered in a low voice: 'Don't you know it is?'

The monstrous thought came into my mind as I perused the fixed eyes and the saturnine face, that this was a spirit, not a man. I have speculated since, whether there may have been infection in his mind.

In my turn, I stepped back. But in making the action, I detected in his eyes some latent fear of me. This put the monstrous thought to flight.

'You look at me,' I said, forcing a smile, 'as if you had a dread of me.'

'I was doubtful,' he returned, 'whether I had seen you before.'

'Where?'

He pointed to the red light he had looked at.

'There?' I said.

Intently watchful of me, he replied (but without sound), Yes.

'My good fellow, what should I do there? However, be that as it may, I never was there, you may swear.'

'I think I may,' he rejoined. 'Yes. I am sure I may.'

His manner cleared, like my own. He replied to my remarks with readiness, and in well-chosen words. Had he much to do there? Yes; that was to say, he had enough responsibility to bear; but exactness and watchfulness were what was required of him, and of actual work – manual labour – he had next to none. To change that signal, to trim those lights, and to turn this iron handle now and then, was all he had to do under that head. Regarding those many long and lonely hours of which I seemed to make so much, he could only say that the routine of his life had shaped itself into that form, and he had grown used to it. He had taught himself a language down here – if only to know it by sight, and to have formed his own crude ideas of its pronunciation, could be called learning it. He had also worked at fractions and decimals, and tried a little algebra; but he was, and had been as a boy, a poor hand at figures. Was it necessary for him when on duty, always to remain in that channel of damp air, and could he never rise into the sunshine from between those high stone walls? Why, that depended upon times and circumstances. Under some conditions there would be less upon the Line than under others, and the same held good as to certain hours of the day and night. In bright weather, he did choose occasions for getting a little above these lower shadows; but, being at all times liable to be called by his electric bell, and at such times listening for it with redoubled anxiety, the relief was less than I would suppose.

He took me into his box, where there was a fire, a desk for an official book in which he had to make certain entries, a telegraphic instrument with its dial face and needles, and the little bell of which he had spoken. On my trusting that he would excuse the remark that he had been well educated, and (I hoped I might say without offence), perhaps educated above that station, he observed that instances of slight incongruity in such-wise would rarely be found wanting among large bodies of men; that he had heard it was so in workhouses, in the police force, even in that last desperate resource, the army; and that he knew it was so, more or less, in any great railway staff. He had been, when young (if I could believe it, sitting in that hut; he scarcely could), a student of natural philosophy, and had attended lectures; but he had run wild, misused his opportunities, gone down, and never risen again. He had no complaint to offer about that. He had made his bed, and he lay upon it. It was far too late to make another.

All that I have here condensed, he said in a quiet manner, with his grave dark regards divided between me and the fire. He threw in the word 'Sir', from time to time, and especially when he referred to his youth: as though to request me to understand that he claimed to be nothing but what I found him. He was several times interrupted by the little bell, and had to read off messages, and send replies. Once, he had to stand without the door, and display a flag as a train passed, and make some verbal communication to the driver. In the discharge of his duties I observed him to be remarkably exact and vigilant, breaking off his discourse at a syllable, and remaining silent until what he had to do was done.

In a word, I should have set this man down as one of the safest of men to be employed in that capacity, but for the circumstance that while he was speaking to me he twice broke off with a fallen colour, turned his face towards the little bell when it did NOT ring, opened the door of the hut (which was kept shut to exclude the unhealthy damp), and looked out towards the red light near the mouth of the tunnel. On both of those occasions, he came back to the fire with the inexplicable air upon him which I had remarked, without being able to define, when we were so far asunder.

Said I when I rose to leave him: 'You almost make me think that I have met with a contented man.'

(I am afraid I must acknowledge that I said it to lead him on.)

'I believe I used to be so,' he rejoined, in the low voice in which he had first spoken; 'but I am troubled, sir, I am troubled.'

He would have recalled the words if he could. He had said them, however, and I took them up quickly.

'With what? What is your trouble?'

'It is very difficult to impart, sir. It is very, very difficult to speak of. If ever you make me another visit, I will try to tell you.'

'But I expressly intend to make you another visit. Say, when shall it be?'

'I go off early in the morning, and I shall be on again at ten to-morrow night, sir.'

'I will come at eleven.'

He thanked me, and went out at the door with me. 'I'll show my white light, sir,' he said, in his peculiar low voice, 'till you have found the way up. When you have found it, don't call out! And when you are at the top, don't call out!'

His manner seemed to make the place strike colder to me, but I said no more than 'Very well.'

'And when you come down to-morrow night, don't call out! Let me ask you a parting question. What made you cry "Halloa! Below there!" to-night?'

'Heaven knows,' said I. 'I cried something to that effect –'

'Not to that effect, sir. Those were the very words. I know them well.'

'Admit those were the very words. I said them, no doubt, because I saw you below.'

'For no other reason?'

'What other reason could I possibly have!'

'You have no feeling that they were conveyed to you in any supernatural way?'

'No.'

He wished me good night, and held up his light. I walked by the side of the down Line of rails (with a very disagreeable sensation of a train coming behind me), until I found the path. It was easier to mount than to descend, and I got back to my inn without any adventure.

Punctual to my appointment, I placed my foot on the first notch of the zig-zag next night, as the distant clocks were striking eleven. He was waiting for me at the bottom, with his white light on. 'I have not called out,' I said, when we came close together; 'may I speak now?' 'By all means, sir.' 'Good night then, and here's my hand.' 'Good night, sir, and here's mine.' With that, we walked side by side to his box, entered it, closed the door, and sat down by the fire.

'I have made up my mind, sir,' he began, bending forward as soon as we were seated, and speaking in a tone but a little above a whisper, 'that you shall not have to ask me twice what troubles me. I took you for some one else yesterday evening. That troubles me.'

'That mistake?'

'No. That some one else.'

'Who is it?'

'I don't know.'

'Like me?'

'I don't know. I never saw the face. The left arm is across the face, and the right arm is waved. Violently waved. This way.'

I followed his action with my eyes, and it was the action of an arm gesticulating with the utmost passion and vehemence: 'For God's sake clear the way!'

'One moonlight night,' said the man, 'I was sitting here, when I heard a voice cry "Halloa! Below there!" I started up, looked from that door, and saw this Some one else standing by the red light near the tunnel, waving as I just now showed you. The voice seemed hoarse with shouting, and it cried, "Look out! Look out!" And then again "Halloa! Below there! Look out!" I caught up my lamp, turned it on red, and ran towards the figure, calling, "What's wrong? What has happened? Where?" It stood just outside the blackness of the tunnel. I advanced so close upon it that I wondered at its keeping the sleeve across its eyes. I ran right up at it, and had my hand stretched out to pull the sleeve away, when it was gone.'

'Into the tunnel,' said I.

'No. I ran on into the tunnel, five hundred yards. I stopped and held my lamp above my head, and saw the figures of the measured distance, and saw the wet stains stealing down the walls and trickling through the arch. I ran out again, faster than I had run in (for I had a mortal abhorrence of the place upon me), and I looked all round the red light with my own red light, and I went up the iron ladder to the gallery atop of it, and I came down again, and ran back here. I telegraphed both ways: "An alarm has been given. Is anything wrong?" The answer came back, both ways: "All well."'

Resisting the slow touch of a frozen finger tracing out my spine, I showed him how that this figure must be a deception of his sense of sight, and how that figures, originating in disease of the delicate nerves that minister to the functions of the eye, were known to have often troubled patients, some of whom had become conscious of the nature of their affliction, and had even proved it by experiments upon themselves. 'As to an imaginary cry,' said I, 'do but listen for a moment to the wind in this unnatural valley while we speak so low, and to the wild harp it makes of the telegraph wires!'

That was all very well, he returned, after we had sat listening for a while, and he ought to know something of the wind and the wires, he who so often passed long winter nights there, alone and watching. But he would beg to remark that he had not finished.

I asked his pardon, and he slowly added these words, touching my arm:

'Within six hours after the Appearance, the memorable accident on this Line happened, and within ten hours the dead and wounded were brought along through the tunnel over the spot where the figure had stood.'

A disagreeable shudder crept over me, but I did my best against it. It was not to be denied, I rejoined, that this was a remarkable coincidence, calculated deeply to impress his mind. But, it was unquestionable that remarkable coincidences did continually occur, and they must be taken into account in dealing with such a subject. Though to be sure I must admit, I added (for I thought I saw that he was going to bring the objection to bear upon me), men of common sense did not allow much for coincidences in making the ordinary calculations of life.

He again begged to remark that he had not finished.

I again begged his pardon for being betrayed into interruptions.

'This,' he said, again laying his hand upon my arm, and glancing over his shoulder with hollow eyes, 'was just a year ago. Six or seven months passed, and I had recovered from the surprise and shock, when one morning, as the day was breaking, I, standing at that door, looked towards the red light, and saw the spectre again.' He stopped, with a fixed look at me.

'Did it cry out?'

'No. It was silent.'

'Did it wave its arm?'

'No. It leaned against the shaft of the light, with both hands before the face. Like this.'

Once more, I followed his action with my eyes. It was an action of mourning. I have seen such an attitude in stone figures on tombs.

'Did you go up to it?'

'I came in and sat down, partly to collect my thoughts, partly because it had turned me faint. When I went to the door again, daylight was above me, and the ghost was gone.'

'But nothing followed? Nothing came of this?'

He touched me on the arm with his forefinger twice or thrice, giving a ghastly nod each time:

'That very day, as a train came out of the tunnel, I noticed, at a carriage window on my side, what looked like a confusion of hands and heads, and something waved. I saw it, just in time to signal the driver, Stop! He shut off, and put his brake on, but the train drifted past here a hundred and fifty yards or more. I ran after it, and, as I went along, heard terrible screams and cries. A beautiful young lady had died instantaneously in one of the compartments, and was brought in here, and laid down on this floor between us.'

Involuntarily, I pushed my chair back, as I looked from the boards at which he pointed, to himself.

'True, sir. True. Precisely as it happened, so I tell it you.'

I could think of nothing to say, to any purpose, and

my mouth was very dry. The wind and the wires took up the story with a long lamenting wail.

He resumed. 'Now, sir, mark this, and judge how my mind is troubled. The spectre came back, a week ago. Ever since, it has been there, now and again, by fits and starts.'

'At the light?'

'At the Danger-light.'

'What does it seem to do?'

He repeated, if possible with increased passion and vehemence, that former gesticulation of 'For God's sake clear the way!'

Then, he went on. 'I have no peace or rest for it. It calls to me, for many minutes together, in an agonized manner, "Below there! Look out! Look out!" It stands waving to me. It rings my little bell –'

I caught at that. 'Did it ring your bell yesterday evening when I was here, and you went to the door?'

'Twice.'

'Why, see,' said I, 'how your imagination misleads you. My eyes were on the bell, and my ears were open to the bell, and if I am a living man, it did NOT ring at those times. No, nor at any other time, except when it was rung in the natural course of physical things by the station communicating with you.'

He shook his head. 'I have never made a mistake as to that, yet, sir. I have never confused the spectre's ring with the man's. The ghost's ring is a strange vibration in the bell that it derives from nothing else, and I have not asserted that the bell stirs to the eye. I don't wonder that you failed to hear it. But *I* heard it.'

'And did the spectre seem to be there, when you looked out?'

'It WAS there.'

'Both times?'

He repeated firmly: 'Both times.'

'Will you come to the door with me, and look for it now?'

He bit his under-lip as though he were somewhat unwilling, but arose. I opened the door, and stood on the step, while he stood in the doorway. There, was the Danger-light. There, was the dismal mouth of the tunnel. There, were the high wet stone walls of the cutting. There, were the stars above them.

'Do you see it?' I asked him, taking particular note of his face. His eyes were prominent and strained; but not very much more so, perhaps, than my own had been when I had directed them earnestly towards the same spot.

'No,' he answered. 'It is not there.'

'Agreed,' said I.

We went in again, shut the door, and resumed our seats. I was thinking how best to improve this advantage, if it might be called one, when he took up the conversation in such a matter of course way, so assuming that there could be no serious question of fact between us, that I felt myself in the weakest of positions.

'By this time you will fully understand, sir,' he said, 'that what troubles me so dreadfully, is the question, What does the spectre mean?'

I was not sure, I told him, that I did fully understand.

'What is its warning against?' he said, ruminating, with his eyes on the fire, and only by times turning them on me. 'What is the danger? Where is the danger? There is danger overhanging, somewhere on the Line. Some dreadful calamity will happen. It is not to be doubted this third time, after what has gone before. But surely this is a cruel haunting of *me*. What can *I* do!'

He pulled out his handkerchief, and wiped the drops from his heated forehead.

'If I telegraph Danger, on either side of me, or on both, I can give no reason for it,' he went on, wiping the palms of his hands. 'I should get into trouble, and do no good. They would think I was mad. This is the way it would work: Message: "Danger! Take care!" Answer: "What Danger? Where?" Message: "Don't know. But for God's sake take care!" They would displace me. What else could they do?'

His pain of mind was most pitiable to see. It was the mental torture of a conscientious man, oppressed beyond endurance by an unintelligible responsibility involving life.

'When it first stood under the Danger-light,' he went on, putting his dark hair back from his head, and drawing his hands outward across and across his temples in an extremity of feverish distress, 'why not tell me where that accident was to happen – if it must happen? Why not tell me how it could be averted – if it could have been averted?

When on its second coming it hid its face, why not tell me instead: "She is going to die. Let them keep her at home"? If it came, on those two occasions, only to show me that its warnings were true, and so to prepare me for the third, why not warn me plainly now? And I, Lord help me! A mere poor signalman on this solitary station! Why not go to somebody with credit to be believed, and power to act!'

When I saw him in this state, I saw that for the poor man's sake, as well as for the public safety, what I had to do for the time was, to compose his mind. Therefore, setting aside all question of reality or unreality between us, I represented to him that whoever thoroughly discharged his duty, must do well, and that at least it was his comfort that he understood his duty, though he did not understand these confounding Appearances. In this effort I succeeded far better than in the attempt to reason him out of his conviction. He became calm; the occupations incidental to his post as the night advanced, began to make larger demands on his attention; and I left him at two in the morning. I had offered to stay through the night, but he would not hear of it.

That I more than once looked back at the red light as I ascended the pathway, that I did not like the red light, and that I should have slept but poorly if my bed had been under it, I see no reason to conceal. Nor, did I like the two sequences of the accident and the dead girl. I see no reason to conceal that, either.

But, what ran most in my thoughts was the

consideration how ought I to act, having become the recipient of this disclosure? I had proved the man to be intelligent, vigilant, painstaking, and exact; but how long might he remain so, in his state of mind? Though in a subordinate position, still he held a most important trust, and would I (for instance) like to stake my own life on the chances of his continuing to execute it with precision?

Unable to overcome a feeling that there would be something treacherous in my communicating what he had told me, to his superiors in the Company, without first being plain with himself and proposing a middle course to him, I ultimately resolved to offer to accompany him (otherwise keeping his secret for the present) to the wisest medical practitioner we could hear of in those parts, and to take his opinion. A change in his time of duty would come round next night, he had apprised me, and he would be off an hour or two after sunrise, and on again soon after sunset. I had appointed to return accordingly.

Next evening was a lovely evening, and I walked out early to enjoy it. The sun was not yet quite down when I traversed the field-path near the top of the deep cutting. I would extend my walk for an hour, I said to myself, half an hour on and half an hour back, and it would then be time to go to my signalman's box.

Before pursuing my stroll, I stepped to the brink, and mechanically looked down, from the point from which I had first seen him. I cannot describe the thrill that seized upon me, when, close at the mouth of the tunnel, I saw the appearance of a man, with his left sleeve across his eyes, passionately waving his right arm.

The nameless horror that oppressed me, passed in a moment, for in a moment I saw that this appearance of a man was a man indeed, and that there was a little group of other men standing at a short distance, to whom he seemed to be rehearsing the gesture he made. The Danger-light was not yet lighted. Against its shaft, a little low hut, entirely new to me, had been made of some wooden supports and tarpaulin. It looked no bigger than a bed.

With an irresistible sense that something was wrong – with a flashing self-reproachful fear that fatal mischief had come of my leaving the man there, and causing no one to be sent to overlook or correct what he did – I descended the notched path with all the speed I could make.

'What is the matter?' I asked the men.

'Signalman killed this morning, sir.'

'Not the man belonging to that box?'

'Yes, sir.'

'Not the man I know?'

'You will recognize him, sir, if you knew him,' said the man who spoke for the others, solemnly uncovering his own head and raising an end of the tarpaulin, 'for his face is quite composed.'

'O! how did this happen, how did this happen?' I asked, turning from one to another as the hut closed in again.

'He was cut down by an engine, sir. No man in England knew his work better. But somehow he was not clear of the outer rail. It was just at broad day. He had struck the light, and had the lamp in his hand. As the engine came out of the tunnel, his back was towards her, and she cut him down. That man drove her, and was showing how it happened. Show the gentleman, Tom.'

The man, who wore a rough dark dress, stepped back to his former place at the mouth of the tunnel:

'Coming round the curve in the tunnel, sir,' he said, 'I saw him at the end, like as if I saw him down a perspective-glass. There was no time to check speed, and I knew him to be very careful. As he didn't seem to take heed of the whistle, I shut it off when we were running down upon him, and called to him as loud as I could call.'

'What did you say?'

'I said, Below there! Look out! Look out! For God's sake clear the way!'

I started.

'Ah! it was a dreadful time, sir. I never left off calling to him. I put this arm before my eyes, not to see, and I waved this arm to the last; but it was no use.'

Without prolonging the narrative to dwell on any one of its curious circumstances more than on any other, I may, in closing it, point out the coincidence that the warning of the Engine-Driver included, not only the words which the unfortunate Signalman had repeated to me as haunting him, but also the words which I myself – not he – had attached, and that only in my own mind, to the gesticulation he had imitated.

The Trial for Murder

I have always noticed a prevalent want of courage, even among persons of superior intelligence and culture, as to imparting their own psychological experiences when those have been of a strange sort. Almost all men are afraid that what they could relate in such wise would find no parallel or response in a listener's internal life, and might be suspected or laughed at. A truthful traveller, who should have seen some extraordinary creature in the likeness of a sea-serpent, would have no fear of mentioning it; but the same traveller, having had some singular presentiment, impulse, vagary of thought, vision (so called), dream, or other remarkable mental impression, would hesitate considerably before he would own to it. To this reticence I attribute much of the obscurity in which such subjects are involved. We do not habitually communicate our experiences of these subjective things as we do our experiences of objective creation. The consequence is, that the general stock of experience in this regard appears exceptional, and really is so, in respect of being miserably imperfect.

In what I am going to relate, I have no intention of setting up, opposing, or supporting any theory whatever.

I know the history of the Bookseller of Berlin, I have studied the case of the wife of a late Astronomer Royal as related by Sir David Brewster, and I have followed the minutest details of a much more remarkable case of Spectral Illusion occurring within my private circle of friends. It may be necessary to state as to this last, that the sufferer (a lady) was in no degree, however distant, related to me. A mistaken assumption on that head might suggest an explanation of a part of my own case, – but only a part, – which would be wholly without foundation. It cannot be referred to my inheritance of any developed peculiarity, nor had I ever before any at all similar experience, nor have I ever had any at all similar experience since.

It does not signify how many years ago, or how few, a certain murder was committed in England, which attracted great attention. We hear more than enough of murderers as they rise in succession to their atrocious eminence, and I would bury the memory of this particular brute, if I could, as his body was buried, in Newgate Jail. I purposely abstain from giving any direct clew to the criminal's individuality.

When the murder was first discovered, no suspicion fell – or I ought rather to say, for I cannot be too precise in my facts, it was nowhere publicly hinted that any suspicion fell – on the man who was afterwards brought to trial. As no reference was at that time made to him in the newspapers, it is obviously impossible that any description of him can at that time have been given in the newspapers. It is essential that this fact be remembered.

Unfolding at breakfast my morning paper, containing the account of that first discovery, I found it to be deeply interesting, and I read it with close attention. I read it twice, if not three times. The discovery had been made in a bedroom, and, when I laid down the paper, I was aware of a flash – rush – flow – I do not know what to call it, – no word I can find is satisfactorily descriptive, – in which I seemed to see that bedroom passing through my room, like a picture impossibly painted on a running river. Though almost instantaneous in its passing, it was perfectly clear; so clear that I distinctly, and with a sense of relief, observed the absence of the dead body from the bed.

It was in no romantic place that I had this curious sensation, but in chambers in Piccadilly, very near to the corner of Saint James's Street. It was entirely new to me. I was in my easy-chair at the moment, and the sensation was accompanied with a peculiar shiver which started the chair from its position. (But it is to be noted that the chair ran easily on castors.) I went to one of the windows (there are two in the room, and the room is on the second floor) to refresh my eyes with the moving objects down in Piccadilly. It was a bright autumn morning, and the street was sparkling and cheerful. The wind was high. As I looked out, it brought down from the Park a quantity of fallen leaves, which a gust took, and whirled into a spiral pillar. As the pillar fell and the leaves dispersed, I saw two men on the opposite side of the way, going from West to East. They were one behind the other. The foremost man often looked back over his shoulder. The second man followed him, at a distance of some thirty paces, with his right hand menacingly raised. First, the singularity and steadiness of this threatening gesture in so public a thoroughfare attracted my attention; and next, the more remarkable circumstance that nobody heeded it. Both men threaded their way among the other passengers with a smoothness hardly consistent even with the action of walking on a pavement; and no single creature, that I could see, gave them place, touched them, or looked after them. In passing before my windows, they both stared up at me. I saw their two faces very distinctly, and I knew that I could recognize them anywhere. Not that I had consciously noticed anything very remarkable in either face, except that the man who went first had an unusually lowering appearance, and that the face of the man who followed him was of the colour of impure wax.

I am a bachelor, and my valet and his wife constitute my whole establishment. My occupation is in a certain Branch Bank, and I wish that my duties as head of a Department were as light as they are popularly supposed to be. They kept me in town that autumn, when I stood in need of change. I was not ill, but I was not well. My reader is to make the most that can be reasonably made of my feeling jaded, having a depressing sense upon me of a monotonous life, and being 'slightly dyspeptic.' I am assured by my renowned doctor that my real state of health at that time justifies no stronger description, and I quote his own from his written answer to my request for it.

As the circumstances of the murder, gradually unravelling, took stronger and stronger possession of the public mind, I kept them away from mine, by knowing as little about them as was possible in the midst of the universal excitement. But I knew that a verdict of Wilful Murder had been found against the suspected murderer, and that he had been committed to Newgate for trial. I also knew that his trial had been postponed over one Sessions of the Central Criminal Court, on the ground of general prejudice and want of time for the preparation of the defence. I may further have known, but I believe I did not, when, or about when, the Sessions to which his trial stood postponed would come on.

My sitting-room, bedroom, and dressing-room are all on one floor. With the last there is no communication but through the bedroom. True, there is a door in it, once communicating with the staircase; but a part of the fitting of my bath has been – and had then been for some years – fixed across it. At the same period, and as a part of the same arrangement, the door had been nailed up and canvassed over.

I was standing in my bedroom late one night, giving some directions to my servant before he went to bed. My face was towards the only available door of communication with the dressing-room, and it was closed. My servant's back was towards that door. While I was speaking to him, I saw it open, and a man look in, who very earnestly and mysteriously beckoned to me. That man was the man who had gone second of the two along Piccadilly, and whose face was of the colour of impure wax.

The figure, having beckoned, drew back, and closed the door. With no longer pause than was made by my crossing the bedroom, I opened the dressing-room door, and looked in. I had a lighted candle already in my hand. I felt no inward expectation of seeing the figure in the dressing-room, and I did not see it there.

Conscious that my servant stood amazed, I turned round to him, and said: 'Derrick, could you believe that in my cool senses I fancied I saw a –' As I there laid my hand upon his breast, with a sudden start he trembled violently, and said, 'O Lord, yes, sir! A dead man beckoning!'

Now I do not believe that this John Derrick, my trusty and attached servant for more than twenty years, had any impression whatever of having seen any such figure, until I touched him. The change in him was so startling, when I touched him, that I fully believe he derived his impression in some occult manner from me at that instant.

I bade John Derrick bring some brandy, and I gave him a dram, and was glad to take one myself. Of what had preceded that night's phenomenon, I told him not a single word. Reflecting on it, I was absolutely certain that I had never seen that face before, except on the one occasion in Piccadilly. Comparing its expression when beckoning at the door with its expression when it had stared up at me as I stood at my window, I came to the conclusion that on the first occasion it had sought to fasten itself upon my memory, and that on the second occasion it had made sure of being immediately remembered.

I was not very comfortable that night, though I felt a certainty, difficult to explain, that the figure would not return. At daylight I fell into a heavy sleep, from which I was awakened by John Derrick's coming to my bedside with a paper in his hand.

This paper, it appeared, had been the subject of an altercation at the door between its bearer and my servant. It was a summons to me to serve upon a Jury at the forthcoming Sessions of the Central Criminal Court at the Old Bailey. I had never before been summoned on such a Jury, as John Derrick well knew. He believed – I am not certain at this hour whether with reason or otherwise – that that class of Jurors were customarily chosen on a lower qualification than mine, and he had at first refused to accept the summons. The man who served it had taken the matter very coolly. He had said that my attendance or non-attendance was nothing to him; there the summons was; and I should deal with it at my own peril, and not at his.

For a day or two I was undecided whether to respond to this call, or take no notice of it. I was not conscious of the slightest mysterious bias, influence, or attraction, one way or other. Of that I am as strictly sure as of every other statement that I make here. Ultimately I decided, as a break in the monotony of my life, that I would go.

The appointed morning was a raw morning in the month of November. There was a dense brown fog in Piccadilly, and it became positively black and in the last degree oppressive East of Temple Bar. I found the passages and staircases of the Court-House flaringly lighted with gas, and the Court itself similarly illuminated. I *think* that, until I was conducted by officers into the Old Court and saw its crowded state, I did not know that the Murderer was to be tried that day. I *think* that, until I was so helped into the Old Court with considerable difficulty, I did not know into which of the two Courts sitting my summons would take me. But this must not be received as a positive assertion, for I am not completely satisfied in my mind on either point.

I took my seat in the place appropriated to Jurors in waiting, and I looked about the Court as well as I could through the cloud of fog and breath that was heavy in it. I noticed the black vapor hanging like a murky curtain outside the great windows, and I noticed the stifled sound of wheels on the straw or tan that was littered in the street; also, the hum of the people gathered there, which a shrill whistle, or a louder song or hail than the rest, occasionally pierced. Soon afterwards the Judges, two in number, entered, and took their seats. The buzz in the Court was awfully hushed. The direction was given to put the Murderer to the bar. He appeared there. And in that same instant I recognized in him the first of the two men who had gone down Piccadilly.

If my name had been called then, I doubt if I could have answered to it audibly. But it was called about sixth or eighth in the panel, and I was by that time able to say, 'Here!' Now, observe. As I stepped into the box, the prisoner, who had been looking on attentively, but with no sign of concern, became violently agitated, and beckoned to his attorney. The prisoner's wish to challenge me was so manifest, that it occasioned a pause, during which the attorney, with his hand upon the dock, whispered with his client, and shook his head. I afterwards had it from that gentleman, that the prisoner's first affrighted words to him were. '*At all hazards, challenge that man!*' But that, as he would give no reason for it, and admitted that he had not even known my name until he heard it called and I appeared, it was not done.

Both on the ground already explained, that I wish to avoid reviving the unwholesome memory of that Murderer, and also because a detailed account of his long trial is by no means indispensable to my narrative, I shall confine myself closely to such incidents in the ten days and nights during which we, the Jury, were kept together, as directly bear on my own curious personal experience. It is in that, and not in the Murderer, that I seek to interest my reader. It is to that, and not to a page of the Newgate Calendar, that I beg attention.

I was chosen Foreman of the Jury. On the second

morning of the trial, after evidence had been taken for two hours (I heard the church clocks strike), happening to cast my eyes over my brother jurymen, I found an inexplicable difficulty in counting them. I counted them several times, yet always with the same difficulty. In short, I made them one too many.

I touched the brother juryman whose place was next me, and I whispered to him, 'Oblige me by counting us.' He looked surprised by the request, but turned his head and counted. 'Why,' says he, suddenly, 'we are Thirt –; but no, it's not possible. No. We are twelve.'

According to my counting that day, we were always right in detail, but in the gross we were always one too many. There was no appearance – no figure – to account for it; but I had now an inward foreshadowing of the figure that was surely coming.

The Jury were housed at the London Tavern. We all slept in one large room on separate tables, and we were constantly in the charge and under the eye of the officer sworn to hold us in safe-keeping. I see no reason for suppressing the real name of that officer. He was intelligent, highly polite, and obliging, and (I was glad to hear) much respected in the City. He had an agreeable presence, good eyes, enviable black whiskers, and a fine sonorous voice. His name was Mr Harker.

When we turned into our twelve beds at night, Mr Harker's bed was drawn across the door. On the night of the second day, not being disposed to lie down, and seeing Mr Harker sitting on his bed, I went and sat beside him, and offered him a pinch of snuff. As Mr Harker's hand touched mine in taking it from my box, a peculiar shiver crossed him, and he said: 'Who is this!'

Following Mr Harker's eyes, and looking along the room, I saw again the figure I expected, – the second of the two men who had gone down Piccadilly. I rose, and advanced a few steps; then stopped, and looked round at Mr Harker. He was quite unconcerned, laughed, and said in a pleasant way, 'I thought for a moment we had a thirteenth juryman, without a bed. But I see it is the moonlight.'

Making no revelation to Mr Harker, but inviting him to take a walk with me to the end of the room, I watched what the figure did. It stood for a few moments by the bedside of each of my eleven brother jurymen, close to the pillow. It always went to the right-hand side of the bed, and always passed out crossing the foot of the next bed. It seemed, from the action of the head, merely to look down pensively at each recumbent figure. It took no notice of me, or of my bed, which was that nearest to Mr Harker's. It seemed to go out where the moonlight came in, through a high window, as by an aerial flight of stairs.

Next morning at breakfast, it appeared that everybody present had dreamed of the murdered man last night, except myself and Mr Harker.

I now felt as convinced that the second man who had gone down Piccadilly was the murdered man (so to speak), as if it had been borne into my comprehension by his immediate testimony. But even this took place, and in a manner for which I was not at all prepared.

On the fifth day of the trial, when the case for the prosecution was drawing to a close, a miniature of the murdered man, missing from his bedroom upon the discovery of the deed, and afterwards found in a hiding-place where the Murderer had been seen digging, was put in evidence. Having been identified by the witness under examination, it was handed up to the Bench, and thence handed down to be inspected by the Jury. As an officer in a black gown was making his way with it across to me, the figure of the second man who had gone down Piccadilly impetuously started from the crowd, caught the miniature from the officer, and gave it to me with its own hands, at the same time saying, in a low and hollow tone, – before I saw the miniature, which was in a locket, – '*I was younger then, and my face was not then drained of blood.*' It also came between me and the brother juryman to whom I would have given the miniature, and between him and the brother juryman to whom he would have given it, and so passed it on through the whole of our number, and back into my possession. Not one of them, however, detected this.

At table, and generally when we were shut up together in Mr Harker's custody, we had from the first naturally discussed the day's proceedings a good deal. On that fifth day, the case for the prosecution being closed, and we having that side of the question in a completed shape before us, our discussion was more animated and serious. Among our number was a vestryman, – the densest idiot I have ever seen at large, – who met the plainest evidence with the most preposterous objections, and who was sided with by two flabby parochial parasites; all the three impanelled from a district so delivered over to Fever that they ought to have been upon their own trial for five hundred Murders. When these mischievous blockheads were at their loudest, which was towards midnight, while some of us were already preparing for bed, I again saw the murdered man. He stood grimly behind them, beckoning to me. On my going towards them, and striking into the conversation, he immediately retired. This was the beginning of a separate series of appearances, confined to that long room in which *we* were confined. Whenever a knot of my brother jurymen laid their heads together, I saw the head of the murdered man among theirs. Whenever their comparison of notes was going against him, he would solemnly and irresistibly beckon to me.

It will be borne in mind that down to the production of the miniature, on the fifth day of the trial, I had never seen the Appearance in Court. Three changes occurred now that we entered on the case for the defence. Two of them I will mention together, first. The figure was now in Court continually, and it never there addressed itself to me, but always to the person who was speaking at the time. For instance. The throat of the murdered man had been cut straight across. In the opening speech for the defence, it was suggested that the deceased might have cut his own throat. At that very moment, the figure, with its throat in the dreadful condition referred to (this it had concealed before), stood at the speaker's elbow, motioning across and across its windpipe, now with the right hand, now with the left, vigorously suggesting to the speaker himself the impossibility of such a wound having been self-inflicted by either hand. For another instance. A witness to character, a woman, deposed to the prisoner's being the most amiable of mankind. The figure at that instant stood on the floor before her, looking her full in the face, and pointing out the prisoner's evil countenance with an extended arm and an outstretched finger.

The third change now to be added impressed me strongly as the most marked and striking of all. I do not theorize upon it; I accurately state it, and there leave it. Although the Appearance was not itself perceived by those whom it addressed, its coming close to such persons was invariably attended by some trepidation or disturbance on their part. It seemed to me as if it were prevented, by laws to which I was not amenable, from fully revealing itself to others, and yet as if it could invisibly, dumbly, and darkly overshadow their minds. When the leading counsel for the defence suggested that hypothesis of suicide, and the figure stood at the learned gentleman's elbow, frightfully sawing at its severed throat, it is undeniable that the counsel faltered in his speech, lost for a few seconds the thread of his ingenious discourse, wiped his forehead with his handkerchief, and turned extremely pale. When the witness to character was confronted by the Appearance, her eyes most certainly did follow the direction of its pointed finger, and rest in great hesitation and trouble upon the prisoner's face. Two additional illustrations will suffice. On the eighth day of the trial, after the pause which was every day made early in the afternoon for a few minutes' rest and refreshment, I came back into Court with the rest of the Jury, some little time before the return of the Judges. Standing up in the box and looking about me, I thought the figure was not there, until, chancing to raise my eyes to the gallery, I saw it bending forward, and leaning over a very decent woman, as if to assure itself whether the Judges had resumed their seats or not. Immediately afterwards that woman screamed, fainted, and was carried out. So with the venerable, sagacious, and patient Judge who conducted the trial. When the case was over, and he settled himself and his papers to sum up, the murdered man, entering by the Judges' door, advanced to his Lordship's desk, and looked eagerly over his shoulder at the pages of his notes which he was turning. A change came over his Lordship's face; his hand stopped; the peculiar shiver, that I knew so well, passed over him; he faltered, 'Excuse me, gentlemen, for a few moments. I am somewhat oppressed by the vitiated air'; and did not recover until he had drunk a glass of water.

Through all the monotony of six of those interminable ten days, – the same Judges and others on the Bench, the same Murderer in the dock, the same lawyers at the table, the same tones of question and answer rising to the roof of the Court, the same scratching of the Judge's pen, the same ushers going in and out, the same lights kindled at the same hour when there had been any natural light of day, the same foggy curtain outside the great windows when it was foggy, the same rain pattering and dripping when it was rainy, the same footmarks of turnkeys and prisoner day after day on the same sawdust, the same keys locking and unlocking the same heavy doors, – through all the wearisome monotony which made me feel as if I had been Foreman of the Jury for a vast period of time, and Piccadilly had flourished coevally with Babylon, the murdered man never lost one trace of his distinctness in my eyes, nor was he at any moment less distinct than anybody else. I must not omit, as a matter of fact, that I never once saw the Appearance which I call by the name of the murdered man look at the Murderer. Again and again I wondered, 'Why does he not?' But he never did.

Nor did he look at me, after the production of the miniature, until the last closing minutes of the trial arrived. We retired to consider, at seven minutes before ten at night. The idiotic vestryman and his two parochial parasites gave us so much trouble that we twice returned into Court to beg to have certain extracts from the Judge's notes re-read. Nine of us had not the smallest doubt about those passages, neither, I believe, had any one in Court; the dunder-headed triumvirate, however, having no idea but obstruction, disputed them for that very reason. At length we prevailed, and finally the Jury returned into Court at ten minutes past twelve.

The murdered man at that time stood directly opposite the Jury-box, on the other side of the Court. As I took my place, his eyes rested on me with great attention; he seemed satisfied, and slowly shook a great gray veil, which he carried on his arm for the first time, over his head and whole form. As I gave in our verdict, 'Guilty', the veil collapsed, all was gone, and his place was empty.

The Murderer, being asked by the Judge, according to usage, whether he had anything to say before sentence of Death should be passed upon him, indistinctly muttered something which was described in the leading newspapers of the following day as 'a few rambling, incoherent, and half-audible words, in which he was understood to complain that he had not had a fair trial, because the Foreman of the Jury was prepossessed against him'. The remarkable declaration that he really made was this: '*My Lord, I knew I was a doomed man, when the Foreman of my Jury came into the box. My Lord, I knew he would never let me off, because, before I was taken, he somehow got to my bedside in the night, woke me, and put a rope round my neck.*'

PENGUIN

LITTLE BLACK

CLASSICS

PENGUIN

LITTLE BLACK

CLASSICS

21. JANE AUSTEN

The Beautifull Cassandra

22. FYODOR DOSTOYEVSKY

The Meek One

23. AESOP

The Cat and Venus

24. CHARLES DICKENS

To Be Read at Dusk

25. JOHANN PETER HEBEL

How a Ghastly Story Was Brought to Light by a Common or Garden Butcher's Dog

26. OSCAR WILDE

Lord Arthur Savile's Crime

27. LEO TOLSTOY

The Death of Ivan Ilyich

28. MICHEL DE MONTAIGNE

How We Weep and Laugh at the Same Thing

29. EMILY DICKINSON

My life had stood a loaded gun

30. WALT WHITMAN

On the Beach at Night Alone

企鹅经典：小黑书　第三辑

21. 漂亮的卡桑德拉

[英] 简·奥斯汀

22. 温顺的女人

[俄] 陀思妥耶夫斯基

23. 猫与维纳斯

[古希腊] 伊索

24. 黄昏之读

[英] 查尔斯·狄更斯

25. 一个可怕的故事是如何被一条普通的屠夫的狗公之于众的

[德] 约翰·彼得·黑贝尔

26. 亚瑟·萨维尔勋爵的罪行

[英] 奥斯卡·王尔德

27. 伊凡·伊里奇之死

[俄] 列夫·托尔斯泰

28. 我们为何为同一件事哭和笑

[法] 蒙田

29. 我的生命是一杆上实弹的枪

[美] 艾米莉·狄金森

30. 独自在黑夜的海滩上

[美] 沃尔特·惠特曼

猫与维纳斯

The Cat and Venus

［古希腊］伊索　著
杨仲舒　译

中信出版集团 | 北京

图书在版编目（CIP）数据

企鹅经典：小黑书．第三辑：汉、英／（英）简·奥斯汀等著；夏星等译．-- 北京：中信出版社，2019.6

书名原文：Penguin Little Black Classics
ISBN 978-7-5217-0407-5

Ⅰ．①企… Ⅱ．①简… ②夏… Ⅲ．①世界文学－作品综合集－汉、英 Ⅳ．①I11

中国版本图书馆 CIP 数据核字（2019）第 072172 号

企鹅经典：小黑书　第三辑
猫与维纳斯

著　　者：［古希腊］伊索
译　　者：杨仲舒
出版发行：中信出版集团股份有限公司
（北京市朝阳区惠新东街甲 4 号富盛大厦 2 座 邮编 100029）
承 印 者：北京楠萍印刷有限公司

开　　本：787mm × 1092mm　1/32　　印　　张：45.75　　字　　数：756 千字
版　　次：2019 年 6 月第 1 版　　印　　次：2019 年 6 月第 1 次印刷
京权图字：01-2018-6477　　广告经营许可证：京朝工商广字第 8087 号
书　　号：ISBN 978-7-5217-0407-5
定　　价：149.00 元（全 10 册）

服务热线：400-600-8099
投稿邮箱：author@citicpub.com

鹰和寒鸦

一只鹰从高耸的岩石上飞下来，猛扑向一只绵羊，用爪子牢牢地抓住了它。一只寒鸦看到了整个过程，十分嫉妒，决定效仿鹰的力道和飞行方式。

寒鸦高高地飞到空中，飞快地俯冲下来，翅膀扇动得呼呼作响，落在一只大公羊的背上。他想要抓起公羊，可是爪子却缠在了羊毛里。尽管他不停地拍打翅膀，也无济于事。

牧羊人目睹了这一切，他跑过来，捉住了寒鸦，剪掉了他的翅膀，晚上带回家给孩子们。孩子们问:“爸爸，这是什么鸟呀？”他回答道:“据我所知，他是只寒鸦，但他想要人们以为他是只鹰呀。”

猫和公鸡

一只猫捉住了一只公鸡，想着找个好借口美餐一顿。他控诉公鸡晚上打鸣，不让人们睡觉。但公鸡却为自己辩护说，他打鸣也是为人们好，让他们能够及时起床劳作。猫回答道:“尽管你在粉饰你的过错，但我也不能饿肚子呀。”于是，猫杀了公鸡，把他给吃了。

山羊和驴

有个男人曾经养了一只山羊和一头驴。

山羊很嫉妒驴丰盛的伙食，于是他对驴说：“你这样被使唤真是可怜呀：有时你要去磨坊里拉磨，有时你又要驮很多重物。”紧接着，他建议驴假装患了癫痫，掉进一个沟里，这样就能够休息一会儿了。驴听从了山羊的建议，掉到了一个沟里，摔得遍体鳞伤。

驴的主人派人去请兽医，寻求他的意见。兽医吩咐他把山羊的肺敷在驴的伤口上。他们立即杀了山羊，然后医好了驴。

斗鸡和鹰

两只斗鸡正激烈地为农场的统治权而战。一只最终战胜了另一只。

被打败的那只逃走了，躲进了一个安静的角落；而胜利的那只飞上了高墙，扑腾着翅膀，用尽他浑身力气得意地鸣叫。一只鹰在高空飞翔，突然袭击了他，用爪子把他抓走了。

被打败的那只公鸡立即从角落里走了出来，无可争辩地成为农场的统治者。

骄兵必败。

渔夫和渔网

一个贪婪的渔夫，抛出了成功的一网，捕到了一大网鱼。他熟练的拉网技巧使得所有的大鱼都留在了渔网里，他将它们成功拖上了岸。但是他无法阻止小鱼从网眼里滑落，逃回大海。

狐狸和樵夫

一只狐狸在狂奔，后面跟着一群猎犬。他突然遇见了一个正在砍橡树的樵夫，就请求樵夫给他找个安全的藏身之所。樵夫建议狐狸藏在他的小木屋里。于是狐狸钻进去，悄悄地爬到一个角落，藏了起来。

不久之后，猎人赶上了他的猎犬，他向樵夫询问狐狸的踪迹。樵夫声称自己没有见到狐狸，但是在他说话时，他的手一直指着狐狸藏身的木屋。猎人没有留意他的暗示，但是相信了他说的话，于是赶紧向前追去。

等他们一离开，狐狸连声招呼都没打，就走了。樵夫高声地责备狐狸："你这个不知感恩的家伙，你欠我一条命，而你现在呢，一句谢谢都不说就走了。"狐狸回答道："如果你言行一致，如果你的手没有出卖你的言辞，那我的确会好好地感谢你。"

狐狸和山羊

一天，一只狐狸掉进了一口深井里，无论如何也逃不出来了。一只口渴难耐的山羊也路过了这口井，看见了井里的狐狸，便问他井里的水好不好。

狐狸用欢快的幌子掩饰了他悲惨的处境。他对井里的水不吝任何赞美之词，说它好得不能再好了，并请山羊自己下来尝一尝。山羊只想着赶紧解渴，其他想都没想，立刻跳进了井里。当他喝足了之后，狐狸和他说了他们所处的困境，并给出了解决之法。“如果，”狐狸说，“你前腿伸到墙上，头弯下来，我就能跳到你的背上，先逃出去，那之后我再来帮你。”

山羊欣然同意了，狐狸跳上了他的背，踩着山羊的角，安全地到达了井口，随即便以最快的速度跑走了。当山羊责骂他背弃诺言时，他转过身，呼喊道：“你这个愚蠢的老家伙！如果你脑子和你的胡须一样发达的话，你是不会在没想好出路前就跳进这口井的，更不会将自己置于如此险境，无从逃脱。”

三思而后行。

熊和狐狸

一只熊在吹嘘自己博爱。他说，在所有动物中，他对人类最温柔，因为他对人类如此尊重，以至于都不愿去触碰死尸。一只狐狸听见他的话，面露微笑地对熊说道:“哦！所以你宁可吃死尸也不吃活人呗。”

青蛙求王

／

青蛙们因没有一位稳定的国王统治而感到十分不满。于是，他们派了一个使者去见朱庇特[1]，请求他赐给他们一个国王。

鉴于他们的无知，朱庇特向湖里投了一根巨大的木头。青蛙被溅起的水花吓到了，他们飞快地游到了池塘最深处。可是渐渐地，他们发现木头一动不动。于是，他们再次浮出水面。消除恐惧之后便爬了上去，轻蔑地蹲坐在木头上。

过了一段时间，他们认为，被赐予这样一个国王，简直是对他们的侮辱。他们又派了一个使者去见朱庇特，请求他再赐给他们一个统治者。朱庇特让一条鳗鱼去统治他们。当他们发现鳗鱼天性温驯后，第三次派使者去

1. 此中文译本译自英文版，因此文中提及众神均属罗马神话体系，朱庇特对应在希腊神话中，便是众神之王宙斯。（说明：本书脚注均为编者注。）

见朱庇特，恳求他再选一个新国王。

朱庇特被这样纠缠得很生气，便派了一只鹭去统治他们。鹭每日以捕食青蛙为生，渐渐地，湖面上便再也听不到青蛙呱呱的叫声了。

大力神与车夫

一个车夫驾驶着牛车在乡村小路上行驶。突然，车轮深深地陷进了车辙里。这位乡下的车夫一下子呆住了，站在那儿看着牛车，什么都不做，只是大声呼喊大力神来帮他。

大力神出现了，对他说："这位老兄，用你的肩膀把车轮扛起来，并吆喝你的牛。在你尽力自助之前，别祈求别人帮你。否则，今后你的祈祷都是徒劳的。"

天助自助者。

猫与维纳斯

一只猫爱上了一位英俊的小伙子，它恳求维纳斯[1]把它变成女人。维纳斯答应了，立马将它变成了一位美丽的少女。小伙子对少女一见钟情，将她娶回了家。

一天，他们俩在房里依偎着，维纳斯想知道那只猫改变了外形后，是否也改变了本性。于是，她在屋子里放了只老鼠。那只猫忘乎所以，从沙发上站起来，捉住老鼠想要吃掉它。维纳斯十分失望，将她再次变回了原来的样子。

江山易改，本性难移。

1. 身为罗马十二主神之一的维纳斯是代表爱与美的天神，对应希腊神话中的阿佛洛狄忒。

农夫与蛇

一年冬天，一位农夫发现了一条冻僵的蛇。出于同情，他捡起了蛇，把它放进怀里。蛇很快暖和了过来，便露出本来面目，冲着恩人的胸口就咬上致命的一口。“哦，”农夫用最后一口气哭喊道，“怜悯一个恶棍，我真是活该。”

最好的善意不会改变忘恩负义之人。

女人和母鸡

女人有一只母鸡，它每天都会为她下一颗蛋。她经常思索，如果一天想得到两个蛋该怎么做。最后，为了达成她的目的，她决定喂母鸡双份的大麦。从那天起，母鸡就长得又胖又圆，一个蛋也下不了了。

海豚、鲸鱼和小海鱼

海豚和鲸鱼在激烈地交战。当战斗进入高潮时，一只小海鱼从海浪中伸出头来说，如果他们愿意接受他做裁判，他可以来劝和。一只海豚回答道：“我们宁愿战斗至死，也不愿让你干涉我们的纠纷！”

水池里的牡鹿

一只热得受不了的牡鹿到水池边喝水。当他俯下身子，看到自己在水里的倒影时，他对自己犄角的尺寸和多样的形状十分满意。但同时，他又嫌自己的腿太瘦弱、太纤细了。

当他在自我欣赏的时候，一只狮子出现在水池边，盯上了他，并发动攻击。牡鹿立刻跑了起来，并加速到最快。在开阔的空地上，他始终保持着领先优势。但当他来到一片森林时，他的角被树枝挂住了。狮子飞快地赶上并捉住了他。

眼见为时已晚，牡鹿自责道："我好悲哀啊！我是如何骗自己的！我鄙视我的腿，但它们可以挽救我的生命；我赞叹我的角，它们却见证了我的毁灭。"

最有价值的东西往往被低估。

两个死对头

两个互为死敌的男人乘坐同一艘船航行。为了能够离对方足够远，他们一个坐在船尾，一个坐在船头。

一场猛烈的暴风雨来临，船有沉没的危险。在船尾的那个人问领航员，船的哪头会先沉没。领航员回答说船头可能先沉下去。这个人说：“我不会觉得死亡是件悲伤的事情，只要我能看到我的敌人比我先死。”

青蛙怨日

很久很久以前，太阳宣布了自己想要娶个妻子的意图。青蛙们提着嗓门大声朝着天空呱呱叫。朱庇特被噪声弄烦了，便问他们呱呱叫个不停是为什么。他们回答道：“当太阳还单身的时候，就已经要烤干我们的沼泽了，迫使我们悲惨地死在干旱的家中。如果他再生下其他太阳，我们未来该怎么办呀？”

骡子

／

一天早晨，一只骡子玉米棒吃多了，因为无事可做，便开始肆意地奔过来跑过去，还自言自语："我的父亲一定是一匹精力充沛的赛马，我的速度和精气神完全随了他。"

第二天，因为经历了一段长途跋涉，骡子感到十分疲惫，于是用沮丧的腔调说道："我一定搞错了，我的父亲可能终究只是个毛驴罢了。"

战马和磨坊主

一匹战马年老体衰，不再征战四方，而是被送到一家磨坊工作。

不过，当他被迫拉磨而不是在战争中服役时，便哀叹起命运的变化，并联想起自己之前的境遇，他说道："啊！磨坊主，我之前的确四处征战，但我从背到尾巴都披着华服，有专人喂我。我现在想不通是什么促使我放弃服役，选择来磨坊的。"

"忍忍吧，"磨坊主对他说，"你一味地对过去喋喋不休，但命运总是起起伏伏的呀。"

骆驼

／

当一个人第一次看到骆驼时，他被骆驼庞大的体型吓得跑开了。

过了一段时间，这个人察觉到骆驼的温驯，便鼓起勇气走近他。

不久之后，这个人观察到骆驼完全没脾气时，便大胆地用缰绳套住了他的嘴，让一个小孩去驱赶他。

核桃树

一棵长在路边的核桃树结出了许多核桃。为了得到核桃，路过的人们用木棍或石头击打它的枝干。核桃树哀怨道:“哦！可怜的我！我用果实取悦那些人，他们却用疼痛来回报我！”

小虫子和公牛

一只小虫子飞落在公牛的一只角上，在那儿待了很长时间。当他准备飞走的时候，弄出了嗡嗡的响动，想以此来问询公牛是否介意他离开。公牛回应道：“你来的时候，我都没注意到；你走的时候，我自然也不会留恋你。”

有些人总是把自己看得比在旁人眼中重要得多。

捉蝗虫的男孩

一个男孩在捉蝗虫。他捉了好多。这时男孩看到一只蝎子，误以为他是蝗虫，伸手想要捉他。蝎子露出了他的刺，说道:“如果你摸了我的话，我的朋友，你不仅会失去我，你也会失去你所有的蝗虫。”

粗心大意，后果严重。

跳蚤和男人

一个男人被一只跳蚤惹烦了，最终捉到了他。男人说道:“你怎么如此大胆，不但敢咬我，还让我费了这么大劲才捉住你?”

跳蚤回答道:“哦，我亲爱的先生，求求你放我走吧，别杀我，我不可能对你造成很大伤害的。”

这个男人笑着回答道:“我现在就要亲手杀了你。因为邪恶是不应被容忍的，无论这邪恶是大是小。”

被狗咬的男人

一个男人被狗咬了之后，想要寻找一个可以医治他的人。一位朋友见了他，弄清楚他的需求后说:“如果你想要伤口愈合，请拿一小片面包，用它蘸你伤口流出的血液，然后把它给咬你的那条狗。”

被狗咬的男人边嘲笑他的建议边说道:“为什么？如果我这样做的话，那我就好像在求全镇的狗都来咬我似的。”

对行恶者施与恩惠只会使他们加倍地伤害你。

恶狗

有一条狗总是悄无声息地走到每个遇到的人脚边，趁其不备张嘴就咬。于是，他的主人便在他的脖子上系了一个铃铛，以便在他出现的时候，给大家提个醒。狗将这个铃铛视为自己与众不同的标记，对此感到特别骄傲，十分得意地在市场里招摇。

一天，一条老猎狗对他说："你为什么要如此炫耀自己？相信我，你戴着的那个铃铛不是勋章，恰恰相反，它是耻辱的象征呀。它提醒所有人你是一条恶狗，要避开你。"

恶名常被误认为是美誉。

狼和小羊

一只狼遇见了一只从羊群中走失的小羊，他决定不急着下毒手，而是想找个证明他有权利吃小羊的借口。他对小羊说：“先生，去年你狠狠地侮辱了我。”

“事实上，”小羊用悲哀的语调咩咩叫道，“我那时还没出生。”

狼又说道：“那你在我的牧场上吃过草。”

“不，好先生，”小羊回答道，“我还从未吃过草呢。”

狼再次说道：“你喝了我的井水。”

“不，”小羊呼喊道，“我从未喝过水，因为我妈妈的奶对我来说，既是饭也是水。”

狼捉住了他，把他给吃了，说道：“好吧！我是不会饿着肚子的，即使你推翻了我的每一种推论。”

暴君总会为他的暴政找借口。

小羊和狼

一只狼在追赶着一只小羊。小羊在一座庙里避难。狼要求小羊从里面出来，并说道:“如果你不出来的话，牧师就会捉住你，把你供奉在祭坛上。”小羊如是说:“谢谢，我想我就待在这儿了，我宁愿被拿去祭祀，也不要被你吃掉。”

因此，一些在学校里似乎有点才能的演说家，一旦进入政治舞台便暴露出了他们的无能。

城里鼠和乡下鼠

一天，乡下鼠邀请他的密友城里鼠来乡下做客并享用乡村野味。

当他们坐在裸露的耕地上，享用小麦和从篱笆上拔出的根茎拼凑出的晚餐时，城里鼠对他的朋友说："你过着蝼蚁一般的生活呀，而在我的屋子里，食物应有尽有。我的四周都是美食，如果你跟我来的话，我也希望你能跟我来，我一定会让你美餐一顿的。"乡下鼠很轻易地就被说服了，和他的朋友一起去了城里。

他刚到，城里鼠就为他拿出了面包、大麦、豆子、无花果干、蜂蜜、葡萄干，最后还从篮子里拿了一块美味的奶酪。看到这么丰盛的食物，乡下鼠热忱地表达了他的谢意，还哀叹了自己悲惨的命运。

当他们正准备开始吃时，有人打开了门，他们飞快地吱吱叫着跑进了一个小洞里，那个洞小得只够他们两个在里面挤成一团。当他们心惊胆战地准备再次用餐时，另一个人走进来从碗橱里拿了些东西。这两只老鼠比之前更加惊慌失措，赶紧躲起来了。

最后，乡下鼠饥饿难耐，他对他的朋友说：“尽管你为我准备了这么丰盛的一餐，你还是自己享用吧。取悦我要面临太多危险了。我更喜欢裸露的耕地和篱笆上的根茎，在那儿我可以安全地、不用担惊受怕地活着。”

墨丘利[1]和工人

一位工人在河边砍树，他的斧头不小心掉进了一个很深的水塘里。他因为没了谋生的手段，坐在河边，哀叹起了自己悲惨的命运。

墨丘利出现了，询问工人哭泣的缘由。在他听了工人不幸的经历后，跳入水中，捞出了一把金斧头，并问工人这是不是他丢的斧头。工人否认了，墨丘利再次潜入水中，捞出了一把银斧头，再次询问他。工人否认了，墨丘利又一次潜入河底，捞出了他丢的那把斧头。工人对斧头失而复得感到十分高兴。墨丘利很高兴他这么诚实，就把金斧头和银斧头也送给了他。

工人回到家后，把他的经历告诉了同伴。其中一个人决定自己也去碰碰运气。他跑到河边，故意在同一个

1. 墨丘利为罗马神话中众神的使者，负责众神间的交流与沟通，罗马十二主神之一，对应希腊神话中的赫尔墨斯。

地方把斧头扔进河里，并坐在河边抽泣。

墨丘利如他所料地出现了。当墨丘利弄清楚他悲伤的原因后，跳进水中，捞起了一把金斧头，问他是不是他丢的那把。工人贪婪地夺过斧头，并声称这正是他丢的那把。墨丘利对他的无赖行径十分反感，不仅拿走了这把金斧头，还拒绝为他寻回原来丢掉的那把斧头。

驴和宠物狗

曾经有个人养了一头驴和一只十分美丽的马耳他狗。

驴住在马厩里，有充足的燕麦和干草享用，过着跟别的驴一样的日子。小狗会耍许多花招，很讨主人喜欢。主人经常爱抚他，每次赴宴归来都会给他带点儿好吃的。相反，驴有许多工作要做，比如磨谷物啦，从森林里运木头啦，或是驮农场上的重物。

他经常哀叹命运的悲惨，并将自己的命运和小狗轻松懒散的生活相对比。直到有一天，他挣脱了缰绳，飞快地跑进了主人的屋子，无拘无束地尥着蹄子，尽他所能地蹦跳着献殷勤。当他看到小狗跳到主人的膝上时，他也想这么做，结果打翻了桌子，摔碎了碗碟。接着，他想要舔主人并跳到他的背上。仆人听到这异常的喧哗，察觉到主人身处险境，飞快地跑去救他，并连踢带打地将驴赶回了马厩。

驴回到马厩时已经被打得半死不活了，他悔恨道：“这都是我自找的！我为什么不能满足于和同伴一起劳作，而非要想着像那只无用的小狗一样整天无所事事呢？”

披着狮皮的驴

一头驴穿上了狮皮，在森林里巡游，以吓唬那些愚蠢的动物为乐。后来，驴遇见了狐狸，也想要吓吓他。但是狐狸一听到他的声音就大声说道：“如果我没听见你的驴叫，或许会真的害怕呢！”

母鸡和燕子

一只母鸡发现了一窝蛇蛋，小心翼翼地为它们保温，精心地将它们孵化了出来。一只燕子发现了她的所作所为，对她说:“你这个蠢东西！你为什么要孵这些蛇呀？当他们长大之后，会危害所有生物，就从你开始！”

鹧鸪和捕鸟人

一位捕鸟人捉住了一只鹧鸪，正要杀了他。鹧鸪恳切地求捕鸟人放了他，并说道："祈求上帝，大人，放我一条生路吧，我会骗更多的鹧鸪飞到您的网里，作为对您的报答。"

捕鸟人回答道："杀你这事儿，我现在更是没什么可犹豫的了。你居然想靠出卖朋友和亲人来换自己的命！"

猴子和骆驼

猴子站起身，跳起了舞，逗得森林里的动物们哈哈大笑。博得大家的欢心后，他在经久不息的掌声中坐了下来。

骆驼对猴子获得的赞赏感到十分嫉妒，也想要以同样的方式得到来宾们的喜爱。轮到他时，他决定也站起身，跳舞为大家助兴。他走动的方式非常滑稽，以至于所有动物一怒之下棍棒交加地把他赶出了集会。

模仿比我们更胜一筹的人总是荒谬可笑的。

鼹鼠和妈妈

鼹鼠是一种生下来就没有视力的动物。有一次，他对妈妈说："我确信我能看见，妈妈！"

为了证明他是错的，他的妈妈在他面前摆放了一些乳香，并问他："这是什么？"

小鼹鼠说道："这是卵石。"

他的妈妈惊呼道："我的儿子，恐怕你不仅看不见，鼻子也不灵了吧。"

墨丘利和被蚂蚁咬的人

一个人曾经目睹了一艘船和它上面全体船员沉没的场景。他严厉地斥责着众神的不公。

“他们根本不关心一个人的品性，”他说道，“只会让好人和坏人一起赴死。”

他站立的地方附近有一个蚁丘，在他说话时，一只蚂蚁咬了他的脚。他把脾气发在了蚁丘上，一脚踩上了蚁丘，数百只无辜的蚂蚁命丧黄泉。

突然，墨丘利出现了，他用他的手杖痛打这个人，并说道：“你这个恶棍，现在你那伟大的正义感哪去了呢？”

骗子

一个人生病了，病入膏肓。他发誓，如果众神能够让他重获健康，他一定会为他们献上一百头牛。众神想知道他会如何履行诺言，就立即让他痊愈了。

现在，他一头牛都没有，于是他用牛油做了一百头小牛，并把它们供奉在祭坛上。他说道：“众神啊，我请你们见证，我信守了我的诺言。”

众神决定报复他一下，于是他们给他托了个梦。在梦中，他被吩咐去海边，去拿回他在那儿发现的一百克朗。醒来之后，他兴奋地跑到海边，却落入了一群强盗手中。他们捉住了他并把他卖为奴隶：卖得的钱刚好是他想要找的一百克朗。

别许下那些自己做不到的承诺。

男人和狮子

一个人和一只狮子结伴旅行。在谈话的过程中，他们开始吹嘘自己勇猛无敌，并声称自己无论在力量还是勇气方面都胜过对方。他们正在热烈地争论时，刚巧途经一个十字路口，这里摆放着一个人勒着狮子的雕塑。

“那儿！”人耀武扬威地说道，“看那个！这不正证明了我比你强吗？”

“别这么快地下结论，我的朋友，”狮子说，“这只是你看这个问题的角度。如果我们狮子也能够制作雕塑的话，你应该会看到大多数雕塑都是人在下面。”

每个问题都有两个角度。

蛇与朱庇特

一条蛇时不时地就会被人和野兽踩到，遭了不少的罪。一方面由于他身体太长，另一方面由于他不能够离开地面站立起来。于是，他向朱庇特抱怨他所要面临的风险。但是朱庇特一点儿都不同情他。“我敢说，”朱庇特说，“如果你第一次被踩时，就咬他的话，其他人就会费点劲儿，看看该把脚放在哪儿了。”

屋顶上的小孩

一个小孩被长在茅草屋顶上的小草和其他东西所吸引，爬上了外屋的屋顶。当他站在那儿四处眺望时，他发现一只狼从下面经过。小孩嘲笑那只狼捉不到自己。狼只是抬头看了看他，然后说道：“我听到你了，我年轻的朋友；但是嘲笑我的并不是你，而是你脚下的屋顶呀。”

蝙蝠、荆棘和海鸥

/

蝙蝠、荆棘和海鸥决定结伴一起出海贸易。蝙蝠为他的冒险活动借了一大笔钱；荆棘储存了各种各样的服饰；海鸥带了一些铅。就这样，他们出发上路了。

没过多久，一阵猛烈的暴风雨突然来袭。他们的船和所有货物都沉入海底。但这三个旅行者都设法回到了陆地上。从那时起，海鸥就在海面上来来回回地飞，不时地把头扎进海里，找寻他丢失的铅。而蝙蝠害怕见到他的债主，于是就在白天躲藏起来，晚上才出来觅食。荆棘则钩住每个过路人的衣服，梦想着有一天能够找回他丢失的服装。

所有人都更关心找回他们丢失的东西，而不是得到他们缺少的东西。

驴和货物

一个小贩有头驴。有一天他买了一些盐，并且尽可能多地装在了驴背上。在回家的路上，驴在渡过一条小溪时，蹄子滑了一下，跌入了水中。

盐全都湿透了，许多都溶解流走了。因此，当驴站起来时，他发现身上的负担轻了许多。他的主人赶着他回了集市，买了更多的盐放进了他的驮篮里。他们再一次出发了。

当他们刚到小溪时，驴立马跌坐在水里，然后像之前一样站起来，身上的负担又轻了许多。他的主人识破了他的诡计，又一次地回到集市，买了许多海绵，把它们堆在了驴背上。

当他们来到小溪时，驴故技重施，但是这一次，海绵吸了大量的水。当他站起来时，发现身上的负担变得前所未有地重。

好牌不能频繁地打。

驴、公鸡和狮子

驴和公鸡一起待在牛栏里。这时，一只几天没吃饭的狮子出现了，正准备攻击驴并吃掉他时，公鸡跳了起来，用力地扑棱着翅膀，发出惊人的鸣叫。

这种情境下，要是有什么还能吓到一只狮子的话，那也就是公鸡的鸣叫了：狮子刚一听见公鸡的叫声，就飞快地逃走了。

驴看到这个场景十分高兴，他想着，如果狮子连公鸡都怕的话，那么他肯定也不可能打得过驴。于是驴跑出去追赶狮子。但是当他们到达公鸡看不到也听不到的地方时，狮子径直扑向驴，把他给吃了。

盲目自信通常导致灾难。

狗和狼

一条狗躺在农场门前的阳光下。这时，一只狼突袭了他，正要吃掉他。但他乞求狼饶他一命，并说道："你看我多瘦呀，现在的我只能给你塞塞牙缝。但是你再等几天的话，我的主人将要摆宴席。那时，所有丰盛的残羹剩饭都会落入我的腹中，我将变得又胖又美味，那才是你该吃我的时候。"

狼觉得这个主意不错，便走开了。不久之后，他又来到了农场，发现狗躺在马厩的屋顶上。"你下来，"他喊道，"该我吃你了，你记得我们的约定吗？"

但是狗冷酷地说："我的朋友，如果你再看见我躺在门口的话，可别再等什么盛宴了。"

一回上当两回乖。

年迈的狮子

一只狮子，随着年龄的增长变得衰弱无力。他不再能够凭借武力获得食物，便决定用诡计给自己弄点食物。他走到山洞里，躺在那儿，假装病了。每当有动物进去询问他的身体状况时，他就一跃而起，把他们吞入腹中。

许多动物都以这种方式丧了命。直到有一天，一只狐狸来到这个山洞。因为怀疑狮子是不是真的病了，所以他并没有走进去，而是站在山洞外，问狮子感觉怎么样。狮子回答说，他感觉很不好。“但是，”他说，“你为什么站在外面呢？请进来吧。”

“我本该这么做，”狐狸回答说，“如果我没注意到这些脚印只有进没有出的话。”

预言家

一位预言家坐在集市里，给那些想要一探究竟的人算命。

突然来了一个人告诉他，他家里遭贼了。他们把所有能找到的东西都抢走了。预言家立即跳起来，冲了出去，扯着自己的头发，诅咒那些恶棍。

路人们都被逗笑了，其中一个人说道：“我们的朋友自称能够预测他人的命运，但他似乎还没聪明到能预测自己的未来呀。”

妻子和醉酒的丈夫

一个女人一直忍受着她酗酒的丈夫带来的屈辱。有一次，当她丈夫喝得烂醉时，她把他送进了存尸房。当她估摸着丈夫应该是时候恢复知觉时，她走开了，然后又回来敲门。

“谁在那儿？”酒徒说。

“一个给死人送肉的人。”女人说。

“朋友，”他说，“还是给我来点酒吧。我想任何认识我的人给我别的东西时，也不会忘了给我酒。”

“好吧，”她说，“这种我所察觉到的情绪已经完全控制了他，成了他的恶习，他已经没救了。”

养成的恶习会成为我们的天性，就好像我们被撕成碎片，然后重新被拼接在一起，仿若被修补过一样。

音乐家

一位嗓音嘶哑的人，有着一间很棒的音乐室。他在那个小房间里练声，回音使他觉得自己的声音很美。他十分骄傲，并想着要在剧院展示一番。但他唱得实在太糟糕了，人们将他轰下了舞台，还朝他扔石头。

一个人可能会很喜欢自己镜中的样子，但公共场合中的世人却无法爱上他。事实上，我们对自己情况的了解很片面，除了从别人的眼中解读自己之外，我们没有其他方式。

PENGUIN

LITTLE BLACK

CLASSICS

企鹅经典：小黑书 第三辑

21. 漂亮的卡桑德拉

[英] 简·奥斯汀

22. 温顺的女人

[俄] 陀思妥耶夫斯基

23. 猫与维纳斯

[古希腊] 伊索

24. 黄昏之读

[英] 查尔斯·狄更斯

25. 一个可怕的故事是如何被一条普通的屠夫的狗公之于众的

[德] 约翰·彼得·黑贝尔

26. 亚瑟·萨维尔勋爵的罪行

[英] 奥斯卡·王尔德

27. 伊凡·伊里奇之死

[俄] 列夫·托尔斯泰

28. 我们为何为同一件事哭和笑

[法] 蒙田

29. 我的生命是一杆上实弹的枪

[美] 艾米莉·狄金森

30. 独自在黑夜的海滩上

[美] 沃尔特·惠特曼

Penguin Little Black Classics Vol. III

21. JANE AUSTEN
The Beautifull Cassandra

22. FYODOR DOSTOYEVSKY
The Meek One

23. AESOP
The Cat and Venus

24. CHARLES DICKENS
To Be Read at Dusk

25. JOHANN PETER HEBEL
How a Ghastly Story Was Brought to Light by a Common or Garden Butcher's Dog

26. OSCAR WILDE
Lord Arthur Savile's Crime

27. LEO TOLSTOY
The Death of Ivan Ilyich

28. MICHEL DE MONTAIGNE
How We Weep and Laugh at the Same Thing

29. EMILY DICKINSON
My life had stood a loaded gun

30. WALT WHITMAN
On the Beach at Night Alone

‘ . . . Until you
have done your
best to help
yourself, or
depend upon it
you will
henceforth pray
in vain.’

AESOP

The Cat and Venus

The Eagle and the Jackdaw

An Eagle, flying down from his perch on a lofty rock, seized upon a lamb and carried him aloft in his talons. A Jackdaw, who witnessed the capture of the lamb, was stirred with envy and determined to emulate the strength and flight of the Eagle.

He flew around with a great whir of his wings and settled upon a large ram, with the intention of carrying him off, but his claws became entangled in the ram's fleece and he was not able to release himself, although he fluttered with his feathers as much as he could.

The shepherd, seeing what had happened, ran up and caught him. He at once clipped the Jackdaw's wings, and taking him home at night, gave him to his children. On their saying, 'Father, what kind of bird is it?' he replied, 'To my certain knowledge he is a Daw; but he would like you to think an Eagle.'

The Cat and the Cock

A Cat caught a Cock, and pondered how he might find a reasonable excuse for eating him. He accused him of being nuisance to men by crowing in the night time and not permitting them to sleep. The Cock defended himself by saying that he did this for the benefit of men that they might rise in time for their labours. The Cat replied, 'Although you abound in specious apologies, I shall not remain supperless'; and he made a meal of him.

The Goat and the Ass

A man once kept a Goat and an Ass.

'The Goat, envying the Ass on account of his greater abundance of food, said, 'How shamefully you are treated: at one time grinding in the mill, and at another carrying heavy burdens'; and he further advised him to pretend to be epileptic and fall into a ditch and so obtain rest. The Ass listened to his words, and falling into a ditch, was very much bruised.'

His master, sending for a leech, asked his advice. He bade him pour upon the wounds the lungs of a Goat. They at once killed the Goat, and so healed the Ass.

The Fighting Cocks and the Eagle

Two game Cocks were fiercely fighting for the mastery of the farmyard. One at last put the other to flight.

The vanquished Cock skulked away and hid himself in a quiet corner, while the conqueror, flying up to a high wall, flapped his wings and crowed exultingly with all his might. An Eagle sailing through the air pounced upon him and carried him off in his talons

The vanquished Cock immediately came out of his corner, and ruled henceforth with undisputed mastery.

Pride goes before destruction.

The Fisherman and His Nets

A Fisherman, engaged in his calling, made a very successful cast and captured a great haul of fish. He managed by a skilful handling of his net to retain all the large fish and to draw them to the shore; but he could not prevent the smaller fish from falling back through the meshes of the net into the sea.

The Fox and the Woodcutter

A Fox, running before the hounds, came across a Woodcutter felling an oak and begged him to show him a safe hiding-place. The Woodcutter advised him to take shelter in his own hut, so the Fox crept in and hid himself in a corner.

The huntsman soon came up with his hounds and inquired of the Woodcutter if he had seen the Fox. He declared that he had not seen him, and yet pointed, all the time he was speaking, to the hut where the Fox lay hidden. The huntsman took no notice of the signs, but believing his word, hastened forward in the chase.

As soon as they were well away, the Fox departed without taking any notice of the Woodcutter: whereon he called to him and reproached him, saying, 'You ungrateful fellow, you owe your life to me, and yet you leave me without a word of thanks.' The Fox replied, 'Indeed, I should have thanked you fervently if your deeds had been as good as your words, and if your hands had not been traitors to your speech.'

The Fox and the Goat

A Fox one day fell into a deep well and could find no means of escape. A Goat, overcome with thirst, came to the same well, and seeing the Fox, inquired if the water was good.

Concealing his sad plight under a merry guise, the Fox indulged in a lavish praise of the water, saying it was excellent beyond measure, and encouraging him to descend. The Goat, mindful only of his thirst, thoughtlessly jumped down, but just as he drank, the Fox informed him of the difficulty they were both in and suggested a scheme for their common escape. 'If,' said he, 'you will place your forefeet upon the wall and bend your head, I will run up your back and escape, and will help you out afterwards.'

The Goat readily assented and the Fox leapt upon his back. Steadying himself with the Goat's horns, he safely reached the mouth of the well and made off as fast as he could. When the Goat upbraided him for breaking his promise, he turned around and cried out, 'You foolish old fellow! If you had as many brains in your head as you have hairs in your beard, you would never have gone down before you had inspected the way up, nor have exposed yourself to dangers from which you had no means of escape.'

Look before you leap.

The Bear and the Fox

A Bear boasted very much of his philanthropy, saying that of all animals he was the most tender in his regard for man, for he had such respect for him that he would not even touch his dead body. A Fox hearing these words said with a smile to the Bear, 'Oh! That you would eat the dead and not the living.'

The Frogs Asking for a King

The Frogs, grieved at having no established Ruler, sent ambassadors to Jupiter entreating for a King.

Perceiving their simplicity, he cast down a huge log into the lake. The Frogs were terrified at the splash occasioned by its fall and hid themselves in the depths of the pool. But as soon as they realised that the huge log was motionless, they swam again to the top of the water, dismissed their fears, climbed up, and began squatting on it in contempt.

After some time they began to think themselves ill-treated in the appointment of so inert a Ruler, and sent a second deputation to Jupiter to pray that he would set over them another sovereign. He then gave them an Eel to govern them. When the Frogs discovered his easy good nature, they sent yet a third time to Jupiter to beg him to choose for them still another King.

Jupiter, displeased with all their complaints, sent a Heron, who preyed upon the Frogs day by day till there were none left to croak upon the lake.

Hercules and the Wagoner

A Carter was driving a wagon along a country lane, when the wheels sank down deep into a rut. The rustic driver, stupefied and aghast, stood looking at the wagon, and did nothing but utter loud cries to Hercules to come and help him.

Hercules, it is said, appeared and thus addressed him: 'Put your shoulders to the wheels, my man. Goad on your bullocks, and never more pray to me for help, until you have done your best to help yourself, or depend upon it you will henceforth pray in vain.'

Self-help is the best help.

The Cat and Venus

A Cat fell in love with a handsome young man, and entreated Venus to change her into the form of a woman. Venus consented to her request and transformed her into a beautiful damsel, so that the youth saw her and loved her, and took her home as his bride.

While the two were reclining in their chamber, Venus wishing to discover if the Cat in her change of shape had also altered her habits of life, let down a mouse in the middle of the room. The Cat, quite forgetting her present condition, started up from the couch and pursued the mouse, wishing to eat it. Venus was much disappointed and again caused her to return to her former shape.

Nature exceeds nurture.

The Farmer and the Snake

One winter a Farmer found a Snake stiff and frozen with cold. He had compassion on it, and taking it up, placed it in his bosom. The Snake was quickly revived by the warmth, and resuming its natural instincts, bit its benefactor, inflicting on him a mortal wound. 'Oh,' cried the Farmer with his last breath, 'I am rightly served for pitying a scoundrel.'

The greatest kindness will not bind the ungrateful.

The Woman and Her Hen

A Woman possessed a Hen that gave her an egg every day. She often pondered how she might obtain two eggs daily instead of one, and at last, to gain her purpose, determined to give the Hen a double allowance of barley. From that day the Hen became fat and sleek, and never once laid another egg.

The Dolphins, the Whales, and the Sprat

The Dolphins and Whales waged a fierce war with each other. When the battle was at its height, a Sprat lifted its head out of the waves and said that he would reconcile their differences if they would accept him as an umpire. One of the Dolphins replied, 'We would far rather be destroyed in our battle with each other than admit any interference from you in our affairs.'

The Stag at the Pool

A Stag overpowered by heat came to a spring to drink. Seeing his own shadow reflected in the water, he greatly admired the size and variety of his horns, but felt angry with himself for having such slender and weak feet.

While he was thus contemplating himself, a Lion appeared at the pool and crouched to spring upon him. The Stag immediately took to flight, and exerting his utmost speed, as long as the plain was smooth and open kept himself easily at a safe distance from the Lion. But entering a wood he became entangled by his horns, and the Lion quickly came up to him and caught him.

When too late, he thus reproached himself: 'Woe is me! How I have deceived myself! These feet which would have saved me I despised, and I gloried in these antlers which have proved my destruction.'

What is most truly valuable is often underrated.

The Two Men Who Were Enemies

Two Men, deadly enemies to each other, were sailing in the same vessel. Determined to keep as far apart as possible, the one seated himself in the stem, and the other in the prow of the ship.

A violent storm arose, and with the vessel in great danger of sinking, the one in the stern inquired of the pilot which of the two ends of the ship would go down first. On his replying that he supposed it would be the prow, the Man said, 'Death would not be grievous to me, if I could only see my Enemy die before me.'

The Frogs' Complaint Against the Sun

Once upon a time, when the Sun announced his intention to take a wife, the Frogs lifted up their voices in clamor to the sky. Jupiter, disturbed by the noise of their croaking, inquired the cause of their complaint. One of them said, 'The Sun, now while he is single, parches up the marsh, and compels us to die miserably in our arid homes. What will be our future condition if he should beget other suns?'

The Mule

A Mule, frolicsome from lack of work and from too much corn, galloped about in a very extravagant manner, and said to himself: 'My father surely was a high-mettled racer, and I am his own child in speed and spirit.'

On the next day, being driven a long journey, and feeling very wearied, he exclaimed in a disconsolate tone: 'I must have made a mistake; my father, after all, could have been only an ass.'

The Charger and the Miller

A Charger, feeling the infirmities of age, was sent to work in a mill instead of going out to battle.

But when he was compelled to grind instead of serving in the wars, he bewailed his change of fortune and called to mind his former state, saying, 'Ah! Miller, I had indeed to go campaigning before, but I was barbed from counter to tail, and a man went along to groom me; and now I cannot understand what ailed me to prefer the mill before the battle.'

'Forbear,' said the Miller to him, 'harping on what was of yore, for it is the common fate of mortals to question the ups and downs of fortune.'

The Camel

When man first saw the Camel, he was so frightened at his vast size that he ran away.

After a time, perceiving the meekness and gentleness of the beast's temper, he summoned courage enough to approach him.

Soon afterwards, observing that he was an animal altogether deficient in spirit, he assumed such boldness as to put a bridle in his mouth, and to let a child drive him.

The Walnut Tree

A Walnut Tree standing by the roadside bore an abundant crop of fruit. For the sake of the nuts, the passers-by broke its branches with stones and sticks. The Walnut-Tree piteously exclaimed, 'O wretched me! That those whom I cheer with my fruit should repay me with these painful requitals!'

The Gnat and the Bull

A Gnat settled on the horn of a Bull, and sat there a long time. Just as he was about to fly off, he made a buzzing noise, and inquired of the Bull if he would like him to go. The Bull replied, 'I did not know you had come, and I shall not miss you when you go away.'

Some men are of more consequence in their own eyes than in the eyes of their neighbours.

The Boy Hunting Locusts

A Boy was hunting for locusts. He had caught a goodly number, when he saw a Scorpion, and mistaking him for a locust, reached out his hand to take him. The Scorpion, showing his sting, said: 'If you had but touched me, my friend, you would have lost me, and all your locusts too!'

Carelessness has consequences.

The Flea and the Man

A Man, very much annoyed with a Flea, caught him at last, and said, 'Who are you who dare to feed on my limbs, and to cost me so much trouble in catching you?'

The Flea replied, 'O my dear sir, pray spare my life, and destroy me not, for I cannot possibly do you much harm.'

The Man, laughing, replied, 'Now you shall certainly die by mine own hands, for no evil, whether it be small or large, ought to be tolerated.'

The Man Bitten by a Dog

A Man who had been bitten by a Dog went about in quest of someone who might heal him. A friend, meeting him and learning what he wanted, said, 'If you would be cured, take a piece of bread, and dip it in the blood from your wound, and go and give it to the Dog that bit you.'

The Man who had been bitten laughed at this advice and said, 'Why? If I should do so, it would be as if I should beg every Dog in the town to bite me.'

Benefits bestowed upon the evil-disposed increase their means of injuring you.

The Mischievous Dog

A Dog used to run up quietly to the heels of everyone he met, and to bite them without notice. His master suspended a bell about his neck so that the Dog might give notice of his presence wherever he went. Thinking it a mark of distinction, the Dog grew proud of his bell and went tinkling it all over the marketplace.

One day an old hound said to him: 'Why do you make such an exhibition of yourself? That bell that you carry is not, believe me, any order of merit, but on the contrary a mark of disgrace, a public notice to all men to avoid you as an ill-mannered dog.'

Notoriety is often mistaken for fame.

The Wolf and the Lamb

Wolf, meeting with a Lamb astray from the fold, resolved not to lay violent hands on him, but to find some plea to justify to the Lamb the Wolf's right to eat him. He thus addressed him: 'Sir, last year you grossly insulted me.'

'Indeed,' bleated the Lamb in a mournful tone of voice, 'I was not then born.'

Then said the Wolf, 'You feed in my pasture.'

'No, good sir,' replied the Lamb, 'I have not yet tasted grass.'

Again said the Wolf, 'You drink of my well.'

'No,' exclaimed the Lamb, 'I never yet drank water, for as yet my mother's milk is both food and drink to me.'

Upon which the Wolf seized him and ate him up, saying, 'Well! I won't remain supperless, even though you refute every one of my imputations.'

The tyrant will always find a pretext for his tyranny.

The Lamb and the Wolf

A Wolf pursued a Lamb, which fled for refuge to a certain Temple. The Wolf called out to him and said, 'The Priest will slay you in sacrifice, if he should catch you.' On which the Lamb replied, 'It would be better for me to be sacrificed in the Temple than to be eaten by you.'

Thus, certain orators who, at school, seem to have some talent, reveal their incompetence as soon as they enter the political arena.

The Town Mouse and the Country Mouse

A Country Mouse invited a Town Mouse, an intimate friend, to pay him a visit and partake of his country fare.

As they were on the bare plowlands, eating their wheat-stocks and roots pulled up from the hedgerow, the Town Mouse said to his friend, 'You live here the life of the ants, while in my house is the horn of plenty. I am surrounded by every luxury, and if you will come with me, as I wish you would, you shall have an ample share of my dainties.' The Country Mouse was easily persuaded, and returned to town with his friend.

On his arrival, the Town Mouse placed before him bread, barley, beans, dried figs, honey, raisins, and, last of all, brought a dainty piece of cheese from a basket. The Country Mouse, being much delighted at the sight of such good cheer, expressed his satisfaction in warm terms and lamented his own hard fate.

Just as they were beginning to eat, someone opened the door, and they both ran off squeaking, as fast as they could, to a hole so narrow that two could only find room in it by squeezing. They had scarcely begun their repast again when someone else entered to take something out of a cupboard, whereupon the two Mice, more frightened than before, ran away and hid themselves.

At last the Country Mouse, almost famished, said to his friend: 'Although you have prepared for me so dainty a feast,

I must leave you to enjoy it by yourself. It is surrounded by too many dangers to please me. I prefer my bare plowlands and roots from the hedgerow, where I can live in safety, and without fear.'

Mercury and the Workmen

A Workman, felling wood by the side of a river, let his axe drop – by accident into a deep pool. Being thus deprived of the means of his livelihood, he sat down on the bank and lamented his hard fate.

Mercury appeared and demanded the cause of his tears. After he told him his misfortune, Mercury plunged into the stream, and, bringing up a golden axe, inquired if that were the one he had lost. On his saying that it was not his, Mercury disappeared beneath the water a second time, returned with a silver axe in his hand, and again asked the Workman if it were his. When the Workman said it was not, he dived into the pool for the third time and brought up the axe that had been lost. The Workman claimed it and expressed his joy at its recovery. Mercury, pleased with his honesty, gave him the gold and silver axes in addition to his own.

The Workman, on his return to his house, related to his companions all that had happened. One of them at once resolved to try and secure the same good fortune for himself. He ran to the river and threw his axe on purpose into the pool at the same place, and sat down on the bank to weep.

Mercury appeared to him just as he hoped he would; and having learned the cause of his grief, plunged into the stream and brought up a golden axe, inquiring if he had lost it. The Workman seized it greedily, and declared that truly it was the very same axe that he had lost. Mercury, displeased at his knavery, not only took away the golden axe, but refused to recover for him the axe he had thrown into the pool.

The Ass and the Lapdog

A man had an Ass, and a Maltese Lapdog, a very great beauty.

The Ass was left in a stable and had plenty of oats and hay to eat, just as any other Ass would. The Lapdog knew many tricks and was a great favourite with his master, who often fondled him and seldom went out to dine without bringing him home some tidbit to eat. The Ass, on the contrary, had much work to do in grinding the corn-mill and in carrying wood from the forest or burdens from the farm.

He often lamented his own hard fate and contrasted it with the luxury and idleness of the Lapdog, till at last one day he broke his cords and halter, and galloped into his master's house, kicking up his heels without measure, and frisking and fawning as well as he could. He next tried to jump about his master as he had seen the Lapdog do, but he broke the table and smashed all the dishes upon it to atoms. He then attempted to lick his master, and jumped upon his back. The servants, hearing the strange hubbub and perceiving the danger of their master, quickly relieved him, and drove out the Ass to his stable with kicks and clubs and cuffs.

The Ass, as he returned to his stall beaten nearly to death, thus lamented: 'I have brought it all on myself! Why could I not have been contented to labour with my companions, and not wish to be idle all the day like that useless little Lapdog!'

The Ass in the Lion's Skin

An Ass, having put on the Lion's skin, roamed about in the forest and amused himself by frightening all the foolish animals he met in his wanderings. At last coming upon a Fox, he tried to frighten him also, but the Fox no sooner heard the sound of his voice than he exclaimed, 'I might possibly have been frightened myself, if I had not heard your bray.'

The Hen and the Swallow

A Hen finding the eggs of a viper and carefully keeping them warm, nourished them into life. A Swallow, observing what she had done, said, 'You silly creature! why have you hatched these vipers which, when they shall have grown, will inflict injury on all, beginning with yourself!'

The Partridge and the Fowler

A Fowler caught a Partridge and was about to kill it. The Partridge earnestly begged him to spare his life, saying, 'Pray, master, permit me to live and I will entice many Partridges to you in recompense for your mercy to me.'

The Fowler replied, 'I shall now with less scruple take your life, because you are willing to save it at the cost of betraying your friends and relations.'

The Monkey and the Camel

The beasts of the forest gave a splendid entertainment at which the Monkey stood up and danced. Having vastly delighted the assembly, he sat down amidst universal applause.

The Camel, envious of the praises bestowed on the Monkey and desiring to divert to himself the favour of the guests, proposed to stand up in his turn and dance for their amusement. He moved about in so utterly ridiculous a manner that the Beasts, in a fit of indignation, set upon him with clubs and drove him out of the assembly.

It is absurd to ape our betters.

The Mole and His Mother

A Mole, a creature blind from birth, once said to his Mother: 'I am sure than I can see, Mother!'

In the desire to prove to him his mistake, his Mother placed before him a few grains of frankincense, and asked, 'What is it?'

The young Mole said, 'It is a pebble.'

His Mother exclaimed: 'My son, I am afraid that you are not only blind, but that you have lost your sense of smell.'

(Translated by George Fyler Townsend)

Mercury and the Man Bitten by an Ant

A Man once saw a ship go down with all its crew, and commented severely on the injustice of the gods.

'They care nothing for a man's character,' said he, 'but let the good and the bad go to their deaths together.'

There was an ant-heap close by where he was standing, and, just as he spoke, he was bitten in the foot by an Ant. Turning in a temper to the ant-heap he stamped upon it and crushed hundreds of unoffending ants.

Suddenly Mercury appeared, and belaboured him with his staff, saying as he did so, 'You villain, where's your nice sense of justice now?'

The Imposter

A certain man fell ill, and, being in a very bad way, he made a vow that he would sacrifice a hundred oxen to the gods if they would grant him a return to health. Wishing to see how he would keep his vow, they caused him to recover in a short time.

Now, he hadn't an ox in the world, so he made a hundred little oxen out of tallow and offered them up on an altar, at the same time saying, 'Ye gods, I call you to witness that I have discharged my vow.'

The gods determined to be even with him, so they sent him a dream, in which he was bidden to go to the sea-shore and fetch a hundred crowns which he was to find there. Hastening in great excitement to the shore, he fell in with a band of robbers, who seized him and carried him off to sell as a slave: and when they sold him a hundred crowns was the sum he fetched.

Do not promise more than you can perform.

The Man and the Lion

A Man and a Lion were companions on a journey, and in the course of conversation they began to boast about their prowess, and each claimed to be superior to the other in strength and courage. They were still arguing with some heat when they came to a cross-road where there was a statue of a Man strangling a Lion.

'There!' said the Man triumphantly, 'look at that! Doesn't that prove to you that we are stronger than you?'

'Not so fast, my friend,' said the Lion, 'that is only your view of the case. If we Lions could make statues, you may be sure that in most of them you would see the Man underneath.'

There are two sides to every question.

The Snake and Jupiter

A Snake suffered a good deal from being constantly trodden upon by man and beast, owing partly to the length of his body and partly to his being unable to raise himself above the surface of the ground: so he went and complained to Jupiter about the risks to which he was exposed. But Jupiter had little sympathy for him. 'I dare say,' said he, 'that if you had bitten the first that trod on you, the others would have taken more trouble to look where they put their feet.'

The Kid on the Housetop

A Kid climbed up on to the roof of an outhouse, attracted by the grass and other things that grew in the thatch; and as he stood there browsing away, he caught sight of a Wolf passing below, and jeered at him because he couldn't reach him. The Wolf only looked up and said, 'I hear you, my young friend; but it is not you who mock me, but the roof on which you are standing.'

Bat, the Bramble, and the Seagull

A Bat, a Bramble, and a Seagull went into partnership and determined to go on a trading voyage together. The Bat borrowed a sum of money for his venture; the Bramble laid in a stock of clothes of various kinds; and the Seagull took a quantity of lead: and so they set out.

By and by a great storm came on, and their boat with all the cargo went to the bottom, but the three travellers managed to reach land. Ever since then the Seagull flies to and fro over the sea, and every now and then dives below the surface, looking for the lead he's lost; while the Bat is so afraid of meeting his creditors that he hides away by day and only comes out at night to feed; and the Bramble catches hold of the clothes of everyone who passes by, hoping someday to recognise and recover the lost garments.

All men are more concerned to recover what they lose than to acquire what they lack.

The Ass and his Burdens

A Pedlar who owned an Ass one day bought a quantity of salt, and loaded up his beast with as much as he could bear. On the way home the Ass stumbled as he was crossing a stream and fell into the water.

The salt got thoroughly wetted and much of it melted and drained away, so that, when he got on his legs again, the Ass found his load had become much less heavy. His master, however, drove him back to town and bought more salt, which he added to what remained in the panniers, and started out again.

No sooner had they reached a stream than the Ass lay down in it, and rose, as before, with a much lighter load. But his master detected the trick, and turning back once more, bought a large number of sponges, and piled them on the back of the Ass.

When they came to the stream the Ass again lay down: but this time, as the sponges soaked up large quantities of water, he found, when he got up on his legs, that he had a bigger burden to carry than ever.

You may play a good card once too often.

The Ass, the Cock, and the Lion

An Ass and a Cock were in a cattle-pen together. Presently a Lion, who had been starving for days, came along and was just about to fall upon the Ass and make a meal of him when the Cock, rising to his full height and flapping his wings vigorously, uttered a tremendous crow.

Now, if there is one thing that frightens a Lion, it is the crowing of a Cock: and this one had no sooner heard the noise than he fled.

The Ass was mightily elated at this, and thought that, if the Lion couldn't face a Cock, he would be still less likely to stand up to an Ass: so he ran out and pursued him. But when the two had got well out of sight and hearing of the Cock, the Lion suddenly turned upon the Ass and ate him up.

False confidence often leads to disaster.

The Dog and the Wolf

A Dog was lying in the sun before a farmyard gate when a Wolf pounced upon him and was just going to eat him up; but he begged for his life and said, 'You see how thin I am and what a wretched meal I should make you now: but if you will only wait a few days my master is going to give a feast. All the rich scraps and pickings will fall to me and I shall get nice and fat: then will be the time for you to eat me.'

The Wolf thought this was a very good plan and went away. Some time afterwards he came to the farmyard again, and found the Dog lying out of reach on the stable roof. 'Come down,' he called, 'and be eaten: you remember our agreement?'

But the Dog said coolly, 'My friend, if ever you catch me lying down by the gate there again, don't you wait for any feast.'

Once bitten, twice shy.

The Old Lion

A Lion, enfeebled by age and no longer able to procure food for himself by force, determined to do so by cunning. Betaking himself to a cave, he lay down inside and feigned to be sick: and whenever any of the other animals entered to inquire after his health, he sprang upon them and devoured them.

Many lost their lives in this way, till one day a Fox called at the cave, and, having a suspicion of the truth, addressed the Lion from outside instead of going in, and asked him how he did. He replied that he was in a very bad way: 'But,' said he, 'why do you stand outside? Pray come in.'

'I should have done so,' answered the Fox, 'if I hadn't noticed that all the footprints point towards the cave and none the other way.'

The Prophet

A Prophet sat in the market-place and told the fortunes of all who cared to engage his services.

Suddenly there came running up one who told him that his house had been broken into by thieves, and that they had made off with everything they could lay hands on. He was up in a moment, and rushed off, tearing his hair and calling down curses on the miscreants.

The bystanders were much amused, and one of them said, 'Our friend professes to know what is going to happen to others, but it seems he's not clever enough to perceive what's in store for himself.'

(Translated by Vernon Jones)

A Wife and a Drunken Husband

A Woman that lay under the mortification of a fudling Husband, took him once when he was dead drunk; and had his body laid in a charnel-house. By the time she thought he might be come to himself again, away goes she, and knocks at the door.

Who's there? (says the Toper)

One, says the Woman, that brings meat for the dead.

Friend, says he, bring me drink rather. I wonder any body that knows me, should bring me one without t'other.

Nay then, says she, the humour I perceive has taken possession of him; he has gotten a habit, and his case is desperate.

Inveterate illhabits become another nature to us, and we may almost as well be taken to pieces, and new put together again, as mended.

Musician

A Man that had a very coarsevoice, but an excellent musick-room, would be still practising in that chamber, for the advantage of the eccho. He took such a conceit upon't, that he must needs be shewing his parts upon a public theatre, where he perform'd so very ill, that the auditory hiss'd him off the stage, and threw stones at him.

A man may like himself very well in his own glass, and yet the world not fall in love with him in publick. But the truth on't is, we are partial in our own case, and there's no reading of our selves but with other men'seyes.

(Translated by Sir Roger L'Estrange)

PENGUIN

LITTLE BLACK

CLASSICS

PENGUIN

LITTLE BLACK

CLASSICS

PENGUIN

LITTLE BLACK

CLASSICS

“我发现，她这时
依然很惊慌，
但我并没有因为
她的情绪而缓和语气，
相反，看到她被吓到，
我说得更直接了。”

PENGUIN

LITTLE BLACK

CLASSICS

*此中文译本译自俄语原文

温顺的女人

The Meek One

[俄]陀思妥耶夫斯基　著
田浩　译

中信出版集团 | 北京

图书在版编目（CIP）数据

企鹅经典：小黑书．第三辑：汉、英 /（英）简·奥斯汀等著；夏星等译．-- 北京：中信出版社，2019.6

书名原文：Penguin Little Black Classics

ISBN 978-7-5217-0407-5

Ⅰ．①企… Ⅱ．①简… ②夏… Ⅲ．①世界文学－作品综合集－汉、英 Ⅳ．① I11

中国版本图书馆 CIP 数据核字 (2019) 第 072172 号

企鹅经典：小黑书　第三辑

温顺的女人

著　　者：[俄] 陀思妥耶夫斯基

译　　者：田浩

出版发行：中信出版集团股份有限公司

（北京市朝阳区惠新东街甲 4 号富盛大厦 2 座 邮编 100029）

承 印 者：北京楠萍印刷有限公司

开　　本：787mm × 1092mm　1/32　　印　　张：45.75　　字　　数：756 千字

版　　次：2019 年 6 月第 1 版　　印　　次：2019 年 6 月第 1 次印刷

京权图字：01－2018－6477　　广告经营许可证：京朝工商广字第 8087 号

书　　号：ISBN 978－7－5217－0407－5

定　　价：149.00 元（全 10 册）

作者自述[1]

我请求读者们原谅，在本期《作家日记》[2]中，我没有采取以往的编排形式，而是只刊登了一部中篇小说。虽然这篇小说的写作占用了我将近一个月的时间，但无论如何，我还是希望大家能够谅解我的做法。

现在我们来谈谈小说中的故事。虽然我称这篇小说

1. 本章节收录于《温顺的女人》同期期刊之前，做解释说明之用，因感觉有助于读者理解作家的创作缘由，所以从俄文译出一并收录，英文部分没有此章节。——编者注

2.《作家日记》是陀思妥耶夫斯基自费出版发行的一份期刊，内容涉及国家政治、外交、战争、法律、宗教、家庭、青年以及文学艺术与往事回忆等。其中，《温顺的女人》刊载于 1876 年 11 月号，占了当期的全部篇幅。（说明：书中脚注除特别标明之外，均为译者注。）

是“幻想的”，但我认为故事本身是非常现实的。由于小说写作过程中确实有幻想的成分，因此我认为，在这里做一些预先说明还是有必要的。

事实上，这篇小说既不是一个完整的故事，也不是一篇手记。试想一下，有这么一位丈夫，他的妻子几小时前跳楼自杀了，现在尸体就放在他旁边的桌子上。他心烦意乱，无法集中精力思考。他在自己的房间里走来走去，试图将刚才发生的事情解释清楚，他想“把自己的注意力集中到一点上”。与此同时，他又是个严重的疑病症患者，还常常自言自语。因此，大家会看到他在自己给自己描述这件事，向自己解释事情的前因后果。尽管他的话看似具有一定的连贯性，但无论在逻辑上还是感受上，都存在一些自相矛盾的地方。他为自己辩护，同时又指责妻子，而且还给出一些与此事毫无关系的解释：其中既有思想和心灵的粗鄙，又有深切的体验。他的确一步步地给自己解释清楚了事情的来龙去脉，也把自己的注意力“集中到了一点上”。他的一连串回忆最终把他引向了真理，而真理又升华了他的思想和心灵。与杂乱无章的故事开头相比，到最后，他的论调都发生了变化。至少他自己认为，对于他这个不幸的人来说，真理已经非常地清晰与明确了。

这就是故事的主题。当然，整个故事的发展持续了几个小时，中间断断续续，形式上也不连贯：他有时是自言自语，有时又好像是在讲给一位不在场的听众或一位法官听。这种情形在现实中也是存在的。如果有一位速记员能听到他的话，并把它们都记录下来，那么这篇记录读起来可能比我写的还要晦涩和不通顺，但我认为，他的心理发展脉络应该不会有太大变化。类似关于速记员记录他讲话（之后我再对记录进行加工）的假设，就是我称这篇小说具有“幻想”特点的主要原因。其实这种创作手法在文学作品中并不鲜见，例如，维克多·雨果在自己的名著《一个死囚的末日》中就使用过几乎相同的方法，虽然没有采用速记员视角，但他进行了更大胆的假设。他想象一个被判处死刑的囚犯不仅在自己最后一天，甚至在最后一小时、最后一分钟都能（而且有时间）写手记。如果他不进行这种幻想的话，大概也就不会有这部在他创作生涯中最贴近现实的杰作了。

一

／

1. 我是谁，她又是谁

……只要她现在在这儿，就一切都好：我可以每隔几分钟就走过去看看她，但她明天就要被人抬走了，一想到就要剩下我一个人，我就有些不知所措。现在她正躺在客厅里由两张牌桌拼起来的桌子上，可是明天，棺材就要来了，一副白色的、铺着雪白那不勒斯绸[1]的棺材。不过我想说的并不是这件事……我在屋子里走来走去，想给自己一个解释，可就是无法集中注意力……六

1. 一种产自意大利那不勒斯的高级绸缎，价格昂贵，质地优良。

个小时过去了，我仍然在走、走、走……事情是这样的。我会按照先后顺序给你们讲。（按顺序！）先生们，你们可能看出来了，我不是作家，不过没关系，我会把我知道的全都讲出来。不过对于我来说可怕的地方就在于，我全都明白。

如果你们想知道，或者说，如果咱们从头开始捋，她只是来我这里当东西，据说是为了付《呼声报》的广告费。她在报纸上登了一条求职广告，广告内容大致是要找一份家庭女教师之类的工作，愿意外出或家内授课等诸如此类的话。起初我没太在意她，感觉她和别的客人没有什么不同之处。但过了一会儿，我发现有些地方不太对劲。她身材瘦削，有一头淡黄色的头发，比一般人稍高点。也许是害羞，她和我说话时，总是显得有点儿迟钝（我猜她在陌生人面前就是这样，不言而喻，我和其他人没什么不同，可能她把我也当作一个陌生人，而不是当铺掌柜）。其他人来当东西时总是不停地吵闹、哀求、讨价还价，就是为了多当些钱，而她则不是，给多少就是多少，拿了钱转身就走，一句话都不说……搞得我一头雾水……嗯……首先，她当的东西很奇怪：一对镀了层金的银耳环和一个破破烂烂的小铜牌，总共只值二十戈比[1]。她自己也清楚，这两样东西值不了多少钱，但我从她的神情中能看出来，对她来说，它们是很珍贵的。后来我才知道，这些就是她父母留给她仅有的遗物。有一次我嘲笑了她当的东西。也只有这么一次，你们看出来了吧，其实我从不允许自己这样放肆，我跟人说话时总是带着一种绅士般的口吻：话不多，有礼貌，又很严谨。“严谨、严谨、再严谨”。但这次她居然拿来了一件兔皮袄的“残片”（说是残片毫不夸张），我没忍住，突然对她说了些貌似讽刺挖苦的话。天哪，她好像发怒了。她那双淡蓝色的大眼睛总是若有所思的样子，但现在仿佛要燃烧起来似的。可她还是没有开口，带着“残片”离开了。正是这次经历让我开始对她有了“特别”的关注，而且还想到了关于她的一些事情，就是那种特别的事情。对了，我对她还有一个印象，你们想听吗？这个印象最重要，能概括其他一切印象：就是说，她真的很年轻，看上去就像十四岁。但实际上她那时还差三个月就十六岁了。不过我想说的那个能概括一切的印象不在于此。第二天，她又来了。后来我才知道，她带着那

1. 1 卢布等于 100 戈比。

件兔皮袄还去过多布龙拉沃夫和莫泽尔两家当铺，但人家除了金子什么都不要，也懒得和她说话。相对地，有一次，我收了她的一块玉石（也是那种不值钱的玩意），但事后想起来，也觉得奇怪：我的当铺也是除了金银什么都不收啊，而我居然让她在我这儿当了那块石头。这应该是当时能让我想到她的第二个念头了，我记得这事儿。

这一次，从莫泽尔当铺出来后，她又来到我这里想当一支琥珀烟嘴，小玩意马马虎虎，喜欢这类东西的人有可能瞧瞧，但对我们来说它毫无价值，因为我们只要金子。由于昨天她带来的那场“骚乱”，我在接待她的时候，显得有点严肃。我的严肃实质上就是冷淡。但在付给她两卢布后，我还是没忍住，说了一句可能刺激到她的话：“我只对您开这个特例，要知道，莫泽尔是绝不会收您这类东西的。”我说话时，特意在“对您”两个字上加重了语气，似乎有了某种“特殊含义”。这么做确实有些恶毒。她听到这句“对您”后，又发怒了，但依然默不作声，也没有扔掉两个卢布，她把钱收下了——这就是人穷志短啊！我还记得，她是那么生气！我知道，我的话刺痛了她。她离开后，我问自己：“花两卢布战胜她，这划算吗？”嘿、嘿、嘿！而且我记得，这个问题我问了两次："划算吗？划算吗？"我笑着给出了肯定的答案。那一刻真是太美妙了，我并没有什么负罪感：我是故意这么做的，我想试探试探她，因为当时我脑子里掠过了一些关于她的念头。这是能让我想到她的第三个念头。

……好吧，从那时起，我们的故事就算正式开头了。不用说，我开始努力从侧面打听有关她的所有情况，然后急不可耐地期盼她的到来。你瞧，我总是能预感到，她很快就要来啦。只要她一过来，我就会极其礼貌地和她攀谈一番。要知道，我受过良好的教育，也很注意举止风度。哼哼，那时我感觉她既善良，又温顺。善良和温顺的人不会总是拒人千里之外，虽然她们不太可能完全敞开心扉，但也不会拒绝一次谈话：她们回答时会非常谨慎，但只要您愿意和她们交谈，而且不会感到厌烦的话，那么她们的话会越说越多。不过她当时并没有和我多说什么。关于《呼声报》和其他事情都是我后来才知道的。那个时候，为了在报纸上登求职广告，她几乎倾尽所有，起初的广告词中还带有一丝高傲的口吻："兹有家庭女教师愿外出工作，条件随函递送"，但没过多久，就变成了"可做任何工作，授课、女伴、管家、病人护理，能缝纫"等众人所熟悉的常见写法！不消说，这些都是不同阶段分别添加进广告内容中的。直到最后，她实在走投无路，连“不求薪酬，只需膳食”这样的字眼也都用上了。但即便如此，她依然找不到事做。那个时候，我决定对她进行最后一次试探：我突然拿出一张当日的《呼声报》，给她看上面的一条广告：“青年女子求职，本人孤儿，可做幼儿家庭教师，中老年鳏夫家庭雇用更佳，可料理家务。”

“您看，这是今天早上登出的广告，晚上大概就能找到工作。广告词就应该这样写！”

她又发怒了，眼睛似乎又要喷出火焰来，一句话没说，转身就离开了。我反倒很高兴。因为此时我已有十足的把握了，一点儿也不害怕：才不会有谁会收她的烟嘴，更何况她现在连烟嘴也已经当出去了。果不其然，三天后她又来了，面色苍白，焦虑不安。我看得出来，她家里应该是出了什么事，而且也的确是出事了。我一会儿再解释到底出了什么事，现在我只想说说当时我是如何在她面前优雅地表现自己，进而提升在她心目中的地位的。这个想法也是突然从我脑子里冒出来的。事情经过是这样的，她拿来了一尊圣像（一看就是下了狠心）……唉，听听！听听！到这里故事才真正开始，我又把它讲得一团糟……我总是想回忆所有事情，每个细节。我本来是想把注意力集中在一点上的，但好像办不到，我脑子里总是千头万绪的……

那是一尊圣母像，圣母抱着圣婴，就是普通人家里供奉的那种，看上去有点儿年头了，披着镀金的衣饰——这东西值……嗯，值六卢布。看得出来，圣像对她来说很珍贵，她没有把圣像上的衣饰拿掉，完整地拿来典当了。我对她说，最好是把衣饰摘下来留在我这儿，圣像拿回去，毕竟那是尊圣像啊。

“难道典当圣像是被禁止的吗？”

“不，可以当，只是您自己可能……”

“那就把衣饰摘下来吧。”

“不，还是别那么做了，我都收下吧，我会把它放在神龛里，”我边想边说，“和其他圣像放在一起，在神灯下面（自从我开当铺起，就一直点着神灯）。”“我直接给您十卢布，就这么简单。”

“我不要十卢布，五卢布就行，我一定把圣像赎回来。”

“您不想要十卢布吗？这圣像值这么多钱。”因为看到她眼睛里一闪而过的亮光，我便补了这么一句。她没作声。我给了她五卢布。

“您可别瞧不起任何人，我也在困境中挣扎过，而且比这还要糟，您别看我现在干这行……我也是经历了种种苦难……”

“那您是在报复社会，对吗？”她突然打断我，言语中带着一丝嘲讽，不过这种嘲讽并无恶意，反倒带着些许的天真无邪（之所以这么说，是因为她当时认为我和其他人没有区别，因而对我说这句话并无恶意）。“啊哈！”我心里想，“原来你是这样的人，性格会自己显露出来的、属于新派的那类人。”

“您看，”我马上半开玩笑又故作神秘地跟她说，“我——我是那常欲作恶，却永远为善的力量的一部分……”

她快速地看了我一眼，眼神中带着孩童般的好奇：

“等等，这是什么意思？是谁说的？我好像在哪儿听过……”

“别费脑筋了，这是梅菲斯特[1]向浮士德做自我介绍时说的话。《浮士德》读过吗？”

“没……没仔细读过。”

---

1. 歌德巨著《浮士德》中引诱浮士德怠惰满足的魔鬼。

“那就是根本没读过。应该读读。不过我看您又面带讥讽地笑话我了。您别以为我没品位到会为了往自己当铺掌柜的身份上贴金，而试图在您面前把自己比作是梅菲斯特。开当铺的就是开当铺的。我们都懂，小姐。”

“您真奇怪……我从来都没那么想过……”

她其实想说的是：我没想到您是一个受过教育的人。虽然她没说出口，但我知道，她就是这么想的；我令她非常满意。

“您看，”我说，“无论干哪一行，人都可以做好事。当然，我不是说我自己，除了坏事，我好像什么都没做过，不过……”

“当然了，无论在何种地位，人都可以做好事。”她一边说，一边用锐利的目光飞快地看了我一眼。“不管处在什么地位，确实如此。”她又突然补充了一句。

啊，我记得，我记得每一个瞬间！我想多说一句，当一个年轻人，一个可爱的年轻人想要说一句睿智而又深刻的话时，她的脸上就会立刻浮现出过于真诚和天真的神情，仿佛是在告诉你：“现在，我，有一句睿智又深刻的话要说给你听。”这不是虚荣心在作祟，和我们不一样。你能看得出来，她自己极为珍视这一切，相信又尊重这一切。而且她会认为，我们和她一样，也尊重这一切。啊，真诚！年轻人就是用真诚来征服别人的，这在她身上得到了完美的体现。

我记得很清楚，什么都没忘！她离开后，我当机立断。就在那天，我进行了最后一次调查，把有关她的其余所有情况都打听得一清二楚，包括眼下的各种细节；过去的事情我早已从卢克里娅那里打听到了。卢克里娅那时还是她家里的用人，几天前我就买通了她。她的情况听上去非常可怕，我不明白，身处这样的恶劣环境中，她怎么还能像刚才那样笑得出来，而且还对梅菲斯特的话充满好奇。但她毕竟是个年轻人啊！我想她的时候，总能感到骄傲和兴奋，正是因为年轻人这种豁达坦荡的态度：即使处在崩溃的边缘，歌德的伟大诗句依然光芒万丈。青春就是这样的豁达坦荡，即使它极其短暂又充满曲折。你们知道，我说的是她，只有她。更重要的是，那个时候我已经认为她是我的了，而且我毫不怀疑自己的能力。要知道，当你不再有任何怀疑时，每个念头都充满了诱人的魅力。

我这是怎么了？这样下去的话，什么时候我才能集中注意力呢？快点儿，快点儿——这些根本不是重点，我的天啊！

2. 求婚

我打听到的“底细”可以用一句话讲清楚：她父母三年前去世了，她和两个名声并不太好的姨妈一起生活。说她们名声不好都是客气的。其中一个是寡妇，带着六个孩子，一个比一个小，另一个是让人厌恶的老处女。两个人都不怎么样。她父亲当过公务员，但只是做文书工作，还有一个非世袭的贵族头衔。总之，一句话：我完全驾驭得了。我的社会地位似乎更高一些：毕竟我是一个退伍上尉，曾在一个有光荣历史的团里服役，我还是世袭贵族，经济独立，等等。至于我的当铺，她那两个姨妈也只有仰视的份儿了。她和姨妈们一起生活的三年过得和奴隶一样，即便如此，她还是坚持了下来，并在某个地方通过了一个考试。她试图从每日残酷无情的劳役中尽力挤出所有的时间来准备考试。这意味着，在她看来，还是有某种更美好的生活值得去追求！可我为什么要娶她呢？不过我的事不重要，一会儿再说吧……问题也不在这儿！她要教姨妈的孩子们识字，要缝补内衣，后来就不仅是内衣了，而且尽管她的肺不好，却还得擦洗地板。她们甚至还动手打她，说她是个吃闲饭的。

最后，打算把她卖了。呸！那些肮脏的细节我就不讲了。后来，她把自己所有的经历都详细地告诉我了。她家邻居中有个胖老板，他不是个普通的店铺老板，而是两家食品杂货店的老板。他观察了一年，把她们家的基本情况都掌握了。他的两个老婆都被他折磨死了，现在又想找第三个，于是就看上了她，说她“安静，出身清贫，可以照顾好我家里那些孤儿”。他家里确实有孤儿。他上门求婚，和姨妈们商量。但毕竟他都五十岁了，把她吓坏了。从那时起，她就不断到我这儿来当东西，急着要在《呼声报》上登广告。最后，她央求姨妈们，给她一点儿时间来考虑一下。她们答应了，但给她的时间也不是太多，等她再请求时，她们没有再给，还假惺惺地说："就算没你这张多余的嘴，我们自己也不知道吃啥。”这些事我都知道了，就在她来当圣像的那天上午，我做了决定。当天晚上，胖老板从杂货店里拿了值半卢布的一磅糖果去了她家。她陪他坐着，我把卢克里娅从厨房里叫出来，让她进屋传话，就说我在大门口等她，有急事要见她。我对自己的决定和行动非常满意。总的来说，那一整天我都对自己感到极其满意。

首先，把她叫出来，在大门口当着卢克里娅的面，对着已经惊呆了的她表白，我觉得这是一种幸福和荣耀……其次，我不想让她对我的举动感到诧异，我对她说："我这个人是直性子，我考虑好了。"我没撒谎，我确实是直性子。嗨，先别管这个了。我说话的时候不但彬彬有礼，显出我是一个有教养的人，而且更重要的是，我说的话都不落俗套。我这么做不对吗？我是想评判一下自己，而且我也这么做了。赞成与反对[1]我都想说，我也这么说了。回想起当时的情况，我觉得很满意，虽然这看上去有点儿蠢：我当时直接表白，并不觉得这有什么不妥。首先我说，我没有什么过人的才能，也不太聪明，可能也不是太善良，而且我还是个非常庸俗的利己主义者（我记得这句话是在去她家的路上想出来的，当时觉得非常得意）。这些非常、非常有可能让我在其他人那里不受待见。说这些话的时候我觉得非常自豪——这种感觉你们都明白。当然咯，我还没有高尚到只坦白自己的缺点，不说优点的地步，我说："但另一方面，我也有很多优点，如此这般，这般如此……"我发现，她这时依然很惊慌，但我并没有因为她的情绪而缓和语气；

1. 原文为拉丁语。

相反，看到她被吓到，我说得更直接了：我告诉她，我能让她吃喝不愁，但出席盛装舞会，去剧院听歌看戏，这些暂时还做不到，除非以后我能达到自己的目标。我缓了缓，接着说，显得随意的样子，我干这一行，开这个当铺，只有一个目的，就是……我似乎有些话中有话。但我有权这么说啊，我确实有自己的目标，但也确实有隐情。稍等，先生们，要知道，我一辈子都厌恶我那个当铺，这方面谁能比得过我，虽然自言自语的时候还故弄玄虚确实有点儿可笑，但我实质上就是在“报复社会”啊，千真万确！所以，她早上嘲笑我“报复”的那句俏皮话并不是不恰当。你们看出来了吧，要是我直接对她说“对，我就是在报复社会”，估计她会哈哈大笑，就像她那天早上一样，不过这也确实可笑。但用一句神秘兮兮的话来进行间接暗示，确实能激发想象力。况且，当时我也什么都不怕了：我知道，无论在哪方面，她都更厌恶那个胖老板，而出现在大门口的我，简直就如同救星一般。这一点我当然明白。唉，人更容易理解那些卑鄙的事！但哪些事是卑鄙的呢？如何去评判一个人呢？那时候我不是已经爱上她了吗？

别急，我还没说完……那个时候我当然不会说什么我有恩于她的话，半句都不会有；相反，我当时说的是："是我，我是那个蒙恩之人，而不是您。"我本来不应该这么说，但没控制住，可能这句话听上去有点儿蠢，因为我注意到她皱了皱眉头。但总的来说，我还是如愿以偿。好吧，既然我把这些肮脏的事情都讲了，那就干脆把我那最后一丁点儿龌龊行为也告诉你们吧：我站在那里，脑子里冒出一句话——你身材高挑又匀称，还受过教育……还有……长相也不难看。这就是当时我脑子里想的。当然咯，最后她在大门口答应了我。不过……不过我还得说一句：她在门口想了好久才说"好"。她就在那儿想啊想……想得太久了，我真想问一句："喂，你怎么想的？"当然，我最后还是没忍住，但很优雅地问了一句："小姐，您意下如何？"

"等一下，让我想想。"

她那张小脸儿是那么严肃，严肃到我都能读懂她在想什么！我当时有种被冒犯的感觉，我想："难道她还要在我和那个老板之间进行选择吗？"唉，那时候我还不明白！那时候我真是一点儿都不明白！直到现在我也不明白！我记得，我转身离开后，卢克里娅在后面追了上来，在街上拦住我，气喘吁吁地说："先生，您要是能娶了我们家这位好小姐，上帝会保佑您的，只是您别和她这么说，她就是太清高了。”

哦，清高！我就喜欢清高的人。清高的人特别好，只要……嗯……只要你能镇得住她们，是吧？唉，我这低贱又愚蠢的人啊！我这是多么地小人得志啊！当初她站在大门口犹豫着是否答应求婚时，我还挺奇怪的，可你们知道吗，说不定那时她就在想：“既然怎么选择都是不幸的，那还不如干脆就选那个最差的，那个胖老板，让他喝多了赶紧把我打死算了！”你们说呢？你们是怎么想的，她有过这样的念头吗？

我现在还是不明白，我现在什么都不明白！我刚刚说她可能想选择最差的，就是说，那个老板。但是那个时候对于她来说，谁才是最坏的选择——我，还是他？是杂货店的胖老板，还是读过歌德的当铺掌柜？这也是一个问题！这是什么问题？看看吧，答案不就在桌子上躺着嘛，你还在想什么“问题”呢！其实我没那么重要！问题也完全不在于我……况且，现在对于我来说，问题是不是出自我这里又有什么意义呢？我根本就解决不了这个问题。还是躺下睡觉吧。我的头好疼……

3. 最高贵的人，但我自己却不相信

我没睡着，感觉脑子里有东西一跳一跳的，就像脉搏那样。我想把这一切肮脏的事情弄明白。唉，这些事啊！唉，是我把她从那肮脏的烂泥里拉出来的啊！她应该明白的，她应该对我感激不尽啊！我喜欢我脑子里的各种想法，例如我已经四十一岁了，而她才十六岁。这种差距感让我着迷，多么幸福，多么甜蜜啊。

再比如说，我想举办一场英式[1]婚礼，只有我们两个人，再加上两个证婚人，其中一个应该是卢克里娅，婚礼结束我们就立刻跳上火车，可以去莫斯科（正好我在那儿有事要办），订一家旅馆，在那儿住上两个星期。但她不同意这个想法，她也不让我这么做。她要我恭恭敬敬地去见她两个姨妈，就像见岳父母那样，然后从她们那里把她娶走。好吧，我妥协了，她那两个姨妈也拿到了应得的东西。我甚至还给了那两个娘儿们每人一百卢布，还做了些承诺。当然，这件事我没有告诉她，以免她为自己曾经的处境而难过。姨妈们拿了钱立刻变得服

1. 此处原文为法语。

服帖帖。在嫁妆问题上还是有些争议的：她几乎是一无所有，但她什么都不想要。不过我还是成功地说服她，一点儿嫁妆都没有是不行的，嫁妆可以由我来准备，因为还有谁能给她置办嫁妆呢？好，先不说我了。当时我把我的很多想法都跟她讲了，至少让她心里有个数。这么做可能有点儿操之过急了。但更重要的是，从求婚成功的那一刻开始，虽然她表面上依旧矜持，但却已满怀爱意地投入我的怀抱了。每次傍晚时分我去看她时，她总是兴高采烈地接待我，少女呢喃般地和我聊天，（多么迷人的天真啊！）讲她小时候的事，讲她老家，讲她父亲和母亲。而我却给她的愉悦浇了一盆冷水。我是故意那样做的。我用沉默，一种善意的沉默来回应她的欣喜，当然……她很快就看懂了，我和她不太一样，我就是一个谜。对，我就是打算要做那个谜！但我这谜面设得是多么愚蠢啊！首先，我太严肃了，严肃地把她娶回了家。虽然我心满意足，但还是定下了一套规矩。这事我做得毫不费力，这规矩是多么天经地义啊！退一步讲，考虑当时的情况，这规矩我能不定吗？这规矩理所应当，我没必要诋毁自己啊！不，听我说，如果你要评判一个人，就要把事情的来龙去脉搞清楚……别说话！

从何说起呢，这事也挺复杂的。而且，当你要开始自我辩护时，就更难了。你们知道，年轻人都鄙视金钱，但我不一样，我更重视金钱，也追逐金钱，这使她变得越来越沉默。她睁着那双大眼睛，看着、听着、沉默着。你们也知道，优秀的年轻人都道德高尚，又充满激情，但有时候不够宽容，一言不合就怒目相对。而我认为，年轻人应该更加开朗豁达，我要让她有海纳百川的心胸，对不对？举个通俗点儿的例子吧，比如说，我是怎么描述我那个当铺的呢？我当然不会直接描述个没完，那样的话，好像我是在请求别人原谅似的。我说过，我为人清高，我用沉默来讲述。我善于通过沉默的方式来表达自己，来讲述我的生活，讲述我承受的种种不幸。我是多么不幸啊！我被大家抛弃，我被人们遗忘，这一切又有谁能理解呢！然而，这个十六岁的姑娘从一些小人那里捕风捉影，听到了一些关于我的事情，她就以为掌握了我的全部情况，但隐情只能藏在这个人的心里！我仍然保持沉默，特别是在她面前，直到昨天——我为什么要沉默呢？因为我是一个清高的人啊！我希望她能够自己去了解这个人，不要来问我，也不要听那些小人的胡言乱语，她应该自己来读懂他，真正地理解他！既然我把她娶进家门，就希望她能充分尊重我。我希望她能为我的痛苦祈祷——这是我应得的。我总是这样清高，要么拥有一切，否则什么都不想要。这就是我无法与人分享幸福的原因，我要完全占有，这也正是为何我要强迫自己如此表现的原因：让她自己来读懂我、尊重我！你们也一定会同意我的想法，如果我自己去跟她解释，然后吞吞吐吐地暗示她要尊重我，这难道不就是在乞求施舍吗……可是……可是，我干吗要说这个呀！

愚蠢、愚蠢、愚蠢，太愚蠢了！我当时对她说的那几句话简直是直截了当且残酷无情（再怎么强调也不为过）：年轻人志向高远，这很好，但它一文不值。为什么这么说呢？因为“志向高远”太容易做到了，它并非来自生活的打磨，而只是“生命的第一印象”，但让我们看看你都做了些什么事？廉价的志向似乎让一切事情看起来都很容易做到，甚至连献出生命也变得很容易了。因为那只是你热血沸腾、精力旺盛，又充满对美的渴望！不信的话，你们可以尝试去做一件高尚的、艰难的、无声无息的事情，它无人喝彩，却有人诽谤，要做出巨大牺牲，又得不到一点儿荣誉。而且当一个光明磊落的人这么做时，当你是这个世界上最真诚的人时，大家将你视为卑鄙下流之徒。您可以试试看，不，我的小姐，您会拒绝的！而我，我就是这么做的，我一辈子都在这样高尚行事。一开始，她还和我激烈争论，但后来就渐渐不作声了，一言不发，只是瞪大了眼睛在那里听着，全神贯注，眼睛越瞪越大。而且……而且我还突然发现她脸上浮现出一丝质疑、冷漠、不怀好意的微笑。这种微笑在我娶她进门的那天也见过。的确，她那时也是无处可去……

4. 计划，全是计划

当初我们俩是谁先开始的？

谁都没有。是这件事自己迈出的第一步。我说过，我娶她进门时很严肃，但其实从一开始我就有所和缓了。她还是我未婚妻的时候，我就对她说过，以后要帮我打理当铺生意，由她来收抵押物和付款，她当时什么也没说（这里提醒大家注意），而且工作起来也是满怀热情。还有，我们的房子和家具也都没有变化，和从前一样。房子有两个房间：一间是前厅，很宽敞，跟当铺柜台是隔开的；另一间是我们的房间，做起居室和卧室，也很大。我的家具很少，甚至还没有她姨妈家的多。我的神龛和神灯放在当铺里；我们的房间里有一个橱柜，里面有一些书，有一个小箱子，钥匙在我这儿；房间里还有一张床，几张桌子和几把椅子。她还是我未婚妻时，我就说过，我要在三年内攒到三万卢布，我、她和卢克里娅（我把她也带过来了），我们每天包括生活费在内的花销不能超过一卢布，否则的话是攒不到这个数的。她不反对，但后来我又把每天的花销标准提高了三十戈比。还有剧院的事。她是我未婚妻的时候我就说过，我们是不会去剧院看戏的，不过后来我还是决定，每个月去一次，而且是预订更体面的池座。我们一起去过三次，看的好像是《追求幸福》和《会唱歌的小鸟》。（这个无所谓！）我们来去的路上都沉默不语。为什么，为什么我们一开始就是这样？要知道，我们刚开始生活时并没有吵过架，但依然是相对无言。我记得，她那时总是偷偷看我，可她越是这样，我就越加沉默。是的，保持沉默的是我，而不是她。她有那么一两次激情迸发，扑过来拥抱我；但我认为这种情绪是病态的，歇斯底里的，我想要的是稳定的幸福，要的是她的尊重，所以我冷漠地回应了她。我的判断没错，每次她激情过后，第二天就是一顿争吵。

要想不争吵，那就只有彼此保持沉默了，但她的样子却越来越放肆。“叛逆与独立”——这大概就是她想要的，只不过她不知道应该如何表现出来。是的，这张温顺的脸变得越来越放肆了。你们相信吗，我在她眼里变得越来越可恶了，这一点我当然清楚。她有时也会为此情绪爆发，这也是自然而然的事。例如，像她这种刚刚摆脱肮脏与贫贱的生活，不需要再刷地板的人，有时竟会突然抱怨起我们太穷了！您知道吗，这不是贫穷，这是节俭，我们的家饰，哪样不是又高级又整洁？因为我以前一直认为，丈夫整洁更能讨妻子欢心。不过，她抱怨的似乎不是贫穷，而是嫌弃我太吝啬了，她仿佛想说的是：“人家可是有坚定目标的。”她突然不再去剧院了，脸上也越来越多嘲讽的神情……而我则继续沉默，更加沉默。

我怎么可以为自己辩解呢？主要的问题是我那个当铺。这么说吧，先生们：我知道，作为一个女人，而且是一个十六岁的姑娘，不可能完全不屈从于男人的意志。女性缺乏独立的见解，这是最简单不过的道理，即使是现在，即使是对于现在的我来说，它都是千真万确的。

她就在那儿，躺在前厅里，那又怎样呢，真理就是真理，即便是密尔[1]本人在这里，他也不能否认这一点！一个被爱情冲昏了头脑的女人，唉，这种女人会把她所爱的人加以神化，神化他的缺陷，甚至是他的罪恶。她为他的恶行所找的借口，他自己是想不出来的。这是女人的宽容与豁达，并不是什么独立见解。缺少独立见解只会毁掉女人。你们指给我看那个躺在桌子上的人吗？我再重复一遍，“那又怎样呢？”难道那就是有独立见解的体现吗？唉！

听我说：那时候我坚信她是爱我的。她有时候会扑到我身上，抱住我的脖子。她爱我，更准确地说是——她希望爱我。不错，当时的确就是这样：她希望爱我，努力尝试着来爱我。更重要的是，我身上没有任何罪恶需要她来找理由为之辩护。当然，你们会说“你是个当铺掌柜”，你们所有人都会这么说。当铺掌柜又怎么了？这只能说明，一定有某种原因，让一个心胸最为坦荡的人成了当铺掌柜。你们瞧，先生们，有些想法……你们知道，有些想法如果用语言能够表达出来，那听上去会

---

1. 约翰·斯图亚特·密尔（旧译约翰·斯图亚特·穆勒，1806—1873），19 世纪英国著名自由主义思想家。

是非常愚蠢的。那会让你自己都感到害臊。为什么呢？不为什么。因为我们所有人都烂透了，我们不愿接受真理，如果这都不是原因的话，那我就真不知道了。我刚才说过的那句“心胸最为坦荡的人”听上去有点儿可笑，但事实就是这样的。要知道，这就是真理，千真万确的道理。那个时候我有权开这个当铺给自己的生活提供一个保障，是的，我这么做：“你们，就是你们，你们全都排斥我，用你们那轻蔑的沉默驱赶我。我对你们满腔热忱，而你们却用对我的羞辱来回应。现在我要和你们一刀两断，我有权这么做，我会攒够三万卢布，去克里米亚终老一生：在南方的海岸边，在山脚的葡萄园，在我自己购买的宅邸中。最重要的是，这能让我远离你们这些人，但我不会怨恨你们，我的灵魂中长存信念，我的心中有挚爱的伴侣，如果上帝赐福，我还会有一个家庭，还要去帮助周围的邻人。”我把这些想法说给自己听是好的，如果当初把这些都绘声绘色地给她描述一遍的话，那就太愚蠢了。这也正是我一直保持清高与沉默，又同她相对无言的原因所在。她怎么会明白我的理想呢？她只有十六岁，如此年轻，我的辩白、我的痛苦，她又能理解多少呢？她鲁莽，不懂生活，拥有年轻人那种廉价的信念，反而对“美好心灵”视而不见，更重要的是——我的当铺，够了！（难道我是个开当铺的恶人吗，难道她不了解我的为人吗，我取过不义之财吗？）啊，世上的真理是多么可怕！这个女人迷人、温顺，如天使一般圣洁，但她却是个暴君，让人无法忍受的暴君，奴役并折磨着我的灵魂。我必须要这么说，否则我就是在诋毁自己！你们认为我不爱她吗？谁能说我不爱她？你们看到了吧，这就是一种嘲弄，是来自命运和造化的恶意嘲弄！我们都是被诅咒的，人类的生命被诅咒了！（特别是我！）我现在终于知道了我错在何处！这里的确存在问题。一切都已明朗，我的计划就像天空一样清晰：“刚毅、高傲，不需要任何道德上的慰藉，默默地承受苦难。”事实如此，我没有撒谎，我没有撒谎！“她以后会明白，这就是宽宏大量，但现在她还不具备读懂这一切的能力——如果未来某一天她能醒悟的话，她将会倍加珍惜我，双膝跪地，对我顶礼膜拜。”这就是我的计划。这里我好像忘了什么东西，或是漏掉了其中一项。有什么事情我没能做成，但够了，已经足够完美了。现在还需要请求别人的谅解吗？都结束了。你勇敢一点儿，不要低头！不是你的错！……

好吧，我要实话实说，我不害怕面对真相：是她的错，她的错！……

5. 温顺的女人反叛了

我们之间的争吵源于她一时兴起，竟然要自己决定付给客人多少钱，而且还高估抵押物的价值，甚至有那么两次还赏脸和我争论起这个问题。我自然是不会同意她那么做。但就在这时，来了一位上尉的遗孀。

老太太拿来了一个吊坠——是她已故丈夫留下的礼物，一看就是件纪念品。我付了她三十卢布。她一边诉着苦，一边央求我们要保管好这东西——我们当然会好好保管咯。但五天后，她又突然回来，想用一个八卢布都不值的手镯把吊坠换回去；我当然是不会同意了。不过她当时可能从我妻子的眼神中看出了什么，后来趁我不在时又来了，换走了吊坠。

我知道这事后，说了她几句，给她讲了这其中的道理，语气温和，但又不失严厉。她坐在床边，眼睛盯着地板，右脚尖敲打着地毯（她习惯的姿势），嘴角边挂着一丝坏笑。我没有提高嗓门，依然心平气和地对她讲，钱是我的，我有权从自己的角度来看待生活；我还告诉她，当初我把她娶进家门时，就没对她隐瞒什么。

她突然跳了起来，浑身颤抖——你们猜怎么着——她居然在我面前跺脚；这是头野兽，这是在发作，这是兽性的发作。我惊呆了，从没想到她会做出这样出格的举动。但我没有失态，我甚至都没有动，依然如往常一样，心平气和地对她讲，从今以后不许她再参与当铺的生意了。她冲我哈哈大笑，走出了家门。

事实上，她无权离开这间公寓。她还是我未婚妻时，我就和她定好了规矩，没有我，她哪也不许去。傍晚时分，她回来了；我一句话也没和她说。

第二天一大早，她又离开了，第三天也是这样。我关了当铺，去她姨妈那儿找她。婚礼结束后我就和她们断了联系——再也没有互相来往过。但她并不在那里。她们好奇地听着我讲的事，然后还当面嘲笑我："您这就是活该了。"对此我并不感到意外。我私下里买通了二姨妈，就是那个老处女，答应给她一百卢布，先付二十五。两天后，她来到我家，告诉我："我听说有一个中尉军官，叶菲莫维奇，过去和您在一个团里服役，他和你们的事有牵连。"我大吃一惊。在军队服役的时候，这个叶菲莫维奇就把我害得够惨。一个月前，他还以当东西为名，恬不知耻地来过我这儿几次，那时他就开始和我妻子有说有笑。我当时就过去警告他，不要再到我当铺来了，还提醒他我和我妻子之间的关系；但我从来没想过会发生这种事，我仅仅以为这人就是个无赖。现在她姨妈突然告诉我，他们早就见过面了，从中撮合的是一个叫尤莉娅·萨姆索诺夫娜的寡妇，曾是一位上校的夫人，是姨妈们从前的老相识。"您家那位太太现在应该就在她那儿。"她说。

长话短说。我为这事儿一共花了三百卢布，两天之内已经做好了安排，我会在隔壁房间虚掩的门后，听我妻子和叶菲莫维奇的第一次单独约会[1]。但在这前一天的晚上，我和她发生了一次小争吵，这对我来说意义重大。

临近傍晚，她回来了，坐在床边，用略带嘲弄的眼神看着我，一只脚敲着地毯。我看着她，突然想起来一件事，在最近整整一个月里，更准确地说是最近的两个星期，她的性格发生了很大变化，甚至可以说完全变了一个人——一反常态：脾气暴躁，无理取闹，行为虽谈

1. 原文为法语。

不上不知羞耻，但也是毫无规矩，而且还有意挑衅。但她温顺的本性还是会在她想变本加厉的时候妨碍到她。她胡搅蛮缠的时候，即使行为再出格，也明显能看得出，她是在有意逼迫自己这样做，天生的纯良品性让她无法克服自己行为本身带来的羞耻感。也正因如此，这样的人有时会控制不住自己行为的尺度，她们的越轨行为可能让你无法相信自己看到的一切。反倒是那些骨子里荒淫无度的人，常常表现得温文尔雅，这种人越是做坏事，就越表现得循规蹈矩、彬彬有礼，而且在别人面前总觉得高人一筹。

“您被军队开除，是因为您不敢和别人决斗，是吗？”她突然问道，眼里还闪闪发光。

“是的，按照长官们的裁决，我必须离开军队，不过，在这之前我就已经递交了退伍申请。”

“是因为贪生怕死才被赶出来的吗？”

“他们是这么认为的。但我拒绝决斗不是因为贪生怕死，而是不愿意屈从那些专横的裁决，我当时并没有觉得自己受辱。您要明白，”说着说着，我有点儿激动，“用行动来反抗专横，并承担一切后果——这要比任何决斗都更需要勇气。”

她又不怀好意地笑了。我有点儿控制不住自己了，这句话好像是在为自己辩解，而她这么做只是想变本加厉地羞辱我。

“之后这三年您就像个流浪汉一样在彼得堡大街上游荡，讨点儿小钱，然后在台球桌下过夜，是吗？”

“实际上我甚至经常在干草广场的维亚泽姆斯基大院[1]过夜。的确，是真的，退伍后我的生活就是那样的，饱尝羞辱，也堕落过，但不是道德上的堕落，因为那个时候连我自己都很厌恶我的所作所为。其实这只是意志和心灵的颓废，是对当时处境的绝望。但这一切都过去了……”

“哦，现在您是个大人物了——是个金融家啦！”

这是在说我的当铺。但我已经冷静下来了。我知道，她非常想让我亲口说出一些自取其辱的话，但我没有给她这个机会。这时，有人摇响了当铺的铃铛，我去了前厅招呼客人。一个小时后，她突然穿戴好准备出门，还在我面前说：

“您结婚前从来没对我说过这些，对吧？”

1. 19 世纪彼得堡市一个收容底层市民的场所。

见我没回应，她就走了。

于是第二天，我站到了那房间的门后，揣着一把左轮手枪，听一听我的命运将如何做出安排。她打扮得漂漂亮亮，坐在桌子旁，叶菲莫维奇坐在她对面，装腔作势。虽然之前我没意识到自己有什么预感，但事情还是和我的事先判断丝毫不差（这里要夸奖一下我自己）。我不知道，我说明白了没有。

事情经过就是这样。我听了整整一个小时，在这一个小时里，我仿佛见证了一位世界上最高贵的女性和一个庸俗的、堕落的、愚蠢的、灵魂卑微的无耻之徒间的决斗。我非常惊讶，我想，这个天真、温顺、沉默寡言的女人是从哪里学会这些话的？上流社会最有幽默感的喜剧作家恐怕都创作不出那种极具讽刺效果的剧本，里面充满了天真无邪的大笑与美德对丑恶的神圣鄙视。她说出的词句是多么华丽，敏捷的回应是多么机智，她的责备声中又饱含着多少真理啊！即便如此，她的话语里也完全不失少女的纯真。她嘲笑他的爱情表白，嘲笑他的腔调，嘲笑他的求婚。他没预料到她会抗拒，因此一上来就表现得十分鲁莽，这下他完全呆住了。起初我还认为，她就是在那儿卖弄风情——“这种行为虽然放荡，但能显得她俏皮可爱，这样可以提高她自己的身价。”但事实并非如此，真相就如同太阳的光芒一样，让猜忌无处容身。她的心智还没有完全成熟，决定赴这次约会只是出于对我的怨恨，突发奇想，有意为之。不过一旦事情开始，她就会立刻清醒过来。她苦思冥想，就是要找出一个能羞辱我的方法来，但真要开始做那种龌龊事时，她又忍受不了。如她这般纯洁无邪又充满理想的人，真的能被叶菲莫维奇或其他上流社会的无耻之徒引诱吗？绝无可能，他只能让她发笑。真理会从她的心灵中涌现，愤怒会激起她发自心底的嘲讽。我再说说当时的情况，那个跳梁小丑最后十分尴尬，皱着眉头坐在那里，几乎一句话也说不出来，以至于我有点儿担心，他会不会出于卑鄙的报复心理去直接羞辱她一番。我还要补充一下：我内心毫无波澜地听完了这场戏，我的表现还不赖。这场面我仿佛似曾相识，我去的原因似乎也正是要重温这一场景。我虽然带了一把枪，但我什么都不相信，什么说辞都不想听——这是真的！我怎么能把她想象成另外一种样子呢？我为什么爱她，我为什么欣赏她，我为什么要和她结婚？当然，那个时候我太执迷不悟了，认为她讨厌我，但我也坚信她是贞洁的。我终止了这场表演，推门走了进去。叶菲莫维奇吓了一跳，我抓住她的手，请求她和我回去。叶菲莫维奇回过神来，高声大笑。

“啊，我不能侵犯神圣的夫权，带她走吧，带她走吧！您知道，”他在我身后喊，“虽然一个正派的人不应该和您决斗，但看在您夫人的面子上，如果您自己愿意冒险尝试……我一定奉陪……”

“听见了吧！”在出门的一刹那我叫住她说道。

回家的路上我们一句话都没说。我挽着她的手，她并没有拒绝。相反地，她看上去有些惊慌，但这也只是在回家的路上。回家后，她就坐在椅子上盯着我看。她面色十分苍白，虽然略带嘲讽地抿着嘴唇，但眼神中已然带着一股郑重其事的挑战意味。似乎她真的相信，我马上会用左轮枪打死她。但我只是默默地从口袋中取出枪，放在了桌子上。她看了看我，又看了看枪。（请注意：她对这把枪并不陌生。当铺刚开张的时候，我就买了这把枪，装好了子弹。从准备开当铺时起，我就决定不养烈性犬，不雇像莫泽尔家的那种壮丁。如果家里有客人来，厨娘会去开门。但是干我们这一行的是不可能不有所防备的，所以我买了这支左轮枪，装上了子弹。她刚嫁到我家时，对这把枪非常感兴趣，缠着我问这问那，我甚至给她讲解了枪的原理和构造，而且还说服她做了一次打靶射击。请注意我说的这些。）我没理会她惊恐的神情，脱了外衣躺在床上，我感到筋疲力尽。已经将近十一点了，她还坐在那里一动不动，大约又过了一个小时，她熄了灯，没脱衣服，躺在了墙边的沙发上。这是她第一次没有和我一起睡——这也应该注意。

6. 可怕的回忆

现在来说一说这段可怕的回忆吧……

我早上醒来时，大概不到八点，房间里早已大亮。我一下子清醒过来，猛地睁开双眼。她当时就站在桌子旁边，手里握着枪。她没注意到我已经醒了，而且还在看着她。我突然发现，她拿着枪朝我走了过来。我赶紧闭上眼，假装熟睡。

我听见她走到床边，站在那里。此时我什么都听见了，虽然房间里一片死寂，但我却能听到这寂静的声音。我突然抽搐了一下，不由自主地睁开了眼睛。她直勾勾地盯着我，看着我的眼睛，左轮枪已经指向了我的太阳穴。刹那间我们四目相对，但很快又移开了眼神。我竭尽全力把眼睛重新闭上，在那一瞬间，我下定决心，不论发生什么，我都不会动，也不会睁开眼睛。

在一般情况下，一个熟睡的人突然睁开眼睛，甚至抬起头看了一眼房间，然后又马上睡过去，这一过程应该是完全无意识的，他什么都不会记住。我和她四目相对，感觉到枪指着我的太阳穴，然后又突然闭上眼睛，一动不动，如同熟睡一样——她一定会认为，我实际上根本没醒过来，什么也没看到。而且，如果一个人看到了当时我眼前的情形，还能那样重新闭上眼睛，是完全不可思议的事。

这的确不可思议。但她可能还是弄不明白，这到底是怎么回事——其实，这就是当时我脑中瞬间闪现的念头。啊，在那一刹那，我脑中的想法和感受如旋风般疾驰而过，如闪电般的人类思维是多么伟大！面对这种情况（我切身感受到的），如果她能认识到我当时已经清醒的话，那么我这种从容赴死的勇气一定会让她感到无比震撼，她的手可能仍旧在发抖。这种非凡的印象可能会改变一个人过去的决断。有这样一种说法，人们站在高处时，总会感觉到好像有一股力量在把他们向下拉，拉向深渊。我想，很多自杀或杀死别人的人完全就是因为他们有枪在手。无底深渊也好，四十五度的斜坡也罢，人们站在这上面不可能不向下滑落，就如同你手中拿着枪，总会有某种不可阻挡的力量促使你扣动扳机。但也许她当时已经意识到，我看见了她在做什么，也意识到我是清醒的，我是在默默等待死亡的到来——正是这种意识阻止了她继续滑向深渊。

房间里的寂静仍在蔓延，而我却突然感觉到一个冰冷的铁器碰触到了我的鬓发，你们会问：当时我真的认为自己不会死吗？上帝见证，我要告诉你们：那一刻我真的不抱任何希望，除非有奇迹发生。我为什么要接受死亡？我也要问问你们：我挚爱的人举着左轮枪对着我，即使她不开枪，我之后的人生还有什么意义？而且，我非常了解我这个人，我知道，那一瞬间，我们是在进行一场战斗，是关乎生死的一场可怕对决，其中一方正是那个被视为懦夫，被赶出军队的人。这一点我很清楚，而且，如果她能看出来我当时并没睡着的话，那么她也会明白的。

可能实际情况并非完全如此，也有可能我当时并不是那样想的，但即使我没有那样想，那一刻发生的事也确实是存在的，因为日后我还能经常回想起当时做的那一切。

可你们还会问：为什么你没有把她从罪恶中拯救出来？是啊，我也不断地问自己这个问题——每次一想起那一刻，我就脊背发凉。但那时我的灵魂已深陷绝望之中：如果连我自己都死了，我还能拯救谁？你们凭什么说，我那时还能想到拯救别人？你们怎么会知道我当时的感受？

那一刻，我思绪翻腾。时间在一秒秒地流逝，房间里依然一片死寂。我感觉她一直站在我旁边——过了一会儿，心底的一丝希望让我突然浑身一颤！我马上睁开眼睛。她已经不在房间里了。我从床上坐起来：我赢了——她永远被我征服了！

我起床去喝茶。我们家的茶炊总是放在前屋，每次都是由她来斟茶。我默默地坐到桌边，从她手里接过一杯茶。五分钟后，我看了她一眼。她面色十分苍白，甚至比昨天还要严重。她也在看着我。突然，突然间——当她发现我看她时，苍白的嘴唇间露出冷冷的一笑，怯生生的眼神里似乎充满了疑问。她好像还是拿不准刚才发生的事，并在问自己：他到底是知道还是不知道，看见还是没看见？我不动声色地避开了她的眼神。喝完茶后，我关了当铺，去市场上买了张铁床和一扇屏风。回家后，我吩咐把床放在前厅里，用屏风把它围上。床是给她买的，但我并没和她说什么。看到这张床，不用说她也应该明白，我“都看见了，也都知道了”，她也不用再猜疑了。晚上我照旧把左轮枪放在桌子上，她也一声不响地睡到了自己的新床上。婚姻关系解除了，“她被征服了，但没得到宽恕”。夜里她不断呓语，第二天早上热病发作，卧床了六个星期。

二

1. 高傲的梦

卢克里娅刚才跟我说，等太太下葬后，她不想继续在我这儿待着了，她也准备走。我已经跪着祷告五分钟了，我原本打算祷告一个小时，但我脑子里一直安静不下来，一直在想各种各样的问题，全是些病态的想法，想得我头疼——在这里祈祷有什么用呢？只不过是个罪过！说来也奇怪，我竟然不想睡觉：一般说来，人在极度悲伤的情况下，特别是在经历了最初的强烈刺激后，总是想睡觉。据说，被判处死刑的人在行刑前夜会睡得非常踏实。这也可以理解，符合人的本性，否则的话那人是熬不住的……我躺在沙发上，但睡不着……

在她生病的六个星期里，我雇了一位受过专业训练的助理护士，加上我和卢克里娅，我们三人日夜照料她。我不心疼钱，甚至想在她身上多花一点儿。我请来的施罗德医生每次的出诊费是十卢布。她清醒过来后，我就很少出现在她面前了。我说这些干吗呢？基本康复后，她就常常坐在我房间里一张专门为她买的桌子旁，一言不发……是的，我们俩基本上不说话；后来才慢慢开始有了些交流，但也仅限于一些日常杂事。我当然是有意不去多说话的，但我很清楚，不用和我说过多的废话让她也很高兴。我认为，她的这些表现都是很正常的：毕竟她受到了极大的震撼，又在和我的斗争中惨败。但我认为，她需要时间去忘记这些事，而且要习惯现在的这种状态。因此，我们就这样彼此保持着沉默，但我时时刻刻都在为自己的未来做着准备。我想她应该也是如此吧，那个时候我最大的兴趣就是猜测她的想法，猜测她心里是怎么看我的。

还有……唉，你们谁也想不到，我为她的病忍受了多少折磨。但所有的一切我都只在内心默默承受，从未表露过，甚至连卢克里娅都察觉不到。我无法想象，甚至不敢去假设，她在一无所知的情况下死去会是种什么情形。在她脱离危险、逐渐康复后，我知道，我也会很快平静下来。而且，我想让现在的状态暂时维持下去，我们的未来终会降临，但我想尽量把它推后。的确，当时我的心理状态有点儿奇怪，总有种特别的感觉……这么说吧，我觉得我胜利了，对于我来说，只要一想到这件事，我就十分满足。整个冬天就这么过去了。而我，从来没有像这个冬天那样，觉得一切如此完美。

你们要知道，在我妻子的惨剧发生前，我的人生中还有过一次可怕的经历——被迫从军队退役，这件事无时无刻不在困扰我，使我声誉受损。总之，我受到了蛮横无理的对待。是的，我的同事们不喜欢我，他们认为我性格阴郁，甚至有些可笑。事情往往就是这样的，有些东西您觉得它是高尚的，值得尊重，您把它深藏心底，但不知为什么，这竟会让有些人发笑。是啊，人们从来都不喜欢我，甚至在学校里就是这样。我总是处处不受欢迎。连卢克里娅都不喜欢我。在团里服役时，有件事可以证明我不受欢迎，虽然它是偶然发生的。有的时候厄运会像飘来的浮云一样凑到一块儿，可能发生也可能不发生的意外都会让一个人毁掉，没有什么事比这更令人反感和难以接受的了。对于一个睿智的人来说，这简直就是有辱尊严。事情的经过是这样的：

有一次我去剧院看戏，幕间休息时去了趟茶点部。这时一个叫阿×的骠骑兵突然走了进来，当着在场军官和其他观众的面，对另外两个骠骑兵大声说，我们团的别祖姆采夫上尉刚才在走廊里大吵大闹，“好像是喝多了”。他们的交谈没了下文，说的也不是真事，别祖姆采夫上尉并没有喝多，也没像他说的那样大吵大闹。几个骠骑兵又闲聊了几句，然后就走了。但第二天，这事传到了我们团里，立刻有人说，当时我们团在茶点部的只有我一人，而且骠骑兵阿×在污蔑别祖姆采夫上尉时，我也没有上去制止他。可我为什么要那样做呢？如果他对别祖姆采夫有恶意的话，那也是他们之间的私事，我干吗要蹚这浑水呢？但军官们认为，这并非只是私人恩怨，而是牵涉到了我们团，因为当时团里的军官中只有我一人在场。我的做法就等于在向其他军官和观众们证明，我们团里可能有军官不重视自己和团队的荣誉。我不同意这样的定论。有人告诉我，虽然现在有点儿晚了，但还是有机会补救的，只要我正式向阿×解释清楚当时的情况就可以了。我不想这么做，而且觉得很气愤，所以就一口回绝了。不久之后，我就退役，离开了军队。这就是事情的整个经过。我高傲地离开，但心理却崩溃了。之后便一蹶不振。恰巧这时，我在莫斯科的姐夫挥霍掉了我们本就不多的财产，其中也包括我的那一小份，致使我身无分文，流落街头。我本可以在私人机构谋个职位，但我没那样做：脱下闪亮的军装，我不想随便到铁路上的什么地方去工作。就这样吧，羞愧、耻辱、堕落，要来就来吧，越坏越好——这就是我当时的选择。种种幽暗的记忆与维亚泽姆斯基大院，填满了我接下来三年的生活。一年半之前，我的教母，一位有钱的老妇人，在莫斯科去世了，有些意外的是，在她的遗嘱中有三千卢布是留给我的。经过一番考虑，我做出了改变自己命运的决定。我打算开一家当铺，这并不需要别人的理解：等赚够了钱，我会去找一个能安身的角落，开始新的生活，远离从前的记忆——这就是我的计划。然而，那段黑暗的往事和永远洗刷不清的羞辱却在时时刻刻折磨着我。后来我结婚了，这是不是偶然的事情——我也不知道。但娶她进家门时，我想，我是给自己找了一位朋友，我太需要朋友了。但我也清楚，朋友间是需要磨合的，甚至是需要征服的。我能立刻向这位对我抱有成见的十六岁姑娘解释清楚所有事情吗？比如说，如果没有那次可怕的“左轮枪事件”，我能使她相信，我并非懦夫，被军队除名也是不公正的吗？但这件事来得是多么及时啊！在经受住了左轮枪的考验后，我彻底洗刷掉了那段屈辱与黑暗的历史。虽然不会有人知道这些故事，但只要她能明白就够了，这对我来说就是一切，因为她对于我来说就是一切，是我理想中未来的全部希望所在。她是我唯一想要的人，不需要别人了——她应该是都懂了，至少她清楚，投奔我的敌人对我来说是不公平的。这种想法让我无比欣慰。她现在可能还会觉得我是个怪人，但起码不会再认为我是个卑鄙下流之徒了。而且，经历了这一切之后，我更加认同：性格古怪并不是缺点；相反，有时候它更能打动女性的心。总之，我是把这件事暂时放下了，并不急于去解决。我感觉自己非常平静，对于我的理想来说，有太多的图景和素材可以利用。我是个幻想家，但这也是我的问题所在：我总是在幻想自己的未来，但对她呢，再等等吧。

整个冬天就在某种期待中过去了。我喜欢悄悄地看着她坐在桌边的样子。她会做一些针线活儿，缝缝补补，晚上有时会从我柜子里拿一本书读读。我的藏书基本上可以证明我的品位和兴趣。她几乎哪也不去。每天午饭后或黄昏前，我会带她出去散步，做些户外运动，我们也不像从前那样互不说话了。我尽量做出我们相处和睦的样子，但正如我前面说过的，我们俩都不会让自己和对方过于亲近。我是有意这样做的，而她呢，我想，还是应该再“给她些时间吧”。让我感到奇怪的是，我自己竟然从来都没仔细想过这种情况。整个冬天里，我一直喜欢悄悄地看她，但直到冬天结束，她都没看过我一眼！我只是认为，她还是太羞怯了，而且病后的虚弱无力让她看上去更加腼腆温顺。不，最好还是再等等吧——“说不定她会突然自己走过来……”

这个想法总是让我兴奋不已。再补充一句：有时我好像是故意让自己这么激动，这似乎也让我完全受制于她。就这样又过了一段时间。我对她的怨恨并没有越积越深，也没有在心底根深蒂固。我自己感觉这就像一场游戏。不错，那个时候我是解除了婚姻关系，给她买了床和屏风，但我从来没把她当成一个有罪之人来看待啊。这并不是因为我对她的过错认识肤浅，而是因为从第一天起，甚至在买床之前，我就决定要宽恕她。这听起来确实有点儿奇怪，因为无论如何，在道德要求上，我是个很严格的人。然而，在我眼中，她已经被征服了，受到了应有的惩罚，精神彻底崩溃，虽然有时候我对她充满怜悯，但有时候也对这种结果感到非常满意。我很喜欢我们之间这种不平等的感觉……

这个冬天里，我有意做了几件善事。我免去了两笔应收的债务，还在没有任何抵押物的情况下，放了一些钱给一个贫穷的女人。我没把这些事告诉我妻子，我这么做也不是为了让她知道；但那个女人自己上门来道谢，就差没给我跪下了。这事传了出去，我想，她也应该很高兴我这么做吧。

春天马上就到了，已经是四月中旬了，双层窗户已经被拿掉，明媚的阳光照进了我们安静的房间。似乎曾有一块障眼布挡在我的眼前，蒙蔽了我的头脑。这致命又可怕的障眼布啊！但不知为什么，我眼前的遮蔽物突然落下了，瞬间一切都变得明朗起来，我恍然大悟！这一天的到来是偶然的吗，是注定的吗，是太阳的光芒让我愚钝的头脑瞬间开悟的吗？不，并不存在什么顿悟，而是那根筋脉，那根已经僵死了的筋脉突然间又跳动了起来，它摇晃着我沉寂的心灵和骇人的高傲，它们复活了，它们又放射出了光芒。我突然感觉到像是从地上跳起来一样。是的，它来得太突然，太出人意料。事情发生在那天下午五点钟，临近傍晚……

2. 障眼布突然落下了

在这之前，我先交代两句。早在一个月之前，我就发现她经常莫名其妙地陷入沉思之中，注意，是沉思，不是沉默。我也是突然发现的。我看她的时候，她总是坐在那里低头缝纫，看也不看我一眼。有时她坐在那里的样子会突然让我感到惊讶，纤细、瘦弱、面色苍白，嘴唇也毫无血色，如果再加上她若有所思的神情，那可真是一幅让人震撼的画面。在这之前，我就常常在夜里听到她小声干咳。有一次，我又听到她在咳嗽，我没和她打招呼，马上起床去请施罗德医生过来。

施罗德是第二天来我家的。她惊讶地看了看医生，又看了看我。

她随即面无表情地冷笑着说："我没生病。"

施罗德没有太仔细检查病情（这种医生总是端着架子，有时看病马马虎虎），只是把我叫到另一个房间，对我说，她这是大病初愈后的常见情况，春天时最好能去海边疗养一下，如果不行的话，去乡间休息一段时间也可以。总之，他也没说出什么来，就是告诉我，她现在身体虚弱，需要休息之类的。施罗德走后，她非常严肃地看着我，还是说：

“我真的一点儿病都没有。”

但说着说着，突然脸红了起来，很明显，她觉得很惭愧。不说我也明白：她之所以觉得惭愧，是因为她知道，我还是她的丈夫，仍然像个真正的丈夫那样在关心她。但当时我没能彻底看清的是，她脸上那一抹红晕可绝不是温顺与谦卑的象征。（那就是一块障眼布！）

就这样，一个月之后，在四月一个阳光明媚的下午，我在当铺里结账，她在房间里干着活儿。当时已经五点多了，我突然听见我们的房间里传出了歌声……是她，她在那儿轻声地唱了起来。这是我第一次听到她唱歌，以至于那歌声给我留下的深刻印象，到现在我都无法完全理解。在那之后我几乎没有听到她唱过歌了，除了她刚嫁到我家的时候，我们还有说有笑，有时候我们会用左轮枪去打靶。那个时候，她的声音还很响亮、清脆，虽然有时忽高忽低，但非常悦耳，而且气力十足。但现在她的歌声是那样的微弱，虽然听上去并不忧郁（她唱的是首抒情歌曲），但她的嗓子就好像被撕裂、折断了一样，似乎不太适合用来歌唱，给人的感觉就像那首歌也生病了一样。她轻轻地唱着，唱到高音时，那虚弱的声音就会挣扎着断开，然后咳嗽一下，继续轻轻地往下唱……

有些人可能会嘲笑我太激动了，但可能永远都不会有人理解，我为什么要那么动情！不，我并不只是为她感到惋惜，除此之外，还有其他原因。起码在刚听到她的歌声时，我觉得有点儿莫名其妙，进而是惊讶不已，感到既可怕又怪异，到最后几乎是一种病态的报复心理：她在唱歌，居然在我面前唱歌！难道她忘了我的存在吗？

我浑身发抖地坐在那里，然后猛地站了起来，不假思索地拿上帽子准备出门，但我根本不知道要去哪里，要做什么。卢克里娅帮我穿好了大衣。

“她在唱歌？”我随口对卢克里娅说。但她没明白我的意思，看了看我，还是没搞懂；我这话说得的确有点儿含糊不清。

“这是她第一次唱歌吗？”

“不，您不在的时候，她偶尔会唱。”卢克里娅回答。

我明白了。我走下楼梯，上了街，开始漫无目的地游荡。我走到一处拐角，站下来想一想我要去哪儿。那里人来人往，不时会有人撞到我，但我毫无感觉。我叫下了一个马车夫，让他带我去“警察大桥”，我也不知道为什么要去那里。可不一会儿我就放弃了这个想法，并塞给他二十戈比。

“打扰了，这些钱你拿着吧。”我冲他茫然地笑了笑，但心里却突然开始一阵狂喜。

我加快脚步，转身回了家。那个颤抖、虚弱、撕裂的歌声又突然在我脑海里响起，几乎让我窒息。障眼布终于落了下来！假如她还能在我面前唱歌的话，那么说明她已经不在乎我了——这一点是很明确的，同时又很可怕。我能感受得到。但我心中的狂喜战胜了恐惧。

这真是命运对我的捉弄！要知道整个冬天我的心里全是这种喜悦的感觉，根本容不下其他任何东西，可我自己在哪里呢？我和我的心灵是融为一体了吗？我匆匆忙忙地跑上楼梯，我不知道，我进门的时候是不是看上去怯生生的。我只记得，地板仿佛波浪一样起起伏伏，而我则像是在水面上漂浮。我走进房间，她还是坐在原来的地方，低头做着针线活，但没有唱歌。她有意无意地朝我这边看了一眼，但目光并没有落在我身上，只是做了个动作而已，平淡又冷漠，无论谁来她都是这个样子。

我直接走了过去，坐在紧挨着她的椅子上。可能是我的举动有点儿反常，她似乎是被吓了一跳，飞快地看了我一眼。我握住她的手，但忘记了和她说的是什么，因为我当时已经完全语无伦次了。我已经控制不住我的声音了，我不知道我说了什么，只记得当时快要窒息了。

“我们聊聊吧……你知道……随便说点儿什么都行！”我好像是说了一些蠢话，可这时候又怎么能仔细思考呢？她哆嗦了一下，立刻把手抽了回去。她吓得不轻地看着我，但眼神中却满是严肃的惊讶神情。没错，惊讶又严肃的神情，它立刻将我击得粉碎。虽然她没有开口，但眼神却在突然发问：“爱情？你也想要爱情？”我能读懂她的眼神，我能读出她眼中的一切。这一切都让我激动不已，我扑倒在了她的脚边。是的，我在她面前崩溃了。她一下子跳了起来，但我用尽全力握住了她的双手。

我完全记得我当时绝望的感觉，对，完全记得！但你们相信吗，也正是在那个时候，我的心中翻滚沸腾，感受到了难以抑制的狂喜，我想，我快要死了。我如痴如醉地亲吻着她的双脚，沉浸在无边无际的幸福之中。没错，这难以言表的幸福就出现在彻底的绝望面前。我一边哭泣，一边想要说些什么，但根本说不出话来。她刚才那惊恐的神情突然变成了一副忧虑的样子，她看我的眼神有些怪异，甚至带有一丝野性，她似乎有一个非同寻常的问题，但很快又把它想清楚了，继而微微一笑。我继续亲吻着她的双脚，她羞涩地把脚移开，我便亲吻她脚下的地板。她看着眼前发生的这一幕，突然笑了（你们也见过羞涩的笑吧）。她笑得越来越厉害，甚至近乎歇斯底里，我看见她的双手在颤抖，但这些我都毫不在意，只是在那不停地对她低语，说我爱她，说我愿意永远匍匐在她面前，“让我吻你的裙子吧……我一辈子都会这样对你顶礼膜拜……”她突然开始号啕大哭，浑身不停地抽搐，犹如陷入可怕的癫狂中一般。是我把她吓到了。

我把她抱到床上。过了一会儿，她逐渐冷静下来，但神色却十分憔悴。她坐在床边，拉着我的手，请求我一定要冷静：“够了，您不要再折磨自己，冷静一点儿吧！”——说完，她又哭了起来。那天晚上我一直陪在她身边，寸步不离。我一直在和她说话，说我要带她去布洛涅[1]，去洗海水浴，马上出发，再过两星期就走；说我听到她的声音还像不久前那样虚弱；说我要关了当铺，把它卖给多布龙拉沃夫；还说要开始新的生活，这是最重要的，要去布洛涅，去布洛涅！她听了我讲的这些，觉得有些害怕，而且越来越害怕。但我并没有太在意她的感受，对于我来说，更重要的是，我发疯似的想要再跪倒在她的脚边，再亲吻她的双脚，亲吻她脚下的地板，膜拜她，我不停地对她说："我再也不会向你索要什么了，不要回应我，不要在乎我，完全不要，我只请求你允许我在一个角落里默默地看着你，把我当成你的一件东西就好，把我当成一条狗……"她又哭了。

"我还以为您不会再理我了。"她脱口而出，说得那么突然，那么不经意，仿佛她自己都没有意识到她说了什么。但对于我来说，这是那天晚上最重要的一句话，无比清晰，正中要害，让我心如刀绞。这句话让我彻底醒悟了，只有她在我身边，在我眼前，我才能对未来充满渴望，我才能感到无比的幸福。啊，那天晚上我让她筋疲力尽，我能理解，但我也不断在想，我要马上做出

1. 全称为"滨海布洛涅"，法国西北部港口城市，临加莱海峡，拥有海滨浴场。

改变。最后，她终于撑不住了，我劝她休息，她倒头便睡。夜里，我不停地起来，穿上鞋走到她床边，静静地看着她。和我想象的一样，她有时会在梦中低声呓语。我一边搓着手，一边看着她，看着这个躺在我花三卢布买来的小铁床上的病人。我跪了下来，但没有亲吻她的脚。（会弄醒她的！）我祈祷了一会儿，然后站了起来。这时，卢克里娅从厨房走了出来，看到了我。我走到她跟前，告诉她可以去睡觉了，从明天开始，就是“另一番光景”了。

我对这一点坚信不疑，甚至到了迷狂的程度。虽然我的眼前不再有任何障碍遮挡我的视线，但当时我正沉浸在那种无边无际的喜悦之中，久久不能平静下来，以至于完全不去理会灾祸降临的某种征兆。我只期待明天马上到来，对，就是明天！要知道，那个时候她还活着，她就在那里，就在我的眼前，就像我在她的眼前一样，一想到这些，我如何能平静得下来呢？“等她明天醒来，我要把这一切都告诉她，她会理解的。”这就是我当时的想法，简单而又明确，我为此狂喜不已！更重要的是去布洛涅的旅行。不知为什么，我总是想着布洛涅，似乎那就是一切，似乎在布洛涅会有某种终极存在的东西。“到布洛涅去，到布洛涅去！……”我狂躁地等待着明天。

3. 我了解得太清楚了

这件事的的确确就发生在几天前，五天，总共只过去了五天，就在上星期二。不、不，如果她能再多等一会儿，用不了多长时间，我就可以驱散阴霾了！难道她的心还没有平静下来吗？第二天她听我说话时，虽然看上去有些心神不定，但脸上已经挂着微笑了……但在过去的整整五天里，她时而心神不宁，时而羞愧难当。她仍然感到害怕，非常害怕。我不会去争辩，也不想反驳，我没有丧失理智，她感到恐惧是可以理解的，她怎么能不害怕呢？要知道，我们彼此早已是陌生人了，相互生疏，形同陌路，但却突然发生了这一切……我并没有注意到她的恐惧，我只看到了美好的新生活！……的确，千真万确，我犯了一个错误。也可能是很多错误。第二天一觉醒来（已是星期三了），一大早我就犯了个错误：我竟然把她当成了自己的一位朋友。我向她坦白了我的过去，甚至连一生中自己都不想直面的事也没有隐瞒，虽然这是有必要的，但我过于着急了——这哪里只是坦白啊！我直接对她说，在这整整一个冬天里，我始终坚信她是爱我的。我向她解释，我当时开这个当铺只是由于意志和心灵的颓废，它既是对我个人意志的鞭挞，也是一种自我夸耀。我还向她承认，当初在茶点部时，我的确是害怕了，这是我的性格所致，我的神经过于脆弱：当时的氛围让我惶恐不安，连茶点部也让我惊慌失措，我甚至在纠结，我要不要赶紧离开，我是不是表现得很愚蠢？我害怕的不是决斗本身，而是在这一过程中被人嘲笑……后来我也一直不愿承认，我是在折磨所有人，我也因此在折磨她，我娶她就是想让她为此感到痛苦。我发疯似的跟她说了这些话。她抓住我的手，哀求我不要再说了："您这说的什么话……您不要再折磨自己了。"说完，又开始号啕大哭，差点再次歇斯底里！她不停地求我什么都别说了，不要再想这些事了。

我没太理会她的请求，继续和她说着关于春天，关于布洛涅的事。那里有太阳，那里有我们的新太阳，这就是我要说的！我要关了当铺，把它转让给多布龙拉沃夫。我又突然向她提议，把我们所有的财产都分发给穷人，只留下我从教母那里继承的三千卢布，我们用这笔钱去布洛涅，等回来后再靠我们的双手开始新的生活。事情就这么定了，她没有反对，因为她什么也没说……只是笑了笑。她的笑似乎更像是出于安慰，只是为了不让我伤心。我看得出来，我让她很为难，你们别以为我又愚蠢又自私，什么都不懂。其实我什么都明白，我比谁都看得透，我已经处在彻底绝望的边缘了！

我把所有事都和她讲了，关于我的、关于她的，乃至关于卢克里娅的。我告诉她，我也哭过……唉，我当然不会多说关于我哭的事，而且有些事情我也是尽量不去提及。我记得，有那么一两次，她和我交谈时也表现得兴致勃勃，对，我记得！你们怎么可以说我什么都不在意呢？如果这件事没有发生的话，那一切都将大不一样。要知道，两天前她还笑着和我讲这个冬天她读过的书，讲吉尔·布拉斯和格林纳达大主教的片段[1]。那是多么纯真、可爱的笑容啊，和她还是我未婚妻的时候一模一样。（时间真是过得飞快！）看到这笑容我是多么高兴啊！不过，她在讲到大主教时的那种状态倒是让我很惊讶：很显然，她在冬天里读那本文学经典的时候获得了

1. 出自法国作家阿兰·勒内·勒萨日（1668—1747）的长篇小说《吉尔·布拉斯》。

内心的宁静和幸福，以至于让她面露笑容。难道她那时真的已经心如死灰，完全确信我将抛弃她吗？因为她星期二的时候还说过：“我还以为您会抛弃我呢！”唉，这可真是十岁小女孩的想法！实际上，她那时的确完全相信，未来的一切事情都会是像她想的那样：我们两个人各自坐在自己的桌子旁，就这么一直坐下去，直到六十岁。但突然有一天，我走到她面前，我是她的丈夫，一个需要爱的丈夫！这是多么深的误解啊，我是多么糊涂啊！

我欣喜若狂地看着她，但这样做不太好，可能会把她吓到，我应该再克制一点。其实我已经很克制了，我控制住自己没再去亲吻她的脚。我从来没表现出过那种样子……就是……我作为一个丈夫的样子——我脑子里从来就没想过那应该是什么样子，我只想膜拜她！但我已经无法再沉默下去了，让我一言不发是完全不可能的。我突然对她说，和她交谈是一种愉悦的享受，我认为她的教养和见识都要远远超过我。她的脸涨得通红，慌忙说，我这是言过其实了。但处在狂喜中的我犯了一个愚蠢的错误，我情不自禁地和她提起了当初躲在门后，听她和那个无耻之徒论战的事，那次清白的论战。而且我还告诉她，我是多么地欣赏她的智慧、机敏和孩童般的纯真。她听了我的话，身体微微颤抖了一下，依然说我言过其实了，但这次声音更轻，而且脸色一下子阴沉了下来，随后便用双手捂着脸失声痛哭……这下我再也控制不住自己了：我又跪倒在她身边，亲吻她的双脚，最后又是以一阵歇斯底里般的发作收场，那场景和星期二时一模一样。这是昨天晚上的事，但到了第二天早上……

第二天早上?！天啊，那不就是今天早上吗，就在不久前，就是刚才！

你们仔细想想：就在我们刚才一起喝茶的时候（就是在昨天的那阵发疯后），她还对我说，她冬天时让我惊讶的那种平静心态是真实的！而我却整夜在为昨天的事担惊受怕。但她突然走到我面前，双手紧紧握在一起，（就在刚才！）对我说，她知道，她是有罪之人，整个冬天她的罪孽都在折磨着她，而且现在也没有停止……她说她非常敬佩我高尚的情操和坦荡的胸襟……“我要做您忠诚的妻子，我会一直尊敬您……”我一下子跳了起来，发疯似的抱住了她！我亲吻着她，吻她的脸颊，吻她的嘴唇，就像一位久别归家的丈夫一样。可我刚才为什么要出门，我就离开了两个小时……我去办理我们的出国护照……哦，我的天啊！我要是早回来五分钟，就那五分钟！……我回来时一群人围在大门口，那些人盯着我，那些目光……啊，主啊！

卢克里娅说（我现在无论如何也不能让卢克里娅走，她了解所有细节，整个冬天她都在，她会把一切都告诉我），大约在我回来前的二十分钟左右，她走进房间去问我妻子一件事，我记不起来是什么事了。她当时看到，圣像（就是前面提到过的圣母像）已被取了出来，就放在桌子上，好像我妻子刚刚祈祷过。“您怎么了，太太？”“没什么事，卢克里娅，你去吧……等等，卢克里娅。”我妻子走到她跟前，吻了她一下。“您现在觉得开心吗，太太？”“是的，卢克里娅。”“先生早就该向您道歉，太太……感谢上帝，你们终于和好了。”“好，卢克里娅，你去吧。”她笑了笑，但看上去有些怪异，怪异到卢克里娅总觉得有什么地方不对劲，十分钟后又返回房间去看她，“她当时站在墙边，离窗户很近，一只手贴着墙，头贴在手上，好像在想着什么事情。她想得太出神了，都没注意到我在门外看她。我看见，她好像在笑，站在那儿一边笑，一边想心事。我站了一会儿，就悄悄走开了，我正在纳闷儿的时候，突然听见窗户被打开的声音。我急忙走回去说，‘外面冷，太太，您可别着凉了’，就在这时我突然看到，她站到了窗台上，窗户开着，她背对着我站在窗户中间，手里握着圣像。我的心扑通一下，赶紧喊‘太太，太太’，她听见了，我以为她会转过身来看看我，但她没有，而是把圣像按在胸前，向前跨了一步，跳了下去！”

我只记得，我刚走进大门时，她还有体温。主要是他们都在看我。一开始他们还在吵吵嚷嚷，但一看到我立刻安静了下来，给我让出了一条路，我看见……她躺在那里，抱着圣像。我记得，当时感觉周围一团漆黑，我默默地走过去，站在那儿看了好久，大家围在我身边，好像在对我说着什么。卢克里娅当时也在，但我没看见她。听别人说，她还和我说话了。我记得，有一个人一直在冲我嚷嚷：“从嘴里流出一小摊血，就一小摊，一小摊！”他还指给我看地面上的血。我的一根手指好像沾到了血，有些弄脏了，我看了看我的手指（这个我记得），而那个人就一直在旁边对我说：“一小摊，一小摊！”

“什么‘一小摊’，你是什么意思？”我用尽全力冲他喊（据说是），然后抡起拳头朝他扑了过去……

啊，荒唐，荒唐！这是个误会！这不正常！这怎么可能！

4. 只晚了五分钟

难道不是这样吗？难道这会是真的吗？难道你们觉得这是有可能的吗？为了什么，究竟是什么原因让这个女人选择了死亡？

你们要相信，我是知道原因的；但她为了什么而死——仍然是个谜。她对我的爱感到恐惧，她一定是认真地问过自己：是否应该接受这种爱？既然回答不了这个问题，那就只好选择死亡。我知道，我知道，其实这没有什么值得伤脑筋的地方：她对自己做了太多的承诺，她害怕无法兑现——就是这样。但有些情况是非常可怕的。

现在我仍然弄不明白的是，她是为了什么目的而死的？这个问题一直在我脑子里挥之不去。实际上，无论她想要过怎样的生活，我都会让她得偿所愿。但她不相信我会那样做，这就是问题所在！不、不，我在撒谎，完全不是这么回事。原因其实很简单，和我在一起就应该坦诚相待：她选择爱我，就会全心全意地爱，而不是像她爱那个杂货店老板那样敷衍行事。她是那么纯洁，那么真诚，她无法接受那位老板想要的那种爱情。她不想欺骗我，她不想用二分之一、四分之一的爱来装模作样地骗我。她就是这样的诚实，就是这样，先生们！那个时候我还想让她更加豁达一些，你们记得吗？多么奇怪的想法。

有些问题我非常想知道答案：她尊敬我吗？我不知道。她鄙视我吗？我不认为她会鄙视我。但奇怪的是，为什么我从来没想过这个问题，整个冬天我都从来没考虑过，她是不是在鄙视我。在她用那种严肃而又惊讶的目光看我之前，我一直都坚信她不会鄙视我。没错，严肃。正是那份严肃让我彻底明白，她鄙视我。但现在为时已晚，一切都无法重来了！啊，让她鄙视我吧，哪怕鄙视一辈子都没关系，只要她活着！刚才她还能走路，还能说话呢。我真想不通，她是怎么从窗户跳下去的！我哪曾想到，这事就发生在五分钟前。我叫来卢克里娅。我现在决不能让卢克里娅走，决不能！

我们还有很多事要商量呢。我们只是在这个冬天才开始彼此疏远的，难道就不能重归于好吗？为什么，为什么我们不能在一起重新开始新的生活呢？我是个坦荡又豁达的人，她也是——这不就是我们之间的契合点吗？我们只要再谈一谈，不需要多久，也许再过两天她就能彻底理解我了。

最让人无法接受的就是这样的事——简单、野蛮、愚昧，让人无法预料。这多么遗憾啊！五分钟，我就晚来了五分钟！我要是能提前回来五分钟，这事就不会发生了，她脑子里也再不会出现这样的念头了。到最后，她一定会理解我所做的一切。可现在，房间又变得空空荡荡，又只有我一个人了。钟摆还在那里嘀嗒作响，它无所牵挂，也没有遗憾。我身边一个人都没有——这就是我的不幸！

我一直在房间里走来走去。我知道，我知道，你们不用提醒我：我抱怨这件不可预料的事，我还抱怨那五分钟，你们觉得可笑吗？但你们要知道，这是很明显的。你们想想：出现这种情况时，一般人都会留一张字条，写着“我的死和任何人无关”，但她什么都没留下。难道她没想过，有的人可能会怀疑到卢克里娅吗？人们会说：“当时只有你和她在一起，一定是你把她推下去的。”如果不是当时有四个人在院子里和厢房窗户中看到她怀抱圣像，自己跳下去的话，那卢克里娅即便无罪，至少也要受一些刁难了。但其他人不也是偶然看到她跳下去的吗？是的，这一瞬间发生的事，完全就是无意识的本能冲动。这就是一场意外，这是毫无理性的行为！但你们会问，她在这之前不是还对着圣像祈祷来着吗？但这并不代表她做的就是死前祈祷。很有可能她就是在十分钟前才做出这种决定的——就在她站在墙边，头靠在手上，面带微笑时。那一刻一定有某种想法钻进了她的脑子，让她神魂颠倒，最终屈服。

你们的想法都存在明显的误解。她是可以和我一起生活的。就算她贫血又怎样呢？难道这是贫血或生命力枯竭所致吗？她从冬天开始就已经很虚弱了，就是这么回事……

我来晚了！！！

躺在棺材里的她是那样的纤细，连她的小鼻子都变得尖瘦了！她的睫毛像平放着的箭一样。她坠落地面后，哪里都没有摔破，哪里都没有折断！只有那“一小摊血”，一个勺子那么多。她是内脏破裂。我又冒出一个奇怪的想法：如果她不下葬会怎样？因为如果她被抬走，那么……不，她几乎不可能被抬走！我当然知道，她应该被抬走，我没疯，也没说胡话，相反，我现在比任何时候都要清醒——只不过家里又要冷冷清清了，又只剩那两个房间，又只有我一个人和那些抵押物在一起了。胡话、胡话，这就是在说胡话！我让她痛苦不堪，就是这样！

走到这一步，你们的那些法律对我来说算得了什么？你们的习俗、你们的文化、你们的生活、你们的国家、你们的信仰对我来说又算得了什么？把我送上法庭吧，让你们的法庭来公开审判我吧，我要说，我没什么好招认的。法官会冲我大喊:“肃静，军官！”我也会回应他:“你有什么权力让我服从你？为什么阴暗的守旧势力要打碎这世上最珍贵的东西？你们的法律为什么要这样对待我？我已经和那些条条框框一刀两断了。”我现在什么都不怕了！

盲目，她太盲目了！她死了，听不到我说话了！她不会知道，我把她置身在怎样的天国之中。天国就在我心里，但愿她已经身在其中！她不会再爱我了——好吧，不过那又怎样呢？万物本该如此，也终将如此。她本可以把我当成一个朋友——那样我们都会快乐，我们会看着对方开心大笑。我们本应这样去生活。如果她爱上了别人——好吧，去爱吧，去爱吧！她会和他走在一起开心地笑，而我会在街角望着他们……啊，不管什么都可以，只要她睁开眼睛，哪怕一次也好！睁开一会儿吧，就一会儿！看看我，就像刚才一样，像她站在我面前发誓要做一个忠诚的妻子那样！只要看一眼她就会全明白了！

旧势力啊！这世界啊！人类孤零零地活在这世界中——这就是不幸！俄罗斯的勇士们在呼喊：“有人活着吗？”我不是勇士，我也这么呼喊，可是无人应答。人们说，太阳赋予万物生命。太阳升起来了，你们看看它，难道它有生命吗？一切都没有生命，到处是一片死气沉沉。只有人是活着的，可他们周围却是一片沉寂——这就是我们的世界！“人们啊，彼此相爱吧！”——这是谁说的？这是谁的训诫？钟摆还在那里漠然地嘀嗒作响，令人厌恶。现在已经夜里两点了。她的靴子还立在床边，仿佛在等着她……不，说正经的，明天她就要被抬走了，我该怎么办？

企鹅经典：小黑书　第三辑

21. 漂亮的卡桑德拉

[英] 简·奥斯汀

22. 温顺的女人

[俄] 陀思妥耶夫斯基

23. 猫与维纳斯

[古希腊] 伊索

24. 黄昏之读

[英] 查尔斯·狄更斯

25. 一个可怕的故事是如何被一条普通的屠夫的狗公之于众的

[德] 约翰·彼得·黑贝尔

26. 亚瑟·萨维尔勋爵的罪行

[英] 奥斯卡·王尔德

27. 伊凡·伊里奇之死

[俄] 列夫·托尔斯泰

28. 我们为何为同一件事哭和笑

[法] 蒙田

29. 我的生命是一杆上实弹的枪

[美] 艾米莉·狄金森

30. 独自在黑夜的海滩上

[美] 沃尔特·惠特曼

Penguin Little Black Classics Vol. III

21. JANE AUSTEN

The Beautifull Cassandra

22. FYODOR DOSTOYEVSKY

The Meek One

23. AESOP

The Cat and Venus

24. CHARLES DICKENS

To Be Read at Dusk

25. JOHANN PETER HEBEL

How a Ghastly Story Was Brought to Light by a Common or Garden Butcher's Dog

26. OSCAR WILDE

Lord Arthur Savile's Crime

27. LEO TOLSTOY

The Death of Ivan Ilyich

28. MICHEL DE MONTAIGNE

How We Weep and Laugh at the Same Thing

29. EMILY DICKINSON

My life had stood a loaded gun

30. WALT WHITMAN

On the Beach at Night Alone

‘I could see that she was still terribly afraid, but I didn’t soften anything; instead, seeing that she was afraid I deliberately intensified it.’

FYODOR DOSTOYEVSKY

The Meek One

A Fantastic Story

Chapter 1

I. WHO I WAS AND WHO SHE WAS

. . . Now as long as she's here – everything is still all right: I'm constantly going over and looking at her; but tomorrow they'll take her away and – how will I ever stay behind all on my own? Now she's on the table in the sitting room, on two card tables that were put together, and the coffin will come tomorrow, a white one, with white *gros de Naples*, however, that's not it . . . I keep pacing and want to make sense of it for myself. Now it's six hours that I've been trying to make sense of it and I still can't collect my thoughts to a T. The fact of the matter is that I keep pacing, pacing, pacing . . . Here's how it was. I'll simply tell it in order. (Order!) Gentlemen, I'm far from being a literary man, as you'll see, well, so be it, but I'll tell it as I myself understand it. That's the horror of it for me, that I understand everything!

If you want to know, that is, if we take it from the very beginning, then quite simply she used to come to me to pawn things in order to pay for advertising in the *Voice*, saying, well, that there's a governess, willing to travel and give lessons in the home and so forth and so on. That was in the very beginning and of course I didn't single her out from the others: she came like all the others and so forth. But afterwards I began to single her out. She was so thin, fair, a bit taller than average; with me she was always awkward, as if she were embarrassed (I think that she was exactly the same with all strangers, and, it goes without saying, I was no different than anyone else, that is, if taken not as a pawnbroker but as a man). As soon as she received her money she would immediately turn around and leave. And all in silence. Others argue, beg, haggle to be given more; but not this one, whatever she was given . . . It seems to me that I keep getting muddled . . . Yes; first of all, I was struck by her things: silver gilt earrings, a worthless little locket – things worth twenty kopecks. She herself knew that they were worth all of ten kopecks, but I could see from her face that for her they were objects of great value – and indeed, as I learned later, this was all that she had left from her papa and mama. Only once did I permit myself to smile at her things. That is, you see, I never permit myself that, I maintain a gentlemanly tone with the public: a few words said respectfully and sternly. 'Sternly, sternly and sternly.' But she suddenly permitted herself to bring the remnants (quite literally, that is) of an old rabbit-skin jacket – and I couldn't resist and suddenly said something to her in the way of a witticism, as it were. Goodness gracious, how she flared up! Her eyes were blue, large, thoughtful, but how they blazed! But she didn't let drop a single word, she picked up her 'remnants' and left. That was the first time that I noticed her *particularly* and thought something of that sort about her, that is, precisely something of that particular sort. Yes; I recall yet another impression, that is, if you wish, the main impression, the synthesis of everything: namely, that she was terribly young, so young, as if she were fourteen years old. Whereas she was then three months shy of sixteen. However, that wasn't what I wanted to say, that wasn't the synthesis at all. She came again the next day. I later learned that she had been to Dobronravov and Mozer with that jacket, but they don't take anything except gold and didn't even bother to talk to her. I, on the other hand, had once taken a cameo from her (a worthless little thing) – and when I gave it some thought later on I was surprised: I also don't buy anything except gold and silver and yet I had taken a cameo. That was my second thought about her then, I remember that.

This time, that is, after going to Mozer, she brought an amber cigar holder – a so-so little piece, for the connoisseur, but something of no worth to us, because we deal only in gold. Since she had come after yesterday's *rebellion*, I greeted her sternly. Sternness for me means dryness. However, as I was giving her the two roubles, I couldn't resist and said with some irritation, as it were: 'I'm doing this only *for you*, Mozer wouldn't take a thing like this from you.' I particularly emphasized the words 'for you', and precisely with a *certain insinuation*. I was angry. Once again she flared up, upon hearing that 'for you', but she held her tongue, didn't throw down the money, took it – that's what poverty is! But how she flared up! I understood that I had wounded her. But when she had gone, I suddenly asked myself: So is this triumph over her really worth two roubles? Hee-hee-hee! I remember that I asked precisely that very question twice: 'Is it worth it? Is it worth it?' And, laughing, I answered this question to myself in the affirmative. Then I really cheered up. But this wasn't a nasty feeling: I had a plan, a purpose; I wanted to test her, because suddenly I began to have some thoughts about her. That was my third *particular* thought about her.

. . . Well, it was from that time that it all started. It goes without saying, I immediately tried to find out all her circumstances indirectly and waited for her arrival with particular impatience. You see, I had a feeling that she would come soon. When she came, I launched into an amiable conversation with unusual politeness. You see, I wasn't badly brought up and have manners. Hmm. That was when I guessed that she was kind and meek. The kind and meek don't resist for long, and although they are by no means very open, they don't at all know how to avoid a conversation: they answer grudgingly, but they answer and the longer it goes on, the more they answer; but if this is what you want, you can't let yourself get tired. It goes without saying that she didn't explain anything to me then. It was later that I learned about the *Voice* and about everything else. She was then mustering every last bit she had to advertise – at first, it goes without saying, presumptuously: 'Governess, willing to travel, send terms by post'; but later: 'Willing to do anything, tutor, be a companion, housekeeping, care for the sick, can sew' and so forth and so on. The usual! It goes without saying that all this was added to the advertisement at different stages, and towards the end, when despair had set it, there was even 'without salary, for board'. No, she didn't find a position! I made up my mind then to test her for the last time: I suddenly picked up today's *Voice* and showed her an advertisement: 'Young female, orphan, seeks position as governess of small children, preferably with an elderly widower. Willing to do light housework.'

'There, you see, this was published this morning and by

evening she's sure to have found a job. That's the way to advertise!'

Again she flared up, again her eyes blazed; she turned around and immediately walked out. I was very pleased. However, by then I was already sure of everything and had no fears: nobody would take her cigar holders. Besides, she had already run out of cigar holders. And so it was, two days later she comes, such a pale, agitated little thing – I understood that something had happened at home, and indeed something had happened. I'll explain straight away what happened, but now I merely wish to recall how I suddenly did something chic and rose in her eyes. A plan suddenly occurred to me. The fact of the matter is that she brought this icon (she had steeled herself to bring it) . . . Oh, listen! Listen! This is where it began, but I keep getting muddled . . . The fact of the matter is that I now want to recall everything, every trifle, every little detail. I still want to collect my thoughts to a T and – I can't, and now there are these little details, these little details . . .

An icon of the Mother of God. The Mother of God with Child, a family heirloom, an antique, with a silver gilt frame – worth – well, worth about six roubles. I see that the icon is dear to her, and she's pawning the whole icon, without removing the mounting. I tell her that it would be better if she removed the mounting and took the icon with her, because after all it's an icon.

'Surely you're not forbidden?'

'No, it's not that it's forbidden, but just that, perhaps, you yourself . . .'

'Well, remove it.'

'You know what, I won't remove it, but I'll put it over there in the icon case,' I said, after giving it some thought, 'with the other icons, under the lamp.' (I've always had the lamp burning ever since I opened my shop.) 'And I'll give you ten roubles – it's as simple as that.'

'I don't need ten, give me five; I'll redeem it without fail.'

'But don't you want ten? The icon is worth it,' I added, after observing that her little eyes had flashed once again. She held her tongue. I brought her five roubles.

'Don't despise anybody – I've been in tight squeezes myself, and even a bit worse, and if you now see me in such an occupation . . . well, you see, after all that I've endured . . .'

'You're taking revenge on society? Is that it?' she suddenly interrupted me with a rather sarcastic gibe, in which, however, there was a good deal of innocence (that is, of a general sort, because she certainly did not single me out from the others then, so it was said almost inoffensively). 'Aha!' I thought, 'so that's what you're like, your character is showing itself, you belong to the new movement.'

'You see,' I immediately observed, half-jokingly, half-mysteriously. 'I – I am part of that part of the whole that desires to do evil, but creates good . . .'

She looked at me quickly and with great curiosity, in which, however, there was a great deal of childishness:

'Wait a moment . . . What's that saying? Where's it from? I've heard it somewhere . . .'

'Don't rack your brains: Mephistopheles recommends himself to Faust in those words. Have you read *Faust?*'

'No . . . not carefully.'

'That is, you haven't read it at all. You should read it. However, once again I see a sardonic grin on your lips. Please, don't suppose that I have so little taste that I wished to paint over my role as a pawnbroker by recommending myself to you as Mephistopheles. Once a pawnbroker, always a pawnbroker. We know that, miss.'

'You're such a strange person . . . I didn't in the least want to say anything of the kind . . .'

She wanted to say: I didn't expect that you were an educated man, but she didn't say it, though I knew that she had thought it; I had pleased her terribly much.

'You see,' I observed, 'one can do good in any walk of life. Of course, I'm not speaking of myself; let's suppose that I do nothing but bad things . . .'

'Of course, one can do good in any position,' she said, looking at me with a quick and penetrating glance. 'Precisely in any position,' she added suddenly.

Oh, I remember, I remember all those moments! And I also want to add that when these young people, these dear young people, want to say something intelligent and penetrating, then their faces suddenly show you all too sincerely and naively: 'Here I am, I'm telling you something intelligent and penetrating.' And it's not at all from vanity, as is the case with the likes of us, but you see that she herself sets great store on all this terribly, and she believes, and respects and thinks that you, too, respect all this just as she does. Oh, sincerity! That's what they win you over with! And it was so charming in her!

I remember, I have forgotten nothing! When she left, I made up my mind at once. That same day I made my final enquiries and learned absolutely everything else there was to know about her present particulars; all the particulars of her past I already knew from Lukerya, who was then their servant and whom I had bribed several days earlier. These circumstances were so horrible that I don't understand how it had been possible for her to laugh, as she had that day, and be curious about Mephistopheles' words, when she herself was faced with such horrors. But – youth! That's precisely what I thought about her then with pride and joy, because, you see, there was also magnanimity about it, as if she were to say: the great works of Goethe shine even on the brink of ruin. Youth is always magnanimous, if only ever so slightly and ever so distortedly. That is, I'm speaking of her, you see, her alone. And the main thing, I then looked upon her as *mine* and did not doubt my power. You know, that's a most voluptuous thought, when you no longer have any doubt.

But what's wrong with me? If I keep going on like this, then when will I collect everything to a T? Quickly, quickly – this isn't the point at all, oh God!

II. A MARRIAGE PROPOSAL

The 'particulars' I learned about her I can set forth in a few words: her father and mother had died a long time ago, three years previously, and she had been left with her disreputable aunts. That is, it's saying too little to call them disreputable. One aunt was a widow with a large family, six children, each one smaller than the next; the other was a spinster, old and nasty. Both of them were nasty. Her father had been a government official, but only a clerk, and a non-hereditary nobleman – in a word: everything played into my hands. I appeared as if from some higher world: after all, I was a retired staff captain of a brilliant regiment, a nobleman by birth, independent and so on, and as far as the pawnshop went, the aunts could only look at it with respect. She had been slaving for her aunts for three years, but nevertheless she had passed an examination somewhere – she had managed to pass it, snatched a free minute to pass it, despite relentless work day in and day out – and that meant something about aspirations for the noble and the sublime on her part. After all, why did I want to get married? But who cares about me, we'll save that for later . . . As if that were the point! She taught her aunt's children, she sewed their underclothes, and towards the end she washed not only these underclothes, but she, with her bad chest, also washed the floors. To put it bluntly, they even beat her, reproaching her for every crumb. It ended with them intending to sell her. Ugh! I'll omit the dirty details. Later she told me everything in detail. A neighbour, a fat shopkeeper, had been observing all this for a whole year, and he wasn't just an ordinary shopkeeper, but the owner of two grocery stores. He had already beat two wives to death and was looking for a third, and had cast his eye on her: 'She's a quiet one,' he thought, 'she grew up in poverty and I'm marrying for the sake of my orphans.' Indeed, he did have orphans. He began to seek her hand, started negotiations with the aunts, and on top of that – he's fifty years old; she's horrified. And that's when she started coming to me to get money for advertisements in the *Voice*.

In the end, she began asking the aunts to give her just the littlest bit of time to think it over. They gave her that little bit, but only one, they didn't give her another; they badgered her: 'We don't know where we'll get our next meal, even without an extra mouth to feed.' I already knew all this, and on that same day, after her visit in the morning, I made up my mind. That evening the merchant came, he had brought from the shop a pound of candies worth fifty kopecks; she's sitting with him, and I summon Lukerya from the kitchen and tell her to go to her and whisper that I'm standing by the gate and wish to tell her something most urgently. I remained pleased with myself. And in general I was terribly pleased with myself that entire day.

Right there at the gate, already dumbfounded that I had summoned her, I explained to her, in Lukerya's presence, that I would consider myself happy and honoured . . . Secondly, she was not surprised by my manner or by the fact that this was taking place by the gate: 'I am a straightforward man,' I said, 'and have studied the circumstances of the matter.' And I wasn't lying that I'm straightforward. Well, to hell with it. I spoke not only decently, that is, by showing myself to be a person of good breeding, but originally as well, and that's the main thing. What, is it a sin to acknowledge this? I want to judge myself and am doing so. I must speak both *pro* and *contra*, and I am doing so. I recalled it with delight afterwards, even though it was stupid: I announced straight out then, without any embarrassment, that, in the first place, I wasn't particularly talented, not particularly intelligent, and perhaps not even particularly kind, that I was a rather cheap egoist (I remember this expression, I had composed it on my way there and remained pleased with it) and that – very, very likely – there was much that was unpleasant about me in other respects as well. All this was said with a particular kind of pride – we know how these sorts of things are said. Of course, I had sufficient good taste, after nobly declaring my deficiencies, not to launch into a declaration of my virtues: 'But to make up for this, I have this, that and the other.' I could see that she was still terribly afraid, but I didn't soften anything; instead, seeing that she was afraid I deliberately intensified it: I said straight out that she wouldn't go hungry, but as for fancy clothes, the theatre and balls – there would be none of that, though perhaps later, when I had achieved my goal. I was definitely carried away by this stern tone. I added, and as casually as possible, that if I had taken up such an occupation, that is, keeping this pawnshop, it was for one purpose only – that is, there was a certain circumstance, so to speak . . . But you see I had a right to speak like that: I really did have such a purpose and such a circumstance. Wait a moment, gentlemen, all my life I have been the first to hate this pawnbroking business, but in essence, you see, even though it's ridiculous to talk to oneself in mysterious phrases, I was 'taking revenge on society', you see, I really, really, really was! Therefore, her joke about the fact that I was 'taking revenge' was unfair. That is, you see, if I had said to her straight out in so many words: 'Yes, I'm taking revenge on society', and she had burst out laughing, the way she did that morning, it would indeed have come out ridiculous. But with an indirect hint and by dropping a mysterious phrase it turned out that it was possible to engage her imagination. Moreover, I wasn't afraid of anything then: you see, I knew that in any event the fat shopkeeper was more repulsive than I and that I, standing by the gate, was her liberator. I understood that, you see. Oh, man understands baseness particularly well! But was it baseness? How is one to judge a man in a case like this? Didn't I love her already even then?

Wait a moment: it goes without saying that I didn't say a word to her about doing a good deed: on the contrary, oh, on the contrary: 'It is *I*,' I said, 'who am being done the favour, and not *you*.' So that I even expressed this in words, I couldn't help myself, and perhaps it came out stupidly, because I noticed a fleeting grin on her face. But on the whole I had definitely won. Wait a moment, if I'm going to recall all this filth, then I'll recall this final bit of swinishness: I was standing there and this is what was going through my head: You're tall, fit, educated and – and finally, to speak without any boasting, you're not bad looking. That's what was running through my head. It goes without saying, she said 'yes' there and then by the gate. But . . . but I should add: she thought it over for a long time, right there and then by the gate, before she said 'yes'. She was so deep in thought, so deep in thought that I was on the verge of asking, 'Well, what is it going to be?' – and I couldn't even help myself from asking with a certain sense of chic: 'Well, what is it going to be, Miss?' – adding the 'Miss' for good measure.

'Wait, I'm thinking.'

And her little face was so serious, so serious – that even then I might have read it! But instead I was offended: 'Is she really,' I thought to myself, 'choosing between me and the merchant?' Oh, I still didn't understand then! I still didn't understand anything, anything then! I didn't understand until today! I remember Lukerya ran after me when I was already walking away, stopped me in the street and said, catching her breath: 'God will reward you, sir, for taking our dear young lady – only don't say anything about it to her, she's proud.'

Well now, proud! I like them proud, I said to myself. The proud ones are particularly nice, when . . . well, when you no longer harbour any doubts about your power over them. Eh? Oh, base, awkward man! Oh, how pleased I was! Do you know, while she was standing there by the gate deep in thought about whether to say 'yes' to me, and I was surprised, do you know, that she might even have been thinking: 'If it's to be misfortune either way, isn't it better to choose the worst straight away, that is, the fat shopkeeper; let him get drunk, the sooner the better, and beat me to death!' Eh? What do you think, could that have been what she was thinking?

And even now I don't understand, even now I don't understand anything! I just now said that she might have been thinking that she should choose the worse of the two misfortunes, that is, the merchant. But who was worse for her then – the merchant or I? The merchant or the pawnbroker who quotes Goethe? That's still a question! What question? You don't understand even that: the answer is lying on the table, and you say 'what question'! But to hell with me! I'm not the point here at all . . . And at the same time, what do I care now – whether I'm the point or not? That's something I'm utterly incapable of deciding. I'd better go to bed. I have a headache . . .

III. THE NOBLEST OF MEN, BUT I DON'T BELIEVE IT MYSELF

I didn't fall asleep. And how could I with that pulse hammering away in my head. I want to absorb all this, all this filth. Oh, the filth! Oh, the filth I dragged her out of then! She should have realized that, you know, she should have appreciated my deed! I was pleased, too, by various thoughts, for example, that I was forty-one years old and that she was only sixteen. That fascinated me, this sense of inequality, it was very sweet, very sweet.

I, for example, wanted to have the wedding *à l'anglaise*, that is, just the two of us, perhaps with two witnesses, one of whom would be Lukerya, and then at once to the train, for example, if only to Moscow (it so happened that I had business there), to a hotel for a fortnight or so. She was against it, she wouldn't have it and I was forced to visit her aunts and pay my respects to them as the relatives from whom I was taking her. I gave in, and the aunts were rendered their due. I even made a present of a hundred roubles each to those creatures and promised more, of course, without saying a word to her, so as not to distress her with the baseness of the situation. The aunts at once became as soft as silk. There was an argument about the trousseau as well: she didn't have anything, almost literally, but she didn't want anything either. However, I managed to convince her that it wasn't possible to have absolutely nothing, and so I arranged for the trousseau myself, because who else would do anything for her? Well, but to hell with me! Various ideas of mine, however, I nevertheless did manage to convey to her then, so that she would at least know. Perhaps I was even too hasty. The main thing is that from the very beginning, however much she tried to hold out, she would throw herself at me with her love; she would meet me when I came home in the evening with rapture, she would tell me in her prattle (the charming prattle of innocence!) all about her childhood, youth, about her parental home, about her father and mother. But I immediately threw cold water on all these ecstasies right then and there. That was the whole point of my idea. I answered her raptures with silence, gracious, of course . . . but she nevertheless quickly saw that we were different and that I was – a riddle. And the main thing is that I had set my sights on this riddle! You see, it was in order to pose this riddle perhaps that I committed all this foolishness! First of all, sternness – it was with sternness that I took her into my house. In a word, even though I was quite pleased with things as they were, I began to create a complete system. Oh, it took shape on its own, without any effort. And it couldn't have been otherwise, I had to create this system on account of one incontrovertible circumstance – really, what is this? I'm slandering myself! The system was genuine. No, listen, if you're going to judge a person, then you should judge him knowing the case . . . Listen.

How should I begin this, because it's very difficult. When you begin justifying yourself – that's when it gets difficult. You see: young people despise money, for example – I hammered away about money; I pressed home about money. And I hammered away so that she began to fall silent more and more. She would open her big eyes, listen, look and fall silent. You see: young people are magnanimous, that is, the good ones are magnanimous and impetuous, but they have little tolerance, as soon as something's not quite right – you get their contempt. But I wanted breadth, I wanted to instil breadth right into her heart, to instil it into her heart's vista, isn't that so? I'll take a trivial example: How could I explain, for example, my pawnshop to a person like that? It goes without saying that I didn't bring it up directly, or it would have looked like I was asking her forgiveness for the pawnshop; instead I acted, so to speak, with pride – I spoke almost silently. And I'm a master of speaking silently – all my life I've spoken silently and I've lived through entire tragedies in silence. Oh, and I too have been unhappy! I was cast aside by everyone, cast aside and forgotten, and no one, no one knows it! And suddenly this sixteen-year-old girl got hold of details about me afterwards from vile people and thought that she knew everything, but meanwhile the secret remained only in this man's breast! I went on being silent, and I was particularly, particularly silent with her until just yesterday – why was I silent? Because I'm a proud man. I wanted her to find out on her own, without me, but not from stories told by scoundrels, but that she should *guess herself* about this man and comprehend him! When I received her into my house, I wanted her complete respect. I wanted her to stand before me beseechingly, on account of my suffering – and I was worthy of that. Oh, I've always been proud, I've always wanted all or nothing! And that's precisely why I'm not for half-measures in happiness, but wanted everything – and that's precisely why I was forced to act as I did then, as if to say: 'Figure it out for yourself and appreciate me!' Because, you must agree, if I had begun by explaining and prompting, being evasive and asking for respect – then, you see, it would have been as if I were asking for charity . . . However . . . However, why am I talking about this!

Stupid, stupid, stupid, stupid! I straight away and ruthlessly (and I want to emphasize that it was ruthlessly) explained to her then, in a few words, that the magnanimity of young people was lovely, but not worth a brass button. Why not? Because it comes cheap, they get it without having lived; it's all, so to speak, the 'first impressions of existence', but let's see you do some work! Cheap magnanimity is always easy, and even to give your life – even that's easy, because that's just a matter of the blood boiling and an over-abundance of energy, one passionately longs for beauty! No, take an act of magnanimity that is difficult, quiet, muted, without splendour, where you're slandered, where there's much sacrifice and not a drop of glory – where you, a shining man, are brought forward before everyone as a scoundrel, when you are the most honest man in the world – come on, try your hand at that sort of deed, no, sir, you'll give it up! While I – all I've done my whole life is to shoulder that sort of deed. In the beginning she would argue – and how! But then she began to fall silent, completely and totally, she would just open her eyes terribly wide as she listened, such big, big eyes, and so attentive. And . . . and besides that I suddenly saw a smile, a mistrustful, silent, bad smile. It was with that smile that I brought her into my house. And it's also true that she had nowhere else to go . . .

IV. PLANS AND MORE PLANS

Which of us was the first to begin then?

Neither. It began on its own from the very first. I have said that I had brought her into my house with sternness; however, I softened it from the very first. When she was still my fiancée it had been explained to her that she would assist in taking in the pledges and paying out the money, and she didn't say anything then (note that). And what's more, she even took to the business with zeal. Well, of course, the apartment, the furniture – everything remained the same as before. The apartment has two rooms: one is a large room in which the shop is partitioned off from the rest, and the other one is also a large room in which we have our sitting room and bedroom. My furniture isn't much; even her aunts had better. My icon-stand with the lamp is in the room with the shop; in the other room I have my bookcase with some books and a trunk to which I have the keys; and there's a bed, tables, chairs. When she was still my fiancée I told her that one rouble a day and no more was allotted for our board, that is, food, for me, her and Lukerya, whom I had enticed away: 'I need 30,000 in three years,' I told her, 'otherwise I won't be able to save up enough money.' She didn't stand in the way, but I myself added to our board by thirty kopecks. It was the same thing with the theatre. When she was still my fiancée I told her that there wouldn't be any theatre; however, I decided that we should go to the theatre once a month, and decently at that, in the orchestra. We went together, three times, and saw *In Pursuit of Happiness* and *Songbirds*, I think. (Oh, to hell with it, to hell with it!) We went in silence and returned in silence. Why, why did we from the very beginning choose to be silent? After all, there weren't any quarrels in the beginning, but there was silence then, too. As I recall, she somehow kept looking at me then on the sly; when I noticed that I increased my silence. True, I was the one who insisted upon silence, and not she. On her part there were outbursts once or twice, when she would rush to embrace me; but since these outbursts were unhealthy and hysterical, and what I required was steadfast happiness, together with her respect, I received them coldly. And I was right to do so: each time the outburst was followed the next day by a quarrel.

That is, there weren't any quarrels, but there was silence and – and on her part a more and more insolent look. 'Rebellion and independence' – that's what it was, only she didn't know how. Yes, that meek face was becoming more and more insolent. Can you believe it? I was becoming repulsive to her – I came to understand that. And there could be no doubt about these outbursts that came over her. For example, after leaving behind such filth and beggary, after scrubbing floors, how could she suddenly begin to grumble about our poverty! You see, gentlemen: it wasn't poverty, it was economy, and where necessary there was some luxury, when it came to linens and cleanliness, for example. I had always dreamed before that cleanliness in a husband attracts a wife. However, it wasn't poverty, but my supposed miserly economy that bothered her: 'He has goals, he's showing his firm character.' She suddenly declined to go to the theatre. And there was more and more of that sardonic grin . . . While I intensified my silence, I intensified my silence.

Surely there was no need to justify my actions? The main thing here was the pawnshop. Come now, sirs: I knew that a woman, especially one who was sixteen years old, couldn't help but submit completely to a man. Women have no originality, that's – that's an axiom, even now it's an axiom for me! Never mind what's lying there in the front room: truth is truth, and even Mill himself can't do anything about it! But a loving woman, oh, a loving woman idolizes even the vices, even the villainy of her beloved being. He would not seek such justifications for his villainy as she will find for him. That's magnanimous but not original. It is this lack of originality alone that has been the undoing of women. And what, I repeat, what are you pointing to there on the table? Is there really anything original about what's there on the table? Oh-h-h!

Listen: I was certain of her love then. You see, she would throw herself on my neck then. That meant she loved me, or rather – she wished to love me. Yes, that's what it was: she wished to love, she sought to love. But the main thing, you see, is that there weren't any villainies for which she needed to find justifications. You say a 'pawnbroker' and that's what everyone says. But what if I am a pawnbroker? That means there are reasons, if the most magnanimous of men became a pawnbroker. You see, gentlemen, there are ideas . . . that is, you see, when some ideas are said out loud, put into words, they come out terribly stupid. They come out so that you're ashamed of them yourself. But why? For no reason at all. Because we're all good-for-nothings and can't bear the truth, or I don't know why else. I said just now 'the most magnanimous of men'. That's ridiculous, you see, and yet that's how it was. You see, it's the truth, that is, it's the most truthful truth of all! Yes, I *had the right* then to want to provide for myself and open this shop: 'You, that is, you people, have spurned me, you have driven me away with your contemptuous silence. You have answered my outbursts of passion with an insult that I will feel for the rest of my life. Consequently, I now am within my rights to protect myself from you with a wall, to amass those 30,000 roubles and end my days somewhere in the Crimea, on the southern shore, amidst mountains and vineyards, on my own estate purchased with that 30,000, and the main thing, far away from you all, but without malice towards you, with an ideal in my soul, with my beloved woman at my heart, with a family if God should send one, and – helping out the neighbouring peasants.' It goes without saying that it's good that I'm telling this to myself now, but what could have been more stupid than if I had described all this out loud to her then? That was the reason behind my proud silence, and that was the reason we sat in silence. Because what would she have understood? Just sixteen years old, so very young – what could she have understood of my justifications, of my suffering? I was dealing with straightforwardness, ignorance of life, cheap, youthful convictions, the blindness of 'beautiful hearts', and the main thing, the pawnshop and – *basta*! (But was I a scoundrel in the pawnshop, didn't she see how I conducted myself and did I charge more than I should?) Oh, how terrible is truth on this earth! This charming one, this meek one, this heaven – she was a tyrant, the unbearable tyrant of my soul and my tormentor! I'd be slandering myself, you see, if I didn't say that! You think I didn't love her? Who can say that I didn't love her? You see: there was irony here, the malicious irony of fate and nature! We are accursed, the life of people in general is accursed! (And mine in particular!) I understand now, you see, that I made some mistake here! Something didn't come out the way it was supposed to. Everything was clear, my plan was as clear as the sky: 'Severe, proud, requires no moral consolation, suffers in silence.' That's how it was, I wasn't lying, I wasn't lying! 'She'll see for herself later on that there was magnanimity here, but she just wasn't able to see it now – and when she does fathom it some day, she'll appreciate it ten times more and will fall down in the dust with her hands folded in supplication.' That was the plan. But I forgot something here or failed to take it into account. I wasn't able to do something here. But enough, enough. And of whom can I ask forgiveness now? What's done is done. Take courage, man, and be proud! It's not you who are to blame! . . .

Now then, I'll tell the truth, I won't be afraid to stand face to face with the truth: *she* is to blame, *she* is to blame! . . .

V. THE MEEK ONE REBELS

The quarrels began when she suddenly took it into her head to pay out money as she saw fit, to appraise things for more than they were worth, and a couple of times she even thought fit to enter into an argument with me on the subject. I didn't agree. But then this captain's widow turned up.

An old lady, the widow of a captain, came with a locket – a present from her late husband, well, you know, a keepsake. I gave thirty roubles. She started to whine plaintively, begging me to keep the thing for her; it goes without saying that we keep it. Well, in a word, suddenly she comes five days later to exchange it for a bracelet that's not worth even eight roubles; it goes without saying that I refused. She must have guessed then something from my wife's eyes, but in any case she came when I wasn't there, and my wife exchanged the locket.

When I learned about it that very same day, I began by speaking meekly, but firmly and reasonably. She was sitting on the bed, looking at the floor, tapping the rug with the toe of her right shoe (her gesture); an unpleasant smile played on her lips. Then without raising my voice at all I announced calmly that the money was *mine*, that I had the right to look at life with *my own* eyes and that when I invited her into my house I had not concealed anything from her.

She suddenly jumped up, suddenly began trembling all over and – what do you think – she suddenly began stamping her feet at me; this was a wild animal, this was a fit, this was a wild animal having a fit. I froze in astonishment: I had never expected such an outburst. But I didn't become flustered, I didn't even move a muscle, and once again in the same calm voice I declared plainly that from that time forward I refused to let her take part in my affairs. She laughed in my face and walked out of the apartment.

The fact of the matter is that she had no right to leave the apartment. Nowhere without me, that was the agreement we made when she was still my fiancée. She returned towards evening; I didn't say a word.

The next day, too, she went out in the morning, and it was the same thing the following day. I locked up the shop and set off to see her aunts. I had broken off relations with them from the day of the wedding – I hadn't invited them to visit me, we didn't visit them. Now it turned out that she wasn't with them. They heard me out with curiosity and laughed in my face. 'Serves you right,' they said. But I had expected their laughter. I then and there bribed the younger aunt, the spinster, with a hundred roubles, and gave her twenty-five in advance. Two days later she comes to me: 'An officer,' she says, 'a Lieutenant Yefimovich, a former comrade of yours from the regiment, is mixed up in this.' I was quite astonished. This Yefimovich had done me more harm than anyone else in the regiment, and a month ago he stopped by my shop a couple of times, and being the shameless fellow that he is, under the pretence of pawning something, I remember, he began laughing with my wife. I went up to him then and told him that, considering our relations, he should not presume to visit me; but no idea of anything like that crossed my mind, I simply thought that he was an insolent fellow. But now suddenly her auntie informs me that she had made an appointment to see him and that this whole affair is being handled by a certain former acquaintance of the aunts, Yuliya Samsonovna, a widow, and a colonel's widow at that – 'It's her that your spouse goes to visit now,' she says.

I'll cut this story short. This business cost me almost 300 roubles, but in two days it was arranged that I would stand in the adjoining room, behind closed doors, and listen to my wife's first *rendezvous* alone with Yefimovich. Meanwhile, the previous evening a brief but for me very significant scene between myself and my wife took place.

She returned towards evening, sat down on the bed, looked at me mockingly and thumped the rug with her foot. Suddenly, as I was looking at her, the idea flew into my head then that all this past month, or, rather, for the past two weeks, she had not been herself at all – one could even say that she had been exactly the opposite: a wild, aggressive being had made its appearance; I can't say shameless, but disorderly and looking for trouble. Asking for trouble. Meekness, however, held her back. When a girl like that starts creating an uproar, even if she does cross the line, it's nevertheless plain to see that she's only hurting herself, that she's egging herself on and that she will be the first who is unable to cope with her feelings of modesty and shame. That's why girls like that sometimes go too far, so that you don't believe your own eyes when you witness it. A soul accustomed to debauchery, on the contrary, always softens it, making it more vile, but in a guise of decorum and decency that claims to be superior to you.

'And is it true that you were driven out of your regiment, because you were too cowardly to fight a duel?' she asked suddenly, out of the blue, and her eyes flashed.

'It's true; the officers rendered the verdict that I was to be asked to leave the regiment, although I had in any case already tendered my resignation.'

'You were driven out as a coward?'

'Yes, they judged me a coward. But I refused to duel not

because I was a coward, but because I didn't wish to submit to their tyrannical verdict and issue a challenge to a duel when I did not consider myself to be insulted. You should know,' I couldn't restrain myself here, 'that flying in the face of such tyranny through my actions and accepting all the consequences took far more courage than any duel would have done.'

I couldn't contain myself, with this phrase I launched into self-justifications, as it were, and that was all she needed, a fresh instance of my humiliation. She burst out in malicious laughter.

'And is it true that for the next three years you wandered the streets of Petersburg like a tramp, and begged for kopecks, and slept under billiard tables?'

'I even spent some nights in the Vyazemsky House on Haymarket Square. Yes, it's true; in my life after leaving the regiment there was much shame and degradation, but not moral degradation, because I was the first to loathe my actions even then. It was merely the degradation of my will and mind, and it was brought about only by the desperation of my situation. But this passed . . .'

'Oh, now you're an important person – a financier!'

That is, a hint at my pawnshop. But I had already managed to hold myself in check. I saw that she thirsted for explanations that would be humiliating for me and – I didn't give them. Fortunately, a client rang the bell just then and I went to see him in the front room. Afterwards, an hour later, when she had suddenly dressed to go out, she stopped in front of me and said:

'You didn't tell me anything about this before the wedding, however.'

I didn't answer, and she left.

And so, the next day I stood in this room behind the door and listened to my fate being decided, and in my pocket there was a revolver. She was dressed up, sitting at the table, and Yefimovich was putting on airs. And what do you know: it turned out (I say this to my credit), it turned out exactly as I had foreseen and supposed, though without realizing that I had foreseen and supposed this. I don't know whether I'm expressing myself clearly.

This is what happened. I listened for a whole hour and for that hour I witnessed a duel between the most noble and lofty woman and a worldly, depraved, dim-witted creature with a grovelling soul. And how, I thought to myself in amazement, how does this naive, this meek, this reserved girl know all this? The cleverest author of a high-society comedy could not have created this scene of ridicule, the most naive laughter and the holy contempt of virtue for vice. And such brilliance in her words and little turns of speech; what wit in her quick replies, what truth in her censure! And at the same time what almost girlish ingenuousness. She laughed in his face at his declarations of love, at his gestures, at his proposals. Coming straight to the matter with a crude assault and not foreseeing any opposition, all of a sudden he had the wind taken out of his sails. At first I might have thought that it was simply coquetry on her part – the 'coquetry of a clever though depraved creature in order to show herself more lavishly'. But no, the truth shone through like the sun and it was impossible to have any doubts. It was only out of hatred for me, affected and impetuous though it was, that she, inexperienced as she was, could have decided to undertake this meeting, but as soon as it had become reality – her eyes were opened at once. Here was a creature who was simply flailing about so as to insult me no matter what, but once she had decided on such filth she couldn't bear the disorder. And could she, blameless and pure, with ideals, have been attracted to Yefimovich or any of those other high-society brutes? On the contrary, he aroused only laughter. The whole truth rose up from her soul, and indignation called forth sarcasm from her heart. I repeat, towards the end this fool was utterly dazed and sat scowling, barely responding, so that I even began to fear that he would venture to insult her out of mean-spirited revenge. And I repeat once again: to my credit I heard this scene out almost without astonishment. It was as though I had encountered something familiar. It was as though I had gone in order to encounter it. I had gone, believing nothing, no accusation, although I did put a revolver in my pocket – that's the truth! And could I have really imagined her otherwise? Wasn't that why I loved her, wasn't that why I cherished her, wasn't that why I had married her? Oh, of course, I was all too convinced that she hated me then, but I was also convinced of her purity. I brought the scene swiftly to a close by opening the door. Yefimovich jumped to his feet, I took her by the hand and invited her to leave with me. Yefimovich found his bearings and suddenly burst out in resounding peals of laughter.

'Oh, I have no objections to sacred conjugal rights, take

her away, take her away! And you know,' he shouted after me, 'even though a respectable person can't fight you, yet out of respect for your lady, I am at your service . . . If you, however, want to risk it . . .'

'Do you hear that!' I stopped her for a second on the threshold.

Then not a word all the way home. I led her by the hand, and she didn't resist. On the contrary, she was utterly dumbfounded, but only until we got home. On our arrival, she sat down on a chair and fastened her gaze on me. She was extraordinarily pale; though her lips had at once formed a mocking smile, she was already regarding me with a solemn and severe challenge, and, I believe, she was seriously convinced those first few moments that I was going to kill her with the revolver. But I took the revolver out of my pocket in silence and laid it on the table. She looked at me and at the revolver. (Note: she was already familiar with this revolver. I had acquired it and kept it loaded ever since opening the shop. When I was getting ready to open the shop I had decided not to keep hulking dogs or a burly lackey like Mozer did, for example. The cook opens the door for my visitors. But people who engage in my trade cannot deprive themselves of self-defence, just in case, and I kept a loaded revolver. During those first days when she had come to live in my house she showed a lot of interest in this revolver, she asked a lot of questions, and I even explained the mechanism and how it worked; moreover, I persuaded her once to shoot at a target. Note all that.) Paying no notice of her frightened look, I lay down on the bed half-undressed. I was very tired; it was already almost eleven o'clock. She went on sitting in the same place, without moving, for almost another hour, then she put out the candle and lay down, also dressed, on the sofa by the wall. It was the first time that she didn't come to bed with me – note that as well . . .

VI. A TERRIBLE MEMORY

Now, this terrible memory . . .

I woke up in the morning, between seven and eight, I think, and it was already almost completely light in the room. I woke up all at once fully conscious and suddenly opened my eyes. She was standing by the table, holding the revolver. She didn't see that I was awake and watching. And suddenly I saw that she had started to move towards me, holding the revolver. I quickly shut my eyes and pretended to be fast asleep.

She came up to the bed and stood over me. I heard everything; although a dead silence had fallen, I heard even that silence. Then there came a convulsive movement – and I suddenly, uncontrollably, opened my eyes against my will. She was looking me right in the eyes, and the revolver was already by my temple. Our eyes met. But we looked at each other for no more than a moment. I forced myself to shut my eyes again and at the same moment I resolved with every fibre of my being that I would not stir or open my eyes, no matter what awaited me.

In fact, it does happen sometimes that a person who is sound asleep suddenly opens his eyes, even raises his head for a second and looks about the room, then, a moment later, he lays his head on the pillow again and falls asleep without remembering a thing. When, after meeting her gaze and feeling the revolver at my temple, I suddenly shut my eyes again and didn't stir, like someone sound asleep, she certainly could have supposed that I indeed was asleep and that I hadn't seen anything, particularly since it was altogether incredible that having seen what I saw I would shut my eyes again at *such* a moment.

Yes, incredible. But she still might have guessed the truth – that was what suddenly flashed through my mind, at that very same moment. Oh, what a whirlwind of thoughts, sensations raced through my mind in less than a moment; long live the electricity of human thought! In that case (I felt), if she had guessed the truth and knew that I wasn't sleeping, then I had already crushed her with my readiness to accept death and her hand might now falter. Her former resolve might be shattered by this new extraordinary impression. They say that people standing on a height are drawn downwards, as it were, of their own accord, to the abyss. I think that a lot of suicides and murders have been committed merely because the revolver was already in hand. There's an abyss here as well, there's a forty-five-degree slope down which you can't help but slide and something relentlessly challenges you to pull the trigger. But the awareness that I had seen everything, that I knew everything and that I was awaiting my death from her in silence – might hold her back from that slope.

The silence continued, and suddenly I felt on my temple, at my hairline, the cold touch of iron. You will ask: did I firmly hope that I would be saved? I will answer you as if

I were before God himself: I had no hope whatsoever, except perhaps one chance in a hundred. Why, then, did I accept death? But I will ask: What need would I have of life after the revolver was raised against me by the being whom I adored? Moreover, I knew with all the force of my being that a struggle was going on between us at that very moment, a terrible duel for life and death, a duel of that same coward of yesterday, driven out by his comrades. I knew it, and she knew it, if only she had guessed the truth that I wasn't sleeping.

Perhaps it wasn't like that, perhaps I didn't think that then, but still it must have been like that, even without thought, because all I've done since is think about it every hour of my life.

But you'll ask me the question again: why didn't I save her then from this treachery? Oh, I have asked myself that question a thousand times since – each time when, with a shiver down my spine, I recalled that second. But my soul then was plunged in dark despair: I was lost, I myself was lost, so whom could I have saved? And how do you know whether I still wanted to save somebody then? How can you know what I might have been feeling then?

My consciousness, however, was seething; the seconds passed, there was dead silence; she was still standing over me – and then suddenly I shuddered with hope! I quickly opened my eyes. She was no longer in the room. I got up from the bed: I had defeated her – and she was forever defeated!

I went out to the samovar. We always had the samovar brought to the outer room and she was always the one to pour the tea. I sat down at the table in silence and took a glass of tea from her. About five minutes later I glanced at her. She was terribly pale, even paler than yesterday, and she was looking at me. And suddenly – and suddenly, seeing that I was looking at her, she gave a pale smile with her pale lips, a timid question in her eyes. 'That means that she still has doubts and is asking herself: does he know or not, did he see or didn't he?' I indifferently turned my eyes away. After tea I locked up the shop, went to the market and bought an iron bed and a screen. When I returned home, I had the bed installed in the front room with the screen around it. This bed was for her, but I didn't say a word to her. Even without words she understood from this bed alone that I 'had seen everything and knew everything' and that there was no longer any doubt about this. I left the revolver on the table for the night as always. At night she silently got into her new bed: the marriage was dissolved, 'she had been defeated but not forgiven'. During the night she became delirious, and by morning she had a fever. She was confined to bed for six weeks.

Chapter 2

I. A DREAM OF PRIDE

Lukerya just announced that she won't stay with me and that she'll leave as soon as the mistress is buried. I prayed on my knees for five minutes, and I had wanted to pray for an hour, but I keep thinking, and thinking, and they're all such aching thoughts and my head aches – what's the use of praying – it's nothing but a sin! It's also strange that I don't want to sleep: in great, in such great sorrow, after the first violent outbursts, one always wants to sleep. They say that people who are condemned to death sleep extremely soundly on their last night. As they should, it's only natural, otherwise they wouldn't have the strength to endure it . . . I lay down on the sofa, but I didn't fall asleep . . .

. . . For the six weeks of her illness we took care of her day and night – Lukerya and I and a trained nurse from the hospital, whom I had hired. I didn't begrudge the money, and even wanted to spend money on her. I called in Dr Schroeder and paid him ten roubles a visit. When she regained consciousness, I started to show myself less often. But why am I describing this? When she was completely on her feet again, she sat quietly and silently in my room at a special table, which I had also bought for her at the time . . . Yes, it's true, we were perfectly silent; that is, we began to talk later on, but only about the usual things. Of course, I deliberately refrained from becoming expansive, but I could see very well that she also was happy not to say a word more than was necessary. This seemed perfectly natural on her part: 'She is too shaken and too defeated,' I thought, 'and of course she needs time to forget and get used to things.' And so it was that we were silent, but every minute I was secretly preparing myself for the future. I thought that she was doing the same as well, and it was terribly entertaining for me to guess: Exactly what is she thinking about now?

I'll say one more thing: Oh, of course, nobody knows what

I endured as I grieved over her during her illness. But I kept my grief to myself and kept the grieving in my heart even from Lukerya. I couldn't imagine, I couldn't even suppose that she would die without learning everything. When she was out of danger and her health started to return, I remember this, I quickly calmed down and very much so. What's more, I decided *to postpone our future* for as long as possible, and for the present to leave everything as it was now. Yes, then something happened to me that was strange and peculiar, I don't know what else to call it: I had triumphed and this thought alone proved to be quite sufficient for me. And that's how the whole winter passed. Oh, I was pleased as I had never been before, and that for the whole winter.

You see: in my life there had been one terrible external circumstance, which until then, that is, until the catastrophe with my wife, weighed heavily on me every day and every hour, namely, the loss of my reputation and leaving the regiment. To put it in a nutshell: this had been a tyrannical injustice against me. True, my comrades disliked me on account of my difficult and, perhaps, ridiculous character, although it often happens that what you find sublime, what you hold dear and esteem, for some reason at the same time makes a group of your comrades laugh. Oh, I was never liked, even in school. I've never been liked anywhere. Even Lukerya cannot like me. The incident in the regiment, though a consequence of this dislike for me, without a doubt bore an accidental character. I mention this because there's nothing more exasperating and intolerable than to be ruined by an incident that might or might not have happened, by an unfortunate chain of circumstances that might have passed over, like a cloud. It's humiliating for an educated man. The incident was as follows.

During the intermission at the theatre I went to the bar. Hussar A—v came in suddenly and began talking loudly with two of his fellow hussars in the presence of all the officers and public gathered there about how Bezumtsev, the captain of our regiment, had just caused a scandal in the corridor 'and he seems to be drunk'. The conversation moved on to other things; besides, there had been a mistake, because Captain Bezumtsev wasn't drunk, and there hadn't really been a scandal. The hussars began talking about something else, and that was the end of it, but the next day the story made its way to our regiment, and at once they began saying how I was the only person at the bar from our regiment and that when Hussar A—v spoke insolently of Captain Bezumtsev I had not gone over to A—v and put a stop to it by reprimanding him. But why on earth should I have done that? If he had it in for Bezumtsev, then it was their personal affair, and why should I get involved? Meanwhile, the officers began to take the position that the affair was not personal but concerned the regiment, and that since I was the only officer of our regiment present, I had proved by my conduct to all the officers at the bar as well as the public that there might be officers in our regiment who were not overly scrupulous concerning their honour and the regiment's. I could not agree with this verdict. I was given to understand that I might still set everything right even now, belatedly, if I should wish to demand a formal explanation from A—v. I did not wish to do so and since I was annoyed, I refused with pride. I then at once resigned my commission – and that's the whole story. I left proud, but with my spirit crushed. My mind and will both foundered. It was just then that my sister's husband squandered our little fortune and my portion of it, a tiny portion, so I was left on the street without a kopeck. I could have found employment in a private business, but I didn't: after wearing my splendid regimental uniform I couldn't go work on some railroad. And so – if it's shame, let it be shame, if it's disgrace, let it be disgrace, if it's degradation, let it be degradation, and the worse, the better – that's what I chose. There followed three years of gloomy memories, even of the Vyazemsky House. A year and a half ago a rich old lady, my godmother, died in Moscow and among other bequests unexpectedly left me 3,000 in her will. I gave it some thought and then decided my fate. I settled on the pawnshop, with no apologies to anyone: money, then a corner and – a new life far away from my former memories – that was the plan. Nevertheless, my gloomy past and the reputation of my honour, forever ruined, tormented me every hour, every minute. But then I married. By chance or not – I don't know. But when I brought her into my house, I thought that I was bringing a friend, I greatly needed a friend. But I saw clearly that my friend had to be prepared, given the finishing touches, and even defeated. And could I have explained anything straight off like that to this sixteen-year-old girl with her prejudices? For example, how could I, without the accidental assistance of the terrible catastrophe with the revolver, have convinced her that I wasn't a coward and that I had been unjustly accused by the regiment of being a coward? But the catastrophe arrived just at the right moment. Having stood up to the revolver, I had avenged all of my gloomy past. And even though nobody knew about it, *she* knew about it, and that was everything for me, because she was everything to me, all my hopes for the future in my dreams! She was the only person whom I was preparing for myself, and I didn't need another – and now she knew everything; at least she knew that she had unjustly hurried to join my enemies. This thought delighted me. In her eyes I could no longer be a scoundrel, but merely a peculiar person, and even this thought, after everything that had happened, did not at all displease me: peculiarity is not a vice; on the contrary, it sometimes attracts the feminine character. In a word, I deliberately postponed the finale: what had taken place was more than sufficient, for the time being, for my peace of mind and contained more than enough pictures and material for my dreams. That's the nasty thing about this – I'm a dreamer: I had enough material; as for her, I thought that *she would wait*.

And so the whole winter passed in some sort of expectation of something. I liked to steal looks at her, when she happened to be sitting at her little table. She would be busy with her needlework, with the linen, and in the evenings she would sometimes read books which she would take from my bookcase. The choice of books in the bookcase should also have spoken in my favour. She hardly ever went out. Every day after dinner, before dusk, I would take her for a walk and we would go for our constitutional, but not completely in silence, as before. I precisely tried to make it look as though we weren't being silent and were speaking harmoniously, but as I've already said we both avoided getting carried away talking. I was doing this on purpose, while she, I thought, needed to be 'given time'. Of course, it's strange that it did not once occur to me until almost the very end of the winter that though I liked to look at her on the sly, I never once caught her looking at me that whole winter! I thought that it was timidity on her part. Moreover, she had an air about her of such timid meekness, such weakness after her illness. No, better to bide one's time and – 'and she will suddenly come to you on her own . . .'

That thought delighted me irresistibly. I will add one thing: sometimes it was as if I had deliberately inflamed myself and really brought my heart and mind to the point that I would feel that I had been wronged by her. And so it continued for some time. But my hatred could never ripen and take root in my soul. And I even felt that it was only some sort of game. And even then, although I had dissolved our marriage by buying the bed and screen, never, never could I see her as a criminal. And not because I judged her crime lightly, but because it made sense to forgive her completely, from the very first day, even before I bought the bed. In a word, this was a strange move on my part, for I am morally stern. On the contrary, in my eyes she was so defeated, so humiliated, so crushed that I sometimes felt tormenting pity for her, even though at the same time I sometimes definitely found the idea of her humiliation pleasing. The idea of our inequality pleased me . . .

That winter it so happened that I deliberately performed several good deeds. I forgave two debts, I gave money to one poor woman without any pledge. And I didn't tell my wife about this, and I hadn't done this so that she would find out; but the woman came to thank me herself, she was practically on her knees. And that was how it became known; it seemed to me that she was truly pleased to find out about the woman.

But spring was approaching, it was already the middle of April, the storm windows had been taken down, and the sun began to light up our silent rooms with its bright pencils of light. But scales hung before my eyes and blinded my reason. Fateful, terrible scales! How did it come about that they suddenly fell from my eyes and that I suddenly could see clearly and understand everything! Was it chance, was it that the appointed day had come, was it a ray of sunshine that had kindled the thought and conjecture in my benumbed mind? No, it wasn't a matter of a thought but rather a nerve began to play up, a nerve that had grown numb began to quiver and came to life and illuminated my entire benumbed soul and my demonic pride. It was as if I had suddenly jumped up from my seat then. And it happened suddenly and unexpectedly. It happened towards evening, at about five o'clock, after dinner . . .

II. THE SCALES SUDDENLY FALL

A couple of words first. A month earlier I had noticed a strange pensiveness in her, not just silence, but pensiveness. I had also noticed this suddenly. She was sitting at her work at the time, her head bent over her sewing, and she didn't see that I was looking at her. And suddenly I was struck by how delicate and thin she had become, that her face was pale, her lips were drained of colour – all this as a whole, taken together with her pensiveness, shocked me all at once in the extreme. I had already heard earlier a little dry cough, particularly at night. I got up at once and set off to ask Schroeder to pay us a visit, without saying anything to her.

Schroeder came the following day. She was very surprised and looked first at Schroeder and then at me.

'But I'm fine,' she said with an uncertain smile.

Schroeder didn't examine her very thoroughly (these medical men sometimes are condescendingly offhand), and merely told me in the other room that it was the remnants of her illness and that come spring it wouldn't be a bad idea to take a trip somewhere to the sea or if that were not possible, then simply to find a place in the country. In a word, he didn't say anything other than that there was some weakness or something of the sort. When Schroeder had gone, she suddenly said to me again, looking at me terribly seriously:

'I'm really, really fine.'

But after saying this, she then and there suddenly flushed, apparently from shame. Apparently, it was shame. Oh, now I understand: She was ashamed that I was still *her husband*, that I was taking care of her as if I were still her real husband. But I didn't understand then and ascribed her blush to humility. (The scales!)

And then, a month later, between five and six o'clock, in April, on a bright sunny day I was sitting in the shop and doing the accounts. Suddenly I heard her in our room, at her table, over her work, singing ever so softly . . . This new development made a tremendous impression on me, and to this day I don't understand it. Until then I had almost never heard her sing, except perhaps in the very first days when I brought her into my house and we could still have some fun, target shooting with the revolver. Then her voice was still rather strong, ringing, though a bit off-key, but terribly pleasant and healthy. But now her little song sounded so feeble – oh, not that it was doleful (it was some romance), but it was as if there was something cracked, broken, in her voice, as if the little voice couldn't cope, as if the song itself were ailing. She was singing under her breath, and suddenly, after rising, the voice broke – such a poor little voice, it broke so pitifully; she cleared her throat and started singing again, ever so softly, you could barely hear her . . .

My agitation may be laughable, but no one will ever understand why I had become so agitated! No, I didn't feel sorry for her yet; it was still something altogether different. At the beginning, for the first moments at least, I suddenly felt bewilderment and terrible surprise, terrible and strange, painful and almost vindictive: 'She is singing and in my presence! *Has she forgotten about me, is that it?*'

Completely shaken, I stayed where I was, then I suddenly rose, took my hat and left, without thinking it through, as it were. At least I didn't know why or where I was going. Lukerya started helping me on with my coat.

'She sings?' I said to Lukerya unintentionally. She didn't understand and looked at me, still not understanding; but I really had been incomprehensible.

'Is this the first time that she's been singing?'

'No, she sometimes sings when you're not here,' Lukerya replied.

I remember everything. I walked down the stairs, went out into the street and set off for nowhere in particular. I walked as far as the corner and began to stare off into the distance. People passed by me, jostled me, but I didn't feel it. I hailed a cab and told him to take me to the Police Bridge, I don't know why. But then I suddenly changed my mind and gave him a twenty-kopeck piece.

'That's for your trouble,' I said, laughing senselessly, but some sort of rapture had suddenly begun to fill my heart.

I turned around and went home, quickening my step. The cracked, poor, broken little note suddenly rang out in my heart again. It took my breath away. The scales were falling, falling from my eyes! If she'd started singing in my presence, then she had forgotten about me – that's what was clear and terrible. My heart sensed this. But rapture shone in my soul and overcame my fear.

Oh, the irony of fate! You see, there had been nothing else and there could not have been anything else in my soul all winter except this very rapture, but where had I myself been all winter long? Had I been there with my soul? I ran up the stairs in a great hurry, I don't know whether I walked in timidly or not. I remember only that the entire floor seemed to be rippling and it was as if I were floating down a river. I walked into the room, she was sitting in the same place, sewing, with her head bent, but no longer singing. She threw me a fleeting and incurious glance, but it wasn't even a glance, merely the usual, indifferent gesture one makes when somebody enters a room.

I walked straight up to her and sat down on a chair right beside her, like a madman. She gave me a quick look, as though she were frightened: I took her by the hand and I don't remember what I said to her, that is, what I wanted to say, because I couldn't even speak properly. My voice kept breaking and wouldn't obey me. And I didn't know what to say, I just kept gasping for breath.

'Let's talk . . . you know . . . say something!' I suddenly babbled something stupid – oh, but was I capable of making sense? She flinched again and recoiled, badly frightened, looking at my face, but suddenly – *stern surprise* appeared in her eyes. Yes, surprise, and *stern*. She was looking at me wide-eyed. This sternness, this stern surprise came crashing down on me all at once: 'So you still want love? Love?' that surprise seemed to ask suddenly, although she was silent as well. But I could read it all, all of it. My whole being was shaken and I simply fell to the ground at her feet. Yes, I collapsed at her feet. She quickly jumped up, but I restrained her by taking hold of both her hands with extraordinary force.

And I fully understood my despair, oh, I understood! But would you believe it, rapture was seething in my heart so irrepressibly that I thought I would die. I kissed her feet in ecstasy and happiness. Yes, in happiness, immeasurable and infinite, yet understanding nonetheless all my hopeless despair! I wept, said something, but couldn't speak. Her fright and surprise suddenly gave way to some anxious thought, some extreme question, and she looked at me strangely, wildly even – she wanted to understand something quickly, and she smiled. She was terribly ashamed that I was kissing her feet, and she kept moving back, but I would at once kiss the spot on the floor where she had been standing. She saw this and suddenly began to laugh from shame (you know how people laugh from shame). Hysterics weren't far off, I saw that, her hands quivered – I didn't give it a thought and kept muttering that I loved her, that I wouldn't get up, '. . . let me kiss your dress . . . I'll worship you like this for as long as you live . . .' I don't know, I don't remember – and suddenly she burst out into sobs and started trembling; a terrible fit of hysteria had set in. I had frightened her.

I carried her over to the bed. When the fit had passed, she sat up on the bed and with a terribly distraught look, seized me by the hands and pleaded with me to calm myself: 'Enough, don't torment yourself, calm yourself!' and she began to weep again. I didn't leave her side all that evening. I kept telling her that I'd take her to Boulogne to bathe in the sea, now, right away, in two weeks, that she had such a cracked little voice, I had heard it earlier that day, that I would close the pawnshop, sell it to Dobronravov, that everything would begin afresh, and the main thing, to Boulogne, to Boulogne! She listened and was still afraid. She was more and more afraid. But that wasn't the main thing for me, but rather that I more and more irrepressibly wanted to lie down again at her feet, and once again, to kiss, to kiss the ground on which her feet stood, and to idolize her and – 'I'll ask nothing more of you, nothing,' I kept repeating every minute. 'Don't answer me anything, don't take any notice of me at all, and only let me look at you from the corner, turn me into your thing, into your little dog . . .' She wept.

'*But I thought that you were going to leave me like that*,' suddenly burst forth from her involuntarily, so involuntarily that perhaps she didn't notice at all how she had said it, and yet – oh, it was the most important, her most fateful word and the most comprehensible for me that evening, and it was as if it had slashed my heart like a knife. It explained everything to me, everything, but as long as she was there beside me, before my eyes, I went on hoping irrepressibly and was terribly happy. Oh, I wore her out terribly that evening and I understood that, but I kept thinking that I would change everything at once. Finally, towards nightfall, she broke down completely; I persuaded her to go to sleep, and she immediately fell sound asleep. I expected delirium, and there was delirium, but it was very mild. I got up during the night every few minutes, and would quietly go in my slippers to look at her. I wrung my hands over her, as I looked at this sick being lying on that pathetic little cot, the iron bedstead that I had bought for her then for three roubles. I got down on my knees but I didn't dare kiss her feet while she was sleeping (against her wishes!). I would start praying to God, and then jump up again. Lukerya watched me closely and kept coming out of the kitchen. I went to her and told her to go to bed and that tomorrow 'something quite different' would begin.

And I believed that blindly, madly, terribly. Oh, I was surging with rapture, rapture. I couldn't wait for tomorrow. The main thing, I didn't believe in any misfortune, despite the symptoms. My powers of understanding had not yet fully returned, even though the scales had fallen, and for a long, long time would not return – oh, not until today, not until this very day! And how, how could my understanding have returned then: you see, she was still alive then, you see, she was right there before me, and I before her. 'She'll wake up tomorrow, and I'll tell her all this, and she'll see it all.' That was my reasoning then, clear and simple, hence the rapture! The main thing was this trip to Boulogne. For some reason I thought that Boulogne was everything, that there was something final about Boulogne. 'To Boulogne, to Boulogne! . . .' I waited for morning in a state of madness.

III. I UNDERSTAND ALL TOO WELL

But this was only a few days ago, you see, five days, only five days ago, just last Tuesday! No, no, if only there had been a little more time, if only she had waited just a little bit longer and – and I would have dispelled the darkness! And hadn't she calmed down? The very next day she listened to me with a smile even, despite her confusion. The main thing was that during all this time, all five days, she was either confused or ashamed . . . She was also afraid, very afraid. I don't dispute it, I won't deny it, like some madman: there was fear, but then how could she not be afraid? You see, we'd been strangers to each other for so long, we had grown so far apart from one another, and suddenly all this . . . But I didn't pay attention to her fear – something new was shining! . . . Yes, it's undoubtedly true that I'd made a mistake. And perhaps even many mistakes. And as soon as we woke up the next day, when it was still morning (this was on Wednesday), I suddenly made a mistake right away: I suddenly made her my friend. I was in a hurry, much too much of a hurry, but a confession was necessary, essential – and much more than a confession! I didn't even conceal that which I had concealed from myself all my life. I told her straight out that I had done nothing all winter long but be certain of her love. I explained to her that the pawnshop had been merely the degradation of my will and mind, my personal idea of self-flagellation and self-exaltation. I explained to her that I had indeed turned coward that time at the bar, and that it was owing to my character, my touchiness: I was struck by the surroundings, I was struck by the bar; I was struck by how I would end up looking in all this and wouldn't it end up looking stupid? I didn't turn coward on account of the duel, but because it would end up looking stupid . . . And then later I didn't want to admit it, and tormented everyone, and tormented her for it as well, and then I married her so that I could torment her on account of it. In general, for the most part I spoke as though I were in a fever. She herself took me by the hands and begged me to stop: 'You're exaggerating . . . you're tormenting yourself', and the tears would begin again, and again there'd almost be a fit of hysteria. She kept pleading with me not to say or remember any of this.

I paid little or no attention to her pleas: spring, Boulogne! There was the sun, there was our new sun, that was all I talked about! I locked up the shop, handed over the business to Dobronravov. I suddenly suggested to her that we give away everything to the poor, except for the initial 3,000 I had received from my godmother, which we would use to travel to Boulogne, and then we'd come back and begin our new working life. And so it was decided, because she didn't say anything . . . she merely smiled. And I believe she smiled more out of a sense of delicacy, so as not to upset me. Of course, I saw that I was a burden to her, don't think that I was so stupid or such an egoist that I didn't see that. I saw everything, everything, right down to the last detail, I saw and knew better than anyone else; my despair was there for all to see!

I told her everything about myself and about her. And about Lukerya. I told her that I had wept . . . Oh, I'd change the subject, you see, I was also trying not to remind her of certain things at all. And, you see, she even livened up once or twice, you see, I remember, I remember! Why do you say that I looked and saw nothing? And if only *this* had not happened, everything would have been resurrected. You see, it was she who told me the day before yesterday, when the conversation turned to reading and what she had read that winter – you see, it was she who told me and laughed, when she recalled that scene between Gil Blas and the Archbishop of Granada. And what a childish laugh, sweet, just like when she was still my fiancée (an instant! an instant!); I was so happy! I was terribly struck, however, by the archbishop: you see, that meant she had found enough peace of mind and happiness to laugh at that masterpiece while she sat there that winter. That means that she had already begun to find herself wholly at peace, that she had already begun to be wholly persuaded that I would leave her *like that*. 'I thought that you were going to leave me *like that*' – that's what she had said then on Tuesday! Oh, the thought of a ten-year-old girl! And you see, she believed, believed that everything would in fact remain *like that*: she at her table, I at mine, and that's how it would be for both of us until we were sixty. And suddenly – here I come forward, her husband, and her husband needs love! Oh, the incomprehensibility, oh, my blindness!

It was also a mistake to look at her with rapture; I should have exercised restraint, because the rapture frightened her. But you see, I did exercise restraint, I didn't kiss her feet anymore. Not once did I make a show of the fact . . . well, that I was her husband – oh, and it didn't even cross my mind, I only worshipped her! But you see, I couldn't be completely silent, I couldn't say nothing at all, you see! I suddenly told her that I enjoyed her conversation and that I considered her incomparably, incomparably more educated and developed than I. Embarrassed, she blushed bright red and said that I was exaggerating. At this point, unable to contain myself, I foolishly told her what rapture I'd felt when I stood behind the door and listened to her duel, a duel of innocence with that beast, and how I had taken pleasure in her intelligence, her sparkling wit, combined with such childlike simple-heartedness. She seemed to shudder all over, murmured again that I was exaggerating, but suddenly her whole face darkened, she covered it with her hands and burst into sobs . . . Here I was unable to hold myself back: I again fell down before her, I again started to kiss her feet and again it ended in a fit, just as it had on Tuesday. That was yesterday evening, but the next morning . . .

Next morning?! Madman, but that morning was today, just now, only just now!

Listen and consider carefully: you see, when we met just

now (this was after yesterday's attack), she even struck me with her calmness, that's how it was! While all night long I had been trembling with fear over what had happened yesterday. But suddenly she comes up to me, stands before me and with her arms folded (just now, just now!), began by telling me that she's a criminal, that she knows this, that the crime has tormented her all winter long, and is tormenting her now . . . that she values my magnanimity all too much . . . 'I'll be your true wife, I'll respect you . . .' Here I jumped up and embraced her like a madman! I kissed her, I kissed her face, her lips, like a husband, for the first time after a long separation. But why did I go out just now, for only two hours . . . our foreign passports . . . Oh, God! If only I had returned five minutes earlier, just five minutes! . . . And now there's this crowd at our gate, these eyes fixed on me . . . Oh, Lord!

Lukerya says (oh, I won't let Lukerya go now for anything, she knows everything, she was here all winter, she'll tell me everything), she says that after I left the house and only some twenty minutes before my return – she suddenly went into our room to see the mistress to ask her something, I don't remember what, and she saw that her icon (the same icon of the Mother of God) had been taken down and was on the table before her, and that her mistress seemed to have been praying before it. 'What's wrong, mistress?' 'Nothing, Lukerya, you may go . . . Wait, Lukerya,' she walked up to her and kissed her. 'Are you happy, mistress?' I ask. 'Yes, Lukerya.' 'The master should have come to ask your forgiveness long ago . . . Thank God, you've made up.' 'All right, Lukerya,' she says, 'leave me, Lukerya.' And she smiled, but so strangely. So strangely that ten minutes later Lukerya suddenly went back to look in on her: 'She was standing by the wall, right by the window, she had placed her hand on the wall, and laid her head on her hand, she was standing like that and thinking. And she was so lost in thought standing there that she didn't hear me standing there and watching her from the other room. I saw that she was smiling, as it were, standing, thinking and smiling. I looked at her, turned around ever so quietly and walked out, thinking to myself, only suddenly I hear the window being opened. I at once went to say that "it's fresh, mistress, you'll catch cold" – and suddenly I see that she's climbed up on to the window and is already standing there upright, in the open window, with her back towards me and holding the icon. My heart just sank then and I cried out: "Mistress, mistress!" She heard, made a move as if to turn around towards me, but didn't, instead she took a step, clutched the icon to her breast – and threw herself out the window!'

I only remember that when I entered the gates she was still warm. The main thing is that they're all looking at me. At first they were shouting, but then they suddenly fell silent and they all make way for me and . . . and she's lying there with the icon. I remember, though darkly, that I walked over in silence and looked for a long time, and they all gathered round and are saying something to me. Lukerya was there, but I didn't see her. She says that she spoke with me. I remember only that tradesman: he kept shouting at me 'only a handful of blood came out of her mouth, a handful, a handful!' and pointing to the blood on a stone. I think I touched the blood with my finger, smeared some on my finger, looked at my finger (I remember that), and he kept saying to me: 'A handful, a handful!'

'And what do you mean "a handful"?' I wailed, they say, with all my might, I raised my arms and threw myself at him . . .

Oh, it's absurd, absurd! Incomprehensibility! Improbability! Impossibility!

IV. ONLY FIVE MINUTES TOO LATE

But is it really? Is it really probable? Can one really say that it was possible? Why, for what reason did this woman die?

Oh, believe me, I understand; but why she died is still a question. She was frightened of my love, she asked herself seriously whether she should accept it or not, and she couldn't bear the question and it was better to die. I know, I know, there's no use in racking my brains over it: she had made too many promises, got frightened that she couldn't keep them – that's clear. There are a number of circumstances here that are quite terrible.

Because why did she die? The question persists, all the same. The question hammers, hammers away in my brain. I would even have left her *like that* if she had wished to be left *like that*. She didn't believe it, that's what! No, no, I'm lying, that's not it at all. It was simply because with me it had to be honest: to love meant to love completely, and not like she would have loved the merchant. And since she was too chaste, too pure to agree to a love like a merchant needs, she didn't want to deceive me. She didn't want to deceive me with half a love or a quarter of a love under the guise of love. She was much too honest, that's what it is, gentlemen! I wanted to cultivate breadth of heart then, do you remember? A strange thought.

I'm terribly curious: did she respect me? I don't know. Did she despise me or not? I don't think she did. It's terribly strange: why didn't it occur to me all winter long that she despised me? I was utterly convinced of the contrary right until the moment when she looked at me then with *stern surprise*. Precisely, *stern*. It was then that I understood at once that she despised me. I understood irrevocably and forever! Ah, let her, let her despise me, for her whole life even, but let her live, live! Just now she was still walking, talking. I don't at all understand how she could throw herself out the window! And how could I have supposed that even five minutes earlier? I summoned Lukerya. I won't let Lukerya go now for anything, not for anything!

Oh, we could still have come to an understanding. It's just that we had grown so terribly unused to each other during the winter, but couldn't we have become accustomed to one another again? Why, why couldn't we have come together and begun a new life again? I'm magnanimous, and so is she – that's the point of connection! Just a few words more, two days, no more, and she would have understood everything.

The main thing, it's a pity that it all comes down to chance – simple, barbaric inertia, chance. That's the pity of it! All of five minutes, I was only five minutes late! If I had arrived five minutes earlier – the moment would have passed by, like a cloud, and it would never have occurred to her again. And it would have ended by her understanding everything. But now the rooms stand empty again and I'm alone once again. There's the pendulum ticking, it doesn't care, it doesn't feel sorry for anyone. There's no one – that's the awful thing!

I pace, I keep pacing. I know, I know, don't try to put words in my mouth: you think it's ridiculous that I complain about chance and the five minutes? But it's obvious, you see. Consider one thing: she didn't even leave a note saying, 'Don't blame anyone for my death', like everyone does. Could she really not have considered that even Lukerya might get into trouble? They might say, 'You were alone with her, so you must have pushed her.' In any event, she would have been dragged away, innocent though she was, if four people in the courtyard hadn't seen from the windows of the wing and the courtyard how she stood there holding the icon and hurled herself down. But, you see, that's chance as well that people were standing and saw it. No, this was all a moment, just one inexplicable moment. Suddenness and fantasy! So what if she was praying before the icon? That doesn't mean that this was before death. The entire moment lasted, perhaps, all of some ten minutes, the entire decision – precisely when she was standing by the wall, with her head resting on her arm, and smiling. The thought flew into her head, her head started spinning and – and she couldn't withstand it.

It was a clear misunderstanding, say what you will. She could still have lived with me. But what if it was anaemia? Simply on account of anaemia, the exhaustion of vital energy? She had grown tired during the winter, that's what it was . . .

I was late!!!

How very thin she is in the coffin, how sharp her little nose has become! Her eyelashes lie like arrows. And she fell, you see – without smashing or breaking anything! Just this one 'handful of blood'. A dessertspoon, that is. Internal concussion. A strange thought: What if it were possible not to bury her? Because if they take her away, then . . . Oh, no, it's almost impossible that she'll be taken away! Oh, of course, I know that she must be taken away, I'm not a madman and I'm not the least bit delirious; on the contrary, my mind has never been so lucid – but how can it be that again there'll be no one in the house, again the two rooms, and again I'm alone with the pledges. Delirium, delirium, that's where the delirium lies! I tormented her – that's what it was!

What are your laws to me now? What do I need with your customs, your ways, your life, your government, your faith? Let your judges judge me, let them take me to court, to your public court, and I will say that I acknowledge nothing. The judge will shout: 'Silence, officer!' And I will cry out to him: 'What power do you now possess that I should obey you? Why has dark inertia shattered that which was dearest of all? What need have I now of your laws? I part company with you.' Oh, it's all the same to me!

Blind, she's blind! Dead, she doesn't hear! You don't know with what paradise I would have surrounded you. The paradise was in my soul; I would have planted it all round you! Well, you wouldn't have loved me – so be it, what of it? Everything would have been *like that*, everything would have stayed *like that*. You would have talked to me only as a friend – and we would have rejoiced and laughed with joy, as we looked into each other's eyes. That's how we would have lived. And if you had fallen in love with somebody else – well, so be it, so be it! You would have walked with him and laughed, while I looked on from the other side of the street . . . Oh, let it be anything, anything, if only she would open her eyes just once! For one moment, just one! If she would look at me as she did just now, when she stood before me and swore to be my faithful wife! Oh, she would have understood it all in one glance!

Inertia! Oh, nature! People are alone on this earth – that's the problem! 'Is there a man alive on the field?' the Russian *bogatyr* cries out. And I cry out as well, though I am not a *bogatyr*, and no one answers. They say that the sun gives life to the universe. The sun will rise and – look at it, isn't it dead? Everything is dead, the dead are everywhere. There are only people, and all around them is silence – that's the earth. 'People, love one another' – who said that? Whose commandment is that? The pendulum ticks insensibly, disgustingly. It's two o'clock in the morning. Her little shoes are by the bed, as if they were waiting for her . . . No, seriously, when they take her away tomorrow, what will become of me?

1876

PENGUIN

LITTLE BLACK

CLASSICS

“她身上有好些
招人喜爱的难得品质，
可是却没法管住
自己不喝醉酒……”

PENGUIN

LITTLE BLACK

CLASSICS

漂亮的卡桑德拉

The Beautifull Cassandra

［英］简·奥斯汀　著

夏星　译

中信出版集团 | 北京

图书在版编目（CIP）数据

企鹅经典：小黑书．第三辑：汉、英 /（英）简·奥斯汀等著；夏星等译．-- 北京：中信出版社，2019.6

书名原文：Penguin Little Black Classics

ISBN 978-7-5217-0407-5

Ⅰ．①企… Ⅱ．①简… ②夏… Ⅲ．①世界文学－作品综合集－汉、英 Ⅳ．①I11

中国版本图书馆 CIP 数据核字 (2019) 第 072172 号

企鹅经典：小黑书　第三辑

漂亮的卡桑德拉

著　　者：[英] 简·奥斯汀
译　　者：夏星
出版发行：中信出版集团股份有限公司
（北京市朝阳区惠新东街甲 4 号富盛大厦 2 座 邮编 100029）
承 印 者：北京楠萍印刷有限公司

开　　本：787mm × 1092mm　1/32
印　　张：45.75
字　　数：756 千字
版　　次：2019 年 6 月第 1 版
印　　次：2019 年 6 月第 1 次印刷
京权图字：01-2018-6477
广告经营许可证：京朝工商广字第 8087 号
书　　号：ISBN 978-7-5217-0407-5
定　　价：149.00 元（全 10 册）

目录

杰克与爱丽丝

谨将本篇小说敬献给在陛下之舰坚毅号上服役的海军候补少尉弗朗西斯－威廉·奥斯汀[1]先生。

他恭顺卑微的仆人

作者敬上

1. Francis-William Austen（弗朗西斯－威廉·奥斯汀，1774—1865），作者的兄长，1786 年进入位于朴茨茅斯的皇家海军学院，1788 年 12 月随英国皇家海军坚毅号前往东印度群岛，并在那里待了四年。据 B.C. 索瑟姆在《简·奥斯汀文学手稿》一书中推测，《杰克与爱丽丝》写于作者 13 岁至 16 岁之间，亦即 1788 年至 1791 年间。（说明：书中脚注除特别标明的之外，均为译者注。）

一

曾几何时，约翰逊先生还不到五十三岁；那之后又过了十二个来月，他就五十四岁了。这事让他欢喜得紧，于是他决定，下一回过生日时他要举行一次化装舞会，邀请孩子们和朋友们来参加，以兹庆祝。因此，在他跨进人生第五十五个年头的这天，庆生化装舞会的入场券便送到了他那些邻居的手中。在他住的这个地方，和他相熟的人并不算多，统共也只有威廉斯夫人、琼斯先生和琼斯太太、查尔斯 · 亚当斯以及辛普森家三位小姐。住在帕米迪德尔[1]的就是这么几位，来参加化装舞会的也是这么几位。

在开始讲述这天晚上发生的事情之前，我应当向读者说一说，您刚刚认识的这些人物有着怎样的尊容，化装舞会上的那些角色又是个什么模样。

---

1. Pammydiddle，据 William Baker（威廉 · 贝克）所著的 *Critical Companion to Jane Austen*（《简 · 奥斯汀的重要伴侣》）中 122 页所述，该地名是作者将“Pam”与“diddle”这两个词合并在一起生造而成，前者是一种以梅花 J（即 Pam）作为王牌的纸牌游戏，后者则是“欺骗”的意思。

琼斯先生和太太的身材都很高大，性情也有些暴躁，不过，就其他方面而言，他俩倒还称得上平易近人、彬彬有礼。查尔斯·亚当斯是个和蔼可亲的小伙子，他不仅多才多艺，长相更是迷人；他的美貌如此耀眼，只有老鹰才敢直视他的面孔。

辛普森家大小姐的模样、举止和性格都很讨喜，唯一的毛病就是野心太大。她的二妹苏姬为人善妒，阴险恶毒，又矮又胖，很难相处。小妹塞西莉亚的相貌倒是无可挑剔，可惜太会装模作样，所以没人喜欢她。

集一切美德于一身的威廉斯夫人是个寡妇，她仁慈而坦率，慷慨且真诚；她虔诚又善良，敬神又可亲；她优雅可爱，斯文风趣。风韵犹存的她继承了丈夫留下的丰厚遗产。

约翰逊这一家人感情很好，尽管有一点贪杯和嗜赌，但他们优点也是不少的。

在约翰逊宅邸那间陈设讲究的起居室里，这么一帮子人齐聚一堂。在一众戴着女性面具的人当中，最引人注目的当数一位苏丹女眷的窈窕身姿。而在男性当中，倾倒众生的则是一个戴着太阳面具的人，他两眼射出的光芒正如阳光一般灿烂，且有过之而无不及，炽烈无比，谁也不敢冒险靠近这双眼睛半英里[1]之内；于是乎，在这间不过半英里宽、3/4 英里长的屋子里，最好的位置便被他一人所独占。这位先生最后终于发现，自己的光芒太过刺眼，给众人带来极大不便，逼得他们只能一窝蜂挤在房间一角，于是他把眼睛半闭起来，人们才看出原来这是查尔斯·亚当斯，穿着他那件素色的绿外套，什么面具都没戴。

大家的惊讶之情稍稍平息之后，注意力却又被两个兴冲冲往前赶的面具客给吸引过去；这两人的个子都很高，除此之外还有不少其他优点。“这两位，”睿智的查尔斯说道，“是琼斯先生和琼斯太太。”事实也的确如此。

谁都想不到那位苏丹女眷是谁！直到最后，她对着一位装模作样斜倚在沙发上的美丽女花神说道：“哦，塞西莉亚，我真希望自己扮谁就是谁。”听到这话，查尔斯·亚当斯认出她就是风度优雅、野心勃勃的卡罗琳·辛普森，他的聪明才智可真是战无不胜。至于她亲自开口与之打招呼的那位，则是她那漂亮又做作的妹妹塞西莉亚，这又让查尔斯给猜中了。

---

1. 半英里约为 805 米，后文的 3/4 英里大约是 1207 米，作者在此处似乎是用了（极为）夸张的修辞手法。

众人现在向赌桌走去，那儿有三位面具客（每人手里都拿着一个酒瓶），正赌得起劲儿呢；不过，有一位扮成美德的女性看到这触目惊心的场面便脚步匆匆地逃走了，而一位化装成嫉妒、略有些胖的女性却轮番坐在那三个赌棍的前头。查尔斯·亚当斯还是一如既往地机智伶俐，他很快就发现赌博的那几个是约翰逊家里的三位，嫉妒是苏姬·辛普森，美德则是威廉斯夫人。

于是所有人都摘下面具，去了另一个房间，那儿已经备好一桌精美的菜肴，大家吃吃喝喝，随后约翰逊一家三口又积极地给大伙儿倒起酒来，结果这帮子人喝得烂醉如泥，全都是给抬回家的，就连美德也不例外。

二

这次化装舞会为帕米迪德尔的居民们提供了足足三个月的谈资；不过大家说得最多最细的人物还要数查尔斯·亚当斯。他那举世无双的容貌、他那光芒四射的双眼、他那聪明睿智的头脑以及其人本身给人留下的整体印象俘获了许多年轻姑娘的芳心，参加化装舞会的六位女士当中总共只有五位不曾被他征服。爱丽丝·约翰逊正是那倒霉的第六个，她没能抵挡住他的巨大魅力，已然对他倾心钟情。读者诸君恐怕要觉得奇怪了，既然他如此出类拔萃、如此值得爱慕，为何单单只有这一位姑娘爱上他？可你们要知道，辛普森家那三位小姐之所以没有倒在他的魅力之下，是因为大小姐有野心，二小姐爱嫉妒，三小姐太自恋。

卡罗琳心心念念想的都是嫁个有爵位的丈夫；对于苏姬而言，要是人家比她优越得太多，那非但不会激起她的爱意，反而会让她嫉恨；至于塞西莉亚，她对自己爱恋至深，旁人都没法儿叫她中意。还有威廉斯夫人和琼斯太太——前者头脑太过清醒，不会爱上一个比自己年纪小这么多的人；后者虽然个子又高、性子又急，不过她很爱自己的丈夫，自然不会去想这档子事。

然而，尽管约翰逊小姐尝尽一切努力想要看出他对自己有感情，可查尔斯·亚当斯那颗冷酷淡漠的心却似乎依然如同原先那般自由自在；他对谁都彬彬有礼、一视同仁，还是那个漂亮活泼、无动于衷的查尔斯·亚当斯。

有天晚上，爱丽丝喝了点酒（这种情形并不罕见），头脑有点发热，于是决定去找冰雪聪明的威廉斯夫人说说话，从而调剂一下她那乱糟糟的头脑，安慰安慰她那饱受相思之苦的心灵。

和平日一样，她在夫人家里见到了她，威廉斯夫人不喜欢外出。她就像那位了不起的查尔斯·格兰迪森爵士[1]，在家时是不屑于谎称自己不在的。现在时兴把不讨人喜欢的客人拒之门外，然而在威廉斯夫人看来，这种行为跟彻头彻尾的重婚罪可是不相上下。

虽然喝了酒，但可怜的爱丽丝情绪却异常低落，她满脑子想的都是查尔斯·亚当斯，说起话来也是一句都离不开他。总而言之，她说得如此直白，威廉斯夫人很快就发现她是在单恋着他，于是对她大为怜悯、深感同情，便说出下面这一番话来。

“亲爱的约翰逊小姐，我听得再明白不过了，你没能抵挡住这个年轻人的迷人魅力，你的心已经为之倾倒，我是真心实意地替你感到可惜。这是你的初恋吗？”

“是的。”

“听你这么说，我就更难过了；我自己就是一个悲惨的例子，伴随着初恋而来的往往都是痛苦，所以我下定决心，将来一定要避免类似的不幸发生。但愿你现在这

1. Sir Charles Grandison（查尔斯·格兰迪森爵士），塞缪尔·理查森所著小说《查尔斯·格兰迪森爵士的历史》中的人物。

么做还为时不晚；亲爱的孩子，初恋非常危险，要是来得及的话，你还是尽力抽身而退吧。第二次恋爱就很少会引起什么严重后果了，所以我对此并不反对。你要保护自己免遭初恋的伤害，却无须担心第二次的到来。”

“夫人，您刚刚提起您曾身受此种不幸所害，所以您好心希望我能得以幸免。不知您是否愿意跟我讲讲您的经历和故事？”

“乐意之至，亲爱的。”

三

“家父是伯克郡一名相当富有的绅士，膝下只得我和其他几个孩子。我年仅六岁时，母亲便不幸离世。当时我年纪尚幼，少不更事，所以父亲并没有送我去学校，而是请了一位能干的家庭女教师，让她在家里教我。我的兄弟们依着年龄进了相应的学校，而我的几个妹妹都比我小，所以依然由她们的保姆照看着。

“迪金斯小姐是一位优秀的家庭女教师，是她指引我走上修习德行之路。在她的教导之下，我的性格变得日益温厚，可是在我十七岁那年，这位可敬的导师却被人从我身边夺走，要不是如此，恐怕我如今已经达到了近乎完美的境界。我从来不曾忘怀她对我说的最后一句话。她说：‘我亲爱的姬蒂，晚安了。’从那以后，我就再也没有见过她。”威廉斯夫人擦了擦眼睛，继续说道：“那天夜里，她跟着管家私奔了。”

“次年冬天，家父的一位远亲邀请我去城里和她小住一阵，这位沃特金斯太太出身显赫，非常富有，还很时髦；人人都说她是个美女，不过我却从不觉得她有多漂亮。在我看来，她的额头太高，眼睛太小，肤色又太重。”

“这怎么可能呢？”约翰逊小姐气得面红耳赤，打断她道，“你觉得可能会有人肤色太重吗？”

“我觉得会，亲爱的爱丽丝，我来告诉你我为什么会这么想；要是人的脸色红得过了头，那么我就会认为他们的脸看起来太红了。”

“可是，夫人，人的脸有可能会太红吗？”

“当然会，亲爱的约翰逊小姐，我告诉你怎么会这样。要是面色太红呢，这人的长相看起来就不如皮肤苍白一些的时候那么好看。”

“夫人，还是请您接着往下讲吧。”

“好的，正如我先前所说，这位夫人邀请我去城里和她小住几个星期。很多上流社会的先生都觉得她很漂亮，可是在我看来，她的额头太高，眼睛太小，肤色又太重。”

“夫人，关于这一点，我先前已经说过，您肯定是弄错了。沃特金斯太太的肤色不可能会太重，因为没人会这样。”

“亲爱的，在这一点上，恕我不能同意你的观点。请容我解释清楚，对于这种情况，我的看法是这样的：要是一个女人脸颊上红色的部分太大，那么她的肤色就太重了。”

“可是，夫人，我认为这是不可能的，任何人脸颊上的红色部分都不会太大。”

“亲爱的，如果有人偏偏就是肤色很重呢？”

约翰逊小姐现在已经失去了耐心，威廉斯夫人越是继续这么强硬冷静，恐怕约翰逊小姐就越是不耐烦。不过，毕竟夫人在某个方面比爱丽丝要强多了；我的意思是，她没有喝酒，要是酒精上头，再一激动，她也是要控制不住脾气的。

她俩到最后越吵越凶，爱丽丝“从动口发展到几乎要动手了”。万幸的是，约翰逊先生来了，虽然费了点力气，但总算是把她从威廉斯夫人这里拉走了，没再继续让她们就沃特金斯太太以及她的红脸蛋纠缠不休。

四

读者诸君也许会以为，经过这么一番吵闹，约翰逊一家跟威廉斯夫人是再也不能亲密无间了，但是你们错了。夫人深明大义，她不会看不出，爱丽丝之所以会这样，自然是喝醉酒的缘故，所以她并不恼火；而爱丽丝是诚心诚意地敬重威廉斯夫人，又非常爱喝夫人的红酒，所以尽力做出了一切让步。

她俩和好几天之后，威廉斯夫人前来拜访约翰逊小姐，提议两人去一处香橼树林里散散步，那树林的一头是夫人家的猪圈，另一头则是查尔斯·亚当斯家的饮马池。爱丽丝觉得威廉斯夫人提议这一趟散步是出于好意，想到最后能看见查尔斯家的饮马池，她是非常满意的，于是便兴高采烈地接受了邀请。她俩走出去没有多远，爱丽丝尚且沉浸在即将降临的幸福之中，威廉斯夫人却开了口，将她从沉思当中唤醒。

“亲爱的爱丽丝，我一直克制着没有将自己的经历说下去，是因为我不愿叫你忆起往事，毕竟当时的情景还是忘记的好（那事可没给你争光，而是让你丢了脸）。”

爱丽丝的脸已经红了，她张口欲言，夫人却看出她的不悦，于是继续说道：“亲爱的姑娘，恐怕我刚才的话对你多有冒犯，不过我向你保证，我之所以旧事重提，并非是有意要让你难受，毕竟往事已矣，无可挽回；总的来说，我并不像许多人那样认为这事是你不好，人在喝醉的时候是没法儿对自己的所作所为负责的。”

“夫人，您说这话我就不能忍了，我坚持认为——”

“亲爱的孩子，别再为此自寻烦恼了，你放心，关于此事我已经全不计较。其实当时我也没有生气，因为我一直都看得出，你几乎是烂醉如泥了，我知道你说出那些奇谈怪论是身不由己。我瞧着你听得又难过了，那我就换个话题吧，希望这事永远也别再提起。你要记住，我已经全都忘了——现在我就接着讲自己的故事。不过我必须要强调一下，我不会再对你描述沃特金斯太太的长相，这只会让往事重演罢了，既然你与她从未谋面，那么无论她的额头是不是太高、眼睛是不是太小，又或者肤色是不是太重，这都与你不相干了。”

“又来了！威廉斯夫人，这可真是太过分了——”

一提起旧事，可怜的爱丽丝又被激得冒了火，要不是她俩的注意力被另一桩事吸引了过去，我真不知道此事会如何收场。有个漂亮的年轻女子躺在一棵香橼树下，看起来非常痛苦，这着实耐人寻味，不由得她们不去注意。于是乎，她俩忘记了自己的争吵，同情地向她走去，和气地跟她搭话。

“这位美丽的姑娘，你似乎正身受某种不幸，我们很乐意把你解救出来，不知你是否愿意告知我们这是怎么一回事。你能给我们讲讲你的经历和故事吗？”

“当然可以，太太小姐们，劳驾您二位坐下吧。”她俩坐了下来，她便开了口。

五

“我出生在北威尔士，也在那里长大，家父是当地一名顶顶出色的裁缝。我们家孩子很多，刚好家母有个姐妹是寡妇，在我们隔壁的村里经营一家啤酒坊[1]，家境很富裕，所以父亲很容易便被说动了心，让她把我带走

1. alehouse（啤酒坊），多为女性经营，出售自酿的啤酒。

并抚养长大。因此过去这八年来，我都是与她同住，在此期间，她请了几位一流的大师来给我授课，凡是我这种地位的女子所应当具备的才艺，我全都学过。在他们的教导下，我学习了舞蹈、音乐、绘画以及好几种语言，如此一来，威尔士没有哪个裁缝的女儿比我更加多才多艺了。谁都不如我这般快活，直到半年以前——不过我本应先告诉你们，在我住的那一片，最重要的一处产业属于查尔斯·亚当斯，您看，也就是那边那栋砖房的主人。”

“查尔斯·亚当斯？”爱丽丝吃惊地喊道，“你认识查尔斯·亚当斯？”

“是的，小姐，我正是为此而伤心。大约在半年前，他来收租金，就是我刚刚提到的那处产业。这是我第一次见到他；小姐，您看来也是认识他的，我就不必向您描述他有多么迷人了。我无法抵挡他的诱惑……”

“唉！谁又能抵挡得了呢？”爱丽丝说着深深地叹了一口气。

“我的姨妈跟他家厨娘关系极好，于是，在我的请求之下，她决定去找这位朋友打探一下，看看他是否可能也对我有情。为此有天晚上她去跟苏珊太太一起喝茶，苏珊太太在谈话中说起她这职位如何如何好、她那主人如何如何好。我的姨妈便借机开始套她的话，我姨妈是很会套话的，没一会儿工夫苏珊就承认说，她觉得她家主人永远都不会结婚，‘因为（她说）他常常对我说无论他的妻子是谁，都必须年轻貌美、出身良好、聪明睿智、人品高洁、钱财丰厚。我曾多次（她继续说道）想要劝他改变心意，让他明白他是不可能遇到这样一位小姐的，可是我说的道理他一点也没听，他的决心丝毫也不曾动摇。’太太小姐们，你们也许能想象出我听到这番话时的痛苦心情；尽管我年轻貌美、聪明睿智、人品高洁，而且还有可能继承我姨妈的房子和生意，可我却担心他会觉得我的出身不够高贵，因而不配成为他的妻子。

“不过，我还是决定要大胆一搏，于是我言辞恳切地写了一封信给他，带着浓情蜜意对他说，我愿将自己的人和心都交给他。可他在回信中却怒气冲冲地断然拒绝了我，我想他这恐怕只是谦逊之词罢了，便再度就此事敦促于他，然而他再也没有给过我回音，而且没过多久便离开了乡下。我一听说他离去的消息，就把信写到了这儿，告诉他我期待着不久之后能有幸在帕米迪德尔与他相见，这封信他仍然没有回复，于是我当作他已经默许，就瞒着我的姨妈离开了威尔士，一番长途跋涉之后，今早才到达此地。我向人打听他家住何处，有人告诉我要穿过这片树林，也就是你们所看到的这一处。我满心欢喜地踏进树林，期待着与他见面的幸福时刻，一路走到这里，却感觉到我的腿似乎突然被人给抓住了，查看以后才发现，原来我踩中了一个捕兽夹，这种东西在绅士老爷们的地界上很是常见。”

“哎，”威廉斯夫人喊道，“我们是何其幸运，竟然遇到了你；不然的话，我们也可能是和你同样的下场。”

“千真万确，太太小姐们，你们真是走运，我只比你们早到了一小会儿。你们不难想象，当时我尖叫起来，一直喊到林子里响起回声，这无情的坏蛋才派个仆人来向我施以援手，将我从这可怕的禁锢中解放出来，然而我有一条腿已经彻底断了。”

六

听到她这伤心的故事，威廉斯夫人那对美丽的眼睛里盛满泪水，爱丽丝也忍不住大声说道：“哦！查尔斯真是狠心，这么美丽的一个人儿，竟然被他伤心又伤腿。”

威廉斯夫人打断她的话，说这位年轻女士的腿应当马上接好，一刻也不能再耽搁。她仔细察看了骨折的情况，然后立刻娴熟地开始接骨，考虑到她以前从未做过这样的事，她的技艺就更显高超了。露西随后从地上站起身来，发现自己已经可以走动，而且毫不费力，在威廉斯夫人的特别请求之下，她便同她们一起来到夫人的宅邸。

露西身材匀称，容颜秀丽，举止优雅，待到夜宵[1]结束与爱丽丝作别的时候，她已经赢得了后者的好感。爱丽丝向她保证，在这世上，除了她的父亲、哥哥、叔伯、舅舅、姑妈、姨母、堂亲、表亲以及其他亲戚，还有威廉斯夫人、查尔斯·亚当斯和另外几十个特别的朋友之外，她最喜欢的就是露西了。

她如此信誓旦旦地表达了自己的喜爱之情，作为被器重的对象，露西本该觉得不胜荣幸，然而露西却清清楚楚地看到，这位性子和善的爱丽丝喝起威廉斯夫人的红酒来可是毫不客气。

---

1. 据 William Baker（威廉·贝克）所著的 *Critical Companion to Jane Austen*（《简·奥斯汀的重要伴侣》）中 537 页所述，supper 指的是一天中最后一餐，并不需要非常丰盛，尤其是已经吃过盛大晚餐（dinner）的情况下。故而本书中 supper 统一译为夜宵，dinner 则一律译为晚餐。

夫人（她的洞察力厉害得很）从露西那一脸了然的表情看出她对此事的想法，所以约翰逊小姐刚一告辞离去，她便对露西说道:“露西，等到你和我们爱丽丝更亲近熟悉一些以后，再看到这可爱的人儿多喝了一点酒，你就不会觉得吃惊了，因为她天天都是这样的。她身上有好些招人喜爱的难得品质，可是却没法儿管住自己喝醉酒。他们一家子根本就是一帮糟糕的醉鬼。尽管很痛心，可我还是要说，我没见过比他们三个更加烂赌的人，尤其是爱丽丝。可她很讨人喜欢。诚然，我见过她大发脾气的模样，她的性情也许不是世上最温柔的，但她依然是个可爱的姑娘。我相信你一定会喜欢她的。我简直不曾见过比她更和气的人。——哦！你是没见到她有天晚上是什么样儿！为了那么一点鸡毛蒜皮的小事，她便破口大骂！她真是个讨人喜欢的孩子！我永远都爱她！”

“照夫人您这么说，她似乎是有很多优点的。”露西回应道。“哦！千好万好,”威廉斯夫人答道，“不过我对她太偏心，兴许是被这份喜爱蒙住了眼，所以对她真正的缺点都视而不见了。”

七

第二天早晨，辛普森家的三位小姐前来拜访威廉斯夫人，夫人极有礼貌地接待了她们，并将露西介绍给她们认识。辛普森家的大小姐对她非常喜欢，到临别时甚至宣称，自己唯一的心愿就是露西次日一早能陪伴她同去巴斯，因为她们姐妹三人正准备去那里小住几周。

“露西，”威廉斯夫人说道，“是完全可以自己做主的，如果她选择接受如此盛情的邀请，那么我希望她绝不要因为对我有任何顾虑而犹豫不决。真不知道我如何能够与她分别。她从未去过巴斯，我觉得她一定会非常享受这次旅行。亲爱的，”她转过头对着露西继续说道，“你愿意跟这几位小姐做个伴吗？你走了我会很难过，不过这趟远足一定会让你非常开心——我希望你能去；要是你去了，我肯定会死的——请你千万要听我的劝。”

露西恳请婉拒这份荣幸，她就不陪她们去了，同时她也向辛普森小姐充分表达了感激之情，感谢她这么客气地邀请自己。

对于她的拒绝，辛普森小姐似乎大失所望。威廉斯夫人坚持要她去——宣称如果她不去，那她就永远不会原谅她，可要是她去了，她也绝不会独活。总之，夫人用如此具有说服力的理由让事情最终有了定论——露西会去的。次日上午十点，辛普森家的几位小姐来接走了她，不久之后，威廉斯夫人便收到她这位年轻朋友传来的好消息，心满意足地得知她们已经平安抵达巴斯。

现在该言归正传说说本篇小说的主人公了，也就是爱丽丝的哥哥。想来我一直都没什么机会提起他，这恐怕在一定程度上要归罪于他那令人遗憾的嗜好——贪杯使得他完全荒废了上天赋予他的才能，所以他从未做出什么值得一提的事情。露西离开之后没过多长时间，他便一命呜呼了，似他那般有百害而无一利的活法，这也是自然而然的结果。他一死，他妹妹便成了一大笔财产的唯一继承人，这让她重新燃起希望，觉得自己又够格做查尔斯·亚当斯的妻子了。想到这一点，她无疑是满意至极的——既然结果这么让人高兴，那起因也就不怎么叫人伤心了。

她发觉自己对查尔斯的爱慕之情一天更比一天强烈，最后终于向父亲吐露了实情，希望他能够向查尔斯建议他们两家结一门亲事。她的父亲欣然同意，于是有天早上便动身去向这位年轻人表明此事。约翰逊先生是个沉默寡言的人，很快就说完了自己该说的话，他得到的答复是这样的——

“先生，您恐怕曾以为，听到您提出的建议，我应当表现得兴高采烈、感激不尽，但我要告诉您，我认为您的提议是一种冒犯。先生，在我自己看来，我是个毫无瑕疵的美男子——您在哪儿见过有人比我的体形更加优美、容貌更加迷人？还有，先生，我认为自己的举止与言谈也是最为优雅的，这样的温文尔雅和独有的温柔可亲无法言表，我从未见过有谁能与我匹敌。撇开这些偏爱不谈，我在各种语言、各类科学、各门艺术以及一切事情上的成就都是无可否认的欧洲第一人。我性情温和，优点无数，无与伦比。先生，既然我有着这样的品格，那么您说希望我娶您的女儿为妻，究竟是什么意思呢？容我简要地描述一下您和她是何等样人。先生，我认为您大体上是个很好的人，诚然您是个老醉鬼，不过我对此倒是无所谓。至于您的女儿，先生，对我而言她既不够美丽也不够温顺，既不够聪明也不够富有。我妻子将会发现我是个完美无缺的人，我希望她也是个完美无缺的人。先生，这就是我的想法，我以此为荣。我有一个朋友，但令我骄傲的是，我只有这么一个朋友。现时她正在为我准备晚餐，如果您愿意见见她的话，她就会来到这里，并且告诉您，我的想法一贯如此。”

约翰逊先生觉得很满意，他对亚当斯先生的赐教表示万分感激，感谢他让他知道了自己和女儿是什么样的人，随后便告辞了。

不幸的爱丽丝从父亲那里听到这桩伤心事，晓得父亲此去是无功而返，她失望得简直不能自已，于是赶紧去借酒浇愁，很快就将这事抛到了脑后。

八

帕米迪德尔的人正在处理这些事情的时候，露西却在巴斯赢得了所有人的喜欢。在那里住了两个礼拜，她几乎已将查尔斯那令人神魂颠倒的模样从记忆中抹消得一干二净——她想起自己从前因为被他迷住所吃的苦头，又记得自己的腿为他的捕兽夹所伤，因而要忘记他也并非难如登天，她便下定决心要把他给忘了；为了达到这个目标，她每天都花上五分钟将他从记忆里赶出去。

在写给威廉斯夫人的第二封信里，她传来喜报说自己已经完成这项任务，她对此十分满意；她还在信中提及某公爵向她求了婚。那位公爵年事已高，极为富有，健康却欠佳，他来巴斯主要是为了疗养身体。她继续写道：

> 我痛苦地发现，自己也不清楚是想答应他还是拒绝他。嫁给公爵的好处数不胜数，除了地位和财富这些次要因素，这桩婚事能给我一个家，这才是我最大的渴望，其他一切都比不上它。夫人您希望我能永远留在您身边，您这番好意既高尚又慷慨，可我如此地爱您、敬您，我无法想象自己成为您的沉重负担。我们即使要承担责任，这责任也只能来自那些为我们所不齿的人——这是我自小就被我那可敬的姨妈所灌输的观点，我在心中一直谨遵她的教诲。我姨妈是一名很出色的女性，我听说她因为我贸然离开威尔士而大发雷霆，故而不欢迎我再回去了。我无比衷心地希望能离开我所陪伴的这几位小姐。辛普森小姐（抛开她的野心来看）待人确实非常亲切，可她那位善妒又恶毒的二妹苏姬太难相处。我在此地这些大人物的圈子

里广受崇拜，相信这已经引起了她的痛恨与妒忌，这并非我的凭空想象，她经常威胁说要杀了我，有几次还试图要动手割我的喉咙。所以，夫人您一定会同意我的观点，认为我想要离开巴斯、想要有个家容身并没有错，我也确有此意。迫切盼望您能就公爵一事给我建议。

对您感激不尽的露西敬上

威廉斯夫人将自己对此事的看法写信告诉了她，信上是这么说的：

我最最亲爱的露西，对公爵的求婚，你干吗还要有片刻犹豫？我打听过他的人品，发现他既无耻又无知。我的露西可不能嫁给这么一个人！他富可敌国，而且财富与日俱增。这钱要是由你来花，那该有多么体面！在众人眼里，你会给他带来多大荣光！人们对他的尊敬会有多少是看着他妻子的面子！不过，亲爱的露西，为了给此事一个了断，你为什么不立刻回到我身边永不离开呢？你关于责任的高尚情怀令我钦佩，可是我请求你不要因此就不再给我带来快乐。如果让你永远留在我身边，我肯定要付出一大笔开销——我承受不起这笔花费，但这跟有你陪伴带给我的幸福如何能够相提并论？我知道这会让我倾家荡产——所以，这些理由一定可以说服你回到我身边的。

你最亲爱的 C. 威廉斯敬上

九

如果露西收到信，夫人的建议会对她产生何种影响，我们已经无从得知了，因为就在这封信到达巴斯的几个钟头之前，露西已经咽下最后一口气，沦为嫉妒与恶毒的牺牲品。苏姬妒忌她魅力超群，于是对她下了毒，让她在十七岁的年纪便离开了倾心爱慕着她的人们。

可爱可亲的露西就这么香消玉殒了，她此生从不曾犯下罪过，除了离开姨妈这一鲁莽之举，她的人生再无瑕疵，认识她的人都诚心诚意地为她的死感到悲伤。在她的朋友当中，最为痛苦的当数威廉斯夫人、约翰逊小姐以及那位公爵；后面这两位对她的关切可是最最真心的，尤以爱丽丝为甚，毕竟她曾经跟露西相处了整整一个晚上，而且从那之后就再也没有想起过她。公爵大人的苦痛也同样不难理解，过去这十天来，他感受到露西的温柔怜爱与真切关心，如今却失去了她。对露西的死，他忠贞不渝地哀悼了两个礼拜，随后却让卡罗琳·辛普森野心得偿，抬举她当了公爵夫人。辛普森小姐最期盼的事情终于做成，自是十分地称心如意。至于她的妹妹——那位背信弃义的苏姬，在此后不久也同样被大伙儿吹捧了几天，她倒也受之无愧，而且就她的所作所为来看，这根本就是她一向的渴望。她的残忍谋杀行为被人发现，尽管亲朋好友纷纷求情，她还是很快被送上了绞刑架。还有美丽动人却装模作样的塞西莉亚，她觉得自己的魅力无人能敌，更何况如果就连卡罗琳都能勾搭上一位公爵，那么她有志要赢得某位王子的青睐也就无可厚非了，不过她知道自己祖国的那些王子基本上都已经“名花有主”，所以她离开了英格兰。据我所知，她如今是莫卧儿[1]大帝最为宠爱的妃子。

与此同时，帕米迪德尔的住户们也大大地吃了一惊，

1. Mogul（莫卧儿帝国），16 世纪至 19 世纪统治印度大部分地区。

而且好奇得紧，因为有传言说，查尔斯·亚当斯打算要成婚了。但那位小姐的芳名却仍旧无人知晓。琼斯先生和琼斯太太猜测是约翰逊小姐；不过约翰逊小姐比他们要清楚，她只担心他要娶他的厨娘。可是叫所有人意外的是，他竟公然娶了威廉斯夫人。

亨利与伊丽莎

谨将本篇小说献给库珀[1]小姐。

她恭顺又卑微的仆人

作者敬上

这天，乔治爵爷和哈考特夫人在监督晒干草的工人干活，见着勤快的便赞许地笑笑，对着偷懒的就打几棍子。恰在此时，他俩看见一垛干草堆底下躺着个漂亮的小女孩，最多不过三个月大，差点就被那茂密的草叶给

1. Jane Cooper（简 · 库珀，1771—1798），作者的表姐兼儿时好友，大约在 1789 年年初的时候拜访过奥斯汀一家。索瑟姆在《简·奥斯汀文学手稿》中推测，《亨利与伊丽莎》的写作时间是在 1787 年至 1790 年。

挡住了。

夫妇俩自己并没有孩子，看到她那可爱秀美的面容，听到她活力十足的儿语，似在回答他俩那许许多多的疑问，不禁深受感动、大为欣喜，于是决定把她带回家，悉心照料，供她念书。

这夫妻俩本身都是好人，所以他俩认为，最首要也是最主要的就是激励她热爱美德、憎恨恶行，在这一点上，他们做得非常成功（伊丽莎的天性本就如此）。待到她长大以后，凡是认识她的人，都觉得她很讨人喜欢。

哈考特夫人宠着她，乔治爵爷疼着她，全世界都爱着她，这孩子一直过得快快乐乐，从未吃过一点苦，直到她十八岁这年。有一天，她那冷酷无情的恩主夫妇发现她偷了一张五十英镑的钞票，便将她逐出家门。对于那些没有伊丽莎这般伟大高尚思想的人而言，要是他们遭逢如此剧变，肯定就只有死路一条，不过伊丽莎知道自己是出类拔萃之人，于是开开心心地自娱自乐起来。她坐在一棵树下，现编现唱了下面这段歌词。

歌

尽管我双脚踏进不幸的阴影，

可我希望自己永远不会缺了友情，
只因我将永葆心灵的无邪，
绝不背离美德的疆界。

她唱着这支歌儿，愉快地想着心事，如此消遣了几个钟头才站起身来，走上通往 M 镇的那条公路。M 是一个小小的集镇，她最要好的朋友就在那里，经营着一家名叫红狮[1]的小酒馆。

她径直来到朋友这里，向她讲述了自己新近的不幸遭遇，同时表明心愿，说她想要去人家家里做个卑微的女伴。

要伊丽莎说，这世上最可亲的人，那就是威尔逊太太了。她刚一知晓伊丽莎的愿望，便在酒馆里坐下来，给她最为敬重的 F 公爵夫人修书一封，信中这样写道：

F 公爵夫人　敬启

1. Red Lion（红狮），英国最受欢迎的酒馆名称。缘自 1603 年，伊丽莎白一世死后无嗣，苏格兰国王詹姆士六世继承英国王位，称詹姆士一世。他下令英国所有重要建筑（包括酒馆在内）均需涂上代表苏格兰的红狮纹章，以象征苏格兰和英格兰的统一。目前全英仍有七百多家酒馆名为“红狮”。

恳请贵府收留一名年轻女子，她的人品高洁无瑕，不想去做女佣，却愿意与您做伴。请快些将她从我的怀抱里带走吧。

萨拉·威尔逊敬上

这位公爵夫人和威尔逊太太友谊深厚，就算为她付出一切代价也在所不惜，现如今这么一个大好机会摆在面前，让她能够为威尔逊太太效劳，公爵夫人自是大喜过望。因此，收到信以后她即刻就启程上路，当天晚上便到了红狮酒馆。F公爵夫人年约四十五六，很容易激动，交了朋友便死心塌地，结了仇恨也绝不会回心转意。她是个寡妇，唯一的女儿眼下正在跟一个极为富有的年轻人谈婚论嫁。

公爵夫人一看到咱们的女主角，就张开双臂搂住她的脖子，宣称自己对她十分喜欢，并决定今后和她永不分离。听到她这一番友情宣言，伊丽莎很是欣喜，她洒泪挥别亲爱的威尔逊太太，次日一早陪着公爵夫人来到了她位于萨里郡的宅第。

公爵夫人将她介绍给女儿哈丽雅特小姐[1]认识，言辞之间尽显殷殷关切。哈丽雅特小姐非常喜欢她的相貌，于是恳求与她以姐妹相待，伊丽莎纡尊降贵地答应了。

哈丽雅特小姐的恋人塞西尔先生常常到公爵夫人家里来，因而也就经常见到伊丽莎。他和伊丽莎互生情愫，塞西尔先开口表白了自己的爱，并劝说伊丽莎跟他私订终身。他没费什么力气便得到伊丽莎的应允，而且，他俩确信，公爵夫人的牧师也深爱着伊丽莎，只要是为她效劳，他什么都愿意做。

有天晚上，公爵夫人和哈丽雅特小姐去参加一个集会，他俩便趁着她们离家的大好机会，在那位倾心于伊丽莎的牧师主持下结为夫妻。

夫人和小姐回到家才大吃一惊地发现，伊丽莎不见了，只留下一张便条，上面写道：

夫人：

我们结婚了，就此别过。

亨利·塞西尔和伊丽莎·塞西尔

---

1. Lady Harriet，公爵之女可称“Lady”。

这封信已经足以将整件事情解释得一清二楚，夫人读完之后勃然大怒，用尽了她盛怒之下所能想到的一切难听字眼大骂他们，舒舒服服骂了半小时。随后派出三百人带着武器去追他们，同时下令说，活要见人，死要见尸，决不允许空手而归。夫人的打算是，如果这些人真的将他俩活着带回来了，她就先把他俩关上几年，再折磨至死。

与此同时，逃跑在外的塞西尔和伊丽莎来到了欧洲大陆。他俩认为在这里比在祖国要安全一些，可以免遭公爵夫人的可怕报复——他们的担心是极有道理的。

他俩在法兰西先后生下两个男孩，只是结婚才三年伊丽莎就成了寡妇，无力养活她自己和两个孩子。自从结婚以来，他们几乎是挣多少花多少，没存下几个钱来。他们每年的花销是一万两千磅，可是塞西尔先生留下的遗产却连这个数字的二十分之一都不到。

伊丽莎深知这摊子事是没法儿理清爽了，丈夫一死，她便乘着一艘装有五十五门大炮的军舰回到英格兰，这军舰还是他俩当初手头比较宽裕的时候建造的。可是她一手牵着一个孩子刚刚踏上多佛尔的海岸，就被公爵夫人派来的军官抓住，送进了地牢。这里地方虽小，倒也温暖舒适，恰似夫人私家的新门[1]监狱，是公爵夫人专为款待她的秘密囚犯而建。

进了地牢之后，伊丽莎第一桩想到的事就是如何离开这里。

她来到门口，门是锁着的。她看看窗户，窗上有铁条。两条路都不通，她好生沮丧，觉得逃跑无望，正在万念俱灰之际，居然瞧见监房一角摆着一把小锯子和一架绳梯，这可真是鸿运当头。她立刻就拿起锯子动起了手，几个礼拜之后，她已经锯掉了所有的铁条，只留下一根用来拴绳梯。

接下来又遇到的一个难题，她想了好些时候才找到解决的法子。她的孩子们年纪还太小，没法儿自己从绳梯上爬下去，而她下去的时候又不可能抱着他俩一起。最后她决定，先把她所有的衣物都扔下去——她多的就是衣服，再严令孩子们切不可伤了自己，然后把他们也扔下去。她自己则轻轻松松地顺着绳梯往下爬，到了底下，她满意地发现两个小家伙都完好无损、睡得正香。

1. Newgate，著名监狱，位于伦敦西门。

如今她觉得，她和孩子们要想活下去，这些衣服就非卖不可了。挥泪告别昔日辉煌仅存的遗迹之后，她用所得的钱财去买了些其他更有用处的东西——给孩子们买了些玩具，又给她自己买了块金表。

上述这些生活必需品刚刚拿到手，她就开始觉得饥肠辘辘，并且有理由相信她的两个孩子也差不多是同样的情形，因为他们正要啃下她的两根手指头。

眼见得大难临头、躲避不过，为了做些补救，她只好下定决心，仍旧回去找她的老朋友——乔治爵爷和哈考特夫人，他二人慷慨大度，她曾多次亲身体会，只盼着如今也能再度亲历。

他们那舒适宜人的大宅距此还有四十英里，她马不停蹄地走了三十英里，发现前方是一座小镇。在从前那段幸福的时光，她常常陪着乔治爵爷和哈考特夫人来到这里，在其中一家客栈里吃顿冷餐。

往事历历涌上心头，她记起自己最后一次开心地这样吃吃喝喝，记起自己从那以后所经历的桩桩奇遇，一时间想出了神，便在一位先生家门前的台阶上坐下了。往昔忆完，她立起身，决心就在那家给她留下愉快回忆的客栈安营扎寨，指望着从进进出出的宾客那里讨些赏钱。

她刚刚在客栈院子里选定位置站好，一辆马车便驶将出来，在转过她所站的角落时停下，以便车夫能有机会欣赏一番她美丽的芳容。伊丽莎于是走到车旁，打算向他们乞求施舍，可是一看到车里的那位夫人，她便惊叫起来。

“哈考特夫人！”

听到这话，那位夫人答道：“伊丽莎！”

“是的，夫人，我正是可怜的伊丽莎。”

乔治爵爷也在马车里，吃惊得说不出话来，他正要请伊丽莎说说她眼下这是什么处境，哈考特夫人却喜不自胜地喊道：“乔治爵爷，乔治爵爷，伊丽莎不仅是咱们的养女，她还是咱们的亲生女儿。”

“咱们的亲生女儿！哈考特夫人，你这话从何说起？你也知道自己从未生过一男半女，求你说说清楚吧。”

“乔治爵爷，你一定还记得，当初你乘船去往美洲的时候，我已经怀孕了。”

“我记得，我记得，请继续说吧，亲爱的波莉。”

“你离开四个月之后，我生下了这个女孩，可我害怕你会不高兴，因为你想要的是男孩。于是我带着她来到一垛干草堆旁，将她放在那里。又过了几个礼拜，你回来了，万幸的是，你并未向我问起此事。我以为自己的孩子过得很好，觉得心满意足，很快就忘了自己曾有过孩子。所以，不久之后咱们在那垛干草底下发现她时，不仅你没想到她是我的孩子，就连我自己都没有想到，尽管我当初正是在那里把她放下的。冒昧地说，本来没什么会让我想起此事，但是刚才偶然间听到她的声音，我忽然意识到，这跟我自己那孩子的声音正是一模一样。”

“这事的来龙去脉你解释得合情合理，令人信服，”乔治爵爷说道，“毫无疑问，她就是咱们的女儿，既是如此，对她当年犯下的盗窃罪行，我便既往不咎了。”

双方就此言归于好，伊丽莎带着她的两个孩子登上马车，回到她已阔别近四年的那个家。

伊丽莎在哈考特庄园重拾往日威势，随即便募集了一支军队，带着他们将公爵夫人那温暖舒适的监狱夷为平地，此举为她赢得了千万人的称道，她心里也觉得自己做得极好。

漂亮的卡桑德拉

/

经奥斯汀小姐[1]许可，特将本篇小说敬献于她，共十二章。

献词

小姐：

您就如同凤凰[2]一般。您品位高雅、情怀高

1. Cassandra-Elizabeth Austen（卡桑德拉－伊丽莎白·奥斯汀，1773—1845），作者的姐姐。本篇作品很可能创作于1787年至1788年之间，因为作者一家曾于1788年8月到访过作品中的背景地伦敦。

2. 作者在献词中将姐姐卡桑德拉喻为“凤凰”，这一点颇令人费解。据R. W. 查普曼编纂的《简·奥斯汀作品集第六卷：次要作品》，这可能是指卡桑德拉像凤凰一样以虚构的形式重现在这篇由十二个章节构成的小说里。

尚、美德无数。您容颜秀丽、体形优美、风姿绰约。您举止优雅、言谈理性、相貌出众。如果下面这篇小说能供您消遣一时，我也就再无所求了。

您最最恭顺卑微的仆人

作者敬上

一

卡桑德拉是邦德街[1]上一位著名女帽制造商的独生女儿。她的父亲出身高贵，和某某公爵夫人的管家是近亲。

二

到了十六岁这年，卡桑德拉已经出落得美丽动人，性子也很和气。她刚巧看上了一顶精致优雅的帽子——这是一位伯爵夫人订做的，她的母亲才刚刚做好。她将

1. Bond Street，伦敦市中心一条著名购物街，自 18 世纪开始，已成为伦敦的时尚购物中心。

这顶帽子戴在自己那漂亮的脑袋上，然后走出她母亲的商店，出门闯荡去了。

三

她遇见的第一个人是一位子爵，这个大名鼎鼎的年轻人不仅德才兼备，而且风度翩翩、相貌英俊。她对他屈膝一礼，随后继续前进。

四

她走进一家糕点店，风卷残云般吞下六份冰激凌，却拒绝付钱，将糕点师打倒在地，然后扬长而去。

五

接下来，她登上了一辆出租马车，命车夫前往汉普斯特德，可是刚到那里，她却又命令车夫掉转车头送她回来。

六

回到了出发时的同一条街、同一个地点，车夫向她索要车钱。

七

她在衣兜里搜了一遍又一遍，却一无所获，一分钱也找不到。车夫强横起来，她便将帽子往他头上一戴，拔腿跑了。

八

跑过一条又一条街道，她一直平安无事，直到经过布鲁斯伯里广场的转角，在这里她遇见了玛丽亚。

九

卡桑德拉吓了一跳，玛丽亚似乎也大吃一惊；她俩颤抖着，脸色由红转白，然后一语不发地擦肩而过。

十

有人和卡桑德拉搭讪，那人是个寡妇，跟卡桑德拉是朋友。她的脑袋小，窗户却更小，她便将脑袋从窗户里挤出来，向卡桑德拉问好。卡桑德拉屈膝一礼，然后继续前进。

十一

又走过四分之一英里，卡桑德拉回到了邦德街上的家里，此时她已经离家近七小时了。

十二

她走进家门，被母亲紧紧拥在怀里。这真是位贤妻良母。卡桑德拉微微一笑，低声自语道:“今天过得可真充实。”

一位处境困难的年轻女子写给友人的信[1]

几天以前，我去参加阿什伯纳姆先生举办的一场私人舞会。因为家母从不出去交际，她便将我托付给格雷维尔夫人照顾，夫人赏光同意顺道来接我，并且允许我面向前方坐着——对于这一优待，我倒是无所谓，尤其是我深知夫人将之视为赐予我的莫大恩惠。“哎，玛丽亚小姐”（夫人看见我朝着马车车门走来，便开口说道），“今天晚上你看起来特别漂亮——我可怜的女儿们在你身旁可就被比下去了。但愿你妈妈别因为让你出门而担心。

1. 本篇出自 *A Collection of Letters*（《书信集》），是第三封信。该书信集由五封风格各异、相互独立的书信组成，均敬献给作者的表姐 Jane Cooper（简·库珀）。

你这是穿了一件新礼服吗？”

“是的，夫人。”我尽量不动声色地答道。

“对嘛，我也觉得这件挺好（她用手摸了摸，因为我是蒙她恩准坐在她旁边的），我敢说这礼服非常时髦，不过我得直说——你知道我总是想到什么就说什么，我觉得这钱花得冤枉。你为什么不能穿你那件条纹的旧礼服呢？我这人不会因为人家穷就横加挑剔，我一向认为，穷人应该被人瞧不起，被人可怜，但不该受人责备，特别是那些身不由己的穷人。可是另一方面我也得说，在我看来，你那件条纹的旧礼服穿在你身上就已经很不错了，跟你说实话吧（我这人向来想到什么就说什么），我想舞会上恐怕有一半的人压根儿就不会知道你有没有礼服，不过我估摸着你是打算今天晚上钓个金龟婿。嗯，那就是越快越好了，祝你成功。”

“夫人，其实我并无此意——”

“谁听过哪位年轻姑娘承认自己想嫁个有钱人啊？”格雷维尔小姐大笑着说，不过我相信埃伦肯定是同情我的。

“你走之前，你母亲已经睡下了吗？”夫人问道。

“亲爱的夫人，”埃伦说，“现在才九点。”

“话是不假，埃伦，但蜡烛是要花钱买的，威廉斯夫人这么明智，她可不会铺张浪费。”

“夫人，我走的时候，她刚刚坐下来准备吃夜宵。”

“她夜宵吃什么？”“我没看到。”“我猜是面包和奶酪吧。”“我觉得这就是最好的夜宵了。”埃伦说道。“这话真没道理，”她母亲反驳道，“你哪天吃得都比这个好。”格雷维尔小姐夸张地大笑起来，她听见她妈妈说俏皮话时总是这个反应。

这便是我乘坐夫人的马车时被迫面临的屈辱境地。我却不敢失礼，母亲总是告诫我，要想立足于世，就须谦卑忍耐。她坚持认为，只要格雷维尔夫人开口相邀，我就不可拒绝。若非如此，我是断然不会踏进她家一步的，也绝不会登上她的马车，因为肯定会不愉快——她总是对我恶语相向，缘由不过是我穷罢了。我们到达阿什伯纳姆府上时已近十点，比预期晚了一个半小时；不过格雷维尔夫人是个时髦的人（或者说她自以为很时髦），自然是不会守时的。舞会尚未开始，专为等着格雷维尔小姐。进屋之后不久，伯纳德先生便来邀我跳舞，我们正要起身，他却记起自己的白手套还在仆人那里，于是立刻跑出去取。就在此时，舞会开始了，走向另一个房间的格雷维尔夫人刚好从我面前经过，她看见我，随即停下脚步，也不管近旁还有好几个人，开口说道：

“你好啊，玛丽亚小姐！找不到舞伴吗？可怜的姑娘！我看你的新礼服怕是白穿了。不过别灰心，今天晚上这舞会结束前，没准你还是能跳上一支舞的。”她一边这么说，一边继续走，尽管我一再保证已经有人邀请过我，她却根本不听，让我因为她在人前如此说我而大为光火——不过伯纳德先生很快就回来了，他一进房间就来到我身边，当着那些老夫人的面带我走向跳舞的人群。这些人刚才可都是听见了她那一席话的，但愿格雷维尔夫人对我人品所泼的脏水可以就此洗清。没过多久，跳舞的乐趣就使我忘却了一切烦恼，我拥有全场的最佳舞伴，并且他还是一大笔财产的继承人。我看得出格雷维尔夫人似乎很不高兴，因为她发现伯纳德先生竟然选了我做舞伴。她打定主意要给我难堪，于是当我们在跳舞间隙坐下休息时，她便带着梅森小姐朝我走来，比平日更加盛气凌人，大声开了口，全场有一半人都能听到她的声音：“请问，玛丽亚小姐，令祖是做哪个行当的？梅森小姐和我对此有点分歧，不知道他究竟是杂货商还是订书匠。”我明白她是想羞辱我，便决心尽量不让她的奸计得逞。“夫人，都不是；他是一名红酒商人。”“是了，我就知道他的工作低贱得很——他破产了不是吗？”“夫人，我想他并不曾破产。”“难道他没有潜逃吗？”“此事我闻所未闻。”“总之他死的时候还欠着债吧？”“从没有人如此说过。”“怎么，难道令尊不是穷得叮当响吗？”“我认为不是。”“他有一回是不是被人给告了？”“我倒不曾见过他出入法庭。”她狠狠地看了我一眼，怒气冲冲地转身走了；我却是喜忧参半，喜的是我没有对她恭敬有礼，忧的是怕旁人会觉得我太过粗鲁。格雷维尔夫人被我气极了，一晚上都不再搭理我了，不过，即便她对我青眼有加，也同样会无视我的存在，因为她喜欢跟一群大人物待在一起，除非是实在找不到人说话了，否则她可不会理睬我。吃夜宵时，格雷维尔小姐跟她母亲那一帮人坐在一起，不过埃伦更愿意和我以及伯纳德一家待在一块儿。我们跳舞跳得很开心，回家的路上格雷维尔夫人一直在睡觉，所以这一路我还是挺自在的。

第二天我们吃晚餐的时候，格雷维尔夫人的马车来到门口停下了，她一般认为就该这个时候来。她叫仆人进来传话，说她“不能下车，但有话要对玛丽亚小姐讲，所以请小姐务必去到马车门口，而且要赶紧去、马上就去”！“妈妈，这话可真是太无礼了！”我说。她却答道：“去吧，玛丽亚。”于是我只得出去，被迫听凭夫人摆布，顶着刺骨的狂风站在那里。

“玛丽亚小姐，我怎么觉得你没有昨晚那么漂亮了——不过我可不是来查看你穿了什么衣裳的，只是想告诉你一声，后天你可以来和我们共进晚餐。不是明天。记好了，明天别来，因为我们要宴请克莱蒙特勋爵和夫人以及托马斯·斯坦利爵爷一家。我后天不会派马车来接你，所以你得委屈一下，要是下雨的话，你就把伞带上——”听到她恩准我不让自己淋湿，我差点就忍不住大笑起来。“还有，请你务必记住要准时，我可不会等着你。我讨厌食物被煮过头。不过你倒也不必提前来。你母亲还好吗？她在吃晚餐是吧？”“是的，夫人，您大驾光临的时候，我们刚好在用晚餐。”“玛丽亚，你恐怕很冷吧。”埃伦说。“是很冷，这东风[1]吹得真是吓人——”她母亲说道，“实话对你说，这窗子开着我都要受不了了。不过，玛丽亚小姐，你已经被风吹习惯了吧，所以你的肤色才会如此红润粗糙。你们这些不常有马车坐的年轻

---

1. 英国的东风系从欧洲大陆北部吹来，类似于我国的西北风，非常寒冷。

姑娘从来就不在意辛苦赶路时是什么天气，也无所谓风吹起裙子露出了腿。我是不会让我的女儿们在这种天气像你这样站在外头的。可是有一种人，要么就是感觉不到冷，要么就是不知道体贴别人。好了，别忘记礼拜四下午五点钟到我们家里来。你千万要叫女仆晚上来接你，那天不会有月光，你走回家这一路会很可怕。替我向你母亲问好。恐怕你的晚餐都要凉了。赶车走吧。”她就这么走了，我却被她气得怒火中烧。她每次都是如此。

玛丽亚 · 威廉斯

一位热恋中的年轻女子写给友人的信[1]

/

我叔叔越来越小气，我婶婶越来越挑剔，而我却一天比一天爱恋更深。如此发展下去，到了年底不知会是何等光景！今天早晨，我有幸收到亲爱的默斯格罗夫写来的信，内容如下：

萨克维尔街：1 月 7 日

自我初见美丽的亨丽埃塔那天起，迄今已有整整一月，这是个神圣的纪念日，必须以某种与之相称的方式记录下来，所以我便写信给

1. 本篇亦出自 *A Collection of Letters*（《书信集》），是第五封。

她。我永远也不会忘记她的美貌第一次展露在我眼前的那一刻——如您所知，时间绝不可能将此刻从我记忆中抹去。我和她相遇在斯库达摩尔夫人家里。夫人何其有幸，住处竟与亨丽埃塔女神的居所相距不足一英里！当这可爱的人儿踏进房间之时，哦！我的感觉是怎样的？见到您，我惊为天人，一脸爱慕地注视着您，您的魅力似乎每一刻都有增无减。不幸的默斯格罗夫未及环顾左右便为您的妩媚所俘虏。是的，小姐，我爱上了您，这是我的幸运，亦是我的不幸，对此我却只有无尽感激。我扪心自问："默斯格罗夫，你凭着哪一点能为亨丽埃塔牺牲呢？你这令人羡慕的凡夫俗子！你为伊人憔悴，伊人却不只为你一人所独钟，有位上校也倾心于她，还有位准男爵为了她举杯祝酒！"迷人的亨丽埃塔，您是多么美丽！我宣布，您就是女神！您并非一介凡人，您是天使，维纳斯就是您。总而言之，小姐，我此生从未见过比您更漂亮的姑娘。您允许默斯格罗夫爱您，给我以希望，您在我眼中便更加美丽动人。

啊！天使般的亨丽埃塔小姐，我是多么热切地期盼着您那可憎的叔父和缺德的婶娘早赴黄泉，此心此情，苍天可鉴。我的佳人非要等他们死了才肯答应嫁给我，因为他们的遗产可以让她过上富足的生活，而我的财产却不足以做到。尽管我的产业还是有可能会增加的，可是狠心的亨丽埃塔决意如此，不肯动摇！我目前和姐姐住在一起，我自己的房子虽好，眼下却有些破败失修，在修葺完毕可以住人之前，我打算一直住在姐姐家里。再见了，我心中温柔可亲的公主，我用这颗心颤抖着签下自己的名字。

您最狂热的崇拜者以及忠实卑微的仆人

T. 默斯格罗夫

玛蒂尔达，这就是一封典型的情书啊！如此富有见地，如此充满感情，思想如此纯洁，语言如此流畅，如此情真意切，全都集于这一张纸上。你从前可曾读过这样的杰作？不，这个问题我可回答不了，像默斯格罗夫这样的人是可遇不可求的。哦！我多么想和他在一起！我打算明天把下面这封信寄给他作为回复。

最最亲爱的默斯格罗夫，来信收到，吾心甚喜，无以言表；我以为自己会喜极而泣，因我爱你胜过爱这世上任何人。在我眼中，你是英格兰最可亲、最英俊的男人，你肯定就是如此。这是我此生读过的最甜蜜的来信，再像这样给我写一封吧，把字里行间都写满你对我的爱。我迫不及待想要见你。咱们怎么才能设法见上一面？我们是如此相爱，分离会要了我们的命。哦！亲爱的默斯格罗夫，你无法想象我是多么盼望叔父和婶娘快点死，简直都等不及了。我对你的爱恋与日俱增，如果他们不早点死的话，我想我一定会发疯的。你的姐姐何其幸福，能够享受到你在家中与她为伴的乐趣；伦敦的众人何其幸福，因为有你在那里。亲爱的默斯格罗夫，希望能很快再次收到你的信，我以前可从未读到过如此甜蜜的来信。

永远最忠于您的亨丽埃塔·霍尔顿敬上

但愿他会喜欢我的回信，我也只能写到这样了，不过跟他的信还是不能相提并论；事实上，我一贯听人说他很会写情书。你知道，我跟他第一次见面是在斯库达摩尔夫人的家里。后来我见到夫人的时候，她便问我对她的表弟默斯格罗夫印象如何。

“哎，不瞒您说，”我说道，“我觉得他是个非常英俊的年轻人。”

“你这么想，我很高兴，”她答道，“因为他已经疯狂地爱上了你。”

“天哪！斯库达摩尔夫人，”我说，“您怎么能说出如此荒唐的话来？”

“这话不仅不荒唐，而且是千真万确，”她答道，“我敢担保，他从见到你的那一刻起就爱上你了。”

“但愿如此，”我说，“一见钟情还是有些道理的，对于其他的种种爱情，我都不屑一顾。”

“好啦，恭喜你，这就把他给征服了，”斯库达摩尔夫人说道，“我相信他已经完全没有招架之力。我表弟是个很迷人的小伙子，见过许多世面，还很会写情书，我读过最好的情书都是他写的，所以你这也算是一场大胜了。”

听了这话，我非常高兴，对我的爱情俘虏更是极为满意。不过我觉得自己还是应该摆摆架子，于是我对她说:“斯库达摩尔夫人，这当然好，不过您也知道，我们这些将要继承大笔遗产的年轻小姐可万万不能委身下嫁身无分文的男人。”

“亲爱的霍尔顿小姐，”她说，“关于这一点，我和你一样确信无疑。而且，我向你保证，不管是谁，要是他没有指望发财，我是断然不会怂恿你嫁给他的。默斯格罗夫先生远远谈不上身无分文，他继承了一笔遗产，每年大约有几百镑的收入，将来可能还会大大增加，他还有一处极好的房产，只是眼下仍需要修葺一番才是了。”

“如果是这样的话，”我答道，“那我就说不出什么来反对他了。要是如您所言，他是个见多识广的年轻人，又写得一手好情书，我相信我没有道理因为他倾慕于我而对他挑三拣四。不过，斯库达摩尔夫人，我恐怕不会因此就嫁给他。”

“你当然不是非得嫁给他不可，”夫人说道，“不过你会心甘情愿听凭爱情的摆布。要是我猜得差不离的话，此刻你已经对他情根深种，只是还不自知罢了。”

“啊呀，斯库达摩尔夫人，”我红着脸答道，“您怎么会想到那儿去呢？”

“因为你的眼神、言谈无一不在泄露你的心事，”夫人说道，“得啦，亲爱的亨丽埃塔，把我当作朋友，跟我实话实说吧，在所有认识的男子当中，你是不是最喜欢默斯格罗夫先生？”

“斯库达摩尔夫人，请不要问我此类问题，”我背过脸说道，“我是不好回答的。”

“才不是呢，我的宝贝，”她答道，“现在你已经证实了我的猜测。可是，亨丽埃塔，你既然是爱得其所，却又为何羞于承认，为何不肯向我吐露实情？”

“我并没有羞于承认，”我鼓起勇气说道，“也并非不肯向你吐露实情，厚着脸皮说一句，我确实爱着您的表弟默斯格罗夫先生，这是真心诚意的爱恋，爱上一个相貌英俊的男子并不丢脸。要是他平平无奇，我也许还有理由对这份感情感到羞耻，因为所爱之人不值得，所以这爱情本身也必定低贱。可是您的表弟有着这样的身材与面孔，还有那么漂亮的头发，如此出众的品质令我印象深刻，我为何要羞于承认呢？”

“我的好姑娘（斯库达摩尔夫人说着就热情洋溢地来拥抱我），在这些事情上头，你的看法可真是周到细致，像你这个年纪的人倒很少有这般机敏的洞察力！哦！你这高尚的情怀令我肃然起敬！”

“夫人，果真如此吗？”我说道，“您真是太热心了。不过，斯库达摩尔夫人，请您告诉我，是您的表弟亲口对您说他爱慕我的吗？如果是这样，那我就会更喜爱他几分，要是连个红颜知己都没有，那他还算哪门子的情郎呢？”

“哦！我的宝贝，”她答道，“你们俩简直是天生的一对。你说的每一个字都让我更加深刻地确信，你们俩意气相投，你们的头脑仿佛受到一股无形的力量驱使，因为你们俩的想法和观点竟是分毫不差。不，就连你们头发的颜色都很相近。是的，亲爱的姑娘，正是可怜又绝望的默斯格罗夫本人对我透露了他的情事。我倒是没觉得吃惊，虽然不知道为什么会这样，但我有种预感，他一定会爱上你。”

“那么，他是如何对您说的？”

“那是在用完夜宵之后，我们围坐在炉火旁，聊着无关紧要的话题，其实基本上都是我一个人在说，他心事重重、一言不发，可就在我话说到一半的时候，他突然打断了我，用一种夸张至极的语气喊道——

‘是的，我恋爱了，现在我才明白

我已拜倒在亨丽埃塔·霍尔顿的石榴裙下——’”

“哦！他这表白的方式，”我说道，“还真是甜蜜！竟然为我作了如此动听的两句诗！只可惜并不押韵！”

“看到你喜欢这两句诗，我也很欣慰，”她答道，“这里头肯定是值得好好品味一番的。‘那么你爱她吗，表弟？’我说道，‘我真替你感到惋惜，尽管你方方面面都无懈可击，有一笔可能大幅增加的可观财产，又有一栋破败失修的漂亮房子，可她是迷人的亨丽埃塔，有位上校向她求过婚，还有位准男爵曾为她举杯祝酒，谁能指望抱得美人归呢？’”

“我曾——”我喊道。

斯库达摩尔夫人却还在往下说。“‘啊，亲爱的表姐，’他答道，‘有这么多人爱慕着她，我也相当确信自己不大可能赢得她的芳心，不需要您再来泼冷水。不过，我想要为她赴死，成为她迷人魅力的牺牲品，相信无论是您还是美丽的亨丽埃塔本人，肯定都会成全我这美好的心愿。待我死后’他继续说道——”

“哦，斯库达摩尔夫人，”我擦着眼睛说，“这么一个漂亮的人儿竟然会说到死！”

“此情此景，的确感人至深。”斯库达摩尔夫人答道，“‘待我死后，’他说，‘请将我抬去放在她的脚边，也许她会收起不屑，在我那可怜的尸体上洒下一滴同情的泪水。’”

“亲爱的斯库达摩尔夫人，”我打断她道，“快别说这个叫人伤心的话题了，我受不了。”

“哦！我可真喜欢你这温柔可人的性子，无论如何我都不会让你太过伤心的，那我就不说了。”

“还请您接着说吧。”我说道。她便继续说了下去。

“‘到了那时，’他又说道，‘啊！表姐，想象一下吧，当我感觉到那宝贵的泪水一滴滴落在我脸上，我该会是何等激动！为了一尝这般狂喜的滋味，谁会不愿赴死呢！等我下葬之后，但愿某个比我幸运的年轻人能得到亨丽埃塔女神的青睐，但愿他亦如不幸的默斯格罗夫一般对她一往情深，待我化为尘土之时，但愿他俩成为幸福夫妻的楷模！’”

“你可曾听过如此感伤的话语？等他死后叫人将他抬到我的脚边，多么可爱的心愿啊！哦！能怀有这样一个心愿，他的思想必然崇高无比！”

斯库达摩尔夫人接着说道：“‘啊！亲爱的表弟，’我对他说，‘任何女人见到你这高尚的行为，无论她生来是怎样的铁石心肠，也一定会被你融化的；要是亨丽埃塔女神听到你这一番对她幸福的慷慨祝愿，似她那般心软的人，我想她定会怜惜你的情意，努力回报于你。’‘哦，表姐，’他答道，‘请不要试图用这种安慰人的好听话来给我希望。不，我不敢奢望能讨得这天使般女子的欢心，除了一死，我已别无他法。’‘真爱总是叫人意志消沉的，’我答道，‘可是，亲爱的汤姆，我还要给你更大的希望，你是有望征服佳人芳心的。你且放心，我密切关注了她整整一天，我看得明明白白，她心中已然对你情根深种，只是她还不自知罢了。’”

“亲爱的斯库达摩尔夫人，”我喊道，“这事就连我都不知道呢！”

“我适才不是说了吗？你对此尚不自知。我继续对他说道：‘我可没有一开始就把这事说出来给你鼓劲儿，意外之喜才更让人高兴。’‘不，表姐’，他说道，声音无精打采的，‘你说什么我都不会相信自己能够令亨丽埃塔·霍尔顿心动，要是你在欺骗自己，就请你不要试图来欺骗我。’总而言之，亲爱的，我劝了这灰心丧气的可怜年轻人好几个小时，说你真的喜欢他；到了最后，他终于不再否认我那强有力的论据，相信了我的话，那一刻他激动不已、欣喜若狂，我简直没法儿形容。”

“哦！亲爱的人儿，”我大声地说，“他爱我爱得多么深情！可是，亲爱的斯库达摩尔夫人，你有没有对他说，我是完全依赖叔父和婶娘过活的？”

“当然，我什么都对他说了。”

“那他怎么说？”

“他大喊大叫，把所有的叔伯姑婶都刻毒抨击了一通；又指责英格兰的法律有问题，明明侄儿侄女缺钱，法律却容许当长辈的将财产抓住不放，还说他要是下议院的议员，就要改革立法机关，消除其一切弊病。”

“哦！这个大好人！他多么有志气啊！”我说。

“他还说，就算他的房子已经一切就绪待你入住，他也不敢自作多情，以为美丽的亨丽埃塔会为他自降身份，放弃已经习以为常的奢华与尊荣，却只换得他那有限的收入所能负担的舒适雅致。我对他说，她是不可能这么做的，如今她有权有势且行事高贵，用手中的权力对同胞中的贫穷民众广施善行，要是你认为她能够仅仅为了成全你和她自己而放弃权势，这对她可不公平。”

“那是当然，”我说，“我确实时不时地会做点善事。默斯格罗夫先生听了这话怎么说？”

“他回答说，他虽然忧伤，却不得不承认我所说的就是事实，所以如果他有这个福分，注定要和美丽的亨丽埃塔结为夫妻，那么不论他有多么迫不及待，他都得下定决心等下去，等待那幸运的日子来临，等到她脱离那些坏亲戚的辖制，等到她能够嫁与他为妻的那一天。”

他是多么高尚的人啊！哦！玛蒂尔达！我是何其幸运，竟然将要成为他的妻子！我的婶婶在喊我过去做馅饼了。再见，我亲爱的朋友。

H. 霍尔顿敬上

一位年轻女子的来信[1]

（她的感情过于强烈，判断力却不足，

因而犯下许多违心之过）

/

亲爱的埃莉诺，我曾有过许多烦恼，也曾历经浮浮沉沉，虽然吃了苦头，但唯一令我觉得安慰的就是，在仔细审视自己的所作所为之后，我相信这些完全是我咎由自取。我很小的时候便谋害了自己的父亲，其后又害死了母亲，现在我打算要去谋杀自己的姐姐了。我的宗教信仰经常变来变去，如今我也不知道自己还相信什么。过去这十二年来，我在每一场公开审判中都做了伪证，

1. 出自 *Scraps*（《涂鸦集》），该集子包含五篇小短文，本文是第三篇。

还伪造了我自己的遗嘱。总而言之，几乎没有哪一种罪行是我不曾犯过的，不过现在我要改过自新了。皇家骑兵卫队的马丁上校向我求婚了，我们不日即将完婚。我俩的恋爱颇不寻常，我来给你讲一讲。马丁上校是已故约翰·马丁爵士的次子。爵爷过世的时候富可敌国，却将大部分财产——大约八百万镑——都留给了现任的托马斯爵士，只给三位幼子留下每人十万镑遗产。凭着他这一点点微薄的收入，上校过了近四个月还算惬意的生活，然后他突然心血来潮，决意将长兄的财产全都夺来。他伪造了一份新遗嘱在法庭上出示，可是除了他自己，再没有别人愿意宣誓，保证这才是真遗嘱，然而他发了太多誓，没人相信他。当时我刚好从法庭门口经过，法官便召我进去，他对上校说我是一位淑女，愿意为了正义的目标见证一切，所以建议他来请求我。简而言之，这桩事件很快便妥善解决。上校和我宣誓说这份遗嘱属实，托马斯爵士只得交出他非法获得的财富。满怀感激的上校隔天便来拜访我，向我求了婚。现在我要去谋杀我姐姐了。

安娜·帕克敬上

少女奥斯汀

——《漂亮的卡桑德拉》译后记

《漂亮的卡桑德拉》这本小集子收录了简·奥斯汀少女时代的六篇作品，其中前三篇勉强可算完整的短篇小说，后三篇就只能算作练笔片段了。这些作品全都创作于 1787 年至 1793 年之间，彼时奥斯汀才不过是个尚未成年的小姑娘，大约相当于如今的中学生。记得曾经看过一部传记电影——《成为简·奥斯汀》，如果说这部电影试着还原了奥斯汀的感情生活，那么这个小小的选集则让读者可以一窥她在创作方面的成长历程。

说实话，翻译时我是吃了一惊的，尤其是前三篇的荒谬与幼稚，其中有些地方甚至不合逻辑到令人难以置信的地步。比如在《杰克与爱丽丝》一文中，作者描写约翰逊家的起居室有“半英里宽、3/4英里长”，这相当于八百多米宽、一千两百多米长，即便是用了夸张的修辞手法，恐也有过度之嫌。再比如在《亨利与伊丽莎》一文中，奥斯汀大笔一挥，让公爵夫人派了三百人带着武器去追捕私奔的亨利与伊丽莎。还有《漂亮的卡桑德拉》，虽然由十二章构成，然而每章只有短短一句话，就连正文之前的献词都比任何一个章节要长。看到这三篇小说里漏洞百出的情节，再想想这些乃是出自一个十二三岁的小女孩之手，我不由得暗笑自己太过较真。她写作一是因为自己热爱，二是为了娱乐家人，不过是些练笔之作，有多少人在这个年纪还在努力消除语法错误呢，她却已经刻画出了个性鲜明的众多人物。

后三篇的书信体片段写作时间略晚一些，笔触也稍显成熟。其中《一位处境困难的年轻女子写给友人的信》是全书我最爱的篇章，格雷维尔夫人身上可不就能看见《傲慢与偏见》中凯瑟琳·德波夫人的影子？她势利专横，自以为是，允许玛丽亚小姐在马车上面朝前方坐着便觉得这是赐予她的莫大恩惠；她认为穷人就不该穿新衣，晚上也不应该吃夜宵，而应当为了节省蜡烛早早睡下；她明知人家家里正是用餐时间，却特地赶在此时到访，可是又不肯下车，叫玛丽亚冒着刺骨寒风听她在马车里絮絮叨叨，还说出了这样的话：“我是不会让我的女儿们在这种天气像你这样站在外头的。可是有一种人，要么就是感觉不到冷，要么就是不知道体贴别人。”鲜活生动的人物形象跃然纸上，对话中的讽刺意味读来令人忍俊不禁，稍加改动便能拍出一集精彩的好剧。

“世界上这一半人的乐趣，那一半的人不会懂。”（One half of the world cannot understand the pleasures of the other.）年届四旬的简·奥斯汀在《爱玛》一书中借由双十年华的女主角之口说出了这句至理名言。不经历少女时代的那些稚嫩可笑，何来成熟之后的睿智洞明？从译近十载，这是我译得最开心的一本书。得遇才华横溢的少女奥斯汀，并穿越时空与她同行一段，我何其幸运。

夏星

2018 年 8 月

PENGUIN

LITTLE BLACK

CLASSICS

conquered only hers, it will be necessary to inform them that the Miss Simpsons were defended from his Power by Ambition, Envy, and Selfadmiration.

Every wish of Caroline was centered in a titled Husband; whilst in Sukey such superior excellence could only raise her Envy not her Love, and Cecilia was too tenderly attached to herself to be pleased with any one besides. As for Lady Williams and Mrs Jones, the former of them was too sensible, to fall in love with one so much her Junior and the latter, tho' very tall and very passionate was too fond of her Husband to think of such a thing.

Yet in spite of every endeavour on the part of Miss Johnson to discover any attachment to her in him; the cold and indifferent heart of Charles Adams still to all appearance, preserved its native freedom; polite to all but partial to none, he still remained the lovely, the lively, but insensible Charles Adams.

One evening, Alice finding herself somewhat heated by wine (no very uncommon case) determined to seek a releif for her disordered Head and Love-sick Heart in the Conversation of the intelligent Lady Williams.

She found her Ladyship at home as was in general the Case, for she was not fond of going out, and like the great Sir Charles Grandison scorned to deny herself when at Home, as she looked on that fashionable method of shutting out disagreable Visitors, as little less than downright Bigamy.

企鹅经典：小黑书　第三辑

Penguin Little Black Classics Vol. III

21. JANE AUSTEN
The Beautifull Cassandra

22. FYODOR DOSTOYEVSKY
The Meek One

23. AESOP
The Cat and Venus

24. CHARLES DICKENS
To Be Read at Dusk

25. JOHANN PETER HEBEL
How a Ghastly Story Was Brought to Light by a Common or Garden Butcher's Dog

26. OSCAR WILDE
Lord Arthur Savile's Crime

27. LEO TOLSTOY
The Death of Ivan Ilyich

28. MICHEL DE MONTAIGNE
How We Weep and Laugh at the Same Thing

29. EMILY DICKINSON
My life had stood a loaded gun

30. WALT WHITMAN
On the Beach at Night Alone

‘She has
many rare
and charming
qualities, but
Sobriety is not
one of them . . .’

JANE AUSTEN

The Beautifull Cassandra

Contents

Jack and Alice

a novel

Is respectfully inscribed to Francis William Austen Esqr Midshipman on board his Majesty's Ship the Perseverance
by his obedient humble
Servant The Author

CHAPTER THE FIRST

Mr Johnson was once upon a time about 53; in a twelvemonth afterwards he was 54, which so much delighted him that he was determined to celebrate his next Birth day by giving a Masquerade to his Children and Freinds. Accordingly on the Day he attained his 55th year tickets were dispatched to all his Neighbours to that purpose. His acquaintance indeed in that part of the World were not very numerous as they consisted only of Lady Williams, Mr and Mrs Jones, Charles Adams and the 3 Miss Simpsons, who composed the neighbourhood of Pammydiddle and formed the Masquerade.

Before I proceed to give an account of the Evening, it

will be proper to describe to my reader, the persons and Characters of the party introduced to his acquaintance.

M[r] and M[rs] Jones were both rather tall and very passionate, but were in other respects, good tempered, wellbehaved People. Charles Adams was an amiable, accomplished and bewitching young Man; of so dazzling a Beauty that none but Eagles could look him in the Face.

Miss Simpson was pleasing in her person, in her Manners and in her Disposition; an unbounded ambition was her only fault. Her second sister Sukey was Envious, Spitefull and Malicious. Her person was short, fat and disagreable. Cecilia (the youngest) was perfectly handsome but too affected to be pleasing.

In Lady Williams every virtue met. She was a widow with a handsome Jointure and the remains of a very handsome face. Tho' Benevolent and Candid, she was Generous and sincere; Tho' Pious and Good, she was Religious and amiable, and Tho' Elegant and Agreable, she was Polished and Entertaining.

The Johnsons were a family of Love, and though a little addicted to the Bottle and the Dice, had many good Qualities.

Such was the party assembled in the elegant Drawing Room of Johnson Court, amongst which the pleasing figure of a Sultana was the most remarkable of the female Masks. Of the Males a Mask representing the Sun, was the most universally admired. The Beams that darted from his Eyes were like those of that glorious Luminary tho' infinitely superior. So strong were they that no one dared venture within half a mile of them; he had therefore the best part of the Room to himself, its size not amounting to more than 3 quarters of a mile in length and half a one in breadth. The Gentleman at last finding the feirceness of his beams to be very inconvenient to the concourse by obliging them to croud together in one corner of the room, half shut his eyes by which means, the Company discovered him to be Charles Adams in his plain green Coat, without any mask at all.

When their astonishment was a little subsided their attention was attracted by 2 Dominos who advanced in a horrible Passion; they were both very tall, but seemed in other respects to have many good qualities. 'These,' said the witty Charles, 'these are M^r^ and Mrs Jones,' and so indeed they were.

No one could imagine who was the Sultana! Till at length on her addressing a beautifull Flora who was reclining in a studied attitude on a couch, with 'Oh Cecilia, I wish I was really what I pretend to be', she was discovered by the never failing genius of Charles Adams, to be the elegant but ambitious Caroline Simpson, and the person to whom she addressed herself, he rightly imagined to be her lovely but affected sister Cecilia.

The Company now advanced to a Gaming Table where sat 3 Dominos (each with a bottle in their hand) deeply engaged; but a female in the character of Virtue fled with hasty footsteps from the shocking scene, whilst a little fat woman representing Envy, sate alternately on the foreheads of the 3 Gamesters. Charles Adams was still as bright as ever; he soon discovered the party at play to be the 3 Johnsons, Envy to be Sukey Simpson and Virtue to be Lady Williams.

The Masks were then all removed and the Company retired to another room, to partake of an elegant and well managed Entertainment, after which the Bottle being pretty briskly pushed about by the 3 Johnsons, the whole party not excepting even Virtue were carried home, Dead Drunk.

CHAPTER THE SECOND

For three months did the Masquerade afford ample subject for conversation to the inhabitants of Pammydiddle; but no character at it was so fully expatiated on as Charles Adams. The singularity of his appearance, the beams which darted from his eyes, the brightness of his Wit, and the whole tout ensemble of his person had subdued the hearts of so many of the young Ladies, that of the six present at the Masquerade but five had returned uncaptivated. Alice Johnson was the unhappy sixth whose heart had not been able to withstand the power of his Charms. But as it may appear strange to my Readers, that so much worth and Excellence as he possessed should have

In spite of the wine she had been drinking, poor Alice was uncommonly out of spirits; she could think of nothing but Charles Adams, she could talk of nothing but him, and in short spoke so openly that Lady Williams soon discovered the unreturned affection she bore him, which excited her Pity and Compassion so strongly that she addressed her in the following Manner.

'I perceive but too plainly my dear Miss Johnson, that your Heart has not been able to withstand the fascinating Charms of this Young Man and I pity you sincerely. Is it a first Love?'

'It is.'

'I am still more greived to hear that; I am myself a sad example of the Miseries, in general attendant on a first Love and I am determined for the future to avoid the like Misfortune. I wish it may not be too late for you to do the same; if it is not endeavour my dear Girl to secure yourself from so great a Danger. A second attachment is seldom attended with any serious consequences; against that therefore I have nothing to say. Preserve yourself from a first Love and you need not fear a second.'

'You mentioned Madam something of your having yourself been a sufferer by the misfortune you are so good as to wish me to avoid. Will you favour me with your Life and Adventures?'

'Willingly my Love.'

CHAPTER THE THIRD

'My Father was a gentleman of considerable Fortune in Berkshire; myself and a few more his only Children. I was but six years old when I had the misfortune of losing my Mother and being at that time young and Tender, my father instead of sending me to School, procured an able handed Governess to superintend my Education at Home. My Brothers were placed at Schools suitable to their Ages and my Sisters being all younger than myself, remained still under the Care of their Nurse.

'Miss Dickins was an excellent Governess. She instructed me in the Paths of Virtue; under her tuition I daily became more amiable, and might perhaps by this time have nearly attained perfection, had not my worthy Preceptoress been torn from my arms, e'er I had attained my seventeenth year. I never shall forget her last words. "My dear Kitty" she said. "Good night t'ye." I never saw her afterwards,' continued Lady Williams wiping her eyes, 'She eloped with the Butler the same night.

'I was invited the following year by a distant relation of my Father's to spend the Winter with her in town. Mrs Watkins was a Lady of Fashion, Family and fortune; she was in general esteemed a pretty Woman, but I never thought her very handsome, for my part. She had too high a forehead, Her eyes were too small and she had too much colour.'

'How can that be?' interrupted Miss Johnson reddening with anger; 'Do you think that any one can have too much colour?'

'Indeed I do, and I'll tell you why I do my dear Alice; when a person has too great a degree of red in their Complexion, it gives their face in my opinion, too red a look.'

'But can a face my Lady have too red a look?'

'Certainly my dear Miss Johnson and I'll [tell] you why. When a face has too red a look it does not appear to so much advantage as it would were it paler.'

'Pray Ma'am proceed in your story.'

'Well, as I said before, I was invited by this Lady to spend some weeks with her in town. Many Gentlemen thought her Handsome but in my opinion, Her forehead was too high, her eyes too small and she had too much colour.'

'In that Madam as I said before your Ladyship must have been mistaken. Mrs Watkins could not have too much colour since no one can have too much.'

'Excuse me my Love if I do not agree with you in that particular. Let me explain myself clearly; my idea of the case is this. When a Woman has too great a proportion of red in her Cheeks, she must have too much colour.'

'But Madam I deny that it is possible for any one to have too great a proportion of red in their Cheeks.'

'What my Love not if they have too much colour?'

Miss Johnson was now out of all patience, the more so perhaps as Lady Williams still remained so inflexibly cool.

It must be remembered however that her Ladyship had in one respect by far the advantage of Alice; I mean in not being drunk, for heated with wine and raised by Passion, she could have little command of her Temper.

The Dispute at length grew so hot on the part of Alice that 'From Words she almost came to Blows' When Mr Johnson luckily entered and with some difficulty forced her away from Lady Williams, Mrs Watkins and her red cheeks.

CHAPTER THE FOURTH

My Readers may perhaps imagine that after such a fracas, no intimacy could longer subsist between the Johnsons and Lady Williams, but in that they are mistaken for her Ladyship was too sensible to be angry at a conduct which she could not help perceiving to be the natural consequence of inebriety and Alice had too sincere a respect for Lady Williams and too great a relish for her Claret, not to make every concession in her power.

A few days after their reconciliation Lady Williams called on Miss Johnson to propose a walk in a Citron Grove which led from her Ladyship's pigstye to Charles Adams's Horsepond. Alice was too sensible of Lady Williams's kindness in proposing such a walk and too much pleased with the prospect of seeing at the end of it, a Horsepond of Charles's, not to accept it with visible delight. They had not proceeded far before she was roused from the reflection of the happiness she was going to enjoy, by Lady Williams's thus addressing her.

'I have as yet forborn my dear Alice to continue the narrative of my Life from an unwillingness of recalling to your Memory a scene which (since it reflects on you rather disgrace than credit) had better be forgot than remembered.'

Alice had already begun to colour up and was beginning to speak, when her Ladyship perceiving her displeasure, continued thus.

'I am afraid my dear Girl that I have offended you by what I have just said; I assure you I do not mean to distress you by a retrospection of what cannot now be helped; considering all things I do not think you so much to blame as many People do; for when a person is in Liquor, there is no answering for what they may do.'

'Madam, this is not to be borne; I insist—'

'My dear Girl don't vex yourself about the matter; I assure you I have entirely forgiven every thing respecting it; indeed I was not angry at the time, because as I saw all along, you were nearly dead drunk. I knew you could not help saying the strange things you did. But I see I distress you; so I will change the subject and desire it may never again be mentioned; remember it is all forgot – I will now pursue my story; but I must insist upon not giving you any description of Mrs Watkins; it would only be reviving old stories and as you never saw her, it can be nothing to you, if her forehead <u>was</u> too high, her eyes <u>were</u> too small, or if she <u>had</u> too much colour.'

'Again! Lady Williams: this is too much—'

So provoked was poor Alice at this renewal of the old story, that I know not what might have been the consequence of it, had not their attention been engaged by another object. A lovely young Woman lying apparently in great pain beneath a Citron-tree, was an object too interesting not to attract their notice. Forgetting their own dispute they both with simpathizing Tenderness advanced towards her and accosted her in these terms.

'You seem fair Nymph to be labouring under some misfortune which we shall be happy to releive if you will inform us what it is. Will you favour us with your Life and adventures?'

'Willingly Ladies, if you will be so kind as to be seated.' They took their places and she thus began.

CHAPTER THE FIFTH

'I am a native of North Wales and my Father is one of the most capital Taylors in it. Having a numerous family, he was easily prevailed on by a sister of my Mother's who is a widow in good circumstances and keeps an alehouse in the next Village to ours, to let her take me and breed me up at her own expence. Accordingly I have lived with her for the last 8 years of my Life, during which time she provided me with some of the first rate Masters, who taught me all the accomplishments requisite for one of my sex and rank. Under their instructions I learned Dancing, Music, Drawing and various Languages, by which means I became more accomplished than any other Taylor's Daughter in Wales. Never was there a happier Creature than I was, till within the last half year – but I should have told you before that the principal Estate in our Neighbourhood belongs to Charles Adams, the owner of the brick House, you see yonder.'

'Charles Adams!' exclaimed the astonished Alice; 'are you acquainted with Charles Adams?'

'To my sorrow madam I am. He came about half a year ago to receive the rents of the Estate I have just mentioned. At that time I first saw him; as you seem ma'am acquainted with him, I need not describe to you how charming he is. I could not resist his attractions;—'

'Ah! who can,' said Alice with a deep sigh.

'My Aunt being in terms of the greatest intimacy with his cook, determined, at my request, to try whether she could discover, by means of her freind if there were any chance of his returning my affection. For this purpose she went one evening to drink tea with Mrs Susan, who in the course of Conversation mentioned the goodness of her Place and the Goodness of her Master; upon which my Aunt began pumping her with so much dexterity that in a short time Susan owned, that she did not think her Master would ever marry, "for (said she) he has often and often declared to me that his wife, whoever she might be, must possess, Youth, Beauty, Birth, Wit, Merit, and Money. I have many a time (she continued) endeavoured to reason him out of his resolution and to convince him of the improbability of his ever meeting with such a Lady; but my arguments have had no effect and he continues as firm in his determination as ever." You may imagine Ladies my distress on hearing this; for I was fearfull that tho' possessed of Youth, Beauty, Wit and Merit, and tho' the probable Heiress of my Aunts House and business, he might think me deficient in Rank, and in being so, unworthy of his hand.

'However I was determined to make a bold push and therefore wrote him a very kind letter, offering him with great tenderness my hand and heart. To this I received an angry and peremptory refusal, but thinking it might be rather the effect of his modesty than any thing else, I pressed him again on the subject. But he never answered any more of my Letters and very soon afterwards left the Country. As soon as I heard of his departure I wrote to him here, informing him that I should shortly do myself the honour of waiting on him at Pammydiddle, to which I received no answer; therefore choosing to take, Silence for Consent, I left Wales, unknown to my Aunt, and arrived here after a tedious Journey this Morning. On enquiring for his House I was directed thro' this Wood, to the one you there see. With a heart elated by the expected happiness of beholding him I entered it and had proceeded thus far in my progress thro' it, when I found myself suddenly seized by the leg and on examining the cause of it, found that I was caught in one of the steel traps so common in gentlemen's grounds.'

'Ah,' cried Lady Williams, 'how fortunate we are to meet with you; since we might otherwise perhaps have shared the like misfortune—'

'It is indeed happy for you Ladies, that I should have been a short time before you. I screamed as you may easily imagine till the woods resounded again and till one of the inhuman Wretch's servants came to my assistance and released me from my dreadfull prison, but not before one of my legs was entirely broken.'

CHAPTER THE SIXTH

At this melancholy recital the fair eyes of Lady Williams, were suffused in tears and Alice could not help exclaiming,

'Oh! cruel Charles to wound the hearts and legs of all the fair.'

Lady Williams now interposed and observed that the young Lady's leg ought to be set without farther delay. After examining the fracture therefore, she immediately began and performed the operation with great skill which was the more wonderfull on account of her having never performed such a one before. Lucy, then arose from the ground and finding that she could walk with the greatest ease, accompanied them to Lady Williams's House at her Ladyship's particular request.

The perfect form, the beautifull face, and elegant manners of Lucy so won on the affections of Alice that when they parted, which was not till after Supper, she assured her that except her Father, Brother, Uncles, Aunts, Cousins and other relations, Lady Williams, Charles Adams and a few dozen more of particular freinds, she loved her better than almost any other person in the world.

Such a flattering assurance of her regard would justly have given much pleasure to the object of it, had she not plainly perceived that the amiable Alice had partaken too freely of Lady Williams's claret.

Her Ladyship (whose discernment was great) read in the intelligent countenance of Lucy her thoughts on the subject and as soon as Miss Johnson had taken her leave, thus addressed her.

'When you are more intimately acquainted with my Alice you will not be surprised, Lucy, to see the dear Creature drink a little too much; for such things happen every day. She has many rare and charming qualities, but Sobriety is not one of them. The whole Family are indeed a sad drunken set. I am sorry to say too that I never knew three such thorough Gamesters as they are, more particularly Alice. But she is a charming girl. I fancy not one of the sweetest tempers in the world; to be sure I have seen her in such passions! However she is a sweet young Woman. I am sure you'll like her. I scarcely know any one so amiable. – Oh! that you could but have seen her the other Evening! How she raved! and on such a trifle too! She is indeed a most pleasing Girl! I shall always love her!'

'She appears by your ladyship's account to have many good qualities', replied Lucy. 'Oh! a thousand,' answered Lady Williams; 'tho' I am very partial to her, and perhaps am blinded by my affection, to her real defects.'

CHAPTER THE SEVENTH

The next morning brought the three Miss Simpsons to wait on Lady Williams, who received them with the utmost politeness and introduced to their acquaintance Lucy, with whom the eldest was so much pleased that at parting she declared her sole ambition was to have her accompany them the next morning to Bath, whither they were going for some weeks.

'Lucy,' said Lady Williams, 'is quite at her own disposal and if she chooses to accept so kind an invitation, I hope she will not hesitate, from any motives of delicacy on my account. I know not indeed how I shall ever be able to part with her. She never was at Bath and I should think that it would be a most agreable Jaunt to her. Speak my Love,' continued she, turning to Lucy, 'what say you to accompanying these Ladies? I shall be miserable without you – t'will be a most pleasant tour to you – I hope you'll go; if you do I am sure t'will be the Death of me – pray be persuaded'—

Lucy begged leave to decline the honour of accompanying them, with many expressions of gratitude for the extream politeness of Miss Simpson in inviting her.

Miss Simpson appeared much disappointed by her refusal. Lady Williams insisted on her going – declared that she would never forgive her if she did not, and that she should never survive it if she did, and inshort used such persuasive arguments that it was at length resolved she was to go. The Miss Simpsons called for her at ten o'clock the next morning and Lady Williams had soon the satisfaction of receiving from her young freind, the pleasing intelligence of their safe arrival in Bath.

It may now be proper to return to the Hero of this Novel, the brother of Alice, of whom I beleive I have scarcely ever had occasion to speak; which may perhaps be partly oweing to his unfortunate propensity to Liquor, which so compleatly deprived him of the use of those faculties Nature had endowed him with, that he never did anything worth mentioning. His Death happened a short time after Lucy's departure and was the natural Consequence of this pernicious practice. By his decease, his sister became the sole inheritress of a very large fortune, which as it gave her fresh Hopes of rendering herself acceptable as a wife to Charles Adams could not fail of being most pleasing to her – and as the effect was Joyfull the Cause could scarcely be lamented.

Finding the violence of her attachment to him daily augment, she at length disclosed it to her Father and desired him to propose a union between them to Charles. Her father consented and set out one morning to open the affair to the young Man. Mr Johnson being a man of few words his part was soon performed and the answer he received was as follows—

'Sir, I may perhaps be expected to appear pleased at and gratefull for the offer you have made me: but let me tell you that I consider it as an affront. I look upon myself to be Sir a perfect Beauty – where would you see a finer figure or a more charming face. Then, sir I imagine my Manners and Address to be of the most polished kind; there is a certain elegance a peculiar sweetness in them that I never saw equalled and cannot describe—. Partiality aside, I am certainly more accomplished in every Language, every Science, every Art and every thing than any other person in Europe. My temper is even, my virtues innumerable, my self unparalelled. Since such Sir is my character, what do you mean by wishing me to marry your Daughter? Let me give you a short sketch of yourself and of her. I look upon you Sir to be a very good sort of Man in the main; a drunken old Dog to be sure, but that's nothing to me. Your daughter sir, is neither sufficiently beautifull, sufficiently amiable, sufficiently witty, nor sufficiently rich for me—. I expect nothing more in my wife than my wife will find in me – Perfection. These sir, are my sentiments and I honour myself for having such. One freind I have and glory in having but one—. She is at present preparing my Dinner, but if you choose to see her, she shall come and she will inform you that these have ever been my sentiments.'

Mr Johnson was satisfied; and expressing himself to be much obliged to Mr Adams for the characters he had favoured him with of himself and his Daughter, took his leave.

The unfortunate Alice on receiving from her father the sad account of the ill success his visit had been attended with, could scarcely support the disappointment – She flew to her Bottle and it was soon forgot.

CHAPTER THE EIGHTH

While these affairs were transacting at Pammydiddle, Lucy was conquering every Heart at Bath. A fortnight's residence there had nearly effaced from her remembrance the captivating form of Charles – The recollection of what her Heart had formerly suffered by his charms and her Leg by his trap, enabled her to forget him with tolerable Ease, which was what she determined to do; and for that purpose dedicated five minutes in every day to the employment of driving him from her remembrance.

Her second Letter to Lady Williams contained the

pleasing intelligence of her having accomplished her undertaking to her entire satisfaction; she mentioned in it also an offer of marriage she had received from the Duke of —— an elderly Man of noble fortune whose ill health was the chief inducement of his Journey to Bath. 'I am distressed (she continued) to know whether I mean to accept him or not. There are a thousand advantages to be derived from a marriage with the Duke, for besides those more inferior ones of Rank and Fortune it will procure me a home, which of all other things is what I most desire. Your Ladyship's kind wish of my always remaining with you, is noble and generous but I cannot think of becoming so great a burden on one I so much love and esteem. That One should receive obligations only from those we despise, is a sentiment instilled into my mind by my worthy Aunt, in my early years, and cannot in my opinion be too strictly adhered to. The excellent woman of whom I now speak, is I hear too much incensed by my imprudent departure from Wales, to receive me again—. I most earnestly wish to leave the Ladies I am now with. Miss Simpson is indeed (setting aside ambition) very amiable, but her 2[d] Sister the envious and malvolent Sukey is too disagreable to live with. – I have reason to think that the admiration I have met with in the circles of the great at this Place, has raised her Hatred and Envy; for often has she threatened, and sometimes endeavoured to cut my throat. – Your Ladyship will therefore allow that I am not wrong in wishing to leave Bath, and in wishing to have a home to receive me, when I do. I shall expect with impatience your advice concerning the Duke and am your most obliged

etc etc – Lucy.'

Lady Williams sent her, her opinion on the subject in the following Manner.

'Why do you hesitate my dearest Lucy, a moment with respect to the Duke? I have enquired into his Character and find him to be an unprincipaled, illiterate Man. Never shall my Lucy be united to such a one! He has a princely fortune, which is every day encreasing. How nobly will you spend it!, what credit will you give him in the eyes of all! How much will he be respected on his Wife's account! But why my dearest Lucy, why will you not at once decide this affair by returning to me and never leaving me again? Altho' I admire your noble sentiments with respect to obligations, yet, let me beg that they may not prevent your making me happy. It will to be sure be a great expence to me, to have you always with me – I shall not be able to support it – but what is that in comparison with the happiness I shall enjoy in your society?—'twill ruin me I know–you will not therefore surely, withstand these arguments, or refuse to return to yours most affectionately–etc etc.

C. Williams'

CHAPTER THE NINTH

What might have been the effect of her Ladyship's advice, had it ever been received by Lucy, is uncertain, as it reached Bath a few Hours after she had breathed her last. She fell a sacrifice to the Envy and Malice of Sukey who jealous of her superior charms took her by poison from an admiring World at the age of seventeen.

Thus fell the amiable and lovely Lucy whose Life had been marked by no crime, and stained by no blemish but her imprudent departure from her Aunts, and whose death was sincerely lamented by every one who knew her. Among the most afflicted of her freinds were Lady Williams, Miss Johnson and the Duke; the 2 last of whom had a most sincere regard for her, more particularly Alice, who had spent a whole evening in her company and had never thought of her since. His Grace's affliction may likewise be easily accounted for, since he lost one for whom he had experienced during the last ten days, a tender affection and sincere regard. He mourned her loss with unshaken constancy for the next fortnight at the end of which time, he gratified the ambition of Caroline Simpson by raising her to the rank of a Dutchess. Thus was she at length rendered compleatly happy in the gratification of her favourite passion. Her sister the perfidious Sukey, was likewise shortly after exalted in a manner she truly deserved, and by her actions appeared to have always desired. Her barbarous Murder was discovered and in spite of every interceding freind she was speedily raised to the Gallows—. The beautifull but affected Cecilia was too sensible of her own superior charms, not to imagine that if Caroline could engage a Duke, she might without censure aspire to the affections of some Prince – and knowing that those of her native Country were cheifly engaged, she left England and I have since heard is at present the favourite Sultana of the great Mogul—.

In the mean time the inhabitants of Pammydiddle were in a state of the greatest astonishment and Wonder, a report being circulated of the intended marriage of Charles Adams. The Lady's name was still a secret. M^r^ and Mrs Jones imagined it to be, Miss Johnson; but <u>she</u> knew better; all <u>her</u> fears were centered in his Cook, when to the astonishment of every one, he was publicly united to Lady Williams—

Finis

Henry and Eliza

a novel

Is humbly dedicated to Miss Cooper by her obedient
Humble Servant
The Author

As Sir George and Lady Harcourt were superintending the Labours of their Haymakers, rewarding the industry of some by smiles of approbation, and punishing the idleness of others, by a cudgel, they perceived lying closely concealed beneath the thick foliage of a Haycock, a beautifull little Girl not more than 3 months old.

Touched with the enchanting Graces of her face and delighted with the infantine tho' sprightly answers she returned to their many questions, they resolved to take her home and, having no Children of their own, to educate her with care and cost.

Being good People themselves, their first and principal care was to incite in her a Love of Virtue and a Hatred of Vice, in which they so well succeeded (Eliza having a natural turn that way herself) that when she grew up, she was the delight of all who knew her.

Beloved by Lady Harcourt, adored by Sir George and admired by all the World, she lived in a continued course of uninterrupted Happiness, till she had attained her eighteenth year, when happening one day to be detected in stealing a banknote of 50£, she was turned out of doors by her inhuman Benefactors. Such a transition to one who did not possess so noble and exalted a mind as Eliza, would have been Death, but she, happy in the conscious knowledge of her own Excellence, amused herself, as she sate beneath a tree with making and singing the following Lines.

SONG.

Though misfortunes my footsteps may ever attend
  I hope I shall never have need of a Freind
as an innocent Heart I will ever preserve
  and will never from Virtue's dear boundaries swerve.

Having amused herself some hours, with this song and her own pleasing reflections, she arose and took the road to M. a small market town of which place her most intimate freind kept the red Lion.

To this freind she immediately went, to whom having recounted her late misfortune, she communicated her wish of getting into some family in the capacity of Humble Companion.

Mrs Wilson, who was the most amiable creature on earth, was no sooner acquainted with her Desire, than she sate down in the Bar and wrote the following Letter to the Dutchess of F., the woman whom of all others, she most Esteemed.

'TO THE DUTCHESS OF F.'

Receive into your Family, at my request a young woman of unexceptionable Character, who is so good as to choose your Society in preference to going to Service. Hasten, and take her from the arms of your

Sarah Wilson.

The Dutchess, whose freindship for Mrs Wilson would have carried her any lengths, was overjoyed at such an opportunity of obliging her and accordingly sate out immediately on the receipt of her letter for the red Lion, which she reached the same Evening. The Dutchess of F. was about 45 and a half; Her passions were strong, her freindships firm and her Enmities, unconquerable. She was a widow and had only one Daughter who was on the point of marriage with a young Man of considerable fortune.

The Dutchess no sooner beheld our Heroine than throwing her arms around her neck, she declared herself so much pleased with her, that she was resolved they never more should part. Eliza was delighted with such a protestation of freindship, and after taking a most affecting leave of her dear M[rs] Wilson, accompanied her grace the next morning to her seat in Surry.

With every expression of regard did the Dutchess introduce her to Lady Harriet, who was so much pleased with her appearance that she besought her, to consider her as her Sister, which Eliza with the greatest Condescension promised to do.

M[r] Cecil, the Lover of Lady Harriet, being often with the family was often with Eliza. A mutual Love took place and Cecil having declared his first, prevailed on Eliza to consent to a private union, which was easy to be effected, as the Dutchess's chaplain being very much in love with Eliza himself, would they were certain do anything to oblige her.

The Dutchess and Lady Harriet being engaged one evening to an assembly, they took the opportunity of their absence and were united by the enamoured Chaplain.

When the Ladies returned, their amazement was great at finding instead of Eliza the following Note.

'Madam

We are married and gone.

Henry and Eliza Cecil.'

Her Grace as soon as she had read the letter, which sufficiently explained the whole affair, flew into the most violent passion and after having spent an agreable half hour, in calling them by all the shocking Names her rage could suggest to her, sent out after them 300 armed Men, with orders not to return without their Bodies, dead or alive; intending that if they should be brought to her in the latter condition to have them put to Death in some torture-like manner, after a few years Confinement.

In the mean time Cecil and Eliza continued their flight to the Continent, which they judged to be more secure than their native Land, from the dreadfull effects of the Dutchess's vengeance, which they had so much reason to apprehend.

In France they remained 3 years, during which time they became the parents of two Boys, and at the end of it Eliza became a widow without any thing to support either her or her Children. They had lived since their Marriage at the rate of 12,000£ a year, of which Mr Cecil's estate being rather less than the twentieth part, they had been able to save but a trifle, having lived to the utmost extent of their Income.

Eliza, being perfectly conscious of the derangement in their affairs, immediately on her Husband's death set sail for England, in a man of War of 55 Guns, which they had built in their more prosperous Days. But no sooner had she stepped on Shore at Dover, with a Child in each hand, than she was seized by the officers of the Dutchess, and conducted by them to a snug little Newgate of their Lady's which she had erected for the reception of her own private Prisoners.

No sooner had Eliza entered her Dungeon than the first thought which occurred to her, was how to get out of it again.

She went to the Door; but it was locked. She looked at the Window; but it was barred with iron; disappointed in both her expectations, she dispaired of effecting her Escape, when she fortunately perceived in a Corner of her Cell, a small saw and Ladder of ropes. With the saw she instantly went to work and in a few weeks had displaced every Bar but one to which she fastened the Ladder.

A difficulty then occurred which for some time, she knew not how to obviate. Her Children were too small to get down the Ladder by themselves, nor would it be possible for her to take them in her arms, when she did. At last she determined to fling down all her Cloathes, of which she had a large Quantity, and then having given them strict Charge not to hurt themselves, threw her Children after them. She herself with ease discended by the Ladder, at the bottom of which she had the pleasure of finding Her little boys in perfect Health and fast asleep.

Her wardrobe she now saw a fatal necessity of selling, both for the preservation of her Children and herself. With tears in her eyes, she parted with these last reliques of her former Glory, and with the money she got for them, bought others more usefull, some playthings for her Boys and a gold Watch for herself.

But scarcely was she provided with the above-mentioned necessaries, than she began to find herself rather hungry, and had reason to think, by their biting off two of her fingers, that her Children were much in the same situation.

To remedy these unavoidable misfortunes, she determined to return to her old freinds, Sir George and Lady Harcourt, whose generosity she had so often experienced and hoped to experience as often again.

She had about 40 miles to travel before she could reach their hospitable Mansion, of which having walked 30 without stopping, she found herself at the Entrance of a Town, where often in happier times, she had accompanied Sir George and Lady Harcourt to regale themselves with a cold collation at one of the Inns.

The reflections that her adventures since the last time she had partaken of these happy Junketings, afforded her, occupied her mind, for some time, as she sate on the steps at the door of a Gentleman's house. As soon as these reflections were ended, she arose and determined to take her station at the very inn, she remembered with so much delight, from the Company of which, as they went in and out, she hoped to receive some Charitable Gratuity.

She had but just taken her post at the Innyard before a Carriage drove out of it, and on turning the Corner at which she was stationed, stopped to give the Postilion an opportunity of admiring the beauty of the prospect. Eliza then advanced to the carriage and was going to request their Charity, when on fixing her Eyes on the Lady, within it, she exclaimed,

'Lady Harcourt!'

To which the lady replied,

'Eliza!'

'Yes Madam it is the wretched Eliza herself.'

Sir George, who was also in the Carriage, but too much amazed to speek, was proceeding to demand an explanation from Eliza of the Situation she was then in, when Lady Harcourt in transports of Joy, exclaimed.

'Sir George, Sir George, she is not only Eliza our adopted Daughter, but our real Child.'

'Our real Child! What Lady Harcourt, do you mean? You know you never even was with child. Explain yourself, I beseech you.'

'You must remember Sir George that when you sailed for America, you left me breeding.'

'I do, I do, go on dear Polly.'

'Four months after you were gone, I was delivered of this Girl, but dreading your just resentment at her not proving the Boy you wished, I took her to a Haycock and laid her down. A few weeks afterwards, you returned, and fortunately for me, made no enquiries on the subject. Satisfied within myself of the wellfare of my Child, I soon forgot I had one, insomuch that when, we shortly after found her in the very Haycock, I had placed her, I had no more idea of her being my own, than you had, and nothing I will venture to say would have recalled the circumstance to my remembrance, but my thus accidentally hearing her voice, which now strikes me as being the very counterpart of my own Child's.'

'The rational and convincing Account you have given of the whole affair,' said Sir George, 'leaves no doubt of her being our Daughter and as such I freely forgive the robbery she was guilty of.'

A mutual Reconciliation then took place, and Eliza, ascending the Carriage with her two Children returned to that home from which she had been absent nearly four years.

No sooner was she reinstated in her accustomed power at Harcourt Hall, than she raised an Army, with which she entirely demolished the Dutchess's Newgate, snug as it was, and by that act, gained the Blessings of thousands, and the Applause of her own Heart.

Finis

The beautifull Cassandra

a novel in twelve Chapters dedicated by permission to Miss Austen.

DEDICATION.

Madam

You are a Phoenix. Your taste is refined, your Sentiments are noble, and your Virtues innumerable. Your Person is lovely, your Figure, elegant, and your Form, magestic. Your Manners are polished, your Conversation is rational and your appearance singular. If therefore the following Tale will afford one moment's amusement to you, every wish will be gratified of

your most obedient
humble Servant
The Author

CHAPTER THE FIRST

Cassandra was the Daughter and the only Daughter of a celebrated Millener in Bond Street. Her father was of noble Birth, being the near relation of the Dutchess of —'s Butler.

CHAPTER THE 2D

When Cassandra had attained her 16th year, she was lovely and amiable and chancing to fall in love with an elegant Bonnet, her Mother had just compleated bespoke by the Countess of — she placed it on her gentle Head and walked from her Mother's shop to make her Fortune.

CHAPTER THE 3D

The first person she met, was the Viscount of — a young Man, no less celebrated for his Accomplishments and Virtues, than for his Elegance and Beauty. She curtseyed and walked on.

CHAPTER THE 4TH

She then proceeded to a Pastry-cooks where she devoured six ices, refused to pay for them, knocked down the Pastry Cook and walked away.

CHAPTER THE 5TH

She next ascended a Hackney Coach and ordered it to Hampstead, where she was no sooner arrived than she ordered the Coachman to turn round and drive her back again.

CHAPTER THE 6TH

Being returned to the same spot of the same Street she had sate out from, the Coachman demanded his Pay.

CHAPTER THE 7TH

She searched her pockets over again and again; but every search was unsuccessfull. No money could she find. The man grew peremptory. She placed her bonnet on his head and ran away.

CHAPTER THE 8TH

Thro' many a street she then proceeded and met in none the least Adventure till on turning a Corner of Bloomsbury Square, she met Maria.

CHAPTER THE 9TH

Cassandra started and Maria seemed surprised; they trembled, blushed, turned pale and passed each other in a mutual silence.

CHAPTER THE 10TH

Cassandra was next accosted by her freind the Widow, who squeezing out her little Head thro' her less window, asked her how she did? Cassandra curtseyed and went on.

CHAPTER THE 11TH

A quarter of a mile brought her to her paternal roof in Bond Street from which she had now been absent nearly 7 hours.

CHAPTER THE 12TH

She entered it and was pressed to her Mother's bosom by that worthy woman. Cassandra smiled and whispered to herself 'This is a day well spent.'

Finis

Letter the third

From A young Lady in distress'd Circumstances to her freind

A few days ago I was at a private Ball given by Mr Ashburnham. As my Mother never goes out she entrusted me to the care of Lady Greville who did me the honour of calling for me in her way and of allowing me to sit forwards, which is a favour about which I am very indifferent especially as I know it is considered as confering a great obligation on me. 'So Miss Maria' (said her Ladyship as she saw me advancing to the door of the Carriage) 'you seem very smart to night – My poor Girls will appear quite to disadvantage by you – I only hope your Mother may not have distressed herself to set you off. Have you got a new Gown on?'

'Yes Ma'am,' replied I with as much indifference as I could assume.

'Aye, and a fine one too I think—' (feeling it, as by her permission I seated myself by her) 'I dare say it is all very smart – But I must own, for you know I always speak my mind, that I think it was quite a needless peice of expence – Why could not you have worn your old striped one? It is not my way to find fault with people because they are poor, for I always think that they are more to be despised and pitied than blamed for it, especially if they cannot help it, but at the same time I must say that in my opinion your old striped Gown would have been quite fine enough for its Wearer – for to tell you the truth (I always speak my mind) I am very much afraid that one half of the people in the room will not know whether you have a Gown on or not – But I suppose you intend to make your fortune tonight—: Well, the sooner the better; and I wish you success.'

'Indeed, Ma'am, I have no such intention—'

'Who ever heard a Young Lady own that she was a Fortune-hunter?' Miss Greville laughed, but I am sure Ellen felt for me.

'Was your Mother gone to bed before you left her?' said her Ladyship—

'Dear Ma'am,' said Ellen, 'it is but nine o'clock.'

'True, Ellen, but Candles cost money, and M[rs] Williams is too wise to be extravagant.'

'She was just sitting down to supper, Ma'am—'

'And what had she got for Supper?' 'I did not observe.' 'Bread and Cheese I suppose.' 'I should never wish for a better supper,' said Ellen. 'You have never any reason' replied her Mother, 'as a better is always provided for you.' Miss Greville laughed excessively, as she constantly does at her Mother's wit.

Such is the humiliating Situation in which I am forced to appear while riding in her Ladyship's Coach – I dare not be impertinent, as my Mother is always admonishing me to be humble and patient if I wish to make my way in the world. She insists on my accepting every invitation of Lady Greville, or you may be certain that I would never enter either her House, or her Coach, with the disagreable certainty I always have of being abused for my Poverty while I am in them. – When we arrived at Ashburnham, it was nearly ten o'clock, which was an hour and a half later than we were desired to be there; but Lady Greville is too fashionable (or fancies herself to be so) to be punctual. The Dancing however was not begun as they waited for Miss Greville. I had not been long in the room before I was engaged to dance by Mr Bernard, but just as we were going to stand up, he recollected that his Servant had got his white Gloves, and immediately ran out to fetch them. In the mean time the Dancing began and Lady Greville in passing to another room went exactly before me – She saw me and instantly stopping, said to me though there were several people close to us;

'Hey day, Miss Maria! What cannot you get a partner? Poor Young Lady! I am afraid your new Gown was put on for nothing. But do not despair; perhaps you may get a hop before the Evening is over.' So saying, she passed on without hearing my repeated assurance of being engaged, and leaving me very provoked at being so exposed before every one – Mr Bernard however soon returned and by coming to me the moment he entered the room, and leading me to the Dancers, my Character I hope was cleared from the imputation Lady Greville had thrown on it, in the eyes of all the old Ladies who had heard her speech. I soon forgot all my vexations in the pleasure of dancing and of having the most agreable partner in the room. As he is moreover heir to a very large Estate I could see that Lady Greville did not look very well pleased when she found who had been his Choice – She was determined to mortify me, and accordingly when we were sitting down between the dances, she came to me with more than her usual insulting importance attended by Miss Mason and said loud enough to be heard by half the people in the room, 'Pray, Miss Maria, in what way of business was your Grandfather? for Miss Mason and I cannot agree whether he was a Grocer or a Bookbinder.' I saw that she wanted to mortify me, and was resolved if I possibly could to prevent her seeing that her scheme succeeded. 'Neither Madam; he was a Wine Merchant.' 'Aye, I knew he was in some such low way – He broke did not he?' 'I beleive not Ma'am.' 'Did not he abscond?' 'I never heard that he did.' 'At least he died insolvent?' 'I was never told so before.' 'Why, was not your Father as poor as a Rat?' 'I fancy not.' 'Was not he in the King's Bench once?' 'I never saw him there.' She gave me such a look, and turned away in a great passion; while I was half delighted with myself for my impertinence, and half afraid of being thought too saucy. As Lady Greville was extremely angry with me, she took no further notice of me all the Evening, and indeed had I been in favour I should have been equally neglected, as she was got into a party of great folks and she never speaks to me when she can to any one else. Miss Greville was with her Mother's party at Supper, but Ellen preferred staying with the Bernards and me. We had a very pleasant Dance and as Lady G —— slept all the way home, I had a very comfortable ride.

The next day while we were at dinner Lady Greville's Coach stopped at the door, for that is the time of day she generally contrives it should. She sent in a message by the Servant to say that 'she should not get out but that Miss Maria must come to the Coach-door, as she wanted to speak to her, and that she must make haste and come immediately—' 'What an impertinent Message Mama!' said I—'Go Maria—' replied She – Accordingly I went and was obliged to stand there at her Ladyship's pleasure though the Wind was extremely high and very cold.

'Why I think, Miss Maria, you are not quite so smart as you were last night – But I did not come to examine your dress, but to tell you that you may dine with us the day after tomorrow – Not tomorrow, remember, do not come tomorrow, for we expect Lord and Lady Clermont and Sir Thomas Stanley's family – There will be no occasion for your being very fine for I shan't send the Carriage – If it rains you may take an umbrella—' I could hardly help laughing at hearing her give me leave to keep myself dry – 'And pray remember to be in time, for

I shan't wait – I hate my Victuals over-done – But you need not come before the time – How does your Mother do? She is at dinner is not she?' 'Yes, Ma'am, we were in the middle of dinner when your Ladyship came.' 'I am afraid you find it very cold, Maria,' said Ellen. 'Yes, it is an horrible East wind'—said her Mother—'I assure you I can hardly bear the window down – But you are used to be blown about the wind, Miss Maria, and that is what has made your Complexion so ruddy and coarse. You young Ladies who cannot often ride in a Carriage never mind what weather you trudge in, or how the wind shews your legs. I would not have my Girls stand out of doors as you do in such a day as this. But some sort of people have no feelings either of cold or Delicacy – Well, remember that we shall expect you on Thursday at 5 o'clock – You must tell your Maid to come for you at night – There will be no Moon – and you will have an horrid walk home – My Compliments to your Mother – I am afraid your dinner will be cold – Drive on—' And away she went, leaving me in a great passion with her as she always does.

Maria Williams

From a Young Lady very much in love to her Freind

My Uncle gets more stingy, my Aunt more particular, and I more in love every day. What shall we all be at this rate by the end of the year! I had this morning the happiness of receiving the following Letter from my dear Musgrove.

Sackville St: Jan^{ry} 7th

It is a month to day since I beheld my lovely Henrietta, and the sacred anniversary must and shall be kept in a manner becoming the day – by writing to her. Never shall I forget the moment when her Beauties first broke on my sight – No time as you well know can erase it from my Memory. It was at Lady Scudamore's. Happy Lady Scudamore to live within a mile of the divine Henrietta! When the lovely Creature first entered the room, Oh! what were my sensations? The sight of you was like the sight of a wonderful fine Thing. I started – I gazed at her with Admiration – She appeared every moment more Charming, and the unfortunate Musgrove became a Captive to your Charms before I had time to look about me.

Yes Madam, I had the happiness of adoring you, an unhappiness for which I cannot be too grateful. 'What,' said he to himself, 'is Musgrove allowed to die for Henrietta? Enviable Mortal! and may he pine for her who is the object of universal Admiration, who is adored by a Colonel, and toasted by a Baronet!—' Adorable Henrietta how beautiful you are! I declare you are quite divine! You are more than Mortal. You are an Angel. You are Venus herself. Inshort, Madam, you are the prettiest Girl I ever saw in my Life – and her Beauty is encreased in her Musgrove's Eyes, by permitting him to love her and allowing me to hope. And Ah! Angelic Miss Henrietta, Heaven is my Witness how ardently I do hope for the death of your villanous Uncle and his Abandoned Wife, Since my fair one will not consent to be mine till their decease has placed her in affluence above what my fortune can procure—. Though it is an improvable Estate—. Cruel Henrietta to persist in such a resolution! I am at present with my Sister where I mean to continue till my own house which tho' an excellent one is at present somewhat out of repair, is ready to receive me. Amiable princess of my Heart farewell – Of that Heart which trembles while it signs itself your most ardent Admirer

and devoted humble Serv[t]

T. Musgrove

There is a pattern for a Love-letter Matilda! Did you ever read such a masterpeice of Writing? Such Sense,

Such Sentiment, Such purity of Thought, Such flow of Language and such unfeigned Love in one Sheet? No, never I can answer for it, since a Musgrove is not to be met with by every Girl. Oh! how I long to be with him! I intend to send him the following in answer to his Letter tomorrow.

My dearest Musgrove—. Words can not express how happy your Letter made me; I thought I should have cried for Joy, for I love you better than any body in the World. I think you the most amiable, and the handsomest Man in England, and so to be sure you are. I never read so sweet a Letter in my Life. Do write me another just like it, and tell me you are in love with me in every other line. I quite die to see you. How shall we manage to see one another? for we are so much in love that we cannot live asunder. Oh! my dear Musgrove you cannot think how impatiently I wait for the death of my Uncle and Aunt – If they will not die soon, I beleive I shall run mad, for I get more in love with you every day of my Life. How happy your Sister is to enjoy the pleasure of your Company in her house, and how happy every body in London must be because you are there. I hope you will be so kind as to write to me again soon, for I never read such sweet Letters as yours. I am, my dearest Musgrove, most truly and faithfully yours for ever and ever

Henrietta Halton

I hope he will like my answer; it is as good a one as I can write, though nothing to his; Indeed I had always heard what a dab he was at a Love-letter. I saw him you know for the first time at Lady Scudamore's – And when I saw her Ladyship afterwards she asked me how I liked her Cousin Musgrove?

'Why upon my word' said I, 'I think he is a very handsome young Man.'

'I am glad you think so,' replied she, 'for he is distractedly in love with you.'

'Law! Lady Scudamore,' said I, 'how can you talk so ridiculously?'

'Nay, 'tis very true,' answered She, 'I assure you, for he was in love with you from the first moment he beheld you.'

'I wish it may be true,' said I, 'for that is the only kind of love I would give a farthing for – There is some Sense in being in love at first sight.'

'Well, I give you Joy of your conquest,' replied Lady Scudamore, 'and I beleive it to have been a very complete one; I am sure it is not a contemptible one, for my Cousin is a charming young fellow, has seen a great deal of the World, and writes the best Love-letters I ever read.'

This made me very happy, and I was excessively pleased with my conquest. However I thought it was proper to give myself a few Airs – So I said to her—

'This is all very pretty, Lady Scudamore, but you know that we young Ladies who are Heiresses must not throw ourselves away upon Men who have no fortune at all.'

'My dear Miss Halton,' said She, 'I am as much convinced of that as you can be, and I do assure you that I should be the last person to encourage your marrying any one who had not some pretensions to expect a fortune with you. M[r] Musgrove is so far from being poor that he has an estate of Several hundreds an year which is capable of great Improvement, and an excellent House, though at present it is not quite in repair.'

'If that is the case,' replied I, 'I have nothing more to say against him, and if as you say he is an informed young Man and can write good Love-letters, I am sure I have no reason to find fault with him for admiring me, tho' perhaps I may not marry him for all that, Lady Scudamore.'

'You are certainly under no obligation to marry him,' answered her Ladyship, 'except that which love himself will dictate to you, for if I am not greatly mistaken you are at this very moment unknown to yourself, cherishing a most tender affection for him.'

'Law, Lady Scudamore,' replied I blushing, 'how can you think of such a thing?'

'Because every look, every word betrays it,' answered She; 'Come, my dear Henrietta, consider me as a freind, and be sincere with me – Do not you prefer M[r] Musgrove to any man of your acquaintance?'

'Pray do not ask me such questions, Lady Scudamore,' said I turning away my head, 'for it is not fit for me to answer them.'

'Nay my Love,' replied she, 'now you confirm my suspicions. But why, Henrietta, should you be ashamed to own a well-placed Love, or why refuse to confide in me?'

'I am not ashamed to own it;' said I taking Courage. 'I do not refuse to confide in you or blush to say that I do love your cousin Mr Musgrove, that I am sincerely attached to him, for it is no disgrace to love a handsome Man. If he were plain indeed I might have had reason to be ashamed of a passion which must have been mean since the Object would have been unworthy. But with such a figure and face, and such beautiful hair as your Cousin has, why should I blush to own that such Superior Merit has made an impression on me.'

'My sweet Girl' (said Lady Scudamore embracing me with great Affection) 'what a delicate way of thinking you have in these Matters, and what a quick discernment for one of your years! Oh! how I honour you for such Noble Sentiments!'

'Do you, Ma'am?' said I; 'You are vastly obliging. But pray, Lady Scudamore, did your Cousin himself tell you of his Affection for me? I shall like him the better if he did, for what is a Lover without a Confidante?'

'Oh! my Love' replied She, 'you were born for each other. Every word you say more deeply convinces me that your Minds are actuated by the invisible power of simpathy, for your opinions and Sentiments so exactly coincide. Nay, the colour of your Hair is not very different. Yes, my dear Girl, the poor despairing Musgrove did reveal to me the story of his Love—. Nor was I surprised at it – I know not how it was, but I had a kind of presentiment that he would be in love with you.'

'Well, but how did he break it to you?'

'It was not till after supper. We were sitting round the fire together talking on indifferent subjects, though to say the truth the Conversation was cheifly on my side, for he was thoughtful and silent, when on a sudden he interrupted me in the midst of something I was saying, by exclaiming in a most Theatrical tone—

"Yes I'm in love I feel it now
And Henrietta Halton has undone me—"'

'Oh! What a sweet Way' replied I, 'of declaring his Passion! To make such a couple of charming Lines about me! What a pity it is that they are not in rhime!'

'I am very glad you like it,' answered She; 'To be sure there was a great deal of Taste in it. "And are you in love with her, Cousin?" said I. "I am very sorry for it, for unexceptionable as you are in every respect, with a pretty Estate capable of Great improvements, and an excellent House tho' somewhat out of repair, Yet who can hope to aspire with success to the adorable Henrietta who has had an offer from a Colonel and been toasted by a Baronet—"'
'That I have—' cried I. Lady Scudamore continued. '"Ah, dear Cousin," replied he, "I am so well convinced of the little Chance I can have of winning her who is adored by thousands, that I need no assurances of yours to make me more thoroughly so. Yet surely neither you or the fair

Henrietta herself will deny me the exquisite Gratification of dieing for her, of falling a victim of her Charms. And when I am dead" – continued he—'

'Oh Lady Scudamore,' said I wiping my eyes, 'that such a sweet Creature should talk of dieing!'

'It is an affecting Circumstance indeed,' replied Lady Scudamore. ' "When I am dead," said he, "Let me be carried and lain at her feet, and perhaps she may not disdain to drop a pitying tear on my poor remains." '

'Dear Lady Scudamore' interrupted I, 'say no more on this affecting Subject. I cannot bear it.'

'Oh! how I admire the sweet Sensibility of your Soul, and as I would not for Worlds wound it too deeply, I will be silent.'

'Pray go on' said I. She did so.

' "And then," added he, "Ah! Cousin, imagine what my transports will be when I feel the dear precious drops trickle o'er my face! Who would not die to taste such extacy! And when I am interred, may the divine Henrietta bless some happier Youth with her affection, May he be as tenderly attached to her as the hapless Musgrove and while he crumbles to dust, May they live an example of Felicity in the Conjugal state!" '

'Did you ever hear any thing so pathetic? What a charming wish, to be lain at my feet when he was dead! Oh! what an exalted mind he must have to be capable of such a wish!' Lady Scudamore went on.

' "Ah! my dear Cousin," replied I to him, "Such noble

behaviour as this, must melt the heart of any Woman however obdurate it may naturally be; and could the divine Henrietta but hear your generous wishes for her happiness, all gentle as is her Mind, I have not a doubt but that she would pity your affection and endeavour to return it." "Oh! Cousin," answered he, "do not endeavour to raise my hopes by such flattering Assurances. No, I cannot hope to please this angel of a Woman, and the only thing which remains for me to do, is to die." "True Love is ever desponding," replied I, "but I, my dear Tom, will give you even greater hopes of conquering this fair one's heart, than I have yet given you, by assuring you that I watched her with the strictest attention during the whole day, and could plainly discover that she cherishes in her bosom though unknown to herself, a most tender affection for you." '

'Dear Lady Scudamore,' cried I, 'This is more than I ever knew!'

'Did not I say that it was unknown to yourself? "I did not," continued I to him, "encourage you by saying this at first, that Surprise might render the pleasure Still Greater." "No, Cousin," replied he in a languid voice, "nothing will convince me that I can have touched the heart of Henrietta Halton, and if you are deceived yourself, do not attempt deceiving me." Inshort my Love it was the work of some hours for me to persuade the poor despairing Youth that you had really a preference for him; but when at last he could no longer deny the force of my arguments, or discredit what I told him, his transports, his Raptures, his Extacies are beyond my power to describe.'

'Oh! the dear Creature,' cried I, 'how passionately he loves me! But, dear Lady Scudamore, did you tell him that I was totally dependant on my Uncle and Aunt?'

'Yes, I told him every thing.'

'And what did he say?'

'He exclaimed with virulence against Uncles and Aunts; Accused the Laws of England for allowing them to possess their Estates when wanted by their Nephews or Neices, and wished he were in the House of Commons, that he might reform the Legislature, and rectify all its abuses.'

'Oh! the sweet Man! What a spirit he has!' said I.

'He could not flatter himself, he added, that the adorable Henrietta would condescend for his Sake to resign those Luxuries and that Splendor to which She had been used, and accept only in exchange the Comforts and Elegancies which his limited Income could afford her, even supposing that his house were in Readiness to receive her. I told him that it could not be expected that she would; it would be doing her an injustice to suppose her capable of giving up the power she now possesses and so nobly uses of doing such extensive Good to the poorer part of her fellow Creatures, merely for the gratification of you and herself.'

'To be sure,' said I, 'I am very Charitable every now and then. And what did Mr Musgrove say to this?'

'He replied that he was under a melancholy Necessity of owning the truth of what I said, and therefore if he should be the happy Creature destined to be the Husband of the Beautiful Henrietta he must bring himself to wait, however impatiently, for the fortunate day, when she might be freed from the power of worthless Relations and able to bestow herself on him.'

What a noble Creature he is! Oh! Matilda what a fortunate one I am, who am to be his Wife! My Aunt is calling to me to come and make the pies. So adeiu my dear freind,

and beleive me yours etc. – H. Halton

Finis

A Letter from a Young Lady, whose feelings being too Strong for her Judgement led her into the commission of Errors which her Heart disapproved

Many have been the cares and vicissitudes of my past life, my beloved Ellinor, and the only consolation I feel for their bitterness is that on a close examination of my conduct, I am convinced that I have strictly deserved them. I murdered my father at a very early period of my Life, I have since murdered my Mother, and I am now going to murder my Sister. I have changed my religion so often that at present I have not an idea of any left. I have been a perjured witness in every public tryal for these last twelve Years, and I have forged my own Will. In short there is scarcely a crime that I have not committed – But I am now going to reform. Colonel Martin of the Horse guards has paid his Addresses to me, and we are to be married in a few days. As there is something singular in our Courtship, I will give you an account of it. Colonel Martin is the second son of the late Sir John Martin who died immensely rich, but bequeathing only one hundred thousand pound apiece to his three younger Children, left the bulk of his fortune, about eight Million to the present Sir Thomas. Upon his small pittance the Colonel lived tolerably contented for nearly four months when he took it into his head to determine on getting the whole of his eldest Brother's Estate. A new will was forged and the Colonel produced it in Court – but nobody would swear to it's being the right Will except himself, and he had sworn so much that Nobody beleived him. At that moment I happened to be passing by the door of the Court, and was beckoned in by the Judge who told the Colonel that I was a Lady ready to witness anything for the cause of Justice, and advised him to apply to me. In short the Affair was soon adjusted. The Colonel and I swore to its' being the right will, and Sir Thomas has been obliged to resign all his illgotten Wealth. The Colonel in gratitude waited on me the next day with an offer of his hand—. I am now going to murder my Sister.

Yours Ever,

Anna Parker

PENGUIN

LITTLE BLACK

CLASSICS

PENGUIN

LITTLE BLACK

CLASSICS

PENGUIN

LITTLE BLACK

CLASSICS